Imager's Intrigue

Tor Books by L. E. Modesitt, Jr.

The Imager Portfolio
Imager
Imager's Challenge
Imager's Intrigue

The Corean Chronicles
Legacies
Darknesses
Scepters
Alector's Choice
Cadmian's Choice
Soarer's Choice
The Lord-Protector's Daughter
Lady-Protector (forthcoming)

The Saga of Recluce
The Magic of Recluce
The Towers of the Sunset
The Magic Engineer
The Order War
The Death of Chaos
Fall of Angels
The Chaos Balance
The White Order
Colors of Chaos
Magi'i of Cyador
Scion of Cyador
Wellspring of Chaos
Ordermaster
Natural Ordermage
Mage-Guard of Hamor
Arms-Commander

The Spellsong Cycle
The Soprano Sorceress
The Spellsong War
Darksong Rising
The Shadow Sorceress
Shadowsinger

The Ecolitan Matter
Empire & Ecolitan
    (comprising The Ecolitan Operation
    and The Ecologic Secession)
Ecolitan Prime
    (comprising The Ecologic Envoy
    and The Ecolitan Enigma)
The Forever Hero
    (comprising Dawn for a Distant
    Earth, The Silent Warrior, and
    In Endless Twilight)

Timegod's World
    (comprising Timediver's Dawn
    and The Timegod)

The Ghost Books
Of Tangible Ghosts
The Ghost of the Revelator
Ghost of the White Nights
Ghost of Columbia
    (comprising Of Tangible Ghosts
    and The Ghost of the Revelator)

The Hammer of Darkness
The Green Progression
The Parafaith War
Adiamante
Gravity Dreams
Octagonal Raven
Archform: Beauty
The Ethos Effect
Flash
The Eternity Artifact
The Elysium Commission
Viewpoints Critical
Haze
Empress of Eternity (forthcoming)

Imager's Intrigue

The Third Book of the
Imager Portfolio

L. E. MODESITT, JR.

A TOM DOHERTY ASSOCIATES BOOK
NEW YORK

This is a work of fiction. All of the characters, organizations, and events portrayed in this novel are either products of the author's imagination or are used fictitiously.

IMAGER'S INTRIGUE: THE THIRD BOOK OF THE IMAGER PORTFOLIO

Edited by David Hartwell

A Tor Book
Published by Tom Doherty Associates, LLC
175 Fifth Avenue
New York, NY 10010

www.tor-forge.com

Tor® is a registered trademark of Tom Doherty Associates, LLC.

ISBN 978-0-7653-2562-4

First Edition: July 2010

Printed in the United States of America

0 9 8 7 6 5 4 3 2 1

CHARACTERS

CIVIC PATROL

Artois	Commander of Patrollers
Cydarth	Subcommander of Patrollers
Sarthyn	Lieutenant, Patrol Judicial Administration
Subunet	Captain, First District
Jacquet	Captain, Second District
	Kethbryd, Lieutenant
Rhennthyl	Captain, Third District
	Alsoran, Lieutenant
Hostyn	Captain, Fourth District
	Barcuyt, Lieutenant
Bolyet	Captain, Fifth District
	Yerkes, Lieutenant
Kharles	Captain, Sixth District
	Walthyr, Lieutenant

HIGH HOLDERS

Almeida D'Alte
   Ruisa D'Almeida [wife]
Apolyan D'Alte [Councilor from Kherseilles]
Ealthyn D'Alte
Fhernon D'Alte
   Gheranya D'Fhernon [wife]
Guerdyn D'Alte
   Cyana D'Guerdyn [daughter]
Haebyn D'Alte

Haestyr D'Alte [Councilor from Asseroiles]
    Alhyral D'Haestyr [son and heir, fiancee is Dhelora D'Zaerlyn-Alte]
Lhoryn D'Alte
    Petryn D'Lhoryn [son and heir]
Nacryon D'Alte
Ramsael D'Alte [Councilor from Kephria]
    Alynkya D'Ramsael [daughter, also fiancee of Frydryk D'Suyrien]
Regial D'Alte [Councilor from Montagne]
Ryel D'Alte [formerly Kandryl D'Suyrien, younger son of Suyrien D'Alte]
    Iryela D'Ryel [wife]
Ruelyr D'Alte
Shaercyt D'Alte
Shendael D'Alte
    Juniae D'Shendael [wife, political activist, and author]
Suyrien D'Alte [Chief Councilor]
    Frydryk D'Suyrien [son and heir]
Taelmyn D'Alte [deceased]
Zaerlyn D'Alte
    Dhelora D'Zaerlyn-Alte [daughter]

IMAGERS

Poincaryt	Maitre D'Espirt [Head of Collegium]
Dichartyn	Maitre D'Esprit [Head of Collegium Security]
Dyana	Maitre D'Esprit
Dhelyn	Maitre D'Structure [Head of Westisle Collegium]
Jhulian	Maitre D'Structure [Justice]
Rholyn	Maitre D'Structure[Advocate/Councilor from the Collegium]
Schorzat	Maitre D'Structure [Director of Field Operations]
Draffyd	Maitre D'Structure [Medical Imager]
Rhennthyl	Maitre D'Structure [Collegium Imago of Solidar]
Ferlyn	Maitre D'Aspect
Chassendri	Maitre D'Aspect
Ghaend	Maitre D'Aspect
Heisbyl	Maitre D'Aspect
Quaelyn	Maitre D'Aspect [Master of Patterns]
Kahlasa	Maitre D'Aspect [Assistant Director, Field Operations]
Baratyn	Maitre D'Aspect [Council Security]
Dartazn	Maitre D'Aspect
Isola	Chorister of the Nameless

EXECUTIVE COUNCIL OF SOLIDAR

Suyrien D'Alte [Chief Councilor, from L'Excelsis]

Caartyl D'Artisan [Councilor from Masonry Guild, from Eshtora]

Glendyl D'Factorius [Councilor and Steam/Engines Factor, from L'Excelsis]

NAVAL COMMAND

Valeun	Sea-Marshal, Chief, Naval Command
Caellynd	Deputy Sea-Marshal, Naval Command
Geuffryt	Assistant Sea-Marshal, Naval Bureau, Chief of Intelligence

FACTORS

Broussard D'Factorius [Agricultural/Produce Factor]

Chenkyr D'Factorius [Rhennthyl's father, Wool Factor]

    Maelyna D'Chenkyr [Rhennthyl's mother]

    Rousel D'Factorius [Rhennthyl's brother] [deceased]

        Remaya D'Rousel [Rousel's wife]

        Reityr [Rousel and Remaya's son]

    Khethila D'Chenkyr [Rhennthyl's sister]

    Culthyn D'Chenkyr [Rhennthyl's youngest brother]

Diogayn D'Factorius [Councilor and Ironworks Factor, from Extela]

Etyenn D'Factorius [Councilor and Cloth Factor, from Westisle]

Ferdinand D'Factorius [Stone/Brick Factor, from L'Excelsis]

Glendyl D'Factorius [Councilor and Steam/Engines Factor, from L'Excelsis]

Reyner D'Factorius [Councilor and Spice/Essences Factor, from Estisle]

Sebatyon D'Factorius [Councilor and Timber/Lumber Factor, from Mantes]

Veblynt D'Factorius [Paper Factor, from L'Excelsis]

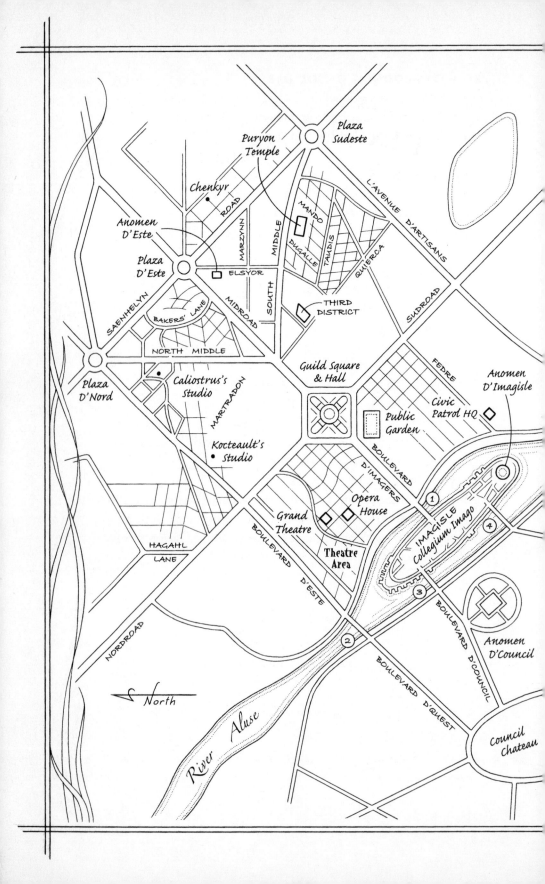

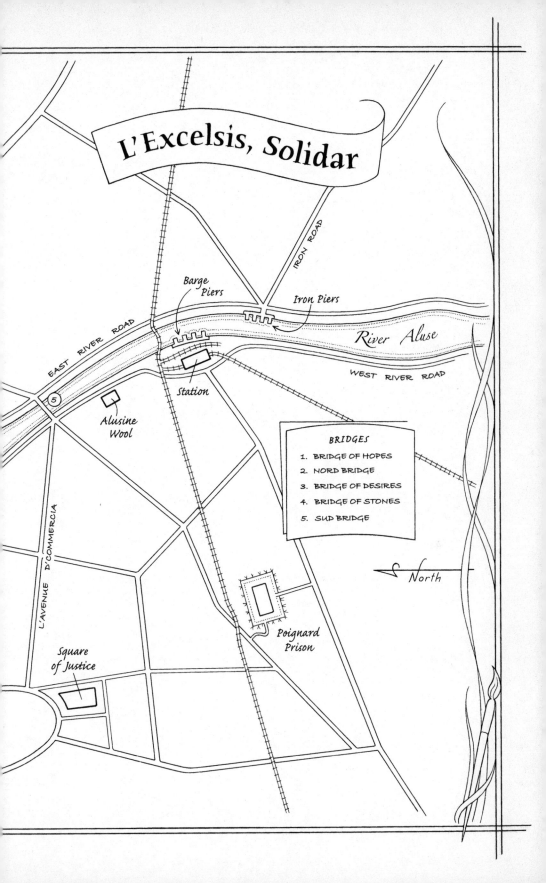

Unlike most people, I hated actually going to sleep and looked forward to waking up . . . in a way. When I'd been a struggling apprentice portraiturist years before, I never would have believed I could have felt that way, but life has a way of changing preconceptions. In my case, it had to do with the sleeping arrangements required of imagers. Although we'd been married for nearly five years—it would be five years on the twenty-first of the coming Fevier—Seliora and I had never slept the entire night together; not that we both wouldn't have wanted to, but the dangers of that were far too high. Even before I'd known I was an imager, I'd lit lamps and imaged things in my sleep, and once I'd even set a chest on fire. Imaging in a nightmare could easily have hurt Seliora . . . if not worse.

So I was pleased to wake, dress in exercise clothes and boots, and leave my discreetly lead-lined bedchamber with its lead glass windows and pad barefoot into the main bedchamber and look at her sleeping there. Then I slipped from the house and ran down the walkways to the exercise area where Clovyl put all those of us assigned to various security-related duties through exercises that ended in a four mille run. After that, I trotted back to the house and showered and shaved, in always cool if not cold water, so that I was clean enough to slip into Seliora's large bed before she actually rose and we got ready for the day.

On this Lundi morning, she was awake, waiting for me, and her arms felt wonderful around me. We didn't get to enjoy that moment for long because a small figure ran in from the adjoining room—meant to be a half-study, but serving as a nursery—and climbed up under the covers to join us.

"Mama, Dada . . ."

Before all that long, the three of us rose, and I washed and changed Diestrya while Seliora showered and dressed. Then Seliora and Diestrya headed downstairs while I dressed in my imager grays. As soon as I sat down in the breakfast room off the adequate but not excessively large kitchen, Klysia filled my large crockery mug with tea, strong tea that I'd likely need for the day ahead.

"More tea, too . . . please?" begged Diestrya from her highchair beside

Seliora and across the table, offering me a winning smile, not that all her smiles weren't dazzling when she wanted something.

Klysia looked to me, then to Seliora. After catching the barest hint of a nod from my black-haired, black-eyed beautiful wife, I nodded. "Just a little, with cream."

Because I was the most junior Maitre D'Structure, a step above the lowest imager master level, Maitre D'Aspect, but below the two senior masters at the Collegium, both of whom were Maitres D'Esprit, our house was a modestly spacious dwelling with an upper level holding three bedrooms, two bathing rooms, the master sleeping chambers, which included my stark sleeping cell and the half-study serving as a nursery, and a main level containing the family and formal parlors, the dining room, the kitchen, the pantry, and a larger study and library, plus, of course, the front entry foyer and Klysia's quarters at the back. I had converted the northern upstairs bedroom into a studio, where I'd done portraits of Maitre Dyana and Master Dichartyn, and where I'd begun the preliminary work on one of Diestrya. That way I didn't have to use the drafty space I'd once been assigned in the Collegium workroom. Fortunately, because my days were rather occupied, no one had changed positions in the Collegium recently, so I wasn't required to paint another Collegium portrait any time soon.

Like all dwellings provided to married imagers by the Collegium, the outside of ours was of gray stone, with a gray slate roof. Inside, the walls were of off-white plaster, except for the main library, which was paneled with cherry and had built-in bookshelves that we had not come close to filling.

With the exception of the formal parlor and the dining room, the furniture in the house was a motley collection of leftovers from the previous maitre and pieces gleaned from sample works from NordEste Design, the business of Seliora's family. "Eclectic" was what Seliora called it, but it was still motley. The formal parlor furnishings, Seliora's bed and dressing table, and the dining room set, with its twin buffets and china cabinets, had all been gifts from her family, as all the linens and woolens had come from mine.

Breakfast was egg toast with berry syrup, sausages, and an oat porridge that Seliora had decided we all needed, particularly Diestrya. I had trouble not making faces in eating the porridge without a surreptitious dollop of the syrup.

"You don't look all that happy, dearest," offered Seliora.

"I'm not." And I wasn't, not when I'd have to spend the morning in one of Commander Artois's monthly meetings of all the District Captains of the Civic Patrol of L'Excelsis. "It's time for Artois's monthly lecture."

"It is the first Lundi in Feuillyt," Seliora said with a smile.

I still found it hard to believe that I'd been married to her nearly five years. At times that seemed more improbable than the fact that I was a master imager—Maitre D'Structure of the Collegium Imago of Solidar—as well as the only imager ever serving as an actual officer in the Civic Patrol, but how all that happened was another story for another time.

We were out of the house two quints before seventh glass. The morning was cool, even cooler than usual for the first Lundi of fall, and Seliora shivered in her cloak.

"Cold?" I asked.

"I should have worn a winter cloak." She smiled at me. "You were out earlier. You could have warned me, except you don't even notice the cold."

"I'll try to be better now that the weather's colder." I grinned at her.

She shook her head, knowing that I'd probably forget.

I carried Diestrya, as we walked southward toward the duty coach area closest to the Bridge of Desires, the stone span that crossed the River Aluse. After Maitre Poincaryt—the head of the Collegium—had worked out the arrangement between the Civic Patrol, the Council of Solidar, and the Collegium that had resulted in my being assigned as Third District Captain, I'd managed to get him to agree to have the duty carriage that took me to the Third District Station every working day make a stop at NordEste Design to drop Seliora off there. After all, it was her family's home and business, and, without her and her family, I'd have died years earlier.

"Moon!" Diestrya pointed to Artiema, full and low in the western sky.

"Yes, that's Artiema." I could also see Erion low in the east, just barely above the granite buildings of Imagisle turned whitish-gray by the white sunlight angling over L'Excelsis.

The first duty coach was the one reserved for us.

"Good morning, Master Rhennthyl. Good morning, Madame," said Lebryn, the driver, who was also an obdurate, immune to the personal effects of imaging on his looks or being.

I opened the coach door for Seliora, then handed Diestrya up while I climbed in, then held my daughter for the ride to NordEste Design.

"What are you working on today?"

"The upholstery design for a Mistress Alynkya D'Ramsael-Alte as a wedding present. Her father might be familiar." Seliora grinned at me. "She came to us because someone once was very kind to her at a dance."

I winced gracefully. That had been one of my early duties in security at the Council Chateau, both to watch for intruders and, as necessary, to make sure that the daughters of High Holders were not without partners. I'd danced with Alynkya at two of the Council's seasonal balls, the first when she'd been pressed to accompany her father, the High Holder and Councilor from Kephria, when her mother was ill, and the second when she had accompanied him after her mother's death. "Who is she marrying?"

"Councilor Suyrien's eldest son, Frydryk."

"She's probably too sweet for him."

"She seems to have a mind of her own."

That was dangerous for any wife of a High Holder, given that High Holders still retained the right of low justice on their own lands—and low justice could include what amounted to perpetual incarceration and other cruelties, even for a High Holder's wife.

Before long, the coach stopped before the building that served Seliora's family as factory, factorage, and dwelling. Located at the intersection of Nordroad and Hagahl Lane, the yellow-brick walls rose three stories, set off by gray granite cornerstones. The wooden loading docks at the south end of the building were stained with a brown oil and well-kept, and the loading yard itself was stone-paved. The entrance on the south side of Hagahl Lane, on the north end, was the private family entrance, with a square-pillared covered porch that shielded a stone archway.

Seliora leaned over and gave me a kiss before she left the coach, and I handed Diestrya down to her. "The newsheets are on the seat."

She always left them there for me to read on the rest of the ride to Third District, and she always reminded me, a ritual that I found somehow reassuring. I followed her down and, holding my shields, walked her up the steps. She used her key to enter.

Then I walked back to the duty coach and climbed in. As Lebryn eased the coach away, I picked up the first of the newsheets—*Tableta*.

The lead headline stated "War Looms in Cloisera." The story was about the increasing tension between Ferrum and Jariola. While the two had reached a truce after the undeclared "Winter War" of 756–757, when the troops of the Oligarch of Jariola had finally pushed the Ferrans back to the pre-war borders and regained control of their coal mines, no peace agreement or treaty had ever been signed. Both nations had armed forces poised along the border, and the two had never resumed diplomatic relations. According to the *Tableta* story, the Ferrans were deploying a new steam-powered land-cruiser, claiming that it could operate in the coldest of winters, unlike earlier models that had broken down in hilly lands of Jariola during the cold winter months.

The story in *Veritum* was similar, but the second newsheet had another story that I found intriguing, not to mention disturbing. The grain warehouse of a wealthy freeholder near Extela had been torched right after harvest, and it was the latest in a series of grain warehouses that had burned across the southeast of Solidar. All the warehouses except one had belonged to freeholders, rather than High Holders.

Then there was a rather cryptic and short story that reported on an explosion of an undetermined nature outside the Place D'Opera on Samedi night after the premiere of *The Trial of Lorien*. The explosion had damaged a coach, killed several people, and injured a number of bystanders.

I frowned. No one had contacted me. But then, the Place D'Opera was in Second District.

Seliora had mentioned the opera because Iryela and Kandryl had wanted to see the premiere, but couldn't because of a dinner at his father's chateau. The dinner might even have been in celebration of Frydryk's and Alynkya's engagement. Or it might not have been, given the social obligations and intrigues that swirled around High Holders.

I'd wanted to see the opera for a different reason, although I was certainly not willing to pay the prices for the premiere. Lorien had been the son of Rex Defou, who'd been removed as ruler and rex of Solidar by Alastar, the first imager to be titled a Maitre D'Image—the most powerful of imagers, of whom there were none at present in the Collegium. Historians had always questioned whether Lorien was strong and temperate or weak-willed and subservient to the High Holders of the time. It would be interesting to see how the composer and the librettist had seen Lorien.

But . . . why weren't there more details about the explosion in the newsheet?

For the moment, I couldn't do anything about it, and I finished reading *Veritum* just before Lebryn eased the duty coach to a stop outside Civic Patrol headquarters.

I stepped out of the duty coach and adjusted the gray visored cap that imagers wore when on duty off Imagisle, a cap similar to those worn by the Civic Patrol, except that mine bore the four-pointed star that symbolized the Collegium. Although the headquarters of the Civic Patrol of L'Excelsis were slightly less than a mille from the south end of Imagisle, my circular trip via NordEste Design had taken four milles. Even had I gone directly from the Collegium, the trip would have been more than two milles because there wasn't a bridge on the south end of the isle that held the Collegium. There really wasn't much difference in distance between going to headquarters and going to my Third District station, although the station was almost two milles northwest of headquarters.

The Civic Patrol headquarters building was of undistinguished yellow brick, with brown wooden trim and doors. There were three doors spaced across the front. The left one led to the malefactor charging area, and the right door was permanently locked. The middle double doors were set in the square archway above two worn stone steps leading up from the sidewalk. I took them and stepped inside and past the table desk, with a graying patroller seated behind it.

"Good morning, Captain Rhennthyl."

"Good morning, Cassan."

I hurried up the time-worn dark oak steps to the second level and turned right, going past one door before stepping in through the open door to the conference room, with its long oval table of polished but battered oak and the straight-backed chairs arranged around it. Three wide windows, both closed, were centered on the outer wall. They offered a view of the various buildings on the north side of Fedre, but not so far enough to see those along the Boulevard D'Imagers. There were no pictures hung on the walls, and only three unlit oil lamps in sconces spaced along the inside wall.

I was the second to arrive. Bolyet, the captain of Fifth District, was already there. He'd replaced Telleryn a year before, when Telleryn had earned out his stipend and moved to Kherseilles with his wife.

"Good morning," I said.

"It won't be for long," the balding captain replied. "Commander's not happy. Something in Second District."

"The explosion?"

He nodded, but before he could say more, Subunet, of First District, entered, trailed by Hostyn and Jacquet, who had dark circles under his eyes. Several moments later, Kharles followed.

Subcommander Cydarth walked in directly behind Kharles. He had black hair and a swarthy complexion. Part of his upper right ear was missing. "The commander will be right here." His voice was so low it actually rumbled, and I recalled how I'd reacted when I'd first heard him speak years before. I'd read of voices that deep, but I'd never heard one until then.

We all remained standing for several moments, until Commander Artois entered and shut the door behind himself. Three or four digits shorter than I was, he was also wire-thin with short-cut brown hair shot with gray. His flat brown eyes never seemed to show emotion. He sat at the end of the table, with Cydarth taking the place at his right. The rest of us sat, those in the first three districts to his left, those in districts four through six on his right, if below the subcommander.

"Good morning, Captains." Artois paused, then continued. "Some of you know we had a problem Samedi evening and yesterday. For those of you who don't, I'll summarize." He tilted his head slightly, looking momentarily at Jacquet, before continuing. "Samedi evening there was a premiere of a new opera at the Place D'Opera. After the opera ended, an explosion destroyed a wealthy factor's coach and killed him, his wife, his eldest daughter, and the coachman. The factor was Broussard D'Factorius of Piedryn. He was visiting a cousin here in L'Excelsis. A message was found pinned to his body after the explosion. The message claimed that the factor had been killed because of his mistreatment of workers on his lands. The signature, if one could call it that, was 'Workers for Justice.' Eight years ago, a High Holder was shot, not fatally, and he received a similar message. There's no other record of such a group."

Jacquet said nothing, but the fingers of his left hand drummed silently on the edge of the table.

"We have another problem," Artois went on. "Broussard's formal coat, cravat, and shirt were shredded. The envelope was intact when found on his chest by the patrollers on the scene." The commander looked to me. "Captain Rhennthyl, is it possible for an imager to stand that close to a blast and then place such a message?"

"No, sir. No imager I know of at the Collegium could do that." I managed a rueful smile. "At one time, I was caught in an explosion when I was a good fifteen yards away. I did survive, but I had broken ribs and couldn't move for days, even with a brace. It was two months before I healed."

Cydarth nodded, thoughtfully, and I wondered why.

"I thought as much," replied Artois. "That means someone who was nearby planted the envelope. It's also likely that whoever it was knew explosives and channeled the blast pattern, then hurried up in the chaos and pinned the envelope." Artois glanced to Jacquet. "The patrollers had been diverted by a fight just north of the building. The man who began the fight escaped, and the man who was attacked was apparently innocent."

Cydarth looked sideways at Artois, not quite questioningly.

"I could be mistaken," Artois said dryly, "but I think it highly unlikely that an elderly and frail chorister emeritus of the Anomen D'NordEste would willingly choose to be involved in such a diversion."

"Yes, sir."

"High Councilor Suyrien has requested that the Civic Patrol and its patrollers exercise special vigilance around locations where wealthy factors or High Holders are likely to be present, except for the area around the Council Chateau, where Council security will exercise such vigilance." Artois's voice was matter-of-fact, as if he'd been requested to deliver such a request, knowing that it was probably close to useless.

Third District had few worries along that line, with more than half of its territory comprising the northeast taudis and adjoining areas where those of only slightly higher means lived and worked . . . although I did have to say that matters in the taudis had improved over the past few years, if far more slowly than I had hoped.

"We may see more of such attempts, and we may not. Right now, Captain Jacquet and his patrollers are looking into all aspects of the matter, and the subcommander or I will let you know of anything that may affect your districts. Now," Artois went on more briskly, "the subcommander will return the proposed budgets and manpower requirements you submitted earlier. I'll go over the revised guidelines. As I told you at the last meeting, you will have your final budget to me no later than next Lundi . . ."

From there on, the meeting dealt with administrative details, and it lasted another glass. When the commander and subcommander finally left, the rest of us stood.

Bolyet glanced across the table at Jacquet. "I have to say I'd rather not be in your boots. Is there anything I can do?"

With Bolyet, I knew, the question wasn't a polite formality.

"Not at the moment. I'll let you know if there is." Jacquet paused, picking up the large envelope he'd received, as had all of the captains, and letting Kharles, Subunet, and Hostyn leave the room. Then he added, "I'll bed every cheap tart in your district, Rhenn, if this is the work of some workers' movement."

"What do you think it is?" asked Bolyet.

Jacquet shrugged. "Too direct for a High Holder, unless it's a High Holder not trying to have it traced to him. The bomb had a directed blast pattern, and that means someone who knows explosives. Could be a retired Navy armorer." He looked at me.

"Some of the imagers at the armory could build something like that, but none of the ones who could build it would be able to use it very well. They'd also be facing an immediate death sentence if they did." I frowned. "If you could send me a report on the bomb, though, I might be able to run it by some armory specialists and find out more about who did build it. I could also use the information to make sure someone didn't reveal something to someone they shouldn't." I didn't mention that I could also eliminate anyone on Imagisle as a possibility . . . or discover if they were.

Jacquet nodded. "I can do that. Might be tomorrow before you get a copy." He looked to Bolyet and then to me. "If you hear about anyone on the shady side suddenly getting flush, it might help."

"We can have the boys keep their eyes and ears open," promised Bolyet.

I just nodded. Then Bolyet and I followed Jacquet out into the upper level hall, down the steps, and out onto the sidewalk.

"Give my best to Alsoran." Bolyet grinned before he stepped into the hack he'd hailed. "I still don't know how you managed to persuade him to go back to Third District."

"I will." I grinned. We both knew that Alsoran had agreed to the transfer because it meant his making lieutenant earlier than otherwise would have been the case, and because he and I got along, which wasn't always the case between district captains and their lieutenants, as I well knew after suffering through three years of working with Warydt, his predecessor.

I hailed the next hack to take me to Third District station. As I rode up Fedre to Sudroad, I couldn't help agreeing with Jacquet that the explosion was a symptom of something far worse, although I couldn't have said why at that moment.

Third District station was located on Fuosta, midway between Quierca and South Middle. The one-story building was hardly impressive. Its once-yellow bricks had turned grayish-tan, and the narrow barred windows in the front on both sides of the double doors of the single entrance added to the grim appearance, clean as the structure was. The doors were battered and iron-bound oak with equally ancient heavy iron inside hinges, and could be barred, although we'd never had the need. The open space inside the doors that could have been called an anteroom was empty, although in the morning, after the day shift arrived, there would have been patrollers checking their equipment and getting the word from the handful of men coming off the midnight to morning shift. Over the past few years, I had managed to get the time-dimmed glass of the windows replaced, and the cracked and ancient floor re-tiled with deep gray tiles, rather than with the dingy light gray that had always looked dirty.

Lyonyt was working the duty desk when I entered the station. He smiled as he looked up from the high and narrow desk set out just far enough from the wall on the right that he could squeeze his stool behind it. "Good morning, Captain."

"Good morning." I smiled back and kept walking to the first door on the right, where I stepped inside. The small study, little more than three yards by four, was typical for a Patrol Captain, and even slightly larger than Master Dichartyn's study at the Collegium, for all that he was the head of all security operations, both in Solidar and worldwide. There was a narrow desk, with a wooden armchair and a worn gray cushion, three creaking wooden file cases against the left wall, and four straight-backed chairs, lined up against the right inside wall for the moment. The two outside windows were barred.

Lieutenant Alsoran followed me into the study. He was the biggest patroller I'd ever run across, standing a good ten digits taller than me, and I was taller than most. His shoulders were also much broader, and there wasn't the faintest trace of extra flesh around his midsection. His black hair was cut short and still faintly curly below his visored cap, and his eyebrows were thick and bushy. "Good morning, Captain. How did the meeting go?"

"As usual, with one exception. Did you hear about the bomb that exploded near the Place D'Opera on Samedi night?"

"Some of the patrollers were talking about it."

"A wealthy factor from Piedryn was killed, with a note pinned to him, signed by a workers' group—Workers for Justice—that no one has heard from in years. Have our patrollers keep their ears open. If someone comes into unexplained golds, I'd like to hear about it."

"I'll let them know." Alsoran paused. "You don't think that's it, do you?"

"Let's say that I think it's unlikely that a workers' group could build, place, and explode a bomb with that much precision."

"What about foreigners? The Ferrans haven't been happy with Solidar ever since the Winter War."

"They certainly could find the expertise, but I can't figure out why they'd target a factor whose lands and wealth come from wheat, corn, and agricultural goods. If they went after a High Holder like Young Ryel, who has factories and mills as well as lands, or after High Holder Shaercyt, who owns most of the port facilities in Westisle . . . that would make more sense. Or especially a factor like Councilor Glendyl, whose works manufacture engines and locomotives." I managed a smile. "Anyway, we're not likely to see anything like that in Third District."

"Even with the rag-paper mill?" Alsoran didn't quite laugh.

"Even with that." I grinned back at him.

The mill was small, housed in a building that incorporated three once-abandoned taudis dwellings a block off Mando, adjacent to Quierca, in what had been the worst part of Third District. It represented an idea Seliora, Mama Diestra, and I had come up with, using the expertise of Factor Veblynt and admittedly, some golds from Seliora's family. Because it wasn't close to any streams, and because the re-used water requirements necessitated more filtration and settling tanks, it was small; but after four years, it reliably produced small runs of high-quality writing paper with special designs that were more and more in demand in L'Excelsis. It also employed some thirty-odd local taudis-dwellers, both full- and part-time, largely women who could not work full-time or young men who wanted to learn the trade. The entire operation usually broke even, but the greater advantage was that it had provided some twenty young men—so far—with the skills to work in Veblynt's larger paper mills, without his having to train them. It also had contributed—along with what Seliora called the "simpleworks"—to improved living conditions in the taudis, and that helped reduce the violence, if not as much as I'd hoped.

"Then, there's the continuing budget problem." I shook my head. "The commander turned down our request for another patroller. I'm afraid we won't get one next year, either."

"We're covering the toughest part of L'Excelsis . . . well . . . what once was the toughest part of L'Excelsis," Alsoran said, "and we do it with fewer patrollers than any other district."

"I told him that, but he said that since we've reduced the number of offenses, we don't have the same priority as Captain Kharles does in Sixth District, with all of his difficulties with the Hellhole taudis."

"We're supposed to do a bad job so we can get enough patrollers that they can work regular shifts like they do in Second, Fourth, and Fifth districts?" Alsoran's tone was gently sardonic.

There was no point in pursuing that. We both knew it. "Before I forget, I'll be in late on Meredi morning. That's if I get a report from Jacquet tomorrow. I'll need to track down some things dealing with the bombing case."

"Be careful, sir. Every time you go off to track down things—"

"I know. Something happens." Seliora offered the same kinds of warnings. "But this might not be quite so dangerous. I'm just looking for information, and I'll be on Imagisle."

The dubious look I received from my lieutenant suggested that I wasn't being terribly reassuring. "Right now, I'm going for a walk, along South Middle, and I'll see if I can run into Smultyn and Caesaro."

Alsoran laughed. "Lyonyt wagered that you'd follow young Santaero up Elsyor." Alsoran laughed again. "Now, I'll have to."

"The scenery's better on Elsyor. Go collect your copper," I replied in a mock-gruff voice.

We both headed out, walking up Fuosta together, past the cafes and the one bistro, if one could call it that, clustered just up from the station. I alternated eating a mid-day meal, when I ate at all, among the various places where I actually didn't get indigestion.

We turned east on South Middle. Just before Dugalle, Alsoran crossed South Middle to take Elysor north. I flexed my imager shields, as much as to make certain that I was holding them as anything, because I'd been forced to develop them early on. They were proof against bullets, and slings and arrows, so to speak, and perhaps small explosions, but not against cannon, falling buildings, and large explosions—as I'd discovered early on as an imager.

Much as I tried not to spend too much time with the patrollers on their rounds, I still felt that, if I didn't spend at least a glass a day with one or more of them, I'd end up out of touch with them and with the district. Besides, if I met with them after their rounds, that took their time, and we were stretched thin, and if I met with them in the station during their shifts, then the district wasn't being patrolled. Also, as I'd discovered early on, I learned more by talking to them on their rounds.

I glanced at the chest-high brick wall to the right, separating the side yards of the taudis-dwellings from the sidewalk and South Middle. At least the bricks were clean. I'd had to lean on Horazt to get that accomplished, but he'd finally managed to take care of it by the expedient of assigning clean-up duties to those members of his gang who misbehaved. That had actually worked better than either of us had thought because the taudis-gang members didn't want anyone else writing on the walls after that.

A block after I crossed Dugalle, still on South Middle, I could see the square structure of the woodworks ahead, on the block before Mando—Seliora's "simpleworks," built from the stones and bricks of the former Temple of Puryon. It had taken two years to construct after the temple had been blown up by the Tiempran fanatics. The taudis-dwellers who worked there produced sturdy, simple, but well-finished benches, tables, and chairs designed for bistros, cafes, and taverns. Since those establishments suffered breakage, there was a continuing market for solid and inexpensive furniture.

Before I reached Mando, I saw Smultyn and Caesaro walking toward me, their eyes scanning the avenue, the side streets, and the yards. They walked not quite casually, alert but relaxed, and that meant the day's rounds had been good—so far.

"Good morning, Captain," offered Smultyn, the short, dark-haired senior patroller of the pair.

"Good morning. Why don't we head back the way you came, and you can tell me what you've seen this morning?"

"Yes, sir."

As we passed the woodworks, I glanced to my right at the long and low building.

"Everything's fine there," said Caesaro. "Fuhlyt said that all the wood was returned."

"Good." I'd just passed the word to Horazt. "Has anyone said anything more about that smash-and-grab at the silversmith's?"

Smultyn shook his head. "Not much. The serving woman at the bistro one door up said that it was a taudis-youth, but one wearing a open jacket with an orange lining, from what she could see."

"Orange? That's one of the Hellhole gangs, isn't it? The Midroad north of the Guild Square is a long ways from the Hellhole."

"It could be a local, using orange," suggested Caesaro.

"Not smart." Smultyn looked to me.

"I'll pass the word to whatever taudischef I see next."

"Jadhyl was looking for you. He said it wasn't trouble."

"Then I'm sure he'll find me."

In fact, less than two blocks past Mando, I saw Jadhyl in his green jacket. For whatever reasons, the taudis-gangs in my district had always worn colored jackets, rather than black ones with colored linings that the wearer had to leave open to show affiliation. The taudischef was talking to a youth under a lamppost. He said something, and the youth hurried off.

"I'll catch up with you," I told Smultyn, before I headed down the side street.

"Yes, sir."

Jadhyl just waited until I stopped, then inclined his head. "Master Captain."

I'd never seen anyone who looked quite like the east-end taudischef, with his faintly golden-tinged skin and his natural golden-brown hair and piercing eyes. He always spoke in a way that I could only have described as slightly over-precise. He'd never said where his parents had come from, only that they'd died when he was young, and he'd avoided answering me the one time I'd asked. I'd never asked again, because there wasn't any point in it.

"Jadhyl." I nodded in return. "I thought you might like to know . . ." I explained about the explosion, then finished, "If you hear anything, I'd appreciate whatever you might wish to share with me." Before he could reply, I added, "There's one other thing. We had a smash-and-grab at the silversmith's— Alaint's place just off the Midroad."

"He's not that friendly," replied Jadhyl. "Kantros wasn't much of an artist, but he'd smile now and again."

"That's true, but one of the serving girls got a look at the thief. He was wearing orange under his black jacket. Now . . . if he was a Hellhole tough out of his territory . . ."

"Thank you. I do appreciate your courtesy, Captain. I don't mention that often enough. Would that your predecessors had been so. I'll talk to Deyalt. If it's someone who shouldn't be wearing orange . . . we'll take care of it." Jadhyl smiled.

His words meant I'd have to tell Horazt.

"On the other matter . . . I have not heard anything, but if I do, you will know. Explosions . . ." He shook his head, then smiled again. "My nephew Gayhlen. You might recall him?"

"He's the one at the woodworks." Among the taudischefs, "nephew" usually meant a son born of a woman not a wife or a permanent companion.

"Yes. Fuhlyt says he could pass the apprentice-level skills for the wood-workers' guild."

I nodded. "Is he truly the kind who will work hard and not cause trouble?"

"I would not ask otherwise, Captain."

"Then he may list me as a referring sponsor."

"Thank you." He smiled. "He's a good boy, and it's best if he leaves the taudis."

What that meant was that Gayhlen was hard-working and gentle-natured, and thus unsuited to his "uncle's" occupation.

After I left Jadhyl, I had to walk quickly for a good block before I caught up with Smultyn and Caesaro. Smultyn looked at me inquiringly.

"He doesn't seem to know about the smash-and-grab, but . . . we'll see. He wanted to see whether one of his nephews who's been taught by Fuhlyt might be considered as an apprentice woodworker."

"Some of those kids are good," said Caesaro. "A couple of them are sell-ing wooden boxes and little things. They're not bad."

"The more of them that get into real work, the better for us," added Smultyn. "We're not seeing near as many elvers anymore."

Part of that was because I'd pressed the taudischefs to avoid selling elve-weed to the younger people. There wasn't any way that those already addicted would change.

I stayed with the two patrollers all the way to the Plaza SudEste and then down Quierca for a ways before I left them. Nearing Fuosta, I saw a short, dark-haired, and all-too-familiar figure ahead. Horazt was the first taudichef I'd met, because his "nephew" Shault had shown imager talents, and I'd been Shault's unofficial preceptor and helped ease the boy—now a youth and a promising imager secundus—into the routine and discipline of the Col-legium. Horazt had a worried look on his face.

What concerned me more than his expression was that he was looking for me. Horazt was the most secretive of the three taudischefs in Third Dis-trict, and I'd been fortunate that he'd had a problem with Shault, or I'd prob-ably never would have been able to work with him.

"What is it?" I asked, pleasantly, but without smiling.

"Elveweed, Master Rhennthyl. The latest batches have something different . . . It's not good."

"Is it poisoned? Is it from some place besides Caenen?"

"The carriers claim it as good as the best Caenenan green."

"As good as? Where is it coming from?"

"It's not from Caenen. It's too fresh, but they say we can't get any other."

Horazt glanced toward the taudis wall, not quite meeting my eyes. "Three long-timers had half a pipe and went screamer. They weren't the type. Deyalt had that happen twice this week. Doesn't look any different. Doesn't smell that way. I've tried to warn all the runners, but they won't go against their dealers. Since you took over, none of them ever come here, and I don't know where their safe houses are. Not now. I've warned the users I know, but most of 'em won't listen or don't care. I thought you might want to let your patrollers know."

Bad elveweed on top of everything else. "Thank you. I will let them know. There are two things you might like to know . . ." I went on to tell him about the smash-and-grab and the explosion.

He just nodded.

I headed back to the station, where I spent the rest of the afternoon occupied with more of the usual duties of a captain—some of which included interrogating two of the taudis-dwellers picked up for assault, revising the patrol schedules for the next two weeks to take into account the promotion/transfer of Charkisyn to Fourth District when we wouldn't get a replacement for three weeks, checking the charging reports against our arrest records, and accompanying Gervayn on part of his round. I mentioned what Horazt had said about the elveweed to Alsoran and told Lyonyt to put a caution in the duty book for all patrollers. Beyond the worry about elver deaths, there was something about it that nagged at me. For one thing, there were only a few areas of Solidar where elveweed would even grow—unless someone was growing it under glass, and that was far more costly than harvesting it in the wild from the jungles of Otelyrn and shipping it half the world away.

The duty coach arrived at half-past fourth glass and proceeded to NordEste Design where I got out and walked to the door, shields in place, and then walked back with Seliora and Diestrya. I carried our daughter. Once we were back at the duty coach stop on Imagisle, Seliora carried Diestrya to the house, while I hurried south to the Collegium Quadrangle and then across it to the administrative building on the east side. Master Dichartyn was in his study, as he usually was between the fifth and sixth glass of the afternoon. I slipped into the chair in front of his writing desk.

"So . . . what can you tell me about the explosion?" He set down the sheets of paper he'd been reading and lifted his dark gray eyebrows.

"I'm supposed to get a full report from Jacquet tomorrow on the details, but it was a bomb with a defined blast pattern, and someone pinned a note on one Broussard D'Factorius after the blast. The note was ostensibly from

'Workers for Justice,' but otherwise unsigned . . ." I went on to tell him what else I knew.

"Broussard's a rather undistinguished factor except for two things," mused Dichartyn. "He's essentially a freeholder, as well as a factor, with close to enough lands to qualify as a High Holder, but he's rejected any approaches along those lines. He's also come afoul of a High Holder named Haebyn. Haebyn has been a fierce opponent of ancillary water rights, especially to freeholders who use them to produce grain in dry years."

"I think I need more of an explanation."

"Think of ancillary water rights as the right to divert excess water in high run-off times. Broussard has obtained considerable such rights on the Piedra River. This infuriated Haebyn, and he has tried to come up with every possible way to give grain shipments from High Holders priority on the ironway. He pressured Glendyl to delay delivery of locomotives to ironway companies that didn't provide that priority. There were even rumors that golds changed hands, and there were apparently some delays. Needless to say, Broussard was less than pleased about such efforts, and he persuaded Caartyl to push through an amendment to the Cartage Code that made granting priority on any commercial transport a matter only of shipping charges, with criminal penalties for violations, both for the carrier and anyone who attempted to obtain such a priority."

"You could only get priority if you wanted to pay for it?" That made sense to me; but then, my father was a factor.

Dichartyn nodded.

"What sort of pressure was Haebyn exerting?" I knew all too well what sorts of tactics High Holders could employ.

"Works engineers who suffered accidents. Delays in obtaining iron plate or tubing. Nothing fatal and nothing easily traceable. All well away from any of our collegia or even from any regionals. It all stopped once the code was amended."

"That suggests Broussard could have a few enemies, possibly beyond Haebyn. And Broussard had to go to Caartyl? I don't see why Glendyl wouldn't want to push such a proposal, and even if he didn't, what about the other factors on the Council, such as Reyner or Diogayn?"

"Glendyl doesn't want to call attention to himself or his manufacturing. He has the rights to the steam turbines all the newer Navy ships use. His engineers developed them, but he's managed to keep the processes to himself . . . as well as all the contracts."

"So he's the sole supplier to the Navy? And a councilor?"

"Solidar is far from perfect, Rhenn."

"But what about the other factors on the Council? Surely, they . . ."

"Do you know of many who go against the High Holders who don't risk their lives, Rhenn?"

"Point taken." I laughed, softly. Once I would have been mortified at the gentle correction.

"The Guild Councilors have more power, in a sense, because targeting a single member won't change matters that much; while individual factors, especially those with competitors, could lose much. Glendyl doesn't want to risk losing contracts worth hundreds of thousands of golds, but pressure on a Guild Councilor is just likely to make the others madder."

I could see that. "How many High Holders would have access to explosives experts?"

"I assume you're going to find out."

"I'll look into it, but since it didn't happen in my district. . . . You know how the Commander feels about that." And Cydarth, but I didn't say that. The subcommander and I tolerated each other.

"That's something Schorzat might know, also. I'll ask him." He paused and offered a smile. "You'll come to dinner on Vendrei night? Sixth glass? Aelys hoped you and Seliora would."

"We'll be there." I wanted to ask who else might be coming, but didn't. Dichartyn was still my superior in the Collegium, since technically I was merely on loan to the Civic Patrol.

Once I finished with Master Dichartyn—I didn't tell him about the elveweed, since there was no point to that, not yet—I hurried back to the house, just in time to sit down at the table in the breakfast room where we usually ate at night with Diestrya when we didn't have company. These days, that was usually the case.

Seliora said the blessing. "For the grace that we all owe each other, for the bounty of the earth of which we are about to partake, for good faith among all, and mercies great and small. For all these we offer thanks and gratitude, both now and ever more, in the spirit of that which cannot be named or imaged . . ."

"In peace and harmony," Diestrya and I replied.

Klysia set a covered casserole dish before me, and I looked to Seliora.

"Ragout paprikash. I had Klysia fix it with Grandmama Diestra's recipe. I had to write it out for her the other day."

"How is she doing? Mama Diestra, I mean? She looked tired when we were there for the dinner for Odelia and Kolasyn's son." I served Seliora some of the ragout, and then put a much smaller helping on Diestrya's plate.

"About the same. She's frail, but there's never been anything wrong with her mind."

I knew that all too well.

"She's already teaching Diestrya plaques. Our daughter can already shuffle . . . a small deck, anyway."

"I like placques," Diestrya affirmed.

"Definitely that Pharsi heritage," I said with a smile, serving myself, and pouring wine for the two of us from the carafe. It was a red Ryelan, courtesy of Iryela and Kandryl.

"The Pharsi heritage on my side," she countered. "I still say your family hid some Pharsi ancestors."

She was probably right about that, appalling as my mother might once have found it. So I just smiled. "Master Dichartyn and Aelys want us to come for dinner on Vendrei."

"We must be getting popular again. Mama and Papa wanted to know if we'd come to dinner on Samedi."

"That's because people have dinner guests more often when it gets cool. I'd like that, but I'll have to come from the station."

"You worked last Samedi."

"I know, but I'm switching with Alsoran, because his niece is getting married on Samedi."

"So long as it's just a switch."

That was a warning. "It is. Alsoran's very fair about that."

"Unlike Warydt," Seliora said, her mouth twisting as she said my former lieutenant's name.

"Something rather odd happened over the weekend . . ." I explained about the Place D'Opera explosion. ". . . and you might ask her if she knows anything about High Holder Haebyn or Factor Broussard."

Seliora shook her head, smiling. "She doesn't know every factor in Solidar. There are thousands of them. There are fewer High Holders, but there are still over a thousand of them, and that doesn't count family."

"A thousand and thirty-seven High Holders at the latest count."

"I'll ask her about both. Even the question from you will make her feel good."

"She might surprise us. Again."

We both laughed.

Mardi was a typical day, beginning with the usual hurry for Seliora and me—my exercises, dressing and getting Diestrya ready for the day, breakfast, the duty coach to our respective places of work, reviewing patroller performances, a glass or so walking with different patrollers. I didn't see either Jadhyl or Horazt, and that meant they hadn't found out anything about the explosion . . . and that they didn't have other problems of the sort that might concern me or the Patrol. Jacquet's report on the specifics of the Place D'Opera bomb arrived by messenger at the station late on Mardi afternoon. It didn't tell me much more than I already knew, except for the precision of the blast pattern.

Both Seliora and I were exhausted by the time we retired to our separate beds. Tired as I was, the time before I dropped off to sleep was the loneliest part of the day.

Meredi dawned gray and blustery, but it didn't rain while I was trying to keep in shape with Clovyl's exercises and four mille run, or even after I walked with Seliora and Diestrya to the duty carriage. Diestyra walked most of the way.

As on this morning, there were times when I couldn't escort them all the way to NordEste Design, but I tried to keep those to a minimum, and the only time they'd really be exposed was the short walk from the duty coach to the door. I hoped that an imager-obdurate driver was watching, and that it would be enough that my past actions suggested extremely high costs for anyone attacking my family. Also, there were few times when I didn't accompany them, which added an element of unpredictability.

Once I saw them off, I headed to the armory building, where I eventually found Shannyr in a small room filled with kegs and small square boxes. He was sitting at a work table with circular thin bronze disks on one side. On the other side were thicker bronze disks, each looking like a slice from a bronze cylinder.

"Master Rhennthyl." The imager second stood quickly, a worried expression on his face.

"Don't look so concerned," I said with a laugh. "I need your help."

"Mine?"

I explained about the bomb and showed him the diagram.

"Sir, I'm not an ordnance designer."

"I know that. I also know you're very observant, and that you probably understand a lot more than many imagers would guess that you know."

"Menyard is really the one who'd know, sir. He's the top ordnance designer."

"I'll talk to him next . . . but what do you think?"

"The pattern is V-shaped, and that means the blast was directed, but it really wasn't a shaped charge. I'd guess it was an ordnance-type powder because no one mentions a lot of smoke, and you'd have that with black powder."

"Thank you. Where would I find Menyard?"

"In the engineering studies on the second level on the south side. I think his is the one closest to the quadrangle."

"How is Ciermya? And the twins?"

"They're all fine, except both the twins are getting over the childpox, and she's had to stay home from work." He laughed. "She's ready for them to get well."

"I can imagine. I hope Diestrya doesn't get it . . . but with children, you can't ever tell."

"No, sir."

With a smile, I left. Shannyr had been a friend to me when I'd first come to the Collegium, and I hadn't forgotten that, although matters between our families were a bit awkward because Ciermya was scared to death of both Seliora and me.

I made my way to the staircase on the end of the building and climbed up. Although Menyard's door was ajar, I knocked.

"Come on in."

I did, and he hurried to his feet.

"Rhenn . . . or should I say Master Captain Rhennthyl? We don't see you very often any more. Kahlasa and I were actually talking about you this morning. She just left."

"Oh . . . I'm sorry I missed her. And . . . Rhenn is fine. I need your help." I handed him the diagram and the report. "Anything you can tell me will help."

As he took the papers, Menyard's only comment was "Hmmmm. Interesting." He sat back down at the broad table that served both as both desk and drafting board and began to study the report.

I didn't say a word, just seated myself in the straight-backed chair set at an angle to the broad desk set before a window looking toward the north end of the Collegium quadrangle.

After a time, he looked up. "I'd say that someone took a four-digit brass shell casing, shortened it, perhaps by half, and then flared it, packed the explosives inside, covered the explosives with metal filings or thin strips, and capped it with a lead cover, probably designed to break into segments. Most likely, the strips came from the part of the casing they cut down . . ."

"The explosive?"

"Some form of guncotton, Poudre B, I'd guess. The device was attached to the rear axle at an angle. They crimped the bracket holding the device in place. They planned for it to detonate fairly soon after they placed it. If they primed it with totally dry guncotton and an inertial friction spring, any jolt or sudden movement of the axle would trigger the primer."

That meant that the device was fixed to the carriage axle while the coachman was waiting to pick up Factor Broussard and his family. Since the coachman had been one of those killed, it was unlikely that he'd been part of the plan. Likewise, Broussard's cousin certainly wouldn't have wanted to lose both his coach, his coachman, and his team. "They must have scouted Lyrique and known where the pavement was rough."

"Seems right. If they used dry guncotton as a primer, they were also experts."

"We don't use it, do we?"

Menyard shook his head. "It's too dangerous. Even imaging it into place could cause an explosion. But guncotton is relatively easy to make, and there's enough Poudre B in the world that the powder wouldn't be that hard to get." He frowned. "The segmenting could have been done in a soft lead cover with the equivalent of a sharp knife."

What Menyard's analysis suggested was foreign assassins or covert agents. But why would they target a mere agricultural factor, albeit a wealthy one? "Is there anything else?"

Menyard shook his head and handed the report back. "Not from this." He paused, then added, "Anyone who could do this, Rhenn, could build a similar device that would shred even your shields."

"I got that feeling," I said dryly. "It's not a pleasant thought."

"Be careful. We've lost too many imagers over the past few years."

"I will."

Just as I left the armory, a young prime whom I didn't know hurried up to me.

"Master Rhennthyl, sir. Master Jhulian wanted to know if you could spare a moment for him."

"I'd be happy to. I'll be right there."

Jhulian was the justice for the Collegium and the maitre who'd pounded Solidaran law into my skull years earlier. What did he want? Sometimes, he also sat as a member of the Solidaran High Justiciary when it reviewed lower justicing procedures. Was there something he wanted to know about the Civic Patrol? Whatever it was, as I walked across the quadrangle, I hoped that it wouldn't take too long. He had a study just down the hallway from Maitre Dichartyn in the administration and receiving building, and his door was open.

"Do come in, Rhenn."

I closed the door behind me and slipped into one of the chairs across the desk from him. "What can I do for you?"

"Let's start with young Shault first, Rhenn. He isn't exactly excelling in will-ingness to understand the role of law and how it applies to the Collegium."

"You'd like me to talk to him."

"It couldn't hurt. At times, he won't really listen to either me or Dichartyn. You're the only one he'll really listen to, polite as he is."

That had been a problem from the first, and after Shault had made secondus, Maitre Dichartyn had become his preceptor instead of Master Ghaend. That had helped a great deal, but not totally. "That's a combination of the Collegium and the taudis."

"Combination or not, he'll end up like Floryn, or in a dead-end armory position."

I still remembered Floryn. He'd been executed by Master Jhulian just weeks after I'd come to Imagisle. "I'll talk to him tonight."

"Good." He paused, then brushed back a lock of his white-and-blond hair, before saying, "I was talking to Rholyn the other day, and he mentioned that, by the end of the year, the Council will have to decide on whether to re-appoint Commander Artois. What has been your experience with the Com-mander?"

"I'm sure that my opinion would be similar to that of Master Dichartyn." If the matter were as straightforward as the question appeared to be, Jhulian wouldn't have even bothered to ask me. He just would have asked Dichartyn.

He smiled, if coolly. "I thought you might say something like that. Might I ask you why you answered that way?"

I offered an off-hand shrug. "If it's as simple as it sounds, you could just have asked Master Dichartyn. This suggests that you or Rholyn want to be able to claim that you didn't talk to Dichartyn about it. That suggests that someone

is unhappy with Artois and knows that Master Dichartyn would support him."
I still didn't know why what I thought mattered in the slightest, especially to
the Council.

"Or it might be that we want to claim that Master Dichartyn didn't influence you."

While I certainly listened to Master Dichartyn, we'd just as certainly dis-
agreed on matters over the years. "My opinion is fairly direct. Artois is an
honest and effective commander who has always put the Civic Patrol above
anything."

"That's a rather sweeping statement, Rhenn."

"The Patrol is his identity. I doubt that he could let anything destroy or
damage it, if it were in his power to stop such damage."

"That could be dangerous, could it not, if he felt someone or some group
were out to disband or replace the Patrol?"

"Who's on the Council who's opposed to my being a Patrol Captain?"

Jhulian laughed. "Maitre Poincaryt said you'd say that. Why do you think
that?"

"Artois doesn't like me. He never has. He does respect my ability and my
concern for the Patrol, and he thinks I'm good for the Patrol at present. So . . .
who is backing Cydarth as his replacement . . . or as the director or head of another civil enforcement agency?" I watched Jhulian closely.

He turned his hands up, simulating helplessness. "I'm sure I don't know
what you're talking about."

I shook my head. "What do you and Maitre Poincaryt want me to watch
out for?"

"I don't believe we've asked for anything. It would, of course, be in the
interests of the Collegium that Commander Artois and the Patrol remain as
they are, at least for the next several years." He stood. "I'm certain you'll wish
to talk to Master Dichartyn, but he won't be back until tomorrow night."

"Do you know where he is?"

"As you should know, Rhenn, he seldom reveals his destinations, except
to the Maitre of the Collegium."

After I left Jhulian, I walked over to the dining hall, and left a note in
Shault's letterbox telling him that I'd meet him in the hallway off the dining
area at half-past fifth glass. Then, since I was on the east side of Imagisle, I
walked across the Bridge of Hopes and caught a hack to take me to the station.
I couldn't justify taking a duty coach, not when I used one so much anyway.
And now I had something else to worry about.

In the hack, I pondered over what Jhulian had asked, what he had hinted, and what he had not said. The implication was clear that someone on the Council, or several someones, didn't want Artois continuing as Commander. Some of that might revolve around me, but certainly not all. Alsoran might know some of the rumors, but he wouldn't know the Council side of matters.

He met me just outside my study. "Captain."

I gestured for him to follow me inside. "Close the door, if you would."

He did. We both sat down.

"Have you heard anything about someone wanting to replace Commander Artois?"

Alsoran didn't say anything for a moment. He wasn't the kind to reply immediately, but rather to think over what anyone said. I appreciated that quality and tried to emulate it, not always very successfully, as I'd shown earlier in dealing with Jhulian.

"Not in anything like those kind of words. Barcuyt—he's Hostyn's lieutenant—mentioned that the Council had to confirm Commander Artois for another five-year term before long. I didn't think much about it. That was after the lieutenants' meeting at headquarters last month."

I waited. Alsoran often took his time.

"All the captains and the subcommander have to be reconfirmed," he added.

"I'll be up for that a year from now," I said.

"The strange thing was that one of the other lieutenants—I can't think of his name, but he's the one from Second District—he was asking Barcuyt if he'd likely replace Hostyn. Not out in the open, but later, when they were alone, outside waiting for a hack, and I was coming down the steps. I didn't think it was any of my business so I didn't even look their way."

"That's interesting," I mused. "Have you heard anything else?"

"No, sir. Not a thing."

After Alsoran left, I went on to the more routine aspects of my day, if anything in the Civic Patrol was totally routine. The next few glasses were as uneventful as any Patrol captain's time might be. That is, there were arrests and malefactors dispatched by wagon to headquarters for charging. There were two muggings on the northern section of the Midroad in Third District, both of shopgirls careless with their wallets. And, of course, both happened while I was on the other side of the district, accompanying Recyrt and Fuast on their rounds along Saenhelyn Road. I also received a dispatch from Sub-commander Cydarth asking if Third District had discovered anything that might shed light on the explosion. That request crossed my earlier report to Commander Artois summarizing what Menyard had told me, although I had merely referred to "ordnance experts at the Collegium."

The only thing out of the ordinary was that Smultyn and Caesaro found two dead elvers dumped in the street near where Quierca crossed Mando. Both elvers' faces were contorted in pain, and they stunk of elveweed. There was no way to tell for certain, but it was likely that they'd had too much of the bad weed that Horazt had warned of, since they had no wounds, bruises, or other obvious causes of death. For a moment, I had thoughts that we might actually have fewer cases of disturbance and assaults by elvers, but that wouldn't happen. Elvers, like all addicts, or most people, for that matter, didn't really think things happened to them. Everyone else, but not them.

Horazt had warned me about the bad elveweed, but there was one question I hadn't thought to ask, and that was whether the dealers in the other taudis were getting the same weed. I doubted he'd even know. Still, it was something to keep in mind . . . and watch.

The duty coach arrived on time, and Seliora and Diestrya were waiting for me in the lower front foyer at NordEste Design. I took Diestrya by the hand as we walked down the steps and out to the coach.

"Did you find out anything about the explosion?" Seliora asked, once we were in the coach and headed to Imagisle.

"Menyard confirmed that it was designed and planted by an expert. I still don't have any idea who would go to all that trouble for a wealthy factor." I couldn't help shaking my head. "If he had High Holders as enemies, they wouldn't use explosives, and neither would a workers' group. It looks like foreign agents, but everyone else would know that as well."

"So it's someone who wants it to look like foreign agents, maybe Ferran agents, since the Council has backed the Jariolans—"

"Only because the Ferrans attacked our warships. Nearly half the Council was very unhappy about having to support the Oligarch, and they won't want to get involved if war flares up again. You're suggesting Jariolan agents pretending to be Ferrans? What about Ferrans pretending to be Jariolans pretending to be Ferrans? That's wheels within wheels."

Seliora nodded. "It's never simple."

She was right about that.

"There's another problem . . ." I explained about the elveweed. "Is there any way some of your family contacts can find out if Third District is the only taudis getting the fresher weed?"

"Grandmama isn't in touch as much, now, but . . . that might be something Mama could ask about. It also wouldn't hurt to let people know she's aware of that. I'll ask her tomorrow."

"How about your day?" I asked.

"Alhyral D'Haestyr sent his bride-to-be to commission a dining set for the town house he purchased. She's actually rather nice."

I recalled Alhyral all too well. He'd propositioned Seliora before we'd been married. "I just can't imagine why he didn't come."

"You're as bad as any Pharsi," she replied with a laugh.

"You've always claimed I had a Pharsi background," I countered. "Is it a good commission?"

"Very good, and Shomyr can do all the turning with his new lathes."

"Who is Alhyral's finance?"

"Her name is Dhelora D'Zaerlyn-Alte. She's from around Rivages." Seliora paused. "She did know who you were. She made a quiet point of that."

"What exactly did she say?"

"Not much. She just said that her aunt had said you were the first master imager ever to serve in the Civic Patrol. She seemed very bright, far better than Alhyral deserves."

"She doubtless doesn't have much choice."

"No. Few of the High Holders' daughters do."

I couldn't help but wonder who her aunt happened to be, but it could have been some relation of Iryela or even of Alynkya D'Ramsael . . . or of Madame D'Shendael or someone I didn't even know.

Again, after we reached Imagisle, as Seliora walked Diestrya home, I hurried back south along the west side of the quadrangle. Shault was waiting by the letterboxes opposite the dining hall.

"Master Rhennthyl."

"We'll use the conference room here. We need to talk."

"Yes, sir."

Shault was as dark-haired as his "uncle" Horazt, but his eyes were hazel, and he was taller. At age fifteen, after six years of training at the Collegium, he was also healthier and in better physical condition.

I sat at the end of the table, and he took the seat to my right.

"I've been talking to Maitre Jhulian. He's not exactly pleased with your progress with the Code."

"It's so dull, sir. That makes it hard to concentrate."

With that, I could sympathize. I'd felt the same way, but it didn't matter. "Let me see if I can make it clearer and provide some motivation. Just what is justice?"

"The rendering of what is right, owed, or due. That's what the book says."

"The root of the word lies in a Bovarian word meaning 'law,' " I pointed out. "What does that tell you?"

Shault looked puzzled. "That law should be just? That's obvious."

"Who defines what is just? Is it the Nameless?"

"Advocates . . . the Council."

"Who writes the laws? Who carries them out?" I pressed.

"People, sir. Patrollers, imagers."

"Laws are made by people, and they're carried out by people. So is it wrong for a master imager or a Civic Patrol Captain to quietly create justice, especially when the laws don't seem fair?"

Shault just looked at me blankly.

"What's the difference between my enforcing justice and when an ancient rex did it?"

"You're both imposing your will," Shault pointed out.

"That's true, but there's a fundamental difference. What is it?"

"Who could remove the rex?"

"And?"

Shault's face brightened. "You have to answer to Master Dichartyn and the Maitre of the Collegium."

"Or, as a Patrol Captain, to Commander Artois and to the laws enacted by the Council. Even, in the end, the Collegium has to answer to the Council. To whom does the Council answer?"

"Well . . . the guild representatives answer to their guilds. The factors represent the other factors, and the High Holders on the Council answer to the other High Holders."

"In total . . . what does that mean? To whom, in general, does the Council answer?"

"The people, I guess," Shault said slowly. "But . . . no one person can tell the Council what to do."

"Let's get back to my question. Is it wrong for a master imager to create justice, as opposed to following or enforcing the law?"

"Aren't they the same?"

"Are they?"

Shault got that confused look on his face again. "No . . . but . . ."

"Is what I think just the same as what you think is just? Or what Horazt thinks is just? Or what a factor in Tilbora thinks is just?"

"They should be."

"Are they?"

"No, sir."

"So why shouldn't I as a master imager and a Patrol Captain do what I think is just if it conflicts with the law?"

"Oh . . ."

I forced myself to wait.

"Are you saying that laws are written to make sure everyone knows what is just?"

"Not quite."

Shault looked blank . . . again.

I repressed a sigh. "Write me an essay explaining in logical terms what any Patrol Captain should do when he finds that what he believes to be just is in conflict with the law. Then explain why he should do that. Leave it in my letterbox here by Vendrei evening."

"Sir . . ."

"It's more than enough time."

"Sir . . . that wasn't what I was going to say. You got me thinking. You're changing the taudis in Third District, aren't you? You're accountable to the Collegium and the Council, and you're trying to make the taudischefs accountable to you so that they'll follow the law more."

"You're right, but the problem is that I'm making them accountable through fear of my abilities, not out of respect for the law itself and the reasons behind it. As a Patrol Captain, I don't have time to make each one of them think." And some of them never would, and would only respect force. I knew that, but it still bothered me. "I can only hope that they'll see that things are better when more people follow the law." I stood. "I need to go home, and I'm sure you have lessons to prepare."

"Yes, sir."

I hoped he would come to understand, sooner or later, the balance between justice and codified law, and the narrow line that imagers always walked.

I hurried back to the house, hoping that Seliora hadn't had too much trouble with a hungry daughter.

On Jeudi morning, after the four mille run, I loitered just enough to catch Baratyn, for whom I'd worked briefly as a member of the Collegium's covert imagers at the Council Chateau some six years earlier.

"How is the Council handling the heating up of the Jariolan-Ferran hostilities?"

"How do they always handle things until they have to act? They're talking and talking. You shouldn't have forgotten that." He laughed, although he was still a bit out of breath.

"Does anyone there even remember me?"

He frowned, paused, then replied, "As a matter of fact . . . the other day, Councilor Caartyl asked how you were doing as a Patrol Captain. He said you'd proved that artisan enterprise was possible, even in the taudis, and that not everything new had to be larger and operated with less skill and craft. I couldn't say anything to that." Baratyn shrugged. "What did he mean by that?"

"Oh . . . I managed to get people interested in building a small paper mill and a woodworks. They barely break even, but it's helped some taudis-youths get apprentice positions."

"You come from a factoring family, don't you?"

I laughed. "I'd never be any good at it. I found other people who are. Has anyone else said anything?"

"No . . . except for Martyl and Dartazn. They'd like to have you back. Dartazn says things are too quiet."

"I don't think they'll stay that way."

"I'll keep that in mind, sir. If you'll excuse me?"

"Of course."

As he trotted off, I managed to collect myself. Baratyn was a Maitre D'Aspect, a master imager in his own right, and I'd once reported to him. He'd been very friendly until I'd made my last comment, and he'd almost frozen, and then hurried off. What had that been about? I'd have to think about it, but I needed to get back to the house and get ready for the day.

Diestrya was already up and active, and that meant dressing and breakfast were the usual rush. We didn't say much beyond the necessary until we were in the duty coach and crossing the Bridge of Desires.

"Have you started working on the design for the upholstery fabric for young Haestyr's bridal dining set?"

"She won't be back to look at the proposed designs until next week."

"How many chairs does he want?"

"Twenty-two side chairs, two end chairs."

"Did I do something wrong?"

"What?" Seliora turned and shook her head. "No. I have a lot to think about in balancing what we've promised. We're either without enough work or swamped with more than we can handle."

I had the feeling those were the two normal states of human affairs. "At least, the twins can help with Diestrya."

"At times, she wears them down as well. Bhenyt's the one who can calm her down, and so can Grandmama, but Diestrya tires her out quickly. Our daughter's at that age where she's bored quickly."

"That's an age all children are at until they have responsibilities of their own . . . and children."

Seliora sighed. "She's your daughter in that."

Unfortunately, I knew that.

Once I'd left NordEste Design, I quickly read through both *Veritum* and *Tableta*. According to a story below the fold in *Veritum*, the Ferrans had not only produced large numbers of their improved land-cruisers, but were moving them up to their border with Jariola. In turn, the Oligarch had canceled all leave for Jariolan troops and moved several battalions west within an easy march of Ferran territory. The Abierto Isles were loudly pleading neutrality, and the Council was debating reinforcing the northern fleet, currently deployed around the coaling station off Jariola that Solidar had acquired from Jariola during the last round of hostilities in partial payment for Solidaran support.

There was a short story in *Tableta* about the increasing number of violent crimes in the taudis areas across Solidar, but no speculation about the reasons, and no mention of tainted elveweed. Another short story mentioned another case of arson—this time the grain warehouses in the area near Piedryn—and an instance where the lower level of another warehouse was flooded by the failure of a retaining wall alongside an adjoining millrace. The story didn't say who owned the warehouses, but I was getting the impression there was a definite problem with grain warehouses.

I'd barely settled into my study at the station when the morning courier run from headquarters brought various documents and reports, as well as a brief note from Commander Artois thanking me for the report on the explosion and asking to be informed of any other developments that might bear on the case. Since I didn't have any, not yet, I could put off replying until I got another officious communiqué from the subcommander.

After that, I reviewed the log and duty books, checking on what had happened since I'd left the station the afternoon before, and then I made a quick inspection. The holding cells were empty, although it was rare to have anyone there from late morning until late afternoon or early evening, since most offenders were picked up from afternoon on, and any offender brought in overnight was dispatched to headquarters for formal charging right after the morning shift change on the headquarters collection wagon.

Next came a review of the station accounts, and various other oversight chores, before I could leave the station.

Jaerdol and Zandyr were the two patrollers on the day shift who had the taudis round just east of the station—the blocks that Horazt called "his." I caught up with them just short of Dugalle a glass after midday.

"Captain, sir."

"What troubles do you have today?" I asked cheerfully.

"Nothing today," replied Jaerdol.

"That's good, too, sir, after yesterday," added Zandyr. "It took the both of us to handle that fellow who tried to cut Musario. Sure made a mess of his bistro, but he's got it cleaned up already."

"He gave you a meal today?" I grinned.

"Well, sir, he did offer, and . . . he said he'd already set it up."

"I hope it was good." I wouldn't have dared to eat the high-spiced Staka-naran food that Musario served. "Just don't let his gratitude become a habit."

"Oh no, sir."

We turned down Mando, which ran northeast to southwest, as did most of the streets between South Middle and Quierca in Third District. I had to admit that the dwellings on both sides looked better than they had five years earlier. Now, none of the windows were boarded up, and most had shutters.

I could still smell hints of elveweed though, much as I'd tried to get the taudischefs to discourage it. The only thing that the three had agreed on was that children still in school shouldn't be allowed to smoke it. It had taken a few beatings and the disappearance of two young dealers several years back—so I'd heard—to make that stick. I'd definitely turned a blind eye—or ear—to that rumor. I didn't see much point in trying to find whoever had gotten rid of someone who wanted to turn schoolchildren into elvers. Besides, I never knew who the missing dealers were, or even where their bodies might be found. But now, as Horazt had pointed out, no one ever saw the dealers, only their runners.

From the alleyway on the right, I heard footsteps, and I turned quickly.

"Master Rhennthyl! Help! Help!" The woman was carrying a child wearing a stained and worn blue jersey and crudely sewn trousers. He looked to be about Diestrya's age, with a thin and angular face, without any baby fat, but he might have been older, because the taudis-children tended to be smaller. The child was convulsing, but not vomiting or choking. His face was contorting in a way that reminded me of the dead elvers.

"He's not choking! There's nothing in his mouth . . ." She thrust the child at me.

I didn't take him. Holding him wasn't going to help the boy. "What did he eat?"

The woman looked at me, fear in her eyes.

"Did he chew on some elveweed?"

"He . . . he . . ."

"Yes or no?" I snapped.

"Maybe . . . I didn't see."

The child spasmed into another convulsion, so violently that his mother barely could hold him.

I'd imaged items and substances into people, with often deadly results, and I'd imaged items in and out of a cadaver, but I'd never tried to image something out of a living person. But unless I did something, the boy was going to die. He might anyway.

I took one deep breath, then concentrated, trying to recall exactly all that Master Draffyd had shown me, trying to visualize removing whatever was in his stomach, without touching the lining or anything else. The quick wave of dizziness that passed over me indicated that I'd done something, and I was almost afraid to look at the boy, but he was still shuddering. So I hadn't killed him outright.

Even as I watched, the convulsions began to subside, but he continued to breathe. I reached out and touched his forehead. It was hot.

The mother looked to me, then down at the boy.

"I did what I could."

We kept watching. Finally, he moaned. "Mama . . . Mama . . ."

She looked at me once again, her eyes wide.

"Don't let him eat anything spicy. Just plain heavy bread for a day or two."

She nodded, but her face was white, although tears oozed from the corners of her eyes.

When she left, cuddling her son, and murmuring to him, I stood there for a moment. I could only hope I hadn't damaged him permanently in some way that wouldn't show up until later.

Jaerdol and Zandyr just looked at me as I rejoined them.

"Sir? What did you do?"

"I tried to image some elveweed he ate out of his stomach. I hope it works."

"He was about to die. He looks better now," Jaerdol said.

"He might have gotten better anyway," I pointed out.

The two looked at each other.

If the boy lived, there would be another story . . . and more problems. Either way, I needed to talk to Master Draffyd, the imager and doctor at the Collegium. If word got around Third District, who knew who else might come running, and for what. It was just another example of why Master Dichartyn and Maitre Poincaryt were always stressing the importance of doing things in a way that looked like you were doing something innocuous. What I really should have done was to have taken the boy, imaged out the elveweed fragments he'd chewed, probably because he wasn't being fed enough, and then thumped him on the back and claimed that he'd just been choking.

But, again, I'd been caught short and hadn't been able to think that quickly.

"You'd think that imagers can do anything." I laughed. "We can't."

That brought dubious looks from both patrollers.

"Come on," I said. "You have a round to cover, and I need you two to tell me what you've seen recently in each block." I pointed to the second house ahead on the right. "What can you tell me about that one?" That was probably unfair, because I knew that the eldest boy was a quartermaster third in the Navy, because I'd gotten him to enlist before a conscription team drafted him, and that he sent a pay allotment home to his widowed mother. The younger brother was a bigger problem.

"She's got one boy still at home," said Zandyr, "and an aunt living with her. The boy's a loose cannon. Horazt won't even touch him . . ."

We continued on the round.

When I finally returned to the station, it was close to a quarter past second glass, and four patrollers were walking toward the duty desk from the holding cells.

"What happened?" I asked.

"A dray horse spooked and pulled a brick wagon into a spirit wagon," offered Alsoran, who was following the four, "on South Middle just west of the Plaza."

"Don't tell me. In the mess, some of the taudis-kids tried to steal the spirits, and the two teamsters got into a fight, and then the avenue got clogged up, and the cutpurses showed up . . ."

I glanced from Alsoran to Smultyn, whose tunic was smeared in grime.

"Close enough, sir. One of the taudis-toughs caused the brick wagon's dray horse to spook. We had to chase him, but we got him."

"How old does he look?"

"Old enough that he can't plead for the Army or Navy."

"And the others?"

"Petty theft, except for one assault. The brick teamster's in there, too. He tried to take a knife to the spirit wagon guard. Guard cold-cocked him."

I couldn't help frowning at that.

"It was a set-up," suggested Smultyn. "He paid the tough to spook the horse, and he guided it so the brick wagon sideswiped the spirit wagon. That's why all the kids were waiting. The guard accused him of that, and the knife came out."

"Do we know if he's the regular teamster? I'd wager he's not." I took a deep breath, because from the Patrol's viewpoint, it didn't matter.

"Oh . . . and there was one other thing," Alsoran added, with a wry smile.

"Both wagons were overloaded for their axle types?"

He nodded. "We had to cite them both. The Patrol teamsters came out and drove them to the holding yards."

That meant another complaint to the Council, because none of the traders and factors liked having to comply with the weight limits. The wagon owners would pay to get the wagons and teams back, but they knew Commander Artois wouldn't ever relent. His niece had been killed by a runaway overloaded wagon. So they petitioned the Council, but the Council had refused to change the law.

The rest of the afternoon, what was left of it, was far less eventful.

Desalyt was the duty driver who picked me up outside the station. As I was about to enter the coach, he handed me an envelope. I didn't open it until I was inside and headed toward NordEste Design.

The single line on the sheet read, "My study before dinner, please." It was signed with a single "D."

I didn't even want to speculate. But . . . was it about the inevitable resumption of war between Ferrum and Jariola? Or some follow-up about the explosion? Or something else entirely? Whatever it happened to be, it would complicate life.

I barely managed to get to the covered portico at NordEste Design before Seliora hurried out with Diestrya, closing the door behind her with a firmness just short of slamming it.

I decided against saying anything for a moment and took Diestrya's hand so that we both walked her to the coach, unseen imager shields protecting all of us.

Once Desalyt had turned the coach off Nordroad and we were headed southwest on the Boulevard D'Ouest toward the Nord Bridge over the Aluse, I finally asked, "What happened?"

"Are you trying to soothe me?"

"No. I can see you're upset about something. I thought you might want to talk about it."

Seliora glanced down at Diestrya, then shook her head. "Later."

After we'd covered another few blocks, I said, reluctantly, "I'm going to have to stop and see Master Dichartyn before dinner."

"Again? You've had to . . ." Seliora broke off the sentence.

"He doesn't ask unless it's important."

"Important to him."

"I know." I offered a helpless shrug. Maitre Dichartyn was my superior in the Collegium.

Once the duty coach came to a halt at its post on the west side of Imagisle, I did hurry down to the administration building.

Master Dichartyn was standing by the window of his study when I entered, but he did not speak until I closed the door.

"You've seen the newsheets, have you not?"

"I have. To which problem are you going to direct my attention?" I didn't feel like guessing.

"Grain warehouses. You might recall that I mentioned a High Holder Haebyn. The two warehouses that were destroyed and damaged were his."

"So we now have a subterranean conflict between eastern High Holders and freeholders? I assume the grain factors are on the side of the freeholders. Are they?"

"Wouldn't you rather deal with a freeholder than a High Holder?"

"Is this because river flows are down, and the freeholders have bought out water rights? Or is it because grain production is up and the freeholders can underprice the High Holders?"

"Something along those lines," Dichartyn replied. "In dry years, the High

Holders have more water, but in good water years the freeholders can under-price the High Holders to the point where the High Holders lose golds."

"That's very interesting, but what's the connection between that and the Collegium and one Civic Patrol Captain?"

"Nothing . . . yet. Except for one thing: the report of Broussart's death was in error. He was apparently called away and let one of his assistants take his wife and daughter to the opera."

"You're suggesting that he planned the explosion to implicate Haebyn? And he killed his own wife and daughter to do it?"

"He and his wife were not on the best of terms. Apparently, his wife and the assistant were."

I could see that Dichartyn had been busy. "You won't find much in the way of proof. Captain Jacquet won't, either."

"No. I don't expect anyone will. I just thought you'd like to know." He smiled. "One other thing, Rhenn. I don't believe your wife has ever been to a Council Ball, has she?"

"No, sir."

"It's time we remedied that." He handed me a heavy parchment envelope. "That's an invitation for you and your wife as a guest of High Councilor Suyrien. You do have formal wear, and I'm certain Seliora will be radiant."

"What am I supposed to be looking for?" I asked dryly.

"If Suyrien and I knew, Rhenn, both you and Seliora wouldn't be there."

"What should I tell her . . . besides that?"

"That's all."

"There's one thing you should know, sir, if you don't. Some of the elve-weed coming into L'Excelsis is tainted or poisoned . . ." I gave him a short ex-planation, but not what I'd asked Seliora's family to find out. Then I left and hurried to see if I could find Draffyd, but he'd already left the infirmary.

When I reached the house, Seliora met me in the front foyer. "Dinner's not quite ready. Klysia said it won't be long. There's an envelope on the re-ceiving tray, but I didn't know who it was for. I thought I'd wait to open it until you got here."

I glanced down to see Diestrya clinging to Seliora's trousers. I reached down and scooped her up. "There! Dada's got you."

She giggled.

Seliora lifted the envelope from the silver tray on the sideboy, then opened it.

I moved closer to Seliora and looked over her shoulder, trying to read the words while maintaining a hold on a very active and squirming Diestrya.

"Dada . . . want to see."

"In a moment, dear . . ." I tried to offer a placating tone as I struggled to catch the words of the note.

> Kandryl and I would very much appreciate it if you would join us for a private
> dinner on Samedi, the twenty-eighth of Feuillyt, with just one other couple,
> his brother and Mistress Alynkya D'Ramsael . . .

"That's sweet of her," offered Seliora, lowering the note. "It's been a while since we've been out to her estate."

"Two busy weekends . . ." I mused.

"Oh . . . ?"

"The following Vendrei we're expected to be at the Council's Autumn Ball," I said, extracting the envelope that Master Dichartyn had given me from my imager grays.

Seliora looked at the envelope and the seal, raising her eyebrows.

"I'm told that's the seal of High Councilor Suyrien. That was why Master Dichartyn wanted to see me."

With only the slightest frown, Seliora opened the envelope, breaking the seal, and extracting the heavy card.

"We're invited as guests of the High Councilor? That's only three weeks away! I don't have anything to wear . . ."

I managed not to choke openly. My darling wife had a dozen outfits that would out-dazzle any that I'd seen at previous balls.

"Why this year?" asked Seliora. "*We* haven't been asked before. You, but not us."

"Master Dichartyn handed me the invitation when I met with him tonight, and I asked him the same thing. He only said that both High Councilor Suyrien and he wanted us both there. Even when I pressed him, he wouldn't say."

"So now I'm supposed to help the Collegium?" Her words were tart.

"You have all along," I pointed out.

"Do you think he wanted us to have the Ball invitation on the same day as Iryela's invitation . . . or at least no later than that? But how would he know? Oh . . . he got the invitation from Suyrien, and the Councilor must have known what his sons were doing."

"He doesn't do much without a purpose. It could be that he didn't want to give it to us tomorrow at his house."

"You don't really think that, do you?"

"No," I admitted.

"Mother will be pleased. Especially if I don't tell her it's to help the Collegium."

"I suspect your grandmother will be even more so. She won't say anything, though."

"No . . . she won't."

A small bell chimed, Klysia's way of reminding us that dinner was ready, and I'd still have to talk to Seliora about what had upset her . . . after Diestrya was in bed.

It wasn't until more than two glasses later, after dinner and getting Diestrya to bed, before Seliora and I sat down in the family parlor, in front of the old iron stove with ornate castings, whose heat was slowly fading, if still radiating warmth into the room. We hadn't lit any lamps, but we could still see each other by the light oozing from the mica lenses at the top of the stove.

"What were you so upset about when you left your family's place this afternoon?" I asked.

"Odelia."

"You two usually get along." In fact, I'd never heard of a time when they didn't. They'd been as close as sisters the whole time I'd known Seliora.

"It's about Haerasyn."

"Kolasyn's younger brother, the problem one? What's he done now?"

"He's an elver. Not too serious, but . . . Odelia heard about some of the elveweed being poisoned. She wanted to know why you couldn't stop the smuggling and the smoking. I told her that you were fortunate to be able to find out about it, and that she or Kolasyn should tell Haerasyn."

"And?"

"She said that Haerasyn didn't listen to his brother or to his brother's family, especially not to Pharsis tied up with imagers."

"That's Haerasyn's problem, not Odelia's or Kolasyn's."

"Haerasyn's never been . . . very practical."

I wondered if that was because everyone had sheltered him, because he could be so charming, the way my own brother had been.

"Haerasyn can be very sweet, like Kolasyn. Odelia likes Haerasyn, and so does Kolasyn. They're worried, and they can't do anything. They think you can." Seliora squeezed my hand, but her eyes were sad.

"So I'm supposed to halt a trade no one has ever been able to stop because suddenly her husband's brother might lose his life because he's addicted to elveweed . . . and it's your fault if I don't?"

"That's about it. She didn't say it. Not that way. She said that it was interesting what you could and couldn't do."

"Oh . . . I can survive bullets and explosions, even if they break my ribs and nearly kill me, and I've worked with three taudischefs for over six years so that I finally know a few things before they get worse, but I'm supposed to stop a trade in a weed that people have been smoking for hundreds of years all by myself . . . when they're the ones choosing to smoke it?"

"I agree with you, dearest," Seliora said gently, "but . . ."

"Odelia doesn't feel that way, and she's your cousin, and she's looking at you as if it's all your fault because your husband won't do something to save poor addicted Haerasyn. No wonder you were upset." I paused. "What does your mother think?"

"She agrees. You know how practical she is. She just tells me to ignore Odelia about the whole thing, but Odelia kept bringing it up yesterday and today, every chance she got."

"Have they found out anything about the fresher elveweed?"

"No. That will take a few days." Seliora yawned. "You're thinking that someone is sending some of the poisoned weed just to the dealers supplying Third District?"

"I couldn't say. It's too fresh to have come from Caenen or Otelyrn, and I don't see how anyone could grow enough under glass or in the Sud Swamp to supply much of Solidar."

"But why would anyone poison just some of the weed? No one important smokes it, and no one with any factoring or holder connections makes golds from it."

"Not that we know."

"Do you really think . . . ?"

I shook my head. "I don't know enough. It might not mean anything at all, but I'd still like to find out."

"What about the Ferrans?"

"They'll attack, sooner or later. They think that the Jariolans are weak and corrupt."

"Are they?" Seliora yawned again.

"They're corrupt. That doesn't mean they're weak." I took her hands and stood. "You've had a long day, and you're about to fall asleep."

"I know . . . but I like the quiet times, talking to you. We don't have that many of them these days."

That was all too true, between my schedule and Diestrya.

Even so, we climbed the stairs hand-in-hand, and then got ready for bed. Once we were in Seliora's bed, holding each other—and more—helped alleviate my feeling that the relative stability and comfort we'd enjoyed for the past few years was about to vanish . . . and not because of anything that either of us had done.

In the end, of course, we kissed and parted, and I returned to my small sleeping room and cold sheets . . . with the hope that my sleep would be pleasant, or at least dreamless.

Fog had settled around Imagisle, and I was walking southward through the dank and thick gray mist from the house toward the quadrangle to meet with Maitre Poincaryt and Master Dichartyn. I could barely see a yard or two in front of me, and I didn't know what they wanted.

Somewhere overhead in the distance, thunder rumbled, then died away.

Ahead, I saw a figure in a cloak. The cloak could have been either dark gray or black, but whoever stood there on the stone walkway did not move as I neared.

"Hello, there," I offered.

There was no response, nor did the figure still move.

I was close enough to make out the hood, but for some reason I couldn't make out the face within it.

A blinding flash dazzled me, leaving glittering flashes in my eyes. Then, a deafening crash numbed and shook me. The figure in the cloak still did not speak, and instead of a face under the hood, I could only see darkness. Suddenly, as I watched, the cloak collapsed into a heap on the stone walk . . . and huge gray stones began falling out of the misty sky, all around me.

I sat bolt upright in bed, sweat pouring from my forehead. I could smell something, but, after I lit the bedside lamp, a quick check of my sleeping chamber reassured me that whatever I'd imaged in my nightmare hadn't set anything on fire.

Rather than wake Seliora, because she'd looked so tired, and we'd stayed up far longer than we should have, I eased out of my bed and walked to the window. When I looked out, I could see that there was no fog. The stars were shining in a clear sky, and Artiema was half full and casting her pearly light on the lawn and walls below.

Fog? Figures that weren't? Stones falling out of the sky?

Why had I dreamed something like that?

I was afraid I knew. Even if I couldn't logically explain it all, I had a definite sense that troubles lay ahead for both me and the Collegium.

Eventually, I did cool down and go back to sleep.

I wasn't totally surprised when I woke on Vendrei to see a dark line etched in the stone of the wall beyond the foot of my bed. It didn't look like much, just a jagged black line. After opening the bedchamber door, I concentrated on imaging the gray stone to its unmarked appearance, and the line vanished. That small bit of imaging did give me a trace of a headache, which I ignored as I dressed in my exercise clothes, and then slipped out of the house to make my way to join Clovyl, who had added some time spent on refresher training in hand-to-hand combat.

When I finally returned to the house, between the effects of exercise, running, and a cool shower, I felt the future might be less foreboding. I was glad to see that Seliora looked more rested when I joined them at the table, but the headache didn't totally disappear until after I ate.

I just concentrated on being cheerful during breakfast and on the trip to NordEste Design. There certainly wasn't anything Seliora could do about worries I couldn't even explain, nor was there anything more I could say or do to address the problem she faced with Odelia. All I could do was to talk to her and Diestrya and make both of them feel special for the time we had together that morning.

Once I had left them safely at NordEste Design, I read through the newsheets quickly. While the stories speculated on what might happen between Ferrum and Jariola, nothing had yet occurred. Nor had there been any more burned or damaged grain warehouses—not reported in the newsheets, anyway. The most interesting story was about the drowning death of a rising young Caenenan priest who had been trying to build a theo-political movement against the High Priest of Duodeus—effectively the ruler of tropical Caenen. Because Solidar had reached a practical and trade accommodation with Caenen, after having removed the previous High Priest, the drowning suggested the fine hand of one of Schorzat's field operatives. The shortest story in *Veritum* nagged at me. Little more than three sentences long, it stated that the Council would be considering revising the Solidaran sales tax structure and imposing a one percent value-added tax on both the bulk sale of agricultural produce and of manufactured goods, on the grounds that the sellers of those goods were effectively exempted from the end-use sales taxes.

After reading the newsheets, I considered the implications of the invitations Seliora and I had received. Certainly, the combination of Iryela's note and the invitation to the Council's Autumn Ball strongly suggested that High Councilor Suyrien had a definite agenda in mind. But what? In addition to being the Chief Councilor of the Executive Council of Solidar, Suyrien was one of the economically most prosperous and powerful High Holders, with extensive lands around L'Excelsis, one of the largest and most modern iron works at

Ferravyl, not to mention the shipworks at Solis, which built most of Solidar's warships. That had been an issue for a time, because, with its location on the shallow Southern Gulf, Solis was barely a deepwater port.

None of that had much to do with me, either as an imager or as a Patrol Captain. Yet it had to, because neither Suyrien nor Master Dichartyn was going to involve me unless they wanted or needed something. I just had to figure out what it might be before I ended up in a position where I didn't want to be.

After I left the coach at Third District station and stepped inside, Lyonyt beckoned to me when I was barely through the doors. His forehead was furrowed. "Sir."

"What is it, Lyonyt?"

"Last night, there were four more elver deaths. They all had that twisted look . . ."

"Bad elveweed?"

"It looks like that, sir."

After I hurried through various details and reports, I went looking for whatever taudischef I could find. Horazt wasn't in any of his safe houses, and I even tried Shault's mother's place, although I was fairly sure Horazt hadn't spent any time with her in years, probably because her son was an imager, and he wasn't certain that she might not tell Shault something that might upset her son. No one had seen him, or they didn't know where he was, or wouldn't tell me. All I could do was leave word that more of the bad elveweed was being run into the taudis.

I finally ran down Deyalt in mid-afternoon. Except I didn't. He found me as I was walking down South Middle just short of Mando and the woodworks.

"Captain . . . word is that you've been saying there's a lot of bad weed out."

"We picked up four dead elvers last night. There were two last week. In over five years, I've never seen more than one in a week."

Deyalt didn't speak for a moment. "It won't stop, Captain. Word is that the weed isn't bad. It's just a lot stronger. Makes 'em feel even better. They'll pay more for it."

That made matters even worse, not better. The elvers might lay off if they thought the fresher elveweed was poisoned, but a stronger smoke would only end up with more dying. "That will mean more deaths."

Deyalt nodded. "We can't do much about that. Jadhyl thought you should know."

"Thank you. I'll make sure the patrollers understand." I paused. "Do you know if the other taudis are getting the same stronger weed?"

"I heard that it started in the Hellhole. Other than that . . . maybe down by the south river piers . . . I couldn't say."

"Thank you." I nodded, and he slipped away.

The afternoon suddenly turned cold and windy, as it often did in fall, and I was happy to get out of the chill when I returned to the station. My relief vanished with the appearance of two separate dispatches from the Subcommander. One requested an update on any information any district captain might have on the Place D'Opera explosion. The second one was directed at me, wanting to know what the decrease in chargings from Third District meant, indirectly suggesting that we weren't doing our job, as if the number of arrests and incarcerations were the only measure of Patrol success.

How exactly could I reply without sounding arrogant? If I said that Third District had fewer chargings because we'd done something to reduce a few of the causes of crime, that was presumptuous. So was pointing out that the local taudischefs really didn't want to get me angry. So was suggesting that because the taudis was quieter, we could shift a few more patrols to the Avenue D'Artisans and along the Midroad, and that cut down on smash-and-grabs and common theft.

All of those were probably true, but I couldn't prove it. All Cydarth cared about was numbers. To him, arrests and chargings were proof of Patrol effectiveness. I didn't want to press my men to make arrests for his numbers.

So I spent more than a glass writing a calm and dispassionate reply that noted a decrease in violence and attributed it to the wise policies promulgated by headquarters . . . and the aftermath of the removal of the disruptive influence of the Tiempran Temple of Puryon.

After that, I went out and accompanied Chualat on his rounds in the area just east of the Guild Square. When I returned to the station, the Collegium's duty coach was waiting, and I was more than ready to leave, but I still was a quarter-glass late in reaching NordEste Design.

Happily, Seliora had had a better day, and our ride with Diestrya back to the Collegium was short and uneventful. Seliora didn't even complain too much about my wanting to talk to Master Draffyd, especially after I told her why.

Draffyd was in the infirmary, but he almost glared when I walked in. Then he recognized me and smiled. "Rhenn . . . I haven't seen you in a while, and you're on your feet."

"I wanted your advice." I explained what had happened the day before with the child who'd swallowed the elveweed. "I didn't know what else to do. I knew it was dangerous. But . . ." I shrugged.

"I'm glad you realized how dangerous it could have been. The child was fortunate you were the imager there. But you were still very lucky. If you could come in after dinner next Meredi, I'd like to work with you then. Don't eat much supper."

"I'll be here."

I hurried back to the house and arrived with enough time to spare that we both spent a half-glass playing with Diestrya before readying her for bed, and then dressing for dinner at the Dichartyns'. I just washed up and brushed my grays. Seliora changed into an outfit consisting of a dark gray shimmering blouse, with a matching long skirt trimmed in a deep burgundy, and a jacket of the same shade of burgundy.

Then we set out, Seliora carrying a basket filled with two bottles of an amber Grisio that her Aunt Staelia had suggested was quite refreshing. Since Staelia owned and very successfully operated Chaelya's—what I would have called a gourmet bistro—her recommendations were worth heeding.

Master Dichartyn's house was two dwellings to the north of ours. We walked past the dwelling of Master Rholyn and then the one of Maitre Dyana. From the outside, all four looked similar: gray stone walls, with dark slate gray roofs, and leaded glass windows. Each had a low stone wall enclosing the space around the house, with raised beds for gardens flanking the walls, and lawn between the raised beds and the stone walkway surrounding each house. Running along the wide spaces between the walls surrounding each house were stone walks, flanked by low boxwood hedges and, except in winter, flower beds. The dwellings' window casements were painted dark gray—with one exception. Not surprisingly, Maitre Dyana had the trim on her dwelling painted two shades of blue, one a dark grayish blue, and other a light mist blue. But then, she always wore a bright scarf with her imager grays, and more often than not those scarves were either blue or contained blue.

Just beyond Master Dichartyn's dwelling was that of Maitre Poincaryt, or more properly, the official dwelling of the Maitre of the Collegium Imago, located on a low flat knoll doubtless raised two yards above the others just to distinguish it from the houses of the other senior masters. It was also half again as large as the dwellings of the senior masters that surrounded it. Seliora and I had only been inside Maitre Poincaryt's dwelling little more than a handful of times, usually at the year-end reception he held for all the masters of the Collegium.

When we reached the door of the Dichartyns, I didn't even have to lift the knocker, because he opened the door, his gray hair backlit by the lamps of the foyer behind him. "Rhenn, Seliora . . . please come in."

He stepped back, and his wife hurried from the hallway behind to join him.

Seliora handed the basket to Aelys. "We thought you might enjoy this."

"Oh . . . you didn't have to . . ." replied the good Madame Dichartyn, as angular as when I'd first seen her at the Imagisle Anomen six years earlier, "but it was so kind of you." With her last words, that angular severity vanished with the warm welcoming smile she bestowed on us. "The girls are at Maitre Poincaryt's, watching over his grandchildren. He and Auralya are entertaining his daughter and son and their spouses. They don't see them that often, since one couple lives in Cloisonyt and the other in Khelgror. But . . . you must come and see my indoor herb garden." Aelys drew Seliora away.

Master Dichartyn said quietly, "I'd like just a moment with you, Rhenn."

I waited for him to speak.

"Yesterday, you were talking to Baratyn. You gave him quite a worry."

"I know. I didn't mean to. He made a pleasantry about things being quiet at the Council Chateau, and I said that they weren't likely to stay that way. All I meant was that, with a resumption of the war between Jariola and Ferrum likely, he'd likely be seeing more assassins and the like, the same way as before."

"Rhenn," Dichartyn said quietly, "please think about who you are. Believe it or not, people will read more into your words than you may mean. This time, there's no harm done, because I told him the same thing this morning, and that was when he said you'd already warned him, but I don't think you meant it in quite the same way, did you?"

"I meant that it was likely . . . not . . ." I wasn't quite certain what else to say.

"Rhenn . . . how many Maitres D'Structure are there in the Collegium?"

"There are five here, and Dhelyn. I don't know if the heads of the two other Collegia besides Westisle—I know they're all really part of the Collegium, but I think of them that way—are all Maitres D'Structure."

"There are only eight, and you are one of those eight. You also are the one who, when Baratyn saw and sensed nothing, stopped the Ferran envoy from poisoning High Councilor Suyrien, managed to create the fortunately fatal accident for the envoy, and survived an explosion that would have killed anyone else. You cannot afford to have your words misunderstood. Neither can the Collegium."

"Yes, sir."

"Good. Now . . . let's join the ladies and enjoy dinner."

Dinner on Vendrei night was warm, friendly, and notable and pleasant for the very fact that we discussed nothing of great worldly import, and nothing involving the Collegium or the Civic Patrol.

I didn't get up before dawn on Samedi to join Clovyl's exercise group, and that allowed us to have a comparatively more leisurely morning before I had to leave for Third District. I did stop by the dining hall to pick up Shault's essay before I took the duty coach. Once I was inside the coach, I glanced from the newsheets to the essay, then decided I'd best read the newsheets first, just in case there was a story that might affect the Civic Patrol.

Neither newsheet carried anything directly affecting Third District, but there was a story in *Tableta* about the failure of an irrigation storage dam southwest of Montagne. The cause was unknown, and the dam was supposedly owned by a freeholders' cooperative. I recalled something about water law, about being first in time being first in line . . . and if the dam weren't there, then in the drier seasons, those with the older water rights would have priority. That meant High Holders disenfranchising the freeholders who had established their water rights later, at least until the dam was rebuilt.

Then I turned to Shault's essay, not without trepidation, although I laughed as I realized that Master Dichartyn had probably often felt the same way about my essays. The first lines were straightforward enough.

> The law sets rules for the people of Solidar. That is so that all of them know what to do. The Civic Patrol is required to enforce that law. Patrol Captains must make sure that their patrollers carry out the law. The law is not flexible, and there are times when applying the law would not be just. When a Patrol Captain comes across a case like this, he must find a way to apply the law without punishing too much the person who breaks the law. If possible, he should warn the person, but not charge them if they have not broken any laws before . . .

In essence, what young Shault was suggesting was letting the offender know that he'd broken the law and not charging him when possible, and then asking the courts for mercy when there was no way to avoid the charging the offender. Where he was weak in logic was explaining why, and we'd have to discuss that, because imagers needed both to understand and to able to explain the reasons for their actions.

Once I got to the station, I went over the logs with Huensyn, who had the duty desk, then checked the holding cells, which held two disorderlies, whom we'd forget to charge once they sobered up, since they hadn't done much besides sing far too loudly in far too public a place, and a theft and assault case. He'd tried to take a knife to the patroller who'd arrested him, and had suffered broken fingers and a lump on the head from a Patrol truncheon as a result. The brand on his hip marked him as a previous offender, and that meant he'd be spending the rest of his life in the workhouse or on a penal road crew, and that life wasn't likely to be all that long.

I was debating which patrollers I should accompany on their rounds when a patroller first hurried through the station doors. "Captain! We've got a problem over on Sleago!" The patroller was Yherlyt, a dark-skinned and seasoned veteran of nearly fifteen years, who was the son of Tiempran immigrants.

"Do we need reinforcements?"

"It's not that kind of problem, sir."

Translated loosely, they needed me, and Yherlyt didn't want to explain in the station.

I grabbed my cloak and visored hat and hurried to join him. Outside the wind was brisk and chill. Occasional white puffy clouds scudded across a sky that might have been clear and crisp, except too many people in L'Excelsis had lit fires or stoves, and a low smoky haze hung over the city. I didn't speak until we were headed down Fuosta toward Quierca and well away from anyone else.

"What is it?"

"A pair of elveweed runners, sir. One's dead, and the other's wounded. He'll probably make it. There's a young elver. He's dead. There's a woman, too. The mother of the dead elver. Her name is Ismelda. She's cut up a bit. Maybe more than that."

I had an idea, but I just said, "I'd like a little more detail, Yherlyt."

"The runners came to deliver to the dead elver . . . or to collect. They didn't know he was dead. The mother killed the collector with a big iron fry pan. She didn't know he had a partner. The partner took a knife to her, but she broke his nose and jaw with the pan. He tried to run and came out of the house and dropped unconscious on the sidewalk. A pair of kids tried to drag the partner off the sidewalk, but Mhort has good eyes, and we caught them."

"Do you know why all this happened?"

"The dead taudis-kid, the elver, couldn't have been more than fourteen. He was still in school. I'm guessing he was a runner, too."

"So he either stole or bought the elveweed, and smoked too much of the new stuff."

"Yes, sir."

When we reached the dingy narrow house, the fourth up from Quierca on Sleago, two other patrollers waited on the front porch that was barely more than a stoop under wide and sagging eaves. They had cuffed the surviving runner. His entire face was bruised and bloody, and his jaw on the left side was crooked and turning purple.

"Sir?" asked Mhort.

"Take him in. Book him for elveweed running and attempted murder. Oh . . . and tell Huensyn to send a wagon here for the other bodies."

"Yes, sir."

The runner mumbled words through his ruined face. ". . . Attacked us . . . didn't do . . . nothing . . . tried . . . knife . . . keep her . . . off me. . . ."

That was doubtless true. It didn't make any difference. There might not be much I could do about elveweed, but I wasn't about to have school-age boys as runners. Besides, the injured runner would live far longer as a coal loader for the Navy or as a quarry apprentice or the like.

"Off with you, sow-scum," ordered Mhort.

He and Deksyn marched the runner down the three crumbling brick steps and then toward Quierca.

I followed Yherlyt into the small front hall where two bodies lay on their backs. One's face was contorted in agony. That had to be the elver boy. The other figure wore a black shirt and trousers, both washed so many times that their color was closer to dark gray than to true black. His face was burned by streaks of something, and the burns hadn't even started to heal.

In the parlor sat a dark-haired and painfully thin woman. Someone had bandaged her arms with strips of cloth, but in places, some blood had soaked through the crude dressings. She looked at me, not questioningly, but not blankly.

"I'm Patrol Captain Rhennthyl."

She nodded.

"Why did you kill the one runner?" I asked.

"Why?" Her voice rose. "He killed my son. He gave him that weed, and Nygeo smoked it, and he died. He died horribly. You saw his face. Then that scum runner came and demanded silvers for the elveweed. He said that terrible things would happen to me and Foyneo if I didn't pay. I have few silvers, just what I earn from helping Ielsa. She is a seamstress on the other side of Quierca. We would not eat . . . and he killed my boy. He took out a knife, and I threw the grease in the pan in his face and then hit him with it . . ."

That explained the burns on the dead runner's face.

"Don't take me away!" she pleaded.

Yherlyt looked to me. I understood why I was there.

"I don't see any reason to take you anywhere," I said. "Two elveweed runners attacked you to collect silvers that they said your son owed them. You defended yourself. Self-defense is allowed." I paused. "We will need to take Nygeo's body."

"He won't need it . . ." Behind the stoic words was an edge, and her eyes were bright, but her voice did not break, nor did actual tears flow.

"I'm very sorry," I said, inclining my head to her.

She just turned away.

Yherlyt and I carried both bodies out of the dwelling and to the sidewalk.

"Thank you, sir," he said as we lowered Nygeo's already stiff figure to the stone.

"You're welcome. I just did what captains are here for. Write up the report the way she said it, but mention that he had a knife when the dead runner asked for the silvers."

"Yes, sir. That's the way Mhort and I heard it, too."

"Is there anything else you need me for, Yherlyt?"

"No, sir." He paused.

"I need to tell Deyalt. They're not supposed to be using schoolboys for runners."

"No, sir." After a moment, he added, "I'd not speak poorly of the dead, but Nygeo was always a problem. Foyneo is a good boy."

"We don't want the dealers getting any ideas." I didn't like having any elveweed in the taudis, but there wasn't any way I could stop the trade. I'd had to use every tool I knew to get the taudischefs to press for the ban on selling to schoolchildren and not using schoolchildren from the taudis as runners.

I spent more than a glass on the streets. I never did find Deyalt, but did run down one of his toughs in the green jackets. There were always a few around, keeping an eye on things.

"Captain, sir."

"You know Ismelda on Sleago? She sometimes works for a seamstress. She has two boys. One of them might have been a runner."

"That'd be Nygeo. Deyalt told him not to run."

"He won't run anymore. He smoked too much. He's dead. Two other runners tried to collect from Ismelda. One's dead, and we're taking the other. I thought Deyalt ought to know." I offered a pleasant smile.

He froze for a moment. "Deyalt told 'em all . . ."

"I'm not blaming anyone. But . . . perhaps Deyalt might put out the word—again—that I don't like elveweed at all. I especially don't like school-boys being sold to or used as runners."

"He don't either, Captain."

"Then we're all agreed, aren't we?" I smiled again, before heading back to the station.

Comparatively speaking, the rest of the afternoon was calm, and I caught a hack on South Middle a little after fifth glass. I couldn't help thinking about poor stupid dead Nygeo, and the devastation I'd felt in his mother. It didn't help that, when I arrived at NordEste Design, I was as worried as I always was when Seliora left Imagisle without me, even if she always carried her pistol and even if she was a very good shot. I hurried up the steps to the covered portico.

The door opened before I could lift the well-polished and shining but battered knocker that was shaped like a stylized upholsterer's hammer.

The twins—Hanahra and Hestya, Odelia's younger sisters—stood there.

"She's already here, Uncle Rhenn." They both smiled slyly, enjoying call-ing me 'uncle' even though I was married to their cousin, not their aunt; but then, they'd always thought of Seliora as an aunt, and now that she had a child, the age difference seemed even greater, although the twins were seventeen and looked older.

"And you're not with Diestyra?" I stepped into the foyer, and Hanahra closed the door.

"Bhenyt is. She wanted 'Uncle Bhenyt,' " Hestya said dryly. "She's already flirting. She's good at it."

That was something else I'd have to worry about in years to come.

Since the sole inside exit to the foyer was the polished oak staircase, I fol-lowed them up the steps. The ample staircase, with its gleaming brass fixtures and elaborately carved balustrades, opened out at the top into a large entry hall, a good ten yards deep and eight wide. Light golden oak comprised the paneled walls. A lush carpet of deep maroon, with a border of intertwined golden chains and brilliant green leafy vines, largely covered an intricately patterned parquet floor. Set around the foyer were chairs and settees of dark wood, upholstered in various fabric designs. There were, however, far fewer than there once had been, because many of the pieces, which had been samples of the work of NordEste Design, had found their way to our house on Imagisle. At the south end of the hall was a pianoforte, well-kept, if seldom played, I had discovered.

Bhenyt sat in a chair on the left side of the hall, several yards away, his legs crossed, with Diestrya riding on his boot while he held her hands. My daughter never glanced in my direction, although Seliora, wearing a light green dress with a dark gray jacket, certainly did, and she smiled. Standing beside her were her father, Shelim, and her brother Shomyr, broad-shouldered, black-bearded, and half a head shorter than I was. Shomyr's wife, Haelya, with short orange-flame hair, was turned facing Seliora. She was expecting their second child in Avryl.

From the far side of the group, Betara walked toward me. Dark-haired and wiry, wearing blue silk trousers and a matching jacket, at a distance she could easily have been Seliora's older sister, rather than her mother. Her smile was identical to Seliora's. "How was your day?"

"Not terrible," I replied, "but I have to say that I've had better." I didn't see several members of the family. "Where's Methyr?" I asked.

"He's upstairs with a fever," replied Seliora as she joined us. "Father just checked on him and Grandmama Diestra."

With her words, I realized I hadn't seen Grandmama. Betara, understandably, often called her Mama Diestra. I didn't see Odelia and Kolasyn, nor Odelia's mother Aegina, but Aegina was often in the kitchen when we arrived. I wasn't looking forward to seeing Odelia.

"Mama Diestra would like a word with you, Rhenn," Betara said. "She's upstairs in the plaques room."

"She won't be joining us for dinner?"

"Her legs are bothering her more than usual."

I looked to Seliora and Betara. "You two should come." I knew Betara would, but Seliora should know whatever Diestra had to say as well.

I followed Betara and Seliora up the stairs, which had a large landing halfway up, and then across the upper hall. As the three of us entered the upstairs plaques room, Diestra looked up from where she sat in front of an array of plaques, then swept them up, shuffled, and stacked them with a fluidity that remained amazing. As I well knew, for all her age, she was a master player of both life and plaques. "You're looking well, Rhenn."

"And so are you."

"The flattery is transparent, but it is welcome, as is your presence." She smiled and waited for us to sit down around the circular table. Her hair had turned from a heavy gray to a silvery sheen over the years since Seliora and I had been married, but it was still thick and well-brushed, and her eyes were bright, if circled by a blackness that suggested increasing frailty.

"The greener or fresher elveweed is appearing all over L'Excelsis," Diestra finally said. "It's stronger than the dried weed from Caenen and Tiempre. One of my contacts said it was like the weed that came from Stakanar years back, before the Stakanarans rooted it all out."

"They're still getting the dried weed in Rivages and Touryl," Betara added.

"That means the supply of the stronger weed is limited," I mused.

"They can charge more in L'Excelsis," Diestra said dryly. "It's a question of golds."

"Can you find out if any other city is getting the fresh weed?" I asked.

"You have an idea?"

"I have several," I temporized. "More information might help."

"There is one other matter," offered Diestra.

I tried not to stiffen. Whenever Mama Diestra brought up something, it was important.

"Several Pharsi families in Solis, Kherseilles, Estisle, and Westisle have had their eldest sons killed over the past month. The men were all married and had children." She looked to me.

"Do you have any idea how many?"

"We know of fourteen."

"I haven't heard about that. It sounds like the killers don't understand Pharsi ways. Someone who's not Pharsi is trying to make trouble."

"That's what we think, but . . . it hasn't happened here."

"Because I'm a Patrol Captain?"

"Can you think of another reason?" countered Diestra.

"The Collegium and the Council are here."

"There are smaller collegia in both Estisle and Westisle," Betara said.

"Every city you named is a port," I pointed out. "L'Excelsis isn't."

Betara and Diestra exchanged glances. Clearly, they hadn't thought about that. I hadn't either. The idea had just popped into my head.

"Do you know if any of the families have businesses or factorages that supply the Navy? Or deal with grain?"

"We'll have to see." Diestra picked up the deck of plaques and shuffled them, then began to lay out a pattern of cards on the felt surface of the table.

The three of us rose and left the chamber.

"I need to check on dinner." Betara hurried down the stairs ahead of Seliora and me.

As we walked down the last few steps and then moved from the staircase to the main hall, Odelia appeared. "You were talking about elveweed with Grandmama?"

"We were," I said. "There seems to be a stronger version that's causing deaths."

"Can't you do something about it, Rhenn?"

I could sense a tightness behind her words.

"I've suggested to the taudischefs in my district that they warn people against using it."

"Suggested? Warned?"

Seliora shot a glance at Odelia that I wouldn't have wanted to receive.

Odelia ignored it and stared at me.

"Odelia . . . I have slightly fewer than four hundred patrollers assigned to Third District. Third District comprises roughly four square milles. It's the eastern quarter of the old city of L'Excelsis, plus the newer areas to the north. If the blocks were regular, and they're not, but it's close enough to calculate that there are somewhere over 1,000 blocks in Third District. At any one time, I have no more than 150 patrollers on the streets. That's one patroller for every seven or eight blocks. Now, we know we don't have to patrol some areas heavily, and we don't. But even in the taudis, which is heavily patrolled, especially in the late afternoon and evening, we can't do better than having a patroller for every third or fourth block on average at any one time. I have managed to keep the dealers out of Third District, but I can't catch all their runners, and runners are a penny a score. We brought in two this afternoon, one dead."

"With all that explaining, I'm surprised you have time to catch anyone." Her tone was scathing.

"We catch people because the people come to us and tell us, and because the taudischefs let me know things. We also catch people because we vary patrol times and routes, so that common criminals don't know when a patroller might be around. We also catch people because many aren't too bright. The elveweed dealers are not common. They're traders in illegal goods, and those who survive are anything but stupid. That's why they don't get anywhere near me, and I can't patrol everyone else's districts, either practically or legally." I paused, then asked, "What do you suggest that I do, Odelia?"

"Stop the trade. It kills people."

"How? I can find the taudis-kids the dealers use as runners. I can put them in workhouses or send them to the Navy as coal loaders. And if I catch them twice, they can die after working themselves to death on the road gangs before they're thirty. And the day after I send each one away, there's another one in his place. The dealers haven't even entered Third District in years. These days, we've got fewer elvers and no dealers there, but your family and I can't build paper mills and woodworks in every taudis in L'Excelsis, and there aren't enough imagers around to do what I do—and even if there were, the people in the city wouldn't accept that many imagers in the Civic Patrol."

"My . . . how eloquent you are. It doesn't change things. People still die, and more are dying."

"Odelia," I said slowly, deliberately, "I know Kolasyn's brother is an elver. I know you're both worried. But he's the one who chooses to smoke it. No one put a blade to his throat and told him to."

"People shouldn't be tempted like that. Not by something that changes the way they think after smoking it once or twice."

I really wanted to tell Odelia that she couldn't save Haerasyn from himself. "The world is filled with temptations that lead to great danger, Odelia. Neither you nor I can prevent even a small fraction of them. You and Kolasyn do what you can. I do what I can."

"That's easy for you to say . . ."

"Odelia." Seliora's voice cut like an ice knife.

The redhead closed her mouth, but I could sense the rage, and that angered me. Odelia wanted to blame everyone except Haerasyn.

"Don't ever do that again." I could feel my own cold steel fury slam into Odelia, for all that I did not raise my voice or move.

Odelia stepped back involuntarily, shrinking away, even though she was nearly my height. "I'm sorry. I'm very sorry." She backed away, then ran up the stairs.

Seliora smiled sadly at me and shook her head. "We'll talk later."

I understood, and we walked back to rejoin the group gathered near the pianoforte.

Dinner was delicious, and, in the Pharsi tradition, no one talked about business or about troubles, but about the good things in life. Odelia's place at the table was empty, and poor Kolasyn just looked bewildered.

Sometime after eighth glass, Bhenyt went out and hailed a hack for us, as he often did, and we left.

"Odelia thinks you can do anything, and that you didn't really want to help Haerasyn," Seliora offered in the darkness of the cab as we headed down the Boulevard D'Ouest.

"I may be a powerful imager, but that doesn't mean I can save people from their own weaknesses and stupidity. I have enough trouble trying not to do stupid things myself."

"She won't ever approach you again," Seliora said. "She'll avoid you for months. It could be longer."

"I tried to be polite, but when she looked at you like that . . ."

"Every bit of you that is the Pharsi heritage that your mother denies came forward. It joined with the part that is imager, and for that moment, dearest, you were truly terrible. Odelia is strong, but no one could have stood against that."

"You could have."

She shook her head. "Why do you think Iryela begged you to be a friend?"

"She asked . . ."

"For a High Holder, what she did was equivalent to groveling. It was bearable to her because she knew you respected her, and because you saved her life, but she knows you could destroy everything she has. She saw what Odelia just saw. Grandmama sensed that in you from the beginning. Why do you think you've been able to turn Third District around."

"It's not turned that far—"

"Rhenn."

"I'd like to think good ideas, and some golds from your family, have helped change things."

"Exactly. They helped. But the real difference is that the taudischefs don't want to cross you, and the patrollers feel more secure. Even the conscription teams are very well-mannered in your district, and they aren't in most."

"Yes, dear." I wasn't about to argue with her.

She still mock-slapped me, her fingers barely touching my cheek.

I would have liked to have held her, but Diestrya was dozing in my lap, and the last thing I wanted to do was to wake a sleeping three-year-old.

Once we got home, we immediately went upstairs and put our daughter to bed, although she never quite woke up. I waited and watched her for a bit, to make sure that she slipped into a deeper sleep. She was sleeping easily when I finally walked back into the main bedchamber to talk to Seliora. At that moment, an image flashed before me.

In the darkness, I was climbing out of a pile of stone and rubble, under the cold grayish-red light of Erion, dust and ashes sifted around me. Then, as suddenly as it had come, before I could make out more details, the image was gone.

It wasn't a daydream, but a Pharsi foresight flash. Seliora had flashes more often than did I, but I'd had one or two, enough to recognize it for what it was, but not enough to be able to seize on key details. For me, unlike Seliora, they tended to foreshadow troubles. Seliora had seen us being married as a foresight flash, as Remaya had seen being married to Rousel, and my dear wife had known I'd become a Patrol officer before I did—except that she'd only seen me standing amid patrollers, not knowing what it foreshadowed. That was unfortunately often the case when it came to understanding foresight flashes.

"What is it?" she asked. "You looked stunned."

"A flash."

She nodded slowly. "Should you tell me?"

"I don't think so." That was another problem with the flashes. Often, Seliora and her family had discovered, trying to change circumstances only made matters worse. The best strategy was to plan for what might happen in the unglimpsed moments that followed a flash.

But . . . surrounded by stones and rubble? I managed to keep from shivering as I began to undress for bed.

8

Solayi dawned bright and clear, but it could have been cloudy and raining, for all I cared, because Diestrya slept a whole glass later than usual, giving Seliora and me time to sleep and be together, and because I had the entire day off, an occurrence that was all too rare.

When we did get up, Seliora and I fixed breakfast and lingered over it, since Klysia was off from Samedi morning until dinner on Solayi. Diestrya was happy enough that we weren't going anywhere that she just scurried around the breakfast room, not getting into too much trouble, only occasionally asking for attention, while we read the newsheets and talked over tea.

There was little enough truly new in either *Tableta* or *Veritum*. War still loomed in Cloisera, but had not actually broken out, perhaps because of an early heavy snowstorm, and the Council had dispatched a flotilla to join and reinforce the northern fleet, along with a communiqué that stressed Solidar's "vigilant" neutrality. Religious upheaval in Caenen had settled down, but a new prophet of some sort was stirring up trouble in Gyarl, and the Tiemprans were reinforcing their border. And . . . there was a brief story in both newsheets about the stronger elveweed.

"The newsheets both mention the new kind of elveweed," Seliora said, setting down her tea, and glancing toward the lower cabinet where Diestrya was pulling out a stack of baking tins. "I don't recall them ever saying anything about taudis-drugs before."

"The last sentence in *Tableta* says why. It's not just a taudis problem. Some of the more adventurous young people are smoking it now."

"Like Haerasyn." Seliora shook her head sadly. "I'm sorry about last night . . ."

"It isn't your fault. It really isn't even Odelia's. Kolasyn wants to save his brother, and his brother doesn't really want to be saved."

"Do you really think that?"

"No. I should have said that the feelings created by the elveweed are stronger than the understanding that the weed will eventually kill him. Death will happen sometime; he doesn't see it as immediate. The intense pleasure is now."

Seliora shivered, although the breakfast room was not cold. "I'd hate to feel like that."

I just nodded. I'd already seen too many elvers, changed into shadows of what they once had been, because they thought that it couldn't happen to them. I might have been wrong, but I thought that the best defense against something like elveweed was the full understanding that it could happen to anyone. Anyone at all, and that was reason enough never to try it.

The rest of the day was blessedly unscheduled, and Seliora and I particularly enjoyed the quiet during Diestrya's afternoon nap before we all had an early supper. We left our daughter with Klysia and took our time walking to the south end of Imagisle and the anomen, arriving just as the junior imagers who formed the choir began to sing the choral invocation, a piece I didn't recognize. Seliora and I took our places standing near the side and rear of several of the other masters and their families. Maitre Dyana nodded to us, as did Aelys. Master Dichartyn was studying the faces of the choir members. Maitre Poincaryt and his wife stood beyond the Dichartyns and their daughters.

When the choir finished, Chorister Isola stepped forward. She had been at the anomen since before I had first come to the Collegium, but her voice was by far the most melodious of all the choristers I had heard in my lifetime, even in the wordless ululating invocation. She finished the invocation with the formal text.

"We are gathered here together this evening in the spirit of the Nameless and in affirmation of the quest for goodness and mercy in all that we do."

The opening hymn was "Not to Name." As usual, I barely sang, because I was well aware of just how badly I did sing. Seliora sang well. After that was the confession.

"We do not name You, for naming is a presumption, and we would not presume upon the creator of all that was, is, and will be. We do not pray to You, nor ask favors or recognition from You, for requesting such asks You to favor us over others who are also Your creations. Rather we confess that we always risk the sins of pride and presumption and that the very names we bear symbolize those sins, for we too often strive to arrogate our names and ourselves above others, to insist that our petty plans and arid achievements have meaning beyond those whom we love or over whom we have influence and power. Let us never forget that we are less than nothing against Your nameless magnificence and that all that we are is a gift to be cherished and treasured, and that we must also respect and cherish the gifts of others, in celebration of You who cannot be named or known, only respected and worshipped."

"In peace and harmony," was the chorus.

Then came the offertory baskets, followed by Isola's ascension to the pulpit for the homily. "Good evening."

"Good evening," came the reply.

"And it is a good evening, for under the Nameless all evenings are good, even those that seem less than perfect . . ."

Isola smiled and held silent for a moment before she continued. "We are all children of the Nameless, but like children we still cling to familiar names. Isn't it easy to refer to the Nameless? Isn't it comfortable? But who calls that entity we call the Nameless the 'Unnamable'? Or the 'One Too Great to be Described by a Name'? Or even the 'One Beyond Naming'? Isn't a casual reference to the Nameless the same as naming? As equating a comfortable pair of syllables to a being of such magnificence that a name is meaningless . . . ?"

From there Isola went on to suggest how the ease of naming the Nameless applied to everything else in life, so that we did not see what lay behind or beyond the names and how that so often led to a lack of understanding. The true sin of naming was not so much the use of names but the use of names in a manner that denied or obliterated the reality that the name represented.

As with all her homilies, it made me think, even if I still questioned whether there really was a Nameless, and if there happened to be, whether the Nameless, so powerful and magnificent, could have cared in the slightest what I thought or did.

After the service, Seliora and I hurried to get back to the house . . . and our daughter, who was doubtless restive, because it was pushing her bedtime.

"I always like Isola's homilies," said Seliora, shivering under a thin cloak, because the evening had turned chill and blustery since we had entered the anomen.

"Why?"

"Because they relate to real life as well as to the Nameless. They would make sense even without the Nameless."

I could certainly agree with that.

9

The best thing about the next few days was that nothing horrible occurred. We did receive a note from Mother on Lundi asking us to come to dinner on Vendrei evening, explaining that Nellica could watch both Diestrya and Rheityr. Seliora penned a gracious acceptance, and I sent it by messenger the first thing Mardi morning. The remainder of Mardi continued without untoward events, except that there was another elver death, with the unclothed body left in an alley off Dugalle. Seliora noted that Odelia was avoiding her, as we both had thought was likely, and that neither Betara nor Mama Diestra had learned anything more about where the stronger elveweed was being sold.

A light and chill drizzle on Meredi morning made exercising and running considerably less pleasant, and Diestrya cranky about wearing a small slicker that was a shade too large for her. I dropped them off at NordEste Design without any more protests from my daughter, read the newsheets and learned little, and left the duty coach without event at the station.

Alsoran and I talked over possible changes in several patroller rounds, and then Zellyn came hurrying into the station and found me as I was taking a quick look at the reports from the night before. A single look at his face told me that the comparative uneventfulness that had been so welcome on Lundi and Mardi was about to end.

"Captain, we've got a problem over on Geusynor Lane. It's a little lane across Saenhelyn where a lot of factors live."

"I know where it is." I should have. It was less than three long blocks from where my parents lived and where I'd grown up. Usually, we had few problems on the north—the northeast really—side of Saenhelyn. "We'll take a hack."

"Yes, sir." Zellyn had been the first patroller I'd done rounds with, and he still had the weathered and reddish face he'd had then. Both his brush mustache and bushy eyebrows were now totally silver, and his pale brown eyes looked sadder with each passing year—not surprisingly for a patroller as good-hearted as he was.

"Lyonyt, if you'd tell the Lieutenant where I am?"

"Yes, sir."

Zellyn and I walked out of the station. There were no hacks in sight, and we walked up to South Middle. Once there, I flagged a hack, but looked to Zellyn.

"Geusynor Lane, a block and a half off Saenhelyn."

"We can go that, sir."

Once we were inside the coach, I turned. "Tell me what you know."

"Dhean and I were patrolling Geusynor. We only hit it every third round or so, but you never know, when we heard someone scream. So we ran down to this house. It's not a chateau, but it's some house, sir. The carriage gate and the front walk gate are closed, but we can see a woman on the carriage way, and she's shaking, and there's a body on the stones. We go in, and the body is a schoolgirl, it looks like, and the woman who screamed is her mother."

"Who is she?" I knew one or two people on Geusynor, or I had, years back. I supposed most of them still lived there.

"Her name is Rauchelle D'Roulet, and her husband is a factor."

"Roulet D'Factorius?" I hadn't heard of him.

"She said he deals in musical instruments, and manufactures pianofortes."

A factor dealing in musical instruments? I'd never heard of one, but that didn't mean such a factorage didn't exist. "What happened to the girl?"

"It looks like one of those elveweed deaths, sir." Zellyn shook his head. "Pleasant-looking girl, too. She would have been, that is, if her face wasn't so twisted up. Looked like she was running for help or something when it hit her."

I was the first out when the hack came to a stop. "How much?" I asked the hacker.

"Be three, sir."

I handed him four coppers. "Thank you."

"My pleasure, sir."

We walked toward the front gate, partly open, and through it I could see Dhean standing on the side porch and the top of a woman's head, as if she were sitting on a bench or chair with a low back. Zellyn's description of the house showed his own background, and my response to his description, when I saw the place, betrayed mine. The dwelling was slightly smaller than my parents', with a mansard roof and slate tiles that had to have been wired in place, given the angle. The walls were mortar over brick, in a provincial style, and the trim was a pale yellow. The carriage house was in the old style, barely large enough for a single coach, with a rear stable.

A white woolen blanket, likely Tilboran prime wool, covered the body lying at the foot of the steps up to the side porch. I bent over and took a corner of the blanket, pulling it back to see the girl's face and upper body. Her face, contorted into a rictus of pain and shock, was narrow and triangular above thin shoulders. She'd only been wearing a filmy white cotton nightdress. I guessed her age at fifteen or sixteen. I eased the blanket back over her.

Zellyn let me go up the steps to the covered porch first. He followed silently.

The woman who rose from the wicker chair with the faded oilcloth cushion was angular, her face similar to that of the dead girl. The mother was the kind who was so nervous she looked like she was always on the verge of shaking all over. Her hair was tinted a shade of henna-blonde unbecoming to someone with white chalky skin, and the redness of her eyes and the blotchy appearance of her face only accentuated the clash between skin and hair.

"Madame D'Roulet, I'm Patrol Captain Rhennthyl." I inclined my head.

She gave me a second look, then a third, before she spoke. "Oh . . . you're the imager. Chenkyr and Maelyna's son. I'm glad it's you."

That could have meant many things, but I just nodded, then asked, "Can you tell me how this happened?"

"I don't know. Jessya didn't feel well at breakfast, and she stayed home from school. I heard her moving around upstairs, and then she ran down the stairs . . . and the porch door opened. I didn't hear anything after that. For a moment, I thought she had run onto the porch because she needed air. I started to follow her, but then I smelled something burning, and I ran upstairs. There was this funny pipe lying there, and it had charred the carpet. It's a very good carpet, a Mantean Forssya. Her whole room smelled like bitter weeds had burned."

"Have you ever smelled that before?"

"I . . . I don't think so."

I let the lie pass. She'd smelled that odor before, but not often, and probably not strongly. "Then what did you do?"

"I ran downstairs and out onto the porch. That was when I saw her . . . lying there . . ."

The patrollers in Third District had found a number of dead elvers outside, some of them nude, and I'd thought that was because their bodies had been stripped and robbed, but it sounded like whatever the weed did to some people led to them feeling hot and needing air.

"Where did she go to school?"

"Jainsyn's School for Girls."

I nodded. My sister Khethila called the fashionable school "Jayne's Sins."

I spent a quarter-glass going over what Madame D'Roulet had seen and done, but it was clear enough that, while she might have suspected her daughter was doing *something*, she hadn't any real idea what. It was also clear that she hadn't tried all that hard to find out because she had no idea where Jessya had gotten the elveweed, except that it was probably from school friends.

As I was getting ready to leave, Madame D'Roulet cleared her throat. "What will you do now?"

"There's not much more we can do for her. We'll keep looking for dealers and runners, and we'll report her death."

"You won't have to take . . . her, will you? I wouldn't want anyone to see her . . . like this."

"No." There wasn't any point in that. "You can make whatever arrangements you like."

"Jessya is such a good girl . . ." Her eyes drifted past me to the blanket-covered figure on the drive.

I didn't point out that the past tense was more appropriate to the dead schoolgirl, and that any schoolgirl who had access to elveweed couldn't have been all that good . . . unless she was truly naïve and had gone along with bad company, but I had my doubts about that. "Sometimes, it's the innocent who get hurt the most, Madame. They really don't understand the dangers, and they think nothing bad will happen to them."

"Why can't . . . you stop . . . things like this?"

"We try very hard. But the people who sell it make a great deal of golds from doing so, and they go to great lengths to avoid us. Those who buy from them also avoid us, and I don't think anyone would want the Patrol intruding into every home and every business continually, trying to root out dealers. Most crimes are solved because people either come to the Patrol and tell us, or because they're willing to answer our questions. Most who buy, sell, or use elveweed don't do either."

"There must be something . . ."

"We keep looking, Madame." What else could I say to a distracted mother who didn't seem to fully realize that her daughter was dead? Especially since there was so little we could really do. "Is there someone who can help you?"

"My sister Neldya . . . she's inside. She sent a messenger to Roulet." She shook her head. "It doesn't seem real."

"Officer?" came a quiet voice from my left. "If you're through . . . Rauchelle might need some tea."

I turned to see a smallish gray-haired woman standing in the porch doorway. "We're through. Would you like the patrollers to carry Jessya inside?"

"If you would."

I glanced to Zellyn, and he and Dhean went down the steps to the drive, wrapped the blanket around the body, and then carried it back onto the porch and inside. The ease with which they handled her suggested she'd weighed even less than I'd thought.

When the two returned, we walked back along Geusynor toward Saenhelyn Road.

"She'd been smoking for a while, sir," offered Zellyn. "Elvers get thin like that."

"Her mother didn't notice?" asked Dhean. "The smell alone . . ."

"Most factors and their families have never smelled elveweed." Certainly, I never had until I found myself as a Civic Patrol Liaison. "I'll have to visit the school."

"Better you than us, sir," replied Zellyn.

When we reached Saenhelyn, I caught a hack. After a short ride, one I could have walked, it stopped before an imposing set of wrought iron gates fronting the parklike setting due north of the Plaza D'Este that contained the Jainsyn's School for Girls.

The single guard in the booth beside the gate looked at me and decided not to say a word. I walked up the stone drive and around the circle that held a fountain. The bronze figure was that of a fully clothed girl holding a book in the right hand and a lamp in the other. Water sprayed upward from the lamp into the fall air. On the far side of the fountain was a building with four square columns.

I walked between them and through the doors. The round-faced woman seated behind a tall desk in the middle of the entry hall revealed a look of horror and disgust—if only for the barest moment—when she caught sight of me.

"This is a private school, Patroller," she said with a cheerful and patently false smile.

"It's Patrol Captain and Maitre Rhennthyl, Madame," I replied with an equally false and cheerful smile. "I'd like a moment with the most senior person here."

Her eyes took in the imager's insignia on my visor cap and the four-pointed star on my grays. "If you would wait a moment, Master Rhennthyl, I'll see if Madame Lagryce is free."

In moments, she returned. "Madame Lagryce will see you, sir."

I followed her down the hall to the left to the first door and stepped into a study about twice the size of mine at the station, and a chamber far more elaborately furnished, with a large desk of ebon, its legs carved into scrollwork, and four wooden armchairs arrayed in a semi-circle before the desk. Each chair had a padded seat upholstered in green velvet, the fabric matching the wall hangings. The single bookcase was also ebon.

Madame Lagryce, even plumper than her guardian goose, sat behind the desk. She did not rise. Her black eyes were as cold as those of a water serpent above a warm smile. "I must admit that I'm at a loss to why a girls' school with such an impeccable reputation as Jainsyn's would require a visit from such a noted Civic Patrol personage."

"It's really quite simple. You have a student by the name of Jessya D'Roulet, I believe?"

"Why yes, we do. She's very talented, especially musically, and she has a fine hand in drawing. Might I ask why you are bringing up her name?" Her dark and artificially accented eyebrows rose quizzically.

"I thought you might like to know that she died this morning from smoking too much elveweed." I smiled politely. "As we both know, the Patrol can require nothing of a private institution unless we have evidence of a crime being committed on the premises. We do not have such evidence, but, given the very sheltered life of Jessya, it is likely that she got the elveweed from a classmate here, and I thought you'd like to know."

"That is preposterous, absolutely preposterous. Our girls would *never* stoop to such . . . degradation."

"One of them already did, Madame." I smiled again. "I also thought you'd like to know that the drug runners are bringing in a more potent variety of elveweed. Deaths are rising throughout L'Excelsis. I won't take any more of your time, but I do believe that you should be aware of the possibilities." I inclined my head. "Thank you, and good day."

If that didn't get her looking, there wasn't much else I could do at the moment.

Once I was outside, I walked back to the Plaza D'Este and caught a hack to the station.

The rest of the day was routine, and I actually managed to accompany Ultrych and Caaryh on their rounds. Even so, by the time the duty coach arrived at the station, I was feeling tired—and I knew I had to meet with Shault before dinner.

Seliora had just landed a solid commission for a High Holder whose name I didn't recognize—Fhernon—and Diestrya had behaved well. So the ride from NordEste Design to Imagisle was cheerful.

Once I helped Seliora and Diestrya from the coach, I hurried south to the quadrangle and to the dining hall, where Shault was waiting. As I walked into the building my eyes strayed upwards to the section of stone that held the name of imagers who had died in service to the Collegium. I always looked for Claustyn's name, perhaps because he was the first that I'd known to die that way.

Then I saw Shault and ushered him into the conference room.

Within moments of trying to discuss his essay, I got the feeling that the most trying aspect of the day might well be trying to emphasize to Shault the need for clarity in explaining matters. After what had happened already during the day, it shouldn't have been. It was.

"Sir, it's right, or it's wrong. Why do I need to be able to explain it?"

For a moment, I wondered if he were being deliberately obtuse, but then realized he was serious. So I asked, "Is it right for a taudischef to kill a taudis-tough if the tough is a member of his gang, but goes off and steals something while wearing the colors of another gang?"

"He has to do that, or beat him up badly, or the whole gang would be in trouble."

"Who else would know that?"

"Anyone in a taudis-gang knows that."

"So you're saying that it's right for a taudischef to break the laws of Solidar and that everyone else should agree with what you think is right, because you think it's right?"

"I didn't say that."

"You didn't?"

"You're twisting my words, sir."

"Am I?"

"It's different in the taudis, sir." He paused. "Well . . . you've made it different in Third District, but the others are the old way."

"What did you just say?"

He looked at me blankly, again.

"A moment ago," I forced myself to speak quietly, "you said something was either right or it was wrong. Now you just said that it was different in the taudis. Aren't you saying that what's right in one place isn't right in another? And if it's different . . ."

I could tell it was going to be a long session.

It was indeed, and I barely got home in time to eat a little dinner before I had to go back down to the infirmary to meet with Master Draffyd.

He was waiting outside one of the surgery chambers.

"Here you go." He handed me a gown to put over my grays. "I have a ca-daver on the surgery table there. I'm going to dissect it, and you're going to learn more about the major organs. You're also going to practice some deli-cate imagery. If you're going to attempt imagining medicine, you need to know this."

I just nodded, then slipped into the gown, and followed him into the sur-gery.

"We'll start with the esophagus." Draffyd pointed to the throat of the male body on the table. "One of the most common problems is simple choking, and there are two physical methods that should be tried before you image anything. The first one you know—several sharp blows between the shoul-ders. If between five to ten don't work, then you can try the other method—an abdominal thrust. Even if it doesn't work—and it usually does—the method provides a good cover for imaging. That is useful. Now . . . I'm going to stand behind you and demonstrate on you . . ."

He clasped his arms around me, and then wrenched them upward in a way that forced me to exhale—whether I wanted to or not.

"Oooofff."

"Exactly. Now . . . I didn't apply full force. That can crack ribs, but you should get a sense of it. Try it on me . . . but gently and slowly. I'd prefer not to have bruised muscles or ribs if you don't have your arms and hands in the right places."

He made me do the procedure slowly three times before I used more force.

"If that doesn't work . . . you can try imaging. Most objects are caught anywhere from the pharynx at the lower part of the back of the mouth." He took a probe and opened the cadaver's mouth, pointing with the probe. "They may be farther down and block the epiglottis . . . I'm going to place a hard roll there . . ."

After three glasses, Draffyd finally let me go, not that he was really through with what he wanted me to know about the more common human organs, but because my guts were having a hard time staying composed. The cool air blowing off the river from the north helped settle my system as I walked across the quadrangle and north to our house.

Seliora was waiting for me, propped up in her bed, reading.

"Diestrya asked for you . . . but she didn't cry." She looked at me. "Do you need something to settle your stomach?"

"I don't think I could eat anything right now."

"Was it as bad as you look?"

I managed to laugh. "I hope I don't look that bad."

"Just sit here and talk to me."

I did, and it helped.

10

I didn't sleep all that well on Jeudi night, but I didn't image in my sleep as a result of a disturbing dreams. The morning routine—and breakfast—helped settle me. That was until I arrived at the station, where a dispatch from Sub-commander Cydarth to all District Captains awaited me. I read it twice.

> Over the week ending on 7 Feuillyt, more than twenty elveweed addicts were reported as dead from elveweed excess in the taudis areas of Civic Patrol District Six. Four other deaths elsewhere in the Sixth District are suspected as being from the same cause. The total number of deaths is doubtless higher, since the taudis-dwellers will have disposed of some bodies without informing the Civic Patrol. Higher levels of elveweed deaths appear to be occurring in all Civic Patrol Districts.

> For the remainder of the year, the Commander requires all District captains to list elveweed deaths separately from other criminal deaths on their weekly reports to headquarters. When possible, list deaths occurring within taudis areas separately from deaths in other areas of each district . . .

A separate elver death report? That the Commander was requesting such information on a regular basis suggested that the number of deaths from elveweed was exceptionally high throughout all of L'Excelsis. Such a tally would be lower than actual elveweed deaths, even if all such deaths in Third District that came to the attention of the Civic Patrol were listed diligently, because some deaths in the taudis would go unreported, with bodies being sneaked into waste wagons and otherwise being disposed of without Patrol notice. And some elver deaths, particularly among the well-off families in L'Excelsis, would doubtless be listed as deaths from illness. In a way, they doubtless were.

Still . . . we needed to do our best to comply, and I walked into the small study next to mine. Alsoran bolted to his feet. I'd tried to tell him that wasn't necessary, but old reactions still overcame my words.

"Sir?"

I handed him the dispatch and waited for him to read it.

He looked up. "I wouldn't want to be in Captain Kharles's boots."

"I'm more worried about our boots. The subcommander is going to notice that not nearly as many of our elvers are dying as there are in the taudis in either District Six or Four. He'll take that as proof that I've got ties to the taudischefs and dealers."

"You talk to the taudischefs. You always have. He knows that. It only makes sense," Alsoran pointed out.

Subcommander Cydarth might well try to use that against me, but I only said, "We're just beginning to get deaths outside the taudis in Third District, and with the taudischefs trying to pressure the runners, we might see a spike in outside deaths. We really have no way of controlling access to elveweed once it gets outside the taudis." Not that we had that much control inside, but we did have a little influence with those who had some influence with the dealers and the runners.

"You think the number of outside deaths will increase that much?"

"Don't you?"

"I'm afraid so, sir."

We didn't have to wait long. After their second round, Zerbyn and Farran reported two more elver deaths, both on the non-taudis side of Quierca. While there weren't any other elveweed deaths discovered for the rest of the day shift, I had no doubts that there would be more that night and over the weekend. The only question was how many.

It was fifth glass when I hailed a hack outside Third District station and took it to NordEste Design, where I got off. There wasn't much point in our returning to Imagisle and then immediately leaving for my parents' house for dinner.

Betara and Seliora met me at the top of the steps, while Hestya played with Diestrya on a settee near the door to the plaques room off to my right.

"We've gotten some word about the elveweed," said Betara. "It sounds like the only places besides L'Excelsis where the fresher and stronger weed is being sold are Estisle, Westisle, Solis, and Kherseilles."

"The capital and the major ports." I paused. "Also, the same cities, except for L'Excelsis, where Pharsi men have been killed. It could be a coincidence . . . but . . ."

"You don't think so," replied Betara.

"I don't, but I don't have the faintest idea why the two would be connected, because, so far as I know, the Pharsi families don't deal in elveweed." Even as I spoke, another thought struck me. "Elveweed's been around for a long time. From what I know, even when Mama Diestra was closer to the taudis, she didn't deal with it. What's the Pharsi attitude toward it? Is there one?"

"No true Pharsi likes it. It slows thought and takes away intelligence."

"Did Mama Diestra lean on the dealers to keep it out or away from children or something like that?"

"She might have. That was when I was very young." Betara's eyes narrowed. "You don't think . . . ?"

"I just wonder if the men who were killed were the types who dealt with the taudis . . . who had those kinds of connections and who felt the same way."

Seliora looked to me. "Those are the most prosperous cities, aren't they?"

"L'Excelsis is. The others are among the more prosperous, but places like Cloisonyt, Mantes, and Khelgror are just as well-off. Extela might be also."

"The four others where the strong elveweed has appeared are ports, you said," added Betara.

Why ports, I wondered, if the fresher weed was being grown in Solidar? It couldn't be because it was coming off ships. "They are, but it doesn't make much sense to me. If someone wanted to cause trouble in the port cities, giving stronger elveweed to taudis-dwellers and the comparative handfuls of others who smoke it certainly wouldn't disrupt much."

Betara and Seliora exchanged glances that suggested they didn't know either.

I glanced around. "Odelia?"

"She's gone," Seliora said. "She's not talking to me any more than she has to."

"I'm sorry."

"It's not your fault. Everyone has to make their own decisions. Haerasyn isn't a child." Betara paused. "I did overhear her telling Hanahra that Haerasyn thought that smoking elveweed would make him an imager, or something even better, and that was why the imagers wanted to stamp out elveweed."

"That's idiotic," snapped Seliora. "Odelia knows better."

"She does. So does Aegina. They both think he's deluded, but . . ." She shrugged.

"That kind of rumor will tempt more young people to try it," I said, "and that's not good. More of them will die."

We began to collect Diestrya and her things.

At half past five, Seliora, Diestrya, and I walked down to the hack Bhenyt had hailed for us and began the ride in along Nordroad to the Guild Square and then out the Midroad. We arrived just before sixth glass. After the hack pulled up and we stepped out and I paid the hacker, I couldn't help comparing my parents' house to that of Factor Roulet's. The two looked similar in style, but the Roulet's dwelling was perhaps a fifth smaller, with far narrower windows.

Even before we reached the front porch, Mother had opened the door. "Diestrya!"

Our daughter was bright enough to discern that grandmothers who received attention were far more likely to reward them with affection, and even more to the point, with treats. Diestrya hurried up the steps and threw both arms around Mother's right leg. "Nana!"

We followed more sedately, allowing my mother her moment of full attention as she picked up Diestrya.

"Every time I see you," Mother said to her granddaughter, "you've grown. You're getting to be such a big girl. Now . . . Rheityr is waiting for you in the nursery, and there are treats for both of you."

At the word "treats," Diestrya smiled and hugged Mother again before Mother set her down and led her into the house.

Seliora and I exchanged a knowing glance. In that respect, it was a very good thing we didn't see my parents too often.

Culthyn, Remaya, and Father were waiting in the family parlor, Father in his usual chair directly facing the stove, which emitted just enough heat for a chill autumn evening. Remaya turned from whatever she'd been discussing with Culthyn.

"What's new with the Patrol business?" Father always referred to whatever I was doing as "business," even when I'd been a journeyman artist.

"More of the usual," I replied as Mother came back down the steps from the nursery.

"One moment, Chenkyr," she interjected. "What would everyone like to drink before dinner? Seliora?"

"The Dhuensa, if you wouldn't mind?"

"That's what I'll have," replied Father, "as if you didn't know already."

"Red Cambrisio," added Remaya.

"The same," I said.

Mother slipped out to the kitchen, where I could hear Kiesela doing something with pots, but returned immediately.

"I ran across a Madame D'Roulet on Meredi," I said. "She knew who I was. At least, she knew I was your son."

Mother laughed, and Father looked puzzled.

"Don't you remember, Chenkyr? It was years ago, when we went to that party of Dacastro's. She was that awful nervous woman who dragged her husband over to try to sell you a pianoforte for Culthyn . . ."

Father frowned, his brow furrowed. "Why would I have done that?"

Culthyn looked at Mother, aghast. "You didn't . . . ?"

Mother ignored Culthyn. "Her name was Rachela or something like that."

"Rauchelle," I supplied.

"How did you come across her?" asked Mother.

"Her daughter died of an elveweed overdose. The mother didn't really know what it was. She knew there was something like elveweed, but not much more. The patrollers called me in."

"How terrible." Mother shook her head. She looked to Culthyn.

"I wouldn't try that." His voice held the assurance all too common to well-off sixteen-year-olds, an assurance that reminded me of poor Rousel, who'd had assurance beyond his abilities. I had, too, but I'd been fortunate enough to survive it. Rousel hadn't been fortunate enough to survive my unwarranted assurance, even though I'd had no idea that my acts would have led to his death.

Nellica appeared with a tray and tendered a goblet to each of us, then retreated to the kitchen or serving parlor.

"Do you know a factor named Broussard?" I asked my father, then took a sip of the Cambrisio.

"The one they thought had been killed in that explosion, except it was his assistant who'd taken his wife to the opera?" Father shook his head. "He's from Piedryn, and we don't sell much there . . . or buy wool. That's grain land. He must be very well off . . . and well-connected. I couldn't afford seats on the lower box row." He laughed. "Even if I could, we couldn't get them. Those are for High Holders . . . or their guests."

"How do you know that, Chenkyr?" asked Mother.

"Veblynt told me that years ago. I doubt things have changed much. They never do where social matters are concerned."

"I meant about where he was sitting."

"Where his assistant was sitting, you mean. I read it somewhere. One of the newsheets, I think. I couldn't make up something like that."

About that, my father was absolutely correct. He couldn't imagine much beyond the here and now, and the logical and direct consequences of the present. That trait made him the solid and prosperous wool factor that he was and had created a reputation for honesty and solidity for Alusine Wool.

"High Holders or not . . ." Mother paused. "Dinner is ready."

Seliora and I carried wine goblets that we'd barely sipped from into the dining room.

After the blessing and after Father sliced and served the crisped roast lamb—always his favorite—conversation died into a lull.

"How is Khethila doing in Kherseilles?" asked Seliora.

"Fine," replied Father. "I wouldn't have thought it, not as a woman that young running a wool factorage, even with my name behind her." He shook his head, as if still amused by the whole idea.

"You didn't tell them!" Mother exclaimed. "She's now a factoria; the factors accepted her as a full factor."

"Oh . . . I thought they knew."

"Chenkyr, who would have told them? Her letter only arrived on Mardi. She was very pleased."

"That's wonderful!" said Seliora. "Is she the only recognized wool factor who's a woman?"

"I suppose so," replied Father.

I didn't say anything, but I was glad that Khethila was recognized as a factor in her own right, as Khethila D'Factoria, rather than just as Father's daughter. I couldn't help but understand her satisfaction, since she'd had to petition the association and face a real board of inquiry, rather than the mere formality that Rousel had gone through. But she'd succeeded. I did smile.

"She bought the adjoining property, too," added Mother, looking at me. "She's going to expand in time. She said you'd made it possible."

"I hope she didn't have to trade too hard on my name."

"No . . . the Banque D'Kherseilles approached her, saying that the owner would like to sell the property at a reasonable price. She wrote that the Banque D'Rivages represented the owner and handled the sale through the Banque D'Kherseilles. She didn't know the owner, but the banker who approached her asked if she was indeed the sister of Maitre D'Structure Rhennthyl. She said to thank you."

"I'm certain that she managed it all on her own," I replied, knowing that reasonable as the price might have been, the first payment had been made in blood by Rousel years before. But it had been thoughtful of Iryela, even if it made me suspicious, given the timing. Very suspicious.

Father cleared his throat, then said, "She did say that the factors in the Abierto Isles—the ones who ship to Cloisera—have cut back on their orders."

"That suggests they think that war will break out and Ferrum will attack any shipping bound for Jariola."

"They did before," interjected Culthyn.

"They also lost much of their fleet," Father replied.

"They've spent a great deal of golds and effort rebuilding the fleet with more modern vessels. They've also developed better land-cruisers. That says that they haven't given up on obtaining the Jariolan coal fields."

"And anything else they can grab," asserted Culthyn.

"Can we talk about something other than war?" Mother smiled broadly and turned to Remaya. "How is Rheityr doing in the grammaire?"

It was my nephew's first year in school, and Mother doted on every episode that indicated Rheityr's potential.

"He's already reading the first primer . . ."

"That's not new," Culthyn said. "You really had him reading before he went to school . . ." His words died away as all three women at the table looked at him.

After that, all the conversation was about family, or food, or the books that Mother and Remaya had read. I had to admit that I missed Khethila's comments on Madame D'Shendael, and Father's dismissals of that most intellectual of High Holders. But Seliora and I did add a few comments about Diestrya. Just a few.

Mother had paid Charlsyn to stay late and use the family coach to take us back. We were halfway to Imagisle when Seliora, rocking Diestrya gently in her arms, asked quietly, "The opera explosion still bothers you, doesn't it?"

"There's something about it. None of it rings true. A wealthy grain factor is assassinated, except he's not. He's sitting where only High Holders are, with seats that are difficult to obtain, and it happens in L'Excelsis, when he's from Piedryn, and that's something like a thousand milles away."

"Maybe he was trying to make a statement, and hedging his wagers."

"Anything is possible," I hazarded. Whatever it was, it didn't seem likely that it would ever involve me, but I hated things that didn't fit.

11

On Samedi morning, I did make the effort to get up early and struggle through Clovyl's exercises, although I didn't have to go to the station, since Alsoran and I had traded Samedis. I'd hoped to see Master Dichartyn there, since, as a member of the security section, even if he headed it, he usually joined the exercise group. Unfortunately, he didn't show up.

After I finished the run and caught my breath, as I walked back toward the house, hoping I'd get there before Diestrya woke, my eyes turned westward, where, occasionally, I could make out the indistinct shape of the Council Chateau in the faintest graying of the night sky that would soon show the light of dawn. Artiema, less than full, hung over the Chateau in the western sky. Erion had set glasses before.

On the section of the River Aluse that flowed along the west side of Imagisle, a steam tug puffed upstream towing three barges. Although it was hard to tell, two of the three looked to be riding higher, as if they were empty or lightly loaded. Most barges only traveled as far as Ferravyl, or if they came as far upstream as L'Excelsis, they usually docked at the barge piers, adjoining the ironway transfer station south of the city, about a mille south of Alusine Wool. The handful that went farther upriver could only go so far as Rivages before the river became too shallow.

Later, a glass after breakfast, I walked over to Master Dichartyn's house. He was actually home and was even the one to open the door. I could hear the voices of two girls, with tones that suggested either a heated discussion or an argument.

He glanced back over his shoulder and shook his head before saying, "This isn't social, is it, Rhenn?" His smile was faint but knowing.

"No, but it won't take long."

He stepped out onto the porch, closing the door. He waited for me to speak.

"You may recall that there's a newer and stronger form of elveweed coming into L'Excelsis, and we're seeing a lot more elver deaths everywhere . . ." I explained what I'd seen in Third District and told him about Commander Artois's directive. ". . . and I found out that the stronger version seems to be distributed only in Estisle, Solis, Westisle, and Kherseilles, and, of course, L'Excelsis. Interestingly enough, in the other four cities, there have been a number of deaths of Pharsi men, married men, far more than would seem natural. All of them were the eldest sons."

"What do you consider more than natural?"

"There have been at least fourteen deaths in the last month, all of oldest sons."

For several moments, Dichartyn was silent. "What do you think?"

"I don't even have an idea, except that they must be connected in some fashion, since the cities involved are the four largest ports and the capital." I stopped. "Oh . . . there's one other thing. There's a story going around that smoking the stronger elveweed will make youngsters like imagers, or even something better."

Dichartyn shook his head. "That rumor comes up every few years. It has ever since I've been here. If it were true, most of the Collegium would have come from the taudis. Still . . . that's troubling, especially now."

"Why now?"

"What do you think?"

He was always turning questions back to me, but I answered anyway. "It's only a matter of weeks before Ferrum finds a pretext—or makes one—to invade Jariola. If we don't help the Oligarch with troops, which I don't see happening, the Ferrans will take the coal fields, along with a large chunk of Jariolan territory. The Council will be split, and if there's more unrest in the taudis, along with the unresolved conflict between the freeholders and the High Holders, the Council won't want to get involved in the Ferrum-Jariola fighting, and that will lead to the eventual decline and fall of Jariola."

"Why would that be bad? I don't think you've ever been a supporter of the Oligarch."

"I'm not, but the Ferrans pose a far bigger danger to Solidar than Jariola ever will. The Jariolans just want to hang on to what they have. The Ferrans want to rule the world, and they'd like it to be a mercantilist empire, with factors as commercial High Holders or the like, without any of the internal restraints present here in Solidar." I paused just briefly. "I've offered my thoughts. What about yours?"

He smiled, ruefully. "I agree with you about the Ferran motives and the likely outcome of war in Cloisera. Our Navy is presently somewhat understrength, and while the Council has debated funding ten additional warships, nothing has happened. Suyrien's works would build them, and Glendyl's manufactory in Ferravyl would supply the engines and turbines, and those details are causing delays. The Naval Command is also complaining that they're having trouble getting enough recruits and that the conscription teams have been restricted in recent years."

"Only in L'Excelsis," I replied dryly.

"It appears that the Civic Patrols in other cities have also decided that the precedent you set is one that keeps the taudis areas more peaceful. The Navy can't argue against that, but they don't like it. Then, there is the grain problem."

I waited.

"The Navy purchases a great deal of grain—flour, actually. They prefer not to deal with a large number of sellers. So they put out orders for bid, and the bidders have to guarantee the quantity, the quality, and the lowest bidder who can satisfy the first two criteria wins the order."

I thought I could see what was coming. "The bids have all gone to High Holders?"

"Until this year. One Broussard D'Factorius assembled a flour cooperative, to which most of the freehold growers and flour factors in the area around Piedryn belong. He built a large mill and storage facility."

"They're undercutting . . . Haebyn," I had to struggle for the name, "and the other High Holders."

"Not so much as they could," Dichartyn went on. "They've had to employ a large number of guards at the facility to prevent thefts and vandalism that doesn't seem to occur at the facilities of High Holders. That cuts into their profits. They're complaining to the various factoring associations, and to the Council. The High Holders are complaining that a flour cooperative is unfair collusion."

"That's why mills and silos and other facilities are suffering damage?"

"No one can prove it. Not yet."

"That can't make Broussard all that popular with the High Holders. Even so, I still don't see why someone would blow up Broussard's carriage. Anyone with enough skill and knowledge to do that surely would have known that his assistant was in it."

Dichartyn shook his head. "Broussard claims he came down with stomach poisoning at dinner just before the performance. He and the assistant were attired in a similar fashion . . ."

"So he knew or suspected that someone was after him, and he let them take care of his domestic difficulties?"

"That's only a surmise, but he is a very, very intelligent man."

"That way, he's still around to point the Civic Patrol and the Council in the direction he wishes." I paused. "Does he have any Ferran connections?"

"Not that Schorzat or I have been able to discover. That doesn't mean they don't exist."

"Are any other factors or freeholders following his example—the idea of cooperatives and the like?"

"Councilor Caartyl is pressing for a change in the laws to declare such cooperatives unable to bid on governmental procurements unless their organizational structure binds them to commitments made by a permanent head of the organization with a fixed term of office that is at least two years and not more than five, who cannot succeed himself for more than one term."

"He doesn't want the Ferran mercantile structure creeping into Solidar under the guise of cooperatives."

Dichartyn nodded. "Not surprisingly, the factoring associations oppose the proposed law. The guilds, of course, support it, and the High Holders are split. Suyrien is leaning to support it as a compromise, but he hasn't said so publicly."

"Has the Ferran envoy commented?"

"In recent years, no Ferran envoy has commented on much of anything. Publicly or privately." He looked to me.

There was no point in replying to that. Envoy Vhillar had more than deserved what he'd gotten. "What else is happening that you haven't told me?"

"Besides the fact that you gave Draffyd pause with your medical imaging?"

"I didn't know what else to do."

"As I recall, when you get into those positions, usually trouble follows."

"That was why I went to Draffyd."

"He was grateful. He did admit you might make a competent imaging medical surgeon, but he wouldn't want to put a scalpel in your hand. You have the dexterity, but not any practice."

"I wouldn't, either." The thought of cutting into people, even for a good reason, wasn't all that appealing. "What else?"

He shrugged. "Everything is very quiet at the moment."

"That's the most disturbing thing you could have said."

We both laughed, and before long I was headed back to our house to spend what I hoped would be a quiet afternoon and evening with my family.

The rest of Samedi was quiet and pleasant. So was Solayi, until I had to stop by Third District station for a glass or so in the afternoon. As I'd suspected might occur, there had been five more elver deaths, three in the taudis areas, and two others, one just off the Plaza SudEste and one in a quiet area only a block from the Anomen D'Este, where my family attended services. There wasn't much to do but record the deaths. The rest of Solayi was pleasant, or as pleasant as it could have been with the drizzle that oozed over the city in late afternoon and turned everything chill and gray.

The beginning of the week was routine, even for Seliora, with only few more orders coming into NordEste Design. As for Third District, on Lundi, Mardi, and Meredi, the patrollers reported another six deaths from elveweed, three in the taudis and three outside. Thefts and assaults were down, and there was only one killing, at a tavern off Sudroad, near the Guild Square. That was also low for half a week, but I wasn't complaining.

When I arrived at Third District Station on Jeudi, my first question to Lyonyt, seated behind the duty desk, was, "How many last night?"

"Just one, sir."

That was about what I'd expected, because elvers tended to come into coin near the end of the week, either through casual labor or from pilfering money from those with whom they lived and who were generally paid on Vendrei.

At that moment, Zylpher, one of the junior patrollers in Third District, rushed through the door. "Captain! There's been another explosion! This one was in the Banque D'Excelsis, the one on the Midroad just south of Plaza D'Este. Khallyn had me take a hack. It's waiting outside."

That branch of the Banque D'Excelsis was in Third District, if barely, and that meant I'd need to look into it, and in a hurry. "Lyonyt, send a messenger to headquarters and have them send an explosives expert to the banque. Also, tell the lieutenant that's where I'll be."

"Yes, sir."

I hurried back out through the door I'd entered moments before, followed by Zylpher.

The hacker took us up Elsyor, but with all the congestion near the Plaza we got out a block away, where I hurriedly paid the driver and then half-walked, half-trotted the distance to the banque.

People had stopped and were looking at the front of the banque. Khallyn and two banque guards had stationed themselves before the entrance to the building. I stopped for a moment to survey the scene. The damage appeared to consist of a set of iron doors bent apart and a great deal of broken and shattered glass scattered everywhere. What I didn't see were metal fragments or anything like shrapnel or grapeshot.

As I stood there, a messenger hurried up to me. He wore the orange and black sash of one of the private services. "Sir? Are you Patrol Captain Maitre Rhennthyl?"

"Yes."

He extended an envelope, unsealed. "This is for you, sir."

"Can you tell me who sent it?"

"No, sir. He didn't give his name. He paid a gold for an anonymous private delivery." With that, the young messenger was gone.

I wasn't sure I wanted to open the envelope, thin as it was, but I eased shields around it as I slipped out the single sheet. The lines were written so perfectly they might have been engraved.

The explosion was to get your attention . . . and that of your superiors. Ask the banque's director about the missing funds in the account of the Portraiture Guild and about the recent drowning of a clerk and the accounts he tended. You might also find certain fund transfers of some interest, particularly those sent to Councilor Caartyl from the Banque D'Solis and a smaller amount from the Banque D'Ouestan to a Cydarth D'Patrol.

Khallyn and Zylpher both looked at me.

"Some information." I slipped the envelope into the inside pocket of my tunic. "Zylpher, if you would take Khallyn's place here?"

"Yes, sir."

When I stepped through the bent doors, followed by Khallyn, another burly guard stepped forward as if to block our way, then took in the uniforms. "Sir . . ."

"Patrol Captain Rhennthyl and Patroller Khallyn." I smiled politely.

"Yes, sir."

"I'd like to see the director about this." I gestured back to the front of the building and the windows that had shattered against their iron bars.

He didn't look very happy, but I hadn't met a guard yet who wanted to turn away a Civic Patrol Captain who also wore the emblem of an imager, although I doubted he knew I was a master imager as well.

As I stepped past him, a thin man in a blue pinstriped jacket and trousers, with a cravat patterned in silver crescents, stepped forward. His face was dominated by sweeping waxed black mustaches and slightly bulging green eyes. "Officer . . . everything is in hand here."

"Captain, Captain Rhennthyl. Also Master Imager Rhennthyl. Physical violence against an inhabited structure and injuries to inhabitants is a criminal offense, even when it involves the interior premises of a private enterprise." I smiled politely. "Perhaps you could tell me exactly what happened here. Oh . . . and you are?"

"Director Tolsynn. This is my branch."

"Good. What happened?"

"We hadn't opened for the day. A wagon stopped in front, and two men jumped out and rammed the door ajar. They forced something between the doors and drove off. It exploded. Some of the clerks were cut by splinters and glass, but no one was seriously injured. A few have cuts and scratches."

"Did anyone see the men well?"

"I only saw that they wore dark brown, with hoods. Cheluryn was the closest clerk. And Mhanyn. He was the guard. He was about to unlock the door."

"If you'd have them talk to Patroller Khallyn . . ." I nodded to the dark-eyed patroller. "I'll need some more details from you."

Tolsynn glanced to his left, toward the guard who had wanted to stop us.

"Khallyn, if you would find out what you can from the guard and the clerk?"

"Yes, sir."

I looked at Tolsynn. "Please continue."

"Captain . . . no one was seriously hurt, and nothing was taken." He shifted his weight from one foot to another.

"A bombing that causes damage to a banque and injury to its employees is not trivial," I said mildly. "It's also against the law, and enforcing the law and finding the perpetrators—and the reasons for their actions—is the duty of the Patrol."

At my mention of reasons, I could sense an increase in tension. "I see you think there might be someone who had a reason to bomb this branch of the bank. Could you tell me who that might be and why?"

"I cannot. I really don't know of any reason."

I had a good idea that he was lying. "I presume, with your location here, that you handle the accounts of some of the Guilds and factoring associations."

"Our client list is privileged, Captain."

"I did not ask who your clients were, Director." I smiled coldly. "I asked if you had clients of that nature."

Tolsynn moistened his lips. "It would be logical to assume that."

"Would that assumption be wrong?"

"No, but I shouldn't say more than that."

"Has any client indicated that you needed to take special precautions?"

"Of course not." His tone bordered on outrage.

"There is one other matter that might be related . . ."

"Oh?" His tone was close to that of dismissal.

"The clerk who was recently found drowned."

His eyes flickered. "I don't understand. What does Kearyk have to . . . What business is that of the Patrol?"

"It could be that people don't believe that Kearyk drowned. Not on his own accord, at least. It just might be that drowning was a convenient way to keep matters from being exposed. So-called accidents and suicides do happen that way."

"That's a serious allegation, Captain."

I smiled again. "I don't believe I alleged anything. Bombing a banque is a serious offense. When a bombing occurs following a drowning of a clerk and the Patrol is informed that the two might be connected, we are obliged to pursue the matter." I waited a moment. "What can you tell me about Kearyk?"

"He was an account bookkeeper. He'd been with the bank for eight years. Very neat. Very well groomed. Very accurate with his figures. He was very reliable."

"Where did he live?"

"How would I know? He was referred to us by the Grammaire D'Martradon. That was years ago." Tolsynn looked past me.

I turned. A squat patroller with a leather case stood just inside the doors. "Excuse me for a moment. We have a few more things to discuss." I walked over to the patroller with the case.

"Captain . . . I'm Chenoyt. You sent for me? With reason, it appears."

"I did. We've tried to keep people clear, but I'd like you to look all this over and tell us what you can."

He nodded.

"If you don't need me at the moment . . ."

"No, sir."

I returned to Tolsynn. "We were talking about your clerk Kearyk. Would you care to give me your thoughts on his drowning and the disappearance of funds from the account of the Portraiture Guild?"

Controlled as he was, Tolsynn still twitched. "There's no problem with the accounts."

One of the many things I'd learned over the years was that the world was far smaller than people realized, and that someone always knew someone else. Most times I had to look to find the connections. Once in a while, as now, I already knew. "You know, or perhaps you don't, that before I became an imager and a patroller, I was a member of the Portraiture Guild. What you probably don't know is that the head of the Guild is the cousin of a well-known Maitre D'Structure. Now . . . we can discuss these matters now, or Master Reayalt and Maitre Schorzat can come and discuss them, doubtless with less courtesy."

"We'd best go to my study." Tolsynn didn't quite sigh, but I could sense the resignation.

I followed him to a study smaller than mine at Third Station. He did not sit behind the narrow desk, but stood beside it, clearly hoping our talk would not take too long.

"After Kearyk's death was reported," he said after several moments, "I immediately audited the ledgers and the accounts he handled. I didn't expect anything unusual. That's just the normal procedure when an employee dies or leaves. It's to make sure that whoever takes over the accounts starts with a balanced and accurate set of records. The accounts balanced, but . . . there was a letter from the clerk at the Guild claiming that the account had one hundred golds missing, and with the letter was a listing of withdrawals and deposits. I checked the daily ledgers and found a withdrawal that was not in the list sent by the Guild, but it was the last one of the day, and the hand was different."

"Someone entered it later?"

"Kearyk was the one who closed the daily ledger that Meredi, but the hand wasn't his."

"He could have disguised it."

Tolsynn shook his head. "I don't think so."

"That suggests someone had access to more records than that one ledger," I pointed out.

"We've checked through all the ledgers. We're not finished, but so far, there seem to be no other discrepancies. We have, of course, returned the hundred golds to the Guild account."

"Might I see one of the daily ledgers?" I asked.

He turned to the case beside the desk and handed a wide ledger to me. While the account book was bound, the binding was secured with brass screws so that pages could be added.

"Could you show me a page that closes the daily transactions?"

Tolsynn turned several pages, then pointed. Right below where the last entry was a stamped ornate foil seal pressed into the paper.

"Who has access to that seal?"

"I do. So does the head clerk. No one else."

"Where is it kept?"

"In the vault at night. It's locked in the head clerk's desk during the day."

I nodded. "I may have some more questions for you later, Director."

"Do you have any idea . . . why?"

"Someone wanted to send a message to the Patrol. I don't think it has much to do with the banque, but it's too early to say. I'll let you know as soon as possible what else we find out." I stepped back and nodded. "Thank you very much."

It was clear enough to me that neither Tolsynn nor the head clerk had anything to do with matters, except as unwitting accomplices, but someone in the banque did, someone who knew the routine, probably poor Kearyk, who had been pressured to switch a single page in the ledger and enter the withdrawal on the Guild account. The entire routine had been designed to call attention to the funds transactions involving Caartyl and Cydarth. The bigger questions were who was behind the gambit and why.

Once I left Tolsynn, I made my way to Chenoyt, who was closing his leather case. "What have you found out?"

He lifted the case, then turned to me. "This wasn't so much a bomb as an explosive. It looks like they used damp guncotton packed in heavy pressed paper with a fuse set to ignite a dry guncotton primer."

"They wanted a big explosion but limited damage?"

Chenoyt nodded.

"If you'd write that up for me . . . and headquarters."

"Yes, sir."

"Thank you."

Before we left, I talked to Khallyn, but he hadn't discovered that much more than we'd heard when we'd first gotten to the bank. So I left the two patrollers and hailed a hack.

When I returned to the station, I stopped at the duty desk. "Lyonyt, send an inquiry to the other districts. See if they have any information on a bank clerk by the name of Kearyk D'Cleris. He drowned recently. Send whoever's on unattached duty to the Grammaire D'Martradon to find out what they can on him. He left school there maybe eight or nine years ago, but they might have records, or someone might remember him."

"Yes, sir."

I headed to find Alsoran and to brief him. I wouldn't write up a report for the commander until I got the rounds report from Kallyn and Zylpher and the report from Chenoyt. I'd also decided that I wouldn't be able to accompany any patrollers.

By the end of the day shift, I had a written report on the banque explosion and some information on the drowned clerk. The drowning had been reported in District One, because it had taken place in the River Aluse a mille south of the Bridge of Hopes. That was where Kearyk's body had been found. I decided against talking to the clerk's family until I had checked with Dichartyn.

When I picked up Seliora, she looked concerned, but I didn't ask about what, just helped her and Diestrya to the duty coach and boosted my daughter inside.

As the coach began the trip to Imagisle, Seliora asked, "What was your day like?"

"Another elveweed death and another explosion. This one was at the Banque D'Excelsis near Plaza D'Este. We'll need to talk about that later, and I'll need to tell Master Dichartyn when we get to Imagisle. What about your day?"

Seliora's eyes widened slightly, but she nodded and said, "Odelia didn't come to work today."

"Do you know why?"

"Even Aunt Aegina doesn't know. She left to go over to Kolasyn and Odelia's place just before you came."

I did know that, after Kolasyn and Odelia had gotten married, less than six months after Seliora and I had, Odelia had moved to the quarters over the small metal-working shop Kolasyn had inherited from his uncle, for whom he'd been an apprentice. "I hope everything's all right."

"It's my fault. Yesterday, she was complaining about Haerasyn again. I said that, if he wanted to destroy his life, she and Kolasyn couldn't do much to stop him. She said that I was cold and hard-hearted, and that she didn't see how you could stand me."

I managed not to swallow. "You didn't tell me that."

"It hurt too much. I wanted to think about it."

I put my arm around her. "You were right about Haerasyn. It's not as though he doesn't know the dangers. He's ignoring them, and he's using Kolasyn's coins to buy elveweed."

"I think Haerasyn's pilfered coins from Odelia's wallet, too. That's from what she's sort of said at times."

"Pilfer . . . pilfer . . ." contributed Diestrya.

"Pilfer means to take from someone," Seliora said. "You shouldn't pilfer. It's not good."

Diestrya nodded. "Not good."

Once we reached Imagisle, I left Seliora and Diestrya and walked swiftly to and across the quadrangle to the administration building. Dichartyn's door was closed. I knocked. "Rhennthyl here."

Master Dichartyn opened the door.

I saw a young imager seated before his desk, as I once had been.

"It's urgent?" He raised his eyebrows.

"Relatively. It's about an explosion at the Banque D'Excelsis."

He turned. "Eamyn . . . we'll have to cut this short. Read the next section of the anatomy text and the next chapter in the history."

Eamyn rose quickly and scooped up his books. He was around seventeen and had just made tertius. I recalled that, because Dichartyn had asked me to spend several glasses with the young man in the spring, telling him about how the Civic Patrol worked.

"Sirs," he said as he left, inclining his head.

I closed the door and launched into briefing the Collegium's head of security, a position listed nowhere. When I finished, I waited for the inevitable set of questions.

Instead, Dichartyn nodded and simply asked, "What do you think?"

"All I can surmise is that the explosion and the alteration of the ledger were set purposely to establish the credibility of the note I received . . . and to create enough of a crime to allow me the legal ability to question the branch director."

"You didn't ask about Caartyl or Cydarth?"

"No. It struck me that a tip about missing funds could have a legal tie to an explosion, enough to warrant questions, but that wouldn't allow me to look for perfectly legal fund transfers." I paused. "I mean that the mechanism of the transfer was legal."

"I understood what you meant." Dichartyn nodded. "There are two possibilities. First, someone wanted you to overreach and to embarrass the Collegium and the Patrol. I doubt it, but that is a possibility to be considered. The second is that the plotter wanted to call the Collegium's attention to Caartyl and yours to Cydarth. Did you enter the note as evidence?"

"I haven't yet." I knew that withholding it was scarcely legal, and that not turning it in represented another possible trap, but so did turning it in, under the circumstances.

"There's some danger in that, but I'd agree. Just keep it safe."

I nodded. "Could it be an attempt to remove Caartyl from the Council for misfeasance or malfeasance?"

"Whether it is either would depend on the source of the funds. What if it's simply an inheritance or the payment of an old debt that someone is trying to characterize as something untoward by linking it to an actual embezzlement?"

"And what if someone, knowing that Cydarth is not among my most favorite of superiors, is trying to get me to act against him?"

"Or . . . both could be true . . . and that is the most disturbing of possibilities."

"Because only the Collegium could discover such and that would drag us into it all?" I asked.

"Precisely. Still, as I told you earlier, Caartyl pushed through the cartage reform bill. I wouldn't be surprised if he received some reward."

"From Broussard? Or from the Ferrans? Or both?"

"Broussard's too smart to pay anything even remotely close to a reward."

"Is he getting support from the Ferrans?" I knew the Ferrans had a longstanding agenda to undermine the High Holders, for philosophical, political, and practical reasons.

"Not a chance. Caartyl hates them as much as the Jariolans and the High Holders."

"That sounds like someone wants to cause trouble for Caartyl."

"Who doesn't?" Dichartyn's laugh was soft and dry.

"We'll never be able to discover who's really trying to do that, let alone prove it."

"That's very true. That's why you're in the Civic Patrol, and why I'm doing what I do in the ways open to us."

There wasn't much else that I could say to that.

Dichartyn shook his head. "There's one aspect of this that bothers Schorzat immensely, and that's the fact that the Ferrans haven't attacked the Jariolans yet."

"They're waiting for something, reinforcements from somewhere? Who would see an advantage in joining them?"

"I was thinking about hostilities elsewhere, as in Otelyrn, so that the Council will be reluctant to get more involved in Cloisera."

"Didn't Schorzat take care of the Caenenan situation already?"

"That doesn't mean that something couldn't erupt in Stakanar or Tiempre or Gyarl. Schorzat doesn't have enough field operatives to cover everything. We've had word that Tiempre has moved troops toward the border with Gyarl. They're claiming that the followers of Puryon are persecuting the Duodeusans in Gyarl. Stakanar is also calling up troops."

That wasn't good, and it certainly would make the Council leery of committing more ships to the northern ocean.

"What do you suggest I do?" I asked.

"What you've been doing. Watch for signs of anything else unusual . . . and be alert for anything that affects either Artois or Cydarth."

"What exactly is going on there?"

Dichartyn paused, then finally said, "Councilor Reyner is pressing to have Artois replaced on the grounds that he has been Commander for too long."

"Fifteen years is a long time."

"You'd want Cydarth as commander?" His voice was wry.

"Does anyone on the Council besides Reyner want Cydarth?"

"Most factor councilors, except they won't admit it."

"Why?"

"Because the Civic Patrol also runs the piers and the river patrol, and Artois enforces things like wagon weight limits and safety rules."

"Any wagon accident, and we have to check for any weight and safety violations." I paused. "The factoring associations are really upset about that?"

"They don't like the Council interfering in trade, and they see that as the first step toward a return of High Holder control, where the High Holders don't get cited because so many of them have ironway stations on their lands, and those stations aren't subject to the local patrols."

"So their right of low justice effectively exempts them."

Dichartyn nodded.

As I walked back across the quadrangle and north to the house, I wondered if Solidar would ever escape from the abusive remnants of the times of the Rex and High Holders.

13

When I reached Third District on Vendrei, I checked the duty logs immediately. There were two more deaths—one a homeless beggar found in an
alleyway off Elsyor and another elver. The old beggar died from "natural"
causes, such as neglect and poor health. Then I began to assemble the information that had come in on the banque clerk.

According to the reports, Kearyk was older than I'd assumed, four years
younger than I was. His father was a baker who had a shop on Sage Lane,
right off North Middle to the east of Martradon, and Kearyk had lived there
with his parents. If I'd gone by the procedures, I should have informed Bolyet,
but the parents weren't perpetrators or suspects, and I just wanted information. So I took a hack out to Sage Lane. The shop wasn't hard to find, since it was
near the corner—not quite classy enough to qualify as a patisserie, nor pedes-
trian enough to be the corner bakery. The name over the window was Bakery
D'Rykker. The air around the shop carried the odor of baking, of fresh loaves
more than pastries.

I stepped inside.

A short but rotund woman looked at me with wide eyes that darted from
the grays to the imager emblem on my visored cap. "Sir . . . ?"

"I'm Civic Patrol Captain Rhennthyl."

Her eyes went back to the imager pin, questioningly.

"I'm also a master imager. Are you Madame D'Rykker?"

"Giseylle D'Rykker."

"Kearyk D'Cleris was your son, then."

"He was. Why are you here, Captain?"

"Did you hear about the explosion at the Banque D'Excelsis? When we
looked into it, we discovered some interesting things that might have involved
your son, and I wanted to talk to you about him."

A man who appeared too angular to be a baker stepped through the archway that led to the rear of the shop and the ovens. He brushed his hands on
his smudged whites, then looked up as if he hadn't seen me before. He started
to glare, then recognized the uniform and glanced at his wife. "What have you
done now?"

"He's a Patrol Captain. He's here about Kearyk. I told you it wasn't an accident. I told you he didn't kill himself. So did Kleinryk."

Why would Kearyk want to kill himself? "Why didn't you think his death was an accident?"

"He didn't like the water. He was always afraid of it. He was a good boy . . . a good man. Handsome as he was, he was kind and gentle," said Giseylle.

"He was the oldest, wasn't he? But you sent him all the way through grammaire. He didn't join you here in the bakery."

"He didn't want to be a baker," Rykker said.

"He did well at grammaire, and he was a very good clerk. He never got married, though, and he lived with you." I had an idea, but I wanted to see if their reaction would support it.

The two exchanged glances.

"He had a very fine hand," I added. "I've seen some of what he wrote. Did he leave any indication that he was discouraged or upset before he drowned?"

"No."

"When did you see him last? The night before he died?"

They looked at each other again. I waited.

"No," she finally replied. "He did not stay here all the time."

"He never stayed here," added Rykker. "He had a friend."

"Do you know her name? I'd like to talk to her. It's important." I doubted strongly that the friend was female, but I could have been wrong.

"His name is Lacques. He's a . . . street artist," replied Giseylle.

"A chalker?" I asked. "Do you know where I could find him?"

"Him?" Rykker snorted. "He practices his . . . art . . . all around the Plaza D'Este."

"Kearyk never told us where he lived," added Giseylle.

"Did Kearyk ever say anything that suggested he might be in any sort of trouble?" I pressed.

"He never talked about his work," replied the mother.

"Numbers and figures . . . I wish he had stayed here," said Rykker. "He was good with the pastries, but he said he didn't like it."

I talked with them for three-quarters of a glass, but I didn't learn any more about why Kearyk drowned . . . or had been drowned. They did show me a miniature portrait of him, and it showed an extremely handsome young man with short curly blond hair and fine features.

After that I walked up North Middle toward the Plaza D'Nord, thinking over what I'd found out so far, and studying the neighborhood. I was a block

from the Plaza when a patroller stepped from a side street—Silvers Lane—
and hailed me.

"Captain Rhennthyl!"

I turned, but didn't recognize the man. "Yes?"

"Sir . . . I just wondered . . ."

"I'm over here to talk to someone who might be a witness in a case that
happened the other day in Third District." I didn't want to explain even that
much, but refusing to say anything would have suggested I was up to no good,
rather than just trying to avoid burdensome procedures.

"Oh . . . yes, sir."

I smiled politely. "If anyone has any questions, they know where to find
me."

"Yes, sir." He stepped away.

I kept walking.

It wasn't hard to find Lacques, a thin blond man with short curly beard
and a receding hairline. Not only was he one of the few chalkers around in late
morning, but he had just finished signing a long mural on the stone in front of
a boarded-up building a half block off the Plaza. He saw the uniform and
stiffened.

"I wouldn't run, Lacques. I'm also an imager. Besides, I only want to ask
you a few questions.

His eyes took in the imager emblem on my cap and the pin on my grays.
He didn't relax, much as he slouched as I walked toward him. I looked over
the chalk drawing of an abandoned building, with a figure peering over broken and uneven stones. The figure had a face that was split into two sides.
One side showed a cherubic blond young man with an innocent blue eye and
a happy half-smile framed with pinkish lips. The other side of the face depicted an angular and hard-eyed young woman with high cheekbones and a
deep-set eye with a black iris. Her hair was swept back and curled over a bare
shoulder, her mouth outlined in slashing red. It wasn't bad.

"Did you ever study with a Guild artist?"

"Those pretenders?"

"Hand me the red and the pink chalks," I said.

He frowned.

"I'll give them back."

After a moment, he handed them over.

It took me longer than I'd thought it would, but when I finished, the female half-face of the figure held a rose, with its green stem caught by white

teeth, a single drop of blood seeming to hang in mid-air above the uncovered shoulder. I handed back the green chalk. "I think that fits in with what you had in mind."

He looked at the rose and then at me.

"Some of the Guild artists aren't pretenders." I couldn't deny that there were some, like Aurelean, who had aspects of pretenders, because Aurelean was a competent artist who pretended he was great.

"You . . . oh . . . you're the one."

I didn't bother to ask for a clarification. We both knew what he meant.

"I understand you were a very good friend of Kearyk. Why did he drown?"

"He didn't drown. I walked all the way down to Patrol headquarters. I told them he was drowned." Lacques's voice turned bitter. "They didn't listen."

"Do you remember who didn't listen?"

"It was a patroller. He said his name was Merolyn."

Merolyn was Cydarth's assistant. "What else did he say?"

"He said he appreciated my concern, but the body showed no signs of anything but drowning. There were no wounds, no bruises." Lacques shook his head. "There wouldn't be. Kearyk was terrified of water. He wouldn't even walk on the river side of the promenade. All anyone had to do was carry him to a bridge or somewhere on the river where the water was deep, and he would have drowned."

"What else did the patroller say?"

"He started asking about why I was interested. I knew what he had in mind. If I pressed, he'd drag me in, say we had a lover's quarrel."

"Did you?"

Lacques shook his head. His eyes were bright. "Kearyk was supposed to meet me for dinner at Felter's. He never showed. I never saw him again."

"Did he ever mention that he had any troubles at the banque?"

The chalker tilted his head, and his brow furrowed. "No . . . well . . . not exactly. He did say something about the director badgering him about a ledger page missing from his desk, but it was a blank page. It bothered him. Little details, those bothered him. Fire could be raining down from Erion, and he'd be worried about whether he'd capped his inkwell tightly enough."

At that moment, I wished I'd actually insisted on looking at the altered page that Tolsynn had mentioned. I'd have wagered that the entire page had been forged, probably carefully and over time. "Did he mention anything else?"

"No. I don't remember anything. I just remembered that because it was so odd. A blank ledger page. Who would even care?" He shook his head again.

As with the Rykkers, I went back over everything and added questions. After half a glass, I hadn't learned anything else.

As I walked away from Lacques, I was debating whether to get something to eat at a bistro near the Plaza because I'd sampled all of those in easy walking distance in my own district. At that moment, a hack pulled up, across the square, and a figure in the bluish grays of a patroller stepped out. He hadn't taken three steps before I recognized Bolyet. So I just waited for him.

The Fifth District captain grinned as he walked up. "Morrsyn sent word that you were headed toward the Plaza D'Nord. I thought it might be a good idea to see what you were following. Do you care to tell me?" His tone was easy.

"You got word about the explosion at the Banque D'Excelsis in District Three, the one just off the Midroad?"

"You're following up?"

"We got a tip that one of the clerks might be involved. The only problem is that he drowned before the explosion. I was talking to his family and friends . . ."

Bolyet nodded. "You'll keep me informed?"

"Of course, but I have to say it's not looking very promising."

"You do have a way of making the unpromising promising, Rhenn."

I shrugged. "I'm just telling you. I will let you know if something turns up." I paused. "Have you heard anything about Cydarth pushing to become Commander?"

Bolyet laughed, sarcastically. "He's never said anything to me, but it's no secret that's what he wants. He's mentioned it to some of the lieutenants, including Yerkes. Yerkes doesn't think I know that. Alsoran mentioned it to me, just before he left to come back to Third District. Good man, Alsoran."

"I know. I was fortunate to get him."

"No . . . Cydarth let you have him because he didn't understand how solid Alsoran is. He thought that Alsoran would be ineffective because he doesn't speak unless he has something to say." After a moment, he asked, "Anything I should know?"

"You might watch out for elveweed among the wealthier students at Jainsyn's."

"That's in Third District."

"It is, but half the students come from Fifth District," I pointed out. "I thought you might like to know, given the subcommander's directives."

"What about things I can do something about, Rhenn?"

I had to think for a moment. "Well . . . that's a problem. There's someone running around setting explosions, but I don't know who or why, except that whoever it is happens to be an expert. There's the stronger elveweed, but I only know it has to be grown under glass or in the south of Solidar, and I have no leads on who's behind that." I shrugged. "I don't know what else."

"What about the banque case?"

"Explosion, but no one stole anything. The only tip we got was that a drowned clerk had embezzled funds. The records show he did."

"That stinks worse than a week-old mackerel in midsummer."

"Tell me about it."

"Someone thinks he was framed," Bolyet said.

"I suspect they do, and what exactly can I do, except watch and try to run down leads?"

He shook his head. "As if we didn't have enough else to do."

I decided against eating in Fifth District and caught a hack back to Third District station. On the way back, my thoughts went back to the picture Lacques had drawn. The side that had been a young man resembled the miniature I'd seen of Kearyk, but the other side suggested something very different. Yet . . . even with that insight, I didn't know what else I could do.

Once I reached the station, I headed for Alsoran's study. He was about to leave.

"Do you have a moment?"

"I do. I was just going to change the night rounds. Joran is going to fill in for Severyn."

"How is he?"

"The slash he took from putting down the brawl at Semplex is finally healing."

"Good." I followed him back into the study, but didn't sit down. "I followed up on the business with Kearyk. He had a lover, not a woman, and the lover thinks Kearyk was drowned. The clerk was terrified of water. But one other thing came up. The lover's a street chalker, and he claims he went down to headquarters to tell them Kearyk had to have been drowned on purpose. Merolyn dissuaded him and offered a veiled threat. So when I talked with Captain Bolyet I asked a bit about Cydarth, and . . ." I looked to Alsoran.

"From the way you referred to the subcommander, sir, I thought you knew. He's been trying to get all the lieutenants behind him for years. I guess he figured most would become captains. He wasn't real pleased when you forced Warydt into a stipend, you know?"

"His displeasure was rather obvious, but I didn't know that was part of the reason. I just thought he didn't like the amount of control I had over Third District."

"No, sir. He doesn't. He's just waiting for your last term to end."

Or until he could find a way to oust Artois.

"What are you going to report on the bank explosion?" Alsoran asked.

"I'm not going to report anything for a bit. We'll leave the case open for now. If nothing turns up in a month or so, I'll report it as a failed robbery. I don't know what else I can do."

"It wasn't ever intended to be a robbery, was it?"

"I strongly doubt it. They want someone to look into things at the banque, matters that involve the dead clerk . . . maybe more." I shrugged. "Without proof, though, I don't know what else we can do."

Alsoran nodded.

The rest of the day was held to a mugging, two thefts, another wagon smash, another elver death, and a husband beating his wife so badly she might not live. All in all, close to a typical Vendrei.

When I reached NordEste Design and Seliora opened the door, I could tell something had happened from the look on her face.

Her first words confirmed it. "Haerasyn stole all of Odelia's jewelry and all their golds. He ran off. No one knows where."

I couldn't say that I was surprised. "I hope it wasn't too much." I stepped inside the foyer and closed the door behind me.

"The jewelry bothers her more than the golds. One of the brooches came from Grandmama's mother."

"He's likely already fenced or pawned it. Or he will soon. If someone gives me a description, I can circulate it to the goldsmiths who handle pawned goods. They'd hold it, but Odelia would have to pay . . ."

"Aunt Aegina would pay . . ."

And that was how the occupational events of the day ended, not that we didn't have to get on with returning home, feeding and getting Diestrya ready for bed, and all the other details of domestic life.

14

Because it was my turn for Samedi duty at Third District, I got up in the darkness before dawn, made my way to the exercise facility, and endured Clovyl's tortures . . . and the run, which was always a relief of sorts, after strenuous exercise, practice in hand-to-hand combat, and defense against weapons. Seliora was still asleep when I returned. I was grateful for that, because we hadn't gone to bed that early. She'd needed to talk about how upset Odelia had been.

I actually had to wake Seliora after I showered and shaved, not that we had time for anything besides a quick embrace, because Diestrya was already awake, and we struggled through the rest of the morning routine, including a hurried breakfast. Because of the consternation created by Haerasyn's thefts, by the time we finished eating Seliora had decided that she and Diestrya would spend the day with her family, and I'd join them after I finished at Third District.

"You already told your family, didn't you?" I asked.

"I told Mother we would, unless you had other plans." She gave me a sideways smile.

I just shook my head as I rose from the table. "I can probably be there by fifth glass."

"We won't eat until sixth."

"I'll try not to be late . . . but it is Samedi."

"Can you do something about the brooch and the other jewelry?"

"I can circulate the word among the goldsmiths in Third District and ask them to pass it to others."

"Do you think it will work?"

I shrugged. "It just depends."

"It would be nice, but we won't count on it."

That was the best attitude, unhappily.

Before long, we hurried out the door, leaving the house to Klysia, who would soon be leaving it even emptier, since she had most of the weekend off and to herself. The duty coach ride to NordEste Design was uneventful, except when Diestrya saw a pair of matched tans, and began to chatter about "pretty horsies."

At that point, Seliora and I just grinned and listened.

After I walked them to the door at NordEste Design, still holding my shields, and then walked back to the duty coach, I scanned the newsheets on the ride to the station, but there was nothing new, except for a report that the Ferrans were sending more land-cruisers to the border with Jariola.

I wasn't looking forward to duty, not at all, but I would be able to start circulating a description of Haerasyn and the stolen jewelry, both to Third District patrollers and to all the other districts. The Third District patrollers were more likely to keep an eye out for him, but it was always possible patrollers in other districts might see him. If Haerasyn happened to be smart about it, he'd stay well away from Third District. But then, stealing from a relative of a Civic Patrol officer wasn't the brightest of acts.

Delanyn smiled as I walked into the station. "Good morning, Captain."

"Good morning. Quiet so far?"

"Yes, sir."

I hadn't expected anything else. Very little happened early on Samedi, except for the business of making sure that the offenders brought in on Vendrei evening were secure for the weekend, since they stayed at the station until Lundi morning, when they'd be sent to headquarters for charging, or quietly released if their only offense had been being too rowdy.

I stood at the duty desk reading the log and round reports. There had been three more elver deaths since I'd left the station on Vendrei, one in the taudis and two in other areas. A tinsmith's apprentice had been found dead in the alley behind the shop, at Sudroad and the Avenue D'Artisans, and the body of a well-dressed young woman had been found seated on a bench in the gardens behind the Anomen D'Este.

The second case seemed odd, and I went over Freasyn's report. There was absolutely nothing that would identify the woman, who was reported as being in her early twenties, but Freasyn had noted that her wrists appeared bruised, and that she barely smelled of elveweed, although a smoked pipe had been found just beyond her hand, and the remnants of elveweed had been the greener and stronger variety.

I looked to the duty patroller. "Delanyn . . . has the body wagon been here yet?"

"No, sir. Should be any moment, though."

I turned and headed toward the rear of the station. "I'm going to look at the woman elver."

"Yes, sir."

The body room was the last chamber in the station, with thick walls, and in fall and winter the barred windows were opened to keep it cool. I opened the door, ready for anything, but the day was early and cool, and the only smells were that of faint decay and stale elveweed. Three bodies lay on the long tables, uncovered. There wasn't any sense in covering them. I moved to the body in the gray woolen suit on the second table.

The woman hadn't been all that much older than my sister Khethila, but she'd been attractive, possibly beautiful when animated by that spirit we call life, with lustrous shoulder-length blonde hair. From the piercings in her earlobes, she'd been wearing earrings, but they were missing. I studied her hair, and there was something like lint in it. A red woolen scarf with a weave pattern I didn't recognize was arranged around her neck. A scarf, and it was still largely in place? I eased it away from her neck, revealing an abrasion on the left side, as if a chain or necklace had been roughly removed. There were ring marks on her fingers, but not where a wedding band would have rested.

Most important, every elver I'd ever run across, dead or alive, had reeked of the weed. This one didn't. Oh, there was a faint odor, but nothing like the overpowering stench that emanated from them. There was another odor, even fainter, that I recognized from my training with Master Dichartyn. That was pitricin—a poison that also sent a victim into convulsions if administered orally. That explained the bruises on her wrists. She'd been restrained forcibly, probably with a towel across her clothes, while someone had squirted the poison down her throat. But why would anyone do it that way? Pitricin could easily be added to wine or other liquids that would mask its taste . . . at least for long enough that the victim wouldn't be able to do much about it.

I could see trying to cover a murder with the idea of elveweed excess, but there was something else about it . . .

I studied the body again. She'd been wearing a long skirt, but I didn't see any shoes or boots. Then I looked at her feet. They were cut and bruised in places. I checked the skirt. The seams near the bottom had been strained and stretched. She'd been running, barefoot.

For all that, there was still something I was missing. Even if I couldn't figure it all out, I had an idea who might be able to help.

I eased the woolen jacket and the scarf off the body and draped them loosely over my arm, then walked from the chill of the body room, closing the heavy door behind me, back to the duty desk.

Delanyn looked up as I stopped in front of the high counter.

"We're going to hold the woman elver's body until tomorrow."

"Sir . . . ?"

"She's not that far gone, and it was cold last night. I need to check on something. Put it down in the logs as my orders."

"Yes, sir." He shifted his weight on the tall stool and looked inquiringly at me.

"She was murdered. Most likely pitricin poisoning. I'm going to see someone who might be able to tell me about her . . . or at least where she might be from."

My words got a nod and a "Yes, sir."

As I headed out to hail a hack, I had no doubt that at least a few patrollers would hear about what I'd said. I'd have preferred not to explain, even as much as I had, but Patrol Captains who did strange things without explanations created rumors more destructive than the disclosure of information could ever be. That had been what I'd observed.

It took me half a glass to get a hack and to travel to Alusine Wool. There were only two carriages waiting outside. I stepped out of the hack, alert and shields held firmly, as they always were from the time I woke until the time I went to sleep.

The factorage remained the same old one-story yellow-brick structure I'd always known, a long building stretching close to eighty yards and fronting West River Road. Khethila had nagged Father to enlarge the covered entry in the middle of the building to make it more impressive, and he'd finally given in, just before he'd agreed to let her take over the factorage in Kherseilles. I still wasn't certain how much of her pressure for improvements had come from a desire to improve the image and the clientele and how much had been part of her stratagem to pressure Father to let her take over running the Kherseilles factorage. Still, even Father had admitted the improvements in the entrance and the more open space just inside the doors seemed to have improved business.

The loading docks were out of sight in the rear, as they always had been. As I hurried up the three steps to the double oak doors, I noted that it was about time to re-varnish them and repaint the dark green casement trim, but I wasn't about to suggest that at the moment. Once inside, I crossed the open space to the racks that held the swathes of various wools. To the left were the racks with the lighter fabrics—muslin, cotton, linen. Despite the factorage's name, Father had always carried a considerable range of fabrics.

"Master Rhennthyl, what a surprise!" Eilthyr was now totally bald, but his smile was welcoming and genuine. After ten years, he remained in charge of the day-to-day work on the floor.

"I was looking for Father." The raised platform at the back, from where Father could sit at his desk and survey everything, was empty.

Culthyn saw me coming and hurried across the floor from behind the racks to the left. "Rhenn . . . what are you doing here?"

"I need to talk over something with Father. About wool."

"He's in the small storeroom in the back."

I was all too familiar with that part of the factorage, since it had been fire-bombed years before in the events that had led to Rousel's death. "Thank you." I turned and nodded to Eilthyr. "It's good to see you again, Eilthyr."

"And you, too, Master Rhennthyl."

I walked to the small storeroom.

Father was indeed there, checking one of the permanent wall racks. He looked up, surprised, then smiled. "I didn't think I'd see you here on a Samedi."

"Patrol business." I held up the jacket and the scarf. "They're not from here, but I was hoping you could tell me something about them."

He stepped forward and took the garments, laying the red scarf across a rack gently, and then began to study the gray wool jacket for several moments, murmuring and mumbling to himself. Then he straightened. "The jacket is southern mountain wool . . . likely from the hills north of Ferravyl . . ."

Ferravyl . . . what was it about Ferravyl, except that it was a major barge and transport nexus? I forced myself back to concentrating on Father's explanation.

". . . We don't buy any of that. It's soft enough, like top Glacian, but it doesn't wear all that well. The only factorage I know that deals with much of it is a place in Ruile . . ." He paused. "Chaeran Woolens . . . that's it. He uses it for the southerners who like things soft and don't wear wool day in and day out."

"Can you tell me anything else about it?"

"It's a one-off, done by a seamstress, probably the second or third one in a High Holder's estate."

"You can tell that?" I had to say I was impressed.

Father shrugged. "That's a guess, but the inside trimming is just a touch off, and the stitching thread is Parmian cotton, the kind that lasts forever. Street seamstresses don't use it. Now . . . I wouldn't swear to the Nameless on that, but that's what I'd judge." After a moment, he asked, "Where did you get it? It smells . . . sort of . . . off."

"The odor is elveweed, and the garments belonged to a dead woman who was supposed to have died of elveweed excess. I don't think she did. She was probably poisoned, but someone tried to make it look like elveweed." I paused. "What about the scarf?"

He handed the jacket back to me and picked up the scarf. After only a moment, he handed it back to me. "That's from Etyenn. He's the only one who uses the arbora red dye. It's cheap, but it fades in a year or two. The wool has his weave, but there are hundreds of scarves like that. It's faded a bit, and it's probably three years old. Sort of scarf someone your sister's age would wear, not that she would. She's got better taste than to wear something so common." He frowned. "The elver woman . . . she wore both of these?"

"They were both with her." I knew what he was thinking, and I didn't disagree.

"Bartering beauty . . . that's a dangerous business." He shook his head.

"You think . . . ?"

My father smiled ruefully. "The jacket was a gift. The scarf she purchased. That would be my guess."

That made as much sense as anything.

"Will you be coming to dinner any time soon?" he asked.

"Not soon. We have a couple of, shall we say, required engagements. A dinner with the Ryels and then the Council's Autumn Ball next weekend. After that . . ."

"I'll tell Maelyna. Namer-damned thing when you have to plan family dinners weeks in advance."

I started to speak, but he held up a hand. "I know. You're working six days out of every seven and many nights as well, and you two are trying to keep two families happy when you scarce have time for yourselves." He smiled. "It's just that it's so good when you come. Could be that bride of yours. You were fortunate there, Rhenn."

"I know. I do know."

"You be careful, now," he added as I turned to go. "The last time a war loomed, you got shot and then some, and more than a few people wouldn't mind your absence."

"Is that your opinion . . . or has Veblynt suggested that?" Veblynt's wife was a relative of Iryela's mother, and had come from a fallen High Holder family. He still had contacts, and his warnings were to be heeded. "Did he say more than to be careful?"

"My thoughts and his . . . if you must know. And no, he didn't. He said he'd just heard rumors."

"Thank him for me."

"I already did."

Since Culthyn was nowhere to be seen when I left the storeroom, I just went out and hailed a hack on West River Road. The hacker took the Sud Bridge over the River Aluse and went up the Avenue D'Artisans.

I considered what I'd discovered. The scarf was common, coming from the factorages of Councilor Etyenn, and the jacket was handmade and of quality wool and tailoring, but sewn by a seamstress personally for the wearer. I couldn't help wondering for which High Holder she'd been a mistress, or more likely a serving maid who was a convenient concubine. I also wondered what she'd done to displease whichever High Holder it had been, and why her body had been dumped in Third District, if less than a block from Fifth District. While I had some scattered thoughts, with what I knew there really wasn't any way to track her farther. Not yet, at least.

The rest of the day was uneventful, for a Samedi in a district Civic Patrol station. I copied a number of descriptions of the missing brooch and had them given to patrollers who covered areas with goldsmiths. I also copied and circulated a description of Haerasyn and his offenses and posted it in the station, as well as dispatched it to the other districts.

We had a rash of grab-and-runs reported near both the Guild Square and the Plaza SudEste. I sent two more patrollers to each, telling them to make themselves very visible, and after that, there were no reports. I'd probably just sent the young thieves into District One or Five, or possibly even Two, but there wasn't much else I could have done. Besides, if the other three boosted their patrollers in the heavily shopped areas, we'd have fewer thefts. Then again, I was shifting patrollers from areas where there weren't many offenses, and I couldn't do that for long . . . or there would soon be crimes there. All of us faced the same problem—not enough patrollers, because the Council was reluctant to increase taxes.

When I left at a quarter past fifth glass, the patrollers had only brought in one disorderly and one assault, but the assault would go to charging and trial. He already had a hip brand, and he'd tried to carve up a bistro bouncer with a dirk. I did have to leave word with the duty desk where I was, but I just hoped nothing serious enough to send a patroller after me would happen.

When I reached NordEste Design, Bhenyt opened the door even before I lifted the hammer-shaped bronze knocker. "Good afternoon, Rhenn. Well, I guess it's evening."

"Good evening." I glanced past him toward the steps.

"Everyone's here," he said with a smile. "The twins are taking turns with Diestrya."

"Is she behaving?"

"She was, but she always does." He grinned. "Mother says she's just like Seliora was at that age."

Betara and Seliora were waiting at the top of the steps.

"Have you heard anything about Haerasyn?"

Betara shook her head.

"I put out the word about the brooch and Haerasyn. So far, no one's reported anything, but it's early for that. How are Odelia and Aegina?"

"We haven't seen Odelia today," Seliora said. "Aunt Aegina is furious. I think she's irritated because Odelia and Kolasyn weren't careful."

I certainly would have been less than pleased, but I'd seen how little elvers cared for anything but a supply of the weed, and it was hard to imagine that unless you'd been attacked by a crazed elver . . . or seen the emaciated and wasted bodies.

"Mama has some news for you," announced Betara.

"She's upstairs?"

They both nodded, and Seliora and I led the way up to the third level. Before long, the four of us were seated around the plaques table, and Mama Diestra had shuffled the deck and set it to the side.

"We have reports of three more Pharsi deaths, all of them in Ruile, this time," said Diestra.

That didn't surprise me, especially after my day. Still . . .

"Does anyone know where the stronger weed is coming from?" I asked.

"What would be your thought?" Mama Diestra looked at me intently.

I couldn't help but see the tiredness in her bloodshot eyes, a tiredness held in check by sheer force of will. "I don't think that anyone could grow as much under glass as we're seeing. That suggests it has to be coming from the Sud Swamp or the lands surrounding it."

"What else does that suggest?"

I took a moment to consider because the implications weren't exactly good. From what I recalled from my study of Solidaran jurisprudence, there weren't any penalties for growing elveweed, only for providing it to smokers directly. I suspected that was because no one had ever grown it in Solidar. "You're suggesting a High Holder, probably one who is either debt-ridden or greedy." If not both.

She nodded. "It's being hidden in grain and other shipments on the ironway from what we can determine. The dealers pay off the loaders."

"But not with the weed," I replied. "Otherwise, we'd have deaths of ironway loaders. Did the deaths in Ruile come after you started sending out inquiries?"

Betara frowned. Mama Diestra nodded.

"So it's likely the weed is coming through the ironway from Ruile and being sent east and west from there. Do you have any proof of why it's only going to the five cities?"

"No. We're only surmising it's those five cities, but there aren't any reports of the strong elveweed in other cities."

That made sense to me, except I couldn't have explained why. It just did.

Mama Diestra looked across the plaques table at me. She smiled, sadly. "Much as has been expected of you, Rhenn, even more will fall onto your shoulders."

As if I needed that . . .

Seliora looked to her grandmother. "Is it anything you can tell him?"

"Only that you must survive stone and fire . . . and that there will be times when no place is safe."

Seliora looked hard at Diestra.

"I have seen you emerging from piled stones with fire in the distance. That is all I have seen."

I tried not to shudder.

Seliora turned to me. "You've seen it, too, haven't you? That night . . ."

I nodded. "That was all I saw, too."

A long silence filled the plaques room.

"Dinner is almost ready." Betara looked at her mother inquiringly.

"I'll have the broth Aegina fixed and the plain noodles. That will be enough."

I could tell Betara wanted to insist that Mama Diestra eat more, but, good daughter as she was, she only smiled. "I'll bring it right up."

Seliora and I followed Betara down to the main level. We did hold hands, and I knew dinner would be tasty and that no one would mention all the problems.

15

I woke up with the sun on Solayi, calm and peaceful, until I sat up and tried not to think too hard about all the scattered and seemingly unconnected things that I felt were somehow linked in a far larger pattern. The problem was that I didn't have enough information to know whether I was correct or whether I was merely wishing that they were all connected.

At breakfast, Seliora and I refrained from talking about Haerasyn. What was there to say?

"Have you decided what to wear to the Autumn Ball?" I managed not to grin.

Seliora raised her eyebrows. "Husbands have been shot for asking that question." But she laughed. "Yes. It's a surprise." Her face turned serious. "What do you think will happen there?"

"I'd be surprised if anything happened there. I'd also be surprised if we didn't learn something that someone wished we wouldn't."

"That's why we were asked?"

I shrugged, then scooped up Diestrya off the chair beside me just before she had managed to climb into position to grab a knife.

"Did you ever find out what the banque explosion was all about?"

"Someone used the death of the clerk to call my attention to a whole raft of things, and I can't believe that transfers and possible payoffs to Cydarth and Caartyl and missing funds to the Portraiture Guild are related, especially given the small amount that was taken."

"A hundred golds? That's not small."

"If you're embezzling from a banque, that's enough to put you in the workhouse for life. You'd be better off stealing a thousand and vanishing." I thought again about the precise writing on the note that I'd placed in the hidden strongbox in my main floor study. That writing suggested something carefully planned . . . but I still couldn't figure out what really had been intended.

Seliora tilted her head. "Maybe they're related in a different way."

"What do you mean?"

She shook her head. "I can't say. It's just a feeling."

"You're probably right, but I wish I could figure it out." I paused. "The dead girl who was supposed to be an elver and wasn't bothers me, too. She didn't die on that bench. She'd been moved from somewhere else. I wish I knew why."

"To get your attention. Because you're the only Patrol Captain who could stand up to a High Holder."

That also made sense. "Someone else was watching the girl, and she was going to tell someone. She was killed, but before her body was found, they moved it?" I almost shook my head. "That's not only far-fetched, but dangerous, if not really stupid."

"Not for another High Holder."

With more than a thousand High Holders, and a good hundred having estates around L'Excelsis, even if Seliora happened to be right, that didn't help matters much, especially since neither the Collegium nor the Civic Patrol had jurisdiction on the lands of a High Holder, except with evidence of a capital crime definitely linking specific people or locations to that crime. I couldn't very well visit every one of them, just on suspicion, even if I had a good idea . . . which I didn't. And whoever moved the body had to know that as well.

Had she been moved all the way from somewhere near Ruile? It was cold enough to use the ironway, and no one would ever open a High Holder's crate or trunk. That possibility gave me a very chill feeling, especially since the stronger elveweed had to come from there. I'd have to talk to Dichartyn about that, since I certainly had no legal authority that far from L'Excelsis.

At that point, Diestrya indicated that certain functions needed to be catered to, and we left the breakfast room.

The morning was sunny, but the clouds swept in from the northwest, and by mid-afternoon a chill drizzle had settled over Imagisle. I fired up the stove in the family parlor, and, after Diestrya's afternoon nap, Seliora and I alternated reading, while whoever wasn't reading was playing with a very cheerful, but very active daughter.

After an early supper, I didn't really want to go to services, but Seliora and I exchanged glances, and our looks told each other that we needed to. We both were hoping for something inspiring from Isola's homily. Leaving Diestrya in Klysia's care, we made our way southward along the stone walk above the west river wall.

"Rhenn . . . I've been thinking. What do you think the point was for the elveweed dealers to attack the Pharsi families in those port cities? The families don't like elveweed, but they've never gone out of their way to stop others, except close to their establishments. Why five cities?"

"It could be the beginning," I offered. "To see if it increases their take."

"Do you really think so?"

"No. But I don't know what it is, except that it can't be just for the elveweed. The dealers can get more coin for the stronger weed, but I have to believe it's harder to grow here in Solidar. If it weren't, we'd have seen it earlier, and we'd be seeing it all over the place."

"Could it be a High Holder who needs coin to keep his lands?"

"It could be a freeholder." I didn't think so, given the wool jacket the girl had worn, but a wealthy freeholder could have had it made.

We didn't reach any solid conclusions by the time we walked into the anomen.

As usual, I suffered through the singing, but Isola's homily wasn't bad, and part of it intrigued me.

". . . the name is not the object nor the action. That is a basic tenet of the Nameless. But there is a corollary to that simple tenet. Mistaking the name for what it represents is the first step toward theft, deception, lying, and intrigue. Theft is the easiest to explain, especially theft of coins. Although coins have value in themselves, if they're silver or gold, they're also a representation of a small part of life. How can that be? Because we work to earn those coins. We spend a portion of life to obtain them. So . . . when one says that something 'is only coin,' they're devaluing the life it took to obtain that coin. Deception, lying, and intrigue all rest on the use and manipulation of names to misrepresent the reality for which the names stand as symbols . . .

"Let us say two councilors are debating the need to raise tariffs, and one states that he only proposes an increase of one copper on a gold's worth of cargo, a mere increase of one part in a hundred. The other councilor immediately replies that merchants will have to pay twice as much. Could they both be accurate? Indeed they could, and yet both deceive, and both can deceive because the cargo does not stand before them, nor the amount of tariff to be paid in either case . . ."

Isola went on to point out that the farther names are removed from that which they represented, the easier deception becomes.

By the time services were over, the drizzle had changed to sleet, and our return to the house was far swifter . . . and colder.

16

Because I really didn't want to try to catch Master Dichartyn after breakfast, as soon as I finished the four mille run in the dimness of Lundi morning, I stopped and waited for him to finish eating. He just looked at me.

"Are you headed back to your house, sir?" I asked.

"Yes. What is it?" He shook his head and started walking.

"I'd mentioned the stronger elveweed. There have been some other strange developments . . ." I quickly filled him in on the young woman, as well as the probability of the stronger elveweed coming from around Ruile. "I can't prove any of this, and there's nothing that I can do about it, but I felt you should know."

Dichartyn didn't speak or look at me, but kept walking. Finally, he said, "I've learned to my regret that when you suggest connections among seemingly unrelated events, improbable as those connections may sound, I ignore them at my own risk. However . . ." He drew out the word. "Could you enlighten me as to what you think they all mean?"

"In specific terms, sir . . . no. I do think that they're all part of something much, much larger, and I feel that it involves at least one High Holder, the freeholders of the southeast, and some Ferran agents. It might be a way of causing unrest in Solidar or increasing the costs of food for the Army and Navy—"

"Are you suggesting that things like that would distract the Council from pursuing action against Ferrum if the Ferrans actually invade Jariola?" Dichartyn shook his head. "Something like that would be counter-productive. If the Council discovers that the Ferrans are trying that kind of sabotage, even those who sympathize with the Ferrans would turn against them."

"Would they, sir? All of them?" Based on what I'd seen, I wasn't so sure. More than a few well-off artisans and factors were less than pleased with the policies and actions supported by the High-Holder-influenced Council.

"Not all of them, but even the greatest Ferran sympathizers certainly wouldn't say anything."

I couldn't argue with that.

As we neared our houses, Master Dichartyn turned to me again. "I won't say that all this isn't linked, but I think we're both missing something, and I'd like you to think it over."

"Yes, sir. I can do that."

But I didn't have time even to discuss it with Seliora over breakfast because Diestrya was cranky and stubborn, and that wasn't like her. Neither Seliora nor I could find anything wrong with her, and she didn't seem to be cutting teeth. Besides, fussiness over teething had never been a problem for Diestrya.

In the end, we all managed to get dressed, fed, and to where we needed to be by approximately when we were supposed to be there. I even read both *Veritum* and *Tableta*. I was vaguely surprised that hostilities still hadn't broken out in Cloisera, and not at all astounded to learn that both newsheets had stories on both the continuing increase in elver deaths and on grain-field fires southeast of Solis, but neither newsheet mentioned to whom the fields belonged . . . or the extent of lands ravaged.

I had just begun to have a chance to mull over Dichartyn's words when I entered Third District station. I didn't have a chance to consider them for long, because I'd barely reached the duty desk when Lyonyt addressed me.

"Sir . . . did you hear about Captain Bolyet?"

I had a sinking feeling with those words. "No. What happened?"

"There was an accident—some wagons got tangled at the intersection of North Middle and Bakers' Lane . . . one woman hurt and so was a teamster. One of those work wagons with a crane, the kind they use to lift things, was one of them. He was trying to get the wagons untangled and the crane or the hoist broke loose and smashed his head. He never knew what hit him." Lyonyt shook his head.

Bolyet was a good captain . . . or he had been, and I'd liked him. Had his death been an accident? Even though I had no other information, I had my doubts. But was that just because after nearly six years in the Civic Patrol, I doubted any coincidence? Was I becoming suspicious of everything, and for no reason? Was I seeing conspiracies and patterns that really didn't exist?

"Thank you," I finally said. "He was a good captain."

After that, the day didn't get any better at all. Since I'd left the station on Samedi evening, the patrollers had discovered three more elver deaths, and had two others reported from outside the taudis. It couldn't just have been Third District, either, because in mid-afternoon a courier delivered a message from Commander Artois, calling a meeting of all District captains for eighth glass on Meredi morning. The subject was elveweed deaths.

Then there was a fire at the tinsmith's off Sudroad, not a block from where I was grabbing a hasty bite to eat at Arnuel's, and in the confusion, three smash-and-grabs went down in other shops nearby. I was just getting ready to leave the station when Helorran and Sonot returned with a swarthy man bound in cuffs. Sonot had a long slash from his ear to his chin—thin, but bleeding—and that required me to sign off on the charges, because they involved an assault on a Civic Patroller.

On more personal matters, none of the goldsmiths in Third District reported finding the gold brooch that Haerasyn had stolen, and none of the districts had found Haerasyn—not that most would have actively looked for him, since they had higher priorities than seeking a low-level elver thief. I was beginning to think Haerasyn had pawned everything within glasses of taking it. But then, maybe he still had the jewelry and was using the stolen golds for elveweed. In that case, there was a chance of recovering the brooch. Not much of one, but a chance.

I finally left the station a good half-glass late, but Seliora just looked relieved when I appeared at NordEste Design.

Once we were in the duty coach headed back to Imagisle, I turned to Seliora. "There's no word in the patrol about Haerasyn, and none of the goldsmiths in my district have come forward. Has anyone in the family heard anything?"

"No." Seliora paused. "Some of Aegina's personal jewelry is missing . . . older pieces she hasn't worn in years. She thinks Haerasyn might have taken them when he was here for the party at the turn of summer."

I almost missed the last of her words, because Diestrya twisted in my arms.

"She's been restless all day, and she's a little warm."

"That's all you need . . . her getting sick, especially with both the Fhernon and Haestyr commissions . . ."

"If Alhyral would just let his bride-to-be deal with it, everything would be fine."

"Is he still trying to proposition you?" I wouldn't have put it past the slime-snake, High Holder or not.

"No . . . except he's always undressing me with his eyes when Dhelora's not looking."

"She has to know."

"What can she do? Even Iryela . . ." Seliora shook her head.

Neither of us needed to say more about the gilded prisons that held the wives of High Holders.

Between Diestrya's squirming and my own concerns about the way the day had gone, I was more than glad when the duty coach came to a halt on Imagisle and we could start to walk back to the house. The cool air felt welcome after the closeness of the coach, and Seliora held Diestrya by one hand, and I held her other. The sky was so clear that even Erion's thin waning reddish disk was sharp, hanging above the Council Chateau.

On the river I saw a steam tug moving steadily upstream, even with the houses of the senior maitres, including ours. The tug towed three barges, and, as with the string of barges I'd seen a week or so earlier, two of the three were riding higher. But there was also a bargeman standing on the rear barge, the one riding the highest, and he looked to have a spyglass, one trained in the direction of Imagisle.

I could imagine that a bargeman might well wonder about Imagisle, but would a bargeman have a spyglass?

"My tummy hurts. It hurts." Diestrya halted, looking up. "Make it stop, Mama."

Seliora knelt, then frowned. "Her stomach is rumbling."

At that moment, Diestrya bent forward and vomited all over the stones of the path.

I turned from the barges and the bargeman with the spyglass to the immediate problem, the one facing all parents with small children at one time or another.

17

Diestrya was sick enough that, on Mardi, Betara and Seliora ended up trading off taking care of her at our house. While Diestrya was better on Meredi, Seliora told me that she and her mother would take care of her the same way, so I ended up taking the duty coach straight to Civic Patrol headquarters for the captains' meeting ordered by Commander Artois. That gave me a little more time to help Seliora before I left. I just hoped that neither Seliora nor Betara caught whatever illness Diestrya had.

Because I got to headquarters more than a quarter-glass before the meeting, I slipped into the charging section, where I'd worked briefly years before. Back then, Gulyart had been the patroller first who had headed the charging section, but he now worked upstairs under Lieutenant Sarthyn, as one of the patroller clerks who dealt with all the administrative requirements for bringing a prisoner to trial. Now the patroller who ran the charging desk was Buasytt, a graying veteran whom I'd never seen smile. He'd finished the chargings for night's prisoners, and the day's offenders hadn't appeared yet, doubtless because very few offenses occurred in the morning.

"Buasytt . . . what was the weekend like?"

The patroller ran a large hand through his thinning short hair. "A real madhouse, Captain. That didn't even count all the dead elvers."

"What about this week?"

"Real quiet. Can't say as how I've seen it this quiet in a long time." He laughed. "Maybe the weekend was enough. Except for the elvers. Captain Sub-unet says we've got reports of a few more last night."

I nodded. "We've all seen more elver deaths." I smiled. "Take care."

"You, too, Captain."

I made my way up the back steps to the second level and then along the hallway, past the doors that held the various officers' studies, including those of Cydarth and the Commander. Only Sarthyn's door was open, and he wasn't there.

Jacquet and Kharles were already in the conference room, standing beside the windows that looked east. They looked up. Kharles had dark circles under his eyes.

"It looks like you've been fighting the Namer," I offered wryly.

"Haven't we all?" replied Jacquet. "Kharles just has more of his disciples in his district . . . although I hear things haven't been good in Fifth District, and you've had fires and other problems."

"It's not what you'd think," Kharles said tiredly. "We haven't caught or charged a taudis-tough in a week. It's all amateurs or the Duodeans or the Puryons . . . or whatever the Tiempran religious types call themselves." He stopped, looking past me.

I turned. Hostyn had just stepped into the room, trailed by Lieutenant Yerkes, who was apparently the Acting Captain of Fifth District. Behind them was Subunet, followed almost immediately by Cydarth and the Commander. The fact that Artois wasn't waiting for his captains to settle in suggested, as much as the meeting itself, that he was more than professionally concerned. Commander Artois looked thin, almost gaunt, not that he'd ever been particularly beefy or muscular, and he sat down quickly, barely waiting for all the captains to take their places at the conference table.

As soon as the last rustle died away, he spoke. "You all know the subject of the meeting. You may not know that the Council has found the growth in the number of elveweed deaths distressing. Appalling, in fact. There have been more elveweed deaths in the past four weeks than in the entire previous year. There is one anomaly in the reports." His eyes turned to me.

So did Cydarth's, as well. I waited.

"Deaths in all districts are up, but in one district they're up less than half the rate in any other. Captain Rhennthyl, I've studied your report, and it's rather . . . remarkable. In addition to a much lower death rate, you have the only district where the elveweed deaths are barely higher in the taudis areas than outside them. Would you care to explain how you obtained that remarkable achievement? Especially in such a short time?"

"Sir . . . it's not because of anything I've done in the past few weeks. When I first became a captain, there was a tremendous elveweed problem in the taudis in Third District, and the patrollers and I made a strong and determined effort to drive the dealers out of the area. We also worked on preventing schoolchildren from being used as runners. This is something that we've pursued for years, and I've made it very clear to the taudis-dwellers where I stand on this. We certainly haven't been able to stamp out elveweed, but we have been able to restrict it."

"Can you be sure that you just haven't neglected the less . . . well-off areas in order to patrol the taudis?" asked Cydarth, his deep voice sounding more sinister than reassuring.

"If you would like to review the patrol logs, Subcommander, I'd be most happy to make them available to you. But I'm most certain that you will find no change in the patrol patterns and times in Third District over the last several years, and very little change from the patterns established by my predecessor."

"If he says it's so, Cydarth," interjected Artois, his voice tired, "it's so."

"Of course. Of course."

Only Cydarth could inject so much doubt into words of agreement.

Should I let him get away with it? I decided against it, this time. "With such doubt in your voice, Subcommander, I really do think you should come out to Third District and go over the logs. I wouldn't want you to have any misapprehensions." I looked at Cydarth and projected total assurance.

He sat back in his chair and did not speak for a moment. Finally, he said, "It's been a rather trying business for all of us, Captain. I did not mean to suggest . . ."

"Good!" snapped Artois. "The question is what the rest of you can do about the problem . . ."

"We don't have Rhenn's . . . special contacts . . ." offered Yerkes.

The acting captain's words confirmed some of my suspicions.

"Oh?" asked Artois. "Exactly what contacts do you think he has, Lieutenant?"

"He is an imager."

"I haven't seen the Collegium patrolling Third District," Artois replied coldly. "I have seen that he has made an effort to discover the taudischefs and talk to them. That is not beyond your abilities, I don't believe. Is it?"

"I think, Commander," added Cydarth smoothly, "that what acting Captain Yerkes means is that the taudischefs are more likely to talk to an imager."

Artois looked to me again.

I smiled. "Like all patrol officers, I started by walking rounds. Admittedly, it was as a liaison, but I did walk rounds, and, like some good officers, such as Captain Bolyet, I have kept walking rounds and talking to the people on the rounds. I have met every taudischef in Third District by walking rounds." Except for the two who had avoided me and were dead. "I don't think this is impossible. Lieutenant Alsoran continues to do the same, and I suspect that there are other Civic Patrol officers who do the same. It is more work. I'd be the first to admit it, and it's hard on feet and boots." I looked at Cydarth, as guilelessly as I could. "The problem is, Subcommander, that if an officer hasn't been doing it all along, then people get suspicious when he starts doing it.

My talent was in listening to the patrollers who were effective on their rounds, and following their example."

Cydarth started to speak.

"Enough," said Artois. "We're not going into a discussion of how captains maintain the peace." His eyes fixed on Yerkes. "Your task, Lieutenant, is to run Fifth District effectively, based on your abilities. Others have certainly done it, and they weren't imagers either. Do you understand?"

"Yes, sir."

Yerkes had paled, but I suspected there was more than a little rage beneath the subservience.

Again, I looked from Artois to Cydarth, the one tense and nervous and stressed, and the other calm, almost serene, and I knew, even if I couldn't prove it, that Cydarth was somehow linked to the problems plaguing the Commander and the Civic Patrol. The problem was that Cydarth had never cared for me. And he'd certainly care a great deal less for me now.

Artois looked at the captains, one by one before he spoke again. "If you have to incarcerate every drug runner in L'Excelsis for the next week, do it. We can't keep that up for long, but it might buy us some time . . . while other measures are being implemented."

We all knew that implementing the Commander's orders wouldn't help much. Since he usually didn't give those kinds of orders, the pressure on him had to be considerable. From there, the meeting dwindled away into a few minor changes in procedures and then a rapid closure.

I took my time rising from the conference table, letting Yerkes and Hostyn follow the Commander and subcommander. Subunet and Kharles followed, but Jacquet lingered slightly, murmuring as he moved away from the table, "Cydarth won't forgive you. Neither will Yerkes."

"I know." I smiled. "But I don't forget, either, and I only forgive honest mistakes."

We both knew that Cydarth forgave nothing.

18

The fourth week of Feuillyt was definitely a time for unplanned meetings, because when the duty coach picked me up at Third District station on Jeudi afternoon, Lebryn had a message requesting my presence at half-past fifth glass in Maitre Poincaryt's study. Then, when we reached NordEste Design, I discovered that Seliora had been through a long day with Diestrya, and the card-reader on one of the jacquard looms had broken. It had taken Seliora the afternoon to rebuild it, and that had meant Betara and the twins had been stuck with a very cranky, if recovering, Diestrya.

Seliora just looked at me after she read the card signed by Master Dichartyn.

"I didn't plan it," I finally said.

"It would be today."

"I'll get home as soon as I can."

"Don't hurry."

I winced. I hated that tone in her voice.

"Rhenn . . ." Seliora said softly, shaking her head. "I'm not upset at you. But don't hurry. If they need to talk to you, it's important. If you're worried about us, you won't be thinking about whatever it is." She leaned toward me and kissed my cheek.

That kiss helped.

After we reached Imagisle, I did have time to cart Diestrya to the house, and that was necessary because she wanted to sit down and dawdle and otherwise show that she was three years old and had a mind of her own. Then I hurried back to the administration building.

Both Maitre Poincaryt and Dichartyn were waiting for me in the comparatively capacious second-level study of the Maitre of the Collegium Imago situated on the southwest corner. I slipped into the vacant seat in front of Master Poincaryt's desk, beside Master Dichartyn.

"We asked you to join us, Rhenn," began Maitre Poincaryt, "because we believe that Solidar faces one of the most potentially dangerous situations in years. There are a number of matters that lead us to that conclusion, and we would like to describe them to you, as well as hear anything from you that may bear on them."

"Yes, sir."

Dichartyn turned to me. "From everything we've been able to determine, the Ferrans should have attacked Jariola before now. They have not, and it is extremely costly to hold large forces in readiness away from their normal bases for weeks. Yet that is exactly what the Ferrans have done, and they have always been conscious of costs."

"Furthermore," added Maitre Poincaryt, "our sources indicate that two Ferran field commanders have been summarily relieved over the past weeks. But there have been no official disciplinary actions taken."

I'd never thought that avoiding war was a bad idea, but both Maitre Poincaryt's tone and the statement itself suggested more. "You think they're waiting for something else to happen? You're concerned that it might be something here in Solidar?"

"Actually, Rhenn," Dichartyn said mildly, "you're really the one who suggested it . . . if you recall. Have you any more information about either factors or elveweed?"

"The number of elver deaths is up, and it's affecting more and more young people outside the taudis. Commander Artois had a meeting of all the District captains yesterday. . . ." After I explained that, as well as mentioning, again, the death of the woman who hadn't been an elver, they both nodded, if as acknowledging something they already knew, if not in detail.

"There have been more fires and flooding of the freeholder grain and flour storage facilities, not only around Piedryn, but across much of the southeast of Solidar," added Dichartyn. "Another grain silo of High Holder Haebyn also caught fire and exploded."

"Are the southeastern freeholders and High Holders turning to arms yet?" My words were sardonic, yet I couldn't help but worry.

"The Council has cautioned both the High Holders and the freeholders, and the 'accidents' have dropped off in the last week." Maitre Poincaryt's voice was dry. "Unfortunately, I just learned from the Naval Command that quite an amount of old munitions, as well three bombards, have been found to be missing from the Army Ordnance Depot outside Ferravyl." Maitre Poincaryt's voice was so calm he might have been discussing the duty maitre's schedule— a task from which I was exempted so long as I served with the Civic Patrol.

Even Dichartyn looked surprised. "When did that happen? Is there anything linking Broussard or Haebyn to the disappearance?"

"There's no link to anyone. Worse is the fact that they've apparently been missing for months. That may explain what was behind the Place D'Opera explosion."

"The munitions make sense, but bombards? Who would want them? They're essentially immobile siege guns. How old are they?" asked Dichartyn.

"So old that no one missed them, initially," replied Maitre Poincaryt.

"How could anyone walk out with one of those?" I asked. *Let alone three.*

"They probably planned it months, if not years ago," replied Maitre Poincaryt. "We don't know, but I'd wager that they posed as an Army or Navy transport team and used official wagons or the like, then transshipped whatever they took in official crates and used the ironway or a river steamer. Several tonnes of older munitions are missing."

"And the Army just found out?"

"A marshal and several generals have been relieved. An investigation is under way." Poincaryt looked to me. "That's another reason why we wanted to talk to you. Dichartyn has said you had an explosion at a branch of the Banque D'Excelsis in your district."

"Whoever did it was an expert. It was designed to bend the outer doors open, but not to injure anyone. So far as I could determine, as I told Master Dichartyn, the entire idea was to get my attention so that I would believe the information handed to me."

Dichartyn nodded. "We have been led to believe that the funds transfers were shifted from commercial accounts in overseas branches."

"Both of them?" I asked.

"So we've been told; but without seeing the actual ledgers, we can't prove whether Subcommander Cydarth and Councilor Caartyl are being set up or paid off." Dichartyn's lips pursed in an expression between disgust and frustration. "Without evidence, we can't question either one."

"Have you seen or heard anything more about the use of explosives here in L'Excelsis?" Maitre Poincaryt asked me.

"No, sir."

"There's one other matter," observed Dichartyn. "No one has shot at you or attacked you, have they?"

"No."

"That's troubling . . ."

I understood why. The last time Ferrum had gone to war, they'd deployed assassins all across Solidar, and more than a score of imagers had been killed. If the Ferrans were considering war against Jariola, and the likelihood that Solidar would oppose Ferrum, then given the fact that the Collegium had created problems for Ferrum in the past, why hadn't there been any resumption of attacks against imagers? But . . . there was one other thing. "Did you hear that Captain Bolyet was killed in an accident by a loose crane on Lundi? His lieutenant is acting captain, and he's definitely a backer of Cydarth."

Poincaryt and Dichartyn exchanged glances, and the Maitre of the Collegium nodded ever so slightly before asking, "Have you heard anything from your other sources?"

"I told you about the Pharsi deaths. I still think they're connected."

"So do we, but we haven't figured out how they fit in and why they'd benefit the freeholders, the factors, or the Ferrans."

We talked a while longer, although they did most of the talking, largely about possibilities and cautions.

"Before you go, Rhenn, there is one other thing." Maitre Poincaryt smiled pleasantly. "You also need several sessions with Draffyd. He's expecting you on Lundi night at seventh glass for the first. If that interferes with your Civic Patrol duties, you can change the day."

"Lundi night will be fine." For me, though not necessarily for Seliora; but the sooner I got through whatever they wanted, the better.

When I met Draffyd for another grisly session of many was, I suspected, up to me; but now that I'd revealed that I had some talent for medical imaging, Maitre Poincaryt was determined it would be developed as much as practicable. And I'd need to fit that in with everything else at a time when both Seliora and I were handling more than either of us had planned on . . . not to mention a daughter who was clearly less than pleased with the diminished amount of attention available from her parents.

19

For all of the worrying and discussion that had taken place on Jeudi afternoon in Maitre Poincaryt's study, absolutely nothing out of the ordinary occurred in Third District on Vendrei, although I had cautioned all the patrollers to be alert for anything unusual and to let me or Alsoran know. Not that there weren't lawbreakers, because there were, including three out-of-work casual laborers who decided to grab at every wallet in sight around the Plaza D'Este. They hadn't been exactly sober, but it took three patrollers and several bystanders to subdue them before they were carted off. Another elver was found dead, and Caesaro had to bring in a tart for blatantly soliciting on the sidewalk on the Midroad, and then for trying to cut him up with a dagger.

After my exercises and run on Samedi, Seliora left me with our daughter and took a hack to NordEste Design so that she could catch up on everything she hadn't been able to do when Diestrya was ill earlier in the week. I couldn't really complain. I'd worked every other Samedi for the past five years.

Even so, by half-past ninth glass, Diestrya was looking and acting restless. So, despite the chill, I stuffed her into leggings and her coat and cap, and we set out on a walk. The wind was light but chill, but the sunlight was bright, although I could see clouds to the northeast, moving toward L'Excelsis, it seemed.

We didn't get all that far—just to the gate to Maitre Dyana's dwelling—where she was trimming the thorn-roses.

"Good morning, Diestrya," she offered.

"Good morning," Diestrya replied. "What are you doing?"

"Trimming the thorn-roses." She set the iron shears on the top of the wall. "How are you doing, Rhenn?"

"I'm fine, but I have to say that I'm worried. I feel like everything is about to explode, and yet there's nothing obvious."

She laughed, wryly, reaching down and easing the shears away from Diestrya's inquiring grasp. "Usually, those are the worst catastrophes. This one looks worse than the Stakanaran-Tiempran disaster."

I'd read about it, when the Stakanarans had tried to invade the south of Tiempre and seize the diamond and gold mines, but I didn't recall it. That wasn't surprising, since it had taken place when I'd been about the age Diestrya was. I'd always wondered what Maitre Dyana did, but her statement suggested something I should have seen earlier. "Was that when you had the position that Schorzat does now?" That was a guess, based on a few observations.

She smiled. "You're doing better every year, Rhenn. As a matter of fact, I'd just taken over from Maitre Poincaryt."

"Dichartyn took over from you, later then, as head of security?"

She nodded.

"But you still get all the reports and advise the Maitre of the Collegium?" I grinned. "Are you the, shall we say, unannounced deputy to Maitre Poincaryt? The heir in waiting?"

"Not the heir in waiting." She shook her head. "Not with this Council, or probably any Council in the near future." She smiled. "Just think about Madame D'Shendael . . . or about how much it took for your sister to be acknowledged as a factoria—after she'd totally turned around the Kherseilles branch of Alusine Wool and increased revenues every year for five years, so much so that she handles most of the wool trade there?"

I managed to nod, as I eased Diestrya away from the pile of thorny cuttings beside the stone wall. I'd never told anyone those facts. Neither had Father; but what Maitre Dyana had said in just a few moments confirmed her position and her access to the covert network that Dichartyn controlled—and that was mentioned nowhere. "Doesn't it get to you, though? Not being recognized or appreciated for what you do?"

"It bothered me greatly when I was younger. It bothered my husband more . . ."

I never realized she'd been married.

". . . but when I look at Poincaryt, Dichartyn, or you, all having to carry full shields all the time, and you worrying about your family every moment of every day . . . I've come to realize that there are worse things than being unknown—or underknown, as you once suggested to Dichartyn."

"Why did you pick the three of us as examples? You didn't mention Rholyn or Jhulian."

"You three are the most visible, much as Dichartyn tries to keep a low profile. You're the designated targets, if you will."

"Were we picked because we have the strongest shields?"

She laughed again. "All of you picked yourselves, you more than the others. I don't think you could keep a low profile in pitch darkness in an abandoned gold mine. That's not without benefit for the rest of the Collegium, because people tend not to look past the others, especially you."

I had to pick Diestrya up and set her down away from the pile of thorny branches. "What do you think will happen next?"

"War. The question is when. Ferrum won't give up, because Jariola gets weaker every year. You can't maintain strong commerce and industry under a hereditary oligarchy. Stakanar is still eyeing the mines in southern Tiempre, and the Abierto Isles want to annex Meritas. The Council really doesn't want to continue building up armaments, although they keep talking about modernizing the fleet. That won't happen anytime soon, and the Ferrans know it."

I picked up Diestrya, because that was easier than continually moving her away from danger. "So who's behind the stronger elveweed?"

"The seeds or cuttings were doubtless supplied by Stakanar, and the funds to grow it—you were right about it having to be in the south—from Ferrum."

"Do you know where?"

"Know? Yes. Be able to prove it, no." She picked up her shears. "I need to get back to trimming these before we get a truly hard freeze. Enjoy your dinner with Iryela and Kandryl."

"I hope to." I'd never mentioned that dinner to anyone at all, except Seliora, not even Maitre Poincaryt.

Diestrya and I continued our walk, all the way up to the park area, and the hedge maze that she was still too young to appreciate, and then all the way back home. The whole way I wondered what I needed to find out from Iryela . . . or Kandryl.

I also wondered why I hadn't picked up on what Maitre Dyana really was before, other than that she'd come from a High Holder family. But when I'd studied with her, she'd revealed nothing and always kept me on the defensive. Ever since then, I'd been with the Civic Patrol and hadn't seen her all that much. When I had, she'd always avoided talking anything but pleasantries. Her recent words hadn't been casual, and that raised yet another set of questions, all of which suggested that even more was at stake than I'd already thought.

At the same time, when it came right down to it, I was only one Civic Patrol captain among a number, and one of a handful of talented imagers, and all of the others with such abilities were far more experienced. Besides, even if war broke out, few events of major impact could occur in L'Excelsis that we hadn't already seen—conscription riots, spies and assassinations, and explosions, to name but a few. Certainly, the Place D'Opera explosion, though startling, was nothing to compare to the explosion that the Tiemprans had set off years before in the Temple of Puryon.

Still, I couldn't help but worry as I fed Diestrya and put her down for her nap. With all the exercise, she slept well.

Seliora walked into the house just after fifth glass, as Diestrya and I were struggling with the usual three-year-old's post-nap crankiness. Somehow we got through the next glass and were ready to depart when the Dichartyn girls arrived to watch Diestrya, since Klysia had Samedis off. I would have been very surprised if Aelys didn't look in once or twice as well. I'd also made arrangements earlier to borrow my parent's coach—and Charlsyn—since Iryela's L'Excelsis estate was a good half-glass north of the Plaza D'Nord, and I didn't feel right about using a duty coach. There wasn't any way to catch a hack back to L'Excelsis, and I didn't want to impose on Iryela, although she certainly could have afforded the imposition.

Seliora wore a red ankle-length dress with a black jacket and a black sash belt, with a black opera cloak, not that we'd been to the opera in years. As always, I was in grays, and we met Charlsyn on the west side of Imagisle, where we usually took the duty coach, at sixth glass. I'd thought that on a Samedi evening, the Boulevard D'Ouest would be thronged, but it wasn't, and less than a quarter-glass later, we were riding through the Plaza D'Nord.

"It's good to be going somewhere by ourselves," said Seliora, "and not with family."

I agreed. "We'll probably get a note from Mother . . ."

"It came yesterday. I forgot to tell you. She's asked us for next Samedi, or the following one, if that's not convenient."

"Which would you prefer?"

"This coming Samedi, the thirty-fifth. Mother was thinking about a dinner for Shomyr's birthday on the seventh."

"Are you up to two nights in a row?" I paused. "We could leave early, saying we were tired because of the Autumn Ball the night before."

"Rhenn . . . they are your family," she said gently.

"I know, but I'll have to work on Samedi."

She just looked at me, and I laughed. "Next Samedi it is."

"They'll be happy." She raised her eyebrows. "After all, would you want to eat dinner with Culthyn every night?"

She had a point there.

Iryela's chateau—technically it was now Kandryl's, even though she'd inherited it and had to marry him to keep it, if only after a fashion—was set on the east side of the main road, a structure a good three hundred yards from end to end laid out in a "Y" shape. The southern section ended at what looked to be a cliff, but which was really a wall down from the terrace. At the end of the terrace there had once been a square stone tower, but Iryela had not had it rebuilt after I'd destroyed it. A gray stone wall a little more than two yards high extended around the grounds, and a single set of iron-grilled gates, without even a crest on them, afforded access to the paved drive beyond that led to the chateau.

The gates opened at our approach. Charlsyn then guided the coach through the walls and up the spotlessly clean stones of the driveway and under the portico. There, a footman in black and silver stepped forward to open the coach door and to extend a hand to Seliora. As I stepped out after her, I saw another coach stationed on the far side of the circle, beyond the fountain and circular garden. The crimson and silver body work, far grander than the brown and brass of our coach, confirmed that Frydryk D'Suyrien and Alynkya D'Ramsael had already arrived.

We hadn't even reached the outer doorway when an older man, in a black velvet jacket with silver piping over a silver shirt and black trousers, stepped forward, inclining his head deeply. "Master Rhennthyl, Madame, welcome."

"Thank you, Fahyl," I replied. "You are looking well, as always."

"Thank you, sir. Madame awaits you in the family salon."

We followed Fahyl inside and down the right-hand hallway off the main foyer. The family salon, although twice the size of our dining room, was the smallest and most intimate gathering chamber in the chateau.

Iryela immediately rose from the settee where she'd been seated. "Seliora! Rhenn!" While she'd filled out slightly after the birth of her twins the year before, she was still slender and very white-blonde.

Kandryl also rose, immediately, as did Alynkya. Frydryk was slower, languid in standing, as if he were the Chief Councilor instead of his father, although I'd observed that Councilor Suyrien always exhibited great courtesy on the occasions when I'd seen him.

"Do sit down," Iryela went on. "Our white Grisio for you, Seliora?"

"Please."

"Your red," I said.

I took the chair beside Iryela, since she had gestured toward it, while Seliora eased onto the other settee beside Alynkya.

"You travel enough that you ought to have your own carriage," said Frydryk.

"For work, I can use the duty coaches, and otherwise," I said with a shrug, "we make do. Besides, where would we keep the coach and coachman?" I turned to Iryela. "How are the twins?"

"Sleeping, thankfully," replied Kandryl dryly from beside her.

"I imagine you're happy they're past the colicky stage," said Seliora.

"Exceedingly," said Iryela.

Frydryk didn't quite sneer, as if to intimate that talking about children and colic was scarcely suitable High Holder conversation.

So I smiled and asked him, "How is your father these days? I've heard that he's rather occupied."

"Ah, yes . . . with all the troubles caused by the freeholders." Frydryk nodded sagely. "I wouldn't be surprised if they were being counseled and paid by Ferran agents."

"Anything is possible in these times," I said, taking a goblet of the Ryel red—a varietal Grisio, really—from a serving girl, and looking to Iryela. "This is one of my favorite wines, and not just because it's from your vineyards."

"We're glad you enjoy it."

Seliora accepted her goblet and took a sip.

"I can tell Seliora and I think the same of the white," said Kandryl. "As does Father."

That offered the opportunity I wanted. "I don't think I've seen your father more than a handful of times since the wedding . . . although he did invite us to the Council's Autumn Ball next Vendrei."

"None of us see him very often," said Frydryk with a laugh. "If he's not dealing with Council business, he's dealing with other High Holders. At the moment, he's in Ruile . . . something to do with Ruelyr. He's got all the lands between Ruile and the Sud Swamp. Ruelyr and Father have been friends for years, but . . ."

"But?" asked Alynkya.

"Ruelyr . . . let's just say that he'd have been more successful as a High Holder several centuries back. Father has had to caution him more than once about the distinction between low justice and Council justice." Frydryk glanced to me. "Or Civic Patrol justice."

Neither Iryela nor Kandryl spoke, and I could sense the tension. Why would Frydryk offer such a pointed remark? To test me? Or to needle Iryela by reminding her that she was subject to Kandryl's enforcement of low justice?

"The Civic Patrol is an arm of the Council," I said with a smile, "and I'm charged with enforcing the laws of the Council. Most High Holders are like your father, very honorable men, who understand quite clearly that distinction. There are always those men, who can be anything from High Holders to taudis-toughs, who think the law is something for others to obey. They're few, but they cause most of the problems in any land, even in Solidar."

"You've handled them well," said Iryela casually, looking to Frydryk, who ignored her glance while not seeming to do so.

"I've had the value of good counsel . . . and luck, but still . . . it's always better when you can deal with those of good manners, whether crafters, factors, or High Holders. Seliora's found that as well." I inclined my head toward the loveliest woman in the room.

"I suppose you do deal with all sorts," said Frydryk, not quite pointedly.

"Who was it," I interjected quickly, "that was so easy for you to deal with, but whose fiance . . . the bride . . ." I knew very well who it was, but I wanted Seliora to bring up her name.

"Oh . . . Dhelora D'Zaerlyn-Alte . . . she's very bright and quite pleasant." Seliora smiled.

"I've never heard of High Holder Zaerlyn," I said, not that such was surprising, given that there were more than a thousand spread across Solidar.

"The family's been very reclusive," replied Iryela. "Their lands aren't far from ours, and I don't think we've met, even socially, on more than five or six occasions. They have a number of gold and silver properties, and one of the largest porcelain works in Solidar."

"That's a polite way of putting it," suggested Frydryk. "They've produced . . . shall we say . . . bathing and other facilities for generations."

"His name never comes up for the Council or anything else," I said.

"His influence is very subtle," said Kandryl. "He has contacts in surprising places, and Father has often consulted with him."

For several long moments, there was silence, before Frydryk spoke up again. "I've often wondered why there are no imager High Holders. Oh, I know, the law is very strict about that, but I'd think that someone like you, Rhenn, would do as well as the average High Holder." After the slightest pause, he added, "If not better."

Seliora offered a pleasant smile, but I could sense the cold iron behind it.

Even Iryela stiffened just the tiniest bit, for all of her upbringing as a High Holder.

I laughed. "I suppose I could, Frydryk, I suppose I could; but if we allowed that, why, all too many imagers would think they could do it, and then what would happen to all the old High Holders?"

Frydryk actually looked puzzled.

I smiled again, then imaged a bullet into his crystal goblet. It appeared in the middle of the white Grisio and then dropped against the crystal with a dull ring. "I can do that. I could image that anywhere . . . perhaps into a heart . . . an artery . . . a return vein to the heart. Some imagers can do that.

Some can't. It's a bit like High Holders. Some understand. Some don't. Just like your father has to remind High Holders of their duties and responsibilities, so there are imagers who remind other imagers of theirs. Even so, the combination of a High Holder and an imager wouldn't be good for Solidar."

Frydryk was still looking at the bullet. He swallowed. "I've never seen that."

I imaged it out of the glass and onto the side table. "I can also remove things. As a matter of fact, some years ago, when your father was giving a toast, I imaged an entire glass of poisoned wine out of his goblet, and the liquid only trembled."

"He never mentioned that."

"I don't know if he was even told. That's part of the security detail that protects Council members while they're at the Council Chateau. I was only on that detail for a season or so, but I stopped several attempted assassinations. So did others, far more quietly. Much of the time, the Councilors don't even see that. Occasionally, they do. It's a very cooperative system. The Collegium protects the Council, and the Council protects the Collegium. It works."

"Why did you leave that duty?" asked Iryela.

I laughed again, with more humor. "Both the Collegium and I discovered that, among other things, I lacked the requisite talent for remaining unnoticed. I have trouble not doing things like that." I gestured to the bullet I'd imaged out of nowhere. "Civic Patrollers don't have to remain invisible." I paused. "I don't mean literally invisible. I mean that a good imager security type always looks like he or she belongs wherever he or she happens to be, so much so that no one ever questions their presence."

"Was that what you were doing when you requested a dance from me the first time?" asked Alynkya.

"Yes," I replied. "That was part of it. Even there, I wasn't very good at being unnoticed. You not only remembered me, but had your father track down who I was. Had I been truly good at it, you only would have vaguely remembered a pleasant young man who was polite and a good but not outstanding dancer."

"There were some . . ." Alynkya mused.

"Exactly."

She smiled, somehow wistfully and warmly, and at that moment, I truly wished that she had found someone else to marry besides Frydryk. Strong as I suspected she was, she was still far too sweet for him, but there was nothing I could do about that.

From there the conversation drifted into talk of wine vintages, about which my knowledge was limited, and into how Iryela and Kandryl had finally finished rebuilding the gardens after the "great freeze," an indirect reference to my actions that had led to Iryela inheriting Ryel and marrying Kandryl, who only used his holding title—Ryel D'Alte—when absolutely necessary.

A glass later, we repaired to the "small" dining room. The food was exquisite, and even Frydryk stopped sneering once he started eating.

20

We didn't get back to Imagisle until midnight on Samedi, and I paid Charlsyn two full silvers. Doubtless Mother had already paid him extra, but there was never any point in being cheap when you asked for special service, and he was appreciative. We did sleep late on Solayi morning, as late as Diestrya would let us, which wasn't quite until half-past sixth glass, but since I was usually up before fifth glass, it was a luxury of sorts.

We had a half-leisurely breakfast—hurried until Diestrya was fed—and then relaxed more afterwards while she played on the kitchen floor. We sat in the adjoining breakfast room, where we could watch her through the archway, and sipped a second cup of tea.

"I like Alynkya." Seliora smiled sweetly. "Even if you did dance with her when you were courting me."

"It was my duty. Besides, the first time, her mother was dying, and the second time, her mother had just died." I quickly added, "You dance far better."

"You didn't mention the second time," Seliora said.

"That was because that was the ball when Iryela was setting me up, and I was much more worried about that . . . if you recall?"

"I seem to recall something . . ." She laughed, but a frown followed. "Last night Frydryk was baiting both you and Iryela. She didn't say anything, but she wasn't happy. He's not the High Holder yet, and he isn't the Chief Councilor. His father is."

"He was trying to find out something. I don't think he did, but I did. The question is whether he was meant to reveal what he did or not. If he intended to reveal that, does it mean that he's not being all that dutiful a son, or that Suyrien wanted him to?"

"Or he's being stupid?" Seliora raised her eyebrows. "I don't think so. He meant to let on all that about High Holder Ruelyr."

"To protect his father? If so, that suggests—"

"Do you think Ruelyr is involved in growing or supplying the stronger elveweed?"

"I wouldn't be surprised at anything; but if Frydryk had to mention it to me, that suggests that Suyrien is having trouble with the High Holders, and that more than a few of them want to take more direct action against the factors and the freeholders." I paused. "It was also a warning to Iryela. She's close to Madame D'Shendael, and others who want more legal rights for women."

"They want women on the Council," added Seliora. "The Nameless forbid."

"More like a scheme of the Namer, I suspect, according to most High Holders."

"Have you noticed that all the scheming in politics is done by the same men who claim women are the devious ones?"

"Men? You have to be jesting." I tried to keep a straight face, but I couldn't help grinning the tiniest bit.

Seliora just shook her head.

After we finished breakfast, I thought about telling Dichartyn, but, with his network, he had to know where Councilor Suyrien had been. Besides, it wouldn't have changed anything.

Later in the day, Seliora was kind enough to write a note to Mother, confirming that we would join them for dinner on Samedi. I'd send it by private courier on Lundi.

We had an otherwise quiet and generally restful Solayi, for which Seliora and I were both grateful, especially when Lundi dawned blustery, with mist-drizzle that froze on my exercise clothes while I was running. I let the long-legged Dartazn, who always finished before anyone else, finish even farther ahead. I was more concerned about not slipping on the icy grass and walks.

Even the inside of the duty coach was still freezing by the time I dropped off Seliora and Diestrya at NordEste Design, and I read the newsheets wearing gloves, awkward though it was.

Most of the articles were insignificant or what amounted to status reports, such as the uneasy situation between Ferrum and Jariola. One story was not. The *Rovaria*—a merchanter loading grain at Estisle—had caught fire and been totally gutted, sinking pierside. The fire had raged across the main cargo pier where it had been tied up, threatening several other vessels before it was put out. The story noted that the *Rovaria* had been bound for Jariola, but didn't mention the ownership or registry of the vessel. There was also a brief story in *Tableta* about the cost of grain production on freeheld lands being cheaper because freeholders didn't have the responsibilities to tenant farmers that High Holders did. Had High Holder Haebyn "encouraged" that story?

Matters didn't get any better after I reached Third District. The ice-rain had resulted in several wagon accidents and two fires, most likely because people hadn't had their chimneys cleaned since last winter, and the Fire

Brigade hadn't been able to save one of the houses. There were more smash-and-grabs because it was harder to chase the thieves. And, to add to my concerns, I got a communiqué from headquarters. I read it twice.

> Patrol Captain Kharles was shot on Vendrei evening by unknown assailants. Their clothing was of the type worn by taudis-toughs known to frequent the taudis area known as the Hellhole. Because the captain suffered severe injuries, until further notice, Patrol Lieutenant Walthyr will be acting captain. In the event Captain Kharles cannot resume his duties, a review of all lieutenants will be conducted to determine his successor . . .

The communiqué was signed by Cydarth. The last words were a strong indication that Kharles was not likely to survive, and that, if he did, he would not be able to continue as District Six Captain. The wording also suggested that Walthyr would not succeed Kharles. That didn't surprise me. Although I'd only met Walthyr a handful of times, he'd impressed me as a tough, no-nonsense, straight-talking, rough-edged patroller who'd come up the hard way. That meant that Artois wouldn't want to deal with him and Cydarth couldn't corrupt him.

I left the communiqué on Alsoran's desk and pulled on my winter cloak and gloves. Much as I didn't really want to walk a round, I needed to, both to get out of the station and to let the patrollers know that I wasn't a fair-weather captain.

Just as I caught up with Kemantyl and Clursyn just east of the corner of Fuosta and Quierca, I got a glimpse of a taudis-kid running down the alley away from the three of us. To which taudischef was he reporting?

"Captain . . ." offered Kemantyl, the swarthy and squat senior patroller.

"Just keep walking and tell me what you've seen recently."

"Yes, sir." He glanced down the alley. "I can't say as I know the taudis-kid, but he just watched us."

"We're in Horazt's territory. He won't do anything."

They both shook their heads.

"He won't, but . . ." offered Kemantyl.

"He's got a problem," I finished, "and that means one for us. Until he shows up, we'll just follow your round."

I started walking, and they stepped up, flanking me.

"Yes, sir." Kemantyl coughed, then spat to the side. "Hate this weather. You remember Sostrys, the crazy tiler?"

"The one whose head got bashed?" As I recalled Sostrys, he'd been calm, but he was one of the few men in L'Excelsis who stood close to a head and a half taller than I did, and I was far from short. Sostrys also had shoulders to match his height. "Has he had one of those fits where he—"

"No, sir. He's gone. No one's seen him around here. But . . . my cousin Elhyr, he's in Sixth District, and he thinks Sostrys went after the druggers."

"The drug runners?"

"No, sir. The dealers in the Hellhole."

"Why would he do that?"

"There was a girl . . . the one we found last Meredi . . . she was his niece."

That meant she was either his daughter or his niece. "Elver?"

"Not that long. She wasn't scrawny and yellow-gray when we brought in her body. Anyways . . . well . . . we heard about Captain Kharles . . . and there was trouble . . . and everyone knows how you feel about the dealers."

"Do you know what happened?"

Kemantyl glanced around, then spat again. "Elhyr says . . . well . . . the word is that Sostrys killed one and banged up another one before they shot him and dumped his body in the east sewers."

That was all I needed—elveweed dealers coming into Third District. My patrollers didn't need to take them on as well, either. "I appreciate knowing that. I didn't have anything to do with it, but things are getting hot with the dealers. Someone outside L'Excelsis is supplying them with the stronger weed, and it could be they're getting more guns as well." That was speculation on my part, but I had the strong feeling that was the way it was. "Just be careful when you see taudis-types you don't know."

"We've been thinking that way, sir," added Clursyn.

Almost no one was outside in the ice-rain, but we covered three blocks, with me listening to their observations on what had been happening on their rounds, before I saw Horazt, standing under a narrow porch roof just outside the doorway of a house he frequented.

"Looks like someone'd like a word with you, sir." Clursyn's tone was deferential, but worried.

"I'll have to see what he has to say." I walked up to the small porch and out of the icy rain, if barely.

"Master Rhennthyl."

"Horazt."

"I've heard a few things."

"Would they have anything to do with the elveweed dealers?"

"They might." He paused. "How is Shault?"

"He's doing well. I expect he'll become an Imager Tertius before too long. He's bright and talented. He is a bit stubborn."

The taudischef nodded. "Sostrys . . . you know him?"

"The big crazy tiler?"

"He left. He won't be coming back. Some others might be. Word is that some of your patrollers might be in for some long sleeps."

"I heard Sostrys got pretty upset."

"He did. Word is that he put a tiling trowel through Dimanche, the dealer in the Hellhole. That was after they shot him four times. Coddyl may never walk straight again, either. Won't be able to sign his name, either. If he ever could."

I'd never known the names of any dealers. No one had, so far as I knew. That Horazt was telling me . . . in that sense, I wished he weren't. "Do you know when we might see visitors? I'll be accompanying the patrols at night, and any word might be helpful . . . for both of us."

"I'll have my eyes and ears watch." He paused, then flashed a brief smile. "But the druggers' strong-arms don't like ice-rain much." He stepped back. "Thought you'd like to know."

The door opened, and he slipped inside.

I walked back to the two patrollers.

My winter cloak was soaked through and coated in ice by the time I got back to the station. So was my visored cap, and my ears burned as they thawed out. Alsoran was waiting in his study, standing by his desk.

"Captain . . ."

"It's worse than that." I told him what I'd learned.

"When do you think?"

"That depends on the weather."

"Why would anyone tell Horazt?"

"I'm sure the dealers didn't. Probably one of the drug runners into Third District. They'd be afraid that they'd get swept up into the workhouses. They're so dependent on the weed that the withdrawal would kill them."

"They'd just find others. That's why we don't try to throw them in the workhouses now, unless they cause other trouble."

"But they know we could."

"What do you plan, sir?"

"Spending some nights here. What else?"

Seliora would understand. She wouldn't like it, but she'd understand.

21

Lundi night, after a hurried dinner, as I stood in the doorway, ready to leave for my session with Draffyd, I said quietly to Seliora, "After I get back, we need to talk. Things are not getting better."

Holding Diestrya on her hip, Seliora nodded slightly, her black eyes fixed on me. "I know. I'll be here." She smiled at our daughter. "Say goodnight to Dada."

"Goodnight." The single word came out cheerfully and with a smile.

"You be good for your mother." I bent forward and kissed my daughter, then stepped out into the chill. Although the ice-rain had stopped, mist rising off the warmer waters of the river drifted across Imagisle. I walked quickly southward toward the quadrangle and the infirmary.

As I reached the middle of the quad, I caught a glimpse of movement to my left, behind the hedge I suspected had been placed to keep young imagers from cutting from sidewalk to sidewalk and wearing a path in the grass. Immediately, I raised concealment shields and eased forward and around the trimmed boxwood, trying to determine who might be doing what to whom . . . and why. Through the swirling mist, in the gloom on the far side of the hedge, I saw three junior imagers standing on the icy grass, two of them clearly trying to intimidate the third.

The single young imager was a girl, and she was only slightly shorter than the two youths. Both youths carried half-staffs. She carried nothing—except confidence, evident from her posture. That worried me, but I listened as I eased forward.

"You think you're so good. You're just a girl. Girls aren't real imagers."

"Maitre Kahlasa is. So is Maitre Dyana," replied the girl.

"They're old," said the other youth.

"They really can't do anything, not like Master Rhennthyl can."

That was all I needed, young imagers acting like bullies, thinking they were emulating me . . . and attacking another junior imager.

The taller boy jumped forward and struck at her with the staff, except that the staff stopped short of her in mid-air and vibrated as it hit her shields.

Then the other youth began to beat on her shields.

I could sense the girl's dilemma. I'd been there. She could hurt them, possibly kill them, but she wasn't skilled enough to figure out a way to disarm junior imagers without inflicting injuries, possibly severe or fatal ones. And her shields weren't developed enough that she could avoid all of the force and pressure of their blows, force that would eventually break her shields. I didn't want to interfere, not immediately, because, if I did, the boys and their friends would likely just wait for another opportunity when no master was around.

It took me a moment to recognize Tomai. Schorzat was her preceptor. She was feisty and able enough to hold her own for a time. I'd just have to hope that, at some point she'd strike back, and I could mute whatever she did just enough that it wasn't fatal, but strong enough to scare the two witless.

Several more blows slammed uselessly against her shields, but they were closer to her, an indication that she was having to contract them to hold them.

"You'd better stop," she said. "I don't want to hurt you."

"You couldn't hurt a rodent."

"You're a rodie yourself, anyway," declared the larger youth.

Abruptly, she released the shields and jumped back, so that their staffs swung down and onto the grass.

I immediately imaged oil under the boys' feet, then cast shields around the two and slammed them to the ground with a blast of air . . . an instant before two wooden mallets slammed into my shields with disturbing force.

Then I dropped my concealment shields and marched toward the three.

"Enough!" I projected a certain amount of force behind the words, releasing the shields that held the two boys. I stopped short of them and glared. "Are you two idiots trying to kill yourselves? Get up!"

The two were shivering, not from the cold. Up close, I recognized both Silmyn and Torgast. "If I hadn't shielded you both, you'd likely be in the infirmary, if not dead. She knocked you both flat and put enough force in those mallets that if they'd hit your head they might have knocked you cold, maybe even cracked your skulls like eggshells." That last phrase might not have been true, but none of the three would know for sure.

I walked over and picked up one of the wooden mallets, the one that had broken in half, and held it up. "This hit my shields with enough force to split in two. If I hadn't protected you two idiots, what would have happened?"

The wide-eyed looks and swallows suggested that they had some inkling.

I turned to Tomai. "You come with us. None of you are to say a word. Not one, and not until either Maitre Schorzat, Maitre Dyana, or Maitre Dichartyn meets us in the administration building."

Tomai looked as stunned as they did, but I didn't want her saying a single word. They followed me to the main reception hall . . . and the duty watch desk. It took a quarter of a glass before the duty messenger found Maitre Dyana and she appeared. I sent Beleart, the duty junior secondus, to tell Master Draffyt I'd been unavoidably delayed.

Maitre Dyana must have hurried, because she was only wearing a foul weather cloak over her grays, and not one of her signature colorful scarves. She looked at the three junior imagers, standing in a line silently, then at me.

"I need to brief you first, Maitre." Then I turned. "You three are to say nothing until Maitre Dyana questions each of you. Do you understand?"

I got three cowed nods, then looked at Beleart. "Make sure they don't."

"Yes, sir."

Only after Maitre Dyana and I were alone in the conference room off the reception hall did she smile. "You put on quite a performance, Rhenn."

"I had to." I explained exactly what had happened, adding, "I don't know how much force she put behind the mallets, but it wasn't insignificant. One of the mallets split when it hit my shields. I can understand her anger. They were taunting her that women imagers couldn't do what men could. Like someone else, years back, I think she needs some training in less lethal ways of protecting herself. You know why I told her to keep quiet."

"Very wise. She knows she might not have struck them, but she will worry that, if you hadn't, if she had, she might have killed them."

"I thought it might be best if you handled it from here."

"I can do that." Her eyes twinkled. "By the way, Rhenn, exactly why were you headed down here at this time of night?"

"Maitre Poincaryt scheduled me for another session with Draffyd. I attempted to use imaging to keep a child from a poisoning death."

"What happened to the child?"

"He's fine. Maitre Poincaryt worries that it might not go so well next time. He's right, but the boy would have died."

She laughed gently. "If those three you terrified only knew . . ."

"They haven't learned enough to know." Just as I hadn't, once upon a time.

Dyana nodded, and we walked back out to the three, where I took my leave and hurried to the adjoining building that held the infirmary.

"Disciplinary actions?" asked Draffyd as I walked into the surgery.

"I ran into two youngsters trying to beat up a young second named Tomai."

"She couldn't have had a better master come along," Draffyd said. "She reminds all the older masters of another young second some years back."

"I thought you might say something along those lines," I said ruefully. "I managed to temper her strikes enough that she didn't kill them."

"Are you sure that was wise?"

"I haven't heard that either Silmyn and Torgast were the kind of bullies like Johanyr or Diazt."

"They've been a bit of a problem, but, you're right, nothing like Johanyr. He had as much raw ability as you did."

"He didn't want to work."

"It's probably better that way."

"Is he still at Mont D'Glace?"

"I suppose so. We would have heard, otherwise." Draffyd pointed to the surgical smock on the peg beside the door and the cadaver on the surgery table. "We need to get to work."

What he meant was that I needed to get to work.

Two glasses later, I washed up and left the infirmary. I might not have looked green, but my internal organs were somewhat unsteady. Still, the mist and cold helped enough that I was merely chilled through when I closed our door behind me.

Seliora appeared immediately. "You must be cold. I have some warm mulled wine for you."

I couldn't help putting my arms around her, and just holding her.

"How was Master Draffyd?" she finally asked.

"He was fine. I'm glad he's the imager surgeon and not me."

"You could do some of that, couldn't you? Now?"

"A little. If someone would die otherwise." I shuddered.

"Go sit in front of the stove. You're freezing."

I took off my cloak and hung it up, then followed her directions, taking one side of the settee directly before the stove in the family parlor.

Seliora reappeared with two mugs and offered me one, then settled beside me. "You're worried. More worried than I've ever seen you."

"Even more than when Iryela's father was after you and my family?"

"More than that," she said.

I held the mug to my lips, letting the cinnamon-clove steam wreathe my face for a moment, then took a small swallow of the wine before I spoke again. "There's more to all of this than just elveweed and friction between freeholders and factors and the High Holders."

"You think the Ferrans have more spies here causing trouble?"

"I don't think there's any doubt about it. But the stronger elveweed comes from Otelyrn. I mean that it originally grew only there, and that points to Stakanar or Tiempre." I took another swallow of the wine. I was beginning to feel warmer. "It's also caused another problem." I had to explain to Seliora why I'd be changing our schedules for a while. She listened while I talked. When I finished, I waited.

"You're as bad as any Pharsi when it comes to protecting your own," Seliora said quietly.

I didn't mention that Mama Diestra had made that point before we were married. But the plain fact was that it would be difficult for taudis-toughs to kill me. Difficult, but not impossible. But . . . if they went after my patrollers, and I wasn't there . . . before long I'd be totally ineffective as a Patrol Captain. "There's another problem. They're putting the word out that Kharles was shot because I meddled in their operations in his district."

Seliora stiffened.

"I didn't. The crazy tiler lost his daughter. Maybe she was his niece . . ." I explained the rest of the story.

"It's all a set-up to get to you," she said. "I wouldn't be surprised if the two dealers Horazt named are being exposed to punish them and that the others let Sostrys get to those two."

"I wouldn't be surprised at that, either, but it doesn't change anything."

"No. If you're there, even if some patrollers do get hurt, your men will stand behind you. If you aren't . . ."

She didn't have to finish the sentence.

Eventually, we went to bed, first to hers, and then, as always, I went to my own—knowing that, uneasy as I was, my dreams might lead, as they occasionally had, to unthought dream-imaging.

On Mardi, I skipped the early-morning exercises and slept later—not all that much later, given Diestrya, but I needed as much sleep as I could get, and I was grateful that my disturbed dreams hadn't led to sleep-imaging. Even so, I didn't head in to the station until close to ninth glass, but the day was still damp and chill.

Lyonyt greeted me with an announcement. "Captain, we just got a report. First District thinks they just picked up the body of that elver you asked about. Red hair . . . same scar along the forearm."

"Thank you." I couldn't say I was surprised that Kolasyn's brother was dead. The only questions that had ever been in my mind were when he would die and whether anyone would find his body. Some elvers could put in a day's work, go home and smoke a weed-pipe or two, got to bed, and get up and go to work. Then, there were the ones for whom smoking the weed was life itself. They died hard and young. Haerasyn had clearly been one of those. "I'll have to go down to First District in a bit." I paused. "We haven't had any word from any of the goldsmiths, have we?"

"No, sir. I'd say it's not too likely now."

"You're right about that."

After checking the logs and the reports and finding nothing out of the ordinary, I walked into Alsoran's study. I didn't close the door.

As usual, the lieutenant was on his feet. "I heard about your relative."

"It had to happen. It's better that it's over. I'll go down there and take care of matters after we're through here." I gestured to the chairs, then took the one facing his desk. "What's happened that's not in the logs, if anything?"

"We'll need to rework some of the rounds tonight. Last night, Vaeryn got his foot run over by a cart, and Socaryt's out with a flux of some sort."

"Is the foot something that will heal?"

"The surgeon thinks so, but it will be weeks, if not longer."

"Can he handle the duty desk on the midnight to morning shift?"

"He should be able to. We can see."

Once Alsoran and I reworked the rounds, I took a hack down to the head-quarters building on Fedre, just a block or so up from East River Road, not because I wanted to be anywhere near Cydarth, but because the rear of the building also held First District station.

I didn't know the patroller on the duty desk, but he clearly knew me. "The body's in the cold room, Captain Rhennthyl."

"Thank you." I walked back to the far corner and opened the heavy door slowly. There was almost no odor, even though there were five bodies laid out. I could tell from body positions that four were elvers.

Once I stood beside the redheaded form, I recognized Haerasyn. His dead face held the contorted expression common to all the elvers who'd died from the stronger weed. I didn't even shake my head.

I walked back to the front desk. "It's him. I'll sign the claim forms and have the crematorium pick up the body as soon as they can."

"We'll hold it." The desk patroller handed the single sheet of paper to me.

I filled it out, signed it, and handed it back.

He looked at me again.

"I'll be making the arrangements right after I leave here."

"Thank you, sir."

I could understand his feelings. No patroller wanted to have a dead body around very long, although it wasn't so bad in late fall or winter.

"Oh . . . I'd sent a request about jewelry and goldsmiths?"

"Yes, sir. No one's reported anything, and with a reward, it's likely that they would if it crossed their counters."

"Thank you."

After I left the First District station I walked around to the charging section of headquarters. As I'd hoped, since it was early afternoon, Buasytt sat unoccupied at the desk.

"Captain . . . what brings you here?"

"Business with First District. I just wanted to hear what the chargings have been like everywhere."

The graying patroller shook his head. "Last glass has been the quietest in weeks. Until now, it was like every tough in every taudis had decided to get busy." He frowned. "Except Third District." After a pause, he asked, "Would you care to tell me why that might be so, sir?"

"All I can say is that we've been working to change things as much as we can in Third District. We cracked down on the taudis-gangs years ago."

Buasytt nodded slowly. "I recall something about that. You took on two of the taudischefs yourself, didn't you?"

I laughed. "I didn't have a choice. They came after me. When that was done, it made sense to finish the job." And I had, but certainly not in the way I made it sound. "Have there been any attacks on patrollers in other districts?"

He shook his head. "Lots more smash-and-grabs, a couple of small explosions out in Sixth District, but away from anything."

That sounded like someone testing something, but I didn't say so. I just smiled. "I appreciate learning what's been happening. Thank you."

"My pleasure, Captain."

From headquarters, I took another hack out to Elsyor Memorials, where, for the appropriate payments, they were happy to agree to pick up Haerasyn's body, prepare it for viewing, and then for cremation, after a family viewing. They even had a courier service so that I could send a message to Seliora at NordEste Design. I wanted her to get the message, because someone with a level head needed to be the one to inform the family.

Then I took another hack back to Third District. Just in dealing with that small part of the mess Haerasyn had left behind, I'd spent three golds. That didn't count the thirty golds worth of jewelry and coin he'd stolen when he'd vanished.

There had been two smash-and-grabs while I'd been gone, not that they wouldn't have occurred even if I'd been there. I did get back in time so that, at fourth glass, when the evening patrollers reported and those on the day rounds returned, Alsoran and I were able to brief all the patrollers on the possibility of violence against them by taudis-types from outside the district.

After that, I stayed until ninth glass that night, accompanying various patroller teams who worked the taudis on their rounds, but the entire afternoon and evening were quieter than normal. Again, I had to walk to find a hack, but only to the Midroad.

Seliora met me at the door. She studied my face, then stepped back and said, "Thank you for dealing with Haerasyn."

I closed the door behind me and took off my cloak and hung it up in the foyer vestibule. "I'm sorry the message had to come to you, but I wasn't certain how Odelia would deal with it."

"She didn't handle it well."

"She wanted to know where I was, I expect, and why I only sent a courier and a message . . . and that I sent it to you and not to her or Kolasyn."

With a wry smile, Seliora nodded. "Mother and Aunt Aegina pointed out that matters are very unsettled in L'Excelsis and that you had taken time to track down Haerasyn and make the basic arrangements for the services and cremation."

"And Odelia got upset and then retreated?"

"You've gotten to know her moods well."

"For better or worse, her feelings come first." I didn't point out that sometimes thought came far later, if at all.

"She's good at heart," Seliora pointed out.

"That's true, but she can be hard on those closest to her." I laughed as we walked into the family parlor. "At times, I suppose, that's true of all of us." The warmth of the stove felt good after a cold night and a colder hack ride back to Imagisle.

"You're aware of that, dearest." She squeezed my hand. "You're cold. Sit down. I have some warm spiced wine for you."

I didn't need much persuasion to settle on the settee in front of the stove, especially since I knew Seliora would be back beside me before long.

23

Meredi followed the same pattern as had Mardi, but late as I stayed at the station that night, there was still no sign of any violence. That left me edgy, but I didn't doubt that some form of attack would occur. I just didn't know when, and I didn't sleep that well on Meredi night.

Jeudi was bright, clear, and cold, even when I reached Third District station just past mid-day. To me, the chill foreshadowed a long and cold winter. Lyonyt looked up from the duty desk as I neared.

"Are there any severe problems this morning?"

"No, sir. Not yet."

"Any dispatches from headquarters?"

"No, sir."

"Is the lieutenant in yet?"

"Yes, sir. He's been here for a glass or so."

I checked the duty logs. The number of elver deaths was about the same—two for the previous evening—but incidents and arrests remained low, and that was as good a sign as any that trouble wasn't far away. Even though that made no logical sense, that was always the way it was. Then I walked into Alsoran's study.

"Still too quiet," I offered.

"It is." He smiled, ruefully. "How long do you think before the druggers' boys start trying to take out patrollers?"

"Tonight will be the second dry night. It looks like it will be clear. I'd say tonight or tomorrow." I shrugged. "Then, it could be Samedi."

"Not Solayi?"

"That's unlikely. Even the Duodeans and the Puryons respect Solayi. Besides, fewer people are out, and that's likely to call attention to strangers. They like to mingle in crowds once they've made a score."

"You're probably right about that. How long will they keep at it?"

"Until they kill at least five or six patrollers or until we stop them. That's a guess, but there's more at stake here than a crazy tiler killing expendable drug dealers."

"You keep saying that, Captain, but you avoid saying what is." Alsoran glanced toward the barred windows that fronted on Fuosta.

"I wouldn't be surprised if the entire future of Solidar isn't."

Alsoran looked at me for a long moment. "I don't think you're jesting. But . . . druggies shooting at patrollers affecting all of Solidar?"

"Oh . . . what happens here is only a small part of what's happening. The stronger weed is hitting the five most important cities in Solidar. Elver deaths are higher than ever before, and half are hitting outside the taudis—among people with shops and golds. There's almost a civil war going on in the eastern grain lands between the freeholders and the High Holders. War is about to break out between Jariola and Ferrum. And Cydarth is scheming to replace the Commander. But it's all going to happen at once."

"I can't say as I've seen you this gloomy before."

I forced a smile. "I could be wrong. All these things might be coincidence."

The lieutenant snorted. "For a patroller, coincidence is a fair-weather friend. We both know that."

After leaving Alsoran, I spent the next several glasses catching up on the various reports required by headquarters, mostly by Cydarth, who thought that more reports equated to more accountability and more effective patrolling. Beyond a certain point, I'd observed in my own experience, greater accountability resulted in less effectiveness because too much time and effort was spent on reports and documentation.

I made my first rounds with Deomyn and Zarcyl, around sixth glass. While they had to handle a drunken husband and catch and tie up a loose swaybacked dray, their round was calm. At a quarter past eighth glass I switched to accompanying Sammyl and Rarydn. Their round encompassed the east end of the district out to the Plaza SudEste, the same one I'd once patrolled with Alsoran years before, and the round I thought likely to see taudis-toughs or strong-arms from the Hellhole.

We'd made one complete circuit and were just two blocks in and a block east of the woodworks, when a taudis-kid gave a low whistle from the alleyway.

"Sir?" asked Sammyl.

"It's for me."

The two patrollers exchanged looks, but said nothing as I slipped away from them and walked up to the alleyway. I waited.

The slender figure studied me for a moment, then nodded. "Jadhyl says four outsiders are moving up the alley west of Fedre. They crossed Quierca by the old silversmith's. They're likely carrying pieces."

"Give him my thanks." I slipped a pair of coppers to the taudis-kid—a girl, I realized after the fact, as she vanished into the darkness.

I had a good idea where the four outsiders were headed, and that was to the forked alleyway west of Fedre just off North Middle, where the lighting offered a clear view of anyone on the south side of North Middle, and where two separate patroller rounds intersected. That section of the alley was also slightly higher, and afforded several escape routes.

Sammyl and Rarydn and I took two side alleys and zigzagged through the taudis until we reached the top of the alley two blocks south of North Middle, just short of the fork and only a block inside the taudis.

We waited less than a tenth of a glass before I could make out movement in the alleyway south of us. Despite the fact that Artiema hung barely over the houses behind me and was little more than a crescent, it wasn't long until I could make out four figures in black jackets, not even moving all that quietly.

"Stay close to me." I kept my voice low.

Both patrollers moved shoulder to shoulder with me as I walked through the darkness toward the shadows, holding my shields around the three of us.

"Halt! Just stop where you are," I called.

The four never said a word. Bullets slammed into my shields.

Two of the guns had muzzle flashes, and I imaged iron into the barrels. Both weapons exploded, and the toughs carrying them collapsed where they stood. The other two turned and started to run. I imaged a sheet of oil onto the pavement in front of them. They pitched onto the stone.

I kept walking toward them.

One of the two on the rough alley pavement didn't move. The other one—the squatter figure—rolled onto his side and lifted a short-barreled, wide-muzzled weapon. He fired twice.

The force of the shells against my shields threw me back, and I nearly fell. I staggered, and, for a moment, I couldn't breathe.

The squat figure started to run. I imaged more oil under his feet, and projected air and a partial shield. Under the combined attack, he went down hard.

"You all right, Captain?" asked Rarydn.

"A little winded, but I'll be fine." I might also be sore, but I wouldn't know that until later.

Still holding my shields, I imaged away the oil, then moved toward the fallen figures. The two patrollers flanked me, truncheons ready to strike, but even the squat black-jacketed strong-arm was out cold.

We checked all four, but the two whose weapons had exploded were both dead. The other two had cuts and some shrapnel wounds, but they were breathing.

"Cuff the two who are still with us. Let's get them both back to the station," I ordered.

They were heavy enough that we ended up dragging all four figures to the nearest pick-up pole, where we waited half a glass for the wagon.

By the time we reached the station, our prisoners were awake, if groggy, and I immediately set the smaller tough in the small room used for interrogation, not that we did much of that, since usually we knew what had happened by the time prisoners were in the station. Most crimes in Third District were obvious. I did have him tied to the chair. He said his name was Grohar. It probably wasn't.

Grohar looked at me. It was fair to say he was anything but friendly.

"You shot at us. Why?"

"Frig you, trolie! Frig you . . ."

I clamped shields around him and began to tighten them. He said nothing. I released them. "Care to tell me who sent you?"

"Frig you."

I tried a number of other techniques, well short of physical coercion, but, needless to say, anything that I could immediately think of that would leave him in one piece and unmarked wasn't going to persuade him to talk. So I had the station patrollers cart him back to the holding cell and bring in the other one, the one who'd given the name of Haddad and who had fired the stronger weapon, something like a twin-barreled blunderbuss.

I'd spent some moments thinking while he was being restrained.

Just because I couldn't do something painful and obvious to them didn't mean I couldn't suggest the possibility. So I held up the belt knife we'd taken from Haddad, then tossed it into the air . . . and suspended it in my shields.

"It's not that sharp a knife," I said conversationally. "Rather dull. I imagine it's going to hurt if I have to use it to find out what I need to know."

"You can't touch me . . ."

"I'm not going to touch you." I glanced to Alsoran, standing beside me. "I'm not even close to you. And it is your knife, not mine. And . . . if we failed to find it, and you slashed your wrists because you didn't like being caught . . ."

His eyes fixed on the knife, seemingly suspended in mid-air. I eased the shields, and the knife, toward him. "It would be a lot easier if you just told us who sent you."

I edged the knife closer.

I could see the sweat beading on his forehead. It was amazing how a knife hanging in mid-air and edging toward him brought out the fear.

I waited, smiling.

"It was Costicyn . . . he was the one. He told us . . . be a gold for every patroller we brought down. Didn't matter which ones, but had to be inside the streets he told us . . ."

"Which streets?"

"North Middle and Quierca, the part east of Fuosta, and west of Fedre . . ."

Basically, the streets were those that bordered the taudis. That made sense, in a way, because any patrol deaths would be blamed on the taudis-gangs and my inability to control the taudis in difficult times.

"Who was there besides Costicyn?"

"He was the only one . . . he was."

"There had to be other dealers involved . . ." I eased the knife forward again.

"Honest . . . he was the one . . . know he works with Sadharyn . . . but he never said . . ."

After I finished getting what I could from him, I had them bring back in the first tough. I had the knife almost in his eyeball before he cracked.

Neither could offer anything beyond than what I'd gotten from the first, except that they had the idea that Third District was the only one being targeted so far. Whether that was just what they were told or whether it was true . . . that I couldn't determine.

When I'd gotten what I could, Alsoran and I went back to the duty desk.

"Sir?" Cemaryt looked up.

"Put it in the orders book that when those two we brought in are transported to headquarters tomorrow, I want four patrollers from here to accompany the wagon."

"Yes, sir."

"I want them to get to headquarters alive," I added, although I had my doubts how long they'd last, given my suspicions. I just didn't want their deaths to occur while they were in Third District custody. "And I don't want anything to happen to them here." I looked hard at the duty desk patroller.

"Neither the captain nor I would want anything to happen," added Alsoran.

Cemaryt swallowed.

We walked back to my study, and I closed the door.

"I don't like doing that, you know."

Alsoran nodded. "I know, but they don't. That's what they'd expect, and they'd get worse in most stations." After a moment, he added, "It won't stop with them."

"I'll be working late most nights, but I won't be here until after ninth glass tomorrow. I have to make a command appearance at the Council's Autumn Ball."

"Command?"

"We were asked by the Chief Councilor himself."

"That's command," Alsoran affirmed.

My night duty didn't even end then, because it was so late that I had to walk all the way to the Guild Square to find a hack to take me back to Imagisle. At least, I didn't have to walk the whole way. Even so, my feet were aching when I finally stepped into the foyer, but Seliora was waiting with warm mulled wine.

24

Because I knew it was likely I'd be facing a very long night, on Vendrei morning I took my time getting up, although no one without a small child would have considered it late when I rose and greeted my wife and very active daughter. Before all that long, we were off to our various duties.

The newsheets both noted that Ferran forces had moved to positions less than a mille from the border in the areas closest to the Jariolan coal fields. Another grain freighter had caught fire, this time in Kherseilles. I could only hope that the fire had been contained on the pier and not spread, because I worried about Khethila. The Alusine Wool factorage wasn't all that far from the piers.

As soon as I'd checked the daily reports and duty logs at the station, I headed out to see if I could find Jadhyl. I finally spotted one of his boy lookouts near the corner of Fedre and South Middle, and asked if he'd carry a message—for the promise of two coppers—that I needed a few moments with the taudischef.

While I waited for the message to be delivered, I walked up to the Plaza SudEste and studied the flow of carriages and wagons, as well as the people walking along the Avenue D'Artisans. I thought the traffic and the number of pedestrians was lighter than usual on a Vendrei, but not that much. Then I walked back toward Fedre, where I waited for another quarter-glass before the green-jacketed taudischef arrived with his lookout, who promptly vanished with the two coppers that I tendered.

Jadhyl addressed me, as usual, with his excessively precise intonation. "Master Rhennthyl."

"Jadhyl, you may recall that I passed word about outsiders creating trouble."

"I heard something of the sort, but I had also understood that they were looking for patrollers. Why might I be interested?"

"Because we caught two of them last night. It took a little persuasion, but they decided to tell us why they were attacking patrollers. They were promised a gold apiece for every dead patroller shot within the Third District taudis . . . by someone named Costicyn. Their instructions were very clear. Only to shoot patrollers within the taudis."

"There were some shots last night, not far from here." A faint smile creased his lips.

"I was with some patrollers. The assassins were not successful. Two of them died. The other two named this Costicyn . . . and someone named Sadharyn."

"I have never heard either name. The last sounds Stakanaran." Jadhyl tilted his head. "They wish to prove you cannot control your taudischefs, it appears."

"That's how it looks to me."

"What do you wish from me, Master Captain?"

"Just send word if you see taudis-types that don't belong here. It seems to me that would be in your interests as well as mine."

Jadhyl smiled, coolly. "Would that others saw matters so clearly. We will see what is possible."

That was as much as he'd ever say, but if his lookouts saw more assassins, we'd likely be told. "I'd appreciate it."

I walked the long way back to the station, back out to the Avenue D'Artisans and southwest on it until I reached Quierca, then along Quierca back to Fuosta and up to the station. I studied every block, but didn't see or sense anything out of the ordinary. One of Horazt's taudis-kids did give me a half-wave from an alley just short of Fuosta.

Again, the afternoon was the same as every other afternoon, if just slightly quieter, and without any major disturbances. Right after fifth glass, I caught the duty coach back to NordEste Design to pick up Seliora and Diestrya, and then to Imagisle. Because the Council's Autumn Ball was on a Vendrei and not a Samedi we could leave Diestrya with Klysia, but we still had to feed our daughter and give her a story, if earlier than usual, before dressing.

I wore the black formal wear of a Maitre, with the only adornment the four-pointed open silver star of the Collegium, an adornment required when imagers weren't wearing their distinctive grays. Seliora had arranged for a gown in black with thin panels of a brilliant crimson, and her formal cloak was also lined in crimson silk. I also wore a black formal cloak, not that I necessarily needed it for the short coach ride to the Council Chateau.

As we walked from the house to the duty coach stop where we were to meet the Dichartyns, I cleared my throat. "You didn't say anything about the memorial service for Haerasyn."

Seliora smiled ruefully. "Kolasyn put his foot down. He said they'd have a small service after the viewing at Elysor Memorials. He said there was no point in conducting a public service that would be a charade."

I nodded. That was certainly for the best, whether Odelia thought so or not. "I'm going to have to leave the Ball early tonight."

"I thought you might." Seliora frowned, but only for a moment. "Because you think the drug dealers know you'll be at the Chateau?"

"That's what I'm wagering." I also thought they'd strike later on a Vendrei, assuming that fewer patrollers would be alert, and that I might well have had too much wine, even if I did hurry back to Third District. "None of this is accidental. It's all planned."

Seliora raised her eyebrows.

"Not that way," I said. "The drug dealers aren't taking directions from whoever is involved with one side or the other on the grain civil war, or from the Ferrans or the Stakanarans, whoever's responsible for growing the stronger elveweed in southern Solidar. The drug dealers will plan the best way to attack Third District, and whoever's behind the elveweed is counting on that, just as the Ferrans are counting on the freeholders to create problems with the High Holders and the Council."

"It sounds like the Ferrans are trying to stir up trouble in Solidar before they attack Jariola."

"I'd wager on it, even on their involving Stakanar or Tiempre, although I think it's Stakanar."

"There's not too much you can do about it, except in handling matters in Third District."

"No, there isn't." And there wasn't, except I had the feeling that matters went well beyond Third District. I also still worried about the Pharsi foresight flash that showed me struggling from beneath or around piles of gray stone, because that didn't seem to fit anywhere. Had it really been a true foresight flash?

We only waited for a few moments at the coach stop before the Dichartyns appeared. Master Dichartyn wore the same imager formal blacks as did I. Under a dark gray formal cloak, Aelys looked to be wearing a pale gold and russet gown, colors that suited her complexion and thin frame.

"Good evening," I offered.

"The same," returned Master Dichartyn with a smile.

Once we were all seated, Aelys smiled at Seliora. "The girls said that Diestrya was very well-behaved the other evening."

"That's because your daughters are firm and because Diestrya likes them. She's still at the age where she'll test limits if she senses any lack of firmness."

"Some youngsters retain that for a long time," added Dichartyn blandly.

"You should know, dearest," replied Aelys sweetly.

I managed not to grin before I looked as Dichartyn. "I'd like to ask for a favor, sir."

"Ask away."

"I'm faced with the likelihood of a difficult situation in my district later this evening, but I'd like to allow Seliora to enjoy the entire ball."

"Of course," he replied.

"Don't make it so formal, dearest," added Aelys. "You can dance with a young and beautiful woman."

"So long as I don't enjoy it too much?"

His ironic tone had us all smiling.

Our carriage arrived at the Council Chateau slightly before eighth glass, and was perhaps tenth in the line leading up to the steps. I was glad that the weather was clear, if chill, because there was no portico or rotunda, just the stone steps leading up to the main floor Grand Foyer. Once the coach reached the steps, and we disembarked, Seliora and I led the way, because Maitre Dichartyn was still senior to me. Once inside we crossed the foyer and passed the ceremonial guards, then ascended the Grand Staircase, past the winged angelia statues. I recalled them all too well and how angry I'd made my father as a boy when I'd commented on the inaccuracies captured in stone.

When we reached the doorway to the Great Receiving Hall, we stepped up to the same balding man who announced all arrivals at every Ball with a deep bass voice so at odds with his stature.

"Captain and Maitre Rhennthyl and Madame Rhennthyl."

"I still don't feel like I should be announced as Madame," murmured Seliora as we stepped toward the three Councilors on the Executive Council, who formed a receiving line of sorts.

"You're young and beautiful enough to be a mistress, but you'd better not . . . except with me," I teased her.

"Rhennthyl," she said in a low voice, "you're impossible."

Beyond the Councilors, I caught sight of the security imagers, Baratyn standing against the east wall of the Hall and Dartazn and Martyl along the west wall.

Behind us came the announcement of "Maitre Dichartyn and Madame Dichartyn."

The first of the Executive Councilors was Glendyl D'Factorius, the manufacturer of various machinery that included everything from steam engines and mining pumps to full-sized ironway locomotives. As a Councilor from the regions around L'Excelsis, he represented the factors from Solis to Rivages. He inclined his head politely. "It's good to see you, Master Rhennthyl, Madame."

"We're glad to be here," I replied.

Next was the hawk-nosed, black-haired Caartyl, the Councilor from Esh-tora representing the various artisans' guilds across northwest Solidar. "Greet-ings, Master Rhennthyl. It's always a pleasure to see an imager from a guild background. And your beauty, Madame Seliora, even exceeds your family's reputation and artistry."

Seliora inclined her head in response. "You're most kind."

Suyrien D'Alte was only slightly above average in height, several digits shorter than I, with thinning brown hair and a receding hairline. The only physical aspect that suggested why he was the Chief Councilor was the in-tensity in his pale green eyes, an intensity not entirely masked by his warm smile and pleasant voice. "Rhenn, Seliora, I'm so glad that you were able to come. Both Kandryl and Frydryk have told me how much they enjoyed spend-ing the evening with you last Samedi. They and their ladies should be here shortly."

"We're very pleased to be here," I replied. "We wouldn't have missed it for anything."

"According to Frydryk . . . I owe you more than I realized."

"Only to the Collegium, sir. If I hadn't been there, doubtless someone else would have been." I truly doubted that, but the Collegium needed the credit more than I did.

"I have my doubts, but I appreciate your efforts and those of the Col-legium."

"As we appreciate yours and those of the Council."

"Enjoy the ball." Suyrien smiled again.

As we moved out into the hall, and toward the music and those danc-ing, I thought the Councilor's smile was more than professional, but with a good politician, one could never be certain. Behind us, the announcements continued.

"Councilor Alucion D'Artisan and Madame D'Alucion!"

"Councilor Reyner D'Factorius and Madame D'Reyner . . ."

We stopped short of the dance floor and to one side, not that far from the sideboards that held various vintages, where uniformed servers already pro-vided goblets to those who wished them.

"Would you like something?"

"Not yet." Without seeming to, Seliora studied the dancers and those around us.

She didn't need to. She was by far the most beautiful. I glanced toward the temporary dais at the south end of the Hall, where orchestra played music for a slower dance, muted enough for both dancing and conversation, although I didn't recognize the melody. But then, music in any fashion had never been my gift.

"Shendael D'Alte and Madame D'Shendael."

"Marshal Geuffryt D'Mer . . ."

I turned slightly to watch as Juniae D'Shendael smiled at each of the High Councilors, her expression gracious and her short-cut mahogany hair without a strand out of place.

"So that's what she looks like," murmured Seliora. "Khethila might be disappointed."

"She's seen etchings and paintings, and she looks like them."

"The Honorable Dharios Harnen, Envoy of the Abierto Isles, and Madame Harnen."

At past Balls, the envoy had brought his daughter, and the much younger woman with him looked more her age, suggesting that he'd recently remarried.

"Ryel D'Alte and Madame Ryel." That announcement seemed wrong, perhaps because the first time I'd heard it had been for Iryela's parents.

"Frydryk D'Suyrien-Alte and Mistress Alynkya D'Ramsael-Alte."

I watched as the Ryels made their way into the Hall and over to the three Councilors. Iryela wore a gown of shimmering blue and silver, the same colors she'd worn at the first Ball where I'd met her—although Kandryl wore the Ryel colors of black and silver.

"Don't move to them," murmured Seliora. "They can join us. They will."

I didn't argue. If they did, it showed one thing, and if they didn't, it showed another.

Matters didn't turn out quite that way, because I could see Juniae D'Shendael was headed in our direction, accompanied not by her husband, but by the Naval officer who had followed her through the receiving line.

"You're going to get Khethila's wish," I said in a low voice.

"I'll make the best of it for her."

Madame D'Shendael's smile was warm as she inclined her head to us. "Maitre Rhennthyl . . . I do prefer that to 'Captain.' I hope you don't mind." Madame D'Shendael smiled and looked to Seliora. "Being a Maitre D'Structure is more distinguished. There are but six in all the world, and there are six Civic Patrol Captains just in L'Excelsis itself."

I didn't correct her, but just murmured, "You're most gracious."

"I'm very pleased to meet you, Madame D'Shendael," offered Seliora.

"Juniae, please . . ."

"I heard so much about your books from Rhenn's sister, and she would be so pleased to know that you are as gracious—and imposing—as your writings."

Juniae D'Shendael laughed. "Imposing? That sounds like a statue. I hope I'm not quite that stiff and formal." She looked to me. "Does your sister still retain her affection for my work, Maitre Rhennthyl, or was that a passing fashion of youth?"

"She still holds the deepest respect for you and your writing, Madame."

A card appeared in the gloved hand of Juniae D'Shendael. "I've written the name of the latest book on the back. With fortune, it should be printed in the next month or so."

I took the card. "Thank you. I'm certain she will get it. I will have to post the card and information to her, though. She is now running the Alusine Wool factorage in Kherseilles. She's made it quite profitable, and as I told you years ago, she credits some of that to you."

"You are both kind, but I'm certain it was mainly through her own ability. She's a full factoria now, isn't she?"

"That she is. One of the few." I didn't want to go into all the difficulties that had created.

"Good for her . . . and for your father in supporting her." She smiled warmly, then inclined her head to the young-faced, but red-and-silver-haired man in the uniform of a Navy Sea-Marshal. "I did want you to meet Assistant Sea-Marshal Geuffryt. His official title is Director of Internal Operations."

I inclined my head to the marshal. "I'm pleased to meet you. Might I present my wife Seliora?"

"Madame Rhennthyl, I'm delighted to meet you." After bowing his head slightly to Seliora he straightened and said with a smile, "It's always a pleasure to meet people who take their obligations seriously, but not themselves. You both have that reputation."

"So does the Navy," I replied.

"We try," he replied with a laugh.

"If you will excuse us?" Juniae D'Shendael smiled again. "I see my husband beckoning."

After she and the Sea-Marshal turned away, I read what she had written on the back of the card—"The Art of Conversation." The writing looked familiar, near-perfect, so much so that it might have been calligraphy. I'd seen it before. I knew I had. Then I almost froze, realizing that the script well might be identical to the message I'd been given at the banque. I'd have to check, but I was certain that the writing was identical.

"What is it?" asked Seliora, leaning close to me and murmuring her words.

"Trouble . . ." The Assistant Sea-Marshal was clearly the head of Naval intelligence—spying, or the like, although I'd have to check with Dichartyn—and the entire purpose of the meeting and the card was obvious. What I didn't understand was why Marshal Geuffryt couldn't have acted on the information I'd been provided in the note at the banque. "I'll have to tell you later."

I half-turned and smiled as Iryela and Kandryl approached.

"There you are!" offered Iryela warmly. "We did want to join you, but Madame D'Shendael and that Navy officer were taking your time."

"She was giving me a card with the title of her new book so that I could tell Khethila. It's called 'The Art of Conversation.' I imagine it will be more than that. Her books go beyond the titles."

Iryela smiled. "You'd never mentioned you'd read her books."

"I haven't read them all—just two, and not all of one of them," I admitted. "It's not that they're not good . . . but . . . there's never enough time."

"With all that you two do, I'm not surprised." Iryela's eyes flicked to Kandryl.

Kandryl looked to Seliora. "I understand you're a marvelous dancer. If you wouldn't mind . . ." He looked to me.

Seliora offered a smile. "I'd love to, and Rhenn can't tell me no."

I shrugged helplessly, then turned to Iryela. "I fear you're getting the worse of this, but might I have the dance?"

She smiled broadly. "That you may."

As we slipped onto the dance floor, I murmured, "Nicely done. I take it you have a concern."

"I do. It's not something I'd want anyone else to know, except Seliora, of course. There are golds missing from a private contingency account, several thousand. It's a coded account in the Banque D'Rivages. So far as I know, only my father had the codes until. . . . Mother didn't even know about them, and she's stayed on the lands ever since. They were always sealed, and the seals weren't broken when . . . after things happened."

"Can't you change the codes?"

"Oh, we did, and that stopped the losses. We can handle a few thousand golds . . . but it's still worrisome."

A few thousand golds, and she could handle it? After five years as a Maitre D'Structure, I made three golds a week. That was more than all but a few people in a hundred made in L'Excelsis—and we did get a good-sized house as well. Even if I counted in the monetary value of the house, my annual earnings were probably less than four hundred golds a year. All that just illustrated the enormous gap in wealth between the High Holders and the rest of Solidar, except perhaps for a few handfuls of freeholders or factors like Broussard. "Maybe someone in one of the banques just guessed."

"It's possible, but we have our doubts. I thought you, in your present position, might keep an eye or ear open, just in case you find something that might shed some light on how it could have occurred."

"I honestly don't know of anything like that, but I'd be pleased to watch for anything bearing on it." I could tell that the possibility of a lack of control bothered Iryela more than did the loss of the golds. That . . . I understood all too well.

"I do appreciate it, Rhenn."

"Frydryk had a talk with his father."

"He always does. That's the burden of being the heir."

"Kandryl should be thankful to you . . . in many ways."

"He is most grateful . . . and attentive." After the slightest pause, she added, "At times, things do turn out for the best. They have for both of us, I think."

She wasn't talking about herself and Kandryl, and I just said, "Yes, they do, and at times, they even lead to happiness amid the disruptions." I paused. "I never thanked you for selling that land to Khethila."

Her eyes sparkled for a moment. "I didn't even know we had it. When I found out, I thought it was the right thing to do. So did Kandryl. We offered it for less than my father paid for it."

I understood. Iryela had made the offer at fair market value. Her father had bought it at a premium so that he could use it against me and my family, but Iryela also knew that outright charity would rankle Khethila.

After a time of silence, she said, "You have improved since the first time we danced. That has to be your wife's influence."

"She's been a good influence."

As the music of that dance died away, I escorted Iryela back to the edge of the dance floor, where Kandryl and Seliora were already waiting.

"If you will excuse us . . ." offered Iryela.

"Of course," Seliora replied.

I just nodded.

"What did she want?" asked Seliora with a smile.

"Besides a dance?" I grinned. "Did you think—"

"I carry the pistol everywhere," she whispered.

"You're a hard woman."

"But I'm yours . . . if you behave."

"As if I had any choice." I laughed, then, after a moment, explained. "Someone withdrew funds from a coded account. She said the amount didn't bother her so much as that no one else knew the codes. It was only several thousand golds." A touch of irony crept into my voice.

"Who would have known the codes? Her mother? She and Johanyr are the only ones left alive besides Iryela."

"According to Iryela, the codes were sealed and unbroken. Her mother didn't even know they existed, and Johanyr hasn't been in L'Excelsis in something like seven years. Besides, he's nearly blind. I doubt if he could even read them."

"I can see why she's worried, then. But there must be a simple explanation."

"There probably is, but I can't think of it. Her mother could be pretending, but given how Ryel ran his holdings, and the way the older High Holders treat their wives, I doubt it."

"I can see that."

"Let's enjoy the dancing before I have to leave."

Her smile was worth that, and we danced . . . and danced—until just past ninth glass, when I left Seliora with the Dichartyns and hurried out of the Chateau, where I persuaded the duty coach driver—Elreyt, who usually drove evenings—to take me to Third District station.

As soon as the coach stopped on Fuosta, I stepped out and hurried into the station and to the duty desk.

"Any trouble yet?"

"No, sir, but . . . Sammyl said one of the taudis-kids warned us to watch the woodworks."

"I'll be heading there."

Cemaryt glanced at the formal cloak and black formal wear.

I grinned. "I won't be as easily seen."

"Ah . . . yes, sir."

I reached the woodworks, where I waited in the shadows close to South Middle for Sammyl and Rarydn. I stood there half a glass before they neared.

They both started when I appeared.

"Sir?"

"I understand we might have trouble here."

"One of the taudis-kids—she was a girl—told me." Rarydn glanced at the darkened building to his right, questioningly.

"If they destroy the building and kill patrollers . . . it hurts the taudis-dwellers and the Civic Patrol," I pointed out. "Let's head down toward the alley across from the south side."

They exchanged glances, but followed me. We stopped short of the corner of the wall that circled the waste yard on the southeast side of the property.

"We'll wait here," I said in a low voice. "We'll have some cover. You watch behind us, Rarydn."

"Yes, sir."

As I suspected, before long, less than a quarter of a glass, there were four figures coming up the alley, but they stopped short of the side street in front of us, and remained in the alley. All of them bore packs, which they eased off and set on the stones. I could see three other figures coming forward, past the four and stationing themselves on each side of the alley. The three wore the shiny leathers of taudis-toughs. The other four wore dark light-absorbing garb.

I was getting a very uneasy feeling about the entire situation, especially after I saw one of the men setting up something like a tripod pointing in our general direction, but likely at the woodworks building. Then another tripod went up, and a third, and a fourth. When the first man set a cylindrical tube on a tripod, I knew. But I waited until all four tubes were in place on their tripods . . . but not a moment more.

Then . . . I stepped around the corner, my back to the wall, and concentrated, imaging fire into all four cylinders and projecting my shields across the alley at an angle.

Light flared everywhere, and a wave of sound slammed me into the wall.

"Sir! Sir!"

Sammyl was helping me to my feet, but loud as he was speaking his words were barely a whisper.

"I'm all right." I thought I was. I was shaking . . . but I could see and walk, if a trace unsteadily. I felt weak, and I couldn't raise any shields. I just hoped that there was no one else around who might want to take a shot at us. "We might as well see what happened." I started across the side street, but I stopped short of the sidewalk on the other side.

The explosion, contained by my shields, had left a hole a yard deep and five across, and that was through the alley paving stones. There were bits of what had been men and gear strewn like leaves across the bottom of the hole, as well as scraps of twisted metal.

I swallowed and turned away.

Behind me, I could hear Rarydn retching.

I walked back to the other side of the cross street and leaned against the wall. A short time later, the two patrollers rejoined me.

"What happened?" Rarydn's voice was unsteady.

"The first four had explosive rockets they were going to fire into the woodworks. Then when you and Sammyl came running, the three taudis-toughs would have shot you."

Sammyl looked to me. "Wasn't that something the Army should have handled?"

"Well . . ." I offered with a grin I didn't feel, "if we'd waited for them . . ."

"Frig . . ." mumbled the older patroller, adding after a moment, "Pardon me, sir, but it doesn't seem right."

"It's not, but how often do we get stuck dealing with what's not right?"

"How do you want us to write it up?" asked Rarydn.

"Just the way it happened. We got a tip. We came to investigate. We must have startled them. Their rockets exploded all at once and dug a big hole and killed all of them."

"How come—" Rarydn began.

"We don't have to guess why it happened that way," I said. "We're just Civic Patrollers reporting on what happened."

"That's right." Sammyl looked hard at Rarydn.

After a moment, the younger patroller nodded.

We turned and began to walk back to the station. Erion had just climbed above the roofs of the houses to the east, half-full and red-shaded. It might be the moon of the great hunter, but I had the feeling I was as much being hunted as hunter.

25

As tired and as cold as I was by the time I got home on Vendrei, I could raise shields, although it was painful. I wasn't sleepy, not after all that had happened. That was probably good, because the moment Seliora saw me step inside the front foyer she asked, "How bad was it?"

"Bad enough. There were four military types with rockets and three taudis-toughs . . ." I began as I walked into the family parlor and dropped onto the settee in front of the stove. In between bits of explanation, Seliora offered me warm spiced wine. That warmed me and loosened my throat.

When I finished, she said, "The four with the rockets had to be Ferran agents, or something like that, didn't they?"

"Ferran or Stakanaran, I'd guess, but I'm convinced they obtained the munitions here, and that's even more troubling."

"You think that the freeholders or factors like Broussard are involved?"

"They're involved in something. Whether they're just causing trouble for the High Holders right now because it's opportune or because they have something else in mind . . . I don't know enough to say."

"What would they gain?"

"At the very least, they'd put the High Holders on notice that unethical or illegal commercial practices and backdoor discrimination can have a far higher price than the High Holders can afford. At most, they might be pushing for a change in the balance of power on the Council."

"The Council can't afford to give in to that kind of pressure."

"The Council can't, but the High Holders might have to. Already, they really can't compete with the larger freeholders in the east in grain and other produce. Not on price. A factor like Glendyl might well be as wealthy as half the smaller High Holders, and more and more factors are getting into manufacturing. I also think the growing of the stronger elveweed represents more than we're seeing."

"More than others are seeing," Seliora corrected me. "You wouldn't say that if you didn't have something in mind. What is it?"

"The deaths from the stronger weed are making more people unhappy because young people especially are dying outside the taudis. That's affecting crafters, artisans, factors, probably even the families of High Holders, although they don't matter to whoever's behind this. The idea is to make people like Odelia and Kolasyn and their families unhappy with the Council and the Civic Patrol. There are probably already rumors circulating that it's all the fault of Suyrien and the High Holders. It's also to raise golds, possibly to fund things like last night, or all the attacks against the High Holders."

Seliora frowned. "But . . ."

I shook my head. "I'm guessing again, but I think the attacks against the High Holders are designed to make them retaliate against the freeholders and factors, the way they've always done, except now some of the factors and freeholders have the resources and expertise to fight back."

"What else?"

"I don't know. I'm missing something."

"You're tired. Maybe you'll think of it in the morning."

I nodded. I was exhausted, and finally beginning to feel sleepy, but I had the feeling it was something so obvious I'd want to beat my head against a wall when I discovered what it was.

When I finally awakened, well after sunrise on Samedi, I seemed to have my ability to hold shields back, without pain, but I didn't raise them then. The longer before I had to, the less strain I'd face in holding them. I showered and dressed, then ate, because I did have to go into the station. I also wanted to stop and talk to Master Dichartyn before I did.

So I found myself knocking on his door before I hurried off to find a duty coach.

He opened the door, barefoot and wearing only old trousers and an undertunic. "Was the situation as bad as you thought it might be? I assume it wasn't good, since you're knocking on my front door rather early. Come on in."

I stepped into the foyer and went through the events of the night before, ending with, ". . . the power of the explosives suggested to me military munitions. They're most likely those stolen from the Army depot."

"You're sure they were that strong, Rhenn?"

I refrained from being as sarcastic as I might have been. "I can't prove anything, but whatever it was pulverized paving stones and dug a hole a yard deep and five across."

"Part of that had to be from the containment of your shields," he pointed out.

"That might be, but . . ."

"I take your point. They have to be military. Schorzat needs to know, and so does Maitre Poincaryt."

"You want me to report it to him personally?"

"No. The way you did it was the way it should be done. For the moment, I don't want to tell Commander Artois anything more than is in your official patrol report."

That alone told me he shared my view of Cydarth.

"Is there anything else?" he asked.

"Outside of the fact that four taudis-toughs tried to shoot two of my patrollers on Jeudi night? No. Or that two of the more honest District captains have been removed by an accident and a shooting? Or that Cydarth is suggesting that the lower number of deaths from elveweed in Third District has to do with my ties to unsavory elements?"

"I don't believe you mentioned those," he commented in a dry tone.

"I might not have."

He nodded as if that confirmed something, then said, "They'll only make it look like they're trying to kill you."

"So that I'll be set up? I wouldn't be surprised." With the depth of intrigue that I'd seen since I'd come to Imagisle, and with what more I suspected, I wasn't certain that anything wasn't possible . . . and even so, I'd still probably end up being surprised by the depth of greed, avarice, and scheming that I'd find.

"You will be. We always are, no matter what we think. If that's all . . ." He glanced toward the family parlor.

"That's all."

I returned to our house, kissed my wife and daughter, and then walked to the duty coach waiting area, where I had to stand for a quint before another coach appeared. It was still early enough that the ride to the station wasn't hampered by Samedi traffic.

Zharyn had the weekend duty, and he bolted to his feet when he saw me enter the station.

"More problems?" I asked.

"Not in Third District, sir. At headquarters."

"What sort of problems?"

"Those two we caught on Jeudi, Captain? They're dead. Someone poisoned them in the main lockup."

I couldn't help but wonder about Zharyn's knowing that. We usually didn't hear what happened to prisoners we'd sent for charging for a week, sometimes longer if justicing were delayed.

"We got a dispatch this morning by regular headquarters messenger, except . . . no one signed it." Zharyn handed the single sheet to me.

There were only four short sentences.

> The prisoners Grohar and Haddad died Vendrei. Poisoning is suspected. Headquarters is investigating. Send any information that might help in resolving the case.

No seal or signature appeared, but I wouldn't have been surprised if Buasytt had sent it. I'd always had the feeling he didn't see exactly eye-to-eye with either the subcommander or Lieutenant Sarthyn. Then again, it could have been a veiled warning from Cydarth as well, and that might well be the more accurate assumption.

Four taudis-toughs had attacked Third District patrollers on Jeudi, and all of them were dead. So were those who'd attacked on Vendrei. Not only did the deaths leave no trail and no way to follow up, but they pointed out what might be construed as ruthless law enforcement in Third District, and that wasn't likely to be terribly helpful to me . . . or to Commander Artois when he came up for review before the Council.

Fortunately, Samedi morning and afternoon were quiet in Third District, or relatively so for a Samedi in fall, with only petty crimes, and the report of but a single elver death.

I left the station a little early, around fourth glass, and took a hack back to Imagisle, but by a quint past fifth glass the three of us were in another hack headed back out to my parents. Seliora and I hadn't had much time to talk, what with her getting ready and my dealing with Diestrya while she did so.

"How did today go?" Seliora asked as the hack headed up the Boulevard D'Imagers.

"Quiet. A few snatch-and-grabs from shop-girls on the Avenue. There usually are on Samedi, and some of the girls never learn. Some of the patrollers are getting edgy, but I'd be surprised if there are problems tonight."

"And tomorrow night?"

"I'd guess Mardi night, but . . ." I shrugged. "It could happen any time. Alsoran's going to be there this evening for a while."

"He should be. You've been there most nights."

"I worry, but I can't be there all the time."

"No . . . you can't. Can you just enjoy dinner tonight?"

"I'll try."

Seliora looked at Diestrya. "Your cousin Rheityr will be there. You will play nicely with him."

"Yes, Mama."

I caught a hint of a gleam in her eye. "Your mother means it, and so do I."

Diestrya dropped her eyes and her lower lip began to protrude.

"None of that, young lady." I tried to keep my voice matter-of-fact, and the lip quivered, but there was no procession into tears.

Seliora and I managed to stifle smiles, as Diestrya finally looked up and declared, "I like Rheityr."

"That's good. He is your cousin." I added in a murmur, "I'm going to try to catch that expression in her portrait." Not that I'd had much time to work on it lately, even with the studio now in our house.

"She'll hate you for it until she has children," Seliora whispered in return.

That was often the way with children, I'd decided.

It didn't seem that long before the hack let us out at my parents' house, and we joined my parents, Culthyn, and Remaya in the family parlor. Diestrya, of course, joined Rheityr in the nursery.

Before Father could ask me how either the Civic Patrol or imager "business" was, I asked him, "How is the wool business these days?"

He shook his head. "There have been times that have been worse, but not in any recent years. We've had problems in getting the raw wool to the carders and spinners. It's not just in any one part of Solidar, either. The shipping delays are the worst in the northeast, and even in the north around Mont D'Glace, and that's a straight ironway run to L'Excelsis."

"You always have problems," Mother said, extending the tray on which rested his goblet of Dhuensa.

"Not like these." Father shook his head.

"The spice trade has almost stopped now," added Remaya. "Father says that little or nothing's arriving from any of the countries in Otelyrn."

"Is someone else paying more for spices?" I asked.

"That couldn't be the reason," Remaya replied. "Father says that the Stakanaran gunboats are blockading the small river ports where the spices are collected. They're fast enough to outrun larger vessels, and Tiempre and Caenen don't want to tie up their warships for a trade that doesn't benefit them that much."

"How can it not benefit them?" asked Seliora.

My father cleared his throat, then looked at Remaya, who nodded. He cleared his throat again. "Spices are cheap in Otelyrn. They grow easily. The profit lies in transporting them to where they don't grow—here. The traders don't want to lose their vessels to the gunboats, and they—and traders like Remaya's family—are the only ones who suffer."

"Our cooking and food also suffers," added my mother.

"So . . . Rhenn," asked my father, "how is the Civic Patrol business?"

"About like the wool and spice businesses." I tried to keep my tone light. "But we won't solve it here, and I'd like to hear what Rheityr's been up to lately." I grinned. "Then, Seliora and I can talk about our wonderful daughter."

Culthyn actually laughed.

After that, and through dinner, we talked about family and food, and children. Seliora and I—and a very sleepy Diestrya—left just after eighth glass.

The late nights all through the week took their toll on both Seliora and me, and we were asleep in our separate chambers in less than half a glass after Charlsyn dropped us off at the Collegium.

A dull rumbling shook me awake. But that was followed by another, and an explosion. The entire house shook. Even in the darkness, I could see stones falling around me—yet they hadn't, not so far.

I ran from my sleeping chamber and across the main bedchamber. "Seliora!" I kept moving, snatching Diestrya from her small railed bed and hurrying back toward Seliora's sleeping chamber, where I sat on the edge of the bed beside her, raising my shields. "Stay close to me."

Seliora didn't question me, but she wouldn't have had time, because a gigantic unseen hammer slammed the north side of the house. Stones toppled into the house, with some fragments and chunks of masonry and stone and tiles sliding off and around my shields, even as all manner of rubble built up in the hallway and rolled into the bedchamber. Glass sprayed against the shields like grapeshot. The house, solidly built as it was, groaned and shifted.

I could sense something—two somethings, I thought—hurtling toward us, toward my shields and in a fit of anger, image-shifted them back to the point from where they had come. At that moment, my entire body felt like it had been squeezed in a vice. That feeling passed, but my eyes blurred, and I felt dizzy.

The house shifted again . . . and more rubble settled.

Then came the sound of another massive explosion, followed by others, right in a row, somewhere to the north.

At that moment, I was so exhausted I could barely move, and my whole body ached, but I knew I had to hold the shields to protect Seliora and Diestrya until we could get out of the house and the rubble around us. I closed my eyes and concentrated for a time longer.

After everything settled, I turned to Seliora. "I'm holding shields. I don't know what will collapse. We'll move to where we can get clothes and boots and then make our way out. I think the south side of the house isn't as badly damaged."

We just grabbed clothing and boots before making our way down the rubble-filled staircase, more like sliding down the balustrade, but the dwelling had been so solidly built that the main level was clear, if dusty.

My head was pounding, and my whole body ached. Donning the basic grays quickly in the front foyer was difficult, and my eyes kept blurring, from the dust, I supposed. When we finally stepped out of the house, I was struck by the diffuse light filling the northern sky, as if something were burning brightly on the River Aluse, and yet droplets of ice fell out of the sky.

Fire and ice? How could that be?

Yet that light, already fading, allowed me to see the devastation around me. Master Dichartyn's house was rubble. So was Maitre Dyana's, as was the larger dwelling that had been Maitre Poincaryt's. I turned, and my entire body twinged, and a wave a blackness swept toward me, but receded, although I could feel that it had not retreated that far. Out of the smoky haze, I could see Maitre Dyana walking toward me, dressed in working grays.

Behind me, Seliora was saying something, but I couldn't hear the words. I felt light-headed, and dizzy, and my entire body tingled, but I pushed that away. I had to know what had happened, what Maitre Dyana knew.

Maitre Dyana stopped in front of me, then said, "Sit down. Now!"

I almost made it before the blackness slammed me down.

The next time I woke up was with gray walls around me, but my eyes wouldn't focus, and I couldn't talk. Someone fed me something soft, and I drank something, and the blackness rose up again. That sort of thing must have happened for a while, because I thought I saw people around, but nothing made much sense.

Then, I finally swam out of that hazy blackness and could actually see, and feed myself, although my entire body remained a mass of soreness and aches. One of the obdurate attendants watched closely, then took the empty tray away. That I'd been watched by an ob all the time suggested I'd been in a bad way.

I took stock of my physical situation. From what I could see, there were purplish-yellow bruises on my arms and my upper chest, and probably on my thighs, from the way they felt. How had all that happened? I'd held my shields and even angled and slipped them the way Maitre Dyana had drilled into me years earlier. Or had it been when I'd imaged back the shells or bombs or whatever had been aimed at the Collegium?

Draffyd appeared, and his eyes were ringed with black. "How are you feeling?"

"Sore and aching all over," I admitted. "But I can see without everything blurring."

"Your eyes were so bloodshot that they were more red than white. You're fortunate to be alive." He paused. "You were imaging behind shields, weren't you?"

"Ah . . . not exactly. I was imaging beyond them."

His eyes widened, but he only nodded. "Maitre Dyana needs to see you, but I've asked her to be brief. You aren't ready to do much right now."

"Seliora?"

"She and Diestrya have been staying in one of the empty rooms here. You can see her after Maitre Dyana."

Draffyd hadn't been gone more than a tenth of a glass before Maitre Dyana walked in—without one of her colored scarves.

She looked tired, but her words were as crisp and cutting as ever. "Some finesse would have made it easier on you, Rhenn, not that finesse comes that easily in the middle of the night when someone is dropping shells on you and your family."

I just looked at her. "The shields and the finesse were the easy part. Imaging those shells back to their firing points was what hurt."

For the only time in the seven years I'd known her, Maitre Dyana didn't seem to have words. She studied me. Finally, she said, "From all the ice on the river, I wondered about that. How did you manage it?"

"I don't know what happened, but, yes, I imaged some shells, two, I think, back to their starting point."

"You never saw them."

"I can do that. I've always been able to. I've done it with bullets before. I never tried it with anything that big. Just ask Draffyd or . . . What happened to Master Dichartyn?"

"Unlike you or me, he had no warning. The first shells hit his dwelling, and then Maitre Poincaryt's. Dichartyn still managed to shield Aelys and the children."

Dichartyn? Dead? How . . . ? I swallowed. "Maitre Poincaryt?" I paused. "Then, you're the Maitre of the Collegium?"

"Apparently, you should be. No one else can image ten-stone shells back a half mille and explode a floating battery. That's the sort of thing that only Maitre D'Images can do, and not all of them." The tired irony vanished from her voice "No one could figure out why the barges that held the bombards would suddenly explode after a handful of rounds. There was enough powder and shells to reduce the entire Collegium to rubble."

"I was angry," I admitted. "I really didn't think."

"It wasn't the best for you that you reacted, but it doubtless saved most of the Collegium . . . Maitre."

I shook my head. "I don't know enough. I don't even know enough to handle what Master Dichartyn did. Let them think you did it. You'll need that leverage anyway."

Dyana actually smiled, if but for a moment. "You won't escape that destiny, Rhenn. You might be able to postpone it . . . but not escape it." Her eyes took in my arms and chest. "It's still a wonder you're alive."

"If any other masters need to know, tell them that it took both of us . . . or better yet, imply that without saying it."

"You'll still have to become a Maitre D'Esprit."

"Can't Schorzat take on . . ."

"No. He knows it. Dichartyn and he already discussed it. His shields won't take the kind of beating yours can. Frankly, I'm not certain anyone else's can."

"Were they using the stolen bombards?"

"We think so. We really don't have the time or the resources to dredge the Aluse to find out. They were set up on barges."

I couldn't help but wonder if the heavier barges I'd seen in the past weeks had carried the bombards upriver. There really wasn't any point in saying anything about that. What was done was done, and the Collegium—or the river force of the Civic Patrol—couldn't have checked every barge on the river for weeks on end.

"What else happened?"

"What do you mean?"

"It was all part of a plan, wasn't it? The stronger elveweed, the Ferran or Stakanaran funding of explosions and violence. I'd guess that the Ferrans have invaded Jariola by now . . ."

"Is this a guess on your part? Did you—"

"I told Master Dichartyn that was what I thought. We've lost two good captains in the Civic Patrol, and I wouldn't be surprised if the subcommander weren't involved as well, not that I could prove anything. Oh . . . and if you haven't already, you might check with a Sea-Marshal Geuffryt. He has some knowledge about payments to Caartyl and Cydarth. Master Dichartyn probably told Maitre Poincaryt about all that, but I left it to them to tell you, and since I only told some of it to Dichartyn on Samedi morning. . . ." I left the sentence uncompleted, feeling slightly tired just from speaking.

"For someone who almost died, you're sounding suspiciously like Dichartyn. And, no, they didn't get around to telling me all of that. What else is there?"

"Did Ferrum invade—" I had to know that.

"Yes . . . we just got word this morning. It doesn't look good for the Jariolans."

"The Council . . . what have they done?"

"Suyrien announced, on behalf of the Council, that the Northern Fleet would blockade all Ferran ports until the Ferran forces returned to their own territory and would regard any attempt to break the blockade as hostile action against Solidar. The Council also declared that the attack on Imagisle was an act of war." Her voice turned wry. "They didn't name who committed the act."

"So we're not technically at war?"

"Not yet. We may never be. The Council hates to do that because it gives more power to the Chief Councilor."

"What about Otelyrn?"

She gave me a sidelong look, then said, "The Stakanarans have invaded the southernmost province of Tiempre, where the gold and diamond mines are. The Tiemprans are appealing for aid. They likely won't get it . . ."

"Is Suyrien all right?"

"Why do you ask?"

"Because he and Artois are obvious targets. I don't know more than that."

"There's one other thing. You remember Johanyr?"

"Of course." How could I have forgotten?

"He disappeared from Mont D'Glace. Several weeks ago."

"You'd better let his sister know." I had the feeling that his disappearance just might be linked to Iryela's missing golds, even if I had no way to explain it.

"I already have."

There were other things I should have asked, but I was getting tired and sleepy, despite wanting to know more . . . and even with all the aches and sorenesses.

Dyana stepped back. "Thank you. All that will be of great assistance."

As soon as she left, Seliora and Diestrya were in the gray-walled chamber.

Seliora set Diestrya next to the bed, then bent over and kissed my cheek. The closeness of her, despite how everything hurt, felt so reassuring. Tears were seeping from her eyes. "I wasn't certain . . . no one was sure . . ."

"I'll be all right." Now . . . or at least in time.

"Dada!"

"Your father hurts all over, sweetheart. Don't touch him."

"You're all right?" I managed.

"We're both fine." She paused.

"What?"

"There have been fires and explosions all over the city."

I nodded, if only slightly. ". . . not surprised . . ."

"Your parents are all right. So is my family, and they all know we're safe. I sent courier messages saying you were recovering from working hard after the explosions on Imagisle."

"Good . . . wouldn't want them . . . to worry."

"They had the memorial services for Maitre Dichartyn and Maitre Poincaryt and Madame Poincaryt last night."

"I . . . would have . . . should have . . . been there . . ."

"Isola spoke so well. You would have liked what she and Maitre Dyana said."

". . . Always . . . speaks . . . well . . ." I was having trouble keeping my eyes open.

Seliora took my hand and held it while the hazy blackness crept up over me.

27

When I finally walked slowly out of the infirmary on Jeudi morning, gray smoke hung over all of L'Excelsis, and that was four days after the attacks. I was headed toward the administration building, thankfully only fifty yards away, to meet with Maitre Dyana before she convened the remaining senior imagers of the Collegium.

Just before I'd dressed, Seliora had told me that the imagers who specialized in construction had already begun repairs to our house. Apparently, ours was the only one that was merely damaged. Those of Maitre Poincaryt, Maitre Dyana, and Maitre Dichartyn had been totally destroyed, and no other dwelling had been touched, with the exception of the Collegium's boat house on the east side of the river, which had also been destroyed. That bothered me, and it took me a while to realize why. Whoever had used the bombards had been very skilled, had great experience, and had clearly measured the distances from where the barges had been anchored—they had to have been anchored—to the masters' dwellings. That required a very professional gun crew, and that meant Naval experience and careful advance planning.

I'd allowed a little extra time because I knew I wouldn't be moving that quickly, and the outer anteroom was empty, except for Gherard, who was sitting at the desk. Both the door to the conference room, to the right, and the door to the Maitre's study were open.

I nodded to Gherard.

"Good morning, Maitre," he replied.

"I hope you're holding up," I said.

"Yes, sir."

I stepped through the open doorway into the study, closed the door behind me, walked to the middle chair of the three facing the desk and eased into it. "Good morning, Maitre."

Maitre Dyana was seated behind the desk in the study that had been Maitre Poincaryt's for the entire time I'd been an imager—until now. I couldn't see that much had changed in the study, but it was definitely hers, with a few small items here and there and touches of colors. Finesse had always been her emphasis. She had recovered—she was wearing a brilliant blue scarf to complement her imager grays—although I had the feeling that her iron gray hair was turning more toward white.

"Good morning, Rhenn, pleasantry though it is. I'm sorry you missed the memorial services, but at the time, no one knew how long it might be before you recovered. I'd hoped you might be able to say a few words."

"I would have liked to. I owe them both more than I'll ever be able to repay."

"We never repay. We only pay for those who follow, and what you did saved others, just as what he did saved you."

There was truth in that, but I would have liked to have acknowledged the debt publicly. Still . . . was that because . . . I almost shook my head. Master Dichartyn wouldn't have cared about the public statements. In fact, he would have asked if I'd have wanted to speak to show my gratitude in order to prove something about myself. He would have been right, I suspected.

"You've been reading the newsheets, I presume?"

"I have." What I'd read had confirmed my worst suspicions, what with explosions occurring all over Solidar, targeting grain facilities, ports and piers, and several main ironway bridges, including the one over the Aluse just north of Solis, which would delay and restrict the shipment of iron to the ship-works there. In the cities that had been receiving the stronger elveweed, riots had occurred in both taudis and non-taudis areas—with the exception of L'Excelsis, but L'Excelsis had suffered half a score of explosions. In Cloisera, the Jariolans had been pushed back fifty milles, and their coal fields were now under Ferran control. In Otelyrn, the Stakanaran army had seized a large section of western Tiempre.

"What is not in the news is that Suyrien was shot yesterday. The assassin fired a sniper's rifle from a distance at his estate. The shooter was never observed. Suyrien may not recover, but if he does, he will not be in shape to act as head Councilor."

"Hadn't Suyrien just returned from visiting High Holder Ruelyr? I'd heard that Suyrien was less than pleased with something Ruelyr had done."

"Oh?"

"I don't know what it was, other than that Suyrien felt it wasn't in keeping with the responsibilities of being a High Holder. I wondered, though, because Ruelyr holds the lands that include some of northern part of the Sud Swamp, and that might be an ideal location for growing the stronger elveweed." I watched Dyana closely as I finished.

She nodded slowly. "That is useful information, of which I was unaware. Thank you."

"You're welcome."

"Another problem is that Caartyl is acting as head of the Executive Council in place of Suyrien. That will not last, one way or the other. Caartyl claimed the post because Glendyl had to go to Ferravyl to deal with difficulties in obtaining iron for his rolling mills."

"How does he stand on the blockade?"

"Caartyl supports it. He and the guilds don't like the Ferrans any more than the Jariolans. He's said that the factors of Solidar would prefer to replace all the guild members with steam-powered factorages manned by low-paid laborers."

There was something about that . . . but I couldn't grasp it.

"The High Holders have already selected Fhernon to fill Suyrien's Council seat," Dyana continued. "They're petitioning the High Judiciary to have Councilor Ramsael take Suyrien's position as head of the Executive Council. They claim that Caartyl was not selected in a formal Council session. To complicate matters more, several factors' associations are petitioning to have the High Holders' petition set aside until the next formal meeting of the Council, which is not scheduled until the eighteenth of Ianus."

That was more than a month away. "They haven't decided to meet formally any sooner?"

"That can only be decided by either the full Council or the unanimous vote of the Executive Council."

I should have remembered that, but it had been several years since I'd last studied the Council's parliamentary procedures. "I can't say I'm surprised." My greatest concern was that matters would get worse, especially without the moderating influence exerted by Maitre Poincaryt. No matter how capable and knowledgeable Maitre Dyana was, even as Maitre of the Collegium, the fact that she was a woman would weigh against her, particularly in dealing with High Holders. She certainly had the knowledge and understanding, because she'd come from a High Holder family, and she was a powerful imager; but she might have to use far more force, or the hidden threat of it, on the Councilors. I only knew that Ramsael was Alynkya's father and had been slightly patronizing to me years before. Fhernon had commissioned several pieces from NordEste Design and had behaved with dignity and restraint, but that didn't really tell me much about him.

"We won't take an official position on any of those issues, except that the Justiciary rule quickly on the law itself. You present another problem. There is no way you can return to being a Civic Patrol captain and take on the duties before you here at the Collegium."

"You don't have to announce that immediately. Tell Commander Artois that I'm needed here for the time being, given the destruction and deaths here, and that in the interests of the Civic Patrol, Alsoran should act in my stead. Artois already has two lieutenants doing that for dead captains. I'm nowhere close to dead."

"Why do you suggest that?"

"To keep Cydarth from replacing Alsoran. If they think I'm coming back, and even if they don't, it will make that harder. Alsoran looks easygoing, but he'll do what's right. I can make it harder for them by dropping in to see Alsoran once. It doesn't have to be for long."

"That seems reasonable, and it will support Artois. Just don't trot out there until you have full shields and full control." Dyana nodded. "Aelys has already removed all of her husband's personal items from Dichartyn's study in the administration building, and it is ready for your immediate use. I suggest you settle in there as soon as possible."

"Is she staying here?"

"No. She could, but neither of the girls is an imager, and she has a sister in Extela to whom she is very close. Also, the stipend she'll receive, while not miserly, will go much farther there. She and the girls are leaving on the ironway later today."

I suspected Aelys would just as happy to be away from Imagisle.

"You'll also have to take over as preceptor for those junior imagers that Dichartyn was mentoring. You've effectively been doing that with Shault, but there are four others. Only Shault isn't a tertius."

I frankly hadn't thought about taking on being a preceptor, since I'd only had to assist with Shault because of the circumstances of his past. Still . . . that wasn't urgent. "Did you find out anything from Sea-Marshal Geuffryt?"

"Nothing anyone can act on. Not yet."

"Would you mind I kept in touch with him?"

"I'd appreciate it if you would."

"You'd like me to build and maintain contacts with the various military types, then?"

"Since Dichartyn did . . ." She raised her eyebrows.

"He didn't mention those contacts. He did mention his liaison with the Civic Patrol. I'd prefer to wait a few days before dealing with Artois and Cydarth, though."

"That might be for the best."

"I'm still concerned about Caartyl."

"You don't care for him, do you?"

"From what I can tell, he's been plotting since I was with Council Chateau security. You might see if Schorzat or anyone knows anything about a factor named Alhazyr—"

She looked at me, and I realized that was my job, among other things that I really hadn't thought through. "More along your lines, Maitre, Juniae D'Shendael has been close to Caartyl—"

"I know. I've already talked to her. She was actually worried about you. She was playing Caartyl as part of her effort to change Council procedures to allow women Councilors."

"You knew her when . . . before."

"Yes." The single word closed further discussion of Madame D'Shendael. After a pause, Dyana continued. "I've been able to avoid specifics about how the barges were destroyed." Her voice turned wry as she continued. "Draffyd already suspected. He merely asked if I wanted the fact that you'd done it not mentioned. I asked him how he'd come to that conclusion. His answer was rather direct. He said you're the only one who could have. He also said that if you weren't a Maitre D'Image already, you would be soon, assuming you took better care of yourself." She stopped, as if waiting for a response.

I nodded politely. There was no reason to point out that, even if my actions had been emotionally driven, taking better care of myself would have resulted in scores more imager deaths and far greater destruction of the Collegium.

"Good. That's the only suitable response. You understand, I presume, what the meeting is all about?"

"To give everyone the opportunity to believe that they could influence what they should not—and that is something that most of them know."

"Who doesn't know, do you think?" she asked gently.

"Rholyn knows, but he would hate to admit that his greatest strength is dealing with the Council on a day-to-day basis. He will have to say something."

"What about Jhulian?"

"He may say something about the legal aspects, but only if he believes that there's a serious problem. He doesn't flyspeck."

"You best go into the conference room and wait. Please leave the door closed after you leave."

I nodded and rose.

When I walked into the conference room adjoining the anteroom, I was the first one there. I took a seat in the middle of the table, but with my back to the windows, although, since it was still morning, those on the east side of the table wouldn't be looking into the sun.

Jhulian was the first to join me. A thin blond figure, he was the Collegium's legal expert as well as its sole justicer. "Greetings, Rhenn. I'm glad to see you're back on your feet."

"I'm just as happy to be sitting for the moment."

Draffyd was next. He looked at me even before sitting down. "No more physical problems?"

"Not so far."

Then came Rholyn, who was the Collegium's Councilor. I'd even painted his portrait years before, and he hadn't changed much since I had. Behind him came Schorzat, who seated himself across from me.

Before anyone could say anything, Maitre Dyana stepped into the conference room and closed the door behind her. The only senior Maitres not attending were Dhelyn, the master in charge of the branch of the Collegium in Westisle, and the heads of the other two regional collegia. There had never been that many imagers who were Maitres D'Structure or higher, but the fact that all of those in Solidar, save three, were gathered around a single table was more than a little sobering.

Dyana took her seat at the north end of the oval table, then let several moments pass before she spoke. "All of you know the situation facing the Collegium, and I see no point in detailing it. There are two matters that merit this meeting. First is the selection of a replacement for Maitre Dichartyn, which should not take long, and second is a discussion of the Collegium's position with regard to the options open to the Council. That may take slightly longer."

I noted that there was absolutely no humor or irony in the second charge to us.

"The head of Collegium security reports directly to the Maitre and is appointed by the Maitre. I would like to hear any thoughts you may have."

After a moment, Draffyd spoke. "I'm certain you have evaluated all possibilities, but in the unlikely event you might consider me, I must decline."

Dyana smiled. "So noted."

Jhulian smiled as well. "I doubt that my expertise would serve the Collegium well in a security capacity. Also, my involvement in such matters, if it ever surfaced, would create great difficulties that it would be best that the Collegium not face."

Maitre Rholyn cleared his throat. "In practical terms, I face the same problem as Master Jhulian. My elimination effectively narrows the choice to Master Rhennthyl and Master Schorzat. Rhenn is certainly talented, and there's no doubt that few, if any of us, are as strong an imager as he is. But his expertise in handling security, particularly . . . ah . . . covert matters, has been limited. Would it not be better to have Schorzat move into handling all of the security duties, with Rhenn as his assistant?"

The faintest smile flickered across Maitre Dyana's face.

"I must decline," Schorzat said quickly. "All my knowledge is at Rhenn's disposal, but I could not have survived what he and Maitre Dyana did, and whoever succeeds Maitre Dichartyn must have that ability. The head of Collegium security, especially now, can show no vulnerability. The only two imagers ever to survive direct hits by bombard shells are Maitre Dyana and Maitre Rhennthyl."

"The position calls for a Maitre D'Esprit," Rholyn pointed out.

"Rhenn's abilities exceed those of a Maitre D'Esprit," Jhulian replied.

That he was the one to reply surprised me, but it made a sort of sense, since he was the Collegium's justicer and expert in legalities.

"It was felt that he should have a minimum of ten years with the Collegium before being granted the rank, even in a concealed status," Jhulian continued.

"Because we are clearly under attack," continued Dyana, "the luxury and grace of allowing Rhenn more time to widen his understanding of the Collegium itself and its relations with the Council is no longer possible."

Schorzat nodded, in relief, I thought.

"There is no doubt, is there," asked Dyana, turning to Draffyd, "of his abilities?"

Draffyd laughed softly. "When barely a tertius, with only moderate shields, Rhenn was shot with a sniper's rifle as a result of the Ferran assassination teams who had killed more than a score of junior imagers. He had the presence of mind, and the ability, to image a block into his chest to slow the bleeding. While with the Civic Patrol, he has weathered the explosion of the Puryon Temple in the taudis and assassination attempt after assassination attempt."

"I might add," interjected Jhulian, "that with more than five years as a Civic Patrol captain, he has a solid knowledge of the laws of Solidar. That is far more than his predecessor had when he assumed the position. Rhenn also served, if briefly, in the security detachment of the Council Chateau."

"He also has access to intelligence sources that were not available to his predecessor, as I have already discovered," added Maitre Dyana.

Rholyn smiled warmly. "I am very glad to know how thoroughly you have looked into the situation, and I will certainly do my best to provide whatever information and support that Rhenn may need."

"I know that you will," replied Maitre Dyana pleasantly, but there was cold iron behind the warm tones of her voice.

It was more than clear that no one wanted the position, including Rholyn, but that he didn't want me to have it. That was likely because he knew I had some contacts among the High Holders and that I would not have to rely on him totally.

"Now . . . the pressing issues are what stand the Collegium should take with regard to the Council, how much we should make known of our position, and to whom in the Council should that information be conveyed."

"We have always conveyed our support of the Council," observed Rholyn.

"That is a given," replied Dyana.

"Might I raise an observation and a question?" I didn't want to, but I wasn't certain anyone else would. I didn't give any of the others a chance to object, not that they would have. So I said quickly, "Over the past few years, we've seen a conflict growing between the freeholders and the larger and wealthier factors and the High Holders. It's become almost open civil war at times, especially over water rights, grain shipments, and the like. There are only a few more High Holders than the minimum required for the balance of power to shift to the factors and freeholders, that is, in terms of who becomes the Councilor in charge of the Executive Council. My question is: Can we afford to ignore this by merely observing?"

"Exactly what do you have in mind, Rhenn?" asked Rholyn dryly. "Having enough 'accidents' occur that there are fewer than a thousand High Holders? That would certainly change matters."

"Actually, I had something else in mind, perhaps letting it be known that the Collegium is opposed to any change in the Council through violence . . . perhaps strongly opposed." I smiled. "A good number of High Holders are already borderline and may not be able to retain lands and assets sufficient to meet the requirements for being a High Holder. The more successful factors involved in fabrication and the larger freeholders are beginning to out-compete them in many areas. So long as the change occurs through economic and social forces, it should be allowed to occur."

"How can you track down the perpetrators of violence?" asked Rholyn. "Either side has the resources to hire agents."

"We don't have to. Just let the Collegium's position be known. Sooner or later, either a High Holder or a freeholder complaint, with evidence, will find its way to us. If it's a legal issue, I'm certain that Maitre Jhulian will find a way to bring it before the High Justiciary of Solidar. And if it's evidence of another kind . . . well, as you noted, illness and accidents befall us all."

"You're rather cavalier about it," suggested Rholyn.

"I'm not at all cavalier about it," I replied. "I've watched, and I've experienced personally the use of unchecked High Holder power to destroy families and individuals. I see no virtue in standing back and allowing High Holders to fight change with their powers and resources until this civil war gets to the point where everyone on both sides is either poisoning or shooting. That will only weaken Solidar and encourage Ferrum and others. What I'm suggesting is a quiet message that says that everyone can compete economically and legally, but that the Collegium is highly opposed to the use of violence by either side."

"Even if you're prepared to do the same?"

"I bow to your expertise in debate, Maitre," I replied, "but since the enemies of the Collegium have already shown that they are willing to strike at individuals, it's not as though I would be the one who first employed the technique." I managed a smile. "As Master Dichartyn once pointed out, if it looks like an accident or a natural death and there is no evidence to the contrary, then it must be an accident or a natural death." That wasn't quite what he'd said, but it was close enough.

Jhulian laughed. "He has a point there, Rholyn. He isn't proposing that we be the ones to start singling out individuals, nor that we use overt violence."

"More to the point, Rholyn," said Maitre Dyana, "do you have a better approach?"

That question led to more discussion, but, in the end, no one did, and Maitre Dyana closed the discussion by saying, "That's settled. Maitre Jhulian, if you would see that the Collegium rolls are changed to reflect that Rhenn is a Maitre D'Esprit. Maitre Rholyn, while I understand that you have some concerns, I trust that they are not major enough that it will prevent you from arranging a meeting for you and me with Caartyl and Glendyl here, and preferably tomorrow or as soon as Glendyl returns from Ferravyl. Meet them and escort them past the ruins of the three senior imagers' dwellings before you bring them here."

"Ah . . ."

She smiled coolly. "I'm certain that you can manage." Then she stood. "That is all. We have much to do."

28

Seliora and Diestrya were waiting in the first floor study in the administration building that had belonged to Master Dichartyn.

"Beleart said this was the best place to find you," said Seliora. "How did the meeting go?"

"As Maitre Dyana intended." I took the chair behind the desk, empty of anything. There were a few books in the bookcase—three volumes on jurisprudence, the legal codex of Solidar, all fifteen volumes, and a black bound book that held Council procedures.

Diestrya investigated the empty shelves. Fortunately, the heavy volumes of the codex were beyond her reach.

"We got another letter back from your mother, by private courier. Beleart gave it to me. She wrote again how much she appreciated my sending that note by courier to let her know that we were all right. She also said that the fires in Kherseilles missed the factorage there, and that Khethila was fine. Oh, Klysia has already begun to clean up the dust and grit in the house. It should be ready by supper time."

"They've repaired it already?" I almost shook my head at the stupidity of my question. Imagers who could form perfect machine parts could certainly re-image a house back into shape, especially in a few days if a score or more of them were involved.

"You're effectively the second-highest imager in Solidar," Seliora pointed out. "You also saved most of them."

"No one's said anything."

She smiled. "All anyone has to do is look. Three dwellings are destroyed. There's a large hole in the fourth. It's ours. Well . . . they see it as yours. Nothing was destroyed after that, and the barges with the bombards exploded immediately. Also, the word is out that you've been made Maitre D'Esprit."

"It is suggestive," I admitted. "Not conclusive, but suggestive."

"More than suggestive," Seliora countered.

"What can you tell me about Fhernon? Anything at all."

Seliora frowned. "Why? We're still working on his commission. You know that."

"Suyrien was shot and badly wounded. He may not recover. The High Holders have selected Fhernon to take his Council seat . . . but not to serve on the Executive Council."

"Poor Kandryl. . . ." Seliora shook her head.

I noticed her sympathy didn't extend to Frydryk, but said nothing.

"Fhernon has always been polite and very formal. He knows I'm married to you, and he knows who you are. I don't think he's all that different from most High Holders, but he did bring his wife to look at the drawings before he approved the upholstery design for the dining chairs. She was cautious, but did recommend a small change, and he agreed. He paid the advance deposit without quibbling."

"What's your impression, even if you can't explain it?"

"He's cautious. He won't go against the other High Holders unless he's fully convinced. I think he could be stubborn, even against the other High Holders. I also feel he has a dislike of open violence. He's doesn't like to be out in front, but he's not a blind follower."

"That sounds like a cautious choice on the part of the High Holders." It also suggested they were aware that they would be wise not to propose any-one too controversial.

"Things are going to get worse, aren't they?" asked Seliora.

"They could. I'm supposed to keep that from happening."

"Dear . . . that may beyond even you."

"Why do you say that?"

"I was at Mama's earlier. She's gotten word that there were anti-Pharsi ri-ots in Westisle and Solis. They all started in the taudis."

"I suppose there are rumors that the imagers and the Pharsis are the cause of all the problems?" I wasn't quite satiric.

"There are some. Mama says some are saying that the imagers and the Pharsis are doing the High Holders' dirty work."

"I wonder who's behind all that." As if I didn't know.

Seliora stood and scooped up Diestrya. "You have work to do, and I want to put the house back in order. As much as I can, anyway."

I stood, walked around the desk, and hugged the two of them. "I'll see you later."

"At home," Seliora declared.

"Yes, Lady." I grinned.

She did smile back.

Seemingly within moments of Seliora's and Diestrya's departure, Beleart knocked on my door. "Maitre . . . ?"

"Come in. What is it?"

He set five folders on the corner of the desk. "Maitre Dyana said you'd need these. They're the preceptor folders. There's one for each of the junior imagers . . ."

"The ones for whom I'll be preceptor?"

"Yes, sir."

"Thank you."

He nodded and was gone.

I had no doubts that before long, more piles of papers and reports would appear. So I quickly looked over the files to get the names: Eamyn, Haugyl, Marteon, Ralyea, and Shault. Then I read the biographies and academic records on each. After that, the files went into the second desk drawer. I just hoped I didn't have to deal with immediate academic, personal, or disciplinary problems for them.

What I needed to do more than anything was have a series of long and detailed conversations with Schorzat about all those matters about which I knew nothing or too little. So I walked to the third door down the hallway. I didn't have to knock because the door was open.

Schorzat stood with a smile. "I thought it wouldn't be very long."

I stepped into his study and closed the door, then sat down in the single chair across from a desk piled with papers.

Schorzat re-seated himself behind the desk. "I don't envy you, Rhenn."

"I don't envy me, either. What are the more urgent matters I should know about and probably don't? I'm sure there are more than I even know about. So you might start with those that are most likely to impact us immediately if we don't do something."

"First, we need to go over what you . . . and I . . . have to work with." He handed me two sheets of paper. The first was a map of Solidar, with numbers at various locations. The second was a listing of names, with a number after each. The numbers corresponded to those on the maps. "Those are our regionals and their locations. You'll need to keep those safe."

I studied the locations and the comparatively short list of names. "Just thirty-one for all of Solidar?"

"If we could find more with the independence and abilities . . ." Schorzat shrugged. "We have ten vacant regional houses right now, and they're not in tiny towns. Places like Alkyra, Ruile, Thuyl, Juvahl. A regional has to be able to hold light shields, be intelligent and discreet, and have the ability to practice another occupation or have an economic reason for support."

"Most are classed as tertius or Maitre D'Aspect?"

"Mostly very bright thirds. It's a good position for an intelligent imager who won't ever have the raw ability to be a master, but they have to be able to blend in and listen and draw conclusions. . . . They reported to Dichartyn, and now . . ."

"To me," I finished. "I assume there are reports somewhere that I can read and catch up on?"

He laughed. "You get a copy of the monthly report from every Civic Patrol Commander in Solidar—from every city big enough to have a Commander, rather than a captain. You also get a monthly report from every regional."

"What about High Holders, or more important factors? Do we have information on them?"

"There are files on the High Holders who serve on the Council, as well as those who have served, and others who have come to our attention. We only have files on fifteen or twenty factors." He shook his head. "We do our best, but there's no way to keep records on more than a thousand High Holders and tens of thousands of factors. The ones we do have are all in the cases in the study. You'll need to image the hidden catches . . ."

I listened as he explained in more detail the regional imager network that I'd known existed, but little more than that.

After a glass, he leaned back. "Any questions about this?"

"No. I'm sure I will, once I read through everything and think about it. What's most urgent that I should keep in mind as I try to get on top of matters?"

Schorzat chuckled, if nervously. "The biggest problem is the Ferran support of the more militant freeholders. That's a guess, of course."

"I assume that we have no proof of an actual connection, since, if we did, you'd already have done something about it."

"We've discovered and dealt with, in one way or another, over twenty agents. So far there's barely circumstantial evidence of a connection with any others we suspect."

"Blast patterns similar to or identical to Ferran demolitions . . . that sort of thing?"

He nodded, then went on. "Here's what we do know. . . ."

I listened as, again, he provided detail after detail, not once repeating himself, for more than half a glass. In the end, though, he had provided a wealth of events, discoveries, and possible connections—yet without a single concrete linkage to either factors or freeholders. I had a far greater breadth of understanding, but the structure looked to be what I'd already pieced together from my own observations as a Patrol Captain and from my reading of the newsheets. At the same time, I had the feeling that there were events and actions that didn't fit—like the grain explosions and the bombard attack on Imagisle . . . and the growth and distribution of the stronger elveweed, which I suspected lay more with Stakanaran origins.

When he finished, I was the one to nod, then say, "Thank you. You mentioned the riots in Westisle, Estisle, Solis, and Kherseilles. I've heard that all have started in the local taudis, and some were sparked by rumors that imagers and Pharsis have been doing the dirty work for the High Holders."

"That I hadn't heard, but it would fit. The Ferrans will use anything."

"So where are the Jariolan agents?"

He smiled sadly. "We don't know for certain, but we've tracked several suspicious persons to the estates and lands of various High Holders."

"Such as Haebyn?"

"He's one. There are several there."

"Haestyr? Shaercyt?"

"Both of them. Also, Nacryon and Ealthyn. There are others, but those are the most likely."

I knew Nacryon was from Mantes and had interests in copper and tin, as well as a new process that created artificial fertilizer from potash and other mineral deposits. I'd never heard of Ealthyn. "Why would the Jariolans want Ealthyn as a supporter?"

"We don't know yet. In fact, I'd never heard of him, either, until we tracked some former sailors to his lands. They made the mistake of cutting through a taudis in Piedryn. They walked out untouched, but there were six bodies in various alleys."

"Do you think Ealthyn and Haebyn are working together?"

"I'm certain they are. We can't prove it." Schorzat shrugged.

"Did Master Dichartyn ever talk to you about the possibility that a trader or factor named Alhazyr might be involved with certain dubious matters involving Caartyl?"

"He did, but we don't have contacts in Mantes right now . . . and what with the way things turned out . . ."

I understood that. "I take it that he's probably more than someone who just wants public representatives added to the Council?"

"Most likely, but he's very careful."

"What about Stakanar?"

"We've found some agents, but Solidar's a little cool for them."

"They might be behind the elveweed."

"They probably are, but if that's so, someone's shielding them."

"Like Ruelyr?"

"That would be hard to find out."

"See what you can do." I laughed. "Along with everything else."

He smiled wryly.

"What can you tell me about Sea-Marshal Geuffryt? And about his relationship with Madame D'Shendael?"

"I understand they're related in some way, but not all that closely. I could give you his biography and his impressive credentials, but that would obscure more than it would reveal. He's a capable Naval officer. He's more than capable in terms of intelligence."

"Why didn't he know more about what was happening with the bombards and the stolen Poudre B?"

"The Army didn't tell anyone. The Depot Commander either didn't know or covered it up. It's likely to be the latter, since he vanished a month ago."

"When did you and Dichartyn find this out?"

"He started probing into it right after Maitre Poincaryt told him . . . you were there, weren't you?"

I had to think for a moment. "That was on the twenty-sixth."

"Then he found out on the thirty-second. It was just short of a week later."

"I think I need to have a private meeting with Geuffryt." I paused. "Is there any reason why I shouldn't? Or would it be better for the two of us to meet with him?"

"He won't say anything if he meets with more than one person."

"So he can deny that he said it, if necessary?"

Schorzat smiled. "So that no denial is necessary."

I could see that. "You're suggesting that I need to meet with him and that I'd best be very careful. Who else should I meet with? Is there an Army counterpart?"

"No. Geuffryt sends reports to the Army Command as well as to his superiors at Naval Command."

"Do I have you request the meeting or have Maitre Dyana do it?"

"They'll expect me to make the request. I did for Master Dichartyn."

"Whom else do you think I should meet?"

"For now . . . probably no one else until you read some of the recent reports and see what Geuffryt has to say." Schorzat smiled. "You may not have to arrange any meetings. By next Lundi invitations will be arriving at your house for various small dinners from High Holders' wives. Doubtless, Glendyl's wife will hurry over to make Seliora's acquaintance as well. A new Maitre

D'Esprit—and one so comparatively young and with such a beautiful wife—is always in demand during the winter social season."

Seliora might like that . . . if only for a while. "Was that one of the reasons you turned the position down?" I asked lightly and wryly.

"Better you than me," he replied with a laugh.

When I returned to my "new" study, I was tired. I closed my eyes for a time, but that wasn't particularly restful. Not with all the various bits of information swirling through my thoughts. So I tried to make sense of it all. Caartyl couldn't be stupid enough to think that he would remain even as acting head of the Executive Council. That meant he needed the position to do something immediate, and it was likely that he'd arranged, or someone had arranged for him, the difficulties that had required Glendyl to go to Ferravyl. What could that be? I was doubtless missing the obvious, and that was because I was tired and aching.

Then I stood and walked over to the two blank-faced cabinets on the north wall, behind and to the right of the desk. It took several attempts before I figured out the image-linked lock catches. The first shock was the dearth of information on High Holders. While there was information on some I didn't know personally, I didn't see much on those, such as Suyrien, that I did know that I couldn't have found out fairly easily. And while there was a presumptive list of High Holders, there was also a note that it was anything but inclusive or current. That bothered me, more than a little.

After spending more than three glasses reading through reports, my head was aching as much as my body. I was beginning to understand why Dichartyn had often looked so tired, and why he'd been less than patient with me years before. Given the lack of reports from whole sections of Solidar, I also understood why he'd spent time traveling as well.

Overall, the reports gave me a far better idea of what was happening in Solidar outside L'Excelsis, and it was clear that the Ferrans—and the unknown Jariolan agents—were concentrating on less than half a score of cities . . . but I still had the feeling that far, far more was happening than had been reported, and that I needed to puzzle through matters more deeply, if only to pose the questions my brain might find answers to once I was more rested.

Another question was where Cydarth fit into the various machinations. Why would anyone be interested in paying off the subcommander of a city's Civic Patrol, even if the city happened to be L'Excelsis? There were no clues to that in anything I'd read.

There was also the relationship between Geuffryt and Juniae D'Shendael.

Relatives or not, why would she have gotten involved in writing the note conveying information about the banque explosion?

When I finally left the administration building, it was still light, but the sun hung low over the river as I made my way north along the west walk.

When I reached the front gate, I stopped and looked to my right. Beyond our dwelling remained the ruins of Master Dichartyn's and Maitre Dyana's houses, but farther to the north I could see that, already, the walls of the Maitre's dwelling appeared to be half-rebuilt. Then I studied the roof on the north side of our dwelling. I couldn't see any difference in the slates that would indicate where the shell had struck.

After a moment, I started for the front door, where Seliora stood waiting.

29

On Vendrei morning, I realized I had another difficulty, one that was insignificant in some respects, and not immediate, but still a problem, since Seliora had decided to stay at the house and work with Klysia to rid the place of more of the grit and dust that continued to settle, seemingly out of thin air. So, immediately after breakfast, even before going to find out what awaited me in my own study in the administration building, I went to see Maitre Dyana.

Gherard wasn't there, and she appeared as though she'd been there very early when I knocked and eased into her study. "What is it, Rhenn?"

"This is going to seem silly, but . . ."

"Yes?"

"For five years, I've been using a duty coach to go to Third District and—"

"You don't want Seliora and your daughter to use hacks regularly, and you don't want her to have to give up her work or to be in danger."

"That's right. I was hoping I could pay . . ."

"As a Maitre D'Esprit, you now receive ten golds a week."

I almost choked. I hadn't realized how much the difference in pay was. "It's not the cost."

"I understand. I have thought about this. A hack ride to NordEste Design runs, what, three to four coppers each way? That's four silvers a week, or two golds a month. A duty coach is better. What if we simply deduct the two golds a month from your pay and transfer it to the transport section?"

"I would suggest three, so that there's no question, and I would appreciate that very much."

"Three a month it will be. I appreciate your concern for not wanting to take privileges you don't feel are appropriate. We also do want to keep Seliora and your daughter as safe as practicable." Dyana smiled. "If that's all?"

"For now, thank you."

I walked back downstairs and toward my own study, although it was still hard to think of it as mine, because it had been Dichartyn's for so long . . . and I hadn't even been able to attend his memorial service.

As soon as I'd settled behind the desk, I picked up the copy of *Veritum* and began to read the lead story on the progress of the war in Cloisera. The Ferran advance had been slowed by fiercer Jariolan resistance and by an early snowstorm, but the newer Ferran land-cruisers were performing far better than those used in the previous war between the two countries. That was apparently offset to some degree by the new Jariolan land-mines. No one had yet tried to break the Solidaran blockade. I wondered how Glendyl and some of the factors felt about that, with their concern for open trade, at least of their products.

The lead story in *Tableta* dealt with the "annexation" of the Tiempran diamond and gold mines by Stakanar. I wondered how I'd missed that, except I realized that it must have happened while I'd been unconscious. What else had I missed? Not too much, I hoped.

The first lines of the next story caught my attention more than the war news had, and I read the story twice, then again, going through the key parts.

The Civic Patrol in Ruile, along with the Freeholder Constabulary in the Sud region, raided the lands of High Holder Ruelyr late on Samedi. The combined forces discovered close to a thousand hectares of land in the swamp regions of the High Holder's lands devoted exclusively to the cultivation of elveweed. "This is the stronger variety. It's the one that's been killing so many young Solidarans over the past months . . ."

High Holder Ruelyr has not been located, but sources suggest he may be in a remote locale on his lands . . .

Councilor Regial D'Alte expressed great concern. "No matter what the purported cause, invading the lands of a High Holder without a judicial order is the first step toward mob rule and the breakdown of the longest and most successful form of civil government in the history of Terahnar . . ."

I'd been right about where the stronger elveweed had been grown, but the story didn't tell me a great deal about who had been the one actually profiting from the growing and selling. The story implied that Ruelyr was the guilty party, but why would a High Holder get involved in that? Did he owe that much? And to whom?

Newsheet in hand, I walked to Schorzat's study, hoping he was in.

He was, and he immediately announced, "You have a meeting with Sea-Marshal Geuffryt at the second glass of the afternoon. At the Naval Bureau, not the Naval Command."

"Thank you."

He grinned at me. "I didn't see you running this morning."

"It's likely to be several weeks before Draffyd will let me pummel my body to that degree." I held up the newsheet. "The elveweed story?"

"After our talk yesterday, I thought you might be asking."

"It doesn't help that we don't have a regional in Ruile." I paused. "Who would know any more about what's happening there?"

"We'll get some reports, but not for several days."

"What do the Ferrans know about our regionals? Would they know that there isn't one in Ruile?"

He shook his head. "That's hard to say. There's nothing anywhere except in your study and mine—and Maitre Dyana's—in a written form that even alludes to a regional network of imagers. People certainly speculate, and it's known there are imagers across Solidar, but . . ."

"They might just be calculating where they wouldn't be, based on . . ." My words broke off.

"What?"

"Maybe this has been going on for much longer. You remember all the killings of junior imagers six years ago?"

"You think that was part of a longer-term plan?"

"I don't know, but with fewer young imagers over time . . ." That was a possibility, but there wasn't much I could do about the past. "What about Ruile and Ruelyr?"

"Ruelyr owes a great deal," replied Schorzat. "We've known that for a while. Most of the notes were held by the Banque D'Ouestan."

"Interesting." It was more than interesting, since that was the banque from which the drafts to Cydarth had allegedly come. By itself, that proved nothing, but I'd always been suspicious of coincidences. "What do you know about the banque?"

"It's the second-largest banque in Ouestan, and tends to handle non-Solidaran trading and factoring accounts, also foreign currencies and bonds. The Banque D'Cote is the one used by most Solidaran factors and the local High Holders there."

"Who owns the Banque D'Ouestan?"

"That's a good question. It's held by private shareholders and has been for over a hundred years."

"That makes it a perfect conduit for funds and blind drafts. I presume it's exceedingly sound financially?"

"It's the only banque on the entire northwest coast that survived the Panic of '17 without being reorganized or bought out."

"Ferran investors?"

Schorzat shrugged. "Maitre Dichartyn and Maitre Poincaryt thought so. We could never prove it."

"Is there any way to determine if the land that the Civic Patrol of Ruile and the Constabulary raided was actually leased to someone else?"

"That was my thought. We're working on it."

"Good . . ." I paused. "How can we find out if an attractive woman is missing from Ruelyr's household in Sud?"

Schorzat frowned.

"The Civic Patrol found a body a week or so ago. She was young and attractive, wearing an expensive wool suit and an inexpensive bright scarf, and she'd been poisoned, but set up as if she'd been an elveweed death. She wasn't an elver. Oh . . . and the body had been moved some considerable distance, and the suit was tailored on a High Holder estate, but not for the holder's family, and the wools were from the area around Ruile. It bothered me at the time."

Schorzat shook his head. "We don't have anyone close to him, and without a regional there . . . Let me think about it."

That meant I'd have to think about it as well. "Thank you."

I walked the few yards down the hallway to my study, thinking. Had Suyrien visited Ruelyr because he'd heard rumors about the elveweed? Or was there something else occurring in Ruile or on Ruelyr's estates? Frydryk might know. I'd have to talk to him as well, although I wasn't certain I wanted to intrude at the moment.

After stepping into the study, I closed the door behind me and walked to the window. How many times had I seen Master Dichartyn standing there? After a moment, I sat down at the desk. I needed to think about what I wanted from Geuffryt and how to approach him, as well as what I could ask or say to keep him off-balance.

I almost laughed. I was more likely to be the one off-balance.

I thought. I took notes. I scratched them out. I thought some more. I checked some of the reports in the files. Slowly, I came up with questions and information I needed to know. Before I knew it, ten bells had rung out noon.

Since I was now officially back at the Collegium, and since Seliora was engaged in furious cleaning, I walked over to the dining hall for the mid-day meal. There were only a few at the masters' table—Kahlasa, Ferlyn, and Chassendri. All were Maitres D'Aspect, and all but Kahlasa had been masters when I'd been a mere secondus.

Ferlyn gestured for me to join them.

"Congratulations," offered Kahlasa with a smile. "You've already impressed Schorzat."

"Only with my ignorance, I fear; but I thank you for the courtesy." As Schorzat's second, she had certainly heard how I was doing . . . or not doing. "How's Klaustya?"

"She's five. Do I need to say more?"

I grinned. "No. I can hardly wait."

"You and Seliora should have another. You two need to be outnumbered, if only to give the children a chance."

"At some point, we probably will be." I sat down immediately to Chassendri's left.

"Not soon enough," quipped Kahlasa.

Abruptly, I wondered where Maitre Dyana was, since she certainly couldn't be eating at her still-demolished dwelling or the yet-unrepaired Maitre's dwelling. Then, she might be meeting with someone.

"Are you going to leave the Civic Patrol?" asked Ferlyn.

"I'm still a captain, but I'm detailed to help with matters here for now."

Ferlyn shook his head, then grinned, but didn't press the question.

As I cut into one of the veal cutlets, I had to admit that the food at the Collegium was better—and far less costly, since I didn't have to pay for it—than the infrequent mid-day meals I'd been having in the various bistros and cafes in Third District over the past five years. Then again, with more eating and far less walking, I'd really need Clovyl's morning exercises and runs.

After several moments, Ferlyn looked at me. "Rhenn, what can you tell us about who was behind the attack on the Collegium?"

I finished a sip of the red wine before replying. "Since the barge carrying the bombards exploded, we have no evidence of who was actually firing the weapons. They were obviously skilled in antique weapons, and they were unfriendly. Unfortunately, we have more than a few enemies at present." I paused, then inclined my head in Kahlasa's direction. "Wouldn't you say so?"

Kahlasa nodded.

Ferlyn shook his head again, then chuckled. "You covert types."

"You've always known that," said Chassendri mildly. "You just like to point it out whenever you can."

"And you like to point out that I do."

After that, we speculated on whether the advanced Ferran land-cruisers and other devices would survive the Jariolan winter, or if the present Cloiseran conflict would end up in the same stand-off as had the first. We came to no resolution, and I headed back to my study, and the reports and the unresolved questions.

At two quints before second glass, I made my way to the duty coach station, where there were two coaches waiting, one specifically for me.

"Maitre Rhennthyl? To the Naval Plaza?" asked Desalyt.

"The Bureau building there," I confirmed, then slipped into the coach.

Desalyt took the Bridge of Desires and then followed the Boulevard D'Council to the Council Chateau and around it, and then half a mille northwest to the Naval Bureau, located in a gray stone building on the east end of the Naval Plaza. The Naval Command was in a larger imposing structure at the west end.

A lieutenant was waiting for me by the guard desk just inside the entry doors. "Maitre Rhennthyl, sir?"

"Yes."

"This way, if you would, sir."

I followed him a good fifty yards back to a wide staircase with polished marble steps and a brass balustrade, and then up to the second floor and back to an outer anteroom, with a senior clerk-rating seated behind a desk. Marshal Geuffryt's spacious corner study had windows on both outer walls. He stood as I entered.

"Good afternoon, Maitre Rhennthyl."

"Good afternoon, Marshal."

Geuffryt gestured to the small round conference table set back from the windows at the north end of the study. There were four chairs. I took the chair that faced the door. He took the one to my right.

"How might I help you . . . and the Collegium?"

"As I am certain you always have, with information." I smiled.

"We always attempt to be of assistance."

"What other potentially dangerous explosives, munitions, or military equipment is missing or otherwise unaccounted for?" I offered the question casually.

"I can't really tell you that," Geuffryt replied.

"I don't mind so much if you you're not allowed to tell me," I said. "But I'm going to be very worried if no one in the Naval Command knows whether such materials are missing. After all, the last batch of missing munitions and equipment had some very unfortunate consequences. Especially for the Collegium."

"I really can't say."

"Should I be worried, then?"

"I can't—"

I image-projected pure fury at the Sea-Marshal. Given the way I felt, it wasn't difficult.

He turned pale.

I smiled. "Let's try this again. The Collegium has the responsibility of protecting the Council and Imagisle itself. The Naval Command has the responsibility for maintaining and safeguarding munitions and equipment. It's rather difficult and costly for us to do our job when we don't have any idea what you and the Army have lost or allowed to be stolen. And if nothing else is missing, then there's certainly no reason to hide that. Your response indicates fairly clearly that other explosives and equipment are missing. I don't think anyone on the Council would want to know that you're trying to hide that."

I had to give Geuffryt credit. Outside of the momentary paling and the slight dampening of his brow, he hadn't reacted.

"You're only surmising," he said with a faint smile.

"No. I know. Proving it might be harder, but I'm an imager, and if I go to certain members of the Council and suggest that's the case, as well as pointing out that the Army Depot Commander vanished and that no one still investigated matters there . . ." I shrugged, then paused. "I'd rather not. You'd rather I didn't. So what exactly is rumored to be missing?"

"We don't know. There's nothing missing on the scale of the bombards. But we have five major depots and some twelve smaller port and fleet depots, with tens of thousands of tonnes of munitions. We have four hundred armed vessels. Some only have three-digit cannon, but those still require munitions." He shook his head. "We're fairly certain we're not missing something on the order of a thousand tonnes, but accounting errors, errors in resupply . . . how do you tell the difference between that and a tonne or so of Poudre B bags or the like that might have been deliberately misrouted or diverted? A few tonnes aren't that much spread across four fleets."

"But they're quite a bit spread across five or ten cities and set in the right place." I nodded. "You could have told me that to begin with. You didn't. That suggests . . . a number of possibilities. How much do you think you're missing?"

"There are two dubious manifests from the main resupply depot for the rework yard at Solis. They're for one and two tonnes of bagged Poudre B for the standard five-digit guns."

"Those are the most common fleet guns, I take it?"

Geuffryt nodded.

"And the manifests are over a year old," I suggested.

"If you already knew . . ."

"I don't, and I didn't. It just had to be that way. All of this has been planned years in advance so that people would tend to forget. Or, as you put it, believe that the discrepancies were merely clerical errors. Are there any other dubious manifests or unaccounted-for munitions?"

"Nothing more than a few stones' worth here and there. Those can add up, but we think it's unlikely that outside agents would try to gather munitions that way."

I had to agree with that.

"Let's talk about a certain note I received, written by a certain lady we both know, which contained information of a suggestive nature." I looked directly at Geuffryt. "You'll find that I am both discreet . . . and direct. As my predecessor noted, I am inclined to weary quickly of hints and indirection." I paused to let him consider the words. "Who do you believe is transferring funds to the Artisan on the Executive Committee and why?"

"We don't know. The transfers are blind."

"Try investigating a factor or trader named Alhazyr, if you haven't already." With only the slightest pause, I asked, "What exactly is your relation to Juniae D'Shendael?"

He smiled politely. "It's not that much of a mystery. I'm a cousin on her mother's side."

"Are you, perhaps, an expert in hunting weapons? Their construction, and . . . their explosive fallibilities?" That was a guess, but I had a feeling about such matters.

"What a truly strange question . . . I scarcely know what to think."

I'd glimpsed enough. "Thank you."

"For what?"

"For answering the question. It explains a great deal."

"You're a very dangerous man, Maitre Rhennthyl, but had Juniae not had demonstrated proof of your good will, you might still be in a precarious position."

"I'd prefer not to be in such a position, or even to have anyone suggest that possibility." I smiled. Now . . . I knew why Juniae had conveyed the message, and how her only male relative who could have inherited had perished years before. What I didn't know was why the message had been given to me long before it was even likely I'd end up with the position that events had thrust upon me. Or had it been designed as a convenient way of getting the information to Master Dichartyn? I almost nodded. That was the most likely answer, not that the method of conveyance mattered so much as the reasons for letting the Collegium know. "Let's talk about the subcommander of the Civic Patrol."

"Is it wise to discuss a superior?" He raised his eyebrows.

I was getting tired of his superciliousness. "You obviously are worried about Cydarth. From a professional point of view or a personal one . . . or both?"

"I won't deny the personal element, but that's secondary to the professional."

The personal is never totally secondary to professional, as I well knew, but the professional had to be the matter at hand. "Why does he want to remove or replace Artois?"

"Artois's mother was the daughter of a High Holder who committed suicide when Haestyr's grandfather ruined him. Cydarth's father was killed by Iryela D'Ryel's father, merely as a demonstration of power to the factor for whom Cydarth's father worked. Cydarth believes Artois is an apologist for the High Holders, and that Artois hopes some day to prove that he is worthy of his background."

That didn't seem to make much sense, so far as Artois was concerned. "Artois has always been impartial. Sometimes harsh, but I've never seen bias. How does Cydarth fit in with the Ferrans? Or the Jariolans, or Stakanarans, or whoever?" I asked.

"He fits in with none of them. He will support—or not oppose—so far as he is able, anyone or anything that will reduce the power of the High Holders. He believes he is totally fair and unbiased in his views of what is best for Solidar."

"Don't many of us feel that way?" I asked softly.

After a moment, Geuffryt nodded. "That's part of the trouble with Artois and Cydarth. Each of them believes what he wants to do is best."

"But . . . ?" I prompted.

"I suspect you already know, Maitre Rhennthyl. Artois believes in the law as it is. Cydarth believes in a 'good' beyond the law. To date, he's stayed within the law . . . so far as anyone knows."

"You're suggesting that those fund transfers may represent . . . what?"

"I don't know. I only have the word from a trusted source that they exist. The source has never been wrong, but there's no proof. The funds in the Banque D'Excelsis account in the branch that suffered the explosion have never been touched."

"So how can you arrange an explosion without a rationale?"

"I don't believe I said anything about arranging something like that. I was merely aware of it, as were you."

There wasn't any point in pursuing that. "I presume that you're watching the Naval yards and piers closely these days."

"Far more closely." He smiled politely. "What else can we do?"

I changed the subject. "Just how capable are the Navy's fleets in limiting the Ferran and Stakanaran . . . adventuring? I understand that there's been some debate in the Council. Do you really have enough capital ships?"

"We do the best we can with what we have. For the past ten years, the High Command has been recommending an expansion of thirty capital ships to deal with the increased numbers of Ferran warcraft. We also need more smaller vessels. So far, although we've been outnumbered at times, our tactics and training have proved superior. We cannot count on that continuing."

"What about the ten capital vessels under debate?"

"They would provide a good beginning for fleet modernization." Geuffryt smiled. "This proposal has been brought up before, and it has been turned down on the grounds that the Council would have to increase taxes to pay for the construction and fitting out."

"And the factors oppose any more taxes on finished goods, while the High Holders oppose Glendyl's value-added tax?"

"The Navy does not take sides on issues before the Council, Maitre Rhennthyl. We only know what it takes to protect Solidar, and we convey that to the Council."

"In short, the Council doesn't seem to be listening?"

"The Council has received our reports and recommendations. It governs Solidar, and it must make the choices on how to raise revenues and how to spend them. We offer our best counsel and live with their decisions."

Polite as his words were, Geuffryt obviously had some concerns with the funding for the Navy.

"Have the Stakanarans been increasing their fleets?"

"They've been building a substantial number of fast, shallow-draft gunboats in order to control the coastline of Otelyrn. They've also added ten or eleven capital ships."

We talked for another half glass, but while I learned a bit more about the comparative strengths of other Naval forces around Terahnar and slightly more about the extent of his duties and sources of information, it wasn't much more than I had already surmised . . . or learned.

When I returned to the Collegium, I put in another three glasses reading reports and trying to get a better feel of what had been happening all across Solidar. By the time I spent all that effort, not that I was anywhere close to being finished, my head was aching, and my eyes were burning, and I was ready to leave and walk home.

I just hoped that Seliora and Klysia were finished with the heavy cleaning . . . and that Diestrya was in a cheerful mood.

When I woke on Samedi morning, I could raise and hold my full shields without pain or extra effort, but I had the feeling that I'd be in more than poor shape if much impacted them. That decided, I lowered them and washed up, gingerly because all too many parts of my body were still sore, although the purple had faded to a faint, if hideous, yellow. Seliora had taken pity on me and had dealt largely with Diestrya for the past few days, but I did help in getting Diestrya dressed before we headed down to breakfast.

We were close to finishing when Seliora said, firmly, just short of sharply, "Rhenn!"

"What?"

"Your mind is somewhere else. I've asked you twice what you're thinking."

"Oh . . ." I managed a sheepish grin. "About . . . things."

She shook her head. "Just finish up and go to your Collegium study and read all those reports you're worrying about. Diestrya and I will be fine."

"Is Shomyr's party still today?"

Seliora looked at me. "Are you sure you should go?"

"Why not? All I've done is talk to people and read reports."

"You're not yourself yet . . . are you?"

"No . . . but I can hold my shields for a bit and do some imaging." I grinned. "Besides, I'll be with you, and you're very good with the pistol."

"Mother would appreciate it . . ."

"In other words, we really should go."

"Then that's settled." She paused, then added, "I'll have a mid-day meal around half-past noon."

"I'll be here. If you don't mind, I'll go back afterwards and work until a bit before fourth glass. That should give us enough time, shouldn't it?"

She did smile.

Even with a break to eat, the day was long, and by the time I set aside the reports and replaced them in the cabinets at a quint before fourth glass, my head was aching again. I did feel that I had a better grip on what was happening in Solidar. Mostly, though, I had an even greater conviction that someone very clever had been working for years to set up and implement a large-scale plan to disrupt everything in Solidar, putting bits and pieces in place one at a time, with no one piece or part indicating much about the overall plan.

Seliora and Diestrya were waiting when I got back from the administration building.

"We're ready."

"Good." We walked from the house across the Bridge of Desires.

We only waited a few moments before a newer hack appeared with a driver who wore a neatly brushed brown wool jacket and matching gloves and boots.

"Where to, sir?"

"Nordroad and Hagahl Lane."

"Yes, sir."

I opened the door and let Seliora climb up and in before helping Diestrya in after her and then following them.

"Did you find out any more that you needed to know?" she asked after the hacker pulled out onto West River Road, heading north to the Nord Bridge.

"Oh . . . I'm still trying to put the pieces together, but it's getting clearer. We'll have to see." After a moment, I asked, "Do you think Odelia and Kolasyn will be there?"

"I'd think so. They were asked. But . . . after everything . . ."

"You have your doubts," I said.

"I do."

"Mama doubts," said Diestrya.

"Yes, she does," agreed Seliora. "You will, too, when you're older."

We crossed the bridge and were a mille up the Boulevard D'Este when the hack turned west onto Lyrique—away from the theatre district.

"He shouldn't be turning here," said Seliora.

"No. I think we're in for some difficulty. Can you deal with the hacker?" I murmured. "If necessary?"

Seliora nodded.

The hack slowed as it jolted over uneven pavement in a narrow alleyway. Then it came to a stop in a what looked to be a vacant loading yard behind a warehouse whose wagon docks were boarded shut. The hacker vaulted down and opened the door, stepping back. "There are some people who wish to see you. I do trust that you won't make this any messier than necessary."

As he spoke, I finally located four men standing in the shadows, dressed in the same light-absorbing garb I'd seen before. I nudged Seliora.

She shifted her weight on the coach seat, if to ready herself to step out, then said, "Oh . . . I wouldn't want to cause you any trouble."

As the brigand hacker started to smile, she fired her pistol. Once was enough, since the bullet went right through the middle of his forehead.

While she was engaged, I imaged small chunks of stone into the hearts of the four brigands with the wide-barreled weapons.

Even so . . . one of them did manage to fire his weapon, and a second weapon went off when the attacker dropped it on the stones before he pitched forward. The explosions were like small cannon . . . or so it seemed. My shields held . . . barely, and what amounted to small grapeshot rattled across the uneven stones of the loading yard. I was so dizzy that I had to put out a hand against the inside panel of coach to steady myself.

"That was . . . big boom," affirmed Diestrya.

"Very big," I managed, trying to blink away the flashes of light in my eyes.

"Are you all right?" asked Seliora.

"I will be . . . if I don't have to handle anyone else for a little bit."

We just sat in the hack for a moment. I was glad that the hacker had set the brakes and that the dray-horse was well-behaved, because I was in no shape to climb up and drive, and while Seliora would have been better at it than I, far better, I really didn't want her exposed.

After a time, half a quint perhaps, the worst of my dizziness had passed, although I doubted I could raise or hold shields for more than the briefest of instants, and I finally stepped down from the hack.

There were still five bodies there, and no one else.

Seliora peered out, but I held up a hand. "Someone's coming down the alley."

"Is there trouble here?" Following the words was a was a beefy patroller, from Second District, since we were still in that part of L'Excelsis.

"There's been some," I called back. "Some brigand took a hack and tried to rob and murder us."

The patroller approached slowly.

I stepped away from the coach, showing open hands, and turning so he could see the insignia on my visor cap and cloak.

He looked at me, then at the dead hacker, and the four bodies in the shadow of the loading dock . . . and the heavy weapons lying there. "Sir?"

"I'm Captain Rhennthyl from Third District. We've had a little difficulty here. These five wanted to rob us and then kill us. I don't know them, and I don't have any idea why."

"You . . . you're the imager captain."

I nodded.

He looked at the bodies again, then at the body of the false hacker sprawled across the driver's seat. His eyes went to Seliora, holding Diestrya by the hand, and looking innocently concerned.

"We'll be happy to accompany you to Second District Station . . ." I offered.

At that point an older patroller appeared, calling, "Skaryt!" He stopped short and looked at me. "Captain Rhennthyl . . . what happened?"

I explained again. Behind me, Seliora was trying to explain to Diestrya why we weren't going to Grandmama Betara's house quite yet.

The older patroller, whom I didn't recognize, shook his head. "Wouldn't want to be a captain these days. Captain Kharles, Captain Boylet, Captain Hostyn . . . and now you."

Hostyn? "I'm sorry. I've been tied up with the mess on Imagisle. What happened to Captain Hostyn?"

"Same sort of thing as they tried with you . . . except Captain Hostyn got shot. They say he'll be fine, but it's likely to be into the new year before he's fully back. Captain Jacquet and Captain Subunet will probably be glad you took care of this crew."

"We didn't plan it that way. I can tell you that. We were just going to a family dinner."

"No, sir. I'd be certain you didn't." He shifted his weight, then looked at the hack. "Skaryt, best you head back and get some help . . . and send the wagon."

The younger patroller hurried off without looking back.

"You ever see any of these fellows before, sir?"

"No." I shook my head. "I should have noticed that the hacker was a little too well-dressed, but I was thinking about a few other things."

He asked all the questions a good patroller should. When he had, and we'd finished answering, there were four other patrollers and a wagon headed down the alley.

"You have many explosions here in Second District last weekend?" I asked.

"Not like Sixth District or Fourth, no, sir. Just two on the south side of Nordroad. That was more than we needed." He paused. "What can we do for you, sir?"

"We'll be needing a hack, since this one didn't finish the trip."

"We'll walk out to the street with you." The patroller gestured to his partner.

As we walked toward Lyrique, escorted by the pair, Seliora looked to me. "Do you really think we should . . . ?"

"We might as well." I forced a grin. "Just keep the pistol handy."

She nodded.

When we reached the street, we didn't have that long before a hack appeared.

As the hacker eased to a halt, the older patroller asked, "Might I ask where you're headed, Captain?"

"Nordroad and Hagahl."

"Would you be minding, Captain, if we rode with the driver?" asked the older patroller. "That's still in Second District, and we'd not want you having any more troubles."

"I don't know about the captain," Seliora said with a dazzling smile, "but Madame Rhennthyl would be honored."

The patroller actually blushed.

"I thank you very much," I added, "and I would appreciate it."

Seliora and Diestrya didn't say anything until we were inside a hack and traveling toward NordEste Design.

"With all this . . . do you still think . . . ?" Seliora asked.

I knew she was referring to Cydarth, but didn't want to say more, not when Diestrya was with us and with patrollers sitting less than a yard or so away.

"It's hard to tell. I'll need to see what else has happened."

She nodded.

We were largely quiet on the rest of the ride, except, of course, for Diestrya's comments about the pretty paper flowers held by a street vendor.

Once we reached NordEste Design, it was clear Bhenet had been watching for us. He had the door open and stood under the portico waiting, even before the three of us were out of the hack.

While I held Diestrya's hand, Seliora slipped out of the hack, then lifted our daughter down.

I stepped out and looked at the two patrollers. "Thank you. It's been a long week."

"Yes, sir." They both were smiling.

"And thank you from me," added Seliora warmly.

This time, they both blushed.

We walked as quickly as Diestrya allowed, across the sidewalk and up to the portico, where Bhenet waited, and then up the inside staircase. As soon as we reached the main hallway at the top of the stairs, the twins scooped up Diestrya to take her upstairs to the nursery with the other children.

Betara stepped forward and hugged her daughter. "You're good to come. Both of you." She turned to me. "You look tired, Rhenn. Are those bruises on your face?"

"Yes," I admitted. "Let's just say that it's been a very long week and the hack ride here was more interesting than either one of us planned. We're looking forward to a meal with family." I paused. "It has to have been upsetting here, too, with explosions . . . and everything."

"We did have everything locked and barricaded here last Solayi and Lundi," Betara said, "but things settled down by Mardi."

"No one was hurt?"

"No. The mob that came down Nordroad avoided us." She smiled. "But they might have taken notice of all the rifles pointed out from the upper-level windows."

That didn't surprise me. There were only a few windows on the street level of NordEste Design, and those were to work-rooms and manufacturing spaces, with bars and heavy shutters.

"We're happy you're here." Betara stepped back. "Dinner's not quite ready. I need to check with Aegina." She hurried off.

Odelia and Kolasyn had been standing behind and to the right of Betara. Odelia moved toward Seliora.

"Seliora . . . Rhenn . . . I'm sorry." Tears streamed down Odelia's cheeks. "I didn't know . . ." She put her arms around Seliora. "I didn't know . . ."

"It's all right," Seliora said. "I know you were upset."

"No . . . I was so mad at Rhenn. . . . thought he wasn't doing . . . what he could . . ." Odelia was still sobbing. "Kolasyn's friend, Caesaro, he's a patroller . . . told him . . . Rhenn went out every night . . . with patrollers . . . faced the weed dealers' killers . . . bombs and rockets . . ."

After a time, Seliora slowly disengaged herself and looked at me. "You didn't mention bombs and rockets."

"I didn't want to worry you."

Then they both looked at me.

All I could do was shrug and offer an apologetic smile. The shrug hurt. In a different way, so did the smile, since I should have said something earlier.

Solayi morning, we slept late, or as late as Diestrya would let us, then stumbled down to breakfast in nightclothes and robes. We needed the robes, because the wind howled outside and sleet pattered against the windows . . . and the stoves in the kitchen and parlor were cold because we hadn't loaded them before we'd gone to bed. The first task was to get some heat. I did hurry things up slightly by imaging flame into the coal. Even that left me with a headache, but the kitchen and parlor began to warm far more quickly than they would have otherwise . . . and Seliora could start cooking sooner.

As we finished eating, Seliora fixed her eyes on me, with that determined look I understood all too well. "You're not going anywhere, not even to your study at the Collegium. I saw how starting the stove hurt you." She paused. "You are resting. You'll never recover if you keep going out and getting into trouble."

"I didn't go out to get into trouble."

"When you go out, you get into trouble, and you're not strong enough to deal with something like yesterday again."

"Dada is too strong," observed Diestrya.

"He is, but he needs to rest."

I took a last swallow of tea that had cooled to lukewarm. I couldn't help but think about what had happened across L'Excelsis and the other larger cities in Solidar—explosions, riots, mobs, Civic Patrol officers being shot, the attack on the Collegium.

"Well?" persisted my dear wife.

"I surrender to your most reasonable proposition."

"Good. You watch Diestrya while I wash up, and I will while you get dressed."

I did clean up the dishes and the kitchen as I kept an eye on our not-quite-wayward daughter, but even that minimal effort took three times as long as it should have, because three-year-olds have insatiable curiosity, usually involving items such as coal scuttles, hot stoves, or grimy pokers followed immediately by dashes toward white table linens.

Once again, I was reminded why Seliora wanted to keep working as a design engineer for NordEste Design and not spend every waking moment with Diestrya. While Seliora didn't dawdle in getting dressed, she also didn't rush. But she did give me a grateful smile when she relieved me, and I carried the kettle of warm wash water up to the bathroom.

When I came back downstairs, wearing older, heavier, and more comfortable imager grays, Diestrya was peering out the window of the family parlor, entranced by the flow of water across the outside of the panes. Pleased with her absorption and hoping it would last, I settled onto the settee beside Seliora.

"You're still thoughtful," she observed.

"I've been thinking about yesterday. The hacker knew who we were. He was waiting. But . . . if they knew so much . . . ?"

"Do you think they knew you weren't up to full strength?"

"They might have guessed, but I think it was designed so that whoever came up with it couldn't lose. They either killed me, or they got killed. If they got me, that weakens both the Civic Patrol and the Collegium. If they get killed, there's no track back to who hired them, and they were using the kind of weapons that certainly would lead to one of those outcomes."

"If Cydarth is involved," mused Seliora, "he might want you to survive. Then he could suggest how strange it was that you are always surviving."

"Another way of undermining me and the Collegium?"

"Well . . . if you get killed, he's rid of you. If you don't, he undermines your effectiveness by suggesting your survival is the result of something sinister."

"My patrollers know differently."

"They do, Rhenn. Who cares what they think, especially in the Council or in the Collegium?"

She had a point there. Even if I wouldn't be returning as captain, those sorts of rumors wouldn't help me, and especially not the Collegium. "There's another aspect to all this. The more I discover, the more complications I find. The gunners on the barges were set up the same way. If they were successful, they'd have just ridden the barges downriver. By daylight, they'd have been fifteen to twenty milles downstream. At some point in deeper water, they could have scuttled them, and no one would have been the wiser, not any time soon." The level of experience of the gunners still bothered me. That was one reason why I hadn't mentioned that aspect of the matter to anyone, especially to Sea-Marshal Geuffryt.

"That took planning."

"All of it took planning . . . and for years. But so many things happened. I can't believe that any one group—even the head of Ferran spies or whatever they're called—could have organized it all and kept it hidden and all on track."

"Then they weren't all done by the same people." Seliora's tone was matter-of-fact as she got up and intercepted Diestrya before she reached the coal scuttle.

Yet it couldn't be coincidence that everything had happened at once. Or had the Ferrans merely analyzed the problems Solidar faced and woven their plot or plots inside problem areas we already had and hadn't resolved? That was more likely, but why hadn't Dichartyn or Poincaryt discovered that? Then again, if their actions didn't involve deaths . . . or if the deaths happened years before . . .

I didn't like those implications any more than the idea of coincidence.

Was I just trying to fit odd circumstances and a few Ferran-implemented acts into a grand scheme that didn't even exist?

"Rhenn . . . what are you thinking? You have the strangest look on your face."

"I'm trying to make sense of things that may not make any sense at all."

"Things always make sense if you look at their patterns and not yours."

I understood what she meant. Too often, I tried to impose what I thought should be the order or pattern of things, rather than seeing what was.

"That's the engineer's way of thinking," Seliora went on. "When you design things, whether it's a card reader for a loom or a design for fabric, you get in the habit of assuming that everyone designs the way you do, or that there's just one designer, like the Nameless, that arranges everything."

"But people aren't like that," I said with a laugh.

"You need to let your mind rest," she said. "Sometimes that's more useful than worrying it to death, especially when you're as tired as you are."

She was right about that, as she was with many things.

Given the cold and sleet, we didn't go anywhere all day, not even to services at the anomen. We stayed home and enjoyed the warmth of the family parlor.

Seliora was right about my not pushing myself, and she'd never said anything about the less than perfect image-repairing by the Collegium of the furniture damaged by the attack . . . although I had managed to re-image her bed back into a better shape, at least the posters and headboard. Imaging just didn't match crafting, unless the imaging was done by a master-crafter. By Lundi morning, I felt far better, at least until I stepped outside the house and again smelled the acrid odor of smoke and coughed at the bitterness in the air. I didn't feel much better when I reached my study at the Collegium and began to read the newsheets.

Both *Veritum* and *Tableta* reported on a pitched battle between the Solidaran Northern Fleet and two smaller Ferran fleets. While the initial reports were sketchy, all three fleets suffered heavy losses, with possibly as many as a third of our vessels either destroyed or rendered incapable of further fighting. The Ferrans had been unable to break the blockade, but the implication was clear that, unless the Northern Fleet obtained reinforcements, another such battle, with similar results, would destroy the blockade.

I thought about Geuffryt's observations on the shortcomings of our fleet, then made my way to Schorzat's study, but he wasn't there. Would Kahlasa know? She might. I walked two doors down to her study and knocked.

"It's Rhenn."

"Come on in."

She had a stack of reports in front of her, but pushed them aside. "You have questions about something?" Her smile was sympathetic.

"How could I not? I know about Council security and Civic Patrol security and not a lot more."

"Whereas I know little about either of those," she quipped back.

"You read the newsheets about the Northern Fleet?"

She nodded. "If you believe them, and I do, it was the kind of victory that's hardly better than a defeat."

"I've heard that the Naval Command has been requesting capital ships for years and that the Council has yet to act on the request. What do you know about that?"

"I know that's true."

"Suyrien is the head of the Executive Council, and he owns the largest shipworks in Solidar . . . yet he couldn't persuade the Council to build ships when the Navy is asking for them?"

"That's a fair statement," she replied. "It's because he does own the shipworks. None of the factors or the artisans want to spend any more on ships when we already have the largest fleet in the world. They see it as another play by a High Holder to enrich himself at everyone else's expense. To build those ships the Naval Command is requesting would require an increase in taxes—"

"Don't tell me. The way the taxes on goods and services are levied means that they fall more heavily on the factors and artisans?"

"That's right. They don't like it, and so long as they vote as a bloc . . ."

"No new ships. Is that why Glendyl has been pushing the value-added tax reform?"

"Exactly."

"But since he supplies the engines and turbines, he's suspect as well?"

Kahlasa nodded. "By everyone, including the High Holders."

"How are we—the Collegium—viewed? Has Rholyn said?"

"He hasn't told me that much, but Schorzat has relayed some things. He'll be back in a glass or so."

"I'll take the relayed information now and talk to him when he returns."

"Because Maitre Poincaryt had to work with Suyrien, we're viewed as allied closely with the High Holders. Something you did, according to Master Dichartyn, left them cooler toward us, but didn't help gain any support from the factors and artisans. You're also known to be friendly with Iryela D'Ryel and Suyrien."

"I'm a former artisan and guild member, and my family are factors. Everyone in my wife's family is an artisan. The Councilors are seeing what they want to see." I shrugged. "If my acts as a patrol officer over the past five years haven't made an impression, it's not likely that anything I say will. Do you think the reports of the battle will change anyone's mind?"

"They'll talk, but it will still come down to how to pay for the ships."

"Have you ever had to work with Marshal Geuffryt?"

"I've talked with him briefly, but usually Schorzat or Master Dichartyn were the ones who met with him."

"What was your impression of him?"

"He's charming and well-spoken. He's well-informed. He'll do whatever's necessary to rise to the top of Naval Command."

I laughed. "I've only met him twice, but nothing I've seen would contradict that. Is there anything else I should know about him?"

Kahlasa shook her head.

"There's one other thing . . ."

A certain wariness crossed her face. "Yes?"

"I've been thinking about barges. Surely, there ought to be some trace of where the barges—and a tug—came from. They had to have been bought, or chartered, or stolen. Not that many people handle large barges like that."

"You want us to find out what we can?"

"I do, indeed." I smiled politely. "If you see Schorzat before I do, would you mention that I was looking for him?"

"I will. Good luck, Rhenn."

"Thank you."

Once I returned to my study, I began to leaf through the back reports in the cabinet, looking to see if there was anything about the allocation of eastern water rights. Something, somewhere, had jogged my thoughts, and I recalled that someone, years before—it might have been Chassendri—had commented about the legal and economic issues and how the conflict between freeholders and High Holders might reduce the number of High Holders to below a thousand, triggering a change in the Council and those in control of the Executive Council.

I hadn't found what I was seeking when Schorzat peered in through the half-open study door. "You were looking for me?"

"I was. If you'd close the door." I gestured toward the chairs. "When I met with Geuffryt last week, he mentioned the need for more ships. This morning's newsheets seemed to confirm that. I talked with Khalasa, and she indicated there was a power struggle in the Council . . ." I sat down behind the desk.

Schorzat took the chair across from me. "It's been that way for years. I do know that the various Sea-Marshals have felt that the Council was sacrificing Soldidaran prosperity and security to petty politics and that the Collegium should use its influence to break the stalemate over financing fleet upgrading and expansion . . ."

"I can't believe the Sea-Marshals said that. Exactly how did they manage to get that across without saying it?"

Schorzat laughed. "I wasn't there. According to Master Dichartyn, Sea-Marshal Valeun said something like, 'It would be for the best if an impartial party with influence could persuade them to move beyond their petty concerns . . .'"

"Power and golds aren't ever petty concerns, especially if you're the one facing the loss or either."

"No . . . but the Naval Command types place a higher priority on control of the oceans than upon squabbles over control of the purse."

I wouldn't have called the struggle over control of the Council a squabble, not when the outcome might change the entire future of Solidar, but I just nodded.

Schorzat shook his head. "In some ways, you're just like Master Dichartyn. When you give that nod, it's acknowledgment without approval. What don't you agree with?"

"We're approaching a turning point. Solidar is changing. The High Holders won't be able to hold on to control of the Executive Council for too many more years. The entire world, and not just Solidar, has a stake in how that change is handled. It's more than a squabble over how to fund our Navy."

"You think the Ferrans don't want a solution?"

"The longer it takes the Council to work it out, the longer before we get new and better ships and the more likely they'll be able to do whatever they want in Jariola."

"Jariola isn't exactly a place where either of us would want to live."

"No," I agreed, "but Jariola is just the first step toward Ferrum supplanting Solidar. I think most of Terahnar would prefer that not occur. Don't you?"

"I wish I could be certain of that," Schorzat replied.

"Remember, the Ferrans killed scores of young imagers, and they've attacked Jariola twice in less than ten years. I don't recall us starting any wars recently."

"You're right. I do worry that all this could get out of hand."

"That's possible," I said. "It's always possible." Personally, I had the feeling that matters were already well out of hand and that we didn't know how far out of control they were.

"Is there anything else?" he asked.

"Not right now. I'm sure there will be . . . as soon as I think of it."

He nodded and slipped out of the study.

I had barely returned to seeking a report that might not have even existed when Gherard appeared at the door. "Sir, Maitre Dyana would appreciate a word with you."

"Thank you." I closed the cabinet, imaged the hidden catches locked, and headed upstairs.

Her door was open. I stepped into her study and closed it behind me, then settled into the center chair across from her desk.

"You wanted to see me?"

"I did. How did your meeting with Geuffryt go?"

"He's concerned about the state of the fleet and worried about Cydarth. He also admitted that the Navy is missing several tonnes of Poudre B." I went on to tell her almost everything—except for my suspicions about why he had a certain hold on Juniae D'Shendael, although I did mention he was a cousin.

"Did he explain any more about Cydarth?"

"No, he didn't. He just said he had a trusted source who'd never been wrong, but that he had no proof."

"Is there anything else I should know?" she asked quietly.

"The Civic Patrol is getting very short of captains . . ." My explanation of the events of Samedi was as brief as I could make it.

"Do you think Cydarth is involved?"

"I have no idea. He would certainly remake the Civic Patrol if he became Commander, but there's no certainty that the Council won't reappoint Artois."

"They don't like change." Dyana's voice was dry.

"Speaking of the Council . . . can you tell me the situation there . . . or should I be arranging meetings with the Executive Council myself?"

She shook her head. "Normally, Rholyn would be briefing you, but he was called away, and I've been meeting with those Councilors still in L'Excelsis. So I thought I'd tell you what's been happening and get your thoughts as well." She cleared her throat, then went on. "The High Judiciary issued an immediate ruling. The rules of succession mandate that Glendyl becomes the head of the Executive Council until the next formal meeting of the Council, at which time the Council can name whoever it wishes to succeed Suyrien. They made it clear that the Charter of the Council does not mandate a High Holder as head of the Executive Council, but that such is the default choice if there is not a unanimous choice, and that, in the event or death or incapacity of the head of the Executive Council, the order of succession follows the precedence set up in the Council Charter . . . until, of course, the Council meets and makes its will known."

"So you're dealing with Glendyl."

"For the next month."

"You look worried," I said. "What else has happened?"

"There were a score of explosions in Thuyl last Samedi. One of the grain freighters caught fire. Half the piers are unusable."

"Thuyl? Is that a High Holder–controlled port?"

She frowned. "None of them are controlled that way."

"Is it one used more by High Holders?"

"I'd judge so. The ironway line south from Cheva to the port is owned by Ealthyn."

"Some sailors suspected of being Jariolan agents have been tracked to his lands, according to Schorzat."

"You're suggesting that their conflict is also being played out here."

"That would be to the advantage of Ferrum."

She nodded slowly.

"Do I dare ask what else has gone wrong?"

"I'm certain there's more, but even with the express trains on the ironway, it takes time for reports to get here."

I rose from the chair, inclined my head politely, and headed back down to my study.

I really wanted to get out to Third District station, but I wasn't recovered enough to hold full-strength shields. Yet I didn't want to meet with either Artois or Cydarth until I'd actually talked to Alsoran and some of the patrollers about what had been going on in Third District . . . as well as to Horazt or Jadhyl, if I could.

Waiting felt like the Namer's game, and I didn't like it at all.

My shields were much stronger on Mardi, and I did manage to get up early enough to partake of a few of Clovyl's exercises, participation motivated by the knowledge that I did need to get myself back into some semblance of physical conditioning. I decided against the four mille run. After breakfast, I saw Seliora and Diestrya off to NordEste Design in the duty coach. Diestrya waved vigorously from the window, and once they were out of sight, I turned and walked quickly to the quadrangle and to my study in the administration building.

There, I sat down and tried to take a fresh look at the situation. I was in charge of Collegium security, and security for the Council, and to a degree not exactly defined anywhere, even for Solidar itself. In more than a few ways, I felt as though I were underwater, with no way to swim to the top. Or perhaps, it was more like always being late in discovering things. Just as I'd figured out why something had happened, something else happened.

I remembered Master Dichartyn telling me, years before, that the key to success lay in anticipation. "You have to know who your opponents are and understand what they want, why they want it, and how they are likely to try to obtain it, if possible, even before they do."

I was certain that the Ferrans were behind all the major difficulties, but had I really considered what they wanted? My initial assumption had been that they had merely wanted to create so much disruption in Solidar that we would be hampered and unwilling or unable to support the Jariolans after Ferrum attacked. I'd also considered that they might be indirectly supporting various factors and their associations in their efforts to gain political supremacy over the High Holders on the Council. But chaos always leads to more chaos, and, as a result, all the problems Solidar and the Collegium faced wouldn't be resolved even if the Ferrans had vanished from Terahnar. There was also a strong possibility that the Ferrans had decided to act against Jariola precisely because Solidar had so many obvious but unacknowledged problems. Logically, it made more sense to deal with the internal problems first, if only to strengthen Solidar and get them out of the way. I had the definite feeling that approach wouldn't work. First, none of the factions in Solidar wanted to change, and they'd all protest that the time to change what had worked for generations wasn't during a war. Second, with the deaths of Maitre Poincaryt and Maitre Dichartyn, and the incapacity of Councilor Suyrien, the Collegium didn't have the established "presence" or the working relations to engineer political and economic changes. Third, even if we could get past the lack of political power, which was certainly possible, even if I had to resort to tactics I'd prefer not to use, there was still the much larger difficulty of getting such changes accepted, particularly by the factors and freeholders.

My thinking was interrupted by a knock on the door.

"Come in."

The door eased open, and Rholyn stepped inside, closing it behind him. "Rhenn . . ."

I was surprised at the hesitation in the salutation, but, given the situation, I realized the awkwardness of it all, even as I stood to greet him. Rholyn was a good twenty years older than I and had been a Maitre D'Structure longer than I'd been an imager. He didn't want to acknowledge the change in relative rank, and yet he didn't want to offend me, either.

"What is it? You look like the bearer of tidings of dubious cheer."

In fact, he looked exhausted, with dark circles under his eyes, and his skin was blotchy. His right eye twitched.

"Maitre Dyana asked me to let you know that Councilor Suyrien died last night. The services will be on Jeudi at the Council Anomen. At the second glass of the afternoon."

"Thank you. I hadn't heard anything. When I didn't, I'd hoped that he might recover."

"It's probably a mercy he didn't. He was shot in the head and in the chest. Draffyd imaged out bone fragments and stopped the worst of the bleeding, but there never was much hope. It was astounding that he lived as long as he did."

That didn't surprise me. I'd seen the determination behind Suyrien's cultivated good cheer and ease of manner. "Will the family be seeing anyone . . . Or do you know?"

"I haven't heard. Neither has Maitre Dyana."

I nodded, then said, "We haven't had much of a chance to talk. If you have a few moments, I'd like to hear your thoughts on some of the problems facing the Council." I gestured toward the chairs, then seated myself behind the desk.

"I have the rest of the morning." He shook his head as he sat. "It might take that long."

"How will Suyrien's death change the Council?" I prompted.

"Not for the better. Ramsael is personally open to some degree of change. He recognizes that change is inevitable and necessary, but he's an even stronger believer in change through consensus. Most of the High Holders don't want change. That's their consensus."

"What might change their minds?"

Rholyn laughed, softly. "Only very convincing proof that they'd absolutely be worse off without change."

"As you pointed out," I replied, "change is inevitable. Managed change is usually less violent and less costly than unmanaged change. In terms of government, unmanaged change equates to revolution."

"They don't believe that the Collegium will allow revolution to occur, because we'd be swept away by it as well."

"That's an open invitation for Maitre Dyana to ally the Collegium with Glendyl or Caartyl."

"We don't want that. Caartyl's more of a reactionary than the High Holders, and Glendyl, given half a chance, would remake Solidar in the pattern of Ferrum."

Rholyn's brief comments were tending to reinforce my thoughts that we might be better off dealing with the Ferran problems first. But then, that was what he doubtless intended.

"Why did Caartyl try to become acting head of the Executive Council? Was he trying to do something in particular?"

"He was," replied Rholyn. "He was trying to make certain that Glendyl didn't issue some statement that might have been conciliatory toward Ferrum. He also didn't want Glendyl to stop the orders transferring ships from the southern fleet to the northern fleet."

"That sounds as though he already knew what had happened in the sea battle that was reported yesterday."

"Anyone who'd followed Naval matters could have guessed that any battle would be bloody. We've lost much of our edge over the past five years."

That, unfortunately, made sense. "What's Caartyl's greatest weakness?"

"His belief that he knows best, and that whatever is best for the artisans and guilds is best for Solidar."

"And his greatest strength is their belief in him?"

At that, Rholyn pursed his lips, clearly thinking. After several moments, he replied. "That's one of his strengths. Another is that he has no doubts. Everything is black and white to him. He understands the need for compromise, and he will, as needed. But compromise for tactical advantage or partial attainment of his goals doesn't change his views or his objectives."

"What about Glendyl?"

"Glendyl thinks, as you must know, that artisans and guilds and the High Holders themselves are all anachronistic relics of a past that should be dispensed with as rapidly as possible. The Council should be controlled by factors and some few freeholders, since they're the ones who produce most of the machinery and goods for Solidar. Those High Holders like Suyrien—or his heir—who are effectively manufacturers should acknowledge the fact and join with the factors. Those who are landholders should be forced to operate under the same laws as the freeholders. All High Holder privileges and rights should be abolished."

"What about the guilds?"

"They shouldn't be allowed to restrict commerce and trade. Otherwise, he doesn't care."

"Will his value-added-tax proposal bring in enough revenue?"

"I asked Jhulian and one of the Collegium's bookkeepers—a third named Reynol—to look into the plan. According to them, the one percent add-on won't be sufficient. Two percent would provide a surplus."

"And what would be Caartyl's reaction?"

"He thinks the High Holders and the factors and freeholders all want to abolish or restrict the guilds and artisans. He'd probably accept some of what Glendyl wants, if only to restrict the power of the High Holders, but he'll stand firm on retaining the restrictions on entry to the various guilds, and he wants what amounts to a laborers' guild for those in the manufactories so that workers have some recourse and don't have to work for what he terms 'starvation wages.' "

"Some of the manufactories already allow guilds," I pointed out.

"But those are the ones located in places like L'Excelsis where the guilds are strong. Glendyl's proposal would result in factors building facilities in small towns along the ironway where they could get cheaper labor and where people would flee the High Holders' estates."

"So it's likely that Glendyl won't get much support for what he proposes?"

"Most likely."

"What if the Collegium proposed some sort of tax reform?"

"Anything that would improve the present system would be voted down . . ."

We talked for another glass, but I didn't find what he said terribly helpful.

As soon as Rholyn left, I took out pen and ink and began to write a letter of condolence. It took me several drafts before I had something suitable. I read it a last time.

Dear Iryela and Kandryl,
I just received word of Suyrien's death, and Seliora and I offer our deepest sympathy for both of you. Although all of us have had loved ones die, death, especially unexpected death, is never easy and falls hardest on those who care the most.
    Suyrien was always open and fair and tried to work out solutions that would bene-fit all those involved. He was warm and gracious to both Seliora and me on the occasion of your wedding, and his cheer and warmth went a long way . . . .

I finally sealed it and set it on the corner of the desk. Then, since my shields still weren't strong enough for me to leave Imagisle, I decided I might as well begin to get better acquainted with the imagers for whom I'd become preceptor. Over the next glass I wrote notes to each, setting a time for them to meet with me in the mornings over the next few days.

A quint before noon, I set out for the dining hall building, where I slipped the letters into the post boxes for the imagers, and posted the letter to Iryela and Kandryl. There were a number of juniors around, but I didn't see any of those for whom I'd become preceptor. So I stepped into the dining hall proper.

Maitre Dyana was at the masters' table, but she had Jhulian on one side and Rholyn on the other. So I sat with Khalasa, Ferlyn, and Quaelyn, the older pattern-master, who was Ferlyn's mentor.

"It's good to see you more often," said Kahlasa.

"It's good to see you . . . and to have edible food," I replied.

"So . . . we're not much better than the food?" Ferlyn grinned as he passed a pot of steaming tea.

"That's an equation of the unequateable."

"How are you feeling?" asked Kahlasa.

"Better. Enough so that I'll probably have to deal with Artois and Cydarth before long."

"You'll manage," said Ferlyn dryly.

"I may well manage the wrong way. There's more going on than I'd like."

"In what way?" asked Kahlasa.

I served myself rice and chicken before I replied. "Artois tends to want to keep order and ignore the taudis except when they create trouble. He's gone along with the changes I've made in Third District because the results have reduced offenses there without requiring more patrollers. Cydarth seems to quietly oppose Artois, but he hasn't cared for my changes."

"That sounds like he's a partisan of the factors," said Ferlyn. "You've been improving the taudis and getting more of the young men trained in various crafts and skills. If others followed your example, there'd be fewer young men available for cheap labor."

Quaelyn nodded sagely, but did not speak.

I shook my head. "That won't happen. After five years, things are pretty much the same everywhere else in L'Excelsis."

"Does that matter?" asked Ferlyn. "What matters is what people worry about, not what actually is or might happen."

I nodded. He was right about that, but did it really shed any light on what Cydarth had in mind and might have been doing? For a time, I just concentrated on the rice and chicken. I was hungrier than I'd realized.

As I finished, I turned to Ferlyn again. "You're dealing with patterns, analyzing them, and the like. What do your patterns say about Ferrum?" I looked to Quaelyn, sitting to Ferlyn's right. "Or yours, Maitre Quaelyn?"

Ferlyn smiled. "You must be very concerned to ask. But I will defer to my mentor."

"I'm worried." I didn't mind admitting that. "I have the feeling we're missing something important. I'm hoping you two might have an insight I can use."

"He's very concerned," Ferlyn said to Kahlasa.

I forced a grin. "I think you've made that point, and I've admitted it."

Ferlyn didn't say anything, but nodded to Quaelyn. "You've studied Ferrum. You've even been there."

That was something I didn't know, and it meant that the now-frail and white-haired Maitre had once been a covert foreign agent.

"That was a few years ago," Quaelyn said softly, "but the patterns of a society don't change, not without great economic shifts or a loss in war or social upheaval or something of equal magnitude, and Ferrum has not seen any of those in generations. The last, shall we say, conflict with Jariola and our fleet was essentially a stand-off, with all the destruction confined to Jariola and perhaps half a Ferran fleet."

I wasn't certain that the short war hadn't had more of an impact, but then . . . he was probably right. From experience, I'd noted he usually was.

"One matter that has been greatly overlooked," the elderly Maitre went on, "is the impact of the Ferran economic and political structure. In Solidar, because we have a far older social structure, we tend not to change quickly and not to make rash business decisions. A factor, for example, can seldom afford to expand quickly, even if he has a better idea or product. That is partly because his customers are set in their ways, and partly because few have enough golds to make major investments out of their revenues. Those who do not have such reserves find it difficult to obtain large amounts of capital to fund expansion of facilities or manufactories. In Ferrum, price is the ruler. People flock to the cheapest goods of equal quality, and many factors compete for customers. Many factors fail every year, and there is a constant turnover in commerce. Obviously, this is not as pronounced in manufactories dealing with iron or heavy machinery, but even a generation ago, Ferrum had four or five manufactories producing locomotives and engines, and ten shipworks. None, of course, rivaled Suyrien's in scope, but they could build more ships."

"Not better ones, though," I suggested.

"Not then, but they compete against each other, and with each passing year, their vessels are better, and so are their other goods. While I have not seen the actual land-cruisers, the newsheet reports note that the ones used in invading Jariola are far, far better than those they had but five years ago. We have nothing like them, because we see no need for such." Quaelyn paused to take a sip of tea.

"What else?" I prompted.

"A second area that is seldom discussed is the comparative physical fragility of Ferran cities and industrial areas. Because their society is based on the greater creation of revenues and profits in the near-term, and because they are always changing things, they tend to build and rebuild all the time. They don't build manufactories to last, out of stone and brick with walls that may last generations. They also do the same thing for housing for their workers. That means, over time, that they tend to waste golds because they have to rebuild more often. Part of that is that there are more fires, and they cause more damage. Their equipment tends to wear out quickly, but often that doesn't matter, because the goods the equipment produces are changed quickly also." Quaelyn took another sip of tea, then nodded, as if to say that he had said enough.

I wasn't sure I liked the idea of almost-temporary housing that burned quickly, but that was their choice. I took a swallow of tea, hot and bitter, then turned to Ferlyn. "How else do you see the patterns of Ferrum as differing from ours? Are there other differences?"

"One Quaelyn didn't mention directly is the legal structure. The Ferran assembly has changed and modified its laws so that the current economic and political patterns are generally consistent at all levels of society."

"What do you mean by that?" asked Kahlasa. "Can you give an example?"

Ferlyn shrugged. "They don't have local laws that are different from place to place."

"We don't either," said Kahlasa.

"But we do," I pointed out. "The laws are the same in any city, but the High Holders retain the power of low justice on their lands, and that means it's pretty much what each High Holder determines, so long as the punishments don't exceed the maximum stipulated by the Council charter. That's a thousand different systems."

"Precisely . . ." said Ferlyn, drawing out the word. "The same thing is true in dealing with manufacturing. In Ferrum, everything is subject to the same levies, or the same scale of levies, where here, we have different taxation structures. There's one for goods produced by guilds and artisans, another for factors, and another for anything produced by High Holders. This is designed to perpetuate the current division, but it's not terribly fair or efficient."

I wasn't so certain about fairness. Because of the restrictions created in each group, taxing them the same might be less fair. "Should efficiency be the overriding goal?"

"That's a political question. You asked about the differences. The Ferrans work toward maximizing efficiency and production . . . and making large profits quickly. Before long, if we don't change, they'll be able to manufacture ironway locomotives in Ferrum, ship them here, and still sell them for less. That's why they'll eventually conquer Jariola, even if they fail this time. They learn and improve. Even in terms of war and destruction, they're trying to be efficient, to create the most destruction with the least use of resources."

"The most destruction with the least use of resources . . ." I mused, half-aloud. "In a way, that's a terrible way of putting it."

"But that's what war is about . . . in terms of patterns. The winner is the one who creates the most destruction for the other while minimizing the destruction he suffers."

Even after I'd returned to my study, Ferlyn's phrase about destruction kept running through my thoughts. There was something about it . . .

34

On Meredi, after a normal early morning, with somewhat more exercise and greater participation in getting Diestrya ready to leave with her mother, as soon as I got to my study, I met with Eamyn, only for about half a glass, just so that I could go over where he was in his studies. Then I read the latest reports from Patrol Commanders and from the various imager regionals. One thing stood out. There hadn't been any attacks or explosions in any large manufactories or shipworks. At least, none of the reports mentioned any attacks on such facilities. That gave me yet another reason to visit Commander Artois.

I took a duty coach to Civic Patrol headquarters, not that I was looking forward to meeting with Artois. I'd already decided that I wasn't about to discuss anything with Cydarth until after I'd spoken with the Commander. I did have the coach wait for me outside headquarters.

I stepped into anteroom outside Artois's private study just after ninth glass. The older patroller who sat at the left-hand desk of the two small writing desks in the anteroom looked up.

"Captain . . . Maitre Rhennthyl . . ."

"I'm here to see the Commander."

"Yes, sir. Let me tell him." The patroller stood, opened the door to the study, and quickly closed it behind him.

In moments, the door reopened, and the patroller stepped out and to the side.

Artois stood behind him, just inside the study. "Maitre Rhennthyl, do come in. I was hoping to see you before too long."

I stepped into the study and closed the door behind me. An ancient walnut desk was set at the end of the study closest to the river. On the innermost wall to the right was a line of wooden cases. On the wall opposite the desk was a tall and narrow bookcase, filled with volumes. Facing the desk were four straight-backed chairs. The two windows, frosted around the edges, were centered on the outer wall and offered a view of the various buildings on the north side of Fedre and some beyond, but not so far as the Boulevard D'Imagers. As had always been the case, there were no pictures or personal items on the desk, in the bookcases, or on the walls.

"You look a bit battered and bruised," offered Artois, moving toward his desk. Somehow, he looked even thinner and shorter than I recalled, although he was probably only four digits shorter than I was.

"It does happen when someone fires bombards at you and stones crash down around you and your family." I settled into one of the chairs in front of the desk, waiting for Artois to sit down.

He did, smiling genially, although his brown eyes remained flat and expressionless. "You may recall I once said that you could be a very powerful imager. Apparently, I was correct."

"Ability does help some in survival." I smiled politely, waiting to see what he might say.

"I understand that you may have other duties now." Absently, one hand brushed back short gray hair that held but a few remaining strands of brown.

"Maitre Dyana is now the Maitre of the Collegium, and she has changed some duties. I will be taking over those handled by Maitre Dichartyn. In that regard, I would greatly appreciate it if I might receive any listing the Civic Patrol has of the structures damaged by explosions."

"We're still compiling that, but I will be happy to send that listing once it is complete."

"Are you aware of any attacks on large manufactories or the barge piers or the ironway stations or freight terminals?"

"I haven't seen any reports on those." He frowned.

"Thank you." I wasn't about to explain. Not at the moment. "It appears that you face some of the same difficulties here, given the injuries to so many Civic Patrol captains."

He nodded slowly. "We have lost some good captains."

"You have some good lieutenants, some of whom would make solid captains."

"You know, Maitre Rhennthyl, I have often asked myself what makes a good Civic Patrol officer. Is it ability? Intelligence? Or dedication? Motivation? Ambition? Ideals?" He paused and looked at me. "You have been a captain for five years. What do you think?"

I offered a smile. "If it were only the case of a single quality. Dedication is important, but it depends on what the captain is dedicated to. Ability is certainly necessary, but it's not enough. Ideals are vital, but which ideals? Intelligence, but only if it is coupled with practicality."

"You accomplished much in Third District, but you did so with abilities and contacts that no other officer possesses, and that leaves a certain problem."

"That is true, and it would be true if you choose to promote another officer to captain over Lieutenant Alsoran."

"Why do you think that?"

I shrugged. "It's known that I favor Alsoran. It's also known that Alsoran believes in patrolling the Third District in the same fashion as I did. Regardless of what my future duties to the Collegium may entail, I still retain certain ties to Third District. Lieutenant Alsoran, were he to become captain, could call on me upon occasion. Because he is a loyal and dedicated officer, he could not and would not do so if he remained as lieutenant under a new captain. If he were to be transferred to another district, the knowledge he has of Third District would be lost. You, of course, are the Commander and will make whatever choice you think is best."

Artois shook his head. "You sound more like your predecessor than the captain of Third District."

"It is your choice, Commander," I pointed out.

He reached into the top drawer of his desk and withdrew a sealed envelope, then extended it to me. "That is his promotion to captain. While I could I do nothing else, I did wish to discuss the matter with you. I assume you would like to present it personally."

"You mean that you wanted some commitment that I would retain an interest in Third District." I took the envelope and slipped it into the inside pocket of my waistcoat.

"Of course." He smiled.

"And in the Civic Patrol," I added. "What is the worst probable fate for the Patrol?"

His smile vanished. "I would have thought—"

"What I think is what I think. You have been Commander for ten years. I would like your views. You have had mine on Third District."

He frowned.

I waited.

"The worst fate?" He paused. "The worst fate for the Patrol would be to accept injustices as a necessary part of life in L'Excelsis. Injustices are often not preventable, but they should never be regarded as necessary for some good."

"You have certainly made that clear. How might the Patrol come to accept injustices as necessary?"

"There are likely many ways. The Council could reduce our funding. That would result in accepting more injustices. Patrollers could become less honest and accept favors and worse. Patrol officers could become beholden to those with golds. All those have happened in the past, and the outcomes were never good for the Patrol or for L'Excelsis." Artois shrugged.

"Or officers could just become more accepting of injustices among those without guild connections or golds?" I suggested.

"That is also possible, and perhaps the most likely if care is not taken."

"It's been suggested that justice in the cities has not always been to the benefit of the High Holders." So far as I knew, I was the only one who had even voiced that, but I wanted a reaction from Artois.

Again, for a moment, he did not speak. "I had not thought of it in that way, but it is likely so. When there is more equal justice in the cities, those on the great estates may well have greater incentive to depart." He paused. "Justice does not lie merely in the law, but in all aspects of life. A patrol officer cannot change what is beyond the law, and he cannot interpret the law differently because of what he cannot change. You understand that. That does not preclude legal action to improve matters. Your actions have shown that. Others have been critical of such actions, you realize?"

"I'm aware of that."

"I shouldn't keep you, Maitre. You might want to have a word with the subcommander before you leave."

"I should. Is Alsoran's promotion effective?"

"It is. As of today."

"Thank you. I'm sure we will talk in the future."

"I would hope so."

After leaving Artois, I made my way down the upper hall to the next study, rapping on the door and then stepping inside.

Subcommander Cydarth rose from behind his desk. "I hear you may be leaving us."

"In the more direct sense," I replied. "I'm replacing Maitre Dichartyn."

"I was sorry to hear about his death, but you have much more hands-on experience with the Patrol. That could benefit both the Patrol and the Collegium."

"I would hope so." I thought about adding something about benefit being in the eye of the beholder, but decided against it. "Have you had any success in tracking down any of those who destroyed so many buildings?"

"No. I can't say that we have. The only ones we've ever caught were the ones you killed and those found dead in Third District. It was a pity you couldn't bring one in alive."

Those found dead in Third District? I'd have to ask Alsoran about that. "I did bring in some of the druggers. They were poisoned here in headquarters. That was a pity, too."

"They wouldn't have said anything."

"We won't know that, though," I replied.

"No, we won't." He laughed in that deep rumbling voice. "There are always things we won't know."

I smiled. "There are things we can't prove. That doesn't mean we don't know them." I smiled. "I just wanted to let you know about the change personally. Oh, Alsoran has been promoted to captain of Third District, and, of course, I'll be advising him as he feels necessary."

"Of course."

"I'm sure I'll see you from time to time." I smiled, nodded, and stepped out of his study, down the hallway and down the steps to the main entrance.

When I left Patrol headquarters, occasional flakes of snow were drifting out of a light gray sky. Even with my heavy gray winter cloak over an equally heavy waistcoat, I was grateful that the duty coach was waiting. Lebryn waited for my instructions..

"Third District station, please."

"Yes, Maitre."

As the coach carried me up Fedre, I could see, just short of Sudroad, an area of rubble to the right. Once there had been a line of rowhouses there. Another of the explosions set by the Ferrans? Why there?

We reached Third District station without difficulty, and, again, I had Lebryn wait. I wasn't about to risk hacks at the moment.

Huensyn was on the duty desk, and he immediately stood as I walked in. "Sir!"

I gestured for him to take his seat on the stool behind the high desk. "Is Lieutenant Alsoran around?"

"The lieutenant stepped out for a moment, Captain. He said he'd be but a quint, and that was more than a quint ago."

"I'll wait. You can tell me about a few things. I noticed some buildings had been blown up in First District. Did we lose any here?"

"No, sir." Huensyn smiled. "We did find a few dead bodies, fellows in black, though."

"They must have run into trouble." That was good and bad. I just hoped the taudischefs had disposed of the explosives, but most likely they'd sold them, not that there was anything I could do about it. I'd have to talk to them, but that could wait, because what was done was done, and even if there had been markings on the explosives, they would have doubtless been Solidaran markings.

"The lieutenant sent a report to the Commander that you'd stopped two groups already, and that another two had apparently run into difficulties."

"I don't imagine he got a response."

"No, sir."

At that moment, the station door opened. Alsoran smiled broadly as he caught sight of me. "Captain! I'd heard that some of the high-ranking imagers' dwellings were shelled. We didn't know . . ."

"I was laid up for a day or so, but here I am." I nodded to Huensyn. "If you'll excuse us, we need to talk over some matters."

"Yes, sirs."

We walked to Alsoran's study. I let him close the door.

"Before we discuss anything, you need to open this envelope." I withdrew the oblong and handed it to him.

He took it, then opened it slowly, as if he feared what might be inside. He unfolded the heavy sheet and read it, then read it again. Finally, he looked up. "You're leaving, then?"

"I don't have a choice. I'm needed at the Collegium."

He nodded. "I didn't ever expect this. Is it your doing, sir?"

I smiled and shook my head. "Commander Artois wrote it before I talked to him or met with him. It was sealed and waiting in his desk when I saw him earlier today. I did tell him that I'd be happy to offer you any advice or expertise you needed."

He was the one to shake his head. "I still don't . . ."

"You're good at what you do, and the taudischefs trust you. They did back when you were a patroller first. They also know that I support you. What other lieutenant or captain could do as good a job here as you can?"

He offered a crooked smile. "No other officer would want to follow you, not so long as you're still with the Collegium. You're in charge of imager security, aren't you?"

"There's no such position, but I have duties along those lines."

"I thought so."

"Does following me bother you?"

"No, sir. I've never thought I was anything but a good solid patroller. I think I can be a good solid captain."

"So do I, and L'Excelsis needs solid captains." I smiled. "I can't stay long, but I'd like to announce the changes to those here in the station."

Alsoran smiled. "I can't stop you."

As I'd suspected, as patrollers had come in for various reasons, either between rounds or to report offenses, they'd managed to remain, and a half-score were scattered not-so-casually in the area around the duty desk. When I stepped out of Alsoran's study, most eyes flicked toward the two of us.

I walked into the middle of the open area. "I have an announcement to make."

The murmurs died away.

"Because of changes at Imagisle, I've been recalled to duty there. I've appreciated the effort all of you, and all those who are not here, have made. But I would like to tell you that from today on, Captain Alsoran will be the one running Third District, as he already has been in my recent absence." I turned and inclined my head to Alsoran. "Captain."

"Thank you, Maitre Rhennthyl." He paused, then added, "We all appreciate what you have done. You will always be welcome here in Third District."

"Thank you . . . all of you."

I wasn't a believer in long farewells, and I'd never put any personal items in the captain's study. So I didn't have to take anything with me when I left a short time later.

Lebryn took South Middle out to the Midroad, then followed it around the Guild Square to where it became the Boulevard D'Imagers. Two blocks past the Guild Square, we passed another pile of gray rubble—where, weeks before, had stood an older three-story structure that had housed L'Excelsis Indemnity. That had to have been a deliberate target. I'd have to check the list Artois had promised, once it arrived, to see if there was a pattern to the buildings that had been damaged or destroyed.

With all the traveling, I didn't get back to Imagisle until the first glass of the afternoon. Beleart caught me before I even reached my study with a request that I meet with Maitre Dyana as soon as I returned. I did hang my winter cloak in my study before I headed upstairs.

Gherard motioned for me to go into Maitre Dyana's study even before I said a word. As always, I closed the door behind me. Dyana was writing something and nodded for me to sit down. I took one of the middle chairs and waited.

After several moments, she replaced the pen in its stand and looked up. "You left Imagisle. Are you up to that?"

"For short periods. I took a duty coach and met with Artois. He's promoted Alsoran to captain to succeed me, and he's promised a listing of the damaged buildings once it's complete. I also met with Cydarth. Is he still pressing the Council to make him Commander?"

"Neither Rholyn nor I have heard anything along those lines."

"He's likely biding his time. He might be waiting for something to discredit Artois."

"While Artois is hoping something will appear to discredit Cydarth," she suggested.

"Will it?"

"That is what you should be telling me," Maitre Dyana replied.

I thought for a moment. "Geuffryt wanted me to reveal the payments to Cydarth . . . and to Caartyl. He didn't say that, but he did insist that his source was trusted and had never been wrong. What he said bothered me then, and the more I've thought about it, the more it bothers me. If the Collegium revealed something like that, even if it were true, the disclosure would create an impression we don't need. Further . . . the funds have never been touched. The Navy wants more ships. Who controls the Civic Patrol shouldn't matter to the Naval Command. Who controls building the ships—or keeping them from being built—does matter. That strongly suggests that the whole business was a ploy to get the Collegium to act in some way to further the Navy's interests. Revealing that we know about fund transfers, even when we don't, would reduce trust in our impartiality."

"That part is clear enough," Dyana replied. "But why would the Naval Bureau want to reduce our influence when we've supplied them with materials and new devices and when we're more inclined to support modernizing the fleet?"

"I don't have an answer to that, but I can't see anything else that makes sense."

"Neither can I. It might be best if you devoted time and thought to seeing what else you can discover that bears on that."

"I'll see what I can do."

"Have you found out any more about the Ferrans?"

"There were two more teams with explosives. They were found dead in Third District. The explosives are missing."

She shook her head. "That's somewhat better than losing people and buildings. You think it was your taudischefs?"

"They're not mine, in that sense, but I'm certain it was. I haven't had time to chase them down." Nor did I want to spend extended times holding full shields when I had the feeling that I wouldn't learn that much.

"Three hundred people died in the explosions here. The numbers are similar in Kherseilles, Solis, Estisle, and Westisle."

I'd noted the numbers, already. They were surprisingly low. "There's another concern. So far, I haven't seen any attacks or explosions affecting large manufactories or shipworks, and there were only two affecting the ironway. Also, with the exception of the agents we've found in Third District, and those killed on the bombard barges, we haven't found a single Ferran agent."

"Every one who has been found is dead, and all the deaths are connected to you," Maitre Dyana pointed out.

"I've thought of that. But some of those deaths occurred when I was in no shape to do anything."

"Most people wouldn't know that." She rose. "That's two concerns for which we need answers, Maitre Rhennthyl."

I stood and inclined my head. There wasn't much point in saying more.

Back in my study, I reviewed the reports, but didn't find much there.

Later in the afternoon, I checked with Kahlasa, but she hadn't found anyone who was missing barges in the L'Excelsis area, and it would take longer to find out from concerns downriver.

I spent the rest of the afternoon with the reports and with maps, trying to find some link that might make sense. My head was aching by the time I walked into the house close to fifth glass.

"Dada!" Diestrya threw both arms around my legs.

"Diestrya." I picked her up and hugged her, although I wasn't so sure that I didn't need the hug more than she did.

Seliora appeared about the time I set our daughter down. "I sent off a note to your mother, like you told me. Are you sure you'll be up to dinner on Vendrei?"

"Physically, I'd be up to it now." My mother's dinner invitation was her way of forcing me to tell her how I really was. "She's never gotten over my evasions when I was severely injured before we were married."

"Mothers do worry."

"True enough." I settled into the big chair in the family parlor, glad to be off my feet, even though I hadn't stood all that much during the course of the day. But it had been a long day. "We didn't have much of a chance to talk last night because Diestrya was so fussy, but something Ferlyn had said the other day struck me. I still can't quite say why."

"You might tell me what he said." Seliora perched on the end of the settee.

"He was talking about the way lands are . . . I guess you'd say . . . structured.

How, unless Solidar becomes more organized, Ferrum will supplant us as the leading land of Terahnar. I almost got the picture of a land filled with manufactories and little else, where even the crops are harvested by machines, perhaps by great steam monsters like the Ferran land-cruisers. Where would that leave places like NordEste Design?"

"We'd survive. We're already a manufactory. We're one that requires great skill, but we use machines for everything that we can. The ones who would suffer would be the carpenters and cabinet makers. It will happen sooner or later, because the same card techniques we use for the looms should be able to be adapted to wood-working, even metalwork."

"Why hasn't it happened already?"

"The guilds have opposed it. That's another reason why we only belong to the guilds as individuals in different fields of artisanship."

"Don't they know?"

"I'm sure they do, but what we do is so costly that it's clear we'd never take away jobs. Father and I already figured out how to design lathes to produce hundreds of simple table legs and tops, but to make it profitable, we'd have to produce hundreds, maybe thousands, every year."

"If you can do it . . ."

"Someone will, sooner or later," Seliora said. "But the laws limiting the number of crafters and artisans under a single guildmaster would have to be changed. So would the requirement for all products for dwellings or buildings to be made by the family or owner or by a guildmaster or his journeymen or apprentices."

"Has anyone in your family heard about Glendyl or anyone on the Council trying to do something to grant more power to the factors? Or to reduce the power of the guilds?"

She shook her head.

"Still . . . it wouldn't happen that way," I mused. "They'd try to bring it about by saying that whatever it was would benefit everyone, and that the guilds were trying to line their own purses at the expense of everyone else."

"Aren't they?" asked Seliora. "We can make a plain chair for much less than the crafters charge. We don't do it because there's no point in it for us. Even the woodworks in Third District could charge far less than it does, if we weren't spending so much on continually training workers. So could the paper mill, and that's with a facility that's too small to be as efficient as it could be. How much longer can the guilds keep the better machines out?"

I fingered my chin, thinking. Was that why Caartyl had often allied himself and the other guild counselors with the High Holders? Because both had a vested interest in keeping matters as they were and had been? I had another thought. If Cydarth in fact happened to be innocent of receiving the funds Geuffryt had directed Juniae D'Shendael to write about and Caartyl was not . . . what would be the political implications if both transactions were revealed?

"What would be the reaction if Caartyl were discovered receiving funds from a High Holder?"

"He'd be forced to resign . . . if something worse didn't happen. Someone else would replace him—"

"Alucion, most likely, and he doesn't care much for the High Holders." Enough, I suspected, that he would rather support Glendyl than Ramsael and the other High Holder Councilors. It wouldn't hurt the stonecutters because there weren't any machines that could cut or sculpt stone effectively. Not so far, anyway. "I need to talk to Baratyn about some of this. I probably should have done so already."

"You can't do everything all at once, dearest," Seliora pointed out, looking hard at Diestrya, who actually caught the look and retreated from the stove. "Especially after what you've been through."

"I may not be able to, but I fear that's what's required."

"You can only do what you can do." Seliora stood. "If you would watch your daughter, I'd like to check on dinner."

"I *can* do that." I scooped up Diestrya and set her in my lap, still thinking about Ferlyn. There was something else . . . not anything he'd said, but an implication of what he'd said. Things had to change, for the guilds, for the factors, for the High Holders . . . but they also had to change for the Collegium . . . and I hadn't even thought about that.

35

For the first two glasses on Jeudi morning, from seventh glass to ninth glass, I met with three of the four remaining junior imagers for whom I had become preceptor—Haugyl, Marteon, and Shault. I didn't have to spend quite so much time with Shault, because I'd been more involved with him from the time Horazt had brought him to Imagisle.

Before he left, though, he did ask, "Will you still watch out for Third District, sir?"

"As I can, but Captain Alsoran also knows the district, and he will do well."

"Yes, sir."

I could tell that didn't totally convince him, and I understood his concern, since Horazt was his "uncle" and his mother still lived in Third District and likely always would, at least until and if Shault attained the rank of Maitre. That was likely years away, since I'd been one of the youngest Maitres when I'd become a Maitre D'Aspect at twenty-six.

Once I'd ushered Shault out, I went looking for Ferlyn, but he wasn't in his study. Asomyd, the duty second in the administration building, couldn't say where he might be, other than he'd left with Quaelyn, the not-quite-ancient pattern-master of the Collegium and Ferlyn's mentor.

After that, I checked with Kahlasa and Schorzat, but neither had any new information, either about events in Cloisera or about leased, sold, or missing barges. As I thought about the afternoon, and the memorial service, where Iryela was certain to be, I realized that I'd never followed up on what might have happened to her brother. He hadn't been mentioned in any of the recent reports from the Collegium at Mont D'Glace, only in the older report that Dichartyn had received. So I drafted a quick inquiry and sent Beleart to post it.

By then it was noon. Since I knew Baratyn would be at the Council Chateau, after a quiet mid-day meal at the dining hall, I took one of the duty coaches and, again, had the driver—Desalyt, this time—wait so that I'd have a ride down to the Council Anomen for Suyrien's public memorial service at second glass.

I did enter the Chateau through the narrow gate at the rear, the one reserved for the security force. Although I hadn't been to the Council Chateau recently, the obdurate guards had clearly been briefed, because the duty sentry outside greeted me by name.

The Council wasn't in session, and the corridors were quiet, but Baratyn was in his study, seated at his desk and looking down at several sheets of paper. The chamber was without decoration except for the two wall hangings. The large hanging on the wall to the right depicted the four-pointed star of the Collegium Imago. The one on the left depicted the Council emblem, a sheaf of grain crossed by a hammer and a sword. The hangings also concealed, I knew from my time in Council security, listening tubes connected to a number of public places in the Council Chateau, although I doubted anyone but Baratyn could have overheard that much from some of the tubes.

"Good afternoon," I offered.

"Maitre Rhennthyl . . . you surprised me. No one visits when the Council is out."

"That's why I'm here." I slipped closed the study door and took one of the chairs opposite him, gesturing for him to sit down. "I need your information and insight."

"That's why I'm here."

"Among a few other things," I replied dryly.

"There are a few."

"You do follow the Council deliberations and debates, don't you?" I was fairly certain he did, but Dichartyn had never actually gone into that with me.

"As I can. I listen more to what is said outside the Council chambers."

That wasn't surprising, given all the listening tubes that fed into his study, and the fact that Baratyn doubtless used personal concealment shields. "Which is more valuable, I suspect."

"Often." Baratyn smiled faintly.

"I have the impression that Caartyl, for all that he may say publicly, tends to ally himself far more with the High Holders than with the factors. Is this so, or am I missing something?"

Baratyn tilted his head slightly, then frowned before he spoke. "I don't know that it's that simple. He's opposed to anything that might give the factors more power. I even overheard him arguing with Alucion several months ago. He told the old stonecutter that having Glendyl in charge of the Executive Council would be even worse than having Haestyr succeed Suyrien. He also said that, for now, Suyrien was the best to head the Council." He laughed softly. "Not that there's much choice now."

"But?" I paused before adding, "You said it wasn't that simple."

"Caartyl's also fought for better working conditions for those on High Holder lands, and he's sided with Glendyl on measures to reduce the scope of punishments allowed under High Holder low justice."

"Did those measures succeed?"

"They finally passed at the end of Erntyn, but they won't take effect until the beginning of the new year. All the factor Councilors and all the guild Councilors voted for them. In the end, Suyrien brought the measure up for a vote and supported them, against the other High Holders, but I think that was to get some concessions."

"What concessions?"

"There were some changes before the final vote by the Council. How many were trade-offs or concessions and how many were technical improvements might be a matter of opinion. One change dealt with justiciary review. Under the original proposal, any complaint of abuse of low justice required witnesses and proof before it could be reviewed by a regional justicer. The change added one more requirement. If a complaint is brought by anyone in the immediate family of the High Holder, it must also be co-signed by an individual who is neither employed by the High Holder nor a member of his immediate family."

"How did they define immediate family?"

"Mother, wife, children, grandchildren, or sibling."

"I can understand why the High Holders might want that. Did anyone speak against the provision?"

"How could they? No one but the Council even knew about the change. I doubt if any factors or guild Councilors really care about what happens in a High Holder's family."

"Would any other change have made a bigger effect than was obvious?"

"There was one . . ." mused Baratyn. "Under the final law, any low justice sentence that results in permanent injury to the malefactor may be appealed to the Solidaran regional justicer for damages. Suyrien insisted that, when appeals were denied, the malefactor be held responsible for a minimum of one third of the costs of the appeal."

"Those living on High Holder lands couldn't afford anything like even a tenth of those costs," I pointed out. "That would greatly reduce the number of appeals, especially for those with families. It might even effectively stop them altogether. And no one in the Council said anything?"

"Councilor Hemwyt objected, and Suyrien pointed out that without some cost-sharing, every case where a malefactor could prove any sort of injury of the most minor sort would end up being appealed. In the end, Suyrien agreed to reduce the cost-share to one fifth, and the measure was passed that way."

"Were there any other 'minor' changes?"

"Some were technical corrections, changes in terms, but there was one other. It required, for purposes of evaluations and levies, that all property be assessed in value at market value on the thirty-fifth of Finitas each year. There was some considerable debate on that, but the factors and the guilds all agreed with Suyrien. Once they saw the language they immediately wanted it adopted."

"The last day of the year has always been the traditional date for assessments and valuations for everyone else," I pointed out. "I imagine that's why they liked the idea."

"Some of the High Holders—as I recall, Haestyr and Regial—protested that it didn't take into account that agricultural goods are valued at harvest prices, and that lands are valued off of crop yields."

There was definitely something there, but I'd have to look into that. Ferlyn might be able to help me. "Who would have been affected by that? Besides Haestyr and Regial?"

"In practice, it would have hurt all the High Holders who only have lands and herds, such as those north of Cloisonyt or in the prairies and woods of the northwest. It might affect those around Asseroiles, like Haestyr."

Certainly every High Holder would have favored the first two changes, but would the third one have angered another High Holder enough to have him break the traditional practice of never using direct violence against another High Holder? Or would one of the wealthier factors or one of the guild representatives have wanted Suyrien dead because he was effective in subtly undermining reforms of the worst abuses by High Holders?

"Do you know why Suyrien wanted the valuation change?"

"He only said that he felt a uniform system of valuation was necessary, one that treated factors, crafters, shopkeepers, and High Holders in the same fashion, and one that didn't include speculation in valuation."

That sounded like Suyrien. "Do you have any ideas about what he really had in mind?"

Baratyn shook his head. "He must have had something in mind, but whatever it was, I never knew."

I could believe that. "I have a duty coach. Would you like to ride with me to the anomen for Suyrien's memorial service?"

"I'd appreciate that, sir."

I stood, and we walked out through the security doors and gate to the coach.

Baratyn said nothing, even after we were moving away from the Chateau.

"Do you have any idea who might have arranged for Suyrien's shooting?" I finally asked.

He shook his head. "It took place at his L'Excelsis estate, not here. I was told that he was walking down to the boathouse on the river."

That made sense, because getting close to a High Holder on his own estate would have been difficult, while the river was open to anyone with a boat. Still . . . someone had to have reconnoitered the estate in order to know from where on the river what part of the estate could be vulnerable to a sniper.

Although we arrived almost a quint before the service was to begin, over a hundred people were already standing in the anomen, and murmurs filled the hall. I eased over to the left, almost against the wall some three yards back from the first line of those who were already there. I didn't see Maitre Dyana, but I hadn't expected her. Maitre Rholyn was in the second rough row back, but on the far side of the anomen from us. I didn't see anyone else from the Collegium, although I did see Glendyl and Caartyl, on opposite sides of the hall. There was no one in military uniform, either.

As the bells struck the glass, the family walked in from the left side and stood in a line facing the front of the anomen.

I didn't know the chorister who stepped up to the pulpit. That wasn't surprising, since I'd never attended services at the Council Anomen. He was tall and thin, with silvering hair. "We are gathered here together this afternoon in the spirit of the Nameless, in affirmation of the quest for goodness and mercy in all that we do, and in celebration of the life of Suyrien D'Alte, High Holder and Councilor of Solidar, a man distinguished in all that he did."

The opening hymn was "The Glory of the Nameless." I sang, but as quietly as possible. Beside me, Baratyn sang even more softly, if that were indeed possible.

Then came the confession.

"We do not name You, for naming is a presumption, and we would not presume upon the creator of all that was, is, and will be. . . ." As the words of the confession echoed through the anomen, I glanced around, my eyes coming to rest on Suyrien's family at the front, a silver-haired woman flanked by Frydryk and Alynkya on one side and by Kandryl and Iryela on the other, with a younger woman, who was probably a sister, beside Iryela.

"In peace and harmony," came the response.

After that came the charge from the chorister. "Life is a gift from the

Nameless, for from the glory of the Nameless do we come; through the glory of the Nameless do we live, and to that glory do we return. Our lives can only reflect and enhance that glory, as did that of Suyrien, whom we honor, whom we remember, and who will live forever in our hearts and in the glory of the Nameless."

Another hymn followed—"Honor Has No Name."

> "No honor bears a name, for in acts alone lies virtue,
> Nameless is the goodness that prompts the best in all they do . . ."

I agreed with the sentiments and words of the hymn, but both the music and the words were strained, as often was the case when philosophy or religion mixed with music.

Then the chorister said, "Now we will hear from Frydryk D'Suyrien, speaking for the family."

The memorial service would be the last time Frydryk would be called that publicly. After the service, he would be Suyrien D'Alte, probably called "Young Suyrien" for a time. As was the custom, Frydryk did not take the pulpit, but the topmost step of the sacristy dais. He faced the more than two hundred people who had come to pay their respects to the family, or more accurately, I suspected, to sign the registry to ensure that their presences were known to the family.

Frydryk had to clear his throat several times before he finally began. "My father, above all, was an honorable man. He believed in honor in word and deed above all else. From the time we were children, he stressed the importance of honor. He believed that even true love was not possible if a man and woman did not enter into it with honor . . ."

I listened carefully as Frydryk catalogued in more than moderate length all the ways in which his sire had been honorable and managed not to sigh in relief when he had finished. I was sure he believed all he had said, and I was equally sure that Suyrien had believed it and that he was more honorable than the vast majority of High Holders. Unhappily, given the way most of them construed "honor" and the fashion in which all too many of them ignored it in practice, Frydryk wasn't saying as much as he thought he had said.

Once Frydryk rejoined his family, the chorister moved to the pulpit again. "At this time, we wear gray and green, gray for the uncertainties of life, and green for its triumph, manifested every year in the coming of spring. So is it that, like nature, we come from the grayness of winter and uncertainty into life which unfolds in uncertainty, alternating between gray and green, and in the end return to the life and glory of the Nameless. In that spirit, let us offer thanks for the spirit and the life of Suyrien D'Alte. Let us remember him as a child, a youth, a man, a husband, and a father, as not just a Councilor, but as a man devoted to Solidar and to the spirit of serving to the best of his considerable abilities, not merely a name, but as a living breathing person whose spirit touched many. Let us set aside the gloom of mourning, and from this day forth, recall the glory of Suyrien D'Alte's life and the warmth and joy he has left with us . . ."

With those words, all the women let the mourning scarves slip from their hair.

Then came the traditional closing hymn—"For the Glory."

> "For the glory, for the life,
> for the beauty and the strife,
> for all that is and ever shall be,
> all together, through forever,
> in eternal Nameless glory . . ."

After a long and respectful silence, people began to slip away, particularly those at the back, who had doubtless signed the register already. More than fifty others remained, because many of them either wanted to offer condolences to Frydryk and Alynkya or Kandryl and Iryela or to Kandryl's sister, whose name I didn't even know.

I needed to speak to several of them, for differing reasons, but I waited for a couple I didn't know to offer their words before approaching Iryela and Kandryl. Kandryl wasn't quite red-eyed, and Iryela looked perfectly composed. I inclined my head to them. "I'm very sorry. While I didn't know your father that well, he was always cheerful and good to me."

"Thank you, Rhenn," offered Kandryl.

Iryela nodded.

"I have sent inquiries, about Johanyr," I added in a much lower voice to her, "but I have heard nothing yet."

"Thank you," she murmured.

Then I waited behind Councilor Alucion and his wife to speak to Frydryk.

When I stepped forward, Frydryk actually spoke first. "I thought you would be here, Rhenn."

"I'm very sorry. He was a good and honorable man and Councilor."

Frydryk studied my face. "You were attacked also, I heard. I can see bruises everywhere."

"There are many more," I replied wryly, "but one can heal from bruises."

He nodded. "I appreciate your coming."

"I don't wish to intrude, but . . . might I call on you tomorrow?"

Frydryk frowned.

"I wish it were otherwise, but it may bear on your father's death."

"Half past ninth glass at the town estate," he finally said.

"Thank you. If matters were not so urgent, I would not have pressed on you."

Alynkya looked to me, then reached out, took Frydryk's hand, leaned toward him, and murmured something.

Frydryk nodded, if almost imperceptibly. "I'm reminded that you have always been thoughtful in times like these, and for you to insist declares that urgency." He offered a faint smile. "Tomorrow."

I inclined my head in reply and stepped away to allow those behind me a chance to offer their condolences. Baratyn had slipped away, and I finally located the duty coach that had brought me amid the forty or so lined up around the anomen and along the Boulevard D'Council.

Ferlyn was in his study when I finally returned to the Collegium. Every digit of wall space in the tiny room was filled with bookcases, and every shelf was overflowing with either books or papers. There were even books stacked on the single windowsill.

"I heard you were looking for me, sir."

"I was. I have a few questions where I thought the skill of a pattern-master might help."

"I think we often raise more questions than resolve any."

"That's possible with anyone, but I'd still appreciate your thoughts." I picked up the books piled on the single chair and stacked them on top of more books on the desk before sitting down. "You know the requirement for a High Holder to be the head of the Executive Council?"

"How could I not? I assume you're asking how many High Holders already do not meet the requirements set forth in the Council compact."

"Do you know?"

Ferlyn shook his head. "No one knows for certain, because there's always been a discrepancy in valuations between those High Holders like Suyrien and Ryel, who have manufactories and industrial facilities, and those like Haestyr and Haebyn, whose wealth lies in land and forests and other agricultural assets. Haestyr has been pressing for a strict interpretation of the original language, in which craft-related assets were valued at half those of land-related assets."

"Then, there's something you should know." I went on to explain about the change in valuations slipped through by Suyrien.

When I finished, for the first time since I'd taken Dichartyn's position, Ferlyn looked truly surprised. After a silence, he said, "It's not surprising that he was shot. It might be surprising that he wasn't shot earlier."

"Because the change in valuation will mean some High Holders won't be able to retain their position and rights?"

"There might be as many as fifty, and Quaelyn has calculated that there are presently 1,034 High Holders. Master Poincaryt knew about those calculations, but whether he told Maitre Dyana or Maitre Dichartyn, I don't know. We did not tell anyone else—except you, now."

I had wondered about the issue of the number of High Holders for some time, but particularly after learning of Suyrien's changes to the "reform" proposals. "Do you happen to know how many High Holders there were when the Council was formed?"

"No one knows for certain. They probably didn't then, either. From the documents we've searched, it appears that there were close to two thousand."

That explained, in some ways, why the High Holders had accepted the thousand holder threshold for the reduction of High Holder power. It had probably been a concession granted because none of them could have envisioned such a reduction in their numbers, even over the hundreds of years since then.

"Does our Naval Command reflect the patterns of the past, or has it changed more toward the Ferran set of patterns?"

Ferlyn blinked, obviously startled by the change in the subject matter of my questions.

I waited.

"We've talked in the past about the goals of warfare, and the patterns involved," he began. "There are two key questions. The first is the overall mission of the Navy, and the second is what force and support structure will best accomplish that mission. Historically, the mission has been a dual one—to assure open and unrestricted trade, and to dominate the oceans in such a fashion that no other land can threaten our merchant and Naval vessels. The problem inherent in such a split mission is that it requires a larger navy than either part of that mission will alone . . . the Ferran mission is limited to restricting the influence and power of our fleets and ships. That means they attempt to develop vessels and weapons systems designed specifically for use against our warships, while we must also have capabilities they do not. For example, we have Naval marines for boarding, as well as high speed launches and gunboats . . ."

I continued to wait, knowing that Ferlyn would eventually get to the point.

"... do not have the range of information that you or Dichartyn possess, but from what I have seen, the recent requests from the Naval Command suggest a re-focusing on ships more capable of engaging the Ferran dreadnoughts ..."

When I finally left Ferlyn, more than a few thoughts, many of them conflicting, were swirling through my mind.

Vendrei morning I actually woke without a headache and with the feeling that, despite all the bruises, some of which were slightly sore to the touch, I might actually be nearing a full recovery. That assumed that I could anticipate troubles before they impacted me personally. Otherwise, I'd end up injured or worse once more. I did do a few more of the morning exercises, and they didn't hurt all that much.

After seeing Seliora and Diestrya off in the duty coach, I hurried to my study, getting there a quint before seventh glass, because I wanted to look over the recent reports to see if I'd overlooked anything about High Holder Ruelyr. I'd barely finished confirming that there weren't any recent reports on Ruelyr when Ralyea arrived. He was the only one of the imagers whom I had not yet met since becoming his preceptor.

Ralyea didn't quite look at me as he came into the study. "Good morning, sir."

I laughed at the timidity of his presence and speech. Dichartyn's notes had indicated that both were a problem. He appeared paralyzed at my reaction.

"Ralyea . . . I don't bite. I don't even nip, and I'm not nearly so clever with words or arguments as Master Dichartyn was. What I'm interested in was what he was interested in. I want you to become the best imager that you can. Do you know what one of the first things he said to me was, years ago?"

"No, sir." His voice still trembled.

"He told me that there were bold imagers and old imagers, but there were no bold old imagers. He was right. But that's only half the story. The other half is that an excessively cautious imager accomplishes absolutely nothing."

The young third said nothing.

"Have you ever watched a turtle walk, Ralyea?"

He frowned. "Ah . . . yes, sir. Not in years, sir, I mean."

"Tell me. Can a turtle go anywhere by keeping its head inside its shell?"

"No, sir."

"And what happens if a giant land lizard or a heron comes upon a turtle in the open, even inside its shell?"

"Ah . . ."

"Yes?"

"It probably flips it over and kills it."

"On the other hand, what happens if the turtle hurries out of the open into shelter before any predators appear?" I smiled. "What's the point of talking about turtles? As applied to you?"

He didn't answer, and I forced myself to wait, just looking at him.

After what seemed a full quint, he finally stammered, "You're . . . saying that even with shells . . . or shields . . . there's a time to move . . . to act."

"And?"

"Sometimes . . . doing nothing behind shields . . ." He looked at me.

"Let me put it simply. Even a turtle has to stick its neck out to get anywhere. An imager who isn't willing to stick his neck out—cautiously, mind you—won't get any place and will end up in as much trouble, if not more, than an excessively bold imager. Keep that in mind."

After that, we went over his assignments and readings, and I asked him to re-read the section of the history dealing with the events leading to the formation of the Collegium and the first Council. When he left, I almost felt as though I'd been doing manual labor, but I had half a glass to check the reports Kahlasa brought me after Ralyea left. There was nothing more on either Ruelyr or Johanyr.

At least the walk across the quadrangle to the duty coach station refreshed me, even with the chill blustery wind.

As I sat in the duty coach, headed northward on West River Road, I realized why Master Dichartyn had often been so hard to find—and I was far from doing all that I probably should have been. Ferlyn's words, or their implications, still nagged at me. The drive took only slightly less than a glass, since the "L'Excelsis" estate of the Suyriens was three milles from Imagisle, although it was closer to one and a half as a raven flew, because both the road and the River Aluse wound their way north. Still, that was far closer than Suyrien's main estate, some fifteen milles south of L'Excelsis, if also on the river.

The "smaller" L'Excelsis estate was located on a hill overlooking the river. Surprisingly, to me, the walls were less than three yards in height, and there was but a single guard in the gatehouse, who opened the gates and waved the gray Collegium coach through for the drive to the mansion—not quite a chateau, since it was a comparatively modest two-story gray stone structure on the hillcrest a mere hundred yards from end to end. The trim was crimson, and the roof tiles well-kept but weathered slate.

A single footman stepped out from the portico to greet me, and Frydryk was waiting in the hexagonal foyer.

I inclined my head to him. "I'm sorry to intrude at this time, but I'm afraid that your father's death will not be the only one if we can't track down those responsible quickly."

"I understand." He gestured to the door on his left, then turned.

I followed him into a study whose front windows, their pale blue hangings drawn back, overlooked the River Aluse and its gray swirling waters. Floor-to-ceiling bookcases covered the inside wall facing the windows. A small writing desk was set before the windows, with three yards of polished parquet flooring between the desk chair and a circular table with four chairs.

Frydryk took the chair facing the windows. I took the one to his right.

"What would you like to know?" he asked.

"Several things. First, when we had dinner with you and Kandryl, you alluded to why your father had paid a visit to High Holder Ruelyr. I'd appreciate it very much if you'd expand on that. You'd mentioned his problems with low justice, but it wasn't just that, was it?"

"It is a High Holder matter, Rhenn."

"Was it about the elveweed traced to his lands? And the fact that his lands were so heavily mortgaged that he had no other way to meet the banque's terms but to accept a questionable lease and turn the other eye?" The last part was only a guess, but I couldn't see any other reason for a High Holder to get involved . . . except by ignorance or stupidity.

"I shouldn't say. Really."

I smiled pleasantly. "There's already an investigation under way, and possibly a justiciary inquiry, you know. It will come out, and you wouldn't want more holders or factors to die when everyone will know before long anyway. Was he gaoling tenants under low justice to keep them from reporting the elveweed?"

"Father didn't know. He had heard that Ruelyr, and some others, had been incarcerating malefactors longer than they should have. He wanted to find out more."

"Did he?"

"He didn't say much when he came back, except that he couldn't help Ruelyr any more. He was worried. He said that Ruelyr blamed him for his troubles. Father didn't say why. He only said that Ruelyr was living in the past, and that he wouldn't listen. He told me to avoid him because Ruelyr's actions would bring him down, sooner or later."

"He didn't say any more than that?"

Frydryk shook his head.

"Isn't most of Ruelyr's worth tied up in land?"

Frydryk nodded. "He has a few manufactories, but they're really just to supply his lands."

"What does Alynkya think about him?"

"Ah . . . I haven't asked her."

"You should ask her . . . about many things. Women often see what we miss. Her eyes may be the only pair besides your own that you can trust." I paused, then asked, "How are the shipworks doing?"

Frydryk blinked, as if disconcerted by the apparent change of subject. "We're doing well enough with building merchanters and the like. We're finishing up a fast frigate for the Naval Command in a few weeks, but it will be the last, until . . ." He shrugged.

"Despite your father's position, he had great difficulty in persuading the rest of the Council of the need for more modern vessels. That's what I understood."

"That's true enough. Father even agreed to a fixed-price contract for the first fast battlecruiser. We would have lost tens of thousands of golds on it, and the Council still wouldn't agree."

That was something I hadn't known. "Who was the most opposed to the contract?"

"Councilor Glendyl, in spite of all he said in public." A touch of bitterness shaded his words.

"Wouldn't he have supplied all the engines and boilers?"

"He had a contract with father, splitting the profits."

"And he would have shared in the losses?"

Frydryk shook his head. "He would have broken even. Father would have taken the losses." He paused. "Just on the first ship. That was so the Council could see how much better it was."

"What did Glendyl say?"

"He said that he'd be Namer-cursed if he'd forgo a profit because the Council was too stupid to do what was right. He told father that he and the other High Holders either had to change the way Solidar was governed or that the realities of modern technology would take care of it, one way or another."

"That sounds like a threat of sorts."

"Father just laughed afterwards. He said that Glendyl understood golds, but not people, and that was why he accomplished so little in the Council."

"Whereas Caartyl understands people, but not golds?"

"I suppose you could put it that way."

"Have you ever spent much time with either Glendyl or Caartyl?"

"No. I've exchanged pleasantries. That's about it."

"Did your father ever deal with Sea-Marshal Geuffryt?"

"I don't know. He never mentioned that name."

"Juniae D'Shendael?"

Frydryk raised his eyebrows. "It wasn't a good idea even to mention her name around father."

From what I'd heard, I wasn't surprised.

Abruptly, he looked at me, then frowned.

"What is it?" I asked.

"I hesitate to say this, but. . . . Rhenn, do you know how many High Holders aren't . . . how should I put it . . . extraordinarily effusive when your name is mentioned?"

I managed a wry smile. "Besides you, Kandryl, Alynkya, and Iryela . . . I'd be amazed if any were even politely effusive."

"Father alluded to matters . . ."

"Your father was a thoughtful High Holder, especially in considering the interests of all the people of Solidar. Intelligent as most High Holders are, few approach his breadth of understanding." I was probably overstating the case, but, if Suyrien hadn't told his sons, except indirectly, how Kandryl had come to be Ryel D'Alte, I wasn't about to. In such matters, I trusted Suyrien's judgment about other High Holders. Unhappily, it meant that the Collegium would have more High Holder resentments to deal with because I was more visible and more senior.

I didn't want to press Frydryk, nor to answer his implied question, and I replied by saying, "There were some High Holder matters that affected the Collegium, and some of them weren't pleased with the way I was involved. Your father felt that I'd done the best I could, given the situation. He was always fair-minded that way."

"Yes, he was."

"Did he ever mention Glendyl being pressured by Haebyn?"

"The only thing I can recall along those lines was when he said Glendyl didn't understand that Solidar wasn't Ferrum, and that he'd have to learn to deal with Haebyn and the others."

I asked a few more questions, and when it was clear that I wasn't learning any more, I stood and thanked him, profusely, and then departed.

By the time I got back to Imagisle and my study, it was second glass.

Schorzat appeared before I had my winter cloak off and hung up.

"Rhenn, after we talked about Geuffryt last week, I got to thinking. I remembered that Maitre Poincaryt had mentioned something about him, and I dug out my notes. It's not much, but I thought you'd like to know. This was two years ago, at a reception here in L'Excelsis. Maitre Poincaryt didn't say where, even when I asked him. Geuffryt was talking to the top Sea-Marshal—Valeun. He only said a few words before Valeun glared at him." Schorzat smiled.

"They must have been interesting words."

"Geuffryt said something to the effect that he was tired of High Holder control and stupidity because they didn't understand either war or economics, and that the Collegium didn't help matters. Valeun said maybe three words. Geuffryt turned pale and left the reception right then."

"I didn't see anything about that in the files."

"Maitre Poincaryt mentioned it to me when Maitre Dichartyn was out of town on an inspection trip. I told Maitre Dichartyn, but I didn't give him a written report."

"I appreciate your tracking that down. Thank you. Have you or Kahlasa found out anything about barges?"

"We probably won't get a report on them until Lundi."

When Schorzat left, I thought about what he'd told me. By themselves, Geuffryt's words meant little, but I had the feeling there well might be more.

I left my study a bit early so that I could ride out with the duty coach to pick up Seliora and have the driver drop all three of us at my parents' house for a dinner that was more obligation than anything else.

Seliora looked tired when I collected them. So I carried Diestrya to the coach and played with her. Seliora closed her eyes. She might have been dozing, or just resting.

Mother was the one who opened the door, and her eyes went straight to me. "Your face—what happened to you?" she demanded.

"A few stones," I replied.

My mother immediately looked to Seliora. "A few?"

"Quite a few. He got bruised protecting us. He couldn't leave Imagisle until a few days ago."

"Let them get in the house, Maelyna," groused Father from the rear of the foyer.

Once we were in the family parlor, where Culthyn waited, Father looked at me. "That was a Collegium coach, and the word is that some senior imagers were killed in the attack on the Collegium."

"I have a new position at the Collegium," I admitted. "I'm no longer a Civic Patrol captain."

"Did you get promoted?" interjected Culthyn.

"Yes. I'm a Maitre D'Esprit now."

"Do you get paid more?"

"I do. Enough." I managed a laugh. "We're here for dinner, not an interrogation."

"Are you sure you're all right?" asked Mother.

"I'm fine," I insisted. Thankfully, Seliora didn't comment on my slight exaggeration.

While I answered Father's and Culthyn's questions about the state of L'Excelsis, Solidar, and the Collegium, Mother slipped away. She returned shortly with a tray of beverages. I was given hot spiced wine—apparently my bruises removed my choice.

Rather than keep answering, or avoiding answering, I took a sip of the wine, then looked at Father and said, "I've been hearing that some of the factors aren't exactly pleased with the High Holders after what's happened here in Solidar and in the war with Ferrum."

My father laughed. "There's no such thing as a happy factor. If times are bad, he worries that they'll get worse. If they're good, he worries that they won't last."

"What do you think about Councilor Glendyl?"

Father snorted. "He just thinks he's a factor. He's wealthier than most High Holders, and he acts worse than they do. The High Holders provide lodging to their tenants and workers. Glendyl pays his workers but a pittance more and provides nothing, and complains about that."

"Councilor Caartyl has hinted at that," I offered.

"He's almost as bad," Father went on after a swallow of his Dhuensa. "To hear him talk, you'd think that everything produced by hand was a work of high art. The artisans just want to keep things comfortable for themselves, like the spinners and the carders did in my father's time. There's a place for solid goods everyone can buy, and a place for art, but most people don't want to pay for art when they buy work-day garments or potatoes. Caartyl thinks the factors should pay higher taxes so everyone can have art . . . the Navy isn't much better . . . some of those Sea-Marshals aren't beyond scuttling their own ships if it would get them a new battlecruiser, and Glendyl would probably sell them the tools to do it. . . ."

I just sipped and listened.

On Samedi morning, I did do nearly the full version of Clovyl's exercises, as well as the run, which I hadn't done before, and the resultant tiredness convinced me, more than Seliora's insistence, that I had a ways to go before I was fully recovered. I didn't tell her that. Then, the way she looked at me when I returned to the house, I didn't have to.

So I was careful over the weekend, although I did spend more than a few glasses in my Collegium study going over reports—and maps—and older reports buried in the bottom drawers of the two cases. I also spent time taking care of Diestrya so that my very tired wife got some rest as well, and during the one time when they both were sleeping, I checked over the repairs that the imagers had made to the rest of the furniture—adequate, but I wouldn't have wanted Shomyr or Shelim to have seen it.

On Solayi, we attended services at the anomen, and one part of Isola's homily had Seliora quietly nodding. I agreed as well, even if I didn't nod.

". . . the Nameless is neither young nor old, but eternal and everlasting. The Nameless is neither finite nor infinite, but stands beyond our measurements. Nor is the Nameless man or woman . . . These descriptions of the attributes of the Nameless have been set forth for centuries. Then, why is it that people think of the Nameless as a powerful male figure? Could not the Nameless be powerful and female? Or powerful and both male and female? Or powerful without gender?

"For all that is said, we bring our own concepts to the anomen, and because the Nameless is powerful and because in our world men are powerful, all too many assume that the Nameless must, in some fashion, resemble a powerful man. Why? Is not a lightning bolt powerful? Are not the storms of the ocean powerful? Are not the rays of the summer sun filled with power and heat? But who of sound mind and common sense would assert that lightning, storms, or the sun are a man of power?"

Isola went on to assert that the Nameless, by definition, was beyond mere human labels and descriptions. That might well have been true, but it didn't stop people from labeling and describing what they had never seen or never might—or describing badly what they had seen.

As we walked back to the house, under the pale reddish light of a full Erion, an image flashed in front of me . . . or in my mind, but it was so vivid I knew it was another Pharsi farsight flash. Yet, in some ways, it was anything but vivid, because all I could see were what looked to be a mille of large stone buildings, and over them to the right, huge hulking cranes rising on the far side of the structures. Nothing flashed. Nothing flared. Stones didn't fall around me. Then the flash was gone.

I had to stop for a moment and check where I was, but I was still on Imagisle, with the River Aluse to my left, and the stone walk leading north to our house before me.

"Rhenn? Are you all right?" asked Seliora.

"I had a flash . . . but it was just a scene, some sort of endless manufactory. Nothing happened. No explosions, no fires, nothing like that."

"Then . . . you saw it just before something could happen. Was it familiar?"

"No." I shook my head. "I've never been there."

"Maybe you need to go there."

Seliora was probably right—except I had no idea where "there" might be.

Later that evening, after Seliora had sung Diestrya to sleep, we sat side by side on the settee in front of the stove in the family parlor.

"Rhenn . . . ?"

I smiled and put my arm around her, but she sat up straight.

"I've been thinking."

"About what?"

"Odelia and Kolasyn. It's more than that." She paused. "We were so close for so long. Even now, she's so wary when we talk."

"I know how close you were." I laughed softly. "I couldn't ever get to be alone with you except on the small terrace at NordEste Design."

"It hurts. I didn't do anything at all."

"She knows that I couldn't do more than I did. But what we know and what we feel aren't always the same. I wouldn't be surprised if she still feels that, if I'd done something more, Haerasyn would still be alive. She may believe that if you'd pressed me I might have changed things."

"You've done more than anyone else. She knows that. She even said so."

"That's not the question, really, is it?" I asked gently.

"No. You're right. What we know and what we feel, deep inside, aren't the same. People are like that. Sometimes it's the ones closest to you—especially the close friends and family—who hurt you the most. But . . . it's so sad. It shouldn't be that way."

"No . . . it shouldn't. But it is. It always is."

"You're thinking of your brother, aren't you?"

"I did what I thought was right . . . and he paid for it, and he never even knew why."

"It was all Johanyr's fault . . . and everyone in his family paid. He got off the easiest."

"And now no one even knows where he is, except that he's likely stolen thousands of golds from his sister."

"Why did he wait so long . . . if he could have done it all along?" asked Seliora.

"Maybe he couldn't have. He can't see well enough even to write a cheque or a fund transfer request, and no one else is missing from Mont D'Glace."

"Will anyone ever find him?"

"Not unless whoever helped him betrays him, and if he managed it alone, he won't be found if he doesn't want to be."

"That seems wrong."

I didn't say anything. I only knew I wouldn't want to be almost blind and in hiding, even with two thousand in golds.

On Lundi, I compromised, doing the exercises and only running a bit more than a mille, and I returned to the house, feeling only reasonably uncomfortable. Once I got to my study at the Collegium, after reading the morning newsheets, which both reported the loss of more ships from the northern fleet, given my conversation with Frydryk on Vendrei and more research and thought over the weekend, I decided that a conversation with the good Councilor Glendyl was definitely in order. While Maitre Dyana had suggested that she and Rholyn would brief me, she hadn't exactly forbidden me to meet with the Councilors. Implied, but not forbidden. So just before eighth glass on Lundi morning, I took a duty coach to the Council Chateau.

While all the obdurate guards were polite and apparently pleased to see me, Baratyn hurried out of his main floor study before I could make my way to the upper level.

"Maitre Rhennthyl . . . I didn't expect you."

I ignored the various implications. "I assume Glendyl is here."

"Why . . . yes. He's been here since before seventh glass."

"Good. I thought he and I might have a few things to talk over."

"He met with Maitre Rholyn just yesterday."

That didn't make me any happier. But I smiled. "Then Glendyl shouldn't be all that surprised to see me."

"He isn't expecting you?"

"He should be. Whether he is or not remains to be seen."

"I'd best escort you, then," Baratyn said. "Otherwise, he might think you're not who you say you are and bolt the door or shoot at you."

"He carries a pistol?"

"Two of them. He's reputedly a very good shot. That wouldn't hurt you, but the Collegium could look foolish."

"He would look even more foolish," I pointed out, "and that would be far worse for the Collegium."

For a moment, Baratyn was silent. Then he nodded and turned toward the Grand Foyer. Since Glendyl's study was on the southwest corner, taking the formal staircase was actually the fastest way there.

"Has anyone from the Naval Command been here to talk to Caartyl or Glendyl?" I asked as I walked alongside Baratyn.

"No. I have the feeling they're waiting for Ramsael to take over the Executive Council."

That Sea-Marshal Valeun would avoid Glendyl in the middle of an undeclared war with Ferrum said something, but what . . . that was another question. It also didn't make sense, and that meant I didn't know something. "Is that because they're afraid that the full Council will undo anything Glendyl does right now?"

"I couldn't say, Maitre Rhennthyl."

"Or is it that Glendyl now has the power to ask penetrating questions if they press him?"

"That's more likely."

"About the conduct of the war or about the organization and structure of the Naval Command?"

"Glendyl wouldn't second-guess fleet commanders."

"So it's likely that he thinks the Naval Command is overstaffed and inefficient."

"There are more than a few high-paid marshals and senior commanders north of here, and, from the point of view of a factor who has to watch every copper, there might be some questions about their necessity."

"Glendyl knows that summoning them to ask such questions would be perceived as too high-handed and would likely backfire because he won't be in charge for that long, and they won't come asking for anything because then he could ask those questions."

"That would be my guess."

I laughed. "It's likely a very good guess." I also suspected that Dichartyn had probably felt the same way, but those sorts of calculations weren't something that anyone committed to paper, even in the Collegium. The problem was that assessments not committed to paper tended to get lost if the assessor died or vanished. And that was another bit of circumstantial evidence, not the kind I could ever bring before the Justiciary or the Council, but real enough.

When we reached the dark wooden door on the southwest corner, Baratyn rapped on it smartly. "Councilor, it's Baratyn. Maitre Rhennthyl is here from the Collegium to see you."

There was a long silence from the other side of the door before Glendyl replied, "Do have him come in."

I opened the door and stepped into the corner study, with windows on both the south and west outside walls. At first glance, standing beside the wide writing desk, Glendyl was totally unremarkable. He was of medium height, with thinning black hair and pale green eyes. A second glance revealed the hardness of the eyes and the set to a more than rugged jaw.

As I stepped forward, for a moment, I felt cooler air, as if Glendyl had opened one of his study windows for a moment, then closed it. Behind me, Baratyn shut the door quietly as he left.

"Good morning, Councilor," I offered pleasantly.

"Good morning. I understand you've taken over Maitre Dichartyn's position. I always thought you'd go far, Maitre Rhennthyl, even when you were first here. Something about you, I suppose. If you hadn't turned out to be an imager . . ." He shook his head. "Guildmaster Reayalt said you could have been one of the great portraiturists, and your sister may well become the most noted factoria of our time." He smiled, but did not sit or gesture toward the chairs before his desk. "What can I do for you today?"

"I thought it might be a good idea for us to talk, Councilor. There are several matters at hand. I'd like your observations about the Naval Command's use of Council funds for its operations and administration . . ."

"The way you phrased that, Maitre Rhennthyl, suggests that you already know my concerns about the administrative structure of the Naval Command. The purpose of a navy is to control the oceans and to make them safe for our merchanters. That doesn't require that every new vessel be bigger than its predecessor. It does require determining how many of what kind of vessels are necessary and building and operating those. Golds spent for purposes other than building, equipping, and operating those ships should be kept to an absolute minimum. Every factor knows that. That's why there are few studies for supervisors in my manufactories. Supervisors should be supervising, or checking accounts, or making certain that materials are ordered and used in a timely fashion. None of those activities require large or luxurious studies or conference rooms. Nor elaborate dining facilities. Nor assistants to the assistants of senior supervisors." He raised his thick trimmed eyebrows. "I note that the Collegium has operated effectively for centuries without separate dining facilities for masters and without coaches and transport reserved for specific masters."

I smiled. "That's very true."

"Need I say more?"

"Do you think matters have gotten worse . . . recently?"

"I would scarce say that they're better."

I nodded.

"What else did you wish to discuss?"

"The more I've looked into Ferran activities here in Solidar, the more I seem to be finding all too many . . . shall we say . . . oddities."

"Everything associated with the Ferrans is odd to people in Solidar. Most here don't think in the same way they do."

"You've obviously thought about it, Councilor."

"It's time for a brisk walk, Maitre Rhennthyl." His right eye twitched, more than I recalled from my time in security at the Council Chateau. "Just around the Chateau grounds. Would you care to join me?"

"I'd be pleased." Whatever Glendyl wanted to say, he didn't want anyone overhearing. While the listening tubes did not go to any Councilor's study, it was clear Glendyl wasn't counting on that.

He pulled on a heavy black wool cloak and moved toward the door. I opened it and stepped out into the corridor, leaving it for him to close.

I said nothing until we neared the steps, when I asked, "How did you get started in the business of making engines and locomotives?"

"My father made pumps for the mines, but the engines were terrible. There was this artisan who made a different engine. It worked well, but it was too expensive and took too long to build. I worked with him to build a better and cheaper steam engine. Since I had the rights, I applied the same idea to everything that I could." He chuckled.

"You make it sound very easy and simple," I replied. "I doubt that it was either." My eyes passed over the twin statues of angelias at the base of the steps, and I couldn't help thinking of Father.

"Good ideas are always simple. Making them work is the hard part. That's like the Council. More than a few Councilors have ideas they think are good, but half the time they don't think about the implications and effects for everyone else." He paused, resting his hand on the curve of the balustrade, before marching toward the main foyer and the outer doors on the south side of the Chateau. "Your sister is hard-working and very practical. I'd rather have her on the Council than half the Councilors now serving, who think that everything should stay the way it's always been. Things never stay the same. If Rex Charyn hadn't had enough sense to see that the time of single hereditary rulers was past, why, we'd be in the same pickle as the Jariolans. He saw that trade was what counted, not lands and who could raise an army with bows and blades. Now and in the years ahead, engines and machines will count more than artisans and craft or trade in raw materials. Too many in Solidar don't see that."

"Or that the Council needs to reflect that change?"

"It'd be best if the Council led that change. It won't. We'll be fortunate if the Council even reflects that change in a generation. By then it may be too late. We'll be buying goods from Ferrum, getting poorer by the year and wondering what happened." He snorted as he walked through the central archway and toward the stone steps, angling his path toward the east gardens.

"The idea of change doesn't come easily," I pointed out. "The thought of women on the Council upsets more than a few."

"That's because they think of women like Madame D'Shendael, who is charming and writes and speaks well and never met a payroll or a production or delivery deadline. Give me a woman like your sister—"

At that moment, as we were halfway down the main south steps, I heard the faintest *crack*. Beside me, Glendyl began to crumple, redness spreading across his chest.

Instinctively, I imaged caustic back along the path the bullet had taken, even as I grabbed Glendyl. I didn't want any more shots coming our way. Then after easing the Councilor onto a wide stone step and quickly studying the position of his wound, I imaged what I hoped was a block around the return vein to the heart.

Nearly instantly, the spread of blood stopped . . . mostly. For a moment, I wondered if that was because I'd killed Glendyl. But he was still breathing, and I could feel a pulse.

"Not supposed to happen," mumbled the Councilor. ". . . Not that way." His eyes fluttered and closed. He was still breathing.

What wasn't supposed to happen that way? Had Glendyl taken me for a walk to get me shot? He should have known better than that, and, besides, I hadn't felt a thing. If a bullet had been aimed at me and had struck my shields, I certainly would have felt it.

I heard boots on stone and glanced up.

Dartazn sprinted down the side steps. "Rhenn! What happened?"

"Someone shot the Councilor. I think I've stopped the worst of the bleeding, and I've got shields around us both. But we'll need Maitre Draffyd as soon as possible. Use my duty coach! It's by the security gate. If you can, tell Baratyn to get someone to look across the square, in the garden in front and to the side of the Hall of Justice."

"Yes, sir!" He was off, and for once I was very glad of those long legs.

Glendyl's eyes fluttered, then closed again, but he was still breathing, and only a little blood was seeping from the wound. I could only hope I'd done the chest imaging right. It seemed like the oozing blood was from the muscles in his chest.

Before long, two obdurate guards in their dark uniforms appeared, and stationed themselves on each side of us.

Even so, it was half a glass before Draffyd appeared, slipped in beside me. "What did you do?"

"I put a block around the return vein. That's all. I was afraid more would strain his heart."

"Good. You did just enough." Draffyd knelt beside the fallen Councilor. "His pulse is still all right. It's not as good as I'd like, but there's not that much blood. With some luck, we'll pull him through."

"Can I do anything else?"

"No."

The curtness of his reply was a clear indication enough that I was super-fluous now. I moved back. As I stood, I saw Baratyn standing a few yards away and walked toward him.

"Will he make it?"

"I don't know, but Draffyd's hopeful."

"I thought Draffyd was the only medical imager."

"He is, but I can do some things. Draffyd gave me some training."

"For that, Glendyl ought to be grateful." Baratyn shook his head. "He won't be."

I didn't dispute that, but before I could have said more, a messenger hurried up.

"Maitres! Martyl's found the shooter. He's over there." The messenger pointed southward to where Martyl stood, waving, by the wall in front of the low garden to the east of the promenade leading to the Hall of Justice.

"I need to look into that," I told Baratyn, nodding before hurrying down the remaining steps and across the ring road to the front of the Justice gardens where Martyl stood waiting.

"He didn't get very far, sir," Martyl said. "What did you do?"

"Imaged caustic back along the track of the bullet."

The security imager tilted his head, quizzically, then pointed. "He's just behind the wall. He was alone. There's only one set of boot-prints."

The body was that of a muscular but slender man dressed in black gar-ments under a tattered light brown cloak. His face, the part that wasn't burned by the caustic, was contorted in agony. A long sniper's rifle lay less than a yard away.

The only items in his wallet were coins, some eight golds, four silvers, and three coppers.

When we finished searching him, I straightened and looked at Martyl. "If you'd take care of the body."

"Yes, sir." He paused. "Do you think he's another Ferran agent?"

"Most likely, but proving it might be difficult." Since he was dead, we didn't have to, and I took my leave of Martyl. I did have to take a hack, since Draffyd had doubtless used the duty coach to convey Glendyl to the infirmary.

When I returned to the Collegium, I gave Schorzat and Kahlasa a quick summary of what had happened and then went upstairs, glad that Maitre Dyana was in her study.

She motioned for me to close the door, not that she needed to, since I was already doing just that. I took the chair on the end, the one closest to her and the one not in the sunlight.

"I hear that someone shot Glendyl. How did that come about, and what, exactly, were you doing at the Council Chateau?"

"It came about because everything that I've discovered doesn't make much sense, and I wanted to see Glendyl's reaction. I also wanted him to see me. First, I asked him about his concerns about the Naval Command's efficiency . . ." I went on to tell her exactly what had happened.

When I finished, she nodded slowly. "Glendyl thought you'd be the target, and he'd been assured that whatever weapon was used would penetrate your shields. But that was never their intention. What haven't you told me about the shooter?"

"Under a tattered brown cloak, he was wearing the same black, light-absorbing clothes that the agents killed in Third District wore. Most likely all were Ferrans, and Glendyl had to have known something."

"Even if that's true, we can't make a charge like that without proof."

"I'm not charging anyone," I pointed out. "I'm merely observing."

"You can't say a word about the implications involved there, not without actual proof."

"I know." I smiled. "But if Glendyl gets better, he won't be able to avoid my questions, not since he's in our infirmary. He should stay there until he's better, don't you think?"

"I would agree to that, but you can't question him until Maitre Draffyd says he's up to it."

"Does this make Caartyl acting head of the Executive Council?"

"In theory. After what's happened to Suyrien and Glendyl, he may not be so anxious."

"If he is, that might say something."

"He's too politically astute to show enthusiasm," Dyana replied.

"But it's a month before the Council is scheduled to convene."

"I've asked Maitre Rholyn to have Caartyl issue a call for a special meeting of the Council a week from today. Caartyl declined, unless the meeting could be two weeks from now."

"The thirtieth?"

"I would have liked it to be earlier, but he felt that they couldn't get a quorum with a week's notice. The call should be on its way tonight." Her eyes hardened. "None of this explains who was behind the bombardment of the Collegium. What else have you found out about that?"

"The barges didn't come from this section of the river. We should know where they did come from in the next few days." *I hope.*

"You aren't telling me everything."

"No, Maitre. I'm only telling you what I know and what I can reasonably suspect."

"You still don't do finesse as well as you should, Rhenn."

"I probably never will, Maitre."

She shook her head. "Let me know whenever you find out anything."

I stood and made my way back to my study.

I was still trying to sort out matters when, at just after half past the second glass of the afternoon, Kahlasa and Schorzat appeared at my study door.

"Come in. You both look grim."

They did, and Kahlasa closed the door. They sat down.

"We have a very good regional in Solis," Schorzat said.

I concentrated to recall who the regional was, then nodded. "Eslyana. She's even a Maitre D'Aspect. I take it that she sent some information on barges."

Schorzat looked to Kahlasa.

She put several sheets on my desk. "Here's her report. There are only three barges and a tug that can't be accounted for. That's of the ones large enough to carry the weight of a bombard. It's not just the weight, but the deck and hold strength for that much weight concentrated in a single spot. They were leased from one Leavytt, a transport factor in Solis. They never returned. Leavytt put in a claim with L'Excelsis Indemnity. They're still investigating, but . . ."

"They have a problem since someone blew up their main building here?" I suggested.

"No . . ." Kahlasa said slowly. "They'll have to pay, but Eslyana managed to find out a bit more. The lease contract was forged. That is, it was a standard Naval Command contract. It was on the right paper and with the correct watermarks, and with the correct names and seals, and the signatures were also apparently by the right people—except they don't match the real signatures. They're close, unless you examine them carefully."

"There's more, isn't there?"

"It's a real contract, and all the formalities and procedures were perfect. Leavytt's been through this for years. He did say that he didn't recognize any of the crew who took the tug and barges, except for the tug captain. He'd seen him before, but he doesn't recall the man's name. Leavytt didn't know the subcommander who handled it for the Naval Command, but the subcommander knew everyone. He even mentioned the last lease and the Commander who had handled it. He said that the Commander was his superior. The contract deposit cleared before they took possession of the tug and barges. It was a draft on the Banque D'Rivages for five thousand golds. Leavytt said lease drafts were usually drawn on the Banque D'Excelsis, but he'd had one or two over the years on the Banque D'Rivages."

"Whoever leased the tug and barges had considerable background in setting up this sort of thing," I said blandly.

"There's no way to prove it, but someone well-placed in the Naval Command or the Naval Bureau had to be involved," suggested Kahlasa. "It's more likely to be the Naval Bureau, because they handle supplies and leases and transport."

Or someone who knows the Naval Bureau well.

"They also had access to five thousand golds, and we'd know if five thousand golds had been recently transferred from Ferrum or elsewhere or converted to a draft by someone . . . unusual . . ." observed Schorzat.

"You mean by someone who isn't a High Holder or a wealthy factorius?" I asked.

"All large fund deposits from foreign sources have to be reported in time of war."

"They could have done it years before."

"That's possible."

After they finished, we all trooped back up to see Maitre Dyana, where I let Kahlasa and Schorzat report what they'd told me. Then she excused them and, after her study door was closed, looked to me. "The Naval Command will deny any involvement."

"I know. I don't plan to talk to them yet, not before I look into other aspects of it first."

"How long will that take?"

"As long as it takes." I offered a smile. "You know I've never been one to dawdle, even when I should."

Once I was back in my study, I just sat at my desk, thinking. If the Naval Command happened to be involved, would Valeun have taken such pains to avoid Glendyl so obviously at a time when it was clear that Solidar needed more ships? Or was the avoidance merely to buy time before something else happened? Or had the Ferrans infiltrated the Naval Command at a lower level years before and transferred those funds equally early?

There was another possibility, and I wrote a quick note to Iryela asking to call on her. She was one source who might be able to answer some questions I didn't want others knowing I was asking, and she wouldn't say a word. I had Beleart send it by special messenger.

After that, I decided there was little enough more I could do, and I left the study.

As I walked back across the quadrangle and turned toward the house, and Seliora, I couldn't help but think about Seliora's words. *The ones closest to you are the ones who hurt you the most.* But . . . closest in what ways? That was another question.

First thing on Mardi morning, I was at the infirmary, looking for Draffyd.

As soon as I walked toward him, before I could speak, the medical imager said, "Clovyl said you're exercising. That's fine, but don't push."

"That's not why—"

"I know. Yes, it's likely he'll recover. No, you can't talk to him. Maybe late tomorrow. Maybe." He paused, then asked, "Is it that urgent?"

"I don't know," I replied honestly.

"If you, of all imagers, aren't certain, it can wait. Besides, he's not awake, and waking him to talk to you would put too much of a strain on him. It would on anyone."

"You're not going to let him leave?"

"Maitre Rhennthyl," Draffyd drew out my name and title, "the most honorable Councilor Glendyl isn't in any shape to go anywhere and won't be for weeks. If you hadn't been beside him and acted in instants, he would have died on the Chateau steps. I will make certain he knows that, when he's awake enough to understand . . . which he is not at present."

After that, I went back to my study, looking to see if I'd received any more reports. There were only two. One was from the Collegium at Mont D'Glace, and that merely confirmed that they knew nothing more about Johanyr's disappearance. The other was from the Civic Patrol Commander in Alkyra, reporting that a grain freighter scheduled to leave for the Abierto Isles had burned at the pier. Unfortunately, there were no details about what had caused the fire or who owned the vessel.

That led me into thinking about the lack of information, especially the lack of consistent information. The Council and the Collegium received reports from all over Solidar, but they varied greatly in the quality and even the types of information. Both the Council and I, and presumably Maitre Dichartyn before me, had to guess and fill in with estimates. Both the Council and the Collegium needed better information. I doubted that the Ferrans had that problem.

And, as for the Ferrans, why, for the sake of the Nameless, would Glendyl have gotten involved with them? He was influential and wealthy, possibly wealthier than even some High Holders. What could they possibly have offered him? That didn't make any sense, either.

A knock on my study door interrupted my pondering.

"A message for you, Maitre," announced a young voice, most likely the duty prime.

"Come in."

"Yes, Maitre." The youngster, perhaps all of ten and looking most serious in his grays, scurried in, bowed his head, slipped a striped envelope onto my desk, bowed again, and hurried out. I only knew that his name was Petrion from the duty roster.

Inside the outer envelope was another envelope with a note card inside. Iryela had written simply that she would be available to see me any day of the present week at any time before the first glass of the afternoon, except on Jeudi, when she would be unavailable after midday.

Since I wasn't getting anywhere by sitting in the study and waiting for inspiration to strike me and since I had no idea where else I might go to find out more information, I immediately pulled on my winter cloak and headed for the duty coach station, stopping only briefly to let the duty secondus know where I was headed.

I crossed the quadrangle against a bitter biting wind from the northwest. Although the sky was clear, I had the feeling we might have snow by evening— or sometime during the night. The inside of the coach was only chill, but I felt sorry for Lebryn, although he was well bundled up. The roads were clear, but it took almost a glass to reach the Ryel estate north of L'Excelsis.

The footman who greeted me at Iryela's estate bowed and said, "Maitre Rhennthyl . . . if you'll be long, there's a place in the carriage house for your coach and driver."

"Thank you. I'll be long enough, and they could stand to get out of the wind." I turned to Lebryn. "They'll direct you to the carriage house."

"Yes, sir. Thank you."

I had to admit that I was surprised to find Iryela, attired in deep blue trousers and tunic, standing in the foyer to greet me. "It's good to see you, Rhenn. Kandryl was pleased that you came to his father's memorial service."

"Suyrien was an honorable man, and he was Kandryl's father." I paused. "And it has been a trying time for you as well."

"It has . . . and for you." After a moment, she added, "The private drawing room is most comfortable in the morning, with the sun and the stove."

"Whatever you think best. I do appreciate your seeing me on such short notice."

"How could I not?" Her tone was light, with seriousness beneath, as she turned to head toward the left-hand corridor. "Besides, it's very quiet here in the mornings, even with the children, since they're at their lessons, and Kandryl is spending the day at the main estate—Frydryk's, that is. They're going over the finer points of their father's bequests and settlement."

I moved up beside her. "That's fairly set, isn't it."

"Oh, the bulk of everything will go to Frydryk, but there are apparently a number of smaller bequests." She smiled. "There's even a small one for Seliora, although it's really for both of you."

That there was such a bequest surprised me as well, but not the fact that it was to Seliora, because, as an imager, I could inherit nothing from anyone, and Suyrien had to have known that. "She will be pleased, if sad that she will receive it so much earlier than she should have."

"You and Seliora impressed Suyrien. He was always pleased that Kandryl and I were married."

"And you?" I asked gently.

She smiled. "It couldn't have worked out better."

I'd always thought that, but I still liked her to say it. "For both of us."

"Indeed, and you make a better friend."

As she entered the drawing room, she gestured to the small table. "Tea will be here shortly I thought you wouldn't mind that on such a chill morning."

I waited to say anything more until we were seated at the table. "I have some unusual questions . . ."

"That means they're most serious, Maitre Rhennthyl."

"Most serious, Madame Iryela D'Ryel." I matched her tone before letting my voice turn serious. "I've been trying to find any traces of Johanyr. You haven't heard from him?"

"No. I have warned all the guards that he's not to be admitted, either here or at the main estates in Rivages. How could he have just . . . disappeared?"

"He wasn't under guard, and he'd lost his ability to image."

"He's almost blind, isn't he? How could he get around?"

I didn't want to answer that directly. "With great difficulty, I suspect. But there are blind people in every town and city."

"He isn't the kind to beg or be helpless. You know that."

I did indeed. "That's very true. Has he ever written you?"

She shook her head.

"Was there anyone he was particularly close to?"

"No. He wasn't even that close to me or to Dulyk or Alynat, and he wouldn't speak or write to them after he . . . after he went to Mont D'Glace.

He never wrote me, either." The door opened, and an older woman appeared with a tray.

The tea was cardomom-flavored and welcome, since I wasn't totally warmed after the coach ride, even with the gentle heat flowing from the drawing room stove. So were the simple morning cakes.

"I had tea sent down to your driver. I'm sorry you had to come out in such weather."

"The sooner the better. Matters are not that good . . . oh . . . I forgot to tell you. An assassin shot Councilor Glendyl yesterday. He almost died, and he's at the Imagisle infirmary, but Maitre Draffyd thinks it's likely he'll recover."

"Was it the same person as shot Suyrien? Did he get away?"

"Ah . . . no. He's dead. I don't know as there's any way to tell."

"Couldn't they capture him . . ." Her words died away as she looked at me. "Did you . . . ?"

"I went to talk to Glendyl. He didn't want to talk in his study and insisted on taking a walk . . ." I gave her a quick description of what happened.

She shook her head. "If only you'd been with Suyrien . . ."

"I don't know it would have helped. They didn't shoot Glendyl in the head." I took another sip of tea and a bite of the morning cake. "Have you heard anything about why anyone would want to shoot Glendyl?"

"Me? A mere wife to High Holder Ryel?"

Behind the self-mocking tone was a certain sadness, I thought. "You've always seen and understood more than anyone else knew."

"Except you." She took refuge in sipping her tea.

I just waited, taking another swallow of tea.

Finally, she said, "There's been talk for years about how he wants to do away with all the High Holders and break up the big landholdings by applying his so-called value-added tax to lands that don't produce revenue. That's foolish when you consider that you can only harvest timberlands once a generation, if that, but he'd tax the land every year when there's only revenue from it once every thirty to a hundred years. I haven't heard anyone who thought seriously about actually shooting him, but there's not a High Holder out there who liked the idea of his being in charge of the Executive Council, even for a month. Even Caartyl would have been better, but I doubt any High Holder would commission an assassination that would hand the Executive Council over to a guildmaster."

"I can see that. But even if Glendyl did head the Executive Council for the next month, he couldn't pass tax or revenue matters. That takes two-thirds of the entire Council." *And right now, the High Holder Councilors and the single Collegium Councilor constitute one vote more than a third of the full Council.* I also had the feeling that Suyrien hadn't seen Ferlyn's figures on the numbers of High Holders.

"What is it, Rhenn?"

I laughed ruefully. "Trouble, of a different kind. I just realized something. I'm sure Maitre Dichartyn knew it, but some of this is very new to me."

"Why?"

At that point, I realized that I'd never told her what had happened, not in terms of my change of position. I'd assumed she'd known, but I'd never mentioned it, and my presence at the memorial service would have been considered normal, even if I hadn't taken over Dichartyn's duties. "Things have changed at the Collegium. Maitre Poincaryt and Maitre Dichartyn were killed in the bombardment. I'm no longer a Civic Patrol captain. The Collegium has recalled me, and I'm now a Maitre D'Esprit."

"Oh . . ." For one of the few times since I'd met her years before, Iryela looked disconcerted. "You're . . . one of the high imagers, then?"

I knew that was so, but I hadn't let myself dwell on it. "By default. Maitre Dyana is now the Maitre of the Collegium."

Iryela laughed. "No wonder Frydryk has been grumbling. A woman heading the Collegium. How did that happen?"

"She was the only Maitre D'Esprit left."

"That means . . . you're the second-ranking imager in all of Solidar. And you're here having tea with me?"

"I said it was important," I pointed out, trying to keep my tone light.

"What does Johanyr have to do with all of this?"

"I don't know. It might be nothing. It's just that he vanished just before all the attacks on L'Excelsis took place."

She shook her head. "You think he's involved, don't you?"

I shrugged. "I don't know. I worry that he is. Do you know if any of his acquaintances have heard from him?"

"Not that I know of. I used to ask, but he never wrote anyone. I'd think they would tell me if he did now, or if they'd seen him."

"Do you know if he was friendly with Geuffryt, one of the Naval Command Assistant Sea-Marshals?"

"Geuffryt?" She frowned. "Geuffryt . . ." Then she nodded. "Geuffryt D'Laevoryn-Alte. He was the youngest son. He was . . . I suppose he still is . . . some sort of relative of Juniae D'Shendael. He was friendly enough to Johanyr when Johanyr was still a boy, but he was a good ten years older. He was like a distant uncle. Then his father . . . he made some bad decisions, and he went sailing one day and never came back. I suppose that was why Geuffryt stayed with the Navy." She paused. "Why did you want to know?"

"I just wondered. I met Geuffryt several weeks ago and found out that he was a cousin of Madame D'Shendael. He seemed to know about your family." That was more than a slight exaggeration. "So I thought I'd ask. I'm trying to think of anyone Johanyr might contact."

"There really isn't. You know he was always above everyone . . . until . . ."

"I was afraid that might be the case." I smiled wryly. "I've also been watching on the other matter. So far nothing has turned up, but we have run across rumors of a few other odd funds transactions, and I can always hope that we can find out what happened."

"I do appreciate it."

"I do have one other odd question."

"Oh?"

"Do you know if there is a complete listing of all the High Holders in Solidar anywhere?"

"The Collegium doesn't have one?"

"If it does, no one knows about it."

"I don't think there is a current list. I remember my father talking about the last complete census of High Holders being done at the turn of the last century. There is a list in the library, and he did annotate it."

"Might I borrow it? Discreetly?"

"Of course." She smiled. "I will ask that you return it personally."

"I can do that."

"If you will excuse me . . ." Iryela rose.

I stood and watched her leave, but she returned immediately, handing a small bound volume over to me. "It's just a listing of names and the locations of the main lands of each High Holder." After a moment, she asked, "Do you have any other unusual questions?"

"No. I wish I did, because it would mean I knew more."

She did laugh, if softly.

"I should leave. I'm sorry I don't have better news."

"You will let me know . . . if anything . . . happens?"

"I will." I inclined my head. "And you will do the same? About Johanyr or Glendyl or anything else you think useful?"

"I will." She stood. "Congratulations. I always knew you'd do well. I'm sorry for you that it happened the way it did."

"So am I. I'm not as prepared for it as I should be."

"No. We never are. That's life. I'll walk out with you."

As we walked down the corridor, she added, "I told Kandryl times were changing, and we've been more careful than ever. He chided me for worrying . . . until all this happened. Now, he doesn't say anything."

"Except 'Yes, dearest,' " I suggested.

"He understands."

I was certain Kandryl did.

At the entry foyer, she turned to me. "Do be careful, and give our best to Seliora."

"I will indeed."

I had to wait half a quint before the duty coach reached the front entry, but that was fine with me. It was half past one by the time I got back to the Collegium, where I immediately sought out Schorzat. He and Kahlasa were in his study, with a stack of papers between them.

They both looked up. Schorzat opened his mouth, as if he were about to ask where I'd been, but then closed it for a moment before saying, "We're glad you're back."

I handed the bound list to Schorzat. "We need this copied, along with the marginal notes."

He glanced over it. "These are rather tightly held."

"I know. I couldn't find one here in the Collegium."

"It's in the locked collection in the library."

"Then get it, and copy the annotations and give me the new annotated copy." I paused only briefly. "What have you found out?"

"We've been working on the large banques. They won't give details, but they've all assured us that none of them have issued fund transfers from unusual sources."

"Is there a local branch of the Banque D'Rivages?"

"No, but Kahlasa sent a query yesterday by ironway, and we got back a reply less than a glass ago. They were kind enough to note that they had no activity of that nature whatsoever, except from their usual sources."

"Was it phrased that way?"

"Why, yes. Why?" Schorzat lifted a single sheet of heavy paper. "You can read it."

I took it and read the words. He was right.

Considering that I was one of the highest-paid imagers, and five thousand golds represented ten years' pay, there couldn't be that many people in Solidar with those kinds of assets—no more than fifteen hundred to two thousand, and probably half of those used banques in L'Excelsis. The fact that the draft had been on the Banque D'Rivages confirmed my suspicions, and so did the banque's reply, not that what we'd discovered was the kind of proof one could put before the Justiciary.

Now . . . the next questions were why Geuffryt had done it, and what I could do about it . . . if anything.

After Schorzat and Kahlasa left, I just sat down and tried to think matters through. That, I was finding, was far harder than doing things. Then I realized that Maitre Dyana needed to know what I suspected about Johanyr and Geuffryt. So I headed upstairs to tell her, even if I couldn't prove a thing, in the legal sense.

Gherard was sorting papers of some sort at his desk, but he immediately straightened. "Yes, Maitre Rhennthyl?"

"Is she in?"

"No, sir. I believe she's at the Council Chateau, meeting with Councilor Caartyl and Maitre Rholyn, sir."

"Do you have any idea when she'll be back?"

"No, sir. She did say that she might not be back here today and that I shouldn't wait past fifth glass for her."

"Thank you."

When I got back to my study, I realized I was angry . . . at more than a few things. I'd had to ask Iryela for something the Collegium already had, something that should have been in Maitre Dichartyn's files, not locked away in the Collegium library. That wasn't a total loss, because I suspected no one in the library had updated the listing. How complete Ryel's updates were was another question. Then, every time I tried to find out something, such as where large sums of funds were coming from, I kept finding that there wasn't any way or system to find out, or not accurately. The Council was squabbling over how to fund ships Solidar needed, and no one really even knew what sort of taxation on whom would raise how much funding, and I suspected that, if I talked to Reynol, he'd tell me that his figures were estimates at best. That didn't mean I didn't need to talk to him.

None of the Civic Patrol Commanders' reports were the same. Some were little more than half-page summaries. Others went into mind-numbing detail, much of which looked irrelevant. And neither Commander of either Westisle or Estisle had ever really addressed the stronger elveweed issue, except in generalities. The newsheets had reported ships being burned over the past two months, but nowhere in any reports were there any figures, either about totals of vessels lost, destroyed cargoes, and their values.

And who had compiled the High Holder listing? When I'd leafed through it and read some of it on the way back to the Collegium, there was no indication who had compiled or printed the small volume, although a single sentence on the second page had indicated that it was the official roster of High Holders as of the year 700 A.L.—more than sixty years earlier. Why wasn't there a more up-to-date listing? Was that because the High Holders didn't want one? Or because they honestly believed more frequent updates were unnecessary?

I'd thought about compiling a rough estimate of the damages created all across Solidar by the Ferrans and their agents, as a tool to persuade the Council to approve building more warships, but I dismissed the idea immediately. First, there was no way to determine the costs of all the incidents. Second, I didn't see any way to separate out incidents arising from the conflicts between freeholders and High Holders from those created by Ferran agents. And third, most of the Council could not have cared less.

Finally, at half past four, I'd had enough, and I left my study and began the walk home through a wind even more bitter than the one that morning. I did see, as I neared our house, that work continued on rebuilding the large dwelling for the Maitre of the Collegium.

Seliora greeted me in the front foyer when I stepped inside and out of the wind. She had a rueful smile on her lips as she held up two envelopes.

"I take it that those are invitations."

"How did you guess?"

"Because you're holding them up." I smiled. "What else could they be? I have no idea why anyone would be inviting us anywhere." I did manage to keep my voice serious, and half-concerned as I took off my cloak and hung it up.

"Rhenn! We will be getting these invitations. You are effectively the second-highest ranking imager in Solidar . . ." She broke off and began laughing. "You knew all along, didn't you?"

"I was told that we should expect them, because we're far too young to be where we are and you're far too beautiful."

"No one said that."

"Oh, yes, they did. Maitre Schorzat did." I didn't mention Schorzat's speculation about Madame D'Glendyl and hoped one wasn't from her, sent before the shooting.

"He's kind."

"He was also telling the truth. Now . . . where are we invited?"

"To a small reception at the salon of Juniae D'Shendael on the sixth of Ianus at her town house, and to a winter ball at D'Almeida Place, hosted by

Almeida D'Alte and Madame Ruisa D'Almeida. That's on the fourteenth of Ianus."

I didn't know anything about High Holder Almeida, except that Master Dichartyn had once mentioned him in passing, and nothing about Madame D'Almeida. "You might wait a day or so before accepting. There might be more."

"I'm afraid you might be right, dear. You're freezing." She guided me into the family parlor and settled me on the settee directly before the stove.

"Before you head off to tell Klysia to start serving, I need to tell you about today. I saw Iryela . . ." While I told Seliora almost everything, I decided against mentioning the bequest. Until she actually received it, nothing was certain, and, besides, Iryela had said it was small. Small to a High Holder might mean as much as a few hundred golds, but until the terms were presented to the Justiciary and approved, there wasn't much point in even speculating on what she might do with the funds.

"So . . . you think Johanyr provided the funds to Geuffryt? Why?"

"How else could he strike back at me? I wouldn't be surprised if Geuffryt promised that our house would be the first one targeted."

"I can see that. What I don't understand is why Geuffryt would want to attack the Collegium."

"I had trouble with that, too. On the surface, it doesn't make any sense. But then, Schorzat told me what Geuffryt had said to Marshal Valeun several years ago about the High Holders playing stupid games and being supported by the Collegium. Iryela mentioned that his father was a High Holder who lost everything . . ."

When I finished, Seliora asked, "Do you really believe he'd turn against Solidar itself?"

"No. But I can see him as the type who would try to weaken or destroy the Collegium because he believed we opposed a strong Navy or supported those who do. I need to see if Maitre Dyana knows more about his background."

Seliora nodded, then asked, "What else?"

"The more I look into the files, the less I find. There ought to be some numbers about . . . well . . . everything, and some way to find them . . ." I went on to tell her about the High Holder list. ". . . and it's that way with everything . . ."

"I think you're hungry and need to eat. Then, we can talk about it all."

She was right about that.

40

A fine snow was drifting out of high clouds as I made my way toward the infirmary on Meredi morning, but there was only a digit or so on the ground. When I got there, Draffyd told me I'd have to wait until that afternoon before talking to Glendyl.

So I went to my study and quickly read through the newsheets.

Tableta reported that the rising price of coal would require the Naval Command to ask for more funding from the Council in order to keep the northern fleet on station and fully operational. The story also noted that newer ships had more efficient boilers and turbines and didn't burn as much coal, but that the Council had not acted on the Naval Command's request for newer ships during any session during the past four years. That story wouldn't make anyone on the Council happy, except Glendyl, and he was in no condition to enjoy it.

Veritum had a shorter version of that story, as well as a brief report that the body of High Holder Ruelyr had been found in a hunting lodge on his lands near the Sud Swamp. There was no mention of the cause of death. There was also a story on the success of the Stakanaran effort to consolidate what they were already calling their new province—what had once been a part of Tiempre, before it had been a province of Stakanar centuries before. That made perfect sense, given the shifting of Solidaran warships from the waters off Otelyrn to the northern fleet.

After I finished that depressing, if enlightening, news, I headed upstairs to see if Maitre Dyana had arrived. She had, and Gherard gestured for me to enter her study.

"Gherard said that you were looking for me."

"I was. Before I go into that, though, I was hoping that you might know why a High Holder named Laevoryn sailed off into the sunset some years ago and never returned."

"That was twenty years ago." She smiled faintly.

"I don't believe that's an answer, Maitre Dyana. But an actual answer might be relevant to one of our problems."

"It was quite a scandal at the time," she continued as if I'd said nothing.

"Laevoryn was handsome, breathtakingly so. He'd had the effrontery to seduce the wife of another High Holder, rather brazenly, and even to flaunt the matter. The other High Holder said nothing. Instead, he arranged for a complex arrangement of land transactions, involving water rights. I can't say I understood exactly how it worked, but the result was to cut off water to a large portion of Laevoryn's lands. Laevoryn reacted by shooting and killing one of the other High Holders. He claimed it was a hunting accident at a shooting party. That was regarded as a severe breach of etiquette, and for three years no High Holder would have anything to do with Laevoryn, either socially or in business, and any factor who did was punished financially. Several were ruined. One attempted to kill Laevoryn but only ended up killing Laevoryn's mistress. Did I mention that Laevoryn had committed his wife to an estate tower, claiming she was mad?"

"I don't believe that you did."

"In the end, Laevoryn left Kherseilles in his yacht, sailing it singlehandedly. The debts left his wife and children little more than well-off artisans."

"Whose wife did he seduce?" I asked.

"The first wife of High Holder Haestyr."

I couldn't help wincing. Seliora had told me all about Haestyr and his son.

"Haestyr wasn't always the way he is now." After a moment, Maitre Dyana said, "I assume what you have to tell me bears on the acts of his son."

"It does. It appears as though matters have become even more entangled." I explained what I had learned from Iryela and how that bore on what Schorzat and Kahlasa had discovered.

When I finished, she nodded. "That is indeed likely, since the Collegium refrained from intervening in the dispute, on the grounds that it was a matter between High Holders."

If I hadn't seen the brutal indirect cruelty of High Holders directed at my own family, I wasn't sure I could have understood how a seduction had destroyed so many people and how the ramifications continued onward and even threatened the security of all Solidar. "So Geuffryt arranged the attack on Imagisle in an attempt to destroy or severely weaken the Collegium to pay it back for refusing to help his father?"

"There have been less understandable motives." Her smile was cold. "The problem is that we have no absolute evidence to bring before either the Council or the Justiciary. Those who could have been witnesses died on the barges, and all we have left is a stack of forged documents. We can't even claim theft, since the lease of the barges and tug were paid in solid golds. For that matter, it would be difficult to dredge up the remnants of the barges to prove that they are the missing ones."

"That doesn't mean something can't be done," I suggested.

"Maitre Rhennthyl, we cannot afford anyone looking askance at the Collegium. Not at the moment. You will not take action against him or have any of the security imagers do so. Or any other member of the Collegium or anyone who is connected to you, your wife, or to the Collegium. Is that clear?"

"That is clear." I did have another idea, but whether it would work depended on what else I discovered.

"Good. Is there anything else?"

"Glendyl still isn't able to talk. I will let you know."

Maitre Dyana rose. "Please do."

I nodded and left her study.

When I returned to my study, there were two copies of the Year 700 list of High Holders set on my desk with a note on the top.

> Some earlier annotations were made on the Collegium copy by Maitre Poin-
> caryt and Maitre Dichartyn. Those are in black ink. I took the liberty of
> adding the High Holder's notes to the Collegium copy in blue.

The signature was Kahlasa's.

Even though the book was sixty years old, I decided to estimate how many High Holders there had been when it had been printed. There were thirty lines for print on each page, and generally about three lines on each High Holder listed, with an empty line between each entry. That worked out to seven entries a page. That was when I noticed that the pages were unnumbered. I also discovered that the High Holders were listed alphabetically, by region, starting with the northwest and those around Eshtora.

So I counted the pages. There were seventy-three sheets with names on them, or one hundred forty-four pages, since two pages were blank. At that point, I knew I had to count every name on every page, very carefully. I counted the names in ten-page segments, marking the segments with long slips of paper. When I was done, I had one thousand and nine names.

Then I counted up the annotations. Maitre Poincaryt and Maitre Dichartyn had noted the loss of ten High Holdings, and Ryel—Iryela's father—had noted some twenty-one names, but the entries in his book dated back forty years, while the oldest date in the Collegium book was 742 A.L., just nineteen years back. Three names had been eliminated by date, as were they all in the Collegium book, after Ryel's death.

By the count in the Collegium book and according to the Council compact, that meant that the High Holders should lose one Council seat. By Ryel's count, that should have happened years ago. Was that why the count had never been updated?

I could see why Maitre Poincaryt would not have acted on the Collegium count. If threatened by the loss of control of the Executive Council, and thus the loss of the power to block spending and taxation measures, even the greediest of High Holders would have agreed to relinquish some assets and lands to create another High Holding or two, or even found a way to elevate a wealthy and pretentious factor. To me, it was clear that Maitre Poincaryt had been waiting until the number of High Holders dropped to the point where that was not possible. If that happened to be so, then why had Suyrien slipped that "reform" valuation provision into law?

At that moment, I understood, and I stood and picked up both small volumes and headed back upstairs.

Gherard looked at me, then at the closed study door. "Maitre Rholyn just left. She's alone, sir."

His tone suggested that I should enter at my own risk.

I smiled. What else was there to do? "I'll try to leave her in a calmer frame of mind." I eased open the study door, stepped inside, and closed it gently, but firmly, behind me.

Maitre Dyana looked at me with an expression that, for all its apparent serenity, would have frozen the River Aluse solid all the way from L'Excelsis to Solis.

"Is this about Glendyl? Or Geuffryt?" Her tone was low, smooth, and cold.

"No. It's about control of the Council."

"Not that again."

"No. Maitre Poincaryt and Maitre Dichartyn didn't have enough information. I borrowed a copy of the year 700 printed roster. It has annotations of twenty-one lost High Holdings dating back to 710. It also does not include the three in the past five years. As of 700, there were only one thousand nine High Holdings."

"Where did you get that roster?"

"From the library of a noted High Holder—with permission. I had that High Holder's annotations added to the Collegium copy."

"You realize what you have there, don't you?"

"The possibility of civil war? It's possible, but the change is also inevitable. Suyrien had to have known that. That was why he slipped in that provision about High Holder valuations. He decided to do it so that the change would be so dramatic that there wouldn't be any question about the change having to take place. He planned on it not taking effect for another year or so, when he would have had a chance to prepare the groundwork with Maitre Poincaryt."

"How do you know that?"

"The changes don't take effect until after the first of Ianus, but the first valuation would be based on land and asset values as of 35 Finitas of next year, and wouldn't take effect until a year from this coming Ianus. Maitre Poincaryt had had more than a few meetings with Councilor Suyrien."

She sat there studying me for a time. "What do you propose we do?"

"Follow, if we can, what they planned to do. The older annotations will make it easier, but you'll have to spend a great deal of time with every High Holder Councilor, as well as those who are powerful and not Councilors."

"Maitre Rhennthyl, you will be at every one of those meetings, but we will not arrange any meetings until after we deal with the Ferrans. For now, we will not speak of the matter to anyone, especially not to Maitre Rholyn, not until after Ramsael becomes Chief Councilor. I also suggest you keep those books in a very secure place."

"I will. What should I know about Maitre Rholyn's position, besides the fact that he is unhappy with me, and that he sides with the militant High Holders against the factors and the freeholders?"

"Do you need to know more?"

"Do I?" I countered.

"Ramsael would like to avoid violence and wants to calm matters down in the east. Rholyn is trying to persuade him, without appearing to do so, that ancillary water rights erode the very basis of Solidaran water law and should be abolished. At the moment, Maitre Jhulian is finishing a brief to refute that. Maitre Rholyn does not know that, nor should he."

Maitre Dyana's words told me more than I really wanted to know, including the fact that she might well be setting Rholyn up. She would only be doing that because Rholyn was openly following her orders and secretly doing otherwise. That confirmed my long-held opinion of him.

"I believe you understand," she said.

I just nodded before I left, the two books in hand.

41

Finally, in the late morning on Jeudi, Draffyd allowed me in to see Glendyl, after cautioning me not to exhaust him. The Councilor was propped up in the infirmary bed at a slight angle, halfway between lying down and sitting up. His head did not move as I stepped up to his bedside, but his eyes fixed on me.

"Good morning, Councilor."

"I wouldn't call it good . . . except . . . compared to the . . . alternatives."

"Sometimes comparisons are revealing," I agreed.

"I understand you saved . . . my life, Maitre. I do appreciate that."

"I kept you alive so that Maitre Draffyd could." That was a fair statement, I thought. "We never did finish our conversation. I don't understand why a Ferran agent would shoot at you." I watched him closely.

I thought I caught a slight stiffening and perhaps a moment of surprise, and I went on. "After all, you are the voice of the factors and the leading advocate for change in Solidar. That is, change in a direction that would be more . . . along the lines of what the Ferrans believe is the proper form of government."

"I have no idea who they were shooting at, Maitre Rhennthyl. They could have been targeting either one of us. I am grateful they were not more successful."

I knew Glendyl was grateful, but I didn't believe for a moment that he thought he'd been the target, and that suggested he knew very well who the shooter represented, at least who had hired and instructed him. "That's possible. But why would anyone be shooting at a relatively unknown Maitre or the temporary head of the Executive Council? Shooting either of us would change little. Also, how would they even know I was coming to the Council Chateau? I didn't tell anyone I was coming until I took the duty coach on Lundi morning. That would suggest that someone believed I'd be there sooner or later and that they were waiting. But who would know that I'd have to come to the Council Chateau?"

"All imagers wear gray. He might well have thought you were Maitre

Rholyn." Glendyl tried to lift his right hand, as if to wave me off, but it trembled so much that he immediately lowered it. His voice was tired, and he didn't really want to talk to me. That was clear enough.

"Then who do you believe hired the shooter?"

"It could be anyone. We all have enemies."

"Has anyone threatened you?"

"Not recently."

"Why didn't you want to supply the boilers and turbines for the modern fast frigate?"

"Because Suyrien wanted to build the ship at a loss, and that would have allowed the High Holders and Caartyl to declare that we could build more with the same margins. We'd have had to fight even harder for a reasonable profit for the rest of the ships, and that would have delayed things even more and reduced profits as well. I'm not in business to lose golds."

"I take it that the Ferrans allow reasonable profit for their shipbuilders?"

"I wouldn't know, but they must. They're building modern ships, and we're not." He glared at me, except he was too tired to make it effective. "You're asking me stupid questions when you ought to be asking all the High Holders why they won't pay their share, and what they intend to do."

"What else would you like me to do, then?" I asked reasonably.

"Whatever you need to, Maitre." He closed his eyes, not that he was sleepy.

"Thank you. Maitre Draffyd will take very good care of you, Councilor. The Collegium certainly wouldn't want anything to happen to you, especially under our care."

His eyes twitched, but he didn't open them, not while I was in the small gray-walled room.

Draffyd was waiting outside. "You were reasonably brief. Did you find out anything?"

"Not yet. What happened to his right hand?"

"It's always been weak, from when he was younger, but he's kept that hidden for years. The angle that the shot took him at damaged some muscles. I don't know that they'll fully knit, and, if they do, it's likely to be months, or longer."

"I didn't catch that."

"You caught enough. He's still fortunate you were there." He nodded, and I headed back to the administration building.

Maitre Dyana appeared at my study door within moments of when I returned. She slipped gracefully into the chamber, closing the door behind her. She was again wearing a scarf, one of brilliant blue edged with pale yellow. "Was your conversation with Glendyl productive?"

"Did he tell me anything that was directly useful? No. I didn't think he would. The way he avoided the questions was indicative of several possibilities. At the very least, he had arranged, or he knew that senior imagers would have to visit him."

"He had to know that we carry shields that are proof against snipers."

"I thought about that, and that's why he's guilty."

Maitre Dyana did not speak for a moment. "I have an idea, but I'd like to hear why you think so."

"Glendyl is anything but stupid. He has to know about imager shields. He's known, possibly even seen, when Dartazn, Martyl, or I deflected bullets or survived explosions. But . . . he also knows that the Ferran agents, some six years back, were successful in killing a number of imagers, generally caught unaware. What if, just if . . . an intermediary let it be known that the Ferrans had weapons capable of piercing imager shields? What does he have to lose? They either succeed or they don't."

"Why would he want imagers killed?"

"Because he believes that we support the continued control of the Council by the High Holders. He may even know, or suspect, that there are no longer even a thousand High Holders, and yet nothing has changed."

"He hasn't brought that up in the Council, but he wouldn't."

"Did you ask Maitre Rholyn that?"

"No. I've studied the proceedings and records," she replied, "and Maitre Poincaryt never mentioned it, either."

"You think Glendyl wouldn't bring up the question because he fears the High Holders?" That suggested Glendyl might be an excellent factorius and businessman, but that he certainly didn't understand fully what had been going on behind the calm front of the Council. All he had to do was to wait a little bit longer than one more year, and he would have been the head of the Executive Council. Suyrien had already laid the groundwork. Instead, Glendyl had failed to see that change was coming, and had tried to use Ferran agents to force that change.

She shook her head. "He wouldn't bring it up for the same reasons that you believe Maitre Poincaryt didn't. There are some factors, notably Etyenn, who would relish the chance to become High Holders and who probably already have the wealth if not the lands. Even talking about it could delay the change."

"Still," I pointed out, "there's more here. Master Dichartyn told me that Glendyl had knuckled under to High Holder Haebyn's demands to delay locomotives and replacement engines to ironways that didn't give preference to eastern High Holder grain shipments. He also said that there were rumors that golds had changed hands, and that Glendyl had delayed shipments. Why would Glendyl, who disliked High Holders, do that . . . unless he needed golds? Not only that, but Glendyl, who has always been trying to reduce the power of the High Holders, wouldn't offer the cartage reform amendment. Caartyl did."

"That may be, but Glendyl has nothing to gain by having imagers killed."

She was probably right, but still . . .

"You have that look, Maitre Rhennthyl. Did you suddenly recall something of import?"

"I'm not certain of its import. I'll need to talk to some people first."

"Then I suggest you do."

After Maitre Dyana left, I pulled my winter cloak back on and left again, trudging through the gray morning to the duty coach stand.

Three quints after I stepped into the coach, Davoryn, who only drove me occasionally, was guiding it up the drive to Frydryk/Suyrien's L'Excelsis chateau. It was a risk, calling on Frydryk without an appointment and unannounced, but where else was he likely to be on a cold winter day? If he didn't happen to be in, I could find out where he was. But I had a strong feeling I needed to talk to him as quickly as possible.

The retainer who appeared at the door took in my grays and the visored cap with the silver imager insignia, then finally said, "Sir . . . I don't believe that . . . High Holder Suyrien was expecting you."

"I'm most certain that he wasn't," I said agreeably. "Is he in?"

"Ah . . ."

"Please tell him that Maitre D'Esprit Rhennthyl needs some time with him, and that I wouldn't spend a glass getting here without an appointment if it were not important."

"Yes, sir." He paused, then added, "If you would come in and wait in the foyer . . ."

Once I was inside, he closed the door, then turned and headed toward the door on the left side of the hexagonal foyer, the one to the study where I had met with Frydryk earlier. After a quick knock, the retainer opened the door, barely enough to step inside, shutting it behind himself.

In moments, the door opened, and the functionary said, "Sir, this way . . ."

"Thank you."

I didn't even have to close the door. It clicked shut behind me.

Frydryk had clearly just stood from behind the writing desk filled with stacks of papers. "Maitre Rhennthyl . . ." He looked bewildered to see me on his doorstep, literally and figuratively. "To what do I owe this unexpected visit?"

I smiled, as pleasantly as I could. "I need the answer to two questions. Two very simple questions."

"Yes?"

"The first is whether you have had a guard force at the shipworks and whether you know if Glendyl does at Ferravyl."

"That's not all that simple," Frydryk replied. "We've always had guards, and Father made sure that they were paid well. Also, when we do build Navy vessels, there are Navy guards as well around those drydocks as well. Glendyl . . . he never said much about it. Father did mention that he didn't like to pay for anything that didn't produce profit, including guards."

"Thank you. The second question is simpler. How much does Glendyl owe you?"

"That's . . ." Frydryk's mouth opened, then shut. "Was he behind it? The shooting?"

"How much?"

"Close to a quarter-million golds."

"And your father was pressuring him to supply the engines and turbines for the first fast battlecruiser?"

"He—Father—just said that Glendyl was being unreasonable, and that he was certain, once they talked matters over, Glendyl would see reason."

"Did they talk matters over? Do you know when?"

"They did, several nights before Father was shot. When Glendyl left, Father came and found me in the billiards room. He was very pleased, and he sent a message to the head of the shipworks to revise the proposal to present to the Council when it reconvened in Ianus . . ." Frydryk paused. "I can't believe . . . Glendyl? Why would he do that?"

"I don't think he did. I think your father was killed and Glendyl was shot in order to stop the shipbuilding project." That wasn't the whole story, but there was no need for Frydryk to know the rest, especially since I wasn't certain of all the details, not yet.

"But who?"

"The Ferrans. Who else? With your father and Glendyl dead, and a huge debt owed by Glendyl, who would know that Glendyl hadn't arranged for your

father's death? Especially since Glendyl would have known that he would become the acting head of the Council."

"That would mean . . ."

"It could mean any number of things," I said quickly. "Oh . . . I was
wondering. Are there plans and specifications for Glendyl's turbines where
you can reach them?"

That brought another frown.

"I don't need to see them. Glendyl almost died. I'd hate to think that all
that work was only in one place."

He did smile. "That was something Father insisted on, given how much
Glendyl owed him. We have two sets in two very different and safe places."

"Good . . . and thank you. I just needed to know about the debt before I
did anything else. I'd appreciate it if you didn't mention it to anyone for right
now . . . except, of course, Maitre Dyana, if anything happens to me."

That surprised him as much as anything I'd said.

"Of course . . . but . . ."

"We still need modern ships, but I don't want all of this coming out until we can track down all of those who are involved. One way or another, it
shouldn't take that long." Why I thought that, I didn't know. The Ferran plot
had been put in place years before, I suspected.

"Thank you." I smiled again. "I do appreciate it . . . and give my best to
Alynkya."

"Oh . . . I will."

With that, I left the study and a still-confused Frydryk.

In the coach on the way back to Imagisle, I tried to fit more of the pieces
together. Glendyl hadn't gone to the Ferrans. That was clear. They'd come to
him, most likely not even as Ferrans, but as someone reputable, and they'd
known about his debts, perhaps as representatives of a banque concern.
They'd also known about his accepting bribes from Haebyn, and they'd threatened to expose everything unless he did a favor for them. That favor had likely
been tied in some way to Suyrien's death, further enmeshing Glendyl. Then
they had suggested that the only way to avoid being discovered was to remove
senior imagers, such as me or Rholyn.

Still . . . there had to be more. Or I was missing something? Or both.

Then I recalled the last Pharsi foresight flash I'd gotten. Had that been a
vision of Glendyl's massive manufactory at Ferravyl? Was that where I was
supposed to go?

Even as I knew it was necessary, a part of me both resented and accepted

the fact that I had no choice but to go on intuition . . . simply because neither the Collegium nor the Council had developed a unified and standardized
system for handling information.

Seliora could come up with cards and card readers that could replicate
designs for fabrics, but the head of security for the Collegium Imago had to
piece together rumors, fragmentary and incomplete information, and old documents, and then rely on intuition and hope. I'd had more information when
I'd been a District Captain of the Civic Patrol. That was an aspect of Ferlyn's
studies of patterns that, apparently, no one had yet understood. Just as the way
of fabricating and building things was changing, so also was change needed
in the means and systems of administering Solidar . . . and in gathering intelligence and data.

But . . . that would have to wait until after I visited Glendyl's manufactory
in Ferravyl and after I resolved the current crises . . . if I could.

Once I returned to the Collegium, I took full advantage of my position as
a senior Maitre and had the duty staff arrange a sleeping compartment for me
on the evening express to Ferravyl. While they were taking care of that, I wrote
out a set of instructions for Anaxyr, the Collegium's regional in Ouestan, and
then took the sheet to Schorzat, who was in his study, writing out something
himself.

"Does this make sense?"

He took the paper and read it. "It makes sense. Whether he can find out
what you want is another question."

"He ought to be able to discover if there are Ferran clients who've made
recent transactions here in Solidar . . . or if there have been withdrawals on
accounts that meet the parameters."

"That's possible," he said.

"Good. I'd appreciate it if you'd take care of having a copy made and
the original sent. I'm trying to get ready to take the night express to Ferravyl."

"Ferravyl . . . something to do with Glendyl?"

"I hope not, but I'm afraid so."

"Better you than me. Train travel isn't all that marvelous for an imager."
Schorzat shook his head sympathetically.

"I can't say I'm looking forward to it."

I returned to my study, where I did some rough calculations. Then, once
Beleart confirmed that I had passage, I headed up to see Maitre Dyana.

She just looked at me when I walked into her study.

"I'll be leaving for Ferravyl on the evening express."

"What's in Ferravyl that requires your presence so urgently?"

I offered a pleasant smile. "I'm not totally certain, but I think it might be part of the answer to some of the problems we've had."

"Which part? Geuffryt's?"

"No. Why Glendyl and Suyrien were shot. Suyrien needed Glendyl's engines and turbines, even for the merchanters he was building. So who else would be likely to loan Glendyl golds, in order to keep the engines coming? I guessed that the costs of developing and building the newer steam turbines for warships cost Glendyl far, far more than anyone knew, but since he had the sole rights to them, Suyrien didn't have any choice. I checked with Frydryk, and they loaned him a quarter of a million golds."

"That doesn't explain why you need to go there."

"I don't think that was all Glendyl owed. He wouldn't have taken what amounted to bribes from Haebyn if Suyrien's funding happened to be fully carrying him. I can't be certain, but I think the answer is in Ferravyl."

"They may not let you in, you know?"

I smiled back at her. "They will." I smiled back at her. "I'm still a Civic Patrol Captain, too. I never got around to offering a resignation, and Artois never asked for it."

"No." She smiled in return. "The Collegium hasn't canceled your assignment there, either. How long will this take?"

"One way or another, I should be back by Solayi evening."

"Be careful. You aren't that indestructible, Maitre Rhennthyl."

"I intend to be very careful."

"Be more careful than that. If you won't think about yourself, your wife, and your daughter, then think about what will happen to poor Schorzat if he has to pick up the pieces."

"Yes, Maitre."

I eased out of her study.

It took another two glasses to make the remainder of my arrangements, which included another visit to Draffyd and arranging for an obdurate to accompany me on the express. Then I hurried home to pack. I'd just finished when Seliora entered her bedchamber and took in the valise.

"You're going where?" she asked. "When?"

"Ferravyl. I'm leaving tonight. I'm fairly sure that's where that farsight flash took place . . . or will take place."

"Why there?"

"Because it's the only place that makes sense." I gave her a quick and condensed version of what I'd found out and thought.

"Going there could be very dangerous." Those were her only words when I finished.

"That's possible. I think not going could be even more so. I don't think anyone—including Maitre Dyana, the Council, and Sea-Marshal Valeun—really understands how much thought and resources the Ferrans put into this."

"You don't think Geuffryt . . . ?"

"No. He has a very different agenda. The sad thing is that he ended up helping them."

"What can you do about him?"

"I've been ordered not to do anything or to have anyone under me do anything."

Seliora nodded thoughtfully. "You have another idea."

"I may, but it will have to wait. Ferravyl is more important."

"When do you have to leave here?"

"In about a glass."

She stepped closer and put her arms around me, then lifted her lips to mine.

42

Ferravyl was close to 450 milles from L'Excelsis, at least by ironway, and even on the express, that was a trip of some nine glasses. Since I was taking the night special, it also meant taking a lead-cloth bed hanging, which I'd obtained from Draffyd, as well as a small bottle of a sleep opiate. Then, too, there was the requirement for an obdurate travel guard. The guard's name was Claudyn, and, except for the black cloak and trousers, rather than livery, he looked like he might have been a High Holder's personal bodyguard.

The L'Excelsis ironway station was on West River Road, about a mille south of Alusine Wool. We arrived at the station by duty coach at half before seventh glass, and then had to wait.

While we stood on the platform, I asked Claudyn, "Have you done this often?"

"Never that much. None of the Maitres have traveled since the Ferrans shelled the Collegium—excepting Maitre Rholyn."

"Where did he go?"

"Only to Asseroiles. High Holder Haestyr had requested his presence."

"When was that? Do you remember?"

"It was after Councilor Suyrien was shot, but before he died. Maitre Rholyn did say something about not wanting to go."

That was interesting, especially since Claudyn had no idea what the two had discussed, not that Rholyn would ever have told him. Had Haestyr been angling to succeed Suyrien . . . or to oppose Ramsael? I'd have to bring that up to Maitre Dyana.

Once the train was opened to boarding, we made our way to the second accommodation carriage and located compartment three. The private sleeping chamber might have been considered commodious by some, but my lead-lined bedchamber was High-Holder spacious by comparison, although the dark oak paneling and deep green hangings and upholstery did help in making the train compartment seem warmer. Once the train was well away from L'Excelsis I prepared for sleep. Even after taking the draught I didn't slumber all that well, but I didn't dream. I did wake with a pounding headache and a much fuller understanding of what Schorzat had meant about train travel for an imager.

The locomotive puffed into the station in Ferravyl just before seventh glass on Vendrei morning. Breakfast in the dining car hadn't been bad, even if the fried cakes had been a touch heavy. Eating had reduced my headache to a dull but faint throbbing. As we departed the train, under a hazy gray sky, Claudyn was cheerful, but kept that cheer to a few remarks and a near-constant smile. Surprisingly, there were more than a few hacks lined up outside the station, and we had no trouble engaging one for the trip to Glendyl's manufactory, known locally, I discovered, as "the big engine works."

After Frydryk's comments, I'd wondered about the security of Glendyl's facility, but, once the hack stopped outside the closed iron gates, I had the feeling he'd never seen it. The two-and-a-half-yard-high stone wall that surrounded the works ran at least half a mille in each direction from the gates. There were two guards at the stone gatehouse on the right side of the iron gates.

One of them stepped forward as I walked toward him. The wind was raw, although not as cold as in L'Excelsis. That rawness might have been because Ferravyl was far damper.

"I'm here to look at the works," I said pleasantly.

"Ah . . . sir . . ."

The other one murmured, "You want to stop an imager? Or that big ob with him?"

I stopped and waited.

The first guard swallowed. "Sir . . . if you wouldn't mind coming with me? I'm certain Director Huesyt would want to show you whatever you need to see."

"I'd be happy to see Director Huesyt."

"This way, sir."

Claudyn and I followed the guard through a narrow side gate. Then we walked across an open stone-paved space from which ran three paved roads, one straight ahead, and the other two paralleling the walls. On the far side of the plaza, if one could call it that, on the left, was a square gray stone building of one story, some fifteen yards on a side, with a single-door entry. The door was iron and squeaked as the guard opened it. The small foyer held two benches and a table, behind which sat a young man in a pale blue coverall.

"Fardyl . . . Maitre Rhennthyl's here to see the director," said the guard.

At that, Fardyl stood immediately, inclining his head to me. "I'll tell him, sir." He turned and headed down the narrow hallway, barely a yard and a half wide.

The works guard did not move, but stood directly in front of the outside door that he had just closed. As I waited, I took in the confined space, with its old but smooth-sanded and varnished oak floors, the oak shutters, the white plaster walls, devoid of any decorations or hangings, and the faint smell of strong oil soap.

In moments, Fardyl returned. "He'll join you in the conference room, Maitre."

"Thank you."

Claudyn remained standing in the foyer as I followed the aide down the narrow hallway to the first door on the right. I entered, and he retreated, leaving the door open. The rectangular conference table was of ancient golden oak, clearly far older than I, and surrounded by twelve straight-backed, armless, and uncushioned oak chairs.

In moments, another figure stepped through the doorway. Huesyt was a narrow-faced grizzled fellow with a short gray and brown beard and a slight paunch, wearing a padded brown leather waistcoat over a pale blue shirt. His trousers were dark blue, or had been before they had faded slightly. He inquired brusquely, "What can I do for you, Master Imager?"

"I don't know that you'd heard. Earlier this week, Councilor Glendyl was shot. He was seriously injured, but it is likely that he'll recover with no lasting effect."

"I hadn't heard. What does that have to do with your being here?"

"Just about everything," I replied. "I was taking a walk with the Councilor, and we had just started to talk about the new turbines and why the Council didn't seem to want to pay for the ships that they'd propel." I paused. "At that very moment, he got shot. Now, the Council and the Collegium tend to get concerned when the High Holder who builds most of Solidar's warships gets assassinated, and then the factor who supplies the new engines nearly gets killed. Oh . . . did I mention that my predecessor was looking into such matters, and he had a building dropped on him? So . . . you can see why I might be here."

Huesyt didn't speak for several moments. Finally, he shook his head. "I can't say as I understand any of it . . . what with all the troubles . . ."

"I understand things haven't gone smoothly here, either . . ."

He snorted. "We're doing all right on boilers and old-style engines for the merchanters . . . or we would be if we hadn't lost so many workers. Must have had to hire almost a hundred over the past year. Doesn't help that the stupid crafters on the Council—pardon me, sir, but not building better ships when your enemy is doing that is stupid. As I was saying, it doesn't help that we've got the best turbines in the world and we got no ships to use 'em."

"Why have you had so much trouble with workers? I've heard that the manufactory here is modern and well-maintained, and I imagine that workers are paid well."

"They're well paid. That they are, but it's been senseless stuff. You get four or five who tried that new elveweed and killed themselves. A handful more got killed or maimed in tavern brawls. Some just disappeared. Maybe family problems, but no one ever heard from them again. A few got careless on the job. No matter how you try to run safe shops, some get careless or don't listen."

I nodded, then asked, "It sounds like you lost a lot more men than in any year before."

Huesyt nodded. "I've been here twenty years. Never seen anything like it. Not all bad, though. Some of the new men are good, better than those that we lost, but it still slows things down. Now . . . if the Council . . ." He shook his head. "Sometimes, I talk too much . . . What can I do for you and the Council?"

"A tour of the manufactory would be helpful, especially the boiler-making and turbine manufacturing. With the war going the way it is . . . things might be changing."

"I can't believe that there's much for an imager to see, but I'd not be arguing with either imagers or Councilors. You mind if we begin right now? I have a meeting here in about two glasses, and even a quick tour will take time."

"That would be good."

Huesyt turned and strode out of the conference room. I didn't rush after him, but I didn't dawdle, either. When we came out of the small building that certainly exemplified Glendyl's belief in limited administration and supervisors, Huesyt turned westward. Claudyn followed, a step or so behind us.

Despite the light and raw wind, the air held an acrid odor that suggested burning coal, hot oil, and molten metal, as well as other smells I couldn't identify. I took several steps, then almost halted, because of what lay before me, on both sides of the wide street paved in gray stone. Manufactory building after building stretched away on both sides, with large cranes beyond several, a sight identical to the farsight image I'd seen weeks before. Perhaps it was identical . . .

"Master Rhennthyl?" Huesyt stopped and half-turned.

"There's nothing like this anywhere else, is there?"

"Not a thing, sir. A real wonder it is, and it should be." He pointed to his right, eastward. "The locomotive shops are over there. The foundry is the building with the wide stacks, and the plate mills are next to it . . ."

I listened, trying to hold the details in my mind.

". . . the boiler manufactory is at the end on the left . . . beyond the turbine works but on the east side. It's near a mille to the boiler yard beyond the manufactory." He began to walk again.

I stepped up beside him, trying to take in everything, as well as attempting to figure out what I should be looking for—or avoiding—and wondering if I were on a fool's errand.

Down the side lane to my left, two workers in pale blue coveralls pushed a waste cart toward a high-sided wagon. Whatever the refuse already in the wagon might have been, it had to have been heavy, because four dray-horses were hitched to the big wagon. Beyond them, another worker in blue stepped out of a long building, glanced at us, then slipped back inside, hurriedly.

"Over there is where we drop forge all the smaller parts." Heusyt gestured to the right.

I followed his gesture. Beyond what looked to be a loading yard was a windowless stone-walled structure, easily as tall as a four-story building. I thought I could feel the stone pavement vibrate beneath my feet, but suspected that was my imagination.

"We can forge and finish parts to a tolerance of better than a thousandth of a digit there . . . what you need for the speed of rotation of things like turbines, even with reducing vanes."

I didn't really understand what he meant, and I was still trying to take in the scope of the works, still wondering exactly what I was looking for—and what I could do if I found it.

"Now . . . up ahead, beyond the settling pond, that's where the turbines are assembled and the one beyond is where each one is finished, tuned, and tested . . ."

Then a single shot ran out, followed by several more, and I staggered back at the impact on my shields, even as I extended them to cover Huesyt and Claudyn.

Two men in the pale-blue coveralls of the works appeared from out of another building on the next side lane to the left. Each carried the wide-mouthed weapons that I'd seen once before.

I immediately imaged stones into their chests, but one managed to trigger his weapon. The impact and explosion threw the three of us backward, and turned a section of pavement at the edge of my shields into shattered rock and gravel.

A single sharp explosion echoed from the stone structure beyond the settling pond, the turbine assembly building that Huesyt had pointed out moments before, and I immediately strengthened my shields, trying to shape and angle them so that whatever came toward us was diverted around us, even as I tried to link the shields to the solid stone pavement blocks and keep them around the three of us.

A second explosion followed, one much larger, so that my teeth rattled, even behind my shields.

I glanced around. Gray clouds billowed from collapsing buildings. Flames spurted from building after building, and black oily smoke poured from at least one structure.

Huesyt stared at me. "It's all your doing! What did you do?"

"They were firing at me, too," I pointed out. "I did nothing. I came here because I was afraid something like this would happen. The problem is that I found out too late. Just why do you think you lost so many workers over the last year? That was so the Ferrans could replace them with their own people."

"You did this!"

I projected absolute assurance—and anger—at him. "I did not. Now . . . go do what you can." *Be grateful I saved your ass so that you can do whatever is possible.*

After a moment, he turned and began to run toward a building where the doors had opened and two fire wagons were being rolled out. One headed toward us.

I motioned Claudyn to the side of the road, stopping short of the sagging stone wall of a building whose function Huesyt had not explained.

"The turbine works!" Huesyt swung up onto the wagon beside the driver.

For a moment, I watched as the fire wagon dashed down the central road toward the farther turbine building, also beginning to show signs of flame and destruction.

The manufactory was far too large and the fires far too extensive for me to do anything. In one sense, I was certain, I'd done more than enough just by showing up. But . . . sooner or later, the saboteurs would have set off their demolition charges.

Amid the smoke, dust, and fire, Claudyn and I walked back toward the manufactory gates. The only thing more I could have done was exhaust myself, and that wouldn't have changed a thing. I didn't like that thought, but I couldn't afford any futile gestures—not after not even fully recovering from the bombardment and after what I'd just witnessed.

Once we were away from the manufactory—and we had to walk nearly a mille to find a hack—I took it back to the ironway station where I wrote out two messages, one to Frydryk and one to Maitre Dyana. I summarized the sabotage for Frydryk and urged him to make certain that similar events did not befall his shipworks in Solis. The message to Maitre Dyana was an account of what had happened, nothing more. Then I dispatched them as urgent.

Once that was taken care of, I took the hack back to the manufactory where I waited in the administrative building for Huesyt to return. I did more than a little thinking while I waited.

It was close to three glasses later, when he trudged into the foyer. More oily smoke and grit followed him.

His mouth opened when he saw me. "You . . . you're still here . . . after all this?"

I stood. "Where else would I be? There wasn't anything I could do after all the explosions and fires."

He looked at me again. "Why? Our own workers fired at us. One of the foremen saw them set the explosions. He couldn't do anything because one of the first blasts broke his leg. Our own workers . . . why?"

"Because they weren't your workers," I said quietly. "They were Ferrans, sent here to destroy the turbine works and whatever else they could damage. When they saw me, they were afraid that I'd do something to stop them, and they immediately did what they could."

"The locomotive works . . . they were mostly untouched."

I just nodded. Whether that section of the works had been spared because they'd run out of explosives or because they'd run out of time, I had no idea. I doubted we'd ever know.

"Do you keep detailed records on your workers?" I asked.

"There's maybe a page on each. Their name, address, their date of birth, their work area and skills, when they were hired, any commendations or warnings, and their pay rate. And their wife or next of kin. That's about it. What else would we need?"

"Once you put the works back together you might check on those you hired in the last year. I'd wager that a number of them will be nowhere to be found."

Huesyt looked at me. "Pardon my shortness, Maitre Rhennthyl. That isn't much help now."

"No, I imagine it's not. I'll be back tomorrow. I'll need to report on what still works here, and how long you think might take to rebuild."

He just looked at me. I looked back, and he eventually looked away.

Then we left.

Claudyn and I found an inn that was acceptable some two milles from the manufactory—and found that it even had an imagers' chamber, for which I was thankful, because I wasn't looking forward to another night of troubled sleep and headaches.

43

When we clambered out of the hack outside the stone walls of Glendyl's manufactory on Samedi morning, a smoky haze blurred the outlines of more distant structures, and the acridity of the air was more than noticeable with each breath that I took. Claudyn and I walked toward the gates, now guarded by four men, but the guard in charge took one look at my imager cap and insignia and waved us through. From what I could see from the gate plaza inside the walls, the buildings that held the turbine assembly and testing were burned-out hulks, as were a number of others. The big drop forge structure seemed untouched, as did the locomotive works, but all of the other larger buildings seemed damaged, in some cases being little more than rubbled heaps of stone. What had doubtless saved some of the buildings was their stone construction and the fact that Glendyl had spaced them far enough apart that the fires hadn't been able to spread easily from building to building.

Even so, given Glendyl's precarious financial position, both the Councilor and Solidar faced close to insurmountable problems and certain and significant delays in building new warships . . . or any other kind of modern vessel.

When I walked into the administration building, Fardyl was again behind the table. He jumped to his feet. "The director was hoping to see you, Maitre. He and the subcommander are in the conference room."

"Thank you." I walked down the narrow hallway, opened the door, and stepped into the chamber.

The uniformed Civic Patrol officer stood easily, if slightly languidly, and, after a moment, so did Huesyt.

"Subcommander Steyfyl, Maitre."

"Rhennthyl, Maitre D'Esprit, from the Collegium in L'Excelsis. I was sent to look into the possibility of problems with the works here. Apparently, we discovered that possibility a little too late."

The subcommander looked to me. "Maitre Rhennthyl . . . you're the imager who's a District Patrol Captain in L'Excelsis, aren't you?"

Huesyt glanced sharply in my direction.

"I was, until Maitre Dichartyn was killed when his house was bombarded.

The Collegium recalled me to take over his duties. That was less than three weeks ago."

"Much has happened since then," said Steyfyl.

I gestured to the chairs and took the one across from the subcommander, leaving Huesyt at the head—or foot—of the table.

"The locomotive works and the drop forge building appeared intact." I looked to Huesyt.

"The foundry didn't suffer much, either. Could have been worse." He paused, then finally added, "I have to say, it probably would have been if you hadn't come. We discovered places in the undamaged buildings where they were beginning to place explosives." After a short silence, he went on. "Would have been better if you showed up earlier, though."

"They would have destroyed the turbine works anyway," I replied. "That was the principal target."

"Because the turbines go to the warships?" asked the subcommander.

"They would have already, if the Namer-flamed Council had ever gotten off its collective rump," snapped Huesyt. "Wouldn't be surprised if the frigging Ferrans had something to do with the delays, too."

I wouldn't have been, either, but I had no proof of that. "I sent an urgent message to the Collegium yesterday, and I'm certain that the Maitre of the Collegium will make certain Councilor Caartyl knows what happened."

"It's not as though he can do anything."

"Since Factorius Glendyl is also at the Collegium, he'll also have learned," I added.

Both men looked confused.

"After he was shot early this week, he was taken to the Collegium infirmary to recover. It was also felt he would be safer there." That was an assumption on my part, but I thought saying so was best to preclude questions.

"Take a lot of golds to rebuild," offered Huesyt.

"I'm certain it will," I replied. "That's something the factorius will have to work out." I wondered how much Huesyt knew about Glendyl's financial situation, but the moment wasn't the time to bring up that question.

"Did you capture any of the saboteurs?" I asked.

Huesyt glanced at the subcommander.

"No. We only found the bodies and the weapons of the two men who attacked you and Director Huesyt. I must say that I've never seen weapons such as those. They fire what look to be miniature artillery shells."

"They used similar weapons in L'Excelsis last week." I probably should have followed up on the weapons when Seliora and I had been attacked, but

I hadn't been thinking as clearly as I should have been, I realized in retro-spect. "Have you found any undetonated explosives?"

"More than enough. Bags of poudre. We stored them away from the other buildings. It's got Army and Navy markings. You have any idea how that happened?"

"Not in detail, but the Navy was already investigating some explosive thefts. Some of them date back a year or so." I paused, then asked, "Is there anything else I should report to the Collegium and the Council?"

The two exchanged glances, but neither spoke.

"Then I'll be returning to L'Excelsis. Best of fortune to you, Director, and you, Subcommander." I stood.

It would be another long trip on the ironway.

44

I couldn't get a compartment on an ironway carriage back to L'Excelsis until the late night express that left at eighth glass. That might have been better, since I was tired enough by then and went to sleep easily enough, but I still woke with a pounding headache at fifth glass, and the dining carriage didn't begin serving breakfast until sixth glass. I wasn't in the best of moods by the time I arrived at the administration building of the Collegium at half-past eighth glass.

After releasing Claudyn, since I was no longer traveling, I went straight to the duty desk. The duty secondus was Cholsyr.

"Yes, sir?"

"Do you know where I can find Maitre Dyana?"

Cholsyr swallowed, then said calmly, "Maitre Dyana has gone to Rivages. She won't be back until Lundi. She left this for you." He extended an envelope.

I took it and opened it. The note was brief.

Dear Maitre Rhennthyl:

I have undertaken a trip to Rivages in the hopes of forestalling yet another disaster.

If you get back before I do, and anything happens, you'll have to make the decisions. I trust that will not be necessary, but one never knows.

The missive was also signed and sealed, and that bothered me. What was she doing in Rivages? That was where Kandryl's and Iryela's main estates were, but there were several other High Holders located in that general area. I didn't know any reason why Dyana would go there, unless she'd discovered something new about the shootings and explosions, but she did nothing without a reason.

"Did she say why she was going, or where she might be found?"

"No, sir. She only said she was visiting relations, if on duty."

Relations? I knew that Maitre Dyana was one of the few imagers to come from a High Holder family, but she had never revealed what that family had been. About all I had ever been able to discover was that she had known Juniae D'Shendael when they had both been younger.

"Who is the duty master, Cholsyr?"

"It's Maitre Chassendri, sir."

"Is she around?"

"She was in the conference room a few moments ago, sir. I don't believe she's left."

"Thank you." I turned and headed toward the conference room—usually where the duty masters stayed on Samedi or Solayi if they didn't have a study in the administration building.

Chassendri stood as I stepped into the open doorway of the conference room.

"I'm glad you're back. When Maitre Dyana told me about the explosions in Ferravyl . . ."

"I was wise enough to just use my shields. Do you know why she's in Rivages?"

"No." Chassendri shook her head.

"What High Holder family does she come from?"

"She doesn't like to let that be known . . . but you should know. Her brother is Zaerlyn D'Alte."

For a moment, the name didn't register. Then I winced.

"What's the matter?"

"Oh . . . it's not . . . it's just that her niece is going to marry Alhyral D'Haestyr."

Chassendri looked at me blankly.

"Let's just say that . . ." I shook my head. "It's none of my business."

She laughed softly. "I'd hate to be the father of anyone who wants to marry your daughter."

"No one will have to worry about that for years. Did she tell you when she might be back?"

"Late this evening. That was all."

"Has anything else happened?"

"Besides some inappropriate imaging of an ice sculpture in the quadrangle . . . no."

"Not by one of those who I've taken over, I hope?"

"No. Young Scammyl attempted to replicate female anatomy that he clearly doesn't know that well."

I just shook my head. After a few more words with Chassendri, I left, reclaiming the valise I'd left by the duty desk before walking through the light snow toward our house.

Knowing that it was possible that Diestrya just might be taking a nap, when I reached the door, I eased it open as quietly as possible, almost tiptoeing inside before gently shutting it.

Seliora was reading in the family parlor, and I could feel the welcome warmth of the stove. I just looked at her for a long moment.

Then she looked up, and the book went down, and I had my arms full of a very beautiful woman.

Somewhat later, we settled before the fire, and Seliora asked me what had happened, since the newsheets had only a short story about an explosion.

"Almost as soon as I got there, when someone caught sight of me, they lit off a series of explosions. Most of Glendyl's works is little more than rubble. Some of the fires burned for almost a full day, and that was in stone-walled and tile-roofed buildings."

"Did he have any indemnity?"

I hadn't even thought of that, although I should have. "I don't know. I'll have to see."

"We do. It's not cheap, either. Years ago, Grandmama worked it out with L'Excelsis Indemnity. She got a whole group of artisans and shop-keepers to go together . . ." Seliora caught the look on my face, and asked, "What is it?"

"One of the buildings that was destroyed here was their building."

"They don't hold their golds there. Their accounts are with several banques."

"You still might want to have your mother look into it, if she hasn't already."

"I'll ask her." She paused, then asked, "Was it the Ferrans? The ones who destroyed Glendyl's works?"

"I'd guess so, but there's no real proof, except the act itself and the way it was planned."

"Where did they get the explosives?"

"It appears as though they were stolen from the Navy depot in Ferravyl."

"That seems rather convenient."

"Oh . . . it's no coincidence. It's probably why they picked that depot to raid. Glendyl has guards, but he didn't ever think—or his director didn't—about the fact that his workers might not be working for him. All the security was directed at keeping outsiders from doing damage, but not much thought was given to those inside."

"That's not something most people think about. Look at Odelia and Kolasyn. The only losses they've had are from his brother, not from strangers."

"That's probably true of Iryela and Kandryl, too."

"Will you ever be able to prove that?"

"I have no idea. No one's seen Johanyr since he left Mont D'Glace. He's vanished."

"That's not like him, from what you've told me."

At that moment came a loud cry from upstairs, and our conversation was postponed.

We did not attend anomen services that night. Perhaps that wasn't showing thanks to the Nameless, but at that point my gratitude was directed to one special other.

45

Much as I disliked forcing myself to get up and exercise on Lundi, I did. But I helped Seliora get Diestrya ready and still managed to be at the administration building before seventh glass. There, I immediately hunted down Schorzat, catching him as he was coming down the corridor.

"The word is that you had a busy weekend," he offered.

"Except for yesterday afternoon, it was." I waited for him to open his study door, then followed him inside and closed the door behind us.

"In a moment, I'm going to see Maitre Dyana . . ."

"As you think best, sir."

"The Ferrans sabotaged and blew up Glendyl's turbine works and most of his manufactory buildings in Ferravyl. I do think we need to discuss the matter and what the Collegium should do next." I smiled. "Don't you?"

"Yes, sir." Schorzat looked worried.

"Before I do, I need to know a few things." I paused. "How many imager agents are there in the northern fleet?"

"No more than a score."

"How many of them can image fire at a distance . . . a half mille, say, if they can see?"

"Half, perhaps."

"How many field agents can you assemble who can do that as well?"

"Fifteen at best."

"How many junior imagers are there in the various collegia who can do the same?"

Schorzat frowned at that. "I wouldn't know. There might be thirty."

"That should be sufficient if we use all of them."

"What do you have in mind, Maitre?" Schorzat asked.

"Winning the war and teaching the Ferrans another lesson." I smiled again. "Now . . . I'd like you and Kahlasa to assemble all the material you have on the barges and the bombards and everything else dealing with the attack on Imagisle. I imagine I'll need it in less than a glass."

"We can do that."

"Thank you. I'd appreciate it if you and Kahlasa remained available until I get back to you. It shouldn't be that long."

"We'll be here."

He didn't sound happy, but, given what had happened over the weekend, neither was I.

For whatever reason, I was in the anteroom before Gherard was, or perhaps he was running an errand. So I knocked and stepped into Maitre Dyana's study.

She looked up from the papers before her, possibly my report, and flipped a brilliant green silk scarf back over her shoulder, not that almost all of her scarves weren't brightly colored. "Do you have anything to add to this?"

"A few things. Did you discover anything in Rivages?"

"Only a few more High Holders who no longer are. As we discussed before, that will wait. Is the damage to Glendyl's works as bad as you initially reported?"

"It's that bad, if not worse. What I didn't report was that an inordinate number of workers suffered injuries, illnesses, and disappearances over the last year, and the majority of those hired to fill the vacancies seemed very well qualified. That was what the works director told me. Just before the first explosion, he and I were attacked by two workers using the same kind of heavy rifles that have been used here in L'Excelsis by those we've suspected of being Ferran agents. The day after the explosions, Director Huesyt told me that they found incomplete installations of explosives in the parts of the works that weren't destroyed." I paused. "Oh . . . I also sent a message to Frydryk—the young High Holder Suyrien—telling him about the attack on Glendyl's works and suggesting that he might wish to take a closer look at his shipworks."

"Not a bad idea."

"We need to talk to Glendyl together when we're finished here."

"That should not take too long."

"It won't."

"You're the head of security," Maitre Dyana pointed out. "What do you propose to put a stop to all of this? Do you think it's possible?"

"It will be hard to stop whatever the Ferrans have already set up, but I do have a plan for putting an end to their meddling."

"That sounds rather grandiose. Even you can't image their country into ruin, Rhenn. More to the point, you aren't leaving Solidar. Preferably not even L'Excelsis."

I had thought of taking the lead on implementing my proposal, but I just replied, "True, but a hundred imagers could destroy every port city in Ferrum. Perhaps even thirty or forty could."

"You aren't serious, I trust?"

"I'm very serious. Let me explain . . . ." From there I laid out what I'd thought out on the way back from Ferravyl and on Solayi afternoon.

When I finished, she looked at me. "From where did you get that idea?"

"From Ferlyn. Indirectly, of course. He made the point that the world was changing, and I realized that the Collegium needed to change. I didn't quite see how until Seliora pointed me in the right direction. The way machines work is by breaking work down into small repetitive steps. This is just an application of that principle."

"The Navy won't want to cooperate."

"They will . . . after we meet with Sea-Marshal Valeun."

She looked at me. "Then we had best deal with Glendyl first."

The air had finally cleared and was cold and clear, with both moons almost lost in the brightness of the winter sky as we walked from the administration building to the infirmary.

Draffyd hurried to meet us, shaking his head. "Maitres . . . The good Councilor has expressed his desire to depart, most forcefully."

"Could he?" asked Dyana. "Safely?"

"I'd prefer he remain another day or two, but . . ." Draffyd shrugged. "If he's careful and keeps the stitches clean and changes the dressing . . ."

"He'll stay," declared Dyana. "That way, he'll more likely recover, and Caartyl will have to be more cautious."

When we entered the chamber, Glendyl was sitting up in the infirmary bed, not looking terribly pleased, but that might have been because he was able to appreciate the severity of his surroundings, as well as the large and immovable obdurate guard stationed outside his door.

"Ah . . . Maitre Dyana and Maitre Rhennthyl, to what do I owe this visit? Do you wish to collect for saving this factor's life? Or to congratulate me for surviving the fare and sparseness of this chamber? Or to indicate that I must suffer yet more tedium amid this grayness?"

"Why, we wished to see to your health, Councilor," replied Dyana. "It does appear that you are recovering in a satisfactory fashion. Your words would indicate as much. Your wound was quite severe, and you will be staying several more days, but only several more days. Unless you do something foolish and impair the healing."

Glendyl did not speak for a moment, then said, "Surely, it does not take the two highest Maitres in the Collegium to tell me that."

"For a distinguished Councilor, nothing but the best," said Dyana lightly, looking to me.

"I have a question for you, Councilor," I said. "Did you have any interest in L'Excelsis Indemnity?"

"No. Why do you ask?"

"Their branch here was bombed and destroyed. I wondered if that would have any effect on your enterprises."

"I don't see why it would. It's no secret that I've always placed my indemnity contracts with Solidaran Indemnity . . . in the Solis branch. They don't have a branch in Ferravyl."

"Might I ask how much your works in Ferravyl is indemnified for?"

"You can ask. That's my business."

I looked to Maitre Dyana. She nodded every so slightly.

"Not any longer. Your works suffered a series of devastating explosions and fires over the weekend, and whether you will have the funds to replace the destroyed facilities, and how soon, are a matter of interest and concern to all Solidar, including the Council."

"How devastating? Why didn't you tell me sooner?" Glendyl lurched upright in the bed. He tried to move his right hand, and he raised it chest high, before he let it drop.

"Because I just returned from there yesterday and wanted to report to Maitre Dyana and you directly. The locomotive works, the foundry, the drop forge, and possibly the boiler fabrication buildings did not seem too heavily damaged. All the turbine works were leveled . . . and most everything else."

"But . . . how?"

"Ferran saboteurs. They've been removing workers for a year and replacing them with their own people. They even shot at me and Director Huesyt as the explosions were being detonated."

Glendyl was paler than before.

"The amount of indemnity?" I pressed.

"All I could obtain was one hundred and fifty thousand golds," he finally admitted.

"If Suyrien the Younger or others extended more funding, you could rebuild?" asked Maitre Dyana.

"I . . . don't know." He shook his head slowly. "Why . . . why me?"

"Because no one else has facilities to build the new turbines for warships," I replied, "and that means years before Solidar can modernize its fleet while the Ferrans build more and more fast ships."

"I tried to tell the Council. So did Suyrien . . ." He swallowed, then let himself lean back against the pillows. "But how . . . ?"

"Because everyone in Solidar has been concentrating on the traditional ways of fighting wars," I said. "You were right, in a way. Once there are more machines and factories of all sorts, and more factors competing with each other, we won't be as vulnerable to a handful of acts of sabotage. Since you were unable to persuade the Council and since many Councilors chose not to understand . . ."

"The High Holders will not—"

"They won't have any options before long, either." *Nor will you or the other factors.* "Now . . . you need to rest."

"Rest? How can I rest?"

"You can't do much else, right now," I pointed out. "You may have to consider Suyrien's proposal for a fast frigate . . . if the funding can even be worked out."

Glendyl didn't quite glare at me. "Suyrien told me about you."

"I'm certain he did." I smiled. "Do try to get some rest, Councilor. Solidar would prefer to use your expertise, but we will have modern vessels, one way or another."

"You've made that clear, Maitres. Good day."

"Good day," replied Dyana pleasantly. "I look forward to your return to the Council."

I just inclined my head politely.

Glendyl's acknowledgment was the smallest of nods.

After we left Glendyl and walked back toward the administration building, Maitre Dyana said, "You weren't all that easy on him, Rhenn."

"You mean I didn't use much finesse? No, I didn't. If he hadn't been so greedy, trying to hold onto the sole production of those turbines, trying to outwait the Council, we wouldn't be in as bad a position. If Glendyl isn't co-operative, young Suyrien does have the plans and specifications, but for him to build a facility will take much longer than if Glendyl rebuilds. We ought to insist on someone else building the turbines anyway."

"With that debt . . . how can Glendyl rebuild?"

"He's fortunate. He has products we all need. I think you should be able to persuade a number of the more . . . solvent . . . High Holders to loan the funds, for a suitable return, of course. Since he's not a High Holder, there's no point in their ruining him by refusing."

"You're presuming I can do that."

"Maitre . . . I know you can do that." I tried to keep my tone humorous and light.

She did laugh.

"We need to find Valeun, but I need to gather some materials."

"I'll have a coach waiting in a quint," she said.

"I won't be that long."

She just nodded, then headed through the doors and upstairs to her study.

True to his word, Schorzat had gathered everything I'd requested, and I slipped all the documents into a leather folder.

"Might I ask where you're headed?" Kahlasa asked, with a smile that bordered on impish.

"To visit—or attempt to visit—the Sea-Marshal in the Naval Command. I'm trusting that he'll see reason. If not, he will anyway."

Kahlasa nodded. Schorzat barely managed to keep from looking appalled.

I walked out swiftly.

Once we were in the Maitre's coach and headed toward the Naval Command, Maitre Dyana turned and fixed her eyes on me. "What you have isn't complete."

"It doesn't matter, not if Valeun wants to remain Sea-Marshal."

"Do you intend to force change on Solidar?"

"No more than the pressures of change and time would have anyway. Seliora pointed out to me that she and her family already have the kind of card-directed lathes that will provide better and less expensive furniture than can the average cabinet-maker. The Ferrans are applying those techniques to everything, warfare as well. There's no way that they could have built all those new land-cruisers without a similar approach. That's what Glendyl was going to do with the turbines, and what Suyrien was trying to do with the fast frigates and battlecruisers." I snorted. "All I'm trying to do is buy Solidar enough time so that we have a chance to make those changes. Suyrien understood the need. He wouldn't have slipped in those reforms if he hadn't."

"Do you think his son is that wise?"

"No. But Frydryk isn't a Councilor. Nor is he stupid. He'll do what he must to retain what he has. All we have to do is to point out what that is."

"You'll have to do that. He's more likely to listen to you."

"That's fine. The Council is more likely to listen to you."

"More likely? Perhaps. They will listen to me because none of them will wish to deal with you any sooner than they have to."

I didn't argue. I was afraid matters would get to that point far sooner than I would have liked.

The building holding the Naval Command was a two-story, yellow-brick structure with gray granite cornerstones and window casements. It looked even higher than two levels. The covered coach portico was also of brick and granite. The two sailors in dress blues who stood guard did not blink an eye when we left the Maitre's coach and went through the heavily varnished golden oak doors whose brasswork was polished so brightly that it outshone gold.

The senior ranker seated behind the desk at the main foyer to the Naval Command building glanced from Maitre Dyana to me and then back to me.

"This is Maitre Dyana. She's the Maitre of the Collegium Imago. I'm Maitre Rhennthyl. I'm certain that Sea-Marshal Valeun will wish to see us." I projected a sense that his life wouldn't be worth much if he didn't convey our presence to Sea-Marshal Valeun.

"Yes, sirs. I'll have to let Commander Daecyn know, sirs." He tugged on something, most likely a bell-pull.

We only waited a few moments before a Commander strode across the foyer. He was slight of build, ramrod straight, and bore an indifferent expression— until he was close enough to recognize the imager grays. Then, he assumed an solicitous expression.

"This is rather unexpected . . ."

"This is Maitre Dyana, the head of the Collegium. We have urgent news for the Sea-Marshal," I said politely.

"I could convey that . . ." His words died away as he took in the expression on Maitre Dyana's face.

I didn't even have to project anything.

"I'll need to escort you to his study. If you would accompany me . . ."

"Of course," said Dyana.

We followed the Commander through the archway at the rear of the foyer, then up a set of marble steps almost as wide as those in the Council Chateau, and then to the double doors at the rear of the building, doors flanked by the Solidaran flag on the right and the Naval ensign on the left. He opened the doors, holding them for us.

The senior ranker at the desk stood immediately. "Sir, Maitres."

"I'd like to tell the Marshal that the Maitres are here," offered the Commander.

"Yes, sir."

The Commander eased through the single oak door, closing it behind him. He reappeared shortly, looking slightly relieved, and held the door open. "Maitre Dyana . . . Maitre Rhennthyl."

"Thank you," Dyana said as she passed.

I also thanked him, and the door closed behind us.

The study of Sea-Marshal Valeun was a good ten yards by six, dominated by an enormous desk, with five chairs facing it. The wall to the right was essentially a small cartographic library, with a center rack on which was displayed a large map of Ferrum. The left wall consisted of bookcases, in the middle of which was a door that doubtless led to an adjoining conference room.

Valeun stood behind the desk, a man of middling height in dark dress blues, with the silver braid and insignia of a very senior Marshal. His blond-and-silver hair was cut short, and he was clean-shaven. He made no effort to step forward. "Maitre Dyana, Maitre Rhennthyl . . . I understand you are insistent on seeing me."

"It is rather necessary," said Dyana.

"Since you are accompanied by Maitre Rhennthyl, I would like to wait until I can summon Marshal Geuffryt," Valeun said pleasantly.

"No . . . you really don't," I said, projecting absolute authority and power. "Not if you wish matters to go in your best interests. If you really wish to include him, it might be far better to hear what we have to say . . . first."

Valeun glanced to Maitre Dyana. Her smile was pleasant, but her eyes were as hard and as cold as frozen granite. The Sea-Marshal smiled politely, but hardly warmly. "Then perhaps we should be seated, and you can convey what you have in mind." He followed his own advice and seated himself in the large leather chair behind the desk.

"We thought we should be the ones to inform you of several matters." After seating herself, Dyana nodded to me.

"First," I began, "it appears likely that any swift action on the part of the Council in dealing with fleet modernization and the building of faster and more capable warships has been dealt a severe setback."

"How so? I was not aware that any action was even being considered, given the current mood of the Council." Valeun's tone was close to smug.

I smiled. I shouldn't have enjoyed what was coming, but I'd never cared for the politely superior attitude of those in positions of power and command. "Ferran saboteurs destroyed a good portion of Councilor Glendyl's engine works this past weekend. The turbine facilities were totally annihilated."

"You did nothing, Maitre Rhennthyl?"

"Oh . . . when it became apparent that such an attack was likely, I attempted to bring the matter up with the Councilor. That did not work out well, because he was shot just as we began to talk . . . as you may recall. So I traveled to Ferravyl myself, and as soon as I appeared, the saboteurs set off the charges they had already placed. They had not completed their work, and the locomotive works escaped major damage, as did a few other structures. The remaining structures did have partial explosives in place." I paused. "That brings up several rather pointed questions. First, exactly how did all these saboteurs happen to reach Solidar? Second, why was the Naval Command unaware of just how many there were? Third, how did they manage to come up with Naval Command explosives? Did I mention that the undetonated explosives bore Navy markings?"

At my last words, Valeun stiffened. "That's preposterous."

"Is it? I had a meeting with one of your more junior subordinates several weeks ago, and he confirmed that several tonnes of Poudre B could not be accounted for. But that also brings up yet another matter."

"Which is?" This time Valeun's voice held a certain wariness.

"The matter of the bombardment of Imagisle—"

"What does that have to do—"

"Oh . . . but it does," I cut him off. "To begin with, the barges and the tug that were employed were leased under a Naval Command contract, by a Navy subcommander, who employed a former pilot known to be a Navy-approved pilot by the lessor. The funds to pay the lease were disbursed by one of two banques known to pay for such contracts. The subcommander knew all of the personnel who had conducted previous leases. Then there is the small matter of the accuracy of the bombards. The very first shell fired struck Maitre Dichartyn's dwelling. Of the eight shells fired, every single one hit a target. Considering that the shells were fired from the River Aluse, in the dark, after midnight, it's more than fair to conclude that the men who aimed and fired those bombards were professionals and that they knew the guns and had exact measurements for the distances from their mooring and firing point to every target. That degree of accuracy requires experienced Naval gunners."

"You're inventing this."

"I didn't invent the damage to Imagisle, or the stolen barges and tugs." I smiled. "I did think you might find this difficult to believe." I opened the folder I carried and took out several documents, then stood and laid them on the desk in front of Valeun, ready to image a shield over them if he were to be so foolish as to try to tamper with them.

He did not. He read through them, then straightened. "They have to be forgeries."

"They may well be," I said, reclaiming the documents. "But that raises another set of questions. All the authorization codes and numbers are correct. All the procedures were followed to the letter. The forms are standard, down to the ink. That means that, either someone high in the Naval Command was involved, or that your procedures are incredibly flawed." I sat down and waited.

"You want something, don't you? You wouldn't be here otherwise."

"Oh . . . we're not done, Marshal. There's another aspect to this. It's the golds involved."

His frown showed a certain questioning.

"The lease wasn't paid on a promise. The lessor received five thousand golds before the tug and barges were released. We've spent considerable time checking with the banques involved. The funds came from your secondary banque . . ."

"The Banque D'Rivages? That's preposterous. If five thousand golds vanished from the Naval accounts there, I'd have known it."

"Exactly. I'm certain that you would. You didn't. However . . . the funds were transferred from a numbered High Holder account. Shortly before this happened, a former heir to the previous holder of that account vanished from an imager collegium. Now . . . what makes this intriguing is that the only friend remaining to this heir was a certain Assistant Sea-Marshal. What makes that even more interesting is that that Sea-Marshal also revealed certain details of banking information to me, well before that fund transfer. Now . . . of course, the former heir is missing . . . and I have grave doubts he will ever be found. There's little doubt that this Sea-Marshal also has little love for the Collegium."

"That's all speculation, the last part," Valeun observed mildly, almost cheerfully.

"No. Not all of it. The fund transfers are not. The relationships are not. The missing and nearly totally blind heir is not. Nor is the written note I received from Marshal Geuffryt. Nor is the fact that disclosure of this information would destroy your career instantly. Now," I said politely, "I am certain that you will find a way to deal with your subordinate in a fashion that does not embarrass the Naval Command nor require the Collegium to act. You do understand that your failure to deal with the matter will result in your being considered an accomplice in treachery after the fact, Marshal? By the Collegium, as well as by the Council, should we be forced to bring the matter up. Obviously, given the dismal Naval situation with regard to Ferrum, we would prefer not to bring it up; but to have you resolve it, quietly but permanently."

"You are rather insistent, Maitre Rhennthyl."

"I know. It's one of my faults. I also have the habit of resolving matters on my own if others don't. That's one reason why Maitre Dyana felt that I should speak to you first. Now . . . let us leave that rather disgusting matter for the moment . . . and your discretion . . . and turn to the problem at hand. The problem of Ferrum."

For just a moment, Valeun's eyes widened, as if he had no idea why I'd changed the subject. That was fine with me.

"You are struggling to hold the blockade of Ferrum, even by transferring more and more ships from the waters off Otelyrn to the northern fleet. You've suffered more losses than have been made public."

"We would not be in this situation if the Council had agreed to our requests . . ."

"That may be, but we need to win this war. Even if the Council had funded all thirty capital ships last year, and even if Glendyl's works had not been destroyed, it would be two years or more before the first ones were ready. We need to look at a different approach." I paused, then asked, "How many high-speed gunboats do you have in the northern fleet? How many more could you get there in the next few weeks?"

Valeun frowned. "Gunboats? They won't stand up to even a Ferran frigate."

"That's not the point. We're not interested in destroying the Ferran fleet. We're interested in winning the war and teaching them a lesson."

"How will you do that without a larger and faster fleet?"

"By using the one thing that the Ferrans do not have." I went on to explain. ". . . But to give the gunboats the best chance of getting close to the ports, they'll need a diversion . . . something like a massed fleet attack on their fleet or main naval base."

"That would undo . . ." He smiled. "You mean for us to mass the fleet in a way that they'll bring in everything they can?"

"Exactly . . . and then you can disperse."

"It might work," Valeun finally conceded. "If it doesn't, then the fleet is no worse off. If it is successful, we will lose some of those gunboats and those aboard. You realize that, I trust."

"I know, but we'll lose more men, and your fleets will suffer much more than that, if the war drags on. And it will, because it will be years before you can get the more modern vessels."

"Also," said Dyana quietly, "using Rhenn's plan will show the Council that you're willing to try other strategies besides spending more and more golds on more and more ships."

"It will take several weeks . . ."

"The fewer, the better," I said. "We don't want to give the Ferrans time enough to change their tactics to try to pick off your mid-sized warships one by one."

Valeun's eyes narrowed for a moment, but he offered a smile. "We wouldn't want that. Not now."

Maitre Dyana stood. She smiled politely. "It was so good of you to see us, Marshal Valeun. We do appreciate your desire to resolve troublesome matters, so that we can concentrate on the real problems facing Solidar, and I'm certain that you and Rhenn will be able to work everything out, without my assistance, from here on in. He'll be in touch with you after you've thought about how to bring your gunboats into position. For me, dealing with the new Council and keeping them focused on the real concerns is likely to take some doing."

I stood as well, inclining my head to Valeun.

"I'm sure you can manage that, Maitre," he said after a moment.

Neither of us spoke until we were in Maitre Dyana's coach and headed back to Imagisle.

"You realize what you've done, you know?" she said quietly.

"I do. It's better than Geuffryt deserves."

"That wasn't what I meant."

"You mean, about Valeun looking for every opportunity to do me in, either directly or politically or any other way? Yes, but I didn't see any other option that would work and be timely. I assume that's why you told him he'd have to work with me."

"That . . . and to let him see, if he will, that crossing you would be unwise. If he can't see that, then we'll need a new Sea-Marshal."

There wasn't much I could say to that, and I needed to think about how to assemble the imagers I needed and what additional training we might be able to provide on a quick basis.

46

According to the old saying, "the Namer's fingers knot the details." As soon
as I returned to my study after returning from the Naval Command, I started
to become far more aware of how long and how clutching those fingers
were . . . and how the details might well come back to bite one. Just to start
implementing my plan, Schorzat, Kahlasa, and I would have to compile the
list of all the junior imagers at Imagisle who had the necessary ability and
strength to image flame at a distance. The Collegium had a listing of all junior
imagers, with their birth date and where they were born. What it didn't have
was any sort of written or recorded assessment of the abilities of each of
those imagers. Only the preceptor of each imager knew that, and not in all
cases. With the exception of Shault, I certainly didn't know any of the abilities of those imagers for whom I was preceptor, and not all of Shault's capabilities. I'd been so occupied in other matters that I hadn't had a chance to
spend more than a portion of a glass with each one.

So I immediately sent off notes to all five of "my" imagers, telling them
to meet me at the Collegium's steamer pier at a quint past fourth glass that
afternoon. After that, to deal with that part of the problem for the entire Collegium and not just the imagers for whom I was preceptor, and to try to obtain some sort of roughly equivalent standards for evaluation, I immediately
drafted an "abilities form," obtained Maitre Dyana's corrections and approval, and had the duty primes begin to set up the letterpress to make enough
copies of the form so that we could then provide a copy with each junior imager's name on it to his or her preceptor with the notation that the completed
form was to be returned to Maitre Dyana no later than noon on Vendrei.

I also had to draft letters for Maitre Dyana's signature to the three heads
of the regional collegia, requesting their cooperation and sending a copy of
the form to them, although it was questionable whether we'd receive the
information from them in time to be useful for the Naval operation against
Ferrum.

While the primes were using the cumbersome letterpress to print off the
forms, just before fourth glass on Lundi, I pulled on my heavy gray cloak and
hurried through the chill air to the Collegium's steamer pier near the north-

east tip of Imagisle. It was cold enough that there were no mothers or children playing in the park north of the various family dwellings.

Shault was already standing on the pier, as were Eamyn and Ralyea, when I neared the foot of the southernmost stone pier of the three. I heard fast boot steps on the stone walk and turned to see Marteon running toward us.

I couldn't help calling out, "You don't have to run. There's time."

"Yes, sir," puffed the muscular and round-faced tertius as he slowed to a walk less than five yards away.

"Just wait here," I told the four, glancing south toward the quadrangle. In the weak late afternoon sun, I saw no sign of Haugyl, but the glass had just emptied four. I walked up the pier, crossed the short plank gangway, and stepped onto the river steamer, a boat of only fifteen yards in length with a single deck, and the steam engine and the paddlewheel in the rear.

Faeldyn, the obdurate pilot, stood outside the wheel-house, set forward of midships. He nodded as I approached. "Maitre . . . what will you be having them do today?"

"Some imaging exercises. I'd like you to take us just off the northern tip of Imagisle, as close to the point of the riverwall there as is safe, and hold there while I have them work on something."

"Water's a bit rough today. We shouldn't get much closer than twenty yards."

"Thirty or forty would be fine."

The pilot and single crewman nodded.

"Let me get them on board." I glanced back toward the pier. Still no sign of Haugyl, but I motioned for the four others to cross the narrow plank to the boat.

At that moment, I saw Haugyl sauntering along the walk, a good hundred yards south of the pier. Even when he saw the other four junior imagers begin to board, he made no move to hurry. I thought about calling out to him, then decided against it, since I had said a quint past the glass. We just waited for him. The moment Haugyl crossed the plank, I pulled it onboard and stowed it in the heavy iron brackets attached to the gunwale. Behind me, I heard a low exchange.

". . . Watch it. Maitre Rhennthyl didn't look too happy."

". . . Made it before the end of the quint, didn't I?"

"You made the rest of us wait . . ."

". . . No real hurry . . ."

I turned and looked at Haugyl. "No, there wasn't a real hurry, but since everyone else was here, we could have started earlier, and finished earlier, and that would have saved five of us some time. Is your time so much more important than that of five others?"

Haugyl didn't meet my eyes.

"Is it?"

"No, sir."

"You might keep that in mind, especially if you ever hope to be more than a tertius." I looked toward the pilot. "We're all ready, Faeldyn."

"If you'd not mind the line, sir?" asked Faeldyn.

"I can do that." I jumped back to the pier, untied the line fastened around an iron cleat, then scrambled back aboard before Faeldyn backed the boat out into the river channel. I quickly coiled the line and headed back aft. As soon as we headed upstream away from the pier, the boat began to hit the uneven river waves, and small gouts of spray sleeted back from the bow. That was why I stood just forward of the pilot house.

We were still several hundred yards from the northern tip of Imagisle when Haugyl leaned over the railing and loosed the contents of his stomach. He was pale when he finally straightened up.

Eamyn tried to conceal an amused expression, while Marteon looked concerned. Ralyea, for all his apprehensive looks at me and at the small white-caps on the gray waters of the River Aluse, stood facing into the light but chill wind and seemed to be almost enjoying himself. Shault only watched, his eyes measuring the distances from the boat to the eastern shore and then to Imagisle.

When we passed the tip of Imagisle, Faeldyn swung the river steamer to port, angling north of the gray granite triangle that marked the northernmost point of the isle. The engine hissed and rumbled slightly as he slowed the paddlewheel, then reversed it to bring us to a stop.

I stepped toward the five. "You see the stone triangle there? When I call you by name, I want you to image something that will burn fiercely and set it on the very end of the stone closest to us, then set it afire."

Eamyn frowned. "Sir . . . you want us to image fire?"

"Fire isn't enough. You need something to sustain it. Like this." I imaged a small pool of lamp oil onto the stone tip, followed by flame.

A burst of red and orange appeared, followed by black smoke, then slowly died away.

"Or this." The second time, I did a lighter oil, then imaged a mist of black powder into the flame. That was more impressive. "Any more questions?"

There weren't any.

I pointed to Eamyn. "You first."

He squared his shoulders and looked southward. After a moment, an oval flame appeared and flickered out.

"You need something more to sustain it," I commented. "If you're going to image flame, there's no point in doing it unless it can last long enough to catch something on fire. Try again."

The second time he had a flame flaring out of a small pool of something, either oil or bitumen or alcohol.

"Much better." I turned to Marteon. "Your turn."

The round-faced imager came up with something that looked like a candle, and only showed a tiny point of flame.

"We need a bigger flame."

Marteon's next effort had a bigger flame feeding off what I suspected was a lump of oil and wax.

The other three also managed sufficient flame images, although Haugyl's was a bit shaky.

When Ralyea finished, I called to Faeldyn. "Take us up short of the Nord Bridge, but where we can see the tip of the isle."

"Yes, sir."

The water got a bit rougher, and Haugyl turned from pale to slightly greenish, suggesting that he might not be suited to any sort of shipboard duty.

Once Faeldyn brought us to a stop some fifty yards south of the bridge, I repeated the whole process again, making sure that I could image a flame large enough to be seen.

"Shault, you go first."

"Yes, sir."

From a little more than a half mille away, four of the five could manage the flame. Haugyl could not.

Then I had Faeldyn take us to the other side of the bridge, positioned where we could see Imagisle through one of the arches. At a mille, only Shault, Eamyn, and Ralyea could manage the flame imaging. Ralyea's face was covered in sweat, and he looked shaky. Shault and Eamyn might have been able to do more, but the river turned more northward, enough so that, given the Nord Bridge, I couldn't have seen the riverwall anyway. So I had Faeldyn head downstream.

On the way back to Imagisle, I had each of them demonstrate their skills in every item on my form, from imaging a ball into an open space in the middle of a hoop to imaging air bubbles into the middle of a curved glass tube.

Shault was the only one to ask, although the others doubtless wondered, "Could you tell us what all this is for, sir?"

"It's because the Collegium needs to know what all the seconds and thirds can do. A number of you may be required to take a trip and use your skills. If you're selected, you'll learn more about it in a few days, and you'll get more training and learn more." *More than you may want.* "That's all I'm going to say right now."

I didn't have to say more, because Faeldyn was easing the boat up to the Collegium pier, and I took the mooring line and jumped to the pier and tied the boat fast. Faeldyn had the plank out, and Haugyl was the first off. His steps were shaky.

"Good day, sir," offered Shault as he stepped onto the pier. He didn't raise any more questions, but I knew the rumors would be flying across the quadrangle and the juniors' quarters within moments after they were out of sight.

"Good evening, Shault."

Once I thanked Faeldyn, I turned and walked southward and then through the gardens and past the hedge maze toward our house. I noted that the imager-builders had finished re-creating the exterior of the Maitre's dwelling. Maitre Dyana's previous house still remained a pile of gray stone and shattered roof tiles, as did what had been Maitre Dichartyn's. I couldn't help swallowing when I looked at that rubble.

Thankfully, after I reached our house, Seliora was preoccupied with both Diestrya and the loss of two commissions as a result of financial setbacks caused by the Ferran bombings in L'Excelsis, and she didn't ask me any detailed questions on my day. I really wasn't ready to explain, although I'd have to soon enough.

47

I was in my study before seventh glass on Mardi morning, to make sure that the duty primes had delivered the forms to every master of the Collegium at Imagisle by eighth glass. Then I read through the newsheets.

Veritum reported that the deaths from the abuse of the stronger elveweed had decreased, but that they were still occurring, especially among younger users, despite the burning of all the weed growing on former High Holder Ruelyr's lands. Fresh elveweed continued to be sold, and in more cities across Solidar. That wasn't about to change, I knew, now that the drug dealers had discovered that it could be grown in the south of Solidar, and provided more profit and less reliance on smuggled dried weed.

Both newsheets noted that the Ferran advances in Jariola had slowed because of winter storms. *Tableta* reported that desertions in the Jariolan army were rising, and that the Oligarch had authorized field executions of deserters. Both also had short follow-up reports on the explosions at Glendyl's engine works, with the observations that neither the Naval Command nor the Council had issued any comments or statements.

I'd just finished considering the implications of the stories when, at a quint past eight, Heisbyl, who had been a Maitre D'Aspect when I'd first come to Imagisle and who still was only that, rapped on my half-open door.

"Come in."

"Thank you." He closed the door precisely and took the chair in front of the desk. Under his dull gray hair, carefully brushed and parted, was a high forehead and a pair of flat hazel eyes. He cleared his throat.

I smiled and waited.

He held up an envelope, one that looked precisely like one of those dispatched to every Maitre. "Maitre Rhennthyl . . . I must protest. This . . . this edict . . . may have Maitre Dyana's name on it, but it bears your fingerprints."

"Assuming that it does . . . what is the problem?"

"What is the problem? What is the problem? The problem is that you are trying to turn imagers into machines. You want every preceptor to assess each ability of every one of his charges, as if imaging could be measured with yardsticks or calipers or weighed with scales."

I frowned. "Having the Collegium know what all junior imagers can do doesn't make them machines."

"Every imager has a different degree of skill. Machines are all alike."

"I'm not asking you to treat them like machines. I'm certain there are great differences among the seconds and thirds you supervise in the armory workshops. All you need to do is to write out what each can do."

"This is just the first step in turning them into machines, Maitre Rhennthyl. We won't even have to fight the Ferrans because we'll end up just like them."

"Maitre Heisbyl, if we don't change matters here, we won't be able to fight them. You're right. There won't be a fight, because we'll already have lost, and then the machines and those who use and build them will find us useless. Before long, there will be machines that make precision parts as well or better, and with far less effort, than our imagers. In Ferrum, there well may be such machines already. Once, a Maitre D'Esprit could stand against any weapon in all of Terahnar. A month ago, a set of bombards proved that is no longer true— and those were antiques, compared to the long guns on a dreadnought."

My words, or something I did, must have affected him, because his defiance wilted, and he just looked old.

"You are destroying everything we stood for. You will regret it." He stood. "I will return your form, under protest, to the Maitre. The Nameless save us all." He stalked out without another word.

I almost didn't have a chance to catch my breath and consider what Heisbyl had said before Ghaend slipped into my study.

"You're not likely to be all that popular by noon." He settled into the chair across from me.

"Then I'd best make an appearance at the dining hall." I'd thought I would anyway, but it was a good line.

"You understand what you've done? Besides upsetting the older masters?"

"I have an idea, but I might well be wrong. Tell me, if you would."

"Imagers have always been apart. Because of what we can do, we have to be. To compensate for that, the Collegium has created the sense that we're special. There are not all that many of us, some five hundred in all Solidar. Each imager is somewhat different from any other. Unique, if you will. By requiring the newer imagers to be evaluated against a standard and categorized, you're suggesting that we're not unique. You're going against a long tradition and very strong feelings."

I nodded. "What else?"

"Does there have to be anything else?"

"No, I suppose not, but your tone suggests that there might be."

"Well . . . what will happen if that information leaks out? Do we really want the Council or everyone in Solidar—or in Ferrum—to know what we can or can't do?"

"I can understand the concern there. I really can, but there's another problem. Maitre Poincaryt and Maitre Dichartyn probably did know most of what I've asked masters to supply. When they died, that information died with them. We need that information now, and I can't learn it all in time without doing something like this. Also, can we afford to keep losing information because we're afraid to have a record except in the minds of one or two senior imagers? As I told Heisbyl a little while ago, once the most powerful imagers could stand against any weapon. Now we can't. That changes matters."

"For most Maitres, that doesn't matter. You're changing their world."

I nodded. "You're right about that. But I don't see any choice if the Collegium is to survive in a way that will still protect imagers."

"The older Maitres don't see it that way, Rhenn."

"Maitre Dyana does, and, I'd be surprised if Maitre Jhulian doesn't as well. How do you see it?"

Ghaend shook his head. "I agree with you, but I don't like it."

"So . . . if we're going to be honest about it, then, that only leaves something like four or five older Maitres who are unhappy."

"And probably a hundred older seconds and thirds, when they find out."

"What difference will it make to them, unless an older Maitre stirs them up and misrepresents things? I would hope . . ." I broke off the words. "Someone will. You're right. No matter how much sense it makes, no matter how much times have changed, people, even imagers, want to believe in their traditional and special place in the world." I shrugged. "But I can't see any other way around this."

"This is part of something much larger, isn't it?"

"It is, and the longer before I have to reveal it, the better."

"I don't think I'd want to be in your boots, Maitre." Ghaend smiled and rose. "I won't press you. Dichartyn told me, years ago, that to press you was both useless and unwise. I trust that the Council sees it that way as well, for all of our sakes."

I stood. I didn't correct him, but only replied, "So do I."

Once he left, I wondered who would spread the word. Certainly, Heisbyl would, and most probably Maitre Rholyn, if in a more indirect fashion.

The next visitor, surprisingly, was Quaelyn, and he was smiling broadly when he arrived after ninth glass and sat down across from me. "Congratulations to you and Maitre Dyana. It's well past time for something like this." He lifted the envelope.

"Not everyone thinks that way."

"Of course they don't. People have a pattern. If they're comfortable, they want things to stay that way, and Imagisle has been comfortable for a long time." He grinned. "Until you came along."

"I can't say I had anything to do with the attacks on Imagisle or Solidar."

He raised his thin white eyebrows. "Don't be so certain about that. People react to what they feel, not what they see or think. You've changed how people feel. It's time for a change. Change for the better, especially, takes power and a crisis to change things. We've needed more systematic information on imagers for years. Now, you've taken the opportunity."

"I heard you talking about the patterns of where imagers were born, years ago. I'd hoped there would be more in the records. There wasn't."

He smiled mischievously. "I'm gratified that you remembered. I tried for years to get Maitre Poincaryt to ask for more information about incoming imagers, but it never happened."

"I think I know why." And I did. I'd thought about it a great deal, even before Ghaend's visit. "He and Maitre Dichartyn were always worried that such information could get out and be used against the Collegium . . . especially since there have always been so few imagers."

Quaelyn snorted. "That's handicapping yourself for no benefit. I told Poincaryt that then. People will always believe the worst when they want to. Facts that don't agree with what they want to believe just get ignored. The only facts they want are those that support what they want to believe. Not having the information you need because other people might find it and use it is like burying your head in quicksand. They don't need it to cause trouble. They never have." He stood, abruptly. "That's all I had. Don't let them change your mind, Maitre Rhennthyl."

After he left, I closed my door and tried to think through what I hadn't done. In addition to determining how many and which imagers needed to go where for transport to the northern fleet, and working out the associated logistics, I still needed to discover—one way or another—a few other unresolved matters, such as how accurate Geuffryt's information about payoffs to Caartyl and Cydarth had been, and what had been involved with that. Also . . . I couldn't help but wonder about the dead young woman who hadn't been an elveweed suicide . . . and the role the freeholder–High Holder water conflicts played . . . or why L'Excelsis Indemnity had been destroyed . . . or . . .

48

The complexity of what I'd planned spiraled ever wider, and by Meredi morning, I realized that the evaluation of seconds and thirds was just the beginning of the detailed difficulties. We still had to get some twenty-odd junior imagers to a Naval port, most likely Westisle, but I needed to work that out with Valeun—something I wasn't exactly looking forward to, but couldn't avoid. I'd already sent a messenger to the Naval Command suggesting a meeting at the fourth glass of the afternoon, but hadn't yet received a reply.

In the meantime, some aspects of the travel had to be taken care of. The nearest port was Solis, two long days by ironway, while Westisle was more than four days by ironway. Either route required overnight travel . . . and far more sleeping cloths than Draffyd happened to have, not to mention the preparation of large quantities of sleeping draughts. Then there was the requirement for lead foil, because gunboats weren't designed to carry imagers, and while that could be imaged, even for imagers, it was a slow and tedious process.

On top of all those problems was an even larger one, and that was why I found myself once more in Maitre Dyana's study before mid-morning.

She just looked at me.

So I launched into the problems at hand. "You've forbidden me to take charge of this in the field—or on the ocean—but there has to be a master in charge who understands what has to be done and who has strong shields and enough confidence to face down Navy Commanders."

She nodded. "Whom do you suggest?"

I had thought about it. "Can I pick anyone?"

"Anyone who's not a Maitre D'Esprit or a Maitre D'Structure."

That didn't surprise me, given how few senior masters there were. "Dartazn. He's dealt with Councilors. He's impressive in stature. He's thoughtful and intelligent, and he's close to being a Maitre D'Structure in imager abilities."

She nodded. "He'd be a good choice . . . if he's willing to put all his effort into it. He can be rather stubborn in a quiet way when he's forced to do things he'd prefer not to."

"I haven't talked to him, but I have the feeling he might relish something like this."

"Dichartyn once said that about someone else, and he was right. I hope you are."

"If he's not interested . . . then I'd suggest Ghaend."

"So would I, but Dartazn would be better." She nodded. "Go talk to him. He has a great deal to learn in the next week. But don't forget to tell Baratyn first."

"He won't be happy, either."

"You expected otherwise?" She raised a single eyebrow.

With a rueful smile, I left, heading back to my study to see if I'd gotten a reply from Sea-Marshal Valeun. As I walked down the steps to the main level, I was definitely getting the feeling that, by the time everything was resolved— if it even could be—no matter what happened, almost no one at the Collegium was likely to be pleased with me.

Valeun had replied. The duty prime had an envelope, and in it was a curt note said that he would be available at half past fourth glass.

My next task was to meet with Baratyn. So I donned my heavy winter cloak and ventured forth into a bitter wind to make my way to the duty coach stand.

Once I reached the Council Chateau, I found the Council's security master standing in the corridor on the main level, just outside the study where the messengers waited between duties.

"Maitre Rhennthyl, what brings you here these days?"

I offered a smile. "I came to talk to you and to get your thoughts on something."

"If it's thinking, we'd best go to my study."

I followed him and closed the door. He didn't sit down, and I didn't suggest it, either. One way or another, the conversation would be short.

"What do you think of Dartazn as a possibility for a position where we need a thoughtful, but enthusiastic and commanding Maitre D'Aspect?"

"It sounds like something dealing with seconds and thirds. Is it?"

"It is."

"He's been good with them." Baratyn smiled. "He's good with everyone. I figured he might not stay here . . . after all that's happened."

"We're short of masters everywhere. But I wanted to talk to you before I talked to him."

"I do appreciate that." He paused. "We'll be short-handed here."

"With what we're doing," I replied, "the entire Collegium is likely to be short-handed, possibly for several months. Once this is over, it's possible that we may be able to start training some replacements."

"When will you need him . . . if he agrees?"

"The moment he does. I have a coach waiting."

Baratyn's face sobered. Then he nodded slowly. "Is it true that the Ferrans detonated Glendyl's engine works right around you?"

"Unhappily . . . yes."

"And you're planning something to take the war more to them?"

"Let's just say that we're planning something." I smiled. "Do you happen to know where Dartazn might be at the moment?"

"He was escorting a visitor to see acting Chief Councilor Caartyl. I don't imagine he'll be that long."

"Has Caartyl had that many visitors?"

"Very few. Just a handful of guildmasters. Word is out that Glendyl is likely to recover, and he can be vindictive."

"He may be preoccupied with rebuilding his engine works." Then, he might not, if I found any hard evidence to link him to the Ferrans and the shooting of Suyrien. I had the feeling that some of my surmises would remain only that, at least from what I'd learned so far.

"That was a bad business."

"More than I can say."

At that moment, Dartazn came down the steps to the north of where we stood and walked toward us.

"Maitre Rhennthyl needs to talk to you." Baratyn nodded to me.

"Yes, sir."

"I need a few moments of your time." The messenger study was empty, and I gestured for Dartazn to follow me in there. I couldn't close the door, because there wasn't one, only an archway onto the main corridor.

"Yes, sir?"

"Maitre Dyana and I need someone for a special assignment. Both of us thought you'd be good in it, and I've already talked to Baratyn. He agrees."

"What sort of assignment?"

"Taking charge of a group of younger imagers involved in a larger task."

Dartazn nodded slowly. "The way you put that, sir, suggests there is a certain amount of danger involved."

"Yes, although part of that will depend on the skill of whoever takes the assignment."

"Can you tell me more?"

"I'd prefer not to, not outside the Collegium. If you're interested, we can go back to the Collegium. I can tell you more there."

He nodded. "Am I the first or the last junior master you've approached?"

"The only one. I'd rather not have to approach any others."

At that, he smiled wryly, an expression that also held a certain boyish charm, for all that he was slightly older than I. "I think I'd like to try."

"Then we should depart. I have a duty coach waiting."

He gathered his cloak, and we left the Council Chateau.

Once we were in the duty coach, I began to explain, beginning with the Ferran and Stakanaran efforts to undermine Solidar itself and then telling him about the problems with the Solidaran fleet. That was as far as I got by the time we got out of the coach, but that was enough for Dartazn to commit to the position. For the next four glasses, with one glass out for the midday meal, I went over the plan, what I expected of him, and answered his questions as well as I could. The one question he didn't ask was why I wasn't doing what I was asking him to do.

That alone suggested he was the right imager for the task.

Then we found another duty coach, and on the trip northward, I filled him in on what he needed to know about the Naval Command. The only thing I told him about Geuffryt was that the Assistant Sea-Marshal was the intelligence head and to be politely avoided where possible and treated with great civility otherwise, and that any request for information was to be handled by saying, "You'll have to ask Marshal Valeun or Maitre Rhennthytl about that, sir."

Dartazn smiled at those instructions.

The duty coach arrived at the Naval Command building almost exactly at two quints past four. By the time we'd been escorted up to Marshal Valeun's study, it was half past the glass.

The senior ranker in the anteroom stood and opened the door to Valeun's study, without a word, although his eyes lingered on Dartazn for a moment. The door closed behind us.

Valeun stood behind his desk. "Maitres."

"Sea-Marshall Valeun, I'd like to present Maitre Dartazn. He is the master who will be directly in charge of the imagers and who will be with the fleet to coordinate our part of the operation."

"I had thought you might be undertaking that task, Maitre Rhennthyl."

"Alas, like you, Marshal, I've been tasked with overseeing a number of Collegium efforts, and the Maitre of the Collegium felt the master imager on the fleet level should be devoted to the operation and to nothing else."

Valeun studied Dartazn, then nodded. "Welcome aboard, Master Dartazn."

"Thank you, sir."

"We have much to discuss." Valeun gestured toward the chairs before his expansive desk, then seated himself.

I took the seat to the side, letting Dartazn sit directly facing Valeun.

"We will have a fast frigate waiting at Westisle by Jeudi, the thirty-third of Finitas, suitable for transport, but she does not have sufficient lead-lined spaces."

I glanced to Dartazn.

"We will supply lead foil—both for the frigate, and for a number of the fast gunboats," replied Dartazn.

"The frigate will join a replacement flotilla that will be leaving shortly from Solis . . ."

From there we got into detail after detail, and it was more than a glass later before we finally left the Naval Bureau. I'd had to talk more than I'd hoped to, but less than might have been. With Valeun, it was hard to tell, but I got the sense that he'd be more than happy to deal with Dartazn, rather than me. He also didn't mention Geuffryt, and that was just fine with me.

I still wanted to resolve the issues dealing with the Civic Patrol, and the possible involvement of the Banque D'Ouestan with the Ferrans, not to mention the very loose ends dealing with Caartyl and Cydarth; but those would have to wait until we had the imagers packed up and on their way to Westisle.

49

When I woke early on Jeudi, four digits of snow covered the ground, and it was falling so thickly and quickly that I couldn't see the wall that surrounded our courtyard. I went downstairs in my nightclothes and loaded more coal in the stoves, then washed my hands in the kitchen and slipped into bed next to Seliora.

"You're not going to NordEste today . . ."

"I'm not?" she said sleepily.

"Not unless you want to walk four milles though snow . . ."

Not that we had that long together before Diestrya joined us and I finally got up.

After breakfast, I still trudged through the snow to the infirmary to check with Draffyd on Glendyl. I had to wait a bit.

"Have you been here long?" he asked as he stepped out of one the surgical rooms.

"Not really long."

He gestured toward the room he just left. "One of the dining hall workers slipped on the snow and fell. She hit her arm on one of the stone walls outside the hall and broke it." He paused. "What can I do for you?"

"Is Glendyl still here?"

"I'd thought to let him leave today, but with this weather . . ."

"That makes it easier for me to talk to him."

"He's not happy with you, or the Collegium."

"He'd have lost even more if I hadn't gone to Ferravyl when I did."

"He doesn't think so."

"Has he said anything to you?"

"Besides complain about everything here in the infirmary? Not much. He hasn't said a word about you or Maitre Dyana, or the Ferrans, if that's what you're asking."

I grinned. "I was."

"He's in the same chamber."

"Thank you." I nodded and walked down the corridor and into the Councilor's room. The walls were the same gray, but Glendyl had obviously sent for items to make his stay more comfortable. He was seated in an armchair that certainly wasn't from the Collegium, and he wore a silken dressing gown. He set down a file of papers and looked at me, but did not speak.

"Good morning, Councilor."

"What's good about it? It's snowing, and I can't leave. My works are falling apart as we speak, and there's nothing I can do about it while I'm stuck here."

"Well . . . you are alive, and you might not be."

"And I may be ruined because of you."

I shook my head. "I didn't have anything to do with your business decisions. I also didn't have anything to do with the decision of the Ferrans to target your engine works."

"I'm sorry, Maitre Rhennthyl, but I have trouble believing that."

"Why would I want your engine works, especially the turbine buildings, destroyed? There's been far too much destruction already."

"They wouldn't have set off the explosions if you hadn't visited the works."

"Oh? That almost sounds like you were in collusion with them."

"That's not what I said. It's not what I meant. If you'd just told me that you suspected that, I could have had my people look quietly, and none of that would have happened."

His answer tended to confirm some of my suspicions. "That's possible. You have to remember that I don't happen to have all the information that Master Dichartyn had."

"I had not thought of it that way." He smiled politely and slightly knowingly.

"Besides Suyrien and Haebyn, how much did you get advanced through the Banque D'Ouestan?"

His eyes narrowed. "That's . . . I don't believe I ever mentioned the Banque D'Ouestan."

He'd been about to tell me that advances from the banque were none of my business, although that one word and subsequent denial scarcely amounted to proof. "I thought it had to be an outland banque."

"You're inventing things, Maitre Rhennthyl."

"Perhaps, but I didn't invent the bombardment of Imagisle or the destruction of your works, or explosions all across Solidar, or a number of funds transfers of a questionable nature, or your debts to High Holder Suyrien."

"Indebtedness, if repaid under the terms agreed upon, isn't a crime."

"I also didn't invent Ferran agents infiltrating your works, and one of them shooting you, and probably Suyrien the Elder."

"I suggest, Maitre Rhennthyl, that the Collegium should work to deal with those problems, and not waste time interrogating those of us who have already suffered enough."

"The Collegium has also suffered, honored Councilor, and it appears as though the problems we and you have suffered are linked to many other people and problems. I'm just a poor imager trying to figure out what is linked to what, because it appears all too many people do not wish to have others know what they have done or what they owe to whom for what. Yet debts and obligations, and struggles over them, can lead to consequences just as deadly as explosions and murders." I inclined my head. "I will not trouble you more at present, and I hope that you will be able to return to your own estate as safely as possible once the snow clears."

He barely nodded in return.

When I left the infirmary, I walked through the still-falling powdery snow to the administration building and my study. When I had time, if I ever did, I wanted to create a standardized form for those reports and a set of guidelines for filling them in. But, like many things, that was going to have to wait.

I found Kahlasa, and we went into Schorzat's study.

He looked up from his desk with an expression of what I could only have termed watchful wariness. "Yes, sir?"

"The Naval Command will have a fast frigate in Westisle by next Jeudi. We'll need to get the imagers we pick on the ironway late on Solayi. Oh . . . and the master in charge of the operation is Dartazn."

That brought another wary look.

"Maitre Dyana refused to let anyone besides a Maitre D'Aspect be considered, and I doubted that it would be a good idea to have Kahlasa go." I smiled. "Given that, and the fact that there's really no one to replace Baratyn, who would you pick?"

"Dartazn's probably the best choice."

"He's a good choice," added Kahlasa. "He's the kind that all the juniors look up to."

Unfortunately, I understood that all too well. Dartazn radiated almost a boyish enthusiasm, along with quiet confidence. That was one reason why I'd thought of him.

"You're asking them to do dangerous duty, aren't you?" asked Schorzat. "Do you think that's a fair thing to do for junior imagers?"

"It's far more fair than letting them be shot by assassins as was the case when I was a second. It's far more fair than eventually letting the Ferrans dominate the world and attempt to destroy us all. But is it fair? No. It's just the only practical alternative now that the Council has managed to put us all in this position."

"Setting fires in Ferrum won't solve the problem, Maitre."

"It all depends on how and where it's done," I pointed out. "For the moment, however, I need you and Kahlasa to make the arrangements for thirty imagers to travel to Westisle on the express leaving L'Excelsis on Solayi evening. There may not be that many, but it's easier to leave spaces than to find them."

"Reynol won't be happy at that large a draw on the accounts," Schorzat pointed out.

"He probably won't be, but that's what we need."

No one was going to be happy, because at least half of the seconds and thirds would probably be drawn from those employed in the armory or workshops in various specialties.

By the time I headed back to my study, Dartazn had arrived and was waiting patiently. "I'm sorry. I had a few loose ends to deal with."

"I can imagine. I was a little late because I had to turn over some things to Martyl. He's going to be very busy once the Council starts meeting next month."

Although that was four weeks away, I wouldn't even have any idea of how well what I was planning had turned out by then, or even if Dartazn and the fleet had been able to execute it. I shook off that thought and opened the study door. "We'd better get started."

I spent close to two glasses working with Dartazn and with maps of Ferrum, especially the one of Ferrial, which was not only the capital, but also a port. After that, we went to visit Chassendri in her laboratory, where she gave us both, but especially Dartazn, more information and demonstrations on various flammables that were easy to image.

Then we had lunch in the dining hall, and afterward Dartazn resumed working with Chassendri, while I took a glass to read through the various reports from regionals and Patrol Commanders that had arrived over the past week. From those reports, it appeared as though nothing out of the ordinary had occurred anywhere in Solidar. That is, no Ferrans exploded anything, and no prominent figures had been assassinated.

On the other hand, elveweed use and deaths were beginning to rise again. Another grain warehouse near Piedryn had burned under suspicious circumstances, and the snow levels in the eastern mountains were exceptionally light for late fall and early winter, suggesting more conflict over water rights in late summer, unless snowfall levels improved.

When I finished reading through the reports, I went to find Rholyn, but he wasn't around. So I left word with the duty prime that I needed to see him and told her to check his study occasionally and let him know if he returned. Then I pondered whether I dared to approach Iryela and Kandryl to see if they could pressure the Banque D'Rivages to reveal more. While Ryel House essentially owned the banque, they didn't take part in the day-to-day operations.

At a quint past third glass, Rholyn knocked and stepped into my study. "You were looking for me?"

"As a matter of fact, I was. I was hoping you might be able to tell me why Haestyr requested your presence in Asseroiles in the middle of all the problems here at the Collegium."

Rholyn settled into the chair across from me. "He wants to be Chief Councilor. He feels that Ramsael isn't strong enough to maintain leadership. He's also worried that you're too young to have as much power and influence as you do."

"I can't imagine that he said that. Exactly how did he convey it?"

Rholyn chuckled. "He suggested that you had demonstrated remarkable acuity for a Maitre who combined such power and relative lack of experience in dealing with the complexities of politics in a land such as Solidar, and that he hoped you would come to realize that friendship with High Holders is based only on their belief that you will further their ends."

"He's certainly right about all of that, except perhaps the 'remarkable acuity.' That's flattery to a purpose." It also suggested that Haestyr was well aware of Seliora's dislike of his son Alhyral, and that Haestyr simply wanted to keep me from being influenced by any High Holder, knowing that was probably the best he could do. "He must know that he'll never be Chief Councilor, and that you know that as well. What did he really want?"

"He never says. He's very indirect."

I waited. I was getting very tired of waiting when people expected me to ask a question, but waiting was far better than asking the wrong question.

Finally, Rholyn smiled. "You and Maitre Poincaryt."

I didn't ask that question, either. I just returned the smile.

"Haestyr believes that the measures that Suyrien slipped into the low justice reforms need to be revisited, particularly the change from harvest valuation to year-end valuation."

"That wasn't too popular to begin with, I understand."

"No . . . but some of the High Holders didn't fully understand."

"I don't see why that makes any difference. All of them but Suyrien voted against the measure." Actually, I did see the difference. They'd pressure the factor and artisan Councilors to change their votes, just the way that Haebyn had pressured Glendyl to cut off engines and supplies to Broussard.

Rholyn shrugged. "He feels strongly about it."

"Did he say why? Or indicate otherwise?"

"He only said that it was a bad idea, badly executed. When I asked him why, he just said that he didn't have to explain."

I nodded, although I didn't believe him. I had to wonder why Rholyn was still the Collegium Councilor. Surely, Maitre Poincaryt had seen through him. I managed not to show any reaction as I realized just why Rholyn was a Councilor . . . and even why I'd been asked to paint his portrait years before. "Did he ask for you to consider any other proposals?"

"No. He did say that he hoped the Council would finally understand the need for more modern warships, now that it was less likely that they would believe that Suyrien had pressed for them solely for his own benefit."

"Did he mention Ruelyr?"

"I don't believe that he did . . ."

We talked for a while longer, but I learned nothing more from Rholyn's words, only what he had wanted me to, which was what I'd expected. Then he left, and I went back to reading the reports I hadn't finished.

The snow was tapering off when I left my study and trudged back toward the house.

50

By midday on Vendrei, under a sunny sky, the walks and streets around Imag-isle and L'Excelsis were clear enough that I could take a duty coach to Third District station. I did so, partly because I owed it to Alsoran to make an occasional appearance, and partly because I realized once again how isolated I could easily become at the Collegium. I also wanted to know what was filtering out of Patrol headquarters to the captains.

Huensyn had the duty desk when I walked into the station.

"Maitre Rhennthyl . . . you're in luck, sir. The captain's in his study."

I stopped. "How are things going these days?"

"It's Third District, sir. Not too much of the strong weed. No deaths this week, either. Been quiet the last week or so except for some smash-and-grabs up on the Avenue D'Artisans near the Plaza. Oh . . . and a brawl at Kornyn's last Samedi."

"No more explosions or hellhole drug dealers?"

"No, sir. Not a one."

I gave Huensyn a smile and crossed the foyer to the captain's study, where I stepped in and closed the study door before sitting down. Alsoran didn't look as tired as he had the last time I'd been there, but there was a large stack of papers on his desk.

He shook his head, then grinned. "Hate all the reports the subcommander wants. Somehow, it's different when you're the one who has to fill them out."

"Is he still asking for the counts on elveweed deaths?"

"Of course. We don't have many—none this week—but when did anything ever get taken off a report? They just keep adding."

"What has he added now?" I asked with a smile.

"Offenses by outlanders."

I frowned. "Who's an outlander? Someone who doesn't speak Bovarian well? Someone with darker-shaded skin, or pale white skin?"

"All of those and anyone else who doesn't fit." Alsoran snorted. "I told the patrollers not to call anyone an outlander unless they can't understand Bovarian. We've got folks whose grandparents came from Stakanar or Gyarl, and they're as Solidaran as you and me."

"Have you heard anything back?"

"I got a query two weeks ago. Cydarth suggested we weren't recording all the outland offenders. I wrote back that we questioned every offender thoroughly, but we didn't seem to have many outlanders." Alsoran grinned sheepishly. "I also said that was probably because the previous captain had removed a large number of the criminal outlanders and no one had taken their place."

I laughed. "Be careful. You'll replace me as Cydarth's least favorite captain."

"Already have, sir."

"Do you have a lieutenant yet?"

"No. I think they're still trying to work out filling the captain's slots in the other districts. So far, that hasn't happened. No one's told me anything."

"You remember the elver girl who wasn't, the pretty one?"

"Oh . . . the one you thought had been dumped in Third District? We never heard anything. I think you were right about her coming from somewhere else."

"Have you had anything else like that?"

"No. I did have a brief talk with Horazt the other day. I told him you and I had talked. All he said was, 'Good.' I think he worries that, without your showing an interest, Jadhyl and Deyalt will take over his section of the taudis."

"They won't. Jadhyl's too smart for that. He's also patient."

"Ah . . . what about the woodworks . . . ?"

"And the paper mill? There's no reason to change things. They bring in silvers. Seliora's family doesn't stop doing things that make coins."

"That's good."

We talked for a while longer, mostly about patrollers and the Patrol, but I didn't learn anything that might bear on the Ferrans or Artois or Cydarth, and I left after another half glass.

I got back to the Collegium at two quints past ninth glass, and checked with Kahlasa. We actually had all the evaluation forms from the Maitres at Imagisle. That meant that we could decide who might be the best for the mission. So she and I went into Schorzat's study and told him.

"How do you want us to do this?" Schorzat asked.

"Each of us makes a list. Then we get together and talk over our choices and the reasons for them. After that, we work out a list we all agree on, and I give it to Maitre Dyana. She approves it or makes the last set of changes. Then we send the notices."

In going over the forms, I found that I trusted the evaluations of some masters—such as Ghaend, Jhulian, and Kahlasa—more than others. From my juniors, I decided Eamyn and Shault had the abilities and determination, even though Shault was younger than I would have liked. I also felt he needed the experience, beyond both Imagisle and the taudis, and that exposure to the Navy might give him a better perspective on the Collegium.

When the three of us got together again after lunch, we discovered that we only had a handful of differences that were comparatively easy to sort out. At a quint past second glass, I handed the list we'd come up with to Maitre Dyana.

She didn't take long to study it. "You have two on the list. Should you have more?"

"Because I'm known to be demanding and a perfectionist, you mean?"

"That has been said."

"No. Haugyl and Marteon simply aren't as good. Ralyea is borderline."

"Would the experience do him good?"

"I don't know. He's almost timid."

"Give him the chance. We've got enough timid ones hiding in the workshops." A wintry smile came and went. "How will you notify the ones on the list?"

"I thought to send each one a notice about their selection and the briefing tomorrow. I'll send another note to any master with juniors, advising them who of theirs have been chosen. I'll have all those out within the glass." I paused. "Unless you'd rather sign them."

"Your signature will be fine, Rhenn."

I understood the reasons for that as well. "I thought you'd open the briefing for those who are going."

"That's at ninth glass, is it not?"

I nodded. "Then I'll say a few words and turn it over to Dartazn for a few more moments. He won't say anything more of a substantive nature except that they'll get more detailed training on board the frigate. He's working with Chassendri today. Her ideas are proving very helpful."

"Even though she has doubts?"

"We all have doubts of one sort or another."

"What are yours, Rhenn?"

"I have two. The first is that we'll buy time, but that we'll create even more Ferran determination to bring us down." I shrugged. "I tell myself they already feel that way."

"They've certainly acted as if they do. What's the second?"

"That we'll provoke all Terahnar into uniting against us. Not immediately, but as they think about what we did."

"We won't have to worry about that unless your plan works. If it does, they'll think twice . . . and fret for years before acting."

"They will act, sooner or later," I pointed out.

"Sooner, and it will be your problem, but you'll have time to consider how to handle it. Later, and you'll have to prepare a successor. All life is solving problems that create other problems requiring yet other solutions." She smiled politely. "Do you need anything else from me?"

While her words were undoubtedly correct, they also suggested why the Maitres of the Collegium had, behind their measured calm, something approaching amusement at the "crises" of daily life.

"No, Maitre."

With Maitre Dyana's approval on the final selections, I went back to my study and began to write. It took close to two glasses to write them all out, but I did have the duty prime take them and place them in the proper letter boxes. After I finished, rather than head home immediately, I went over to the dining hall to see if Ralyea, Shault, or Eamyn might be there.

Shault and Ralyea were. In fact, they were standing opposite the letter boxes, already with the notices in hand. They both looked up when they saw me. Neither moved.

I motioned for them to join me.

"Can you tell us more, sir?" asked Shault.

"You'll find out more at the briefing tomorrow, at the same time the others who were selected do. I will tell you that Maitre Dartazn will be in charge of you, and that I expect you two, and Eamyn, to learn everything you possibly can from him, no matter how strange or difficult it may seem. Is that clear?" I looked sternly at Shault.

"Yes, sir."

"Good. I'll see you at the briefing tomorrow." I offered a pleasant smile, and then left them standing there.

The air had gotten far colder, and my ears and face were almost numb by the time I stepped into the foyer of our house, only to have Diestrya launch herself at me and wrap her arms around my legs.

"Dada! Play plaques with me!"

That was a request to which I could gladly accede, even as I wondered how many of those junior imagers would return . . . and how many had once been young and trusting like my daughter.

51

My sleep on Vendrei night was scarcely sound. I awoke twice in chill darkness from nightmares where lists swam out of the blackness, and each name was written in fire and blood that burned my hands when I tried to blot out the flames. When I finally roused myself on Samedi morning, I was relieved to see that at least I hadn't imaged fire or letters into the stones of the wall, although some heat would have been nice, since the windows were thoroughly frosted. Each breath puffed steam into the air. With their construction designed primarily to protect everyone else in the house from inadvertent nightmare or dream imaging, imagers' sleeping chambers were not designed primarily for warmth.

I did slip out and hurry down to the exercise building, but not before I loaded the stoves. While I managed Clovyl's entire work-out, I decided against running on the icy ways and walks, except for a careful and gentle jog back to the house.

Seliora and Diestrya were in the breakfast nook of the kitchen when I returned.

"I'm glad you didn't run in this weather." Seliora poured me a mug of steaming tea.

I just held it up to my chin and let the steam wreathe my face. "I ran back . . . carefully."

"We haven't talked about Year-Turn."

"We went to my parents' last year. That means we're going to yours this year . . . if they'll have us."

"I told Mother that, but . . . we hadn't actually talked." Seliora poured herself a second mug of tea.

"We'll have to have dinner with mine the next Samedi, I imagine."

"We can do that. On Year-Turn day, do you want to attend services with the family or here before we go?"

"Whatever you prefer."

"Are you humoring me, dearest husband?"

"No. It's your choice."

She smiled. "Isola does an afternoon service on that Solayi, and it's much shorter. That would be better, since we'll have Diestrya."

I nodded. I didn't mention that Isola also offered better homilies than the chorister at the anomen attended, if infrequently, by Seliora's family. We had a more leisurely breakfast than was usually the case, before I had to leave for the junior imagers' briefing.

At the ninth glass of the morning on Samedi, twenty-seven seconds and thirds sat at the long tables in the dining hall. Maitre Dyana, Dartazn, and I stood at the head of the table, with her in the center. Ferlyn, Kahlasa, Ghaend, and Chassendri stood against the wall behind the masters' table, observing.

Maitre Dyana began. I couldn't help but notice that she was not wearing a brilliant scarf, but one of a gray so dark it verged on smoky black.

"You have been selected to help defend Solidar. Some of you may have grasped what is not in the newsheets and understand that a great deal is at stake. For those of you who have not, I would like to point out that our northern fleet has suffered heavy losses over the past months. Here in Solidar we have suffered attacks by Ferran agents, and most recently, their attacks destroyed the only significant engine works in Solidar. This means a delay of at least a year before we can even begin to build more ships to replace those that have been lost. There have been other attacks and events as well, and unless the Collegium acts, these will increase. You will join the northern fleet to take part in a unique operation designed by Maitre Rhennthyl and Sea-Marshal Valeun. Maitre Dartazn, here, will be your immediate superior from this moment until you return to Imagisle . . ."

As Maitre Dyana finished her brief speech, I studied the faces of the junior imagers I knew. We'd only excluded one imager for reasons other than lack of ability, and that was Tomai. While she was one of the most accomplished seconds, putting a female on any Navy ship would have created too many problems. Even Kahlasa agreed with me on that, but we both regretted it.

". . . And now Maitre Rhennthyl has a few words." Dyana stepped back.

I moved forward. "Some of you may ask why you were selected. You may also ask why you have to face dangers at an age far younger than those who came before you. Unfortunately, that is not true. The older ones among you may recall that almost a quarter of the younger imagers were assassinated by Ferran agents in the years 755 and 756. The difference between them and you is that you will know and face the dangers before you. You will have an opportunity to confront, if indirectly, those who have brought war and destruction to our shores and lands. You will be led and trained by Maitre

Dartazn, and you will be leaving L'Excelsis tomorrow evening on the iron-way. He will give you the details, particularly what you will need to pack in the duffels you will pick up outside the dining hall when you leave. I will leave you with one thought. You are imagers, and you are fortunate enough to live in a land where imagers are respected, even protected; and for that po-sition, we should be both grateful and understanding. For in much of Ter-ahnar, imagers are little more than criminals, if not executed on the spot. Appreciation, however, is not enough. Throughout your lives, each and every one of you will be called upon to repay the faith the people of Solidar have in you. At times, we are called to do more than repay that faith on an indi-vidual basis. This is one of those times."

I eased back and let Dartazn take over.

Dartazn smiled, then started to speak. "While some of you may know this, many of you do not. Maitre Rhennthyl just spoke of the need to back faith with acts, and even with one's body and life. Unlike most of us, he, and Maitre Kahlasa as well, have defended the Collegium, the Council, and Solidar with both. He has broken more ribs than any of you have, and lost more blood than flows in the veins of any three men. He walked the streets of Solidar as a com-mon Civic Patroller, and he has saved Councilors and imagers alike, often suf-fering near-fatal injuries. This is true of every Maitre D'Esprit who has ever served the Collegium. Why am I telling you this?" Dartazn paused.

I was stunned. I hadn't realized he was going to mention me.

"I'm telling you this so that you don't even begin to think of feeling sorry for yourself. As imagers, we have a better life than most, and all advantages and privileges must be paid for. Our payment—and yours—is to defend the only land in all Terahnar that has respected and supported us." He stopped, again for a long moment. "There are duffels outside, as Maitre Rhennthyl said. I'm about to tell you what to pack. Before you get aboard the coaches to take you to the ironway station tomorrow, I will inspect each duffel. Anything that is missing will be supplied at our next destination, but you will have dou-ble the amount it costs deducted from your imager pay, as well as a one-gold fee. Do you understand?"

The one-gold fee definitely grabbed their attention.

Dartazn was a good speaker, and he held their attention.

Afterward, as Maitre Dyana and I left, I asked her, in a very low voice, "Where did he learn all that about me? I never told him."

"I did. He needed to know, in detail, so that he understands that you're not asking anything of him that you haven't suffered, if under differing cir-cumstances."

"So have you, and Maitre Dichartyn . . ."

She offered an amused smile. "Unlike the officers of the Navy, as imagers rise in rank and responsibility, the level of personal dangers also increases. That may be why only the most cautious and very best die of old age."

It might also be why the Maitres of the Collegium were seldom arrogant, also unlike the senior Naval Commanders.

For the next several glasses, I remained in the background, helping Dartazn and his juniors as necessary. Then I went home.

Needless to say, on Solayi evening, neither Seliora nor I attended services at the anomen, because I was at the ironway station to see off Dartazn and his charges.

The first imager I went to see was Shault. Although he stood confidently beside Ralyea, the eyes of both juniors darted from the train carriages that had not been opened to boarding to Dartazn and then to me as I approached.

"Maitre Rhennthyl, I thought you weren't going," offered Ralyea.

"I'm not. I came to see you all off."

"Where are we going?" asked Shault.

"On the ironway." I paused, then added, "This is the express to Westisle." I pointed. "It even says so on the carriage sign." After a moment more, I went on. "Both of you need to practice your shields when you're not working with Master Dartazn. Remember to do that in the open. You can hurt yourselves if you work too hard inside places like train compartments. No, they're not lead-lined, but there's enough metal there to drain you more than you realize."

"Yes, sir."

"I expect both of you to do your best." With a nod, I turned and eased down the platform to where Dartazn stood.

"Good evening, Maitre," he offered.

"Good evening. You seem to have everything well in hand."

"They're still shocked. Most of them anyway."

"They will be for a time. They're not used to sudden changes, but when you're training them, try to upset them so that they get used to it, and practice as much as you can at night."

"I'd thought so."

I stepped closer and lowered my voice, so that none of the juniors ranked to his left could hear. "Remember, you have to make sure that the gunboats get close enough. Marshal Valeun understands that. He knows we'll lose some, and we'll lose imagers. You'll have almost two weeks onboard the fast frigate to give them instruction in how to image to a target most effectively. Just make sure they're imaging over water."

"Yes, sir."

"And make certain that your sample cases get on the frigate as well."

Dartazn looked at me and offered his boyish grin. "You have a hard time when you have to order someone else into danger, don't you, Maitre?"

"How could you tell?" I replied dryly.

He laughed, and then, so did I.

Before long, the train carriage doors opened, and they boarded, and I departed, trying not to think of all that could go wrong.

Once again, on Solayi night, I didn't sleep all that well. I'd told myself that, while I couldn't help but be worried about Dartazn and all the juniors, I'd done what I could do. Either my plan worked, or it didn't. If it didn't, my name might well go down as the most inept and misguided Maitre D'Esprit in the history of the Collegium, but I still couldn't do more about it. None of that helped. Neither did exercise and running early on Lundi. Nor did a good breakfast and a cheerful wife and daughter. The plain fact was that I'd launched a plan that was a tremendous gamble. That Solidar really had few other options didn't matter, because what I'd done was designed to deal with a long-term problem before it got worse, and possibly unresolvable, rather than an immediate crisis. If my plan worked, people were going to be furious, and if it didn't, they'd be even angrier . . . and for far longer.

After spending a glass or so in my study catching up on the latest reports from across Solidar, I walked to the duty coach stand, where I took one to the Council Chateau. The Council was meeting more than three weeks before its normally scheduled date, and Baratyn was short-handed and might need some help. I also wanted to see what I could find out, even if I had no precise idea of what I sought.

I hadn't even gotten much through the side door used by Collegium security before I was face to face with Baratyn.

"Maitre Rhennthyl," he said with a wry smile, "I should be surprised to see you here, but I find that I'm not."

"I thought it wouldn't hurt to be here today, especially after I left you even more short-handed than usual."

"We'll work it out somehow. Dartazn needed new challenges. But . . . I'd appreciate it if you'd keep your eyes open for a good third."

"After all this is over, there might be several who are suitable. We'll have to see. Are there lots of petitioners waiting outside at the gate?"

"Not that many. Most of those who might wish to ask something of a Councilor know that today's meeting will deal with officially choosing a new Chief Councilor and seating Councilor Fhernon."

"Is Glendyl here?"

"He isn't here yet."

"He may not come," I suggested, "but I'd wager that Caartyl's here."

"He was here before seventh glass."

"Is ninth glass still the time they'll meet?"

Baratyn nodded.

"Is there anything I can do?"

"I hope not," he replied with a laugh.

I couldn't help smiling. "Then you don't mind if I just sort of wander around?"

"That might help Ramsael."

"He's still in his old study, then?"

"He's not Chief Councilor yet. The Council does try to follow its own rules . . ."

The way he let the sentence dangle suggested what we both knew. I nodded and headed for the north circular steps up to the upper level where the Councilors had their studies. Outside the Councilors' lounge, I saw two men talking. One was High Holder Ramsael. I didn't know the other, but since I did know all the Councilors by sight, it was almost a certainty that the other man was High Holder Fhernon, the one who would replace Suyrien on the Council. Since he had not, as of yet, he was doubtless in the awkward position of having neither study nor clerk, but only for less than a glass.

". . . Find the Council a very different place . . ."

"So I hear."

Ramsael saw me and gestured. "Maitre Rhennthyl, I thought it might be possible that you would be here. Have you met Councilor Fhernon?"

Why did everyone think I would be at the Council Chateau? Because Master Dichartyn had been . . . or because rumors were beginning to swirl around about me?

I stepped forward. "I have not." I turned to Fhernon as I halted. "I have heard of you and your scrupulous fairness, however." That was close to what Seliora had said.

"You see, Fhernon," said Ramsael with a laugh, "your reputation precedes you. Because the Collegium is less than forthcoming, I might also point out that Maitre Rhennthyl is now the second-ranking imager in all Solidar."

That was definitely a pleasant warning to Fhernon.

"I had not heard." Fhernon inclined his head. "I am certain, then, that we will be seeing more of you."

"Not too often," I replied. "You're far more likely to see Maitre Dyana or Councilor Rholyn. They are the ones who speak for the Collegium."

"While you act for it," added Ramsael.

"Only occasionally," I said lightly, "and when I have, it's often been for the benefit of various Councilors."

Ramsael nodded to Fhernon. "If you will excuse us, Fhernon. Since I see Maitre Rhennthyl so seldom, I'm going to prevail upon him for a few moments of his time." Then he turned back to me. "If you would not mind?"

"It would be my pleasure." I wasn't certain that it would be, but there was little else to be said, and I'd learn something. Whether it would be useful to my own interests was another question.

Ramsael gestured, and I walked alongside him toward the study that would become Fhernon's in a few glasses, when Ramsael became Chief Councilor and took over the large corner study that had been Suyrien's.

"I was sorry to hear that the Collegium was shelled." He opened the study door. "I presume it was by Ferran agents."

"Since we have not found those who did it," I replied as I followed Ramsael into the study and closed the door, "all we know for certain is that they were accomplished gunners."

Ramsael did not seat himself behind the desk, but stood beside the closed window.

I could feel a slight draft that suggested the window was not so tightly fitted as it might have been.

"You may not know this, Maitre Rhennthyl, but I was not the heir to Ramsealte. So I took a commission as an officer and spent four years at sea." He turned from the window. "The more I've learned about the bombardment of the Collegium, the more concerned I've become. The most senior and able of the imagers were targeted. As you noted, the gunnery was excellent. More than excellent. Outstanding, I would judge." He paused. "Could that have been done by an imager? Certainly, there were no vessels remaining in the area."

"The shells were fired from barges north of Imagisle. Quite a few people saw the barges burning and exploding before they sank. As for an imager creating that destruction . . . no. The best of imagers might be able to create and detonate one or two shells in that fashion, but there were something like eight fired quickly."

"I thought as much, but it is best to ask. I must confess that I do not understand the motivation behind such an attack." He held up a hand. "Oh, I can understand how the Ferrans well might wish to cripple Solidar by striking a blow at the Collegium, but by far the best way to do so would be to have tar-geted the quarters of your junior imagers. They represent the future, and one could kill far more of them with each shell. Whoever was behind the attack wanted to take out the leadership of the Collegium."

"That is very clear," I agreed. "But there have never been that many senior imagers, and I have no doubts that Ferrum knows that."

"Might I ask what you intend to do about that and these other attacks on Solidar?"

"Might I ask why you're asking me, rather than Councilor Rholyn or Maitre Dyana?"

"You could indeed. The truth is that you're known not to imply one thing while meaning another or to say nothing at all in most elegant phrases."

"I might not say anything at all."

"You might not, but you will not waste my time."

"Let us just say that the Collegium is well aware of the need to act."

"Will the Naval Command support you in whatever you plan?"

"They will . . . either in the near-term . . . or later."

"Your words contain implications . . ." He cocked his head slightly.

"All words do, Councilor."

"Pardon me if I am unseemly in my bluntness, Maitre, but when might we know of the . . . implications?"

"As we both know," I replied politely, "we are effectively at war with Fer-rum. Until the Ferrans are dissuaded, that conflict will continue. We are work-ing on such dissuasion. At the moment, I would prefer not to say more."

"You are every bit Dichartyn's successor." Ramsael laughed. "Let me change the subject to another that will affect us all, if not quite so immedi-ately. Like all the High Holders who are Councilors, I opposed the 'reforms' that the late Chief Councilor managed to have enacted in the last session of the Council." Ramsael smiled politely at me. "I presume you understand the measures to which I'm referring."

"If you're referring to those contained in the low justice changes, I do." I didn't see any point in denying that I knew very well. First, to do so would have been lying, even if I did so by evasion, rather than by outright prevarica-tion. Second, all that would do would be to delay matters, and not for all that long, while irritating Ramsael. And third, it would just make the eventual res-olution more difficult.

"These changes could have far-reaching effects. I trust you understand that as well." He looked at me directly.

"The changes would come, regardless of those provisions," I pointed out.

"How will the Collegium act if efforts are made to reverse those so-called reforms?"

"I can't speak for the Collegium, Councilor."

"I would have expected no other response, you understand? Yet, I had to ask."

"If the Collegium speaks or acts, Maitre Dyana will be the one with whom you will deal . . . and no one else."

Ramsael frowned. "Given that, as a friend of my daughter and her husband, then, how would you advise me?"

That made it difficult. "Let me just say that I suspect your efforts would be better directed elsewhere."

He nodded slowly. "How much time do we have?"

"You know what the law said. I would judge, and it is only my opinion, that if the Council follows the law and the original charter, the Collegium would see no reason to speak or act."

"That will not set well with some."

"Not following the law and charter will set less well with even more, I fear."

"The Collegium stands where?"

"Behind the law. Where else could the Collegium and its Maitre stand?"

"Not all laws are for the best, some would say."

"I would agree. I would also say that a land that does not live by its laws will not long endure. It may change those laws, but to flout them will destroy it far more quickly than following bad laws."

"You have me there, Maitre Rhennthyl, and best we leave it at that. Is there anything I might be able to help you with?" Ramsael did not smile, but his voice was quietly earnest.

"Several matters, possibly. What can you tell me about the Banque D'Ouestan?"

"Very little directly, except that they've recently opened branches in Kherseilles and Estisle. They also appear to be offering favorable terms for loans to factors." Ramsael seemed relieved at the change in subject, even though he'd brought up the initial questions.

"They wouldn't be touting the fact that they're not beholden to or owned by High Holders, would they?" I asked.

The faintest hint of a smile crossed the Councilor's face, then vanished. "There are rumors to that effect."

"Do you know what factors of import might have had dealings with them?"

"Know? No. There was word that Veblynt played off the Banque D'Excelsis against them to finance his new paper mill south of Rivages. Glendyl avoided talking about them, and that suggests he knew more than he wanted to reveal. Reyner warned everyone to avoid them because they were backed by outland golds. Someone suggested that troublemaker Broussard had dealings with them . . ."

I asked a few more questions, listened, and then took my leave. I was intrigued that Ramsael was familiar with Veblynt, but then the paper factor had come from a High Holder family, and because he was a friend of my father's, I could certainly talk to him . . . when I had some time. In the end, I stayed at the Council Chateau through the opening glass, while the votes were taken to confirm Ramsael as Chief Councilor and to seat Fhernon as the High Holder Councilor replacing Suyrien.

Rholyn made an eloquent speech in support of Ramsael, but the only words that stuck in my memory were: "Like any good Chief Councilor, Councilor Ramsael will be mindful of our heritage. He will understand and accept the present, while planning for a better future that neither rejects the past nor blindly embraces change for the sake of change . . ."

I couldn't help feeling that Rholyn was trying to be all things to all Councilors.

When I finally got back to the Collegium a quint or so after the first glass of the afternoon, I knew I had to concentrate on the links between Glendyl and the other factors and the Banque D'Ouestan.

53

On Mardi, I took the duty coach with Seliora and Diestrya and dropped them off at NordEste Design, then had the driver take me to the Banque D'Excelsis on the Midroad just south of Plaza D'Este, the branch that had been bombed.

As I got out of the coach, I turned to Desalyt. "If you'd wait?"

"Yes, sir."

The guard outside the banque doors glanced at me—or my grays—but decided against saying anything as I entered. I hadn't been able to remember the name of the director of the banque, but I had written it down right after the explosion and locked it into the hidden safebox in my home study, along with the note I'd received and, later, the card I'd gotten from Madame D'Shendael at the Autumn Ball. So I'd taken a moment earlier that morning to open the safebox and copy the director's name—so I wouldn't forget again.

The second guard—the one inside the banque—must have been there on the day of the explosion, because he clearly recalled me. He stepped forward. "Master Captain?"

"I'm here to see Director Tolsynn."

The guard turned toward one of the clerks behind a bronze framed cage. "The Maitre and captain is here for the director."

I only waited a few moments before Tolsynn appeared. I might not have remembered his name, but I couldn't have forgotten the waxed black mustaches and bulging green eyes—or the air of self-importance that made him seem to bulge out of his black pinstriped jacket.

"Maitre Captain." His acknowledgment was a polite statement of the fact that he didn't want to see me.

"There are a few items we need to discuss, Director. Your study would be most convenient."

Tolsynn didn't quite sigh. "I trust this will not be too long."

"Only long enough to go over what we need to."

I followed him to the small study with the narrow uncluttered desk and took the chair farthest from the door. He looked at me, the door, and finally seated himself, waiting.

"You may have noticed that there have been more than a few explosions in L'Excelsis over the past month. In the course of our investigations, the Collegium has come across a variety of indications that the Banque D'Ouestan has been used to convey funds from Ferrum to L'Excelsis, and to other banques, as well as to individuals who may be connected to those explosions." I smiled at Tolsynn, projecting both forthrightness and a certainty that he certainly wouldn't wish to hide anything from me.

He didn't say anything.

I raised my eyebrows and tilted my head slightly, signifying that I was waiting for a response.

"For most of our clients, we seldom deal with the Banque D'Ouestan. Out of all our clients, there are less than a hundred factors and other commercial enterprises who regularly receive funds from that institution. They have done so for years."

"So you haven't noticed anyone receiving large sums from there in just the past year? Someone who didn't before."

"I couldn't say if someone received one or two fund transfers, but I can assure you that no significant funds were transferred to any client over the past year who had not already been transacting business for some time before that."

"Has the Banque D'Ouestan ever sent representatives here for any reason?"

Tolsynn frowned, then he nodded. "They do have a local representative. At least, he represented himself as such. I have his card here." He turned in the chair and lifted an ebony card box, opening it, then riffling through it. "Here . . ." He handed me an engraved card.

The name read:

Vyktor D'Banque D'Ouestan
880 Avenue D'Theatre
L'Excelsis

"What did he want from you?" I studied it for a moment, then handed the card back.

"He didn't seem to want anything. He gave me his card and said that if I had any troubles or questions regarding transactions or transfers that I should let him know immediately. We never have had those problems."

"When did he give you the card?"

"Sometime in Harvest, late Agostos, as I recall."

I asked more questions about the Banque D'Ouestan, but Tolsynn didn't know any more. So I changed the subject. "I'd like to know if you observed anything else about Kearyk. I've seen a miniature of him, and he seemed extraordinarily handsome."

"More like . . ." Tolsynn paused, then said, "almost pretty. He was always well-dressed. I once asked him if he spent all his earnings on clothes. He laughed. He said he didn't have to."

"What did you think of that?"

"I wondered for a time, and I watched. But several times he was picked up by someone in a stylish carriage. More than several times."

"Did you notice anything about the carriage?"

"No. Just that it was black with brass trim. Very conservative. With two matched grays."

"Did you see who was inside?"

Tolsynn shook his head.

"I take it Kearyk had a fine hand, his writing, I mean."

"Yes."

"Did he draw?"

"How would I . . ." He broke off. "Come to think of it, I did see a few . . . well . . . doodles . . . on a scrap of paper once. Very graceful . . . very fine."

"Graceful enough that he could have forged the entire ledger sheet with the off-entry in it?"

"I suppose. I hadn't thought of it. He seemed so gentle and kind. Why would he have done that for such a small sum . . . comparatively, that is?"

I didn't have an answer for that question, although I was beginning to get a glimmer of one. "I have no idea." I laughed softly. "That's why I had to come back to talk to you. This branch doesn't handle the Civic Patrol accounts, I take it?"

"No . . . those are all at Council Square."

"Did you know Captain Bolyet? He was a friend of mine . . . a good officer."

Tolsynn nodded. "I met him a few times . . . and, of course, his widow. It was an accident, I heard."

"One of those freak things that you never think can happen. Any patroller thinks he might be shot at, or attacked, or even have trouble with a runaway hauler's team . . . but to get hit by a loose crane? Even Subcommander Cydarth found that hard to believe."

"He said something like that."

"He's been a client for a long time, I imagine."

"Longer than I've been director here."

"I wonder if he'd know this Vyktor D'Banque D'Ouestan. I'd heard he or his wife had relatives there." I shook my head. "Probably not. When you hear that someone's from someplace or has relatives there, you always think that they'll know people you do, and usually they don't."

Tolsynn nodded. "He's never said anything about that, but we've not passed more than a few words ever." He paused and looked at the door. "Is there anything else?"

"Not at the moment. Thank you." I stood.

After I left the banque, I instructed Desalyt to take me to the Plaza D'Nord. Despite the fact that chalkers worked in places where there were pedestrians, it took nearly a glass for us to find Lacques. He was a block down from the Plaza, on the corner of Milner Lane and Saenhelyn Road, and he looked to have just started a small wall painting on a narrow stretch of stone between a café that looked to be closed and a millinery shop.

I had the coach stop a few yards back and then got out and walked toward the chalker.

He turned and said, "It's not finished . . . sir." For a street artist, he was well-turned out, with dark trousers and polished boots, and even a red cravat.

"Lacques, you might remember that we talked about Kearyk several weeks ago."

"I told you everything I knew . . . sir."

"No. You told me the truth about everything I asked. I've been thinking. That chalk you did, the one of the half-man, half-woman. That was Kearyk, in a way, wasn't it?"

The chalker didn't answer for a moment. Then he smiled crookedly. "Yes. Kearyk had that handsome angelic look, but sometimes he could be a manipulative bitch. He could be so sweet and dear . . . and then . . . other times . . ." Lacques shook his head.

"You don't happen to have a black coach with brass trim, do you?"

"A chalker? With a coach?"

There was an edge to his voice, and I pressed. "But you know who it was, don't you?"

"I don't know his name. Kearyk never said. He told me I didn't own him. I only saw him once, from a distance. He had to be a wealthy swell, but not what you'd expect. Clothes like a High Holder, but dark, and his hair was cut short—like yours."

"Did you see what color his hair was?"

"A mixture of red and silver gray, I thought. He was years older than me. But he had golds, and Kearyk loved golds and clothes."

·

"Kearyk received clothes from this . . . friend?"

"I don't know where else he would have gotten them." Lacques's voice turned bitter. "I'm the one who taught him how to dress and present himself. He was turned down for several clerkships until I showed him what to wear."

"Why didn't you become a guild artist?"

"It's not a matter of talent. You have to have golds to get a master to take you . . . or have them take a special interest in you, and . . . I didn't have the golds, and I was never handsome enough." He shrugged. "I manage to get by, what with the art and being a server a few places."

"Did Kearyk ever say anything about his friend?"

"No. I asked, but he said he was just a friend. He was lying, and he knew that I knew that, but if I'd pressed it, he would have left."

"He didn't say anything at all about him?"

"Just that he knew all the people in the salons, like Madame D'Shendael and Madame D'Almeida. Kearyk liked to think he could have conversed with them. He'd go to the bookshops and read her books a chapter at a time."

"That was all?"

"You think this swell had something to do with his death?"

"I don't know." I thought that he did, but I didn't know.

"But . . . why? I can't believe that Kearyk was anything but . . . a plaything to a swell like that. I even told him so."

"What did he say?"

"He just said that it wasn't like that at all, and he enjoyed the culture. He said if I asked more, he'd leave. I didn't."

I spent another quint with Lacques. I didn't learn much more, but I'd learned more than enough to end up even more puzzled about why matters were turning out as they seemed to be.

By the time I returned to Imagisle, I had enough time to check with Schorzat and Kahlasa, and to write down the name and address of Vyktor D'Banque D'Ouestan. Neither Schorzat nor Kahlasa had anything new to report, and Maitre Dyana wasn't looking for me. So I went over to the dining hall, which contained noticeably fewer junior imagers, unsurprisingly. I sat between Chassendri and Isola.

I'd barely taken a sip of tea before Ferlyn immediately asked, "Most honored Maitre Rhennthyl, might you be able to explain where so many of the juniors have gone?"

"I could. They've been sent on a journey. They're currently somewhere on the ironway."

"Would it be too much to ask where they are going and why?"

I smiled. "In fact, for the moment, it would be."

"Could you give Ferlyn some idea?" asked Chassendri.

She was really suggesting that he'd continue to press unless I gave a better answer, because, after her work with Dartazn, she certainly had some ideas about what we had planned for them to do, if not where and how.

"I think it's fair to say that we're trying to come up with a way to stop all the Ferran attacks and explosions here in Solidar." I immediately took a mouthful of the fowl and rice casserole, because I was hungry and because I wanted to slow down the questioning.

"That's singularly uninformative," interjected Heisbyl, who was sitting farther down the table with Ghaend and Quaelyn, all of whom seldom ate at the dining hall, suggesting that they were there as much to see what I might say as for the culinary excellence of the fare.

Kahlasa, between Ferlyn and Ghaend, smiled faintly.

"True enough," I admitted after another sip of tea. "That's because we're dealing with singular times and events."

"I've said this before," Ferlyn said, his voice not quite edged, "but those of you in the covert branch seem to suspect everyone. You try to hide everything, even from other masters."

"Do you suggest that we send out newsheets to all Terahnar announcing what we plan?"

I could feel Isola wince at my words.

"Surely, surely, you could convey something more to the Maitres of the Collegium," suggested Heisbyl in a reasonable tone.

"There are already rumors afoot that the Collegium is diverting Navy ships for an absurd project of some sort," added Ferlyn.

"That's interesting," I replied. "Might I ask the source of these rumors?" Neither Schorzat nor Kahlasa knew the details of the plan, and Maitre Dyana wasn't about to tell anyone. Of those left in L'Excelsis, that left Sea-Marshal Valeun and whomever he'd told. I suspected that Valeun had let that rumor loose, trying to distance himself from the plan, in case it failed, in which circumstances he could claim that he'd been against it from the start—with witnesses who could back up his assertion.

"You could," replied Ferlyn, slightly archly.

Ferlyn was bright enough, but he could also be infuriating, because he confused his ability to analyze patterns with the understanding of what they meant. That gave him an inflated sense of importance. But then, I doubtless had an even more inflated sense of self-importance.

"Since I have, why don't you tell us? Or was this a rumor that began with your reporting it here?"

"I'm led to believe that it came from the Naval Command, or perhaps the Naval Bureau. You know that to me the Navy types and bureaus are really all the same."

"Now why would anyone there start a rumor that suggests that the Navy is agreeing to an absurd plan by the Collegium?" I asked. "Unless there is such a plan and that someone believes it will fail and he will profit by letting the world know that he was right from the beginning. Of course, anyone who would release that information for purely personal gain probably isn't anyone that should remain in the Navy."

"Unless it really is an absurd plan," countered Heisbyl, "and one that more . . . experienced master imagers should have reviewed."

"That's always a question that the most senior imagers must consider." I emphasized "most" just slightly. "At this point, however, revealing what the Maitre has approved would only endanger those involved without providing any other benefit . . . besides personal satisfaction at the possible cost of lives."

That generally ended the discussion, and the ensuing silence did allow me to finish the casserole and the fresh-baked dark rye bread.

The first thing I did after lunch was to write a short note to Juniae D'Shendael, requesting permission to call on her. I could have shown up, but that could have been awkward, and it wouldn't have had the effect that the note would. Besides, I wanted her to have advance notice.

Then I found another duty coach and directed the driver to take me to Glendyl's L'Excelsis dwelling, which turned out to be a modest mansion a mille north of the Council Chateau. His four-level hillside dwelling some sixty yards across the front, set in a small park a quarter mille on a side, was modest only in comparison to the estates of the wealthier High Holders. It was also far enough outside L'Excelsis that it wasn't under Civic Patrol jurisdiction, which was the only way a factor could obtain the equivalent of personal security that extended to all High Holders through their privilege of low justice. Of course, Glendyl couldn't punish anyone, and if a crime occurred on his lands, he—or someone else—could petition the regional justiciary for punishment of the guilty party—assuming he could come up with proof and the person of that party.

The gate guard looked dubious, but clearly wasn't about to refuse a Collegium Maitre. When I walked through the portico and reached the double doors of the dwelling itself, I came face to face with a pair of guards.

"Maitre Rhennthyl to see the Councilor," I announced.

"He won't be seeing anyone today," announced the shorter and broader guard.

That seemed odd, but I persisted. "Is he here?"

"That he is, but not to anyone."

"I'd appreciate it if you—or someone—would convey my presence to him."

"That we can do, but he won't see anyone." The taller guard yanked on a bell-pull.

Shortly, a tall graying functionary opened the right door. He looked at me. After a moment, he spoke. "Maitre, the Councilor is not seeing anyone. He was specific. If you would like to leave a card . . ."

I didn't feel like being shunted off by Glendyl's functionaries. So I just raised concealment shields, and then imaged a pillar of flame in the middle of the stone portico behind me.

While they were gaping, I yanked open the door and stepped past the bewildered servant in his green livery.

Then I stepped to the side of the foyer, still concealed, and waited.

The flame died away quickly enough, and the functionary retreated, glancing this way and that. I followed him along the corridor to the right to a set of open double doors that filled an archway.

He stopped, cleared his throat, and spoke, "Sir . . ."

"I said I wasn't to be disturbed by anyone." Glendyl's voice was cold and curt.

I stepped around the bewildered functionary and dropped the concealment, but held my defense shields. "Thank you." I nodded to the servant. "You may close the doors. Now."

He was shaking, but he did as I commanded. Then I stepped into the study. Although it had two large bookcases, there were too few volumes for the chamber to be a proper library.

Glendyl looked up from the armchair and the ledger in his lap. To say that he happened to be irritated would have been an understatement. His face was flushed, and his jaw was tight. The fingers of his left hand were white, so hard was he clutching the ledger.

"Maitre Rhennthyl . . . this is unbelievable . . . unacceptable . . . unprecedented . . ."

"Also unavoidable," I said quietly.

"I will report this to the Council. I will have you charged with breaking and entering . . ."

"You won't. First, I broke nothing. I announced myself and I didn't force my way in." I slipped in, but I really hadn't used force. Surprise, but not force. "Second, I've taken nothing and will take nothing. Third, the last thing you want is to confront me before the Council." I smiled. "I don't have time for the niceties, and neither do you. I was hoping that you'd see that your story was not believable, but I see no sign that you intend to do anything but try to cover up your misdeeds."

"Misdeeds? You're the one—"

"Quiet." I projected pure force at him, pressing him back into his chair. "Now . . . was Vyktor the one from the Banque D'Ouestan who came to you, or did he merely introduce you to the others . . . or suggest the others would be in touch with you?" I watched him intently as I dropped Vyktor's name. There was enough of a reaction there.

"I don't have the faintest idea what you're talking about."

"But you do. I intend to bring the whole sorry mess in front of the Council. I thought you ought to know. I've already confirmed the business of the bribes from Haebyn and the debts you owe Suyrien House, not to mention the explosives in your works. The bribes alone will have you removed from the Council, because the artisan and guild Councilors will vote for your removal, as will the Collegium Councilor, as will the High Holders. Of course, they'll also have to discipline Haebyn because Ramsael won't want to give the impression that they'll stand for that sort of thing. With those votes, do you really think Etyenn, Diogayn, Sebatyon, and Reyner will stand up for you?"

"If you're going to do that . . . why are you even here? You need something from me." He reached out, his left hand holding the ledger awkwardly, and slid it onto the table adjoining the desk, which held little, except for a pen to the right of the leather blotter.

"You're right. I do, and I've gotten it."

That confused him, if only for a moment. "Oh?" A sardonic smile crossed his lips.

"I don't like seeing Solidar being crippled because of one factor's greed. I don't like seeing poor workers being killed. I don't like seeing the Chief Councilor being assassinated. I don't like being lied to, and I don't like being made a target."

"That's a rather long string of assertions, Maitre."

"No. They're facts, honorable Councilor, and any one of them is enough to have you removed." I paused.

Glendyl just glared.

"Besides, I really don't have to do anything. You can't repay Suyrien, and that means he'll get the engine works and the plans for the turbines. Oh, and

I might point out that his brother is Ryel D'Alte, in case you've forgotten, and Ryel is a very good friend of mine. Of course, your failure was what your friends the Ferrans had in mind. That was why they set the explosives. For all their talk about wanting to further the cause of the factors, here all they wanted to do was hamper Solidar. Each of you wanted to use the other. You'll both lose." I smiled. "Good day."

Then I walked to the door, making certain my shields were tight, and opened it. But there was no one in the corridor, and I walked out unhindered and down to where Desalyt and the coach waited.

Glendyl was right, in that I couldn't bring up all the charges before the Council, but Frydryk wouldn't hesitate to call his notes, once I pointed out that it was the only way he could possibly recapture a portion of his losses. No High Holder was going to be left bailing out a failed factor.

The only question was how exactly matters would play out. In that sense, Frydryk was fortunate that he was engaged to Alynkya and that Kandryl had married Iryela. That left Glendyl with few options.

Unfortunately, I still had to deal with Geuffryt, and I had no doubts that would be more difficult, because I had absolutely no proof and no real direct leverage on him. My only leverage had been on the Naval Command as a whole . . . and upon a very disgruntled Valeun.

I had barely walked into the administration building when Sorlyt, the very, very junior duty prime, hurried up to me. "Maitre Rhennthyl, Maitre Dyana would like to see you."

"I'll go right up." I hoped that something else hadn't gone wrong.

On the way, I left my winter cloak in my study. Once I entered the outer anteroom, Gherard waved me toward the half-open door to the Maitre's study. I closed it behind me.

Maitre Dyana set down the folder before her. "You've been rather involved today."

"Is anything else the matter?"

"Not that I know of. That's why I wanted to see you. Is anything?"

"It's been an interesting day." I went on to tell her almost everything that I'd discovered during the day, but not what I suspected.

"You still haven't linked all of this together," she pointed out.

"Oh . . . I have. With Glendyl."

She nodded. "You realize that you've just handled Glendyl in the same way any High Holder would have."

"Is that so wrong?" I asked. "His greed has set up a situation where we'll lose junior imagers, even if they're successful in what we've planned, where the Navy will lose ships and men, and where all of Solidar has suffered to one degree or another."

"I didn't say it was wrong. It's more effective . . . but it won't help your relations with the Council. You've been head of security for the Collegium less than a month, and your actions have made your predecessor look mild by comparison." Her smile was sympathetic. "Some of that is the times. Some is not."

"I'm still worried about Valeun and Geuffryt."

"You should be. You've forced Valeun into supporting your plan, and no Sea-Marshal likes that, and you've demanded that he deal with a subordinate who has some allies among the High Holders."

"He has contacts. I'm not certain about allies. If I'd waited to act, or acted more . . . temperately . . . more lives would be lost, and more damage done."

"That is quite true. That is also why you avoid politics and the Council as much as you possibly can. They're far more interested in accomplishing matters without upsetting the Navy and those who put them in power. They always have been, and they always will be."

"Even if it costs everyone else more?"

"Rhenn . . . it's never been any other way. You know that."

I stifled a sigh. "I know, but I'd rather not do things that way."

"That is obvious. Can you not create any more havoc until we know how the action goes against Ferrum?"

"I don't know. It will be two weeks before they'll be in Ferran waters."

She looked evenly at me.

"I'll see what I can do."

"That will be all, then."

As I walked out, I understood her position. The Council was unsettled. The Naval Command wasn't happy, and we still had who knew how many Ferran agents in Solidar and L'Excelsis, and I'd dealt largely with those in Solidar that they'd corrupted, not the agents themselves.

And I still worried about Geuffryt and Cydarth.

54

Much as I'd hoped for an early reply from Madame D'Shendael, I didn't get one, not on Meredi or on Jeudi. I'd planned to spend some time at the Council Chateau, helping Martyl and Baratyn, but I didn't have to because once Ramsael was approved as Chief Councilor, he'd set the next meeting of the full Council for 18 Ianus. That was when the Council would have met anyway. On Meredi, I'd also taken a duty coach out to Veblynt's paper mill south of L'Excelsis, only to discover he was somewhere north of Rivages, trying to work out an agreement for wood scraps and pulp timber. I left a note for him, saying I'd like to meet him, but because the mill was on a side stream south of Iron Road, the trip had wasted almost two glasses. I'd also had Schorzat set up a meeting with Sea-Marshal Valeun, but that wouldn't be until the following Mardi afternoon because he was at the Naval yard in Solis.

The rest of Meredi and Juedi I spent catching up on all the odds and ends I'd neglected, including long session with Haugyl and Marteon, both of whom wanted to know why they hadn't been selected and what the others who had were doing.

Vendrei morning dawned cold and windy under gray skies with light flakes of snow fluttering down, but the clouds were light enough that I doubted we'd get much snow. I checked the newsheets when I got to my study. *Veritum* reported an inconclusive naval skirmish off Ferrial that apparently resulted in our losing a frigate, and the Ferrans losing two ships. *Tableta* didn't have that story, but did report that several fires had broken out at the shipworks in Solis, but that they'd been contained, and that the guards had captured several of the perpetrators.

I was glad to see that Frydryk had been right about his guards and security, but couldn't help but worry where the next set of fires and/or sabotage might take place.

It had been over three weeks since I'd met with Commander Artois, and Dichartyn had met with the Commander weekly, sometimes more often. I needed to keep in touch with Artois more, no matter how awkward it might be. So I took a duty coach to Patrol headquarters. Even if he didn't happen to be there, the gesture would help. I was going to need help, because too many problems were turning out to be the kind that imaging couldn't solve. I supposed that had always been the case; I just hadn't had to deal with those much. Now there wasn't anyone else.

With that not-exactly-consoling thought I pulled on my gray heavy winter cloak and made my away across the quadrangle to the duty coach stand. The clouds had lightened some, and the snow had stopped, although the dusting on the grass had not melted. As I rode toward Civic Patrol headquarters, I tried to think of statements or questions that would lead Artois toward areas where I needed to know more without admitting totally my ignorance.

The Commander was in, and he even smiled and stood, if but for a moment before seating himself, as I entered his study and closed the door behind me.

"Greetings, Maitre. I'd thought I might be seeing you before long, now that you've settled back into the Collegium." He paused. "I must admit that I've been pleased with the performance of Captain Alsoran. That has been a bright spot in a rather grim winter."

"He was always very solid for me." I sat down across from him. "What should I know about this grim winter for the Patrol?"

"I imagine you know some of it. The stronger elveweed is creeping back into the hellhole and the surrounding areas in Sixth District. Cydarth and I agreed on promoting Yerkes and Walthyr to captain, and we'll have to see how that works out." He fingered a chin that looked more pointed than I recalled, perhaps because he was even more gaunt than the last time I'd seen him, not that he'd ever been other than slender. "We still haven't found any more Ferran agents, dead or alive . . . except for the one you killed that shot Councilor Glendyl. There haven't been any more explosions in the last week or so, but there's been a rash of counterfeit silvers—some sort of lead-tin alloy washed with silver. They're always passed at crowded taverns or bistros. The workmanship is good, too."

"Silvers . . . that makes sense. Everyone looks closely at golds."

"You don't think they're the work of a renegade imager?"

"No. If the workmanship is good, it wouldn't take any more effort to image real silvers, and an imager who could do that would be far better off copying jewelry and pawning it."

"I thought as much, but I wanted your opinion."

"I have run across something a bit . . . odd." I smiled ruefully. "You remember the explosion at the Midroad Banque D'Excelsis? Well . . . there was a clerk there who drowned several weeks before the explosion, and I'd asked if there might be any connection. The director couldn't find any, except that, after the clerk died, when his ledgers were audited as a matter of procedure, they discovered that he'd apparently embezzled a hundred golds. I was looking into something involving the Collegium, and I ran across the lover of the dead clerk, and he told me that the poor clerk was absolutely terrified of water, but that when he'd come down here to tell the Patrol, some patroller named Merolyn had threatened to charge him with murder."

Artois nodded slowly. "That sounds . . . unlikely."

He could have meant anything by that, but I just smiled. "Unlikely on all counts. A guilty lover wouldn't try to get an accidental drowning classified as a murder if he'd done it, but I can't see why Merolyn would need to threaten him, either." I shrugged. "But it seemed so odd that I thought I should pass it on. Oh, the dead clerk's name was Kearyk D'Cleris."

"Kearyk D'Cleris . . . I don't recall anything on that."

"The other coincidence is that the subcommander is a client there. The director knows him by sight."

"We all have to banque somewhere, Maitre Rhennthyl."

"That we do. That we do. How is the subcommander?"

"As always," replied Artois dryly.

"Does he have relatives in Ouestan?"

"Not that I know of. Why do you ask?"

"We've run across several strange connections to the Banque D'Ouestan, and one suggested a Cydarth D'Patrol. It's nothing that I could verify, but I did wonder."

Artois nodded. "You never know with that kind of information whether it's real or a ploy to put one in a difficult situation."

"That was my thought exactly."

"Tell me, Maitre Rhennthyl. Do you think we'll see more Ferran agents in L'Excelsis?"

"Like you, I don't know. I have the feeling that those who might remain, if any do, are more likely to be involved in indirect attacks on Solidar. I don't think we've seen the end of the events they may have set in motion or difficulties that may come from those events." I shrugged. "You heard about the explosions at Councilor Glendyl's engine works? Young High Holder Suyrien's guards thwarted similar attacks in Solis."

"I read that. You think others may occur?"

"I'd be surprised if they didn't."

"You have no idea where or when?"

"I wish I did." And I certainly did.

We talked a bit longer, and then I took my leave. Artois did not suggest that I stop and see Cydarth, and I didn't.

Lebryn pulled the coach up as I left headquarters.

"On the way back," I told him, "I'd like to make a stop at 880 Avenue D'Theatre."

"Yes, sir."

The address, despite the street, was actually closer to Nordroad than to the theatre area or to the opera, and when the coach came to a halt, it was outside a yellow-brick structure only ten yards wide, if four stories high, sandwiched between two larger buildings, one of which proclaimed itself the River Association Building. I had no idea that there was a River Association, much less what it might do.

I made my way to the door and rapped on it with the slightly tarnished brass knocker. Although I waited for a time, no one answered.

From there, I had the coach take me all the way out to Frydryk's "local" estate. He wasn't there, but in Laaryn, tending to various legalities and property transfers. The chef d'chateau expected him back on Mardi. On the way back to Imagisle, it began to snow again.

I finally got back to the house at close to fifth glass. I'd barely stepped inside, dusted the light snow off my cloak and hung it up, when Seliora appeared, one hand firmly holding Diestrya's left hand. Diestrya didn't look at me.

"What did she do?"

"She threw her tea at the stove to hear it hiss, and when I took her mug away, she went into the wash room and got water from the pitcher to throw it at the stove. She broke the pitcher as well."

"Someone is going to bed before dinner."

Seliora nodded. "Oh . . . we received another invitation."

"From whom? When?"

"It's from Councilor Fhernon and his wife, on the thirteenth of Ianus. We're going to that ball at the Almeida's the next night." She looked at me. "You need to be at both. I asked mother if Diestrya could spend the night on Vendrei and Samedi. There's really no one here, now, to look after the girls, and Klysia has that Vendrei night off and the weekend."

"Is that all right with your mother?"

"She was fine with it, and so were the twins. So was Aegina. She said the girls needed to see just what dealing with an active three-year-old was like for more than a few glasses. After this evening, I'm more than happy to give them the experience." Seliora turned, then looked back. "The invitation is on the card tray. I'll be back down shortly."

Diestrya didn't say a word as she trudged up the stairs beside her mother.

55

As planned, we went to services at the Imagisle Anomen on Year-Turn afternoon, and then took Diestrya to NordEste Design for the family dinner. Even Odelia was cheerful. We had a good dinner and enjoyed ourselves thoroughly. I tried not to think too much about Dartazn and his charges steaming their way toward Ferrum and what awaited them.

On Lundi, after reading the newsheets that held nothing new, and a few scattered reports from across Solidar that also told me little, I finally received a response from Juniae D'Shendael that said she would be happy to receive me on Mardi at half-past ninth glass of the morning. That wouldn't conflict with my meeting with Valeun at second glass. The rest of Lundi was quiet, and that bothered me. Quiet often foreshadowed trouble, as with a three-year old who was getting into trouble and didn't want her parents to know.

I'd only been in my study for a half-glass or so on Mardi morning when Gherard appeared at my door. "Maitre Dyana would like you to join her and Maitre Dhelyn in her study, sir." The young imager smiled politely.

"Maitre Dhelyn? From the Collegium at Westisle?"

"Yes, sir. He arrived a quint ago."

I rose. The odds were that Dhelyn was less than pleased, and I had a good idea why. "Then we'd best go and meet with him."

The door to her study was open, and that told me that my suspicions were correct. Dyana didn't have to nod for me to close it. She did stand, briefly, before she gestured to the chairs before her desk. "Rhennthyl, you know of Maitre Dhelyn."

Dhelyn nodded but did not stand.

"That I do." I inclined my head politely, and took the seat opposite the other end of the desk so that there was an empty chair between us.

"Now . . . Maitre Dhelyn," Dyana said pleasantly, "you were saying?"

"Rhennthyl, I suspect you know why I am here." Dhelyn had one of those smooth and deep voices, soothing and just short of boring, the kind that could lull you into complacency before he undercut you.

"Perhaps you should tell me. I'd rather not make assumptions based on suspicions."

The faintest trace of a smile creased Maitre Dyana's face, but she said nothing.

Dhelyn smiled politely. "Very well, I will. While it is doubtless a waste of time, at this point a few more moments will make little difference." He paused. "Last Jeudi, some thirty imagers from here boarded a Navy fast frigate in West-isle. In less than four glasses, the ship steamed out of the harbor. Within several glasses of its departure, I received a number of inquiries. As you well know, I could not offer an explanation. My ignorance did not help the Collegium, nor the position of imagers. I do believe, with the exception of Maitre Dyana and Maitre Jhulian, I am the most senior imager in the Collegium, and I was informed of nothing. I would very much appreciate an explanation, and I came to request one from Maitre Dyana. She informed me that it would be best if both of you were here."

I'd thought of being conciliatory, but the arrogance beneath his smooth tone put me off, and I wanted to squash him. That wouldn't help matters. So I smiled before saying a word. "My dear Dhelyn, I understand the position in which our actions may have placed you, and I'm deeply sorry that you felt blindsided. The situation which all Solidar faces, however, requires a drastic solution, and the greatest secrecy. Even now, the exact details of the plan we are implementing are known to exactly two people. Even Maitre Dyana does not know all the details. Nor does Sea-Marshal Valeun. Now . . . why do we need such secrecy? First, are you aware that the Ferrans are perilously close to breaking our blockade, if not destroying a large portion of the northern fleet? Second, because of the damage inflicted by Ferran agents on the engine works in Ferravyl, there is no way that Solidar will be able even to begin to build any replacement vessels for a year, if not more. Third, Ferran agents were behind the series of explosions that took place all across Solidar, as well as behind the murder of Chief Councilor Suyrien and the near-assassination of acting Chief Counselor Glendyl. Fourth, the Stakanarans have unofficially allied themselves with the Ferrans and are the ones behind the growth and distribution of the stronger elveweed that has killed thousands of users in the past few months."

"I understand all of that, but urgency is no excuse for not informing one of the most senior imagers of the greater Collegium," protested Dhelyn.

"Indeed," I agreed, "urgency itself is not. But the greater the number of people who know the details of the operation, the greater the possibility that the Ferrans will find out its nature and take steps against it. I can tell you that, once the operation is concluded, for better or worse, and it is extremely risky, you will be informed, and you will be among the first to know."

"I cannot believe you are telling me this." Dhelyn turned to face Maitre Dyana. "You are letting him ignore long-standing tradition and seniority."

"Maitre Dhelyn," replied Dyana calmly, "as Maitre, I am responsible first and foremost for the safety of the Collegium. If Ferrum is not stopped, and soon, there will be no land anywhere on Terahnar where imagers are safe. This attempt to stop Ferrum requires secrecy. I have not pressed Maitre Rhennthyl for details." She smiled politely. "If I, as Maitre, do not need to know those details, I trust you can accept that you do not need to know them either."

"You would trust his word on something such as this, whatever 'this' is?"

"No. I do not trust his word. I trust him. He has been the recipient of more attacks than any senior imager in generations, with the possible exception of Maitre Dichartyn, and his acts have always benefited the Collegium. He has also earned the Collegium much respect in his years as a common Civic Patroller and as a Patrol Captain."

Maitre Dyana was stretching matters a trace in saying I'd been a common patroller, although I had walked the rounds with common patrollers and just like one, but I was getting the feeling she didn't like Dhelyn much better than I did.

"Still, Maitre . . . I must protest . . ."

"Maitre Dhelyn, you have every right to protest, and I have heard your protest." She smiled. "I do deeply appreciate your concern for the rules and the need to stick by them, and I think you would serve the greater Collegium even better if you took charge of the Collegium at Mont D'Glace. Matters there of late have been lax, and I'm certain that—"

Dhelyn twitched, and I could sense that he was about to image.

I clamped full shields around him, not to hurt him and giving him a full yard on each side, but to restrict any attack. Where he stood was suddenly a pillar of ice two yards across. I dropped the shields and a gout of steam a yard wide flared into the plaster ceiling overhead, removing the plaster all the way down to the laths beneath. A shower of whitish and grayish dust and fragments spray-sifted down into the chamber. When the steam cleared, there were fine dark water droplets everywhere, but nothing more of Maitre Dhelyn, except a sour-bitter odor that permeated everything.

Maitre Dyana shook her head.

"Was I wrong to shield him?"

"No. You were kinder than I would have been. If he had not tried to attack, nothing would have happened to him. In effect, he destroyed himself. We will, of course, have to report this to the full gathering of masters. Dichartyn brought him here years ago to warn him, and he held his peace." She walked to the window and forced it full open, ignoring the gust of chill but fresh air that surged into the study.

"Until Maitre Poincaryt and Maitre Dichartyn were gone."

"He always believed he should be Maitre of the Collegium. He was more interested in what he thought he deserved than what he could do for the Collegium and for Solidar."

"Who will take over there?"

"We don't have to decide yet. It would be better not to for a time, until matters settle."

"Until we discover whether Dartazn is successful?"

"He's likely to succeed, but the cost is another matter. Few of those junior imagers are anywhere near as capable as either of you. How many do you think we'll lose?"

"We could lose three out of four," I admitted. "I'd be relieved if we only lost one in three." Not happy, but relieved.

"Valeun won't be happy to lose three out of four gunboats, or even one of three."

"Better the gunboats than the entire fleet, which will happen if we don't succeed."

"He'll still blame you and the Collegium."

"We'll have to see how that turns out as well," I pointed out.

"Indeed. Is there anything else I should know?"

"Not at the moment. I'm still trying to track down some loose ends. I met with Artois yesterday. Strong elveweed use is up in the hellhole and Sixth District, but not anywhere else . . . so far. There haven't been any more explosions or Ferran agents found, but there's been a rash of high quality lead-tin counterfeit silvers. He asked me about imaging. I pointed out why that didn't make sense. He seemed satisfied."

"If that's all . . . ?"

"That's all." I nodded and departed.

After checking with Schorzat and Kahlasa, I donned my winter cloak and made my way to the duty coach stand, where I had to wait for a quint for Davoryn and another coach to take me to Madame D'Shendael's.

Juniae D'Shendael's town-dwelling—and it was hers in the same fashion that Ryealte really belonged to Iryela—was by far the most modest High Holder dwelling I'd seen, a three-story structure a mere thirty-five yards across, behind a walled front garden and before equally walled rear grounds. On the south side of the property was a drive that led to a covered portico, and that was where the duty coach came to a halt.

A young woman in livery, rather than a footman, opened the coach door. "Welcome, Maitre Rhennthyl. Madame is expecting you."

Another young woman in livery opened the door to the dwelling and escorted me to the small study on the north side of the foyer.

Juniae D'Shendael stood beside a high straight-backed armchair upholstered in a pale blue velvet. At an angle to it was another identical chair, with a low marble-topped table between the two. She wore pale green velvet trousers, a cream blouse, and a darker green velvet jacket. "Greetings, Maitre Rhennthyl. To what do I owe the honor of this call?" She gestured to the chair adjoining hers.

I inclined my head politely, before I replied with a smile, "To your grace and intelligence, of course. And to your writings."

"You do me great honor, and offer excessive flattery." She settled into the armchair.

"The honor is deserved, and some of the flattery." I took the other chair.

She laughed, almost girlishly. "I am certain you did not come here to flatter me. You could do that on Vendrei. In fact, I would be pleased if you did. What did you have in mind for today?"

"To learn what I could from you."

"From another, I might ask how you could learn from a mere woman. Given your wife and your handling of the Ryel affair, I will not."

"The Ryel affair? I had not realized—"

"Oh, most have forgotten, because it is convenient, but I found it rather interesting that the series of incidents that befell that family left the only even-headed and competent heir, and considering that heir was a woman, and considering that only one person had both the ability and motivation to orchestrate those events . . ."

"You would understand all of that, of course," I replied. "And that brings up the matter at hand, which is why you offered that opening."

Her face presented a pleasant, almost insipid smile, but there was a glint and a hardness in her eyes. "You may continue."

"You may recall some weeks back, there was an explosion at the Midroad branch of the Banque D'Excelsis. When I was investigating I received an unsigned message in an exquisitely calligraphed hand. I've seen that same hand twice since, but the message suggested I investigate several fund transactions of purportedly dubious nature. Two I could not, for various reasons, but when I began to look into the circumstances surrounding the death of the clerk associated with an apparent embezzling, I came across several interesting facts." I looked evenly at Juniae.

"You do have an interesting way of putting matters, Maitre Rhennthyl. From what you have said, one could not possibly discern what, if anything, you might require of me, or even if you do."

"The clerk was deathly afraid, terrified, in fact, of water, so much so that he would not even walk the river promenade. Yet he drowned. He also had two lovers, both of whom were men. One of them had red-and-silver hair cut in a military fashion, and often picked him up in a severe black carriage trimmed in brass. This older lover also lavished clothing on the clerk. Now, only a clerk or someone highly placed in the banque would have known the details of certain funding transactions, but at the time I received those details, the clerk had been dead for some time." I smiled.

She nodded slowly. "You do not seem to need me in the slightest."

"No . . . but there is somewhat more to this, and were it merely an intrigue to embarrass or remove a possibly corrupt Councilor or subcommander, I would consider letting matters lie. Unhappily, there is another aspect to this . . . and one far more serious. The attacks on Imagisle itself do not appear to have been the work of Ferrans but of those within Solidar. The funding used to lease the barges and tug that carried the bombards came from a numbered account. I cannot go into the details, but that account required two people to access it, and one of them was an individual with red-and-silver hair. The other individual has vanished without a trace. In addition, though the barge lease was counterfeit, all the forms and authorizations were authentic, as were the procedures, and the munitions were Naval issue." I shrugged. "You can see why I might be concerned, and why I am trying to discover if the individual in question is operating out of personal motivation or whether he has ties to the other explosions and attacks that have been confirmed as Ferran in nature."

"You do face an interesting dilemma, and, from your approach, one might guess that, certain as you may be, elements of your evidence are less than iron-clad in their solidity."

"There is also the possibility that not all of what has been presented to me is accurate in terms of the implications of financial transactions involving those in the Council and the Civic Patrol."

"You still have not indicated what I might contribute to this . . . situation."

"Madame . . . I would prefer not to press you." I emphasized the word "prefer" ever so slightly. "Yet any information you might provide that would assist me in dealing with matters would be appreciated."

Juniae smiled politely. "Let us say that, were I to write a novel, not that I would ever stoop to anything so frivolous, I might posit as a villain of sorts a character of great charm and wit, one whose hair might be that mixture of fire and age that can so lead men astray. As with all too many who end up deviating from their heritage, this villain's family would have fallen from high places, through cruelty and villainy of another and through no fault of his own. He believes that, because no one offered mercy or assistance to his mother and her children, he is under no obligation to reciprocate to others. He places himself where he can learn much about everyone, and he charms men and women alike, generally using them gently, often so gently that they do not know they are being used. Some who do not bend to his whim face ruin if they reveal what they know, yet they are powerful enough that he cannot destroy them without risking his own position, and useful enough that there is no reason to try. Yet never are there any firm links back to him. It pleases him to use seduction equally on men and women, as if to illustrate his control, and those he has seduced range from young and potentially powerful High Holders to clerks, and all tend to regard him with fondness. Such a villain, of course, cannot be brought before the bar of justice, because he has compromised so many that were such even contemplated, either the villain or the accuser, if not both, might well soon be found dead." She paused. "Do you not think that such a fiction would result in a marvelous villain?"

"I do indeed. Except . . . what would motivate such a villain? Most villains seek wealth or positions of power, yet . . ."

"Oh, such a villain would be wiser than that. Wealth and position are merely means to controlling others. Few suspect one who serves his land faithfully and never seeks to stand in the light, even as he destroys those he views as enemies."

"Who would he see as enemies? Everyone?"

"Oh, no. Perhaps an officer of the Civic Patrol who receives a regular . . . retainer . . . for once not looking into certain irregularities, but who may not remain . . . bought . . . or a Councilor who is a supporter of that officer's superior . . . or an imager who pursues the patterns that few others see and whose revelations, were they to come to light, might destroy all he has wrought."

"Would such a villain have allies, not just those whom he controls, but others with coinciding interests? How could he?"

Juniae D'Shendael shrugged. "Everyone, even villains, thinks they have friends and allies. I suppose such a villain might seek allies among those with similar interests or those associated with outland banques or investment houses. Or flatter his superiors into thinking they are friends."

"Have you any other thoughts about such a marvelous villain?"

"One has many thoughts, but none that bear on such a villain."

"Have you thought, were you to write such a novel, what might happen to such a villain?"

"That is why I do not write fiction, Maitre Rhennthyl. In fiction, some improbable hero would charge up to such a villain, attack, and destroy him, and all would live happily ever after. In life, such charges usually result in the death of the would-be hero, and the continued success of the villain in his devious ways. Yet, if an author were to have the villain merely . . . disappear, the readers would feel deprived of some sort of moral victory, voyeuristic and improbable as that victory might be. Alas, in real life, such open confrontations result in wounds for all involved, sometimes worse than the defeats and degradations already suffered." She smiled politely once more. "Those are the other reasons why I do not write fiction."

"I can see that you have a more realistic view of life than most."

"I doubt that it differs markedly from yours, Maitre Rhennthyl, not if even a fraction of the rumors that surround you are correct."

"If they are rumors, their truth is false, and their deception true."

"That is a lovely phrase. I might just borrow it."

"But not for fiction," I replied with a laugh.

"Of course not. Perhaps for an essay on rumors."

While we shared another half quint of polite conversation, she had said what she would say, and my other hints were turned aside gently. As she had implied, I had limited leverage.

After I departed from Madame D'Shendael's, I returned to Imagisle where I was late to lunch at the dining hall. Interestingly, not a single Maitre mentioned Maitre Dhelyn . . . or much of anything concerning the Collegium, although there was much speculation about how long our northern fleet could maintain the blockade of the Ferran ports. I refused to comment, just saying that I did not know enough to make an accurate judgment.

When I returned to my study, I found a budget report on my desk, from Reynol, detailing security expenditures for the previous year and requesting an estimate for projected expenses for the coming year. I didn't have time to read it in any detail before I had to leave for my meeting with Valeun. Budgets, yet. At least, I'd had some considerable experience as a district captain.

After more than a half glass in the duty coach, I arrived at the Naval Command and was escorted up to Sea-Marshal Valeun.

He rose but slightly from behind the wide desk as I entered and the door closed behind me. "Greetings, Maitre."

"Greetings, Marshal." I took the middle chair across from him.

"I thought you might be interested to know that I received word the first thing yesterday morning that the Lyiena left Westisle ahead of schedule, due in part to the organization and the leadership of Maitre Dartazn."

"He is most capable."

"He's older than you, is he not?"

"By two years or so," I replied.

"I wouldn't be surprised to see more of him. The communique mentioned his ability to communicate effectively and smoothly."

"He's very good in that respect, and in others." I understood exactly what Valeun implied, but what the Sea-Marshal didn't understand was that dealing with me was far easier than dealing with Dartazn would have been, because Dartazn was far more adept in the skills of intrigue and diplomacy. Ten years in the Council Chateau had honed those abilities. "How long before the Lyiena reaches Ferrum?"

"If she doesn't encounter heavy weather or a Ferran flotilla, sometime late tomorrow or early on Jeudi."

"And several days to get the imagers to the gunboats after that?"

"And as much as a week to get all of them into position."

"As we discussed, they don't all have to attack at the same time."

"No. I've made it quite clear that the timing is between the senior imager on each gunboat and the ship Commander."

I nodded to that.

"You realize that this operation will reduce our effectiveness in Otelyrn?"

"You were transferring ships from there before we developed this plan," I pointed out. "That was bound to happen, especially with the destruction of the engine works."

"Why is it, Maitre Rhennthyl, that no one has been able to capture Ferran agents alive? That they either escape or end up dead?"

I laughed. "Every operation has been developed so that, if they succeed, they escape, and if they don't, they set themselves up to be killed or destroyed. It's fairly clear that they've been working on these plans for years, since the truce ending the war that never was."

Valeun tapped his fingers on the desk. "And the Collegium never discovered anything about any of this?"

"Maitre Poincaryt or Maitre Dichartyn might have known, but . . ."

"Most convenient."

"But far more effective," I replied. "There's always a trade-off between open communications and effectiveness, as you certainly have shown."

After that, we discussed ship deployments, bemoaned the Council's past

lack of understanding about the need to modernize the fleet, and were cour-
teous to each other.

I'd thought about mentioning Geuffryt, but decided against it. If Valeun
didn't deal with that matter, I might have to . . . but I didn't want to do anything until the Ferran operation was concluded, one way or the other.

When I left the Naval Command, I had Davoryn take me out to Frydryk's
town estate, since I was more than halfway there, and since his chef d'chateau
had indicated he'd be back.

Once the coach came to a halt, I hurried out and walked up to the front
doors. Before I reached them, one door opened.

Alynkya stood there. "Rhenn . . . I thought it might be you."

"I've been trying to get in touch with Frydryk. What are you doing here?"

"We wanted to do some redecorating before the wedding, so that everything's different when I come here. I was looking at the drawing room and
the master bedchambers."

"When will he be back?"

"He sent a note. He went from Laaryn straight to Solis."

"Because of the fires?"

Alynkya nodded. "He hopes to be back on Vendrei."

"I'd like to see him on Vendrei . . ."

"I'll leave a note in his book that you'll be here at the first glass of the
afternoon. That way, if he can't see you, we can send a message before you
leave."

"Thank you . . ." I paused. "Have you talked to your father about all this?
The fires and the destruction of the engine works?"

"He doesn't like to say much. He's not pleased with the Ferrans, or with
Councilor Glendyl's failure to take better precautions. He thinks you're a strong
imager, and one that the Council and Collegium need now . . ."

"But he worries about my lack of experience?"

"He didn't say that."

I laughed softly. "I worry about my lack of experience, especially in dealing with all the intriguing."

"Frydryk doesn't. Neither do I." After a moment, she went on. "I'd like to
redo the master suite. Do you think . . . Seliora? I wouldn't want to impose."

"I think Seliora's family would be pleased, but the way to do it is to first
talk to Betara—Seliora's mother. Tell her what you told me, that you don't
want to impose on friendship and that's why you're contacting her. She'll understand."

Alynkya nodded. "Thank you."

A gust of wind swirled around us, and I realized she wasn't even wearing a cloak. "You'd best get inside before you freeze."

"Thank you. Give my best to Seliora."

"I will." I waited until she was inside before I turned.

As I rode back to the Collegium, I wasn't sure what I'd accomplished in a long day, except to confirm two suspicions, still without proof, and destroy one senior Maitre whose death I could have probably avoided, with a bit more forethought.

Except . . . Maitre Dyana had already known about Dhelyn's pride.

I shook my head. Once again, I'd been played like a plaque, but so had Dhelyn.

56

Maitre Dyana had informed all the masters of the Collegium in L'Excelsis of a mandatory meeting at eighth glass on Meredi morning in the Maitre's conference room. I was there a quint early, as were Dyana and Jhulian, because she'd asked me to be.

Dyana turned to Jhulian. "I will tell what happened. Rhenn will affirm or correct the details, and you will tell them how our acts fall within the Collegium procedures . . . or how they fail to comply."

Jhulian nodded, and so did I.

"We might as well take our places," she suggested.

The first of the remaining masters to arrive were Chassendri and Baratyn, followed by Quaelyn and Ferlyn, then Heisbyl and Ghaend. Draffyd slipped in behind Kahlasa and Schorzat, followed by Isola. Several moments later came Rholyn, always one for the entrance. The only one missing was Dartazn, and that left fourteen of us around the long table, six on each side, with Maitre Dyana at the head and Isola at the foot, and Maitre Jhulian seated to Dyana's right, and me to her left.

Once everyone was seated. Maitre Dyana waited several moments before speaking. "I've called this meeting because of a serious occurrence yesterday here in my study." She paused. "As some of you know, Maitre Dhelyn appeared yesterday morning. He appeared most civil initially, but he wanted to know why thirty imagers had been sent to Westisle under another master without the courtesy of informing him why they were there and what their purpose was. Since their purpose involved Maitre Rhennthyl, I suggested that, before we proceeded, Maitre Rhennthyl be asked to join us. He did. Immediately, Maitre Dhelyn began a verbal assault on Maitre Rhennthyl, insisting that, as the most senior imager in all Solidar, excepting me, he should have been informed . . ." Dyana went on to detail exactly what had happened, all the way to Dhelyn's attempted imaging attack and the unfortunate results. Then she turned to me. "Maitre Rhennthyl, do you have any additions or corrections to what I have said?"

"Only a few points. Maitre Dhelyn was extremely discourteous when I entered the Maitre's chamber, and when Maitre Dyana pointed out that even she did not know all the details of the planned operation against Ferrum, and stated that, if she did not see the need to know the details, she trusted that he did not need to know them either. She then suggested that with his interest in rules he might be better suited to take charge of the Collegium at Mont D'Glace. At that point he stiffened in what I thought was rage, and I clamped protective shields around him, nothing that would injure him, or that he would necessarily even feel if he intended no harm. I made certain that they were a full yard away from his person on all sides. Even so, he summoned so much power that he turned into a pillar of ice, and when I released the shields, a gout of steam flared into the ceiling and ripped away all the plaster down to the laths."

Ferlyn winced, but I was more worried about the frown on Rholyn's face.

"Before we discuss this further, or answer questions," Maitre Dyana added smoothly, "I would like Maitre Jhulian to offer his observations on any rules or precedents that may apply."

Quaelyn nodded at that, but Rholyn frowned even more deeply.

"The rules governing the Maitres of the Collegium are few and comparatively simple," began Jhulian. "All offenses that can be placed in front of the Collegium Justiciary must be so handled. In the event of immediate danger, where such a trial is not feasible or possible, the Maitre has the absolute power to discipline any member of the Collegium, including other Maitres, but any discipline that results in more than superficial physical injury must be placed before the council of all available Maitres for review in no less than one week from the date of the punishment. Those present will hear of the events and may ask questions before any action on a decision is taken. Unless eight out of every ten Maitres present, and there must be ten or more able to vote, disapprove of the punishment, the punishment stands. The Maitre and any other Maitre involved may not vote. There are fourteen Maitres here, and two cannot vote. A quorum is present. Are there any questions on the procedures?"

No one said anything.

"Are there questions on the events?"

"Did Maitre Dhelyn offered any verbal threats?" Quaelyn asked.

"No threats were uttered," Maitre Dyana said.

Quaelyn looked to me.

"As Maitre Dyana has said, he did not offer any threats, but he was very politely belligerent. Several times, he invoked seniority and insisted that as a senior Maitre his right to know was more important than other considerations. Even after she stated that he would be among the first to know the details of the operation when it was appropriate, he flushed and stated quite firmly that he could not believe that Maitre Dyana would deny him the right to know. She stated that her first priority was the safety of the entire Collegium, but he persisted."

After a moment, Rholyn cleared his throat. "But there were no threats?"

"No."

"Why did you feel compelled to place shields around him, then?"

"I was worried. He was not interested in what Maitre Dyana said. He dismissed every statement she made, and his tone got sharper with each question or demand that he be informed. I did not place tight shields around him. They were set a good yard away from his body, yet the ice filled them."

"A good yard?" Rholyn turned to Dyana. "Is that correct?"

"That would seem to be about right. I didn't have time to measure. There was a column of ice close to two yards across. The steam that followed was in the center of that."

"I beg your pardon," Rholyn said, "but to hold shields of that strength against a Maitre D'Structure suggests far more than—"

"Exactly," interjected Draffyd quickly. "You might recall that Maitre Rhennthyl erected shields against ten stone shells and hurled them back close to a mille. He also possesses the ability to image things back to the point from where they came without seeing their path." He looked hard at Rholyn.

The Collegium Councilor paused then nodded. "I had not thought of that. I have no more questions."

Heisbyl coughed, and Rholyn glared at him.

The older Maitre murmured, "No questions."

I had understood what had happened, and I thought I knew why, but I wasn't about to raise those questions, not in an open meeting.

"Then the matter comes to a vote," announced Jhulian. "Maitre Rhennthyl and Maitre Dyana may not vote. All others will do so. All who agree that Maitre Dyana's actions were within the purview of a Maitre of the Collegium please raise their hands."

Twelve hands went up instantly.

"Thank you," Dyana said quietly. "Maitre Jhulian, if you would document the meeting and place the record in the sealed archives."

"Yes, Maitre."

"You may all leave."

Those were her words, but the quick glances to me and to Jhulian indicated that we were to linger, preferably without making a show of doing so.

I dawdled, and so did Jhulian, not that it was particularly difficult, be-cause most of the others seemed all too ready to leave, and in moments, the three of us were the only ones remaining in the conference room.

"You seem to know what happened here, Rhenn, but I'd like some con-firmation," Dyana said pleasantly.

"I'm going by recall, but as I remember the rules of the Collegium, the Maitre is always either the most senior of the highest rank, or selected among those with the highest rank, with the consent of the most senior. It would appear that the shields I erected around Dhelyn, along with the ability with the shells . . ." I decided not to voice more.

"Those skills are, frankly, those of a Maitre D'Image," Jhulian said. "You may or may not have all of them, but Rholyn does not wish you to become Maitre, and he doesn't want the issue opened."

"I don't want to be Maitre. It takes more than imaging ability. Nor would it be good for the Collegium or for me." Skills of a Maitre D'Image? That was far more worrisome than encouraging.

Jhulian chuckled and looked to Dyana. "I told you so."

"Are you renouncing any claim to be Maitre?" asked Dyana.

"No. I'm agreeing with what you indicated earlier, that I'm not ready for any higher position at the moment. I don't even know enough about what I'm doing now."

The two nodded.

"There's another reason why it would not be wise for you to become Maitre," Jhulian offered. "Do you know what that might be?"

"I have several thoughts on that. Do you wish to hear them?"

"It might not a bad idea," suggested Maitre Dyana dryly.

"First, if people suspect that I might be the next Maitre, they're likely to be more reasonable with Maitre Dyana. Second, trying to remove Maitre Dyana resolves nothing. Third, there's a certain deniability. In crises, I can act, and Maitre Dyana can either ask if they'd like to deal with me or offer to step down. There may be others, but those the ones that come to mind."

"There's one other," offered Jhulian. "You'll have more freedom to act in your current position, and fewer people will be questioning and watch-ing you."

"More people are already watching me."

"More than you know," added Dyana. "But less than watch the Maitre."

That wasn't exactly comforting.

57

Over the rest of Meredi and all Jeudi, not a single master made mention of the meeting, not even with allusions or hints. It was as though it had never happened, or that no one wanted to remember that it had happened. I mentioned it to Seliora.

Her response was simple. "You've just proved, without question, that you can destroy any of them. If you were in their boots, would you want to dwell on it, or offend you? Or even talk about it?" Then she had added, "You're going to need to work very hard on convincing people that you want their honest views, because too many people with power only look for others to agree. You don't want that, because it's no help at all."

She was right on both points.

I still did the morning exercises and was back to almost full speed on the run, but I had to push myself there, because Dartazn was no longer there to lead the way, and I was faster than most of the others. Both days were cold, and the ground frozen, but clear, since none of the recent snow had stuck.

On Vendrei morning, after meetings with Marteon and Haugyl, I met again with Schorzat and Kahlasa, because she was receiving reports from the covert imagers in Otelyrn that Caenenan forces were being mustered and trained for something—possibly an annexation of Gyarl, since Tiempre was so involved in trying to hold the line against the still-advancing Stakanaran invasion that the Tiemprans had moved most of their troops to deal with Stakanar. The shifting of ships from the Solidaran southern fleet to deal with Ferrum was another factor. We decided that there wasn't much we could do—or advise them to do—except watch and report.

Right after that, I received a letter from Veblynt, informing me that he would be in L'Excelsis on Mardi, and that he would plan to meet me at ninth glass at the Collegium administration building, so that I would not have to drive so far south, unless he received word to the contrary from me. Although I was more than pleased not to have to make another trip to his paper mill, I half-suspected that he might well intimate, at least in places where he thought it might do him some good, that he was being consulted by the Collegium.

I smiled. It was true, and if that did him good, so be it. That was a price one paid for seeking information. Besides, he'd helped my father when times weren't what they could have been.

Since I received no message from either Alynkya or Frydryk, I skipped the midday meal at the dining hall and took a duty coach out north to Frydryk's "town" estate. He was waiting for me in the study when I arrived, just before first glass.

"Greetings," I offered as I stepped inside after leaving my cloak with the footman. "You've been traveling more than you'd planned, I heard."

Frydryk offered a rueful smile. "Much more. The advocates in Laaryn made matters more complicated than they needed to be, and then there was the business at the shipworks. By the way, I need to thank you for that. Right after you mentioned all the problems with the Ferrans, I sent word to the shipworks about the possibilities. They found some indications, and they were ready."

"I'm glad." At least I'd helped to save part of the Solidaran shipbuilding industry. "Have you heard anything from Glendyl?"

"He sent a long and laborious letter."

"And?"

"He wants me to hold the debt, without requiring interest, until the Council acts on the measure to fund the capital ships. He was very insistent."

I was getting more than a little tired of Glendyl's arrogance and machinations.

"You have the plans, don't you, and the right to build the turbines if he defaults?"

"You had said . . ."

"I was wrong. I thought he was more reasonable. I've since talked to him twice, and each time he has been less tractable."

Frydryk laughed. "For that admission alone, Rhenn, I'd call the notes." He paused. "I did follow your advice and talked to Alynkya. She said I was being too forbearing."

"I also have some indirect indications that he may owe others, so you might want to register the lien with the judiciary before you notify him. But if you do so in person, don't do it when he's near a weapon of any sort. He's not the kind to be indirect, like a High Holder."

"I appreciate the advice on that."

"Have you heard anything about High Holder Haebyn?"

"Is he the one who's been making all the fuss about the eastern water rights?"

"Among other things."

"That's all I've heard."

We talked for a time, and then I took my leave and had another cold ride back to the Collegium. I left the administration building a little before fourth glass because we had to go to Juniae D'Shendael's reception.

When I reached the house and went upstairs, Seliora was in her chamber debating whether to wear red and black or black and silver. I didn't have to debate. I either wore grays of formal blacks, and since it was an evening affair, I'd be in black with a silver imager pin.

"I think the black and silver," Seliora announced.

"You look good in both," I said.

"I like red," declared Diestrya firmly.

Seliora shook her head. "With you two . . ."

"Want to go with you," Diestrya announced.

"This reception is for adults," Seliora said. "Tomorrow night you're coming with us to Grandmother Maelyna's and Grandfather Chenkyr's. Your cousin Rheityr might even be there . . . and your Uncle Culthyn."

"Want to go tonight."

"Where you're going now is down to supper." I picked up Diestrya and carted her downstairs, ignoring the short-lived wailing and the small fists beating on my shoulders. She did settle down, and I fed her the meal that Klysia had waiting. Then I went back upstairs and dressed in formal blacks.

We arrived at the residence of High Holder Shendael at a fraction before seventh glass in a Collegium coach—social engagements were considered duty, provided they were not excessive, and with the unspoken agreement that the driver received one or two silvers, an arrangement that Elreyt appreciated more than many, because he had three children. The timing seemed appropriate, since a cream-and-silver coach had just arrived, and the footman who opened the coach door was the same young woman who had greeted me earlier in the week.

"Welcome, Maitre Rhennthyl, Madame."

"Thank you."

As we walked along under the covered portico to the main entrance, Seliora murmured, "You didn't mention the woman footman."

"I didn't. I forgot. There are several."

Once we entered the mansion, another liveried woman took our cloaks, and we were escorted to what looked to be a drawing room, modest for a High Holder, a chamber paneled in white birch with pale blue hangings, a mere ten yards by eight or so.

Juniae D'Shendael turned from where she stood talking to a white-haired woman in a flowing emerald-green gown, accompanied by a man in the uniform of a Sea-Marshal, and walked toward us.

"Madame D'Rhennthyl, you look as beautifully formidable as ever, and you, Maitre, so unassuming."

"And you as beautifully brilliant as always," returned Seliora.

I wasn't about to claim I was or wasn't unassuming, which was the point of her greeting.

"You must join me and Sea-Marshal Caellynd and his wife Rowlana." With that she eased us toward the other couple.

I was trying to place the silver-and-blond-haired Sea-Marshal, whom I'd never met, then realized from his name that he was Valeun's deputy, the second-in-command of the entire Naval Command. Did Juniae D'Shendael know every senior officer in the Navy? She well might.

"Rowlana, Caellynd, I'd like you to meet Maitre Rhennthyl and his wife Seliora."

"Ah, yes, I've heard of your beauty, dear lady, but the descriptions do not do you justice . . . and the redoubtable Maitre Rhennthyl." Caellynd smiled warmly.

I had to admit that I liked him instantly, although I wondered if that just meant I should trust him even less. After the reception, I'd have to ask Seliora what she felt. "Hardly redoubtable, but pleased to meet you."

"You're far too kind," said Seliora sweetly, "but after a long day, I will take the compliment."

Rowlana smiled. "You must have young children."

"I do, but I also work as a design engineer in the family business. You may have heard of it—NordEste Design."

Rowlana inclined her head slightly, then offered an empathetic smile. "You're doing far more than I would ever have tried." Her eyes turned to me, and her smile became more wary. "You're the one who's been giving Sea-Marshal Geuffryt fits."

"Oh, no, Madame. He's been the one giving me fits. No one could do that so well as he."

Caellynd laughed. "I'm afraid Maitre Rhennthyl has the right of that, dear. Marshal Geuffryt is very good at what he does, but it can be a bit wearing on others." He turned more to me. "Before I forget, I want you to know that I did send a communique to Fleet-Marshal Asarynt, instructing him to give all possible assistance to your Maitre-in-Command. All of us with fleet experience would like to see a quick resolution to this conflict." He shook his head. "We can't even call it a war, since no one on either side wants to declare it one."

"I do appreciate that." I definitely did, but why had he mentioned that he'd sent the communique, unless to suggest that Valeun had done nothing of the sort . . . and that Valeun didn't fully appreciate the situation?

He glanced at his wife and then back to me, before saying with a laugh, "I think we'd best not talk any more about the Naval Command or the Collegium."

I grinned. "Don't you think we're looking at a colder winter than we've had in years?"

"Absolutely," he agreed.

"There is warm spiced wine at the serving table," suggested Juniae.

"How is your latest book selling?" I asked. "The latest is *The Art of Conversation*, is it not?"

"It is. The publisher says that it's selling as do all my books . . . slowly, but with just enough copies that they might publish another. If I don't finish it too soon." Juniae raised her left eyebrow, an ironic effect, before continuing. "Rowlana, have you finished that watercolor? Did you know that Maitre Rhennthyl is also a noted portraiturist?"

From the momentary surprise in Madame D'Caellynd's eyes, it was clear that she had not known.

"For all of his military-like appearance, Rhenn has an artistic side, as does his wife, whose fabric designs grace many of the best salons in L'Excelsis."

It became apparent, very quickly, that we were the exhibit of the evening.

Shortly, we were eased over to meet one of the high justices, Symmal D'Juris, and his wife Maedlynaie, a petite woman who barely topped Seliora's shoulder and was most likely less than five years older than Seliora, who was the youngest of all the guests. Later in the evening, we met Madame D'Lhoryn, but High Holder Lhoryn was away dealing with estate matters, and Seliora and I both gained the impression that he was always "away" for Madame D'Shendael's salon receptions.

By the time we left, my head was aching from the dual effort of being pleasant to all too many people I did not know, all of whom had heard about us, and trying to remember as much as I could. The only good sign about it all was that in the cold clear winter air, both Erion and Artiema shone down nearly full as the coach carried us back to Imagisle.

58

Dinner at my parents' house on Samedi evening was quiet, and that was a relief. Since Khethila hadn't traveled from Kherseilles, not that I expected any such travail, I didn't mention much about the reception, except the feeling of being on display.

"That comes with the perquisites, Rhenn," my father had replied, not quite brusquely. "Too bad you couldn't ask about wool contracts from those Navy types."

Mother had looked sharply at him, and the conversation had turned quickly to children.

The remainder of the weekend had been mostly quiet, although I did embark on beginning the actual painting of the portrait of Diestrya. That would take a number of short sittings, because she certainly couldn't sit still for long. By Lundi morning, I couldn't help but think that Dartazn and the imagers should be in the process of deploying to begin the attacks on Ferrum. What if what we had planned so meticulously didn't work out? What if too many of the young imagers froze and couldn't do what had been asked of them?

I did ask Schorzat what he knew about Caellynd.

His response was close to what I'd expected. "He's been recently posted to the Naval Command. He was the senior Fleet-Marshal for close to seven years, and the one who was so successful in the first Ferran conflict. The Council picked him as Valeun's deputy and successor."

"Was that Suyrien's doing?" I'd asked.

"Maitre Dichartyn never said anything. Neither did anyone else, but Caellynd was a successful Fleet-Marshal who pled the case for more modern warships before the Council."

There was nothing in the records or files, and, again, all I had were suspicions. I was worrying even more about Dartazn and the imagers by Mardi morning. As soon as I'd entered the administration building, I'd asked Beleart if we'd received any dispatches. We hadn't, of course, and I knew we shouldn't have, but I'd still hoped and dreaded what might have arrived.

The reports that flowed in didn't tell me anything new, but reminded me that I not only needed to standardize them, but to find a way to require Patrol Commanders to provide more details, and that would require Council action. I could require those changes of regionals and the collegia heads, but without improved Patrol data, there wouldn't be a significant change.

Finally, at just before ninth glass, Ayma, one of the newest primes, knocked on my study door to inform me that a Factorius Veblynt had arrived.

I hurried out to the reception hall, where he was waiting. Every time I saw Factor Veblynt, I was surprised, because he made an impression in memory larger than his actual height. He was slender, although his carriage was perfect, and he was even a touch shorter than Seliora. He smiled, showing perfect white teeth. This time, the corners of his eyes lifted, as if he were truly glad to see me. Often they didn't. "Rhenn! I understand that you're a Maitre D'Esprit."

"Due to the misfortunes of others," I demurred.

"Nonsense. You may hold whatever position you do in the Collegium for that reason, but even I know that the ranks of the Maitres are due to ability alone."

We walked from the reception hall back to my study, where I closed the door.

Veblynt surveyed the chamber, then settled into the chair in front of the desk. "Such surroundings aren't designed to let you take yourself seriously."

"No, but whether by design or custom or both, I have no idea." I added quickly, "You are most kind to come here, and I appreciate it."

"Anytime the son of a friend travels to my mill to see me, especially when he's one of the highest imagers, it merits a return call." He smiled. "Especially when I was already going to be less than a mille away."

"It was kind, nonetheless, and appreciated."

"You obviously had something in mind."

"I did. I'd heard rumors that you sought competing bids for a loan in order to build your new paper mill."

Veblynt shrugged. "I could have built it with my own capital, but that wouldn't have left any reserves. Even so, the Banque D'Excelsis didn't want to offer favorable terms, and I'd have been a fool not to seek other terms. They don't like it when they can't make more on their loans than the enterprises they fund make on their operations. Once I did get another commitment, they became more reasonable. By the way, I must congratulate you and Seliora on the training you provide the apprentices at your taudis mill. Some of them will be working at our new facility."

"Thank you. Facility? It's not a paper mill?"

"It's a mill and a printing facility. We've been making blank documents for factors, everything from ledger sheets to printed forms for banques, but the demand was more than we could handle at the old facility. The new one will just make document paper, and the rest is for the printing side."

"And you went with another banque to get the funds?"

He looked sharply at me. "Rhenn . . . are you after me for something?"

"No. I'm after information. From what I heard, you know some things that might fill in pieces of the puzzle."

"Given what I've done for your father, I'm going to trust you on this."

"I know. You helped him through a hard time with some Navy contracts. He didn't tell me, either."

He smiled wryly. "I might have known you'd figure that out. What are you looking for?"

"I'd heard you used the threat of going to an outland banque. I'm interested in that banque."

"That's not much of a secret. It couldn't be if the threat were to work. It was the Banque D'Ouestan, but you already knew that, or you wouldn't have asked."

"They don't have a branch here, though."

He nodded slowly. "I dealt with a Vyktor D'Banque D'Ouestan. He has a place of business on the Avenue D'Theatre."

"How did you find out about him?"

"From one of Glendyl's clerks." Veblynt smiled with a certain satisfaction. "Unlike some factors, I talk to more than a few clerks."

"Do you know if they make many loans or advances here in L'Excelsis?"

"Very few, I suspect. Just enough to provide cover for Vyktor, I would guess. He was happy enough to write out a commitment, as if he knew he wouldn't necessarily have to make the loan. He could have, but he's no more a true banque representative than I'm a High Holder. He wasn't in the slightest interested in buying forms, even at a very reduced price."

"An interesting comparison," I observed.

"But accurate."

"How widely is that known, do you think?"

"Not all that widely, I would judge. He is knowledgeable enough about finance, and he does make loans and handle other funding transfers through the Banque D'Ouestan's corresponding arrangements with the Banque D'Rivages and the Banque D'Kherseilles, and doubtless one or two others. He is often gone for periods of time, and I've never known a banque that allowed its representatives to be out of touch so much. I'd judge that he's also a representative of either Ferrum, Jariola, or Stakanar. That's just a judgment on my part." He looked directly at me. "I don't think I'm telling you much you don't already suspect."

"Do you know any others with whom he's had dealings?"

"There are rumors that Broussard received funding through him, and I mentioned Broussard's name in passing." Veblynt offered a crooked smile. "Vyktor doesn't like him. I couldn't tell why from his reaction."

"What do you know about Broussard?"

"He's a freeholder. He's also extraordinarily wealthy . . . and he would squeeze the last drop of water from a sponge in the desert and try to sell it to a man dying of thirst. He'd betray his first-born son or an infant daughter for a single gold."

I found myself fingering my chin. "I haven't heard anything about him since that explosion at the Place D'Opera."

"That's true. I hadn't thought about that. It's certainly not like him to be so quiet."

I couldn't help but wonder if Broussard had taken funds from Vyktor and double-crossed him in the process. I'd always worried about why a High Holder would use explosives against a factor. That simply didn't follow the High Holder traditions of dealing with their enemies, as I'd discovered; but if Vykor happened to be representing Ferran interests . . .

I was also beginning to worry about Geuffryt. I'd heard nothing from Valeun, nor from any other source, and it would have been a grave mistake to have mentioned his name at Juniae D'Shendael's reception. I'd never managed to arrange it so that I was alone with either Caellynd or Juniae, in the latter case certainly because she wanted to avoid any hint of personal closeness.

"Rhenn . . ." Veblynt interrupted my musing. "You have the strangest look."

"I was wondering about Broussard," I evaded, "and how he escaped being killed in the explosion."

"He was looking for a way to do in Estyelle, anyway." Veblynt shrugged. "You're thinking that Vyktor had something to do with that?"

"I have suspicions."

"Vyktor's capable of it, I'd judge, but, if he did, Broussard outwitted him and turned matters his own way."

"If Broussard did," I asked, "then why has he been so silent?"

"You think he's afraid of what's behind Vyktor?"

"Broussard can't be stupid." I pointed out the obvious to see what Veblynt would say.

"He's anything but stupid. He's likely waiting for someone to act against Vyktor."

"That would mean he either knows someone will or has a way to push someone into doing so. I haven't seen either."

"You're looking," Veblynt said with a faint smile.

"Looking doesn't mean acting. Neither the Collegium nor the Civic Patrol is inclined to act if there isn't some sort of evidence of wrongdoing. Suspicion isn't enough. Nor is knowing. We have nothing to tie Vyktor to the Place D'Opera explosion or anything else, or even to Glendyl."

Veblynt nodded. "That is often the problem with pure knowledge. You've gotten around that in the past, Rhenn. I'm certain you will this time."

"It's harder when everyone is watching you." My words came out sardonically.

He laughed. "Then set it up so that they're watching someone else."

I couldn't help but laugh myself, as I realized that he'd given me an idea for a solution. It was just too bad that it was for a different problem. "I will take your words to heart, and I thank you for coming."

"If I find anything of value to you," he said as he rose, "I'll send it."

"Thank you." I stood as well.

"And keep on distrusting Cydarth. He's tied up in it all somehow as well. I don't know how, but . . ." He shrugged, then smiled. "It is a pleasure to see how well you've done after so much adversity has come to your family."

"Friends help."

"True friends help," he replied.

I couldn't disagree with that.

After I walked Veblynt to the main doors of the administration building and made my way back to my study, I thought about his last words. I'd always distrusted Cydarth, and Veblynt had always been right, if often veiled, in his assessments. Yet Geuffryt had tried to get me to attack Cydarth. Why? If . . . if Geuffryt happened to feel himself a "patriot" who was out to destroy the influence of the Collegium, was the idea to show that Cydarth had been spitefully wronged by Artois's allies, such as the Collegium? That seemed rather frail. Yet . . . if Cydarth did happen to be getting Ferran funds through the Banque D'Ouestan, and Geuffryt had discovered that through Kearyk, was there any connection at all between Geuffryt and Vyktor? Or was Geuffryt trying to expose Cydarth as a Ferran plaque through me, because he couldn't reveal how he'd found out about the transfers? Much as I disliked and distrusted Geuffryt, that appeared the most likely possibility . . . and that bothered me greatly.

59

For the remainder of Mardi, I did my best to concentrate on duties that would not lead to greater consternation with the Council and the Collegium. That meant, among other things, that I read a number of reports, said little at the midday meal in the dining hall, and ended up going home through an ice fog more than a little dissatisfied.

Exercise on Meredi morning helped . . . somewhat.

I was still stewing and trying to determine what else I could do when Beleart knocked on my study door at a quint past eighth glass and carried in a large envelope, marked in the stripe that indicated urgent private delivery. He slipped away, closing the door.

I opened the envelope. Inside were a single sheet of paper, printed on both sides, and a folded note card. The document was also signed and sealed at the bottom. I read through it twice. It was a loan and a secondary lien on Glendyl's engine works, executed by Viktor D'Banque D'Ouestan on behalf of the bank for 25,000 golds, and it was dated almost a year earlier, the thirty-second of Fevier. The provision that interested me most was the one allowing unannounced inspections of the subject property by designated agents of the lender.

I opened the note card and read the two lines written there.

> *"Obtaining this last year was far too easy. Be most careful."*

Under the words was an ornate "V."

The package raised yet another question. How had Veblynt obtained it? For what purpose? And why had he sent it? What role was he playing in the swirl of intrigue? The warning suggested he'd been "allowed" to take or steal the document, but he'd obtained it before I'd left the Civic Patrol, and that suggested a different agenda. What that was, I didn't know, but I didn't want to do anything with the document until I knew why.

Instead of straining to figure out items about which I hadn't enough information, I decided to try to tie up another loose end and go find Maitre Jhulian. He was in his study and welcomed me in.

"What can I do for you, Rhenn?"

"You're the expert on law and water rights, and I'm hoping that you can clarify exactly what's going on between the eastern High Holders and the freeholders around Piedryn."

"The law is clear. Nothing else is." His smile was wintry. "Precedence in water rights is based on seniority. The oldest right rights come first, regardless of where they are exercised on the watercourse. This creates a practical problem when a junior rights-holder is located upstream of a senior rights-holder and there is insufficient flow to satisfy both rights. The historic manner of resolving the claim has been through the courts, but courts do not move so fast as water does. So the justicers in the area have taken to issuing preemptive allocations based on flow levels."

"And since the senior rights-holders are mainly High Holders, the allocations are considered as favoring them?"

"Exactly. There's one complication. In peak flow years, or at times when water can't be used, some can be diverted under ancillary rights. Broussard bought a single hectare-foot of absolute water-rights on the Piedra River, at a point just before it flows into the Chela, and then applied for ancillary rights. He was using those ancillary rights to fill a storage lake, and in dry years, he was irrigating crops from it."

"At a time when others couldn't and crop prices were high, I presume."

Jhulian nodded. "So Haebyn applied for ancillary rights, which he'd never needed before, and Broussard brought the matter up to the Justiciary, pointing out that his ancillary rights preceded Haebyn's, and, since excess water couldn't be diverted near the headwaters without prejudicing other rights-holders, Haebyn shouldn't be allowed to divert until Broussard had exercised his rights. The justicer upheld Broussard, pointing out that the law was clear on precedence and that precedence applied to ancillary rights as well."

"That was probably the reason why Broussard's impoundment dam 'failed,' then?"

"That was effective for this year, but Broussard still holds the rights and will doubtless have the dam repaired before the spring run-off."

"What's the situation before the Council? Will Haebyn attempt to change the law?"

"He's been working hard to persuade Councilors. It's a very bad idea, especially now, because what it would do is send the message that the law is only immutable when it benefits High Holders and will be changed if its precedents can be used against them."

When I left Maitre Jhulian, I understood the political and legal implications of the water issues. To me, the question was whether the Ferrans had gotten involved there as well. Had Broussard borrowed from Vyktor to rebuild the dam and impoundment? Or to build grain warehouses? Or had he steered other freeholders to Vyktor? Would I ever know?

I was beginning to doubt that I'd ever find out everything about anything, and I still had nothing truly linking Cydarth to Vyktor or the Banque D'Ouestan—except Geuffryt's note written by Juniae D'Shendael. Perhaps I would pay a courtesy call on Subcommander Cydarth. It might provoke a reaction of some sort. Then, too, I realized, it might make me more of a target. Yet, I probably was anyway . . . or, more properly, I still was.

As I was about to step into my study, Kahlasa came down the corridor. "Rhenn . . . do you have a moment?"

"For you, always." That was true, because Kahlasa never wasted my time or anyone else's, and she was always effective. I held the door for her, then followed her in and closed it.

She set a folder on the desk and sat down.

So did I. "What is it?"

"Most of the explosions in Solidar over the past months have been on piers or near water. Your questions about the tugs and the barges got me thinking. I've made more inquiries, and the regionals have helped. I'd like you to look at the charts there and tell me what you think."

It didn't take long to figure out what she'd determined. In more than half the cases, two transport factors were involved. One was Cholan Freight and Transport, and the other was Mahrun Barge and Cartage. "Did you find out anything about these two?"

"There aren't any records of any contracts older than four years. They always paid in advance, and their funds were always transferred from the Banque D'Ouestan through another banque. They also never defaulted, and always returned leased equipment in good condition. According to Eslyana, the regional in Solis, Cholan Freight rented a building in Solis. It was largely a warehouse with one clerk. He sent all invoices and remittances to a Vyktor D'Cleris."

"How did she find that out?"

"From the very upset widow of the clerk."

"He died in an accident, of course?" My tone was sardonic.

"Of course."

"Did she find out where this Vyktor D'Cleris was located?"

"Only that he was in L'Excelsis. No address, nothing more."

I nodded. "The address would have been useful." I suspected I already had it. "What was the name of the Cholan clerk?"

"Ebslun."

I wrote that down. "What else?"

"From the weights and packing, it's likely that some of the explosives were sent by ironway under the name of Mahrun Barge and Cartage, but we haven't yet located any actual address for Mahrun, except at the Mahrun Ironway Station. They've never leased space there, but at times, someone would pick up messages or packages there. Not often."

"So they basically got accepted by sending or handling small shipments, always paid in advance, before they leased heavier equipment. That's how they moved the Poudre B . . ." I looked to Kahlasa. "You've put together an outstanding report here."

She actually smiled.

By the time we had finished going over the details, it was time to eat, and the two of us walked over to the dining hall. Maitre Dyana was there, sitting with Chassendri and Quaelyn, with Ferlyn peering past the older pattern-master, as if trying to make out Quaelyn's words and Maitre Dyana's responses.

After the meal, I went straight to the duty coach stand, and asked Desalyt to take me to Patrol headquarters. Once I arrived, the duty patroller—Cassan—just nodded as I walked past him and up the steps to the second level.

Cydarth's clerk-patroller looked up from his desk in the anteroom. "Maitre Rhennthyl! Was the subcommander expecting you?"

"No. I just hoped to catch him. Is he here?"

"He's somewhere here in headquarters. I'm sure he'll want to see you. If you wouldn't mind . . . I'll go find him."

"I'll wait."

The patroller hurried out.

I ended up waiting half a quint before the patroller returned. "He was inspecting the holding cells, sir, and it took me a bit to find him. I thought he was down in charging. He said he'd be here shortly."

Shortly turned out to be another half-quint.

"Maitre Rhennthyl," offered Cydarth with a smile as he entered the anteroom. "I do apologize. I hope I didn't keep you waiting too long."

"It happens when you arrive unannounced." I followed him into his study. The patroller shut the door behind us.

"Might I ask the reason for the visit?"

"I was passing by and thought I should stop in and see you."

"Maitre Rhennthyl, that is most kind of you . . . although I must observe that you seldom act merely on the impetus of the instant."

I smiled. "Seldom does not mean never, but you are correct. In addition to realizing that I had not stopped to see you when I last visited the Commander, a matter did come up of which I thought you should be apprised."

"Please." Cydarth gestured to the chairs in front of his desk.

"As you may surmise, at times, the Collegium does receive information which can not be substantiated and whose origin cannot be traced. Recently, I did receive an unsigned missive that suggested you received significant funds through the Banque D'Ouestan. Knowing of your integrity, I did nothing with the missive, because such a report either had to be fallacious or something perfectly innocent, such as a bequest or an inheritance. The more I thought about it, though, the more I realized that I should let you know that someone was circulating this sort of information about you."

The subcommander nodded slowly. "I would have expected nothing less of you, Maitre Rhennthyl. You have always been circumspect and scrupulously fair. Might I ask the context of the missive?"

"The context of the missive dealt with transactions from the Banque D'Ouestan that the writer considered suspicious, because there was an implied suggestion the Collegium look into the matter."

"And did you?"

"The Collegium does not have access to banque records. That is a matter for the Council, and it's certainly not proper to ask them to investigate on the basis of an anonymous note. For all I know, it could be a ploy to create problems for a banque that has a solid financial record, simply because that banque has a number of outland investors. Since I have not made such a request and do not intend to, I did think you should be informed."

Cydarth smiled warmly, even with his eyes.

I didn't trust either his mouth or eyes, but I smiled pleasantly and waited.

"You know, Master Rhennthyl, when you first came to the Civic Patrol, I had my doubts that you had the determination and the restraint to deal with the stresses of day-to-day patrolling without immediately resorting to some form of imaging, whether that imaging was warranted or not. I had my doubts when you became a District Captain. Yet . . . I must confess that your performance was outstanding. You turned Third District from a competent district into one where offenses of all sorts were minimal, especially for an area holding a taudis known for trouble. You accomplished this using the same patrollers . . ."

Cydarth went on for a quint, reiterating what I'd done as a District Captain. On the one hand, I was both amazed and flattered that he'd recalled it all so well and in such detail. On the other, I worried about it. Exactly why was he taking so much time, when usually he wanted to be rid of me as quickly as possible?

". . . And, in the end, while you have created a standard that Third District is thus far maintaining, the Civic Patrol will miss you, possibly more than the Collegium will gain." He smiled again, then laughed. "I apologize. I've taken far too much of your time, but over the years, we've seldom talked at any length."

"That's true, and I do appreciate your kind words." I stood. "I hope what I conveyed will prove useful, and that the matter does not come up again, but I did want you to know."

"You're most kind, Maitre Rhennthyl."

With that, I took my leave and headed downstairs and out of headquarters.

With the cold wind, gray skies, and occasional flakes of snow, I was glad that the duty coach was still waiting for me.

"You missed the row, sir," offered Desalyt.

"Row?"

"Two fellows came out of the alleyway just up there. They starting fighting. One tried to smash the bistro windows over there. Patrollers came out from here. Stupid to start a fight across from a Patrol station. Always stupid folk."

I nodded. "Sometimes you wonder."

"That you do, sir. Where to?"

"Back to Imagisle."

"Yes, sir."

I climbed up into the coach.

Desalyt had waited with the coach headed away from the river on Fedre. So he drove up two blocks and turned right and went three blocks before he came back down Raegyr. I suspected that was so he didn't have to handle the steep hill on Flaekan. As he turned onto the part of East River Road that ran almost due north, I glanced toward the river, and something struck me. The promenade between the road and the river wall was extremely narrow, no more than three yards, and the low retaining wall was little more than a yard. Could this have been the place where Kearyk drowned? A coach could have stopped, and he could have been carried that short distance and thrown into the river in instants. Late at night, it would have been unlikely that anyone would even have seen the coach stop—especially a black coach.

At that moment, the duty coach came to a halt. I glanced forward, but I couldn't see what had blocked us.

"Wagon loose! Master Rhennthyl!"

I glanced to my right just in time to see a huge black wagon rumbling backward down Flaekan and across East River Road—right toward the duty coach. There was no way to get out of the coach in time. All I could do was strengthen my shields before the heavy wagon struck.

My shields held, but they didn't stop the wagon from pushing the lighter coach right over the narrow river promenade to the low wall. Then, with another sickening crunch, the coach's wheels ripped loose, and the remainder of the coach plunged down toward the gray water. I couldn't help but brace for the impact. There wasn't much of one, because the river below the wall was deep enough that once the coach struck the water it just kept descending, and icy water began to pour into the crumpled space around me. Both doors were jammed shut, and so were the window mechanisms.

I took a deep breath, then concentrated, imaging out the window glass from the door that seemed to be the one closest to the surface. More icy water poured over me, filling the entire inside of the coach, which seemed to be bobbing along under water or bouncing up from the bottom. I held my breath and grabbed the edges of the window fame, levering myself out, except my left boot became stuck and I found myself being caught and stretched as the current pulled me downstream and the sunken coach held me fast.

Somehow, I managed to pull my boot free, but my lungs felt like they were bursting by the time my head finally broke above the water. After a moment, I located the river wall. Then I started to swim toward it. That didn't do much good, because all that was there was a sheer expanse of icy smooth stone stretching upward some five or six yards, and the current was carrying me southward.

I must have been swept two hundred yards downstream before I managed to locate one of the ladders, even if there wasn't a platform at the bottom. I lunged and grabbed it, then got my boots on the bottom rung. It didn't get any easier. The iron ladder was icy and slippery, and after I'd climbed three or four rungs, my hands were numb. I kept forcing myself up. I finally pulled myself over the wall and took several steps away from the river. I was shuddering almost uncontrollably.

As I stood on the still narrow river promenade, a thought occurred to me. Could I image the water out of my garments? Then I shook my head. They needed some residual water, or they'd likely turn to dust, and, with the water on my skin, and my exhausted state, I might end up injuring myself.

"Sir! Sir!" A patroller came running toward me. "Are you all right?"

"For the moment. If I don't get out of these clothes, I'll turn into an icicle."

"This way, sir!"

Less than half a quint later, I was wearing borrowed baggy brown wool trousers and a blanket, standing in the kitchen of Aelys's—a bistro I'd never known even existed.

"Can you tell me what happened, sir?" asked the patroller.

"What happened to my driver?" I worried about Desalyt.

"We haven't found him, sir. One of the women who saw it said he went into the river."

"Why didn't the horses go into the river?"

"The traces broke, we think, sir. We had to put one of them down. Could you tell me what happened, please, sir?"

Along with my questions, that took almost a glass, enough that my boots, set near the stove, were only damp, as opposed to soaked. Then, after I took a hack to Imagisle, I had to tell the duty second about the accident, and then meet with Ghaend, who was in charge of transportation, so that he could tell Desalyt's family, and Reynol, who handled losses of property for the Collegium. I also left a brief note for Maitre Dyana, who was at the Council Chateau, presumably meeting with Chief Counselor Ramsael.

It was nearing a quint past fourth glass before I finally left the administration building and made my way across the quadrangle and northward. As I walked swiftly up the front walk to the house, I caught sight of the Maitre's dwelling, where Maitre Dyana would eventually take residence, and realized that the exterior looked to be complete. Work had slowed considerably, given the imagers who had left Imagisle to accompany Dartazn, but there were still enough, obviously, to continue with the repair and rebuilding.

Klysia stepped into the hall and looked at me, wrapped in a patroller blanket and baggy trousers, and carrying soaked grays and my winter cloak. In escaping from the coach, I'd lost my visored cap.

"Master Rhennthyl!"

"I took an unplanned swim in the river."

By the time I had handed off the soaked garments, washed up, and donned fresh garments and dry boots and sat down in front of the family parlor fire for a quint or so, Seliora and Diestrya arrived. I stood and went to the foyer.

"Rhenn . . . you're home early."

"That's because I took an unplanned swim in the River Aluse."

"What? How did that happen?"

"Dada went swimming?" asked my daughter.

"I did. The water was cold. It wasn't a good idea." I turned to Seliora. "Let's get Diestyra settled in the kitchen for her dinner, and then I'll tell you."

Seliora understood.

Once the two of us were back in the parlor, I went through the whole thing, grateful that, by the end of my tale, the combination of hot tea and warmth from the stove finally lifted the last lingering chill from my bones.

Seliora said quietly, "Cydarth wanted you dead."

"That's likely, but the way it was set up will make it difficult, if not impossible, to prove it. There are also a number of people who might want me dead, and all of them would know enough to pick ways that would be hard for an imager to escape."

"Most imagers wouldn't be able to image away a widow under water and swim through an icy river."

"Oh . . . all of those Clovyl trains could do that part."

"What? All ten of you? And who knows that?"

"Very few," I had to admit.

After a long silence, she asked, "Will it always be like this?"

"For a time," I temporized. "Until it becomes clear there are other powerful imagers."

"That could be a very long time, dearest."

Unless I could do something about that . . .

60

On Jeudi morning I woke up only sore in a few places, not enough to change
my morning routine, a routine that had doubtless contributed to my surviving the events of the previous day. I did hurry to the administration building,
since I wanted to brief Maitre Dyana as soon as possible. I was there before she
was. So I sat in her anteroom with Gerard reading the morning newsheets.

Both reported on the story of my river swim, but on the second page.
The front page of *Tableta* featured a story based on "unauthenticated information" that suggested that the northern fleet was preparing for a major offen-
sive against the Ferran fleets. A number of highly placed sources suggested
that such an effort, if indeed true, was incredibly risky in midwinter, given
the potential for storms and high seas. The lead story in *Veritum* was about the
military situation in Otelyrn, and how the lack of Solidaran fleet presence
had allowed Stakanar, an ally in all but name of Ferrum, to seize the most
valuable territory of Tiempre.

The story about my accident was short and direct in both newsheets.
A coal wagon had been stolen right on the streets of L'Excelsis, the driver
coshed and trussed up, but somehow, the hitches had been loosened and the
wagon released and hurtled downhill into the Collegium coach. The team
had been found a block away, largely unharmed. Civic Patrol Captain Subunet
of First District suggested that the thieves had panicked after the wagon had
gotten away and headed downhill. The damage had been limited to the coal
wagon and to the imager coach and its occupants. The single passenger in the
coach had been thrown into the river with the coach, but had escaped and
swum through the icy waters to safety. The driver was still missing and possibly drowned.

I couldn't help but feel guilty. Once again, as had happened too often in
the past, an innocent man had died because people were trying to kill me. Yet,
with all that was at stake, I didn't see that my becoming a recluse on Imagisle
was in anyone's interests, except Cydarth's and Vyktor's . . . and the Ferrans'.

At a slight cough, I set down the newsheets and rose to greet Maitre
Dyana. "Good morning, Maitre."

"Good morning, Rhenn. Do come in."

I did follow her into her study. I also made sure the door was firmly closed.

She set several folders on the desk, then looked at me. She did not sit down, but flipped the end of the gold and green scarf back over her shoulder. "I am glad you left a note, Rhenn. It would have been rather disconcerting to discover those events in *Veritum* this morning."

"Since escaping from a coach in icy water, swimming a quarter mille in that water, and climbing an ice-encrusted iron ladder does have a tendency to exhaust and chill one, I trust you might understand why I did not choose to wait for you, especially since Gherard had no idea when or if you would be returning, and especially since I had already waited almost a glass."

"It must be the position. If I closed my eyes, I could easily have been talking to Maitre Dichartyn." She sighed and seated herself. "You might as well sit down."

I took one of the chairs before the desk.

"Please tell me what was not in the note."

I did, all about Cydarth and his sudden and out-of-character cheerful stalling and the link to the Banque D'Ouestan.

When I finished, she said, "You're doubtless correct, but there's no proof at all. Exactly what do you have in mind?"

"Looking farther. I need to see if I can find out more about the Banque D'Ouestan, especially about their agent here. I have some indication that he lent Glendyl 25,000 golds almost a year ago."

"Is there anyone Glendyl doesn't owe?"

"I don't think he owes the Banque D'Rivages or the Banque D'Excelsis," I replied dryly.

"Glendyl isn't likely to hold onto his works or anything else, except he won't let go of anything willingly, and that won't be good for Solidar or the Navy."

"From his behavior and attitude . . . it shouldn't be surprising if he loses everything. Besides, it might be better if someone else took over the engineworks."

Dyana shook her head. "Nothing good is going to come of that. Be very careful."

"I don't intend to do anything else dealing with Glendyl." I didn't point out that I'd already done all I could.

"That would be best."

"Oh, there is one other matter concerning the Banque D'Ouestan. This was discovered by Maitre Khalasa . . ." I went on to summarize the findings Kahlasa had presented to me.

"What do you intend to do?"

"I'd like to look a little farther. Like so many things, there's little enough direct proof."

"Isn't it always? Let me know when you find out more." Dyana shook her head, ruefully. "I trust you read the other stories in this morning's newsheets?"

"I did."

"How would you interpret them?"

"As an indication that the retirement or ill-health of Sea-Marshal Valeun might be beneficial to all Solidar."

"What good would that do if his successor feels the same way, or, more important, that most of the junior marshals feel that way?"

"Then I need to determine what our options are." I could be wrong, but, after having met Deputy Sea-Marshal Caellynd, I had the feeling he had to be an improvement over Valeun, but that was another thing I needed to determine.

"Or if we have any. Change for the sake of change is not a particularly good policy, especially if it creates even greater distrust of the Collegium."

"Greater distrust would not be good." I nodded politely, even as I worried about keeping what we had when it didn't seem to be doing that much good for either Solidar or the Collegium.

After I left Maitre Dyana, the first thing I did was have Schorzat send a message requesting a meeting with Sea-Marshal Valeun for Vendrei, suggesting a certain urgency. Then I met with Kahlasa and asked her if she could check what she had discovered with the false transport companies to see if there happened to be anything in common with the false barge lease for the vessels used in the attack on Imagisle.

Next, I went back to my study to think.

61

On Vendrei morning, *Veritum* featured a story about the northern fleet and about how the fast frigate delivered to the Navy last week from the Suyrien shipworks was the only half-modern ship in the fleet, and how even the Collegium, once known for its concern about matters military, was silent on the need for fleet modernization. There were also a few lines about how the lack of better ships required a greater reliance on innovative and often desperate tactics, tactics that could only go on for so long. I thought that touch was particularly clever on Valeun's part. I couldn't help but wonder how Maitre Dyana was taking it all.

Then I found a note from Maitre Jhulian that said High Holder Haebyn had filed a motion to stop Broussard from rebuilding his impoundment dam, on the grounds that such reconstruction prejudiced Haebyn's ancillary water rights. Jhulian had added that Haebyn's legal actions were obviously the beginning of a salvo designed to keep the dam from being rebuilt until after the height of the spring runoff.

I could only shake my head.

Moments later, there was a knock on the door, and Schorzat stepped inside. "We did receive a reply from his highest excellency Sea-Marshal Valeun." His voice was emotionless.

"Does he condescend to see me?"

"Only at the first glass of the afternoon, and only for two quints. He will expect you then, unless you send a messenger declining. He can see you on Mardi or Jeudi next week."

"He's playing position gaming. I'll see him today. Timing's more important than bureaucratic maneuvering."

"If it were anyone but you, I'd suggest not seeing him until two weeks from now."

"Waiting only benefits him, and he knows it. That's what he's playing for." I couldn't help shaking my head—again. I was doing that all too often. "Thank you for setting it up. I'll let you and Kahlasa know what happens."

When he left, I went and checked with Ghaend about Desalyt, but so far no one had reported any sign of him or his body. It was a certainty he was dead, and Ghaend had already talked to his wife, most likely his widow.

"It wasn't exactly an accident, was it?" he asked.

"I don't think so, but I don't have any proof, either about whether it was or about who might have done it."

"You were leaving Patrol headquarters, weren't you?"

"I was. I'd just paid a call on Cydarth."

"There are all sorts of rumors about him."

"I know, but I've never found a single shred of proof to support any one of them."

"Be nice if the Namer finally claimed him."

I could agree with that.

When I left the Collegium in the duty coach at two quints past tenth glass, heading out to the Naval Command, I had a fairly good idea of what awaited me. I wasn't that far off. When I reached the anteroom of the Sea-Marshal's study just before first glass, I had to wait. Not long enough to be truly insulting, perhaps less than half a quint, but just enough, and when the door opened, a junior ensign emerged.

Valeun appeared behind the young officer, beaming. "Maitre Rhennthyl, I had no idea you were waiting."

"Neither did I," I replied with a smile equally false.

"Do come in!"

"Thank you."

Once I was inside the study, the aide closed the door, and I didn't bother with being invited to sit. I just took the middle chair across the desk and waited for Valeun to seat himself.

"What can I do for you, Maitre Rhennthyl?"

I waited a few moments. "What news do you have from the northern fleet?"

"I received a dispatch this morning. The *Lyiena* arrived in good stead on the evening of the fifth, and dispersal of imagers began on the morning of the sixth." Valeun smiled politely. "If we assume that dispersal and positioning are on schedule, the attacks could have begun on Mardi. But we don't know the weather or the state of Ferran defenses. It may be that Fleet-Marshal Asarynt will need to wait or that he commenced earlier."

I nodded politely. "What about matters with Assistant Sea-Marshal Geuffryt?"

"That is a most delicate situation. You must understand that situations such as those cannot possibly be rushed, Maitre Rhennthyl. If there were more concrete evidence . . . it might be easier." Another smile followed. "I had hoped that by now you might be able to present such."

"You did receive considerable indication of the involvements and difficulties created for the Naval Command." I kept my voice pleasant, almost dispassionate.

"Ah . . . but as you well know, Maitre Rhennthyl, those difficulties and involvements pose a problem only if they become known, whereas the replacement or removal of an Assistant Sea-Marshal only upon the recommendation of the Collegium might be construed as infringing on the prerogatives of the Council."

"Not necessarily, and not if the Sea-Marshal did so on his own initiative."

"To do so on his own initiative requires cause. Cause requires proof. In cases such as policy differences, the affected Assistant Sea-Marshal would be able to raise other issues, and the Sea-Marshal would be required to justify his actions to the Council. I do trust you understand."

I did indeed. What Valeun was saying was that if he removed Geuffryt without hard evidence, he'd be questioned, and the questions would raise issues that would have him removed as well. Therefore, he had no intention of doing so without hard evidence. I could indeed force the issue, but forcing it would reveal that the Collegium was directly infringing on the Council's territory. He was also implying that Geuffryt couldn't be removed over differences in policy, because Geuffryt had no compunctions about bringing Valeun down.

"And I do understand," Valeun went on smoothly, "that the Assistant Sea-Marshal has pointed out that he is in excellent health and most unlikely to suffer any natural ailments."

"He is most astute, as I have known." I smiled politely. "Perhaps we should defer such matters until after events in Ferrum have taken their course."

"That would seem the wisest of courses."

We passed a few more pleasantries before I departed.

When I returned to the Collegium, I went up to see Maitre Dyana, but she was out, and I headed back to my study. It wasn't that long before Gherard appeared.

"Maitre Dyana can see you now, sir."

"Thank you." I left the latest reports unread.

Maitre Dyana remained behind her desk as I walked into her study and closed the door. "You went to see Valeun, I heard."

"I did. He's stalling on Geuffryt, and strongly suggesting that he needs some hard evidence. He doesn't believe that we'll let people know about all the strange occurrences that have involved the Naval Command."

"We'd be better off if we didn't."

"He also made the point that Geuffryt has spread the word among the Councilors that he is in excellent health and very unlikely to suffer any strange or sudden illnesses. I have the feeling that Geuffryt may know things about Valeun."

"That's very possible." She raised an eyebrow. "What will you do?"

"Nothing . . . not for a bit. We agreed to defer dealing with Geuffryt. It's unlikely we'll get any news on what's happening in Ferrum for another week. It could be more. The imagers arrived safely and were being shifted to the fast gunboats at the time of the last message."

"Do you think he was telling the truth about that?"

"Yes. That's one thing he has no reason to lie about, and I don't think he's the type to lie without a reason that benefits him."

She nodded. "Keep me informed."

I would, although it was clear that I would have to take a different tack in dealing with Valeun, since he had once more proved that he was not to be trusted, not that I'd had any great faith in him to begin with, but that meant re-thinking a number of things.

Nothing of great import happened during the rest of the afternoon, and I was home by fifth glass, just after Seliora. For a moment, I almost called for Diestrya, before realizing she was spending the weekend at NordEste Design.

I had to admit that I took some time embracing her, enjoying the lack of interruptions. She definitely didn't seem to mind, although she did finally disengage herself.

"I do need to get ready for tonight's reception. Arriving disheveled is not a good idea."

It was a very good idea, actually, but not for a reception.

As we walked upstairs, I broached another subject. "Dearest . . . I hate to ask yet another favor of your family . . ."

"I think we can manage that." Her tone was wry.

"I need a Navy officer's sidearm, one in good condition, with a full magazine."

Seliora stopped at the top of the stairs and frowned. "You're thinking about something very dangerous. Imagers don't need sidearms."

"I am. I hope I won't need it, but . . . I have this feeling that it may be necessary."

"For what?"

"As evidence."

"It might take a few days, since we won't see anyone until Lundi."

"Whenever you can."

"Do you want to tell me why?"

"Not unless I have to use it."

That was all she asked, and we got dressed. Seliora wore green and black, and I wore black, not that I had much choice. We did take the Collegium coach I'd reserved—that was another three silvers from my pay, plus another for Elreyt.

We arrived at High Holder Fhernon's town home, located on the highest point in Martradon, just behind a gray coach with brass trim. The three-level dwelling—and the high walls around it—had to have been more than a century old, since most High Holders' dwellings were outside L'Excelsis. The fluted green marble columns echoed the elegance of that time.

The various servants all wore white-collared maroon livery, and we were ushered into the main floor receiving room. Madame D'Fhernon stood at the doorway.

"Maitre Rhennthyl, Madame D'Rhennthyl . . . it is so good that you could join us this evening. You must try the vintages that Fhernon had brought from Faemyra. I do recommend the white." She smiled conspiratorially. "Even if Fhernon insists the red is better."

"We may try both," I replied.

"Thank you for including us," added Seliora.

As we entered the room, I glanced up. The ceiling was all off-white plasterwork, with a maroon and gold border separating the ceiling from the aged walnut panels and maroon and gold hangings that flanked the wide windows.

Standing by the window looking down on the Theatre District, were Frydryk and Alynkya. Alynkya's face held a strained and polite smile, and I belatedly recognized the couple across from them as her father, Chief Councilor Ramsael . . . and Cyana D'Guerdyn, dressed in pale blue. From the way that Cyana positioned herself, I had the feeling that she was now Madame D'Ramsael, and that might well have explained the strain in Alynkya, since Cyana could not have been more than five or six years older than Alynkya. The former Ferran envoy to Solidar had once escorted Cyana to a Council Ball, and that she was apparently now Madame D'Ramsael disturbed me slightly.

Ramsael turned as we moved toward them. "Oh . . . Rhenn . . . and this must be your wife." He inclined his head to Seliora. "You are indeed as so many report."

"You're very kind," Seliora replied.

"I'd like you both to meet my wife Cyana."

We both nodded politely, and I said, "I've been so occupied with other matters that I had not heard of the happy event."

"It was a quiet affair, overshadowed by what happened afterwards," offered Cyana.

"If you will excuse us," said Ramsael, "I do believe we are being summoned."

I could sense the relief in Alynkya as her father and her stepmother moved away.

"Rhenn, if I might have a word with you?" Behind Frydryk's pleasant look was something more.

"Of course." I looked to Seliora. "If you will excuse us, ladies?"

Seliora smiled. "I've so wanted to talk to Alynkya . . ."

I winced, as I was expected to.

They both laughed.

Frydryk eased us toward the corner, between the pianoforte that no one was playing and two unoccupied armchairs. "I'm so glad you two came at that moment."

"I could see Alynkya was less than pleased."

A bitter chuckle was his response. "Cyana is manipulative and then some. That's not why I needed to talk to you." He paused. "Have you heard about Glendyl?"

"No." I had a feeling the news wasn't good.

"I'd better tell it as it happened. After we talked, I decided to meet with Glendyl to tell him that I was calling the notes. He said that calling the notes was a poor idea, and went on to suggest that you were behind all of his difficulties, that you wanted to destroy him . . . that you were worse than any High Holder."

"He clearly doesn't care for me," I replied, since I sensed Frydryk wanted some response.

"No, but I trust your judgment. Before I went to see him, Alynkya insisted that I hold firm, that extending him more time or credit would only harm us both. He went on to tell me that I could call the notes, much good it would do, and that he'd be there to laugh at any attempt to get anything from him. Still, it was my privilege and that his advocate would be in touch with mine. Then he ushered me out, saying he had another urgent appointment." Frydryk shook his head. "Then, just before we left for this engagement, I received a message that he'd killed himself. It doesn't make sense."

"Who sent the message?"

"Kandryl. He'd been meeting with Lhoryn, because Lhoryn had expressed an interest in some properties in Mantes that Iryela and Kandryl wanted to sell—they're too far from anything else, something her father had picked up as a settlement on a debt. A messenger delivered the message to Lhoryn. Kandryl sent me the message because he knew I'd met with Glendyl."

"How did he do it? Did Kandryl's message say?"

"Apparently, sometime shortly after I left, he shot himself with a heavy pistol, through his right temple. That's what Kandryl wrote. Quite swift, but rather messy."

That stopped me, but I didn't say anything for a moment.

"I can see you're as stunned as I am," Frydryk said.

"I'm definitely stunned." But not for the same reason as Frydryk. "I don't know what to say." After a pause, I added, "We should rejoin our wives before they divulge too much about us."

Frydryk did smile at that.

Both Alynkya and Seliora held glasses of an amber white vintage when we returned.

Seliora smiled, wickedly, at me. "Alynkya has been telling me how you two met."

"Absolutely harmless," I said cheerfully, "and in the course of duty."

"You didn't mention that you asked her to dance *twice*." Seliora was smiling broadly, definitely enjoying herself. "At two separate balls."

"Totally innocent." I knew she was teasing, because I'd already told her that.

"I'll accept almost totally innocent."

I could see that Alynkya was trying hard to suppress either a smile or laughter. Frydryk was doing a better job.

A server stopped, with a tray holding wine goblets, and I took one holding the red. So did Frydryk. I took a small swallow and had to admit that it was quite good. I was about to say so when I glanced past Seliora and saw that the server to whom Fhernon was talking was about to leave. "I'll be back shortly." I slipped the wine goblet onto a side table.

My timing was adequate, and I managed to reach Fhernon just after the woman eased away and before anyone else appeared.

"Maitre Rhennthyl, are you enjoying yourself?"

"Most certainly. What can you tell me about a factor named Veblynt?"

Fhernon did not reply, looking as if I'd shocked him.

"I realize that discussing the mundane at such a delightful gathering is, shall we say, less than refined, but, alas, we are indeed rather short-handed at the Collegium, not to mention short of time." Not to mention that I was likely to get put off for days, the way I had with Madame D'Shendael, and I was getting the feeling, especially after Glendyl's death and the attempt on my own life, that I might not have days before something else happened.

"It is most irregular." He paused. "We do have a moment or two yet before dinner." He nodded and I followed him from the receiving room down a wide hallway to the library, lit by a single wall lamp. He closed the door, then turned. He did not move to seat himself.

I waited.

"The name 'Veblynt' came from his mother's family. He took it after the death of his father in a steeplechase accident. His father was Taelmyn D'Alte. His death was no accident. Taelmyn was a notoriously poor rider, and even poorer in stewarding his holdings. He made the ride as a wager to clear debts against Ryel D'Alte—the previous Ryel."

That explained some matters. "Veblynt's wife bears a resemblance to Iryela D'Ryel."

"They're second cousins, once removed. She married Veblynt anyway, and she did have a dowry that funded his first mill. He's far more of a success than his father was or ever could have been. He's very thorough. When he began, he was known to have made investments with borrowed funds, based on his knowledge of various High Holder families. To his credit, he always paid them back, usually early and with some extra, as if to compensate for the means of obtaining them. Thankfully, once he was established, that practice vanished, although I am told that his agents continue to collect information." The slightest sniff that followed Fhernon's words suggested a definite lack of approval of Veblynt and his methodology.

"Do you know whether he had any dealings with Glendyl?"

Fhernon offered a sardonic smile. "Outside of the legal actions, you mean?"

"Those must have been before my time."

"They took place more than ten years ago. Glendyl claimed Veblynt had copied certain processes from his engines, involving some sort of drive mechanism, and sought damages. Veblynt proved that the mechanisms had been in use for centuries in other equipment, if more crudely applied. He sought expenses for defending himself. The courts granted him a third of what he claimed. Neither was happy. So far as I know, they've never spoken since. That's close to the total I know about Veblynt."

"I do appreciate your taking the time." I smiled. "Is there anything else I should know?"

"Only that it is far better to have Veblynt in your debt than the other way around. I doubt, given events, that he would ever regard you as indebted to him. For that, you are fortunate."

As we walked back to the receiving room, I could see why, given Fhernon's explanation, Veblynt had been seeking information on Glendyl. Still, the loan agreement itself did not necessarily tie Glendyl to the Ferrans, only to Vyktor and the Banque D'Ouestan.

I doubted I'd find out more during the course of the evening, but I did hope that Seliora and I could enjoy the company and the various delicacies. Still, every time I turned around, or so it seemed, I discovered something that I should have known—and didn't—and of which there was no record anywhere.

62

On Samedi, Seliora and I were totally decadent. I skipped the early morning exercises and running, and we enjoyed each other and had a leisurely break-fast all by ourselves, for the first time in I couldn't remember how long. It didn't matter that the day was chill and gray. We even walked across the Bridge of Desires and had a late midday meal at Patryce's, one of the better small bistros just off the Boulevard D'Council.

Before we knew it, we were dressing for the winter ball of High Holder Almeida. This time, Seliora was in red and black, in a sleeveless gown with a crimson top over a not-quite-full black skirt and a black silk jacket, trimmed in crimson, with black lace sleeves. She wore long black gloves and a black formal cape, necessary for the walk from the house to the coach stand.

The Almeida estate was situated west of the river and to the north of L'Ex-celsis, not all that far from Frydryk's "city" estate, but a half-mille closer to L'Excelsis. There were a good ten coaches lined up on the drive when we ar-rived at what was truly a chateau, with stone carvings, and antique crenelated parapets topping the garden walls. It took more than a quint before we dis-embarked and went through the removal of cloaks and being escorted to a ballroom comprising most of the west wing of the chateau. Everyone was an-nounced, of course, and I was slightly surprised to hear "Rhennthyl D'Imagisle, Maitre D'Esprit, and Madame D'Rhennthyl." That was the older and more for-mal address, and not much used anymore.

Beyond the ballroom door was the receiving line, consisting of High Holder Almeida and his wife Ruisa, and their eldest son and his wife. As we entered the ballroom, I could see close to a hundred people, not that the ball-room looked at all crowded. I caught a glimpse of Kandryl and Iryela danc-ing, but they were obscured by others. I did see Justicer Symmal and Chief Councilor Ramsael, not that I really wanted to talk to either man or his wife.

"Would you like to dance, dearest?"

"I thought you'd never ask."

The orchestra was on a permanent low dais, framed by octagonal faux marble pillars with deep green velvet hangings, trimmed in gold, clearly an attempt to replicate the decor of the Charynan Period. As we began to dance,

I had to admit that the musicians were far better than those who played for the Council Balls.

After we had enjoyed several dances, when the music paused, I asked, "Are you ready for something to drink?"

"Are you tired already?"

"No, just thirsty."

"So long as this wasn't the last dance," she said teasingly.

"It wasn't." It wouldn't be, not given how much I enjoyed dancing with her.

As we walked toward one of the sideboards, Seliora nudged me. "There's Alhyral and his fiancee, in the off-blue."

Knowing her feelings about Alhyral and given mine about his sire, we eased toward the sideboard farther from them, easily enough, since they were talking to another couple. I did see Juniae D'Shendael, but not Geuffryt. I didn't see any uniforms. That did surprise me.

As we neared the sideboard with an array of wines and crystal goblets, and a server in green and cream livery, a thin man in formal blacks turned, and I recognized Artois. "Good evening, Commander. I don't believe you've met my wife, Seliora."

Artois smiled warmly and inclined his head. "I have not, but it's a pleasure, and I can see why your husband has always been careful and dutiful."

"I'm pleased to meet you, Commander. Rhenn has always commented on your dedication to the Civic Patrol."

"He was equally dedicated, and we will miss him greatly. The Collegium's gain is our loss. If you will excuse me, my wife is waiting." He inclined his head once more, then slipped away, carrying two goblets of the white vintage.

I secured two goblets of the white, a Grisio, and offered one to Seliora. We both took several swallows.

"Not bad," I said.

At that point we were joined by Iryela and Kandryl.

"Good evening," he offered.

"The same to you," I returned. "I saw you dancing, but you disappeared."

"You two didn't," returned Iryela. "Everyone was watching you."

"Oh?" I had to admit I hadn't noticed.

"You dance well, Rhenn," Iryela said, "but Seliora is incredibly impressive, and you two are such a handsome couple. When beauty, grace, and power appear on a dance floor, people will watch."

"She does have all three," I said blandly. "I just accompany her."

"Be careful, Seliora," cautioned Iryela. "He's verging on the difficult."

"For that, dearest," said Seliora, "you may dance with Iryela." She handed me her goblet and turned to Kandryl. "If you would?"

Kandryl bowed, and as he straightened, offered me a quick and knowing smile.

As they entered the swirl of dancers, Iryela looked at me holding the two goblets and said, "At our wedding, I did tell you that she was more than a match for you."

"Every time I forget that, she reminds me." I took several steps and handed both goblets to a server passing with a tray. "Since we are abandoned, would you honor me with a dance?"

"Why, of course. Who would dare to refuse a Maitre D'Esprit?"

"Between the two of you, there's no way to escape the Namer's clutches."

"It's good that you see that."

We moved out to join the other dancers in a stately waltz.

"I can't say that I know more than a handful of people here," I said with soft laugh.

"No, but more than a few want to see you. That's why you were invited. A handful or more will find ways to put themselves in your path as the evening progresses."

"I can hardly wait."

"Frydryk's worried, you know. So is Kandryl."

"Because of Glendyl's death?"

"You didn't call it suicide, I notice," Iryela murmured.

"I'm not sure it was, but I don't think Kandryl and Frydryk have anything to worry about. The damage is done. It will be years before Frydryk's shipworks can complete a modern fast battlecruiser, even if the Council gets around to agreeing to build more ships. Slowing down fleet modernization was what the Ferrans intended."

"You're not finished, are you, Rhenn?"

"Iryela, dear, how could you possibly ask that?"

"Because you don't leave things undone."

"I'm not having the best of fortune. I still don't know anything about Johanyr. No one we've contacted does, either."

"That may be for the best."

I couldn't help but agree, but I wasn't about to say that.

"I hated to send Kandryl to deal with Lhoryn, but he did well. The man makes Dulyk look like the Nameless."

Considering the vices of her late younger brother, that was quite a statement, although I'd never heard much good about Lhoryn. "You were selling some land?"

"Only a thousand hectares, but we still wanted a fair price."

Intellectually I understood that a thousand hectares was small for a High Holder, but emotionally was another matter. "That was when Kandryl found out about Glendyl's death."

Iryela nodded. "He said that Lhoryn smiled."

How many people had Glendyl alienated? I didn't dwell on that. "How are the twins?"

"Kyana takes more after her father . . ."

When the music ended, I escorted Iryela back to Kandryl, who had obtained two goblets of the red wine. I turned back toward Seliora, who was talking to Juniae D'Shendael, when a man with a supercilious smile and back silk formalwear appeared in front of me. Unfortunately, I recognized him.

"Maitre Rhennthyl . . . I apologize for the intrusion, but I've wanted to make your acquaintance for some time. I'm Alhyral D'Haestyr."

"You come from a noted lineage, and I understand that your fiancee has excellent taste."

"Ah, yes, and I hear that you're a most deadly fellow."

The jocular informality grated on me, as I was certain Alhyral intended. "I'm certain that's overstated."

"I've been thinking, Maitre." There was the slightest emphasis to my title, one that bordered on scorn, and I wondered how much he'd already had to drink . . . or if he happened to be that obnoxious without the aid of wine. "Sea-Marshal Valeun was saying that the Navy needs more modern vessels."

"That's true. Assistant Sea-Marshal Geuffryt has also voiced the same concerns. Has he mentioned them to you?"

After the tiniest hesitation, Alhyral replied, "Only in passing. If that is true, as you seem to indicate, why is the Collegium so opposed to spending on them?"

"We're not opposed at all. Might I ask who would think we'd be opposed to that when we lost two of the highest-ranking imagers to Ferran machinations?" I smiled.

"Yet you have done nothing."

"The Council does not meet until next week, and we have but one vote of fifteen in the Council. It might well be that the Council's votes will change after the Councilors begin to meet next week. Not your sire's, of course, since he has always supported better ships."

"Do you expect me to believe that anything will change?"

"I have no expectations for your beliefs at all. What will be, will be. Some Councilors opposed building new ships when Suyrien the Elder was Councilor because they thought he would take advantage. Others thought Councilor Glendyl might . . ."

"Terrible thing, there, with Glendyl . . . but that's what happens when one gets too ambitious . . . or too greedy."

". . . And too overextended," added another voice, that of another man I didn't know.

"Oh, this is Petryn D'Lhoryn, my friend."

"Pleased to meet you," I said pleasantly.

"The same." Petryn offered a minimal nod. "There are those who believe that the Collegium supports the factors, discreetly, notwithstanding the fact that the current Maitre comes from a High Holder background. Your background is from factoring, as I recall."

"My family is in factoring; I was a portraiturist."

"My condolences," offered Alhyral.

"And mine," added Petryn.

"That portraiture training has enabled me to read beyond words and faces, and to realize that ability often has little relation to the grace with which words are uttered, or the indirectness of the insult couched as flattery or condolence. But then, not having had training in verbal hypocrisy, I am afraid that my comments are hopelessly direct. I do hope you enjoy the ball, both of you. Good evening." I offered the barest hint of an inclined head, as taught by Maitre Dyana years before, and turned, still holding shields on the off chance that one of them might stoop to physical violence. They had enough sense not to.

After departing Petryn and Alhyral, I returned to Seliora and Juniae D'Shendael.

"Greetings," offered Madame D'Shendael. "Your wife is most charming, as well as perceptive."

"Far more so than I."

"You are both observant, I think." Juniae smiled. "What do you think of those here?"

I waited to let Seliora speak, but she glanced to me. So I replied, "It would seem an odd grouping. Among others, I've noted the Chief Councilor, a high justicer, the Commander of the Civic Patrol, several heirs of impeccable breeding and with courtesy less than that . . ."

"Not to mention the second-highest-ranking imager in Solidar, and the youngest ever to hold that position," added Juniae. "There are also no Sea-Marshals present, although several were invited, but not, of course, Caellynd."

"He seemed quite pleasant the other night," Seliora offered innocently.

"He is intelligent and exceedingly perceptive. The former is forgivable; the latter is not."

"I only thought that being concerned about the state of the fleet and those serving in it was unforgivable," I countered.

"All Sea-Marshals are concerned about the state of the fleet. Did you not know that, Maitre Rhennthyl?"

"I must have misunderstood. I was under the impression that concern went beyond mouthing words."

The faintest smile crossed Juniae D'Shendael's lips as she looked to Seliora. "You are most courageous, Madame, to appear in public with him."

Seliora laughed softly. "But he is so much better behaved in public, especially when others are watching."

"You two are so well matched," said Junaie to Seliora. "His other name could well be Erion . . . to match yours."

"My family has noted that," replied Seliora, "as has Rhenn's sister-in-marriage."

I didn't wince at the Pharsi references that linked the daughter of the greater moon to the red moon, the one that symbolized conquest and unrest—or truth and power—although my mother wouldn't have been able to avoid such a reaction, and Remaya had made that very same observation the first time she'd seen Seliora and me together.

"Truth and power are a dangerous combination," observed Juniae.

"For whom?" asked Seliora lightly.

Madame D'Shendael laughed gently. "I will not take more of your time, as I see my husband fretting, but it was very good to spend a few moments with you."

After that conversation, I immediately eased Seliora onto the dance floor where I took refuge in her charms.

"When you were talking to Alhyral," she said, "you had that slight stiffness that suggests you'd like to be done with the matter."

"I couldn't escape immediately without being excessively and unpardonably rude, and then they were so obnoxious that I was anyway, in the politest manner of which I was capable. I can see why you detest him. From what I can tell, he's worse than his father, although Madame D'Shendael told me that Haestyr wasn't as difficult as he now is before Geuffryt's father seduced his first wife."

"If the father was a fraction as bad as the son, I doubt much seduction was required." Seliora's voice was syrupy sweet.

"Are you suggesting that I need pay more attention to you?"

She laughed. "No, and today has been wonderful."

As we continued to dance, this time to a pavane, I just hoped life would remain that way . . . even as I knew that was most unlikely.

63

By Lundi morning, I still didn't have any better ideas than to actually visit Vyktor D'Banque D'Ouestan. I would have liked to have known exactly who had visited Glendyl after Frydryk, but short of driving out to his estate, there wasn't any way to determine that. Then I laughed. Why not try? All that could happen would be that I'd be turned away at the gates.

Less than a glass later, I was walking toward the front of Glendyl's mansion. I hadn't even had to argue with the gate guard.

As I neared the main entrance, a footman stepped forward. "The family won't be seeing anyone, Maitre. If you'd care to leave a card . . ."

"I can understand." I paused. "Were you here, the day it happened?"

"Yes, sir."

"Did the banque representative come right after Suyrien the Younger left?"

"Don't know as he was a banque man, sir. He wasn't right after, maybe a quint or two."

"And when did it happen?"

"I couldn't say, sir. No one could. The Councilor had the study proofed when he was selected to be on the Council. Said he didn't like eavesdropping. The staff heard the study door open and the visitor say good-day and the Councilor tell him to be on his way. Then the door slammed, and the fellow left angry-like. Maybe a glass later, when the Councilor didn't answer the bell, Carlysa opened the study door and found him. Must have happened after the fellow left. They both sounded angry, Carlysa said, when they parted. She could scarce tell their voices apart."

It wouldn't do for evidence, but learning more details wouldn't change anything. So very convenient. Glendyl's estate was outside L'Excelsis, and that meant he was responsible for his own security, and that the Civic Patrol had no jurisdiction. Who would petition the Justiciary when there was no real way to prove anything? I extended a card. "If you would leave this . . ."

"I can do that, sir."

"Thank you." I walked back to the waiting Collegium coach.

As I was riding back to Imagisle, I realized something else. The security laws were another pressure that the High Holders and the factors used to keep people either on the estates or in the towns and cities. I hadn't thought of it in that way because I'd grown up in L'Excelsis.

Once I got back to the Collegium, I just had the coach wait outside the administration building while I hurried inside and found Schorzat.

He looked up from his desk. "You're obviously going somewhere."

"I'm going to pay a call, I hope, on one Vyktor D'Banque D'Ouestan. His place of business is at 880 Avenue D'Theatre."

"What do you hope to learn from him?"

"Something that I can use to prove that he's a Ferran agent who's been behind more than a few things. On Vendrei, Glendyl told Frydryk—Suyrien the Younger—he'd never let go of anything, even if Suyrien called in the notes he held. I found out that right after that, Vyktor visited Glendyl, and then Glendyl supposedly killed himself. The only problem is that Glendyl used a heavy pistol at his right temple, and his right arm was too weak to hold it or aim it. I doubt anyone besides Draffyd and I—and now you—knew that. We may have to get a medical opinion from Draffyd before this is all over."

"What about the Civic Patrol?"

"Let's just say that there are complications with that approach." Such as the possibility that Cydarth was involved with Vyktor. "I thought you should know before I left."

"You don't want any company?"

"That would just alarm dear Vyktor."

"I'd suggest strong shields and a stronger degree of caution."

"I'd thought the same, but we need to get this resolved." With a nod, I turned and headed back to the coach.

The streets weren't too crowded, and in less than a quint Lebryn came to a halt outside 880. I sat for a moment in the coach and studied the buildings. The gray stone structure to the right was a good six levels high and looked to be a century old, if not older, built more like a fortress than some commercial establishment. On the left, the River Association Building was of a grayish brick, or perhaps pale yellow brick grayed by time and smoke and almost as high as the gray stone structure. There looked to be a lamp or light of some sort coming from one of the second level windows of Vyktor's establishment. He might even be in.

I stepped out of the coach. "I don't know how long I'll be."

"I'll have to circle here, sir," said Lebryn. "I can't stop on the avenue."

"Can you wait around the corner?"

"I'll try that, sir. If not, I'll come by every half quint."

"Thank you." I walked up to the door and dropped the tarnished brass knocker, twice, then a third time.

From the second level window came a voice. "The door's unlatched. Just go into the waiting room, and I'll join you in a moment."

The door was indeed unlatched, and I opened it. Beyond was a narrow foyer. At the end of the foyer was a door, and an archway to the right opened into a sitting room. The archway to the left was closed by the kind of doors that slid out of recesses. I touched it, but the two doors were locked together. I could have imaged out the lockplate, but I didn't see that such would be helpful. The door at the end of the foyer, presumably leading to stairs, was also closed, and most probably locked, which made sense if the front door were habitually left unlocked.

I stepped into the sitting room, dimly lit by two wall sconces. Where the front window had once been was filled with a heavy built-in bookcase, and the shelves were filled with books. Just out from the rear wall was a green leather couch, with a low table before it, on which were newsheets, neatly stacked. Out from the right wall were two green leather armchairs, set at slight angles to the table. The floor was of dull black tile, largely covered by a cream and green Khelgroran carpet. There were no windows, and the walls were paneled in oak. The only entry or exit was through the archway.

As I turned back toward the foyer, I saw two doors slide into place, sealing me into the room. While I had expected a less than completely friendly reaction, an immediate imprisonment was something I hadn't anticipated.

"The chamber in which you find yourself is entirely lead-lined. Even you can't do much in a lead-lined room, not without killing yourself, Master Imager Rhennthyl." The words echoed softly around me.

I turned, trying to locate the source of the slightly hollow-sounding words that had to come through a speaking tube. As I did, I thought of Maitre Dyana, and the words she'd always spoken when I'd first come to the Collegium— *Finesse, dear boy . . . Finesse.* "I don't see what you get from this, Vyktor. The Collegium will—"

"Don't talk to me about Maitre Dyana or the Collegium. Without you, the Council and the Collegium will crumble, and so will the High Holders and the artisans and guilds. Now that Dichartyn and Poincaryt are dead, *you* are the Collegium."

I couldn't help smiling ironically at the words. I wasn't the Collegium. I was the last thing from being the Collegium. I, as Dichartyn had been before me, was almost the anti-Collegium, whose acts freed the Collegium to be what it was, and if I didn't escape this trap, Dartazn or Shault or some other imager would come along to fill the role of designated target or lightning rod. Still . . . continuing as the lightning rod or the equivalent was far better than the alternatives. "You overestimate me. I presume that your decision to decline to advance funds to Glendyl was what finally determined his ruin."

"You determined that, I believe."

"Hardly. You'd already advanced him funds and led him to believe that you would continue to do so." I thought I'd located the speaking tube, and it provided a way, narrow as it might be, to image beyond the chamber. "Just like you put Broussard in touch with those who enabled him to strike back at Haebyn and the other eastern High Holders. Except he crossed you, and then escaped the explosion. Still, you got what you wanted. He's been rather silent."

There was silence.

"So . . . what will you do when I depart?"

"You won't depart. If you could, you already would have."

"Not necessarily."

"You will not escape this time. Good-bye—"

Before he finished, I imaged pitricin up through the speaking tube, visualizing his position with his lips near the tube opening and spraying it across his brain.

Whatever else he might have said was lost, and the entire building shook. I dashed for the northeast wall, recalling that as the side adjacent to the sturdier gray stone building without a name. I almost made it before the full force of the explosion rocked the building.

The ceiling shuddered. Chunks of plaster dropped. Then the ceiling split and a beam smashed down. I waited just a moment longer, hoping that the destruction had ripped enough holes in the lead lining of the room, and then tightened and strengthened my shields into the smallest area possible to protect me, as I flattened myself against the outside wall.

More sections of the building dropped around me. Dust swirled up, so thick that it coated the outside of my shields. The number of objects impacting my shields began to decrease, and I could feel myself getting light-headed. That suggested there was still a great deal of lead around me. I released the heavy shields and was immediately showered with dust and plaster fragments.

While I tried not to breathe any of it, the dust was so pervasive that I couldn't help inhaling a little, and I immediately began to sneeze. When I stopped sneezing, I tried to make out what was around me, but my eyes were watering so much that for several moments, everything was a blur. Even before I could begin to see, I began to smell smoke, although I didn't feel any heat.

When I could finally see, I discovered that I was standing between two fallen beams, and under another that had sagged, but remained anchored into the wall. Under the beams were bricks, plaster, broken laths, and other debris that left no space to crawl beneath and toward the front of the building. I peered over the top of the beam to my left, and under another beam, in the direction of the street, where I could make out a glimmer of light, possibly where the window that had been filled by the bookcase had been.

The smell of smoke was stronger.

Could I crawl over the beams and through the debris?

The first problem was that I couldn't move my left foot. I wiggled my toes. They moved. I tried to lift my foot again, and I could tell that my leg and foot moved. The boot didn't. After considerable struggle in a very cramped space, I managed to pull my foot out of my boot. Then I levered myself up over and along the beam to my left.

Each movement raised dust, and I kept sneezing. I also smelled more smoke, and that didn't help with the sneezing. I could hear yelling and bells, but none sounded all that close.

I crawled across the rubble beyond the first beam and gained another yard toward the light, but there were splintered and twisted timbers in front of me. The intertwined timbers looked anything but stable. At the same time, the smoke was thicker, and I could feel gusts of cool and very warm air. So I tried to wiggle to the left some, to get around the timbers. My right boot— my only boot—struck something, and the mosaic of debris above me shifted, and plaster and laths and everything else trembled, then creaked and began to shift.

I imaged a timbered block above me, and the shifting stopped.

Unfortunately, for a moment, so did I—or so it seemed. I couldn't see anything at all, and I felt like I couldn't move even my fingers.

Slowly, all too slowly, I could feel sensation returning to my limbs. I could also smell the smoke. I forced myself to extend one arm, then the other, then pull myself forward through the narrow space ahead. I kept going until, suddenly, my head was in open air.

"There's someone there!"

A patroller ran forward, and so did another one.

I let them help me out through the shattered frame, broken glass, and mangled drapes of the false window that had been in front of the bookcase. I was careful where I put down my unbooted foot, and I stood on the stone walk for a moment, trying to let the lightheadedness pass.

"Are you all right, sir? We need to move back. There's a fire somewhere in there."

"That's Captain Rhennthyl!" someone else called.

"Sir?"

"I'm not a captain any longer. I had to go back to Imagisle, but I'm Rhennthyl." I managed to gesture toward the building. "I think there are some wall lamps that are burning."

"The fire brigade is on the way."

We took several steps back toward the street before I spoke again. "You might want to send a patroller to Commander Artois—directly to the Commander," I emphasized, "and tell him about the explosion and that the man who did it might have been behind some of the other explosions. Most important, tell him it's worth his time to come here immediately."

Weak as I was, I must have had enough strength to project command, because the patroller first just said, "Yes, sir."

Then the first wagon of the fire brigade rolled up, followed by a second, a pumper wagon.

I glanced back toward the building. While a thin line of black smoke rose from the right side, it didn't seem to be growing. In moments, the firemen had unreeled a hose and had the nozzle pointed in the direction of the smoke. Then the steam pump kicked in and a thin line of spray arced toward the smoke. The nozzleman was careful, hoarding and playing his water carefully, but there was enough water in the tank that the smoke was gone—at least for the moment—close to the time the tank was empty.

That didn't take all that long, but I just stood with the patrollers, answering their questions with what had happened, and avoiding any and all speculations.

Behind the yellow cords the patrollers had strung, the number of bystanders grew, and I could hear some of their murmurs and comments.

". . . must be something . . ."

". . . more Ferran saboteurs . . . has to be . . . patrollers and an imager . . ."

". . . know what was there?"

"Clear the way!

At that command, I turned to see Subcommander Cydarth step out of a hack. I'd asked for Artois. Had the Commander ignored the message? Had he even gotten it? I just stood and watched Cydarth, waiting to see how he reacted.

When he caught sight of me, for just the slightest moment, the subcommander looked stunned. Then he made his way toward the yellow cord, lifting it, and ducking underneath, before walking toward me and my escorts.

"Good afternoon, Subcommander," I offered.

"Good afternoon, Maitre Rhennthyl. Might I ask what you were doing here?"

"Oh . . . that." I did manage a smile. "I was tracking down the banque representative who might have created the means by which Ferran agents obtained access to the engine works of the late Councilor Glendyl. Before we could properly discuss matters, the building exploded. I had some difficulty in extricating myself."

"I do believe you're the only man I know who's escaped having two buildings explode around him."

"I didn't exactly plan either one," I said as dryly as I could. "I'd barely been inside half a quint when it exploded."

"But you had some difficulty getting out, it appears."

"The door was blocked, and the window in front was false. There was a bookcase wall behind it."

Cydarth looked skeptical. I really didn't care.

"That's against the building codes."

"It may be against the codes, but that's the way it was. There's enough left there that you can see it's so."

"Who else was in the building?"

"I don't know. I knocked, and someone called down from the second level to enter and to wait in the front foyer. I did, and before anyone arrived, there was an explosion and the building came down around me."

"You're fortunate you're an imager."

I didn't answer that.

"Out of the way . . . Out of the way!"

Both Cydarth and I turned to see Commander Artois move through the crowd and under the cord. He immediately turned toward us and strode stiffly toward me, but when he stopped, his eyes landed on Cydarth. "Excuse us, Subcommander." Artois's glance at Cydarth was cold enough to have frozen the entire River Aluse.

I limped slightly after the Commander until he stopped in front of the corner of the River Association Building, still inside the cordon line, but back from the crowd that was beginning to disperse, since nothing more seemed to be happening, I suspected.

"Maitre Rhennthyl . . . it was strongly suggested that I be here. Why, might I ask?"

"So that any papers that are recovered from the ruins go to your hands and not into the hands of the subcommander. If you are not here, that is not likely to happen."

He looked at me, then back to where the fire brigade still pumped water from another tanker over the one smoking spot in the rubble. "What do you want?"

"To look at any papers or documents you find. It's likely that they'll show to whom Vyktor lent golds . . . and perhaps did more than that."

"Vyktor?"

"Oh . . . he is—or was—the ostensible agent for the Banque D'Ouestan here in L'Excelsis. They should find a body in there. It might be his."

"You think he was behind all the explosions in L'Excelsis?"

"That . . . I don't know. It's likely that he supplied the golds to various agents, and that he was receiving those funds through the Banque D'Ouestan. It's also likely that he lent golds, most likely supplied by Ferrum, to various factors and others who opposed High Holders, some of whom are Councilors. I thought you might wish to see those papers first. I would like to see them, all of them, as well, but it's been a very trying afternoon, and I have to confess that I'm not at my best."

"I can understand the Collegium's interest." He looked at me. "Unless you have other reasons, I doubt you need to remain. Do you need a hack?"

"I hope not. I think I have a coach around the corner."

He nodded, then gestured to a patroller.

"If you'd escort Maitre Rhennthyl to his coach."

"Yes, sir."

I inclined my head politely, then walked back along the cordon line, accompanied by the patroller, toward where I thought the coach might be. The stone was cold, and I walked awkwardly, trying to be careful where I placed my unbooted foot. Thankfully, I did find the duty coach nearby, and I limped up into it, with one foot clad only in a very soiled stocking. Lebryn did stare for a moment. I was glad that he hadn't been able to wait in front of the building.

When we reached Imagisle, I had Lebryn drop me at the administration building, where I made my way to see Maitre Dyana—after sending the duty prime to get some rags or something I could wrap around my nearly bare foot.

Her door was ajar, and Gherard just nodded, as if he didn't even want to ask why I wanted to see her.

"You look somewhat the worse for wear," observed Maitre Dyana as I stepped into her study and closed the door behind me. "Only one boot?"

"Just one, and I am." I sat down and proceeded to recount the salient events of the day, from my confirmation of Glendyl's not-suicide to the explosion and what followed.

After I finished, she looked at me for a time before asking, "Exactly what has all this accomplished, do you think?"

"We've temporarily removed one source of funding for Ferran operations here in Solidar. It's fair to say that we have more evidence to bring before the Council on the larger danger Ferrum represents, and possibly on the need to modernize the fleet . . . as well as to undertake a few other changes. Artois may find more."

"Summoning him was a deft touch. The fact that he found Cydarth already there may result in more disclosures. If he does find evidence, it will be his doing, not the Collegium's."

We talked a bit longer and then I left. Rather than search for boots or try to image one that fit, which would have required more effort than I thought I should make, I just wrapped rags and cloth around my unbooted foot and clumped out across the quadrangle and north to our house.

I'd barely stepped inside and shut the door when Diestrya ran toward me, saying, "Dada!" I scooped her up and held her tight. I found my eyes burning when I finally put her down.

Seliora stood in the archway from the parlor. "Your grays and cloak are dusty, and there are smears and smudges on your cheeks, and your foot is wrapped in rags. Is it hurt? What happened?"

"The rags are because my other boot was caught inside the building that another Ferran agent exploded around me."

"Rhenn . . ." Her mouth opened.

"It's all right. He's dead."

"What have you been doing?"

"Why don't you get me some hot tea, and we'll all sit down in the parlor, and I'll tell you. It's been a very long day, and I'm very glad to be home. I can't tell you how glad."

64

I let myself sleep a little later on Mardi morning. It didn't help that much. I dreamed of buildings exploding and falling down around me, feeling helpless in a lead casket, where I couldn't breathe. I woke up less than a half glass later than I usually did. I was sore all over, although I didn't find too many bruises. I wondered if I should have stayed and watched while the Civic Patrol went through the rubble of Vyktor's place.

Given that I was still feeling exhausted, and that I was only able to hold very light shields without feeling dizzy, that probably wouldn't have been a good idea. Besides, events were conspiring to illustrate that I couldn't do everything I wanted to do, much less everything that needed to be done. So I decided to trust Artois, at least so far as to what the Civic Patrol might find, and once I got to the administration building, I thought about how I might handle my problems with Valeun, Geuffryt, and the Naval Command. That wasn't terribly useful, because I kept thinking about what Artois and the Civic Patrol might have found . . . or the fact that they might have found nothing useful at all.

I went through reports and then spent the remainder of the morning with Kahlasa and Schorzat, where we talked over how we could improve the reports we received from regionals and from all the Civic Patrol Commanders across Solidar. They had suggestions far better than mine about what we needed on the reports. None of us had very good ideas on how to get the Council to adopt requirements so that the various city Civic Patrol Commanders would actually be required to supply the information.

Just before noon, Schorzat went to meet his brother in the city, and Kahlasa headed off to eat with her daughter. I went to the dining hall and almost reached the masters' table when I heard a cheerful voice from the other end.

"Rhenn . . . I heard that another building exploded around you," Ferlyn offered cheerfully.

I sat down to the left of Chassendri before replying. "More on me than around me." I shrugged. "What can I say?" Then I turned to Chassendri. "If you wouldn't mind passing the carafe of the red wine?"

"I'd be delighted," she said, almost impishly, for all that she was a good fifteen or twenty years older than me.

"You covert types . . ." Ferlyn laughed. "Never a straight or informative answer."

"That is what covert means," replied Chassendri.

"You're always defending them."

"That's because they're always defending us, Ferlyn. You might try the red wine. It is rather good for a midday meal."

Chassendri and I talked about my junior imagers, particularly Haugyl and Marteon, who were having trouble grasping the concept that being an imager required continual work.

After I ate, I headed back to my study and fretted over how exactly to fit in all the changes we had discussed for the revised report forms, until, slightly before second glass, a young patroller arrived at the administration building looking for me.

"Maitre Rhennthyl, the Commander hoped you could join him at your earliest convenience."

"I'd be happy to."

With that, after I donned my lighter cloak—the heavier one was being fullered—I guided him out of the administration building and to the duty coach stand. We rode back to Civic Patrol headquarters in a Collegium coach. There, I went upstairs alone.

Artois was waiting in his study, but he didn't speak until I closed the door. "You're looking better today."

"Thank you. I'm feeling better as well. I assume you found some items of interest." I sat down across the desk from him.

"We did. There was only one body in the building. From what we can tell, it was Vyktor D'Banque D'Ouestan. He'd rigged the place with explosives, but there were two fuse systems, one above the front room . . . and one just inside the rear door to the alley."

"So he could destroy the building and depart."

"Most likely." Artois looked at me. "We found two lockboxes. Do you have any idea what was in either?"

"There might be a note for 25,000 golds owed to the Banque D'Ouestan by Councilor Glendyl. There might be documents with other names on them. One of those names might be Mahrun Barge and Cartage. Another might be Cholan Freight and Transport."

Artois nodded. "A fair number of golds were transferred to both of those names, and there were also remittances to the Banque D'Ouestan from them. I take it that you believe them to have been Ferran facades?"

"That appears likely. You will make those available, if it becomes necessary?"

"Of course." After a slight hesitation, Artois added, "One of the other names was that of a Civic Patrol subcommander, but the documents involving him weren't notes, but the record of a series of payments to one Vyktor D'Cleris from that subcommander. I thought you might wish to look at it." He extended a small thin book across the desk.

I opened it and scanned the entries in the miniature ledger. Most of them were outlays to names I'd never heard of, but there were occasional receipts. The only regular entries were from "Cydarth D'P., in gold."

"To Vyktor? Not to the banque? Can you check the amounts against withdrawals or transfers from his account at the Banque D'Excelsis?"

"I already did. The banque was cooperative, for once. For the most part, they match withdrawals, but the payments were made in actual golds, as you can see." Artois offered a tight smile. "Although we cannot prove for what the payments were made, there is enough proof to dismiss the subcommander for improper behavior in transferring funds to the agent of a foreign power. He could contest the dismissal before the Justiciary, but that would make matters very public, and that would not be in his interests."

I had a very good idea why Cydarth had paid Vyktor. There had been too many "accidental" deaths of Patrol officers who opposed Cydarth. Again, there wasn't any way to prove that.

"Even more interesting," continued Artois, "is the fact that the subcommander took the ironway somewhere last night. Do you know where?"

"It's likely that he took an express straight to Ouestan, but that's a guess."

"He'll be on a vessel outbound before we can get word there." Artois reclaimed the ledger and extended a file holding loose papers. "I thought you might like to see this as well."

I opened the folder and studied the sheets there. In addition to the original note to Glendyl, there was another note, marked paid, for ten thousand golds from one Broussard D'Factorius and yet another that extended fifty thousand golds to High Holder Ruelyr. The second showed no indication of having been paid. There was a small note card. I read it twice.

Mtre Rh. knows you. He will come after you sooner or later.

The letter underneath was an ornate "L." In the bottom right hand corner, a different hand had added, "10/11/762."

The later hand was doubtless Vyktor's, but who would sign a note with a "L"? Abruptly, I knew, useless as it was, unless I could compare handwriting.

"Most interesting. I assume you have no objection to my retaining this for a time."

"None whatsoever. None relates to offenses here in L'Excelsis."

I'd hoped that there might have been something more directly involving or implicating Geuffryt, but . . . if there didn't happen to be anything, then there wasn't anything.

After a moment, Artois added, with a glint in his eye, "There was also a strongbox buried in the rear of the lower level. It held some four thousand golds." He paused. "Nothing else. Just golds. Except they were Ferran minted golds."

"If you wouldn't mind sending Maitre Dyana a report of that?"

"I'd be pleased to do so." He did not stand, but finally said, "You never trusted Cydarth, did you?"

"No. I never did."

"Why?"

"There were too many little things that bothered me."

Abruptly, Artois laughed. "That's why you were a good Patrol officer, and why you'll do well with what you're doing." He did stand. "We should meet often."

"We will." I stood as well.

The duty coach was waiting outside, with Lebryn ready to return me to Imagisle. And I while I had another piece of proof about Geuffryt, it was anything but conclusive.

65

When I got to my study on Meredi morning, there was nothing in either *Tableta* or *Veritum* about Cydarth, and neither newsheet mentioned anything about our northern fleet. While Valeun might be the first to receive news about fleet actions off Cloisera, I was confident that he wouldn't be able to keep it from appearing in the newsheets. Because there wasn't any news, it was unlikely that any communiqués had yet reached L'Excelsis, but I had no way of knowing whether Dartazn had been successful or whether he'd even been able to conduct the operation. I was definitely getting worried, but there was little I could do about it.

Later that morning, the Council convened for its first true session for the new year. I was there to help Baratyn . . . and to see if anything interesting was reported or occurred. Nothing happened out of the ordinary, not even an attempt on the lives of one of the Councilors, and that often happened on the first day the Council met. There wasn't any news circulating there, either, about the war or—as Deputy Sea-Marshal Caellynd had called it—the "conflict."

The factor's assembly was still considering a replacement for Councilor Glendyl, although they had already agreed that the new factor Councilor on the Executive Council would be Sebatyon, the current timber and lumber factor from Mantes. No one wanted another Councilor associated even indirectly with shipbuilding, and that eliminated Diogayn, the most senior factoring Councilor, because he owned several ironworks.

I did get home not much after Seliora. Because Diestrya was tired and cranky because she hadn't taken a nap, we didn't get to talk until after I had rocked her to sleep while Seliora sang lullabies. Then I eased her into the high-sided small bed, and we tiptoed downstairs.

We just sat down on the settee in the family parlor and sighed, almost simultaneously, loudly enough that we looked at each other and laughed.

"Sometimes . . ." I offered.

She just nodded.

"Would you like some wine? We do have a bottle of Dhuensa in the cooler."

"That would be good."

So I went and got it and poured us each a goblet, and we sat next to each other and had several swallows each.

"I didn't have a chance to tell you earlier," Seliora finally said. "Shomyr came up with the sidearm this afternoon. He didn't know whether you'd need the holster and belt, but they're both there in case you need them, as well as a small box of bullets. I put them in the high strongbox in the study."

"The one our little climber can't reach?" Even if she could, it was locked.

Seliora nodded.

"Thank you . . . and Shomyr."

"Can you explain what you can?" she asked quietly.

"It has to do with Valeun and Geuffryt. I've told you about how I'm convinced that Geuffryt was the one who arranged the bombardment of Imagisle . . ."

"I can't believe anyone could do that just because he thought Maitre Dichartyn and Maitre Poincaryt might be sometimes supporting the High Holder Councilors—even if he wanted revenge. The Collegium only has one vote on the Council."

"There's more to it than that, but I don't know everything. Valeun is protecting Geuffryt, and I have a good idea just who it was that let Vyktor know that I would be visiting him, well before anyone else could have known that it would happen. Even if I could prove that Geuffryt wrote the warning note, it's only another piece of circumstantial evidence . . ." I couldn't help but shake my head.

"So you have to come up with a way to resolve this?"

"Unfortunately, and I'll have to meet with both Geuffryt and Valeun, and that will be anything but pleasant. Oh . . . they'll both be so solicitous and polite and so willing to be cooperative with the Collegium, and if I leave it to Valeun, nothing will happen because he doesn't want any of it to come out, and Maitre Dyana would prefer not to have anything more come out because discrediting the Naval Command will just make getting Council support for rebuilding the fleet harder, and no one will think it's urgent, especially if Dartazn's mission is successful, because they'll think Solidar has plenty of time."

"That's not true, is it?"

"No. Frydryk has the drawings and designs and rights to produce the steam turbines for a new class of warships, but it will take a year, perhaps as many as three, to rebuild the facility, and the Council will want assurances that it can be done, and the shipworks can only build so many at once. It might take ten or fifteen years . . . and if the Council waits several years before acting,

because they want to be sure that the Naval Command is being run cor-
rectly . . ." I shrugged.

"You'll do what has to be done." Seliora reached out and took my hand.
"That's all you can do."

And that was what I feared.

66

I was back to exercising and running on Jeudi morning, and that helped my mood, at least until I got to the administration building after seeing Seliora and Diestrya off. Even so, there was no sense in putting matters off. So I went to find Schorzat. I found him in Kahlasa's study. Both of them looked up, not quite apprehensively.

"Yes, sir?"

"I've been thinking . . . I'd like you to arrange for me to meet with Sea-Marshal Valeun and Assistant Sea-Marshal Geuffryt. I'd prefer later today but tomorrow would be acceptable. Stress that it is urgent, because we've received more evidence of Ferran activities that bear on the Naval Command."

"Do you want me to mention the notes to Ruelyr and Broussard?"

"Don't give them any details. Just say that because it involves both the fleet and intelligence. I need to meet with them both—and only them at first. Then they can decide who else, if anyone, needs to know."

Kahlasa grinned at me. "You know, Rhenn, you're sounding more and more like a cross between Maitre Poincaryt and Maitre Dichartyn."

"What? Trying to ask politely for the impossible?" I let wryness creep into my voice.

"Oh, you know it's possible," she countered. "Just extremely difficult. It's a good thing you've survived so much."

I had a good idea what she was driving at, but I only said, "There are more than a few others, like you, who've been through things I wouldn't want to have done."

"Not many. And you've lost people you've loved because you're an imager."

That surprised me, because I'd never mentioned Rousel's death to anyone but Dichartyn.

Schorzat cleared his throat. I could tell we were making him uncomfortable, with the allusions to the death of Rousel and of Claustyn, Kahlasa's husband, so soon after they'd been married. "I'll have to go out to the Naval Command. Otherwise, they'll stall you."

"I'd appreciate that, and I'll leave you two to continue doing the almost impossible." I smiled as warmly as I could.

Once I returned to my study, I went through the newsheets. *Veritum* reported that the Stakanarans had repulsed a massive Tiempran counter-attack and then slaughtered close to half the Tiempran troops. *Tableta's* lead story was yet another variation on the theme that innovative Naval tactics and superior training could only go so far, citing how much the new Ferran landcruisers had changed the results in winter warfare in Cloisera and how the Stakanaran use of similar vehicles had played a part in the success of the annexation of Tiempran territory.

I couldn't help but wonder if Valeun had some information suggesting that Dartazn's imagers were having early successes against Ferrum.

It wasn't until well into the afternoon that Schorzat knocked on my study door. "Half-past second glass tomorrow afternoon. The Sea-Marshal wasn't pleased. I just asked his clerk-rating if the Sea-Marshal really wanted to put off the second-highest imager in all Solidar. Then I said I'd wait for an answer."

"You leaned hard."

"It wasn't what you said, sir. It was how you said it. You don't want to wait until next week. That was clear."

"Something's in the works, and I need to put the Sea-Marshal on notice."

Schorzat smiled. "I'd love to be there."

I shook my head. "They don't talk unless they're where they can deny what they've said." After a moment, I added, "Thank you. I do appreciate it."

"Better you than me, sir." He stepped back and closed the door.

What with one thing and another, and a late afternoon meeting with Marteon, I didn't get to the house until after fifth glass.

Seliora and Diestrya were sitting in the family parlor where Seliora was reading aloud to a slightly fidgety daughter.

Diestyra looked at her mother. "No more reading, please."

So we talked and played with her until it was time for her to eat.

We headed downstairs after putting her to bed for our own dinner, but Seliora stopped at the foot of the stairs and turned to me. "I received a notice of a bequest today. It came to NordEste Design."

With all that had happened, and my decision not to tell her, I'd almost forgotten that she would get the notice. "A bequest? From whom?"

"From the estate of the late Suyrien D'Alte. Rhenn . . . it's for ten thousand golds. I didn't tell anyone the amount. I didn't want to until I talked to you."

I had to swallow at the sum of the bequest. Iryela had said that it would be small, but I hadn't really accepted what was considered small to a High Holder. I'd have to work for more than twenty years to earn ten thousand golds—and I was one of the highest paid imagers in the Collegium—and to save that amount would have been impossible. Even my father had put by only a fraction of that amount, at least from what I knew.

"You're as surprised as I am," she said. "I wondered if you knew."

"Iryela had mentioned that she thought that you might get a very small bequest. That's why I didn't mention it. She emphasized that it was very small, and I'd thought it might be something like fifty or a hundred golds. I didn't say anything because she said she wasn't sure."

Seliora laughed softly. "Small means something very different to her."

"Every time I deal with High Holders, it seems as though I'm reminded of that."

"What will we do with it?"

"Put it in the Banque D'Excelsis in your name. It has to stay in your name. Talk to your mother and grandmother. Then we'll discuss it. Some of it should go for private tutors for Diestrya if she turns out not to be an imager, although that's not likely."

Seliora's mouth dropped open. "Do you think she will be? You've never said that before."

"If you weren't from a Pharsi background, I'd say it was unlikely, but with an imager father and a Pharsi mother, Kahlasa told me years ago that there are two chances in three for a daughter to be an imager. If both the mother and father are imagers, it's two in three for a boy, and almost always for a girl. I could be wrong, but I have the feeling that Diestrya will show up with the ability."

"Kahlasa has always known that Klaustya will be an imager?"

I nodded. "It may not show up for a time, but she will be."

"She knew that before she had her daughter?"

"She said she felt that it was a gift she had to pass on, like the Pharsi heritage." Kahlasa hadn't compared it to the Pharsi heritage, but her words had held the same import.

"Do you know why Suyrien made the bequest?"

"I can only guess. He never talked to me. Iryela said that he once mentioned that he owed Kandryl's happiness to us."

"So . . . it's a thank-you of sorts."

"That's my guess, but it's only a guess."

Seliora tilted her head slightly. "I'm not sure how I feel about that . . . but that will relieve Mama. She's always worried about the future."

"NordEste Design is doing better than ever, you said."

"Pharsis never stop worrying. We may try to live for the day, but we plan endlessly for the morrow." She smiled warmly at me. "You know that."

I did indeed.

67

Vendrei morning found me in Maitre Dyana's study by half-past eighth glass. She wore a gray and silver scarf trimmed in black, and again there were dark circles under her eyes.

"What do you intend to get out of this meeting with Valeun and Geuffryt? Unless there's something I missed, you still don't have much hard evidence to prove what we all know Geuffryt's been doing."

"I do have an interesting note that I have every reason to believe is in his handwriting, if somewhat disguised. It's a warning to Vyktor that I'll be looking into his operations, and dear late Vyktor was kind enough to add the date of receipt, as pointed out by Commander Artois."

"Artois's seen the note, then?"

"He's the one who found it, but he doesn't know the writer, and I didn't tell him."

"Geuffryt will deny it's his writing."

"I'm certain he will, but I intend to present all the evidence to the two of them and ask them exactly what they intend to do. Their reaction will be most illuminating."

Dyana shook her head. "Are you fully recovered?"

"I have full shields, but I trust it won't come to that." And it wouldn't, if things worked out the way I'd arranged them. That was something that Maitre Poincaryt had stressed—never have a meeting unless you had set it up so that events transpired the way you intended.

"You sound like Dichartyn again."

I just shrugged.

"I'll be here until late. Let me know when you get back."

That—and the fact that she didn't ask for details—told me that she was worried . . . and that she didn't have any better ideas. "I will."

I kept myself busy for the rest of the morning and the midday meal, and then returned to my study where I organized everything—and re-organized it—for the meeting at the Naval Command.

At two quints before second glass, I slipped the loaded sidearm in its holster into the larger inside pocket of my waistcoat, then donned my recently cleaned winter cloak. After that, I picked up the leather folder that contained what evidence I had, all of it indirect, but certainly more than suggestive. There was also a blank notecard on top, as close a match as I'd been able to find to the one that held the short message signed with the "L."

With all my preparations made, I left my study and walked through the chill and windy afternoon across the quadrangle to the duty coach station on the west side of Imagisle. Once I reached the Naval Command building, I had to wait for an escort, and then cool my boots some more in the anteroom outside Valeun's study. I didn't see Geuffryt, and that led me to believe that he was already inside talking with the Sea-Marshal.

A small bell chimed, and the clerk-rating at the desk in the anteroom rose. "Maitre?" He stepped forward and opened the study door.

I rose, leaving my winter cloak on the chair beside the one where I'd been waiting, and walked through the door into the Sea-Marshal's capacious study. Through the windows, I could see the same gray clouds that had hung over L'Excelsis for the past two days.

Valeun was seated behind his desk, with Geuffryt seated on the left. Neither rose as I entered the chamber.

I waited until the door closed before speaking. "Good afternoon, Sea-Marshal," I said, adding, "Geuffryt," as if as an afterthought. I took the chair to the right of Geuffryt, setting the leather folder on the desk before me and moving my chair forward so that I could reach it, and the materials in it, easily.

"You requested this meeting, and the Collegium insisted that it was urgent. Quite urgent." Valeun's voice was smooth, calm, and modulated. His eyes were cold.

So were Geuffryt's.

That didn't bother me.

"It's very urgent." I smiled. "I don't tell anyone something is urgent unless it is." I reached forward and eased back the leather flap that protected the contents of the folder. Then I paused. "Oh . . . I do have a request, a very small request. Before we begin, would you write your name and the word 'visit' on this piece of paper, Geuffryt?" I leaned forward and eased the pen stand away from the end of Valeun's blotter, then slipped the blank notecard onto the desk.

"What does that have to do with anything?" asked Valeun.

"Oh, it's just a way of making certain of the relevance of what's here in the folder." I smiled again, waiting.

"Why not? We might as well get on with whatever you and the Collegium have in mind." Geuffryt's tone was arrogantly dismissive. He leaned forward and extracted the pen, writing the single word and then signing his name below, before sliding the card across the polished wood to me.

"Thank you." I replaced the pen stand before picking up the card and blowing on the ink lightly until it was dry. Then I looked at what he had written and nodded. Superficially, the script was different from the note in my leather, but I could see that there were certain similarities that could not be totally disguised. Again . . . not quite enough proof, except for me.

"Now . . ." I drew the word out. "I briefed Sea-Marshal Valeun on the materials which strongly suggest that Assistant Sea-Marshal Geuffryt had a part in the bombardment of Imagisle." I turned to Geuffryt.

He didn't look surprised, but he didn't say anything.

"From your reaction, I can assume that he has at least summarized the findings."

"There's absolutely nothing there," replied Geuffryt offhandedly.

I had to admire his ability to dismiss the matter, but I just smiled. "Oh . . . I disagree strongly, and so does Maitre Dyana, and so will the Council, especially when combined with the documents that Commander Artois and the Civic Patrol discovered in the building that the latest Ferran agent to be discovered exploded around me." I touched the folder. "It truly is amazing how far the Ferrans penetrated into Solidar and even into L'Excelsis itself. The subcommander of the Civic Patrol vanished the night these documents came to light, as it were."

"What are these documents?" asked Valeun, not quite idly.

"There was the note for twenty-five thousand golds to the late Councilor Glendyl, another for ten thousand golds to Factor Broussard. Then there were all the payments to the two Ferran front organizations, Mahrun Barge and Cartage and Cholan Freight and Transport, and we've verified that they shipped the explosives they stole from the depot to various points across Solidar." I smiled again. "Some of these operations had been running for at least four years. This does bring up the question of how a handful of imagers could discover all these connections in a few weeks when Naval Intelligence apparently was unable to discover them."

"You are the one with the answers, Maitre Rhennthyl, pray tell us." Valeun's voice remained calm.

"In a moment. In addition to those, of course, was the hidden chest with over four thousand Ferran-minted golds in it."

That brought a momentary frown to Valeun's otherwise placidly smooth forehead.

"Oh . . . I'm not under any illusions, Marshal. I have no doubts that Naval

Intelligence knew about much of this for some time. In fact, I have a note in the folder here, initialed and dated, that proves just that, and, in fact . . ."

I coughed and bent forward, easing the sidearm out of my waistcoat even as I extended light shields against all four walls of the room for long enough to do what I needed to prepare. That didn't affect the light inside, just the ability of anyone to observe, since I was going under the assumption that some-one might be watching. "You see, Geuffryt," I said, straightening, but keeping the weapon concealed, beneath the level of the desk and on the side away from Geuffryt, "the Sea-Marshal knows you used your position to strike against the Collegium, but he's covered up for you."

"Oh, you can't—

At that moment, I raised the sidearm and fired.

The single shot—aimed by imaging—went through Valeun's forehead, as I dropped the light shields.

Geuffryt gaped and started to lunge from his chair toward me.

That was long enough for me to image pitricin into his brain and fire the pistol into the floor. As soon as he hit the carpet, between the chairs, I knelt and placed the weapon in his fingers, and let them release it. I checked to make sure he didn't have a sidearm, but he didn't. I hadn't thought he would, because they weren't worn inside the Naval Command or in non-combat situations, but it was best to make sure.

Then I straightened, and imaged the traces of powder off my grays and onto his sleeves while calling, "Help! The Marshal's been shot!" I also dropped the light shields and rushed around the desk to where Valeun lay back in his heavy chair.

The door opened, and the clerk-rating and a guard armed with the same kind of pistol I—or Geuffryt—had used rushed in. Behind them came a smooth-faced junior commander, most likely the officer detailed to observe from hiding.

"Marshal Geuffryt . . . he shot the Sea-Marshal." I tried to look bewil-dered before pulling myself together. "I didn't think he'd react like that."

The two ratings looked blankly at me. That was fine. The commander's eyes were narrowed and wary.

"Is the Deputy Sea-Marshal around?"

"Ah . . ." The clerk-rating gaped.

"If he is, summon him at once."

The commander nodded to the clerk-rating, who hurried off.

I stepped away from Valeun's body, but I kept holding full shields.

The commander stepped forward.

"What is it, Commander?" I asked politely.

He started to speak, then shook his head. "Nothing, sir. This . . . it was so unexpected."

I shook my head in return. "Treachery always outs, and it's never pleasant when that happens." Then I looked squarely at him.

"No, sir." He straightened.

Neither of us, nor the guard, spoke after that, not until Deputy Sea-Marshal Caellynd hurried into the study. His eyes took in the scene. Then he looked to the guard. "You can leave. Close the door."

"Yes, sir."

Once the door shut, Caellynd turned to me. He was obviously surprised, if not totally shocked.

"What happened?"

"I came to present evidence that Geuffryt was involved with the Ferrans and particularly with the bombardment of Imagisle. The Sea-Marshal had seen some of the evidence earlier, but he was not convinced, perhaps because he could not believe a trusted high Navy officer was involved. When I began to mention a note found in the ruins of the Ferran agent's building, Geuffryt shot Valeun and then turned the gun on me. I was so surprised that I stopped him with imaging. The gun went off anyway. If I'd had a moment longer . . . but he was standing so close to me that if he'd actually fired, my shields wouldn't have been that effective."

Caellynd gestured to the commander. "Is that correct?"

"Sir . . ."

"The Maitre's not ignorant, Commander. He has to know you were watching or listening."

"Yes, sir. The conversation was exactly the way the Maitre reported it. The shot happened so quickly I only saw the Sea-Marshal jerk back and the other two move the way the Maitre said."

Caellynd nodded. "You may go. Before you do anything else, write up exactly what you saw and heard."

"Yes, sir."

After the commander departed, and the door closed behind him, Caellynd asked, "Why do you think Geuffryt reacted as he did?"

"I can only surmise. It could be that the Marshal had told him of the previous evidence, and that he didn't believe it was sufficient to implicate him. The Sea-Marshal had declined to act unless the Collegium could provide more proof. You may have heard, on Lundi, a building exploded around me. That building housed a Ferran agent, and the Civic Patrol found more information linking him to the explosions. They also found a note warning this Vyktor that I was looking into his operations. The handwriting was disguised to some degree, but too many letters looked like Geuffryt's, and when I started to bring this latest evidence out, Geuffryt shot the Marshal and tried to shoot me at close range. He knew that imager shields aren't nearly so effective close to a weapon."

"You have all this evidence?" Caellynd's voice was skeptical.

"Most of it's in that folder." I nodded toward the desk. "Some of the background is not, but you can certainly check that yourself if you have doubts." I went on to explain about the barges, and about the funds transfers with the Banque D'Rivages, and the forged documents. Then I let him take his time going through what I had brought.

After looking through the materials, Caellynd looked up. "I can see why you reached the conclusions you did. It's unavoidable. There's one thing that puzzles me. I can see the resemblance in the handwriting of the note, but the initial isn't his."

"It is. Had his father lived and held on to his holding, Geuffryt might well have been High Holder Laevoryn." At least, after he'd removed his older brother, which I had no doubts he would have tried. "That's one reason for his actions. He felt that the High Holders and the Collegium were the reason why he and his family lost everything. He's taken other actions against High Holders in the past."

"Such as?"

I shook my head. "They didn't happen recently, and they're not relevant here. Unearthing them now would only hurt innocents."

"Will you leave that evidence?"

"No. You may view it any time you wish. If you wish to go over it now, I'll wait. Or if you want to have anyone copy from it, I'll be happy to wait as well."

Caellynd nodded slowly. "Given what I've heard and seen, I can see your reluctance to part with it. I can't blame you. We will need to copy parts of it, especially the barge lease contract details."

All in all, I was at the Naval Command for more than a glass before I was finally able to return to the duty coach and begin the ride back to Imagisle.

Maitre Dyana was indeed waiting, even though I didn't get back to the Collegium until two quints past fifth glass.

"What happened?" Her words were cool.

"I offered the evidence. Geuffryt denied it. Then he shot Valeun in the forehead and tried to shoot me. He was less than a yard away. I imaged pitricin into his brain. His shot hit the carpet."

"His study was doubtless under observation."

"A junior commander observed almost everything. His report verified what I told you. Deputy Sea-Marshal Caellynd went over everything with both the commander and me. After that, I presented the evidence to Deputy Sea-Marshal Caellynd, and he went over it thoroughly. He decided that there was no way to hush up everything, but that he would make a statement that apparently Geuffryt shot the Marshal when he realized that his personal ties to a Ferran banker and agent would be revealed and that he would have been demoted and dismissed."

"What about the Civic Patrol?"

"They don't come into it. The Naval Command is a military establishment. They handle their own offenses. In the cases of capital crimes tried by court martial, cases can be appealed to the high justiciary."

"Maitre Dichartyn would be proud of you," she said.

"No. He'd have been telling me there was another way. There probably was, but I couldn't find it, and we were running out of time. Besides, the Navy doesn't need to reveal what Geuffryt really did. They'd never get the ships they need, not for years, and it would be years before the suspicions settled down. Caellynd is the kind of Sea-Marshal all the senior officers want and the kind that the Council can deal with."

"He's not stupid."

"Neither was Valeun, but he still didn't see the dangers. Caellynd is basically honest, but he's also a realist."

Maitre Dyana nodded. "I need to think about this. See me first thing in the morning. Since it's Samedi . . . half past eighth glass."

"I'll be here."

She just looked at me, and I looked back.

"Good-night, Rhenn."

"Good-night." At least, she hadn't made a fuss about my disobeying her instructions about Geuffryt, but that might have been because there wasn't any point to it and because matters would only have gotten worse with the Naval Command if I hadn't acted. Besides, she had once mentioned that we might need a new Sea-Marshal if Valeun proved uncooperative, and he'd proved not only uncooperative, but corrupt.

As I left Dyana's study, I shook my head. One of the aspects of it that bothered me the most was that Valeun would most likely end up venerated and respected, his death thought to be a tragedy.

I returned to my study and locked away the evidence folder, then left and walked slowly back toward the house.

Seliora met me in the foyer. She gave me a sad smile. "You're late. I had to put Diestrya to bed."

"That's probably better." I took a deep breath, then took off my cloak and hung it up. Then I walked over to her and put my arms around her. I held her tightly for a while, then finally released her.

"It was hard, wasn't it?"

"Yes . . . I had to do what needed to be done. Do we have any wine?"

"I brought up the Cambrisio. I thought you might need something."

I didn't say more until we were sitting in the parlor in front of a stove that was barely emitting any heat. Then I began. "You knew I was meeting with Valeun and Geuffryt. I told you how Valeun never wanted to deal with Geuffryt, and how Geuffryt killed the clerk and probably Johanyr, though that's something I can't prove . . ." From there I told her the "official" story, ending with, "and while you know how things really are, there's no point in even talking about that. Sometimes, it's just better to leave things the way people see them, because they don't want to hear or see what really happened. Just like Valeun. He didn't want to admit that he'd made a mistake with Geuffryt. He'd rather have let the man continue to do all sorts of evil things than have any of it come out. I'm not much better, because I don't want some of it to come out because it will hurt Solidar and the Council and the Collegium and accomplish nothing."

"There will be enough of the truth out there that people will be satisfied." Her smile in the dim light was ironic. "They never want the whole complicated truth. Never. They say they do, but they always run from it."

And I was afraid she was right about that as well.

68

Before I went in to see Maitre Dyana on Samedi morning, I did read the new-sheets so that I'd know how the incident was being presented.

Veritum and *Tableta* both had stories on the deaths of Geuffryt and Valeun. *Veritum* reported the "Navy" version, but speculated that Geuffryt had been about to be removed for incompetence, because of his failure to discover all the Ferran infiltration that led to sabotage and explosions. *Tableta* noted that a high-ranking imager had been present and suggested that the Collegium had been demanding Geuffryt's removal because of his failure to stop the Ferran bombardment of Imagisle. Both stories showed Caellynd's ability to deal with the newsheets.

Gherard wasn't in the anteroom, and the door to the Maitre's study was open. So I walked in and sat down.

"Caellynd sent me a note." Dyana wasn't wearing a scarf of any sort, and those were her first words. "By Navy courier."

"Might I ask what he had to say?"

"You can. It was very polite. He wrote that he appreciated your tactful handling of what could have been a difficult situation for the Naval Command, and that he hoped that the Collegium and the Naval Command could resume working together constructively and cooperatively." She leaned forward and handed me the heavy notecard with the Navy seal.

I read it slowly and carefully, but what Maitre Dyana had said was almost word for word what Caellynd had written, except for the last words, which were:

> I have always held the Collegium in the highest respect, and, even more, I
> continue to do so.

"You doubtless understand what lies behind the words," she went on, "but I feel compelled to point it out. He understands fully that you, and the Collegium, will not allow the Naval Command to hide behind procedural niceties to avoid acting when acting is necessary." A brief and wintry smile followed. "That creates a secondary problem. Would you care to describe it for me?"

I would have preferred not to, but some things had to be faced. "We can't afford to be wrong about anything for a long, long time. Otherwise, we'll become feared for our power alone, and everyone will turn against us."

"Exactly, and that will limit what we can do. That may mean that at times we will have to let minor offenses against imagers or others go unpunished, especially if there is no hard evidence, or if punishing the offender will create the impression of unbridled or arbitrary power on our part. What else?"

"I need to become even less visible."

"How do you plan to do that? You haven't been noticeably successful thus far."

"I've thought about that. If matters in Ferrum go well, I intend to follow the example set by my preceptor some years ago."

"You seem rather confident," Dyana said. "What if your plan doesn't work?"

"That's not the question. The question is how well it's worked and how many junior imagers and gunboats we've lost."

"If it has worked poorly?"

"It might be best if I took Dhelyn's position in Westisle."

"That would be acceptable." A wry smile followed. "Not perfect, but acceptable. If . . . just if . . . Dartazn succeeds in implementing your plan in Cloisera in a moderately successful fashion, what would you suggest I recommend to Caellynd and the Council?"

"Send two communiqués—one to the Ferrans and one to the Oligarch of Jariola."

"I assume the one to Ferrum should state that they surrender immediately or face greater consequences and the one to Jariola should tell them to reclaim their own territory and nothing more . . . or face the consequences."

"Something like that."

"You know that over time, Ferrum will try for the coal fields again."

I nodded. "But if they kept the coal fields, then they'd try for something else."

"I can't take anything like that to the Council yet," Dyana pointed out. "Not until we know the results."

"I know, but I thought you'd like my thoughts before you have to act."

"Rhenn . . . we don't need any more action."

I merely nodded. I knew we didn't, but sometimes what one needed wasn't what life, and survival, permitted. Maitre Dyana, for all her words, knew that as well, and knew I knew it.

I stood. "Unless something else comes up, I'll see you on Lundi."

"I hope it's Monday. I'm moving to the Maitre's dwelling this weekend."

"The rebuilding is finished?"

"Mostly. The main floor and the bedrooms are completed. That's more than enough for me, and the Collegium needs the symbol of the lights in the Maitre's domicile." She rose from behind the desk.

"Do you need help? We could—"

"What you could do is spend time with your wife and daughter."

I didn't argue.

69

Enjoying Diestrya and Seliora was harder than it should have been over the remainder of the weekend. I kept wondering what had happened with Dartazn and the imagers, as well as whether Caellynd—or the newsheets . . . or someone—would decide to press the issues around the deaths of Geuffryt and Valeun . . . and whether I'd still have to testify before a Navy court martial. Lundi came and went, and I heard nothing more.

On Mardi morning, I had barely walked into the administration building when Beleart ran toward me. "Maitre Dyana is looking for you."

I dropped my cloak in my study and hurried upstairs, where Gherard motioned me into her study, then closed the door behind me.

Maitre Dyana stood, brushing a pale blue scarf back over her shoulder. "Sea-Marshal Caellynd just sent over a copy of the communiqué he received late last night." She extended the single sheet of paper to me. Her face was somber as she sat back down behind the desk.

I felt like wincing, but I just said, "Thank you." I sat down in the middle chair and read.

> To: Sea-Marshal, Naval Command
> From: Fleet Marshal, Northern Fleet
> Subject: Imager Incendiary Attacks
> Date: 16 Ianus 763
>
> Pursuant to Naval Command instructions, on 11 Ianus, deployment of imagers under the command of Maitre Dartazn was completed. Twenty-eight fast gunboats and one fast frigate composed the strike force. The main fleet body concentrated near Ferdelance Point, as a diversion. The Ferran fleet attempted engagement. The northern fleet conducted a measured withdrawal, with the loss of two corvettes and one Condaign-class frigate. Best estimates of Ferran losses are four frigates and one light cruiser.

Strike force attacked 15 port cities and three non-port industrial works over four days. Destruction of all targets in excess of 90% of structures. Ferran casualties unknown, but expected to exceed tens of thousands. Strike force casualties: eight gunboats lost with all hands; two sunk, but with some survivors recovered; two with light damage and minimal casualties.

Imager strike force survivors returning on *Lyiena*, estimated arrival in Westisle on 23-24 Ianus.

As directed by provisional instructions, we have sent a request for unconditional surrender and immediate withdrawal of all Ferran forces from Jariola. No reply yet received.

I lowered the sheet and looked at Dyana.

She looked back at me. "Your methods were effective, Rhenn."

"I'd thought they would be. My concerns were getting the imagers close enough to be able to image the targets . . . and whether too many would be killed in the attempt."

"You were even right about the casualties. It would appear that the Collegium lost close to twenty promising young imagers."

"We lost that many imagers. Some of them might have been fleet imagers."

"The fleet imagers expect that possibility. The young ones don't understand. Not really." She paused. "I'll make a statement at the midday meal."

Neither of us spoke for a moment. Finally, I said, "More than a few older imagers are going to feel that the whole operation was a terrible waste of young imagers."

"Do you?"

"It wasn't a waste. It was a sacrifice of blood and youth on our part because the High Holders and the factors couldn't bear to pay the cost of remaining strong. It was a terrible waste of life in Ferrum because they couldn't understand that we would pay that price."

Dyana shook her head. "No . . . you decided that the price had to be paid. I agreed, and, in retrospect, so will the Council and the Navy, but you decided, and, had the operation failed . . ."

"I'd be fortunate to spend the rest of my life as an isolated regional or in Mont D'Glace."

"No one could force you, Rhenn, but if that had happened, you'd find no one would spend more than moments in your company."

"Some won't, anyway."

"Not most imagers, but few Councilors will." She paused. "You will accompany me to the meeting tomorrow with Ramsael, Sebatyon, and Caartyl. I doubt it will be pleasant."

"You want me to press them on change."

"Only on the need for change."

I couldn't help smiling, if wryly. I was to be the reminder of the need for change, and then Maitre Dyana could seem oh-so-reasonable.

"Speaking of the Council," I pointed out, "Dartazn can't go back to the Chateau."

"That's true. What do you suggest?

"Make him a Maitre D'Structure and the direct Collegium liaison to the fleets. Give him Dhelyn's position in Westisle and have him train all the fleet imagers in the tactics and weapons he developed. If any of the juniors showed a real flair for that, make them his assistants."

Dyana raised an eyebrow.

"If they're that good at destruction, they're better off dealing with the fleet and some of the senior officers. It also might head off the kind of problems we had with Geuffryt and Valeun."

"That's similar to a rationale I heard years ago."

I shrugged. "There's no reason not to steal from the best."

"He would have been both appalled and proud of you."

"He always was appalled. I'm not sure about proud."

"He was proud of you as well."

I had my doubts, but I just nodded.

"There's one other matter."

"Yes?"

"The Naval Board of Inquiry has found that Valeun was murdered by Geuffryt, that Geuffryt attempted to murder you, and that your actions were justified in self-defense."

"I'm relieved to hear that." What was ironic about the board's findings was that they were all accurate . . . just not in the way they doubtless had thought in making those findings.

"I thought you would be."

After I left Maitre Dyana, I went to find Schorzat and Kahlasa. They needed to know before Maitre Dyana informed the entire Collegium. I found

Kahlasa leaving the conference room where she'd been talking to Aismeya, one of the youngest female imagers, and asked her to join me in Schorzat's study.

When all three of us were gathered there, I said, "I just read the communiqué from Fleet Marshal Asarynt. It appears that the operation was successful, but casualties were high. Maitre Dyana will be making a statement at noon in the dining hall."

"How high?" asked Schorzat.

"Ten out of twenty-eight gunboats carrying imagers were lost, eight with all hands."

Schorzat winced. Kahlasa nodded slowly, if sadly.

"What do you mean by successful?" Schorzat's tone was hard.

"There's not much left of the fifteen largest coastal cities in Ferrum, according to Asarynt."

"That seems a little hard to believe, don't you think?" Schorzat's doubt was clear.

I shook my head. "We taught most of them to image a mixture of jellied lamp oil, etherperoxides, and dry guncotton . . . as well as some other incendiaries Chassendri and I worked out." That wasn't quite true. I'd asked Chassendri to work those out with Dartazn, but it had been my idea, and the blame, or some of it, needed to come back to me. "Ferrum's heavily forested, and they're a factoring and profit-seeking nation, and that means they use much more wood in their cities than we do. Asarynt said that Ferran casualties were high. He's asking for complete surrender."

"Did he say how high?"

"No." But Ferrial held more than a million people, and with eighty percent destruction or more in a day or so, I didn't see how the death toll couldn't have been less than a hundred thousand, not that anyone was going to be able to count accurately, which might be for the best. That didn't count the other fourteen cities with populations greater than fifty thousand.

"Will the Ferran fleet surrender after that?" asked Kahlasa.

"I'm sure that their initial reaction will be to continue to fight. That won't last. They have no place left to resupply or refuel."

"You've definitely taken a scorched earth stance, Rhenn," Schorzat said, his voice flat.

"There wasn't a practical alternative. Between them, the Council and the Navy left the rest of us in an impossible long-term position. We had Ferran saboteurs all over Solidar, and I have no doubts that many are still here." I could tell that Schorzat really didn't understand. Like so many, he believed that once you fell behind it was always possible to catch up. The problem was that every advance in engines and ships, in manufacturing and in trade, fueled yet another advance, and the only way to catch up was to sacrifice comfort and personal wealth, in part by allowing greater competition and change—and neither the factors nor the High Holders had been willing to do that. That failure was why Ferrum had overtaken us in warship design and construction and would have as well in manufactures and machinery. "You heard how they infiltrated the engine works, the Banque D'Ouestan, and worked with the Stakanarans to bring the nastier elveweed to Solidar. They blew up buildings all over the country, and killed thousands. That doesn't include what they did in Jariola. Exactly what did the Jariolans do to merit being invaded—except to possess coal fields and mines that the Ferrans wanted? Or was it because they have a form of government the Ferran factors dislike?"

"The Jariolans aren't exactly paragons of the Nameless."

I looked directly at Schorzat. I didn't say anything. I just looked.

Abruptly, he swallowed. Then he forced a laugh. "You know, Rhenn, while you act for the best of the Collegium, there are times when you make Bilbryn look peaceful, kind, and sympathetic."

That was all I needed, to be compared to the warrior imager champion of Rex Caldor, the man historians claimed was responsible for the bloody unification of Bovaria half a millennium before Rex Regis unified all Solidar the same way. All too often, I'd heard Bilbryn described as Namer-evil-incarnate. I managed a smile. "I'm not sure that comparison is fair to poor Bilbryn. He's not here to defend himself." I paused.

Kahlasa smothered a brief smile.

Schorzat looked appalled.

"Life isn't neat and orderly, Schorzat. It's messy and bloodier than anyone would like. Politics and personal agendas make it worse than that at times. I cut through all that, and I've managed to give us a chance to tidy up things. The only problem is that, like with everything, there's a cost, and most people want to pretend that there isn't. Pretending that there isn't a cost to maintaining what is good only results in matters getting worse. That's how all this happened. No one wanted to pay, and everyone wanted to keep their personal advantages and the restraints on those who might compete with them, from the artisan guilds to the High Holders. Even in the Collegium most imagers didn't want to pay, and the irony is that the two who did—Maitre Poincaryt and Maitre Dichartyn—were the first ones killed. They were both probably too good. I'm not. I'm no martyr. I'm young enough and arrogant enough to want to share that cost." I smiled broadly. "So that's the way it's going to be."

After I walked out of his study, leaving him to think over what I'd said, I laughed, softly and bitterly. Now all I had to do was overhaul the entire economic and political structure of Solidar before Ferrum recovered.

70

Just before eighth glass on Meredi, Maitre Dyana and I stepped from the duty coach and walked through the security entrance into the Council Chateau and up the east circular staircase to the second level and from there to the larger study of the Chief Councilor. All three members of the Executive Council were seated around the circular table. The chairs were arranged so that the three Councilors sat on the south side, with Ramsael in the center, Caartyl on his left, and Sebatyon on his right. Maitre Dyana took the leftmost of the two chairs on the north side, leaving the one to the right to me.

"Greetings, Councilors," she offered. "I believe you all know Maitre Rhennthyl."

"How could we not?" asked Ramsael genially. "Greetings."

Sebatyon and Caartyl merely nodded.

"I trust you've all read the communiqué from Deputy Sea-Marshal Caellynd," began Maitre Dyana.

"I thought he was acting Sea-Marshal," said Sebatyon.

I managed not to wince.

"He is acting Sea-Marshal," Ramsael agreed. "His official title is still Deputy Sea-Marshal. Once the Council votes tomorrow to confirm his position, he will be Sea-Marshal in name as well as fact."

"A mere formality," sniffed Sebatyon. "With the Ferrans under control, we won't need to rush back into those tiresome discussions about new ships for the Navy. We should be able to reduce taxes on goods and return to more prosperous times."

Ramsael glanced to Caartyl.

The guild Councilor cleared his throat. "There are other priorities to consider, Councilor."

"Such as what? I can't imagine anything more important than enhancing Solidaran prosperity. Why tax ourselves for ships that are now unnecessary?"

I glanced at Maitre Dyana. She continued to smile pleasantly.

Ramsael frowned, but appeared disinclined to speak.

So I did. "Councilors, I hate to be contrary, but if what Councilor Sebatyon is saying represents the view of the Council, what we've just endured will be nothing compared to what happens in twenty years."

"Why, Maitre Rhennthyl? Ferrum will not be a danger for years, it would appear from Marshal Asarynt's communiqué." Sebatyon's smile was ingratiatingly unpleasant.

I smiled as cold a smile as I could. "Perhaps I should put it in another way. We leveled more than half the cities in Ferrum. We may have killed millions. We destroyed most of their industry. Thousands more, perhaps tens of thousands, will die of lack of shelter and the inability to get or pay for food. What will motivate the Ferran people for a generation or more to come? They weren't our friends to begin with. Do you think they've forgotten how to build good ships and weapons? Or to rebuild their manufactories? Their farmland is still untouched, as are their mines. As are manufactories away from the coast. What will happen to your children when our fleets are falling apart twenty years from now and the brand-new Ferran fleet masses for revenge? Or do you plan to spend millions of golds to raise an army we don't have to occupy Ferrum so that doesn't happen? Do you propose we continue the same taxing and licensing restrictions on new machinery that hamstrung us so much that Councilor Glendyl mortgaged his entire future in an attempt to avoid what he saw was coming? Do you think it was an accident that both Suyrien the Elder and Glendyl were targeted for assassination by the Ferrans?"

"Maitre Rhennthyl," said Sebatyon pleasantly, "I would that you would spare us the lectures."

I looked at him, and projected pure power at him, as well as anger, literally pinning him in his seat. "Councilor . . . do not patronize me . . . or the Collegium. We sacrificed close to a third of our most promising young imagers to stave off the Ferran threat. We lost our two most senior imagers to a bombardment. You sacrificed nothing. Neither did most High Holders. You are both interested in merely gilding your profits, rather than investing in the future. You will not do so on the bodies of dead imagers, dead sailors, and Solidarans who died from Ferran explosions, Stakanaran elveweed, and treachery. You will devote yourselves to reforming the tax structure, modernizing the fleet, and reforming the licensing laws so that an inventor of new processes must license them to others, for a fair royalty, after a brief period of exclusivity."

I turned to Ramsael. "You are a fair man, Chief Councilor. I trust I will not have to remind you that the needs of all Solidar come before the need for excess profits." I inclined my head politely. "I am not a politician, and I am less than skilled in reasonable and gentle language. I lack the diplomacy of

Maitre Poincaryt, or the patience and experience of Maitre Dyana. I would that I had her measured iron determination, but I think it best that I leave now that you have heard what I have to say. That does not mean I will not follow what you do, nor does it mean that I will not hold you personally accountable. For I will."

Then I left, and walked downstairs to wait outside Baratyn's study.

He immediately came out. "I thought you were with Maitre Dyana."

"I was, but then Sebatyon started in with some nonsense about not needing new ships and returning to the old ways. I expressed my views on his idiocy, suggested that the time was overdue for change, and that I'd hold them all accountable . . . personally. Then I departed and left Maitre Dyana to be politely unyielding."

"You didn't make things easy for her." Baratyn shook his head.

Actually, I thought I had. I'd let them know that they really had no choices, and now they could work out how to do what needed to be done with Maitre Dyana. "With Sebatyon's views, what else could I do?"

"Sebatyon wasn't a good choice. They all knew that, but none of the others would spend the time, not when their factorages are so far from L'Excelsis. Sebatyon's son really runs things. The factor representative on the Executive Council needs to be from L'Excelsis."

"None of the other factors on the Council are from L'Excelsis, and the factors' associations haven't even agreed on a successor to Glendyl yet, have they?"

"That will be weeks away, at best."

"There's one other matter," I offered, since it was my responsibility, and not Maitre Dyana's. "Dartazn won't be coming back to the Chateau."

"I'd thought as much." Baratyn nodded.

"I will be talking matters over with him to see if any of the imagers who were under him on the operation might have shown potential for security duties."

"Do you know who'll be coming back?"

"Not until they return with Dartazn. That's likely to be several days yet."

Baratyn and I must have talked for another quint before Dyana came down the circular east staircase. She smiled at Baratyn. "Greetings. You're looking well, given all the extra work we've piled on you."

"Thank you. Rhenn has said you'll be looking for someone to replace Dartazn."

"He will indeed." She inclined her head politely, then looked to me.

We walked out together, but I didn't say anything else until we were in the coach on the way back to Imagisle.

"Was there too large an outburst after I left?"

"A mixture of cautious indignation and self-pitying righteousness, clothed in protestations of honesty, fairness, and duty." Dyana laughed. "I let them say all that they had to say, and then I spoke to them gently."

"What did you tell them?"

"I simply pointed out that you had all the skills of a Maitre D'Image, which you do, and that you were my designated successor, and that you were only following what the previous Chief Councilor had already planned to undertake. Then I pointed out that no one had achieved much success in opposing you, from previous powerful High Holders, to Ferrum itself, to the former Sea-Marshal, to innumerable assassins, and even to large bombards on barges fired at point-blank range. I also pointed out that you had done a quiet and admirable job as a District Patrol Captain until the Ferrans dropped shells on your house and got you rather angry, and, if we wanted a quiet and uneventful future, that it would be best if they didn't go out of their way to make you angry, the way Sebatyon had, and that we needed to put an end to the dithering and get on with working out the details."

"And . . . ?"

"The next sessions of the Council will discuss the points you raised, and everyone will complain and say how unfair and unreasonable it is that Solidar has been forced to act against the old and honorable traditions. Some will complain about the high-handedness of the Collegium, and Rholyn will be forced to defend our actions by pointing out that the Council's failures had left little choice. Then, when the inevitable finally is forced upon them, Ramsael will point out that the least painful choice will be to address the more important matters, and he will ask each Councilor to provide his recommendations over the following weeks." She smiled. "By the beginning of summer, there might even be a proposal for the necessary changes in taxation."

It was a start.

After Maitre Dyana and I returned to Imagisle, I decided to follow her indirect suggestion and work on matters of a quieter nature, beginning with the design of the report format and the information I wanted conveyed by the Collegium regionals and by the Civic Patrol chiefs across Solidar. I'd been working about a glass when Kahlasa knocked on the door, and then slipped into my study.

"Rhenn . . ." She slid a single sheet onto the desk. "You should see this immediately."

I didn't ask why. If she said so, she had more than enough reason. I began to read the Civic Patrol report from Laaryn . . . about a body found frozen in the ice of a canal. The dead man had been wearing imager grays. He had short curly brown hair and broad shoulders. He'd been shot once in the back of the head. The only item in his wallet, tucked inside a hidden inside oilskin pocket, was a duplicate banque fund transfer slip for five thousand golds drawn on the Banque D'Rivages. The body was being kept on ice pending instructions from the Collegium.

I looked up and nodded.

"It's Johanyr, isn't it? Geuffryt shot him, didn't he?"

"There's no one else it could be, but there's no way to prove it. Not now."

"He got Johanyr to withdraw the golds by telling him that the gunners would take you out . . . or something like that."

"Most likely." It was also clear that Johanyr had known the sealed codes. He might even have imaged them out and memorized them while he was still at Imagisle and visiting his family. Maitre Draffyd had indicated he'd had considerable raw ability.

I rose and walked to the peg holding my winter cloak, still holding the report. "I need to deliver this to the family."

Kahlasa nodded.

The wind had picked up and was gusting all around me as I crossed the quadrangle to the coach station, although the sky remained clear. The ride out to Iryela's seemed longer than the slightly more than two quints that it actually took, and the gate guards didn't hesitate to let me in.

I only had to wait a few moments in the front foyer before Iryela appeared, dressed as informally as I'd ever seen her, in dark green woolen trousers and a matching sweater, with her white-blonde hair pulled back away from her face, giving her a more severe look.

"Rhenn . . . what are you doing here?"

"Is there somewhere we can talk unheard?"

"The private drawing room is empty. Would you like tea?"

"Just tea . . . if you'll join me."

Iryela gestured and a serving woman appeared.

"Tea in the drawing room."

The woman inclined her head and turned down the left-hand corridor, then descended the service steps. I walked with Iryela down the same corridor past the steps. Our boots echoed in the empty hallway. The drawing room door was open, and there was heat from the stove. I did close the door behind us, escorted her to the table, seated her, and took the chair across from her.

"You look very serious, Maitre Rhennthyl."

"I am. Unhappily. I have a report you need to read."

"It's about Johanyr, isn't it?"

"I think so." I eased the report across the pale green linen cloth. I waited while she read.

She looked up. Her eyes were clear, although there was a slight mistiness there, I thought. Then, I might have been imagining it.

She cleared her throat. "I feared something like this. Do you know who did it?"

"I don't know, but I have a strong suspicion."

"You asked me about Marshal Geuffryt. Is he the one?"

"He might well have been, but we'll never know . . ." I went on to give the official explanation of what happened, except I never finished.

"That's the official explanation, isn't it?" she said, interrupting me.

"Yes."

"Thank you." She gave the slightest shiver. "Can we take care . . . of him?"

"Of course. I'll send an official release from the Collegium to the Civic Patrol in Laaryn, and a copy to you."

"It seems so strange . . . it's almost as if I've known for years that something like this would happen . . . but . . ."

"It's still a shock when you find out." I could remember exactly how I'd felt when I'd gotten the letter from Khethila about Rousel.

"You would know," she said softly.

And I did, because we'd each lost brothers, all because Johanyr had tried to destroy me when I'd first become an imager.

In the silence, there was a knock on the door.

"You may bring in the tea," said Iryela.

The server slipped into the drawing room with the silver tray holding a tall green and white porcelain teapot with two matching cups and saucers. She set it on the end of the table closest to the windows and departed as silently as she had come.

"You will join me?"

"Of course."

She poured two cups, then raised hers and took a sip, before asking, "Would you tell me about Diestrya?"

"If you'll tell me about the twins."

She did smile, for a moment.

We talked for a quint, only about the children.

Once I returned to the Collegium, the rest of Meredi went by quietly, and there were few interruptions.

71

Jeudi was quiet, and so was Vendrei, but that did give me a chance to think. At every step, I'd been hampered by the lack of information, from what was happening across Solidar in any meaningful way, to what was being manufactured where in what quantities, to how many High Holders there were. So I asked Ferlyn to join me in my study, and I told him the problem and showed him what I had in mind.

He laughed.

I waited.

"Didn't you know?" Ferlyn looked surprised. "Quaelyn and I created a whole set of forms over two years ago, for the artisan guilds, the factoring associations, and the High Holders. Maitre Dichartyn told us to refine them, but that it wouldn't be possible to get the Council to implement the requirements for High Holders and freeholders to comply. He said we'd have to wait for a crisis to prove they were necessary . . ."

And I'd believed no one had thought about the problem. In what else had Dichartyn anticipated me? After a moment, I said, "Could you get me a set to look over?"

"I'll have it for you in less than a quint. You don't mind if it has some of Master Dichartyn's comments in the margins, do you?"

"Hardly." His comments were likely to be better than any I'd have.

After Ferlyn returned with a folder containing pages of suggested forms, I read through them, comparing my drafts to the older ones. I could see the need for change in theirs, but also a number of things I hadn't considered. I hadn't finished when Gherard rapped on the door.

"The Maitre would like to see you, sir."

"I'll be right there." I left all the forms on my desk and followed Gherard back up to Maitre Dyana's study.

She was standing by the window, looking out across the quadrangle, when I entered. For a time, she continued to stare out the window, even as I walked toward her, stopping short of her desk. Then she turned and walked to the side of the desk. She did not seat herself.

"I've just received a communiqué from Fleet Marshal Asarynt and a message from Dartazn. He's been delayed a day because there wasn't space for all of them on the first express. They'll be arriving on Solayi morning."

"Did he mention who's coming back?"

"He wrote that he didn't feel comfortable putting the names in writing when he couldn't give them to another imager. He didn't say much of anything except that they were all glad to be back in Solidar and that he would report to you and me as soon as he arrived." She handed me the single sheet of heavy paper.

I read it, but she'd summarized it accurately.

"What about Asarynt?" I asked.

Before I could finish asking, the two page communiqué was in my hands. Several phrases and sentences stood out.

". . . superb organization and discipline of imagers by Maitre Dartazn . . ."

". . . extremely effective targeting, particularly in the strike force attacking Ferrial under Maitre Dartazn's direct supervision, reduced the Ferran capital and entire cities to ruins and forced complete Ferran capitulation . . ."

". . . professionalism on all levels by the Collegium a major contribution to the effectiveness of the operation . . ."

At the end, I looked up. "Dartazn did well. That's more than clear."

"Caellynd sent some other materials. The Assembly of Ferrum—what remains of it—has surrendered. They didn't have much choice. Caellynd intends to take the best ships in their fleet and scuttle the rest." Maitre Dyana looked at me. "I can see why Dichartyn spent so much time with you. He was afraid of what you might do, you know?"

There wasn't much to say to that.

"You have this tendency to solve problems completely, regardless of the cost."

"I've never been given much choice."

She shook her head, clearly ignoring my reply. "Fifteen port cities in ashes . . . tens of thousands starving . . ."

"There wasn't any other way, not at the end," I pointed out. "They're the ones who started the conflict by invading Jariola and by trying to cripple Solidar. We never had the resources to respond in kind. Not in a timely fashion, and after the destruction of Glendyl's engine works, the longer the conflict dragged on, the worse our position would have become."

"You can see that and act on it. Most people, even imagers, will try to cope within the world that they know."

"I use what's in the world," I pointed out.

"You use it in ways no one else seems to have considered. You always have, from the moment you first realized you were an imager, Dichartyn said."

"If I hadn't, someone would have."

"Who?" she asked.

I couldn't think of anyone. Dartazn had obviously carried out my plan effectively, and Chassendri had been vital in coming up with the incendiaries, but I'd had to explain what I had in mind to them. That had been true with Dichartyn as well on several occasions.

"You see?" Dyana asked dryly.

I wanted to protest that others in my position might have done what I'd done . . . except it didn't matter. I'd been where I'd been, and I'd done what I'd done. Asking whether an imager made the times, or the times made the imager was a fool's question. In the end, what was . . . was. When you could play the plaques, you did, or you lost, and when you were the one who was played by the times and others, all you could do was survive as best you could.

"I also received a proposal from Caellynd that he intends to submit to the Council," Maitre Dyana added. "He wants to shift fleet headquarters to West-isle. The water is deeper there, and the port is better."

"That sounds like a good idea. It didn't happen before because Suyrien would have opposed it?"

"I suspect so."

I couldn't help but think that there would be many, many changes in the months and years to come, some that none of us could foresee.

72

By Samedi morning, the news about Ferrum was everywhere, with stories in *Veritum* and *Tableta*, both hailing the daring strike operation that combined high-speed Naval vessels with brave imagers who risked their lives to bring Ferrum to its knees and to end the conflict. *Tableta* even had an entire paragraph on Dartazn, praising him as the tactical genius who was the key to the operation's success. It also mentioned that he belonged to the little-known part of the Collegium that protected Solidar through various covert methods, and that section was reputedly headed by an imager who had long experience as a Civic Patrol District Captain. They didn't mention my name. Even so, when Seliora read that part, she frowned.

Still, there was little I could do, and we spent the day together, with a family dinner at NordEste Design. On Solayi, I was up early, if not quite as early as on the rest of the week, so that I could go down to the ironway station and meet Dartazn and the returning imagers.

When we left Imagisle at a quint past eighth glass, I was in the lead coach of the seven that proceeded down West River Road to the ironway station. The station wasn't that crowded, unsurprisingly for morning on Solayi, and there was plenty of space for the coaches across the entry plaza from the main entrance.

I made my way toward platform three, the one for the expresses, and received scarcely a look from the scattered handfuls of people coming and going. Then I ended up standing and waiting almost a quint in the still chill of the late morning, under the spread roof that covered the platform, but not the space above the tracks. The miasma of burning coal hung in the air, giving an edge to each breath I took, before the express slowly steamed into the station and came to rest at the platform with a last hissing and a dull clunk.

Once the doors opened, it took me but a moment to spot Dartazn's tall figure and make my way toward him.

"Maitre Rhennthyl. I thought you might be the one to greet us." He offered an open smile, one that carried a certain relief, as he lowered his duffel to the stone tiles of the platform.

"Welcome back . . . and congratulations," I said warmly. "You did an outstanding job of leading and coordinating the attack on the Ferran ports. Fleet Marshal Asarynt sent a glowing dispatch praising your leadership, initiative, and tact. We'll talk about that later. I have seven coaches waiting across from the station."

"Thank you." He turned. "Imagers! On me!" His voice dominated the platform, and people turned to watch as the gray-clad figures lined up with duffels at their feet.

I counted sixteen seconds and thirds, and I did see both Shault and Eamyn. I didn't see Ralyea anywhere, and I wondered if I'd been wrong to agree to send him. Then Shault caught sight of me and smiled. I nodded in return. Still . . . we'd lost over a third of those I'd sent out. That was the side that people like Sebatyon never considered. Between covert duties and circumstances such as the incendiary operation against Ferrum, the Collegium suffered greater losses on a proportional basis than did either the Navy or the Civic Patrol. Yet revealing such figures was a double-edged blade, because they also demonstrated our comparatively small numbers and our vulnerability.

"Maitre Rhennthyl has coaches arranged across from the station. You can situate yourselves in any but the first . . ." Dartazn began to explain.

I listened, waiting, and when he was finished, we walked back through the station.

When we were in the coach headed back to Imagisle, I asked, "Can you tell me more?"

"The Navy was surprisingly cooperative. They seemed to know they needed help as soon as we started to board the *Lyiena.*" He snorted. "Just as we were casting off, an imager ran up the pier, demanding to talk to the senior imager. He yelled something about the master in Westisle needing to know what we were doing. I told him he'd have to make that inquiry of the Collegium Maitre. He didn't seem too pleased, but I wasn't holding up our departure."

"Maitre Dyana and I took care of that later. Go on."

"There's really not too much to say. I had them practice some on the trip outbound, but seawater doesn't have very good concentrations of what they needed to image. So I had them work on projection imaging of water, just to strengthen their abilities. When we reached Ferran waters, the Navy ferried me to the flagship. I met with the Fleet Marshal himself and explained the general plan. He pointed out where it wouldn't work, and then we came up with some revisions. We briefed all the gunboat commanders, and they put me on a fast frigate, and dispersed the others among the gunboats." Dartazn shrugged. "We did the best we could."

"I don't think it was anywhere close to that easy or simple."

Dartazn smiled sheepishly. "I listened intently, agreed politely, and then did what needed to be done. I told everyone that I was following orders . . . and it worked out. I couldn't have done it without all the preparation you and Chassendri gave me." His face sobered. "We lost more than we should have. Some of them were too brave. Ralyea was one of them. He destroyed the naval base and shipyards at Greissyn. He had the gunboat captain make a last run so that he could try a final imaging at the magazines. He was successful, but the explosions were so devastating that some of the shells and shrapnel shredded his boat and turned it into an inferno. The other boat reported that. Was it worth it?" He paused. "What Ralyea did deprived their fleet of a good portion of their reserve munitions and destroyed the second largest naval station. Fleet Marshal Asarynt was very pleased when he heard that."

Sitting there in the coach, at that moment, he looked much older than I.

"It was devastating, wasn't it?"

"It was awful. With the sea winds, the fires spread everywhere. The shore was filled with flame and smoke as far as we could see when we headed back to the fleet. You could smell it milles offshore, days later." He paused. "Things exploded, in places where you wouldn't have thought there was anything. At times, the snow turned to steam."

For a moment, he didn't speak. Then he asked, "How did you know their cities would burn so much?"

"Patterns. Quaelyn's and Ferlyn's patterns. Ferrum is heavily forested so that timber and planks are much less expensive. All their commerce is based on competition among factors and merchants, and they want high profits in a short time. Solid stone and brick buildings are costly and take time to build. I wasn't certain, but it seemed likely that their cities would be likely to burn. It also seemed they wouldn't spend as much on fire brigades or have as many of them."

"I don't think they do . . . or they did." After another pause, he asked, "You *knew* it would be like that, with fire everywhere, and people dying, didn't you, sir?"

"I did. I would have taken your position . . . if I could have, but Maitre Dyana refused to consider it, almost before I brought it up."

Dartazn shook his head. "With Master Dichartyn gone, you couldn't. Even I saw that."

That might have been, but, especially after seeing what lay behind Dartazn's eyes, I couldn't help but feel guilty. Yet, in a way, feeling guilty on my part was also an indulgence. So I plowed on. "You're now a Maitre D'Structure, and you won't be going back to the Council Chateau."

"A Maitre D'Structure, sir?"

"Maitre Dyana and I already agreed on that."

"What will I be doing, sir? I only know security . . . and what . . . what we did."

"We need to have a closer relationship with the Naval Command, the way I once did with the Civic Patrol. Not exactly the same, but you'll be the master in charge of dealing directly with the fleet and reorganizing the use of imagers on board warships. After all this, I think we'll be able to persuade the Sea-Marshal to grant you an equivalent rank, something like a submarshal, high enough that you'll outrank any vessel commander." I paused. "So far as I know, you haven't married."

"No, sir, but . . ."

"There is a lady?" I smiled.

"Yes, sir."

"Do you think she would mind living at the Collegium in Westisle? I understand that the Naval Command will be moving fleet headquarters there, and due to events here in Solidar while you were gone, we'll need a new Maitre of the Collegium there. You would have senior master quarters, very spacious quarters, I understand. You would have to come back here, several times a year, though."

He smiled slowly. "I haven't talked to Veroniqua, obviously, but I think I . . . we . . . would like that."

I had to be fair. "There's one other thing."

"Sir?" His eyes narrowed.

"You're a bit of a hero, and people will likely be watching you."

He nodded slowly, then grinned. "So you want me to act the part?"

"It would be helpful, given all the Collegium has been through in your absence."

"Oh?"

"Councilor Glendyl died after you left, and Assistant Sea-Marshal Geuffryt killed Sea-Marshal Valeun and tried to kill me . . ." I gave him a quick summary of events, including the role of Vyktor and what we'd discovered about the various Ferran fronts and agents.

When I was finished, he looked at me. "Those are the official versions, I take it."

I nodded.

"I thought as much." After a momentary hesitation, he said, "I didn't mention it to you, because it was obvious you knew, but I never had that good a feeling about Sea-Marshal Valeun. Fleet Marshal Asarynt, though, he was always very solid, very direct."

"So far, I've found Sea-Marshal Caellynd the same way."

"Asarynt said that he had orders from Caellynd to give us every consideration."

"I think you'll find working with the Navy much easier than you might have otherwise, but you will have to work to instill a bit more discipline and respect in the Collegium in Westisle . . ." I explained about Dhelyn and what had happened.

When I finished, he shook his head. "I promise you. I won't do anything like that."

"We already knew that. That's why Maitre Dyana thought you'd be good there."

The coach came to a stop at the west duty coach station on Imagisle, and I opened the door and stepped out. Dartazn followed, then retrieved his duffel.

"I won't keep you. I imagine you'll want to share your news with the young lady."

He grinned at me. "She'll be pleased. I hope she will be."

"You might also tell her that she may have to accompany you a few places over the next few weeks before you leave for Westisle."

He raised his eyebrows.

"I'm guessing at this point, but I expect you'll be attending the Council's Winter Ball this coming Vendrei—as a guest, not as a security imager. I can't imagine that the Council would not want to see and congratulate the hero who ended the conflict."

"I hadn't thought about that."

I had. "You're fortunate in a way, because everyone will want to meet you, and then you'll have the perfectly acceptable departure for your position in Westisle, and that will leave the Council with a lasting favorable impression." And that just might mute less favorable impressions they had of the Collegium as a result of my acts.

"That's only because they didn't see what Ferrum looked like after we finished."

"Of course," I agreed. "Isn't it always that way? Now . . . go and find your lady."

He didn't need any more urging.

I walked past the other coaches as they drew up and then slowly along the riverwalk on the west side of Imagisle, back toward our house, thinking as I did, not that I came to any earth-shattering conclusions.

Seliora and I spent the rest of the day with Diestrya, until Klysia returned to watch Diestrya, and we walked through the early evening and to the anomen for Solayi services.

Isola's homily could have been targeted at me, and perhaps it was.

"We often praise the glory of the Nameless, and that is right and just so to do, but praising our own glory is only an exercise in naming. When we do, we become disciples of the Namer. There are many definitions of glory, such as exalted reputation, worshipful praise or adoration, but seeking glory, especially for the sake of praise by others, can all too often result in pettiness and egotistical self-praise, if not in death and destruction. In our history, which has been bloodier than the Nameless ever could have wished, often the greatest glory has been bestowed on those who achieved their ends with blades and bullets, rather than upon those who accomplished their goals with quiet and constructive building of cities and societies that cherished cooperation and peaceful resolution. Yes, there are times, such as those through which we are now passing, where there is no substitute for force, but those times should be recalled not with praise and glory but with regret that no other solution was possible. They should be followed by sober reflection on how to avoid situations that require the so-called glory of destroying an enemy . . ."

Isola was right there, too, I realized. The reason we had been forced to act as we had was because we had neglected to build our strength constructively. Had we had more than one engine works, better and more modern warships, and more modern manufactories, Ferrum would never have dared to invade Jariola. Our failure to achieve, as Isola put it, "quiet and constructive building," had led to war, and in that sense the "glory" that had come from it was ill-deserved.

I glanced across the anomen, where Dartazn stood with a tall dark-haired woman, a thoughtful expression upon his face as he watched the chorister.

". . . and in the end the only glory of worth belongs to the Nameless, for all earthly glories are based on the exaltation of naming, the wish to have one's name greater than one's achievements. There are great achievements and those that are less great, but those achievements of worth are those whose legacies outlive the names of those who accomplished them . . ."

After the final words of dismissal, Isola and I left the anomen and headed back home, moving bit more quickly than we had come, because the wind had picked up and the air had gotten far colder.

"That homily was intended for you and Dartazn," observed Seliora.

"You think so?" I laughed softly. "How could you tell?"

"Because she didn't look at you, and you nodded and were very thoughtful-looking as she spoke. So was Dartazn, and she looked at him."

"She was right in what she said."

"You already knew that."

I did indeed, but that wasn't the question. The real question was whether I'd remember it and live by it.

As I had suspected, invitations to the Council's Winter Ball did arrive . . . or rather a note from Ramsael did, stating that as the second highest ranking imager I was considered a member of the Council for purposes of Council Balls. Interestingly enough, although the Maitre of the Collegium was also considered as such an "honorary" member, in accord with tradition, the Maitre never attended unless the Chief Councilor was unable to do so.

With the note were five invitations for me to use or not, as I chose. Since Suyrien's death meant neither Frydryk nor Kandryl would necessarily receive invitations, I offered invitations to both, but Frydryk had already been invited as a courtesy by Fhernon. Iryela and Kandryl accepted, as did Dartazn. My parents declined, but since there wasn't time to get an invitation to Khethila, I did write and tell her that I expected her to be in L'Excelsis for the Spring Ball so that she could meet Madame D'Shendael. I also offered an invitation to Commander Artois, and he and his wife also accepted. Had my parents accepted, I would have invited the Veblynts as well. Instead, I invited no one else.

Vendrei evening was freezing, and felt colder because of a bitter wind, but without snow, and after feeding our daughter and giving her a story, if earlier than usual, we dressed and then made our way to the duty coach station. I was in the formal blacks of a Maitre, with a formal black cloak. Seliora was in black and shimmering green, a gown she'd worn before but not to a Council Ball, also with her formal cloak.

Dartazn and the tall young lady were waiting for us. He wore the same imager formal blacks as did I. Under a dark blue cloak, she was in deep blue.

"Good evening," I offered.

Dartazn bowed. "Might I present my fiance, Veroniqua D'Semaelyn. Veroniqua, Maitre Rhennthyl and Madame D'Rhennthyl."

"Seliora, please," interjected my wife.

"I couldn't . . ."

"She means it," I said with a smile, "and I never cross her when she means it."

Dartazn barely managed to avoid smiling.

I opened the coach door and offered a hand to Seliora. Once we were on our way, I looked to Dartazn.

"I have told her," he admitted. "Can you tell me how long before I'm expected to be in Westisle?"

I smiled. "How long do you need? You could easily stay here three weeks to a month. Longer than that might require that you travel to Westisle."

He looked to Veroniqua.

She smiled shyly, then leaned toward him and whispered.

"She says a month would be lovely. We'd already planned tentatively for the twenty-seventh of Fevier."

"Is your family from here?" asked Seliora.

"Yes . . . Seliora." Veroniqua blushed. "I feel so strange using your first name. I always loved the name, but to know . . ."

"You're acquainted with its meaning?" I asked.

Veroniqua nodded. "My father's side is all Pharsi." She looked to Seliora. "My aunt . . . she saw you once, with a pistol in your hand, and she said that you were truly the Daughter of the Moon." Her eyes went to me, but she said nothing.

"Yes," said Seliora, "he is."

I knew what she meant. More than once we'd been compared to the ancient Pharsi legends—the Daughter of the Moon and Erion, the hunter and the lesser red moon. Whether the comparison was apt or even accurate was another question, but there were some things about which I wasn't going to contradict Seliora. Besides, I'd seen her with the pistol, too.

Because it was so chill, when we arrived at the Council Chateau, there were close to fifteen coaches lined up before us. Once we disembarked, while we didn't rush up the open stone steps, neither did we tarry. Dartazn and Veroniqua led the way, in deference to my seniority, in through the Grand Foyer and past the ceremonial guards and the winged angelica statues I recalled all too well, before ascending the Grand Staircase and then leaving our cloaks with the functionary off to the side of the top of the steps. At the doorway to the Great Receiving Hall, Dartazn and Veroniqua stepped up to the same balding man who announced all arrivals at every Ball.

His deep bass voice boomed out, "Dartazn D'Imagisle, Maitre D'Structure, and Veroniqua D'Semaelyn."

The murmurs died away, and most of those in the crowd turned toward the entrance of the Great Receiving Hall.

As we waited to be announced, Seliora leaned toward me and whispered, "You wanted him to stand out like that, didn't you?"

"I'd hoped for it. They all need to focus on a hero, the one who ended the war."

"You're the one who ended the war."

I shook my head. "I made it possible. He did it. He deserves the credit."

When we stepped up, the announcement was simpler: "Maitre Rhennthyl and Madame Rhennthyl."

"I still don't feel like I should be announced as Madame," murmured Seliora as we stepped away and toward the three Councilors on the Executive Council.

"You said that at the last Ball."

"It's still true," she whispered back.

"That's because you're young and beautiful."

"You said that before."

"It's still true," I murmured in the same tone as she'd used.

"Rhennthyl," she said in a low voice, "you're more impossible than ever."

Beyond the Councilors stood Baratyn, just out from the east wall of the Hall, while Martyl stood along the west wall.

Behind us came the announcement of "Councilor Reyner D'Factorius and Madame D'Reyner."

The first of the Executive Councilors was Sebatyon, who inclined his head politely and stiffly. His voice was cool. "Good evening, Master Rhennthyl, Madame."

I smiled broadly. "A very good evening."

Another stiff nod was his only response.

Next was the hawk-nosed, black-haired Caartyl. "Greetings, Master Rhennthyl. Greetings, Madame Seliora. You're more beautiful than ever."

"As always, you're most kind," replied Seliora

Ramsael bowed slightly even before we could speak. "You honor us, Maitre, Madame."

"The Council honors us," I replied.

"Few will admit it," he said, his voice lower, "but resolving the differences between the Councilors will be far easier now." He straightened slightly and said in a normal voice, "Do enjoy the Ball."

"We intend to."

As we moved out into the hall, and toward the music and those dancing, I thought Ramsael's words and smile held a certain relief.

The announcements continued to boom out across the hall.

"Councilor Alucion D'Artisan and Madame D'Alucion!"

"Fhernon D'Alte and Madame D'Fhernon . . ."

Since I didn't see anyone that I knew, and since Dartazn and Veroniqua had stopped to talk to Martyl, I led Seliora right onto the dance floor. As we danced, others continued to arrive.

"Shendael D'Alte and Madame D'Shendael."

"The Honorable Dharios Harnen, Envoy of the Abierto Isles, and Madame Harnen."

"Ryel D'Alte and Madame Ryel."

"Suyrien D'Alte and Madame Suyrien."

Seliora and I finished the dance and slipped to the side of the floor, knowing that, this time, Iryela and Kandryl would come to find us immediately.

They did. Iryela wore silver trimmed in black, but with a blue scarf that kept the silver from washing her out, and Kandryl again wore the Ryel colors of black and silver.

We half-turned and waited as Iryela and Kandryl approached.

"Thank you again for the invitation," offered Iryela. "We couldn't resist, especially after I heard what you said to that mule Sebatyon."

"Where did you hear that?" I hoped it wasn't that widespread.

"Juniae D'Shendael heard it from Caartyl. He said he was glad you didn't hide behind useless traditions. He also said it was clear there would be change, and that it was about time."

"I'd appreciate it if you kept that fairly close."

"Oh . . . we only told Frydryk and Alynkya. She was amused. He was a bit concerned."

I could see why. He would have to license some of the rights he'd paid dearly for, but I wasn't about to make exceptions for friends, not when it affected everyone's future.

"He'll get over it," said Kandryl.

"Oh," added Iryela, "Frydryk won't tell you this, but Alynkya was exceedingly grateful for the invitation to the Ball."

Seliora nodded knowingly.

It took me a moment to understand why, and then I nodded. "I will be happy to do so again, and you can tell her that."

"That will please her no end, and Frydryk as well." Iryela's eyes flicked to Kandryl.

"Might I have a dance?" Kandryl asked Seliora.

Seliora offered me a knowing smile. "I'd love to."

As they swung out onto the dance floor, I offered a hand to Iryela. "Might I?"

She nodded. Once we were dancing, she said, "Thank you for setting up everything about Johanyr."

"I'm sorry it had to end that way."

"Given Johanyr, I'm not sure it could have ended any other way."

"How is your mother taking it?"

That brought a bitter laugh. "How would I know? She keeps her own house at Ryealte. I sent her a letter, but she never replies to anything. We haven't spoken in years. She won't see me, and I won't force it."

"I'm sorry."

"I've discovered that sometimes women are the worst of all in thinking that men should be in charge of everything. When it's your own mother, it's unbearable."

I couldn't help but think that Khethila and Seliora were both very fortunate in that regard.

"I've been seeing Juniae lately. Much as people deride her, I think she's right." Iryela looked up at me, not quite confrontationally.

"So do I. I've read several of her books, you know? My sister introduced me to her work."

"It's too bad more men don't listen to their sisters and wives."

"Kandryl does, you said."

"You and he do. Sometimes, Frydryk does, but that's only because Alynkya is quietly willful, and her father is Chief Councilor. Most men don't."

That was another statement I couldn't really dispute, either, not for most men, although I had no doubts that Betara was always listened to.

As the music died away, I escorted Iryela back to Kandryl, and then reclaimed Seliora.

"What did she want?" asked my wife.

"To thank me for arranging to let them claim Johanyr's body, and to complain about the fact that too few men listen to their wives and sisters. She's begun to talk to Juniae D'Shendael."

"Good."

"Maitre Rhennthyl, Madame," came a voice from our left.

I turned to face Commander Artois, accompanied by his wife, a muscular woman with iron-gray hair, almost as tall as her husband.

"Berthe and I wanted to pay our respects and offer thanks for the invitation."

"The Commander of the Civic Patrol certainly belongs here," I said cheerfully.

"As you are the first to know," Artois said with a faint smile, "what should be and what is are seldom the same. We do appreciate your sense of propriety."

"You are too kind," I replied.

"That's a word seldom applied to me," said Artois.

Berthe turned to Seliora. "You are most beautiful, as always."

"Thank you."

"I understand that the Council may be making some changes," ventured Artois. "Might any of them apply to the Civic Patrol?"

"Anything the Council does applies to everyone," I said with a slight laugh. "It's likely that all Civic Patrol Commanders will eventually be required to submit more standard reports to the Council. The Ferran sabotage revealed a certain lack of information."

"If the Council limits it to that, we can all deal with it." Artois nodded. "A pleasure to see you both looking so good. We will not keep you."

After they stepped away, Seliora looked to me "There will be more of that."

"So long as it's that circumspect . . ." I laughed softly and took her hand.

We danced for a while longer, and then, just before ninth glass, joined the others gathered around the table where the Chief Councilor would make the traditional toast. I could hear murmurs around us.

". . . think he'll say something different?"

". . . Suyrien never did . . ."

". . . you talk to Maitre Dartazn?"

". . . seems likable enough . . . impressive in a quiet way . . ."

I nodded at the last.

As the bells of the glass began to strike, Chief Councilor Ramsael eased away from where he was talking to Haestyr and Regial and their wives. He stepped toward the table, and the music stopped. Then came the drum roll and a quick trumpet call.

A uniformed server brought three bottles to the table, still corked and sealed, as was traditional. The Councilor said something, then gestured. The server removed the foil and cork from the bottle Ramsael had pointed out, then set a goblet down and poured the sparkling white wine into it.

Ramsael picked up the goblet, raised it, and declaimed, "First, with special thanks to Maitre Dartazn, without whose skills and courage this would be a far more somber occasion, and second, for Solidar, for the Council, and in thanks for a successful end to conflict!" Then he lowered the goblet and took a small swallow.

"For Solidar, for the Council, and in thanks for a successful end to con-

flict!" came a low echo from the bystanders. The response was far more enthusiastic than at past balls, perhaps because of the relief at the way the war—
officially only a conflict—had ended.

Ramsael turned from the toasting table, and his eyes fixed on me. He
nodded ever so slightly, then moved on, smiling at his young wife, and then
at Alynkya, whose smile in reply appeared strained, at least to me. Frydryk
seemed not to notice.

"He did that on purpose, that part about Dartazn," observed Seliora. "Did
you . . . ?"

"No. I said nothing to him." Maitre Dyana might have, but I hadn't.

We turned to move away from the toasting table, but then I could see Junaie D'Shendael was headed in our direction, unaccompanied by her husband.

Madame D'Shendael's smile was warm as she inclined her head to us.
"Maitre Rhennthyl . . . Seliora."

"I'm very pleased to see you once more, Juniae," offered Seliora.

"And I both of you. How is your sister?"

"The last I heard, she was doing well. I'm hoping she'll be able to attend
the Spring Ball. By then she will have read your latest."

"That would be wonderful!" Her words and expression showed that she
meant it. "Caartyl told me that you insisted on change for the Council."

"I did try to stress the need for it."

She laughed, harshly but softly. "He said that, without actually saying so,
you informed Sebatyon that if he opposed change he was likely to follow
Glendyl."

"I didn't say a thing."

"There are times, dearest," interjected Seliora, "when words are unnecessary for you." She smiled at Juniae.

They both nodded.

Since they were clearly conspiring, I didn't feel so bad about asking a question I'd pondered for some time. "Why did Geuffryt do it? So many years ago,
that is?"

Juniae smiled sadly. "He wanted me to love him. I couldn't do that. That
was why he kept threatening to reveal things."

"Why did you let him threaten you?"

"The longer I could play him off, the more I could do to change things. The
books have been one way. That was my reasoning." She offered a sad smile. "I'd
like to think that those small efforts made a difference to your sister."

"They did, and to me, as well."

"And to many other women," added Seliora.

"You are both kind."

"I've not been accused of that much, especially recently," I replied.

"You didn't try to restrain Geuffryt, I heard." The implication was clear. She believed I could have, and she was correct.

"No. It would have been more dangerous, and he had already destroyed enough lives." All that was absolutely true.

"I think he feared you from the beginning," she said in a low voice. "He said you were the most dangerous man in L'Excelsis. He was wrong. You offer the most promise to Solidar, but you are also the most dangerous man in Solidar, perhaps in the entire world."

What could I say to that?

She turned to Seliora. "Our future lies in your hands and words."

In a way, it did. Who else could I trust?

Juniae straightened "We will have you to dinner, and before long." Then she smiled and slipped away.

Seliora reached out and took my hands. "We should dance."

And so we did.